INTIMATE MEMOIRS

Georges Simenon

INTIMATE MEMOIRS

including
Marie-Jo's Book

Translated by Harold J. Salemson

A Helen and Kurt Wolff Book
Harcourt Brace Jovanovich, Publishers
San Diego   New York   London

I apologize to my readers for certain cuts in this book, on pages 532 and 779, which, by order of the President of the Court of Justice, dated November 9, 1981, were made at the demand of Madame Simenon-Ouimet. Only one of these deleted passages, six lines, was written by me. The others were taken from a heartrending message of my dead daughter, Marie-Jo.

HBJ

With the permission of the author, a number of minor cuts were made in the translation, none of them substantive; no cuts other than the legally required ones were made in "Marie-Jo's Book."

Library of Congress Cataloging in Publication Data
Simenon, Georges, 1903–
Intimate memoirs.

Translation of: Mémoires intimes.
"A Helen and Kurt Wolff book."
1. Simenon, Georges, 1903–   —Biography.
2. Novelists, French—20th century—Biography. I. Title.
PQ2637.I53Z46913   1984   843'.912 [B]   83-18679
ISBN 0-15-144892-2

Designed by Dalia Hartman

Printed in the United States of America

First edition

A B C D E

INTIMATE MEMOIRS

1

My tiny little girl,

I know that you are dead, and yet this is not the first time I am writing you. You would have liked to go out quietly, without disturbing a soul. But your death touched off legal and other mechanisms, so that even now lawyers and counselors are trying to work out the problems created by your mother's obstinacy, which may sooner or later have to be settled in court.

Our friend Dr. Jean Martinon, of Cannes, whom you were supposed to speak to by phone, was the one who gave the alarm. Martinon called over and over again, and finally found out that the line had been disconnected. He called Marc, the one of your brothers who lives closest to Paris. Marc and Mylène rushed to the Champs-Elysées and found the door to your apartment locked from the inside. The concierge did not have a duplicate key, so they had to call the police, who came right away and got a locksmith.

Your apartment was impeccably orderly and clean, as if, before leaving, you had given it a thorough going over, including laundering and ironing your clothes and linens. Everything was in its place. And you lay on the bed, with a small red hole in your chest.

Where did that single-shot .22 pistol come from? Who bought the cartridges?

A judicial investigation was started: coroner, public prosecutor, police laboratory specialists, and, from my little house in Lausanne, I watched all the legal brouhaha I had so often described in my novels.

Once the on-site investigation was over and your body was taken to the morgue, I was able to get them to skip the autopsy, but I phoned and asked the police superintendent to put seals on both your doors.

They were removed for a few hours about a month ago, to permit an official inventory to be drawn up by an appraiser, in the presence of a notary, a court clerk, the neighborhood police superintendent, two lawyers, your mother's and the one representing us, as well as your three brothers, and of course your mother, and Aitken, who was representing me because I can no longer travel, all of them hovering about near your bed, which was just the way it had been found almost two years ago.

After which the seals were affixed again, and I have no idea when they will ever come off. It's a little as if your body were still warm, after all those days!

Since I was unable to, Aitken was the one who sat beside the driver of the hearse and brought you back to Lausanne, as you wished. I was waiting for you, and you were laid out in a room at the city undertaker's, where, bereft, I spent nearly an hour alone with you.

I scrupulously carried out your last wishes, found on your bed. No ceremony. The next day, just a few people gathered before your casket while an organist played some of the Johann Sebastian Bach music we both loved. Flowers galore. Mine were armfuls and armfuls of white lilacs, which, in my view, harmonized with the laughing little girl I had known.

In the front row to the left, four men shoulder to shoulder: your three brothers, Marc, Johnny, and Pierre, and me beside the narrow aisle.

On the other side, your mother and a woman I don't know.

Behind your brothers and me, Mylène, Boule, and Teresa, followed by two or three of your friends whom you had asked me to invite.

Twenty minutes of motionlessness and music. At the signal of the funeral director, I left first, after making a date with your brothers for the following day. Teresa was waiting for me outside and she brought me home, staring vacantly, as if I had suddenly become a very old man.

Sitting on either side of the fireplace, she and I knew that at the same moment, your body was being cremated. I had made certain, as you had urgently asked of me, that the wedding ring you had begged me to buy for you when you were about eight years old, and which you had had enlarged a number of times, was not taken off your finger.

The next morning, early, the undertaker's man brought us the box with your ashes, and, once we were alone, I fulfilled your last wish: to have those white ashes strewn over the little garden of our pink house.

· · ·

A little later, your brothers came in. The sun was bright, the grass a fine green.

For the last time, I was sleepwalking as I had done in my childhood, but, as I kept looking out on the garden, the violent pain that had kept me doubled over during the long week of waiting gave way to a feeling of tenderness, which I still experience every time I see that garden and the birds pecking in it, and, considering the position of my armchair, which you know so well, that happens a hundred times a day.

I've gotten into the habit of saying good morning to you when the shutters are opened, and good night in the evening when they are closed, as well as talking inwardly to you.

It took me a long time to get used once again to living like everybody else.

On the white shelves, alongside my desk, large file boxes began piling up, one on the other. The hundreds of letters of yours and mine, your first childish compositions, your intimate diaries and innumerable pictures, your datebooks, your jottings, your memos to yourself—everything concrete that remained of my little Marie-Jo was there, before my eyes, and I was waiting for the moment when I would be able to touch it.

It took almost two years for me to feel strong enough to plunge into your past, your whole life, and, by the same token, into my own past too, in which, as I then realized more than I ever had before, you occupy so great a place.

Your confidences, when we sat facing one another, each in his own armchair, when you read me your disquieting poems, when, accompanying yourself on the guitar, you sang, to tunes we both liked, songs you had made up, with English words; the last cassettes you sent me, some of them so heartrending; everything that had made up the essence of your pathetic life, I now began to understand, should not ever be scattered about. I understand, my little girl, your desire that these records of your radiant existence, your dark hours and your struggles, should not disappear.

I told you one day, and I think I even wrote you, that a being is not completely dead so long as he remains alive in the heart of another. And you are still alive within me, so alive that I can write to you and speak to you as if you were going to read and hear me, answer me while looking at me with your eyes brimming with confidence and love.

The more I live in your intimacy, the more certain I am that you were an exceptional being, of rare lucidity, moved by an almost cruel determination to discover the truth. So that your death has become a quasi-heroic action, and, as you well know, as you so shyly let me understand, all of that cannot go to waste.

That is why, after thinking it over a great deal, and having taken the measure of my strength, I am starting today, in pen and ink, in school notebooks very much like the ones you used, which I ordered especially, to write the story of a being whom I cherish and who will no longer be dead to anyone.

This book will be not mine but yours.

You had an almost painful need to express yourself, whether in writing, painting, dance, theater, or the movies. Your true vocation was writing. You felt that later on and you acted on it. And you also brought Marie-Jo back to life much better than I ever could.

Until tomorrow, my little girl.

2

> He was tall
> He was skinny
> With his big feet and his big nose
> He looked starved
> So tall
> So skinny
> How ridiculous he was!

Always looking a little starved, to be sure, like all Belgians who were not rich and could not buy their rations on the black market. I was a little over fourteen years old, and our family doctor had told me—as I was later to be informed erroneously about myself—that my father had only two more years before him. That time, it was correct; he had been suffering for a long time with angina pectoris, for which at the time there was no cure.

And yet that poem, of which I can't remember the rest, which I had scribbled on a bit of paper in the attic, where I hid away in spite of my immense admiration and almost adoration for my father, had a sprightly little lilt to it.

That was in the summer of 1917, and since I knew I would not be able to continue studying at the Jesuit school on Rue Saint-Gilles for the two years remaining before my *baccalauréat*, I wandered, for the most part early in the morning or late at night, through the crowded working-class streets or the greenery of the hills.

I was hungry, yes, hungry for everything, for traces of sun on the houses, for trees and faces, hungry for all the women I passed whose wiggling hips were enough to give me almost painful erections. How many times did I not satisfy that hunger with young local girls older than I in the doorways of houses on dark streets. Or else I would furtively sneak into one of those houses with a window in which a more or less fat and desirable woman sat placidly knitting, until she drew the yellowish curtain as soon as a customer came in.

Other curtains made me dream at night, when, behind their barely luminous screen, I could make out the moving shadows of a man and woman coming and going as if the couple they formed were thus sheltered from the world and its realities.

I was hungry for life, and I wandered through marketplaces gazing here at the vegetables, there at the multicolored fruit, elsewhere again at the displays of flowers.

"Big nose," yes, my little Marie-Jo, for I was inhaling life through my nostrils, through my every pore, the colors, the lights, the odors and noises of the streets.

I have already told all of this, at a different age, in another context, and this time I am evoking it for you, in whom, I am sure, it will cause certain fibers to vibrate, and for your brothers too, who knew me less well than you did.

We were poor. Not really poor, not at the very bottom of that social scale the bourgeois, the haves, the rich invent everywhere in the world, which moved me to indignation: Weren't we all human beings?

At the very bottom of the scale at that time were the factory workers, whose children my mother called "hoodlums" when they played noisily in the streets. One rung above were the artisans, for they also worked with their hands and also got dirty. We were on the rung above that, the third one. My father was a clerk, a bookkeeper, always dressed in dark clothes, dignified and immaculate. Today such people are called "white-collar" workers. In those days they were called "brain workers," because they earned their living through their minds. Had he not, contrary to what was true of his brothers, passed his Latin-Greek *baccalauréat*?

Those brain workers were, in point of fact, poorer than the artisans and the blue-collar workers. You could easily see that by going through the streets on the children's holiday, the feast of St. Nicholas, whom the Americans have turned into Santa Claus, that white-bearded Father Christmas driving his reindeer-powered sleigh across the rooftops.

In the working-class streets, I saw kids proudly playing with cars that had nickel-plated pedals, bicycles their own size, complicated building sets, whereas all I had got, in addition to the traditional gingerbread and the fruit dish with the orange in the middle, were some new tubes of paint, to replace the used-up ones in my paintbox, which dated back several years. Like you, I was crazy about painting, but all I ever did was unimaginatively copy picture postcards.

Now do you understand why, so much later, when you and your brothers opened your sumptuous Christmas presents, I sometimes involuntarily smiled nostalgically? You were rich. Nothing caused you wonderment, so you were less lucky than I had been. I was often afraid for you. I even sometimes pitied you. After all, it's lucky to be born poor and be able to appreciate a simple orange at its true value.

I worked as a clerk in a bookstore and was not ashamed to have to wait on my school chums from the Collège Saint-Servais. I became a cub reporter and was finally able to buy the bike I had been dreaming of since earliest childhood. True, my means were still very limited; I still wore clothes that looked elegant on the dummies in the store windows but began to shrink the minute it rained, so that my pants were too short, my shoulders too tight.

That was only a slight shadow cast over life, which I was embracing to the full, a life in which everything was important, the silhouette of a woman scarcely seen, the faces that went by like those of paintings in an exhibit, the yellowing of the leaves and the silky green of grasses in the sun.

Did you, did any of the four of you, know any of that, in the huge gardens that surrounded our houses and our châteaux? I would not swear to it, and I feel somewhat guilty about it. A chauffeur drove you to school and brought you back home. A nursemaid or governess was there to greet you, ready to satisfy all your desires.

What would my fate be? I did not know, and the question often filled me with distasteful anxiety.

Yet, the four of you were to know that question too. In my case, it was not attributed to "genes," but just heredity. The book written by a professor who scoured three provinces to root out my origins later informed me that my earliest known ancestors, back in the seventeenth century, were people of the land, not prosperous farmers, but laborers who rented out the strength of their arms by the week, the month, or the year.

Those are your ancestors too, at least on your paternal side. The maternal ones are important too, but, as far as my first wife, Tigy, and my second wife, from Canada, are concerned, I know much less about them.

You met Tigy at Marc's house, my little girl, and like your brothers you affectionately called her Mamiche. You probably visited her in her house at Nieul-sur-Mer, in the Charente-Maritime, near the city of La Rochelle. Do you know, my sons and my daughter, that I fixed up that very old house, which centuries before had been a priory, with the idea that one day my grandchildren would spend their vacations there? That is more or less what happened, but I am no longer there to see you, since Tigy and I got divorced, even though we remain the best of friends.

I met her . . . Well, that would seem to concern only Marc and his children, but in reality it concerns all four of you, for I am convinced that our environment and all of the contacts we have during our childhood and adolescence have an influence on our characters and our destinies.

As a reporter on the *Gazette de Liège*, I had by chance fallen in with a bunch of young art students, painters just graduated from the Academy or about to be graduated. Through them, I met a girl, Régine Renchon, whose first name displeased me, so I renamed her Tigy, which has no real meaning, certainly not that of queen.

She was rather tall, wore a brown coat of no special shape and low-heeled shoes. On her hair, which was brown too, parted in the middle and rolled into buns, a brown hat of the same material, shaped like a Basque beret. No lace, no embroidery, no frills or furbelows. She walked with long determined steps, looking neither to left nor to right, her eyes, under their heavy eyebrows, gazing straight ahead.

She had a lively intelligence, wide knowledge, especially of art, and within the small group that her friends and I made up everyone was impressed by her sharp retorts, always jolly but sometimes tinted with unmalicious irony.

Was it love at first sight? No, but I did seek out her company. I still dreamed of two shadows behind a slightly lighted blind, and it occurred to me that it would be nice some evening to be with her in the shelter of that blind, to be one of the two shadows.

Three months later, after having spent an evening a week at her studio, I got into the habit of waiting for her at nine at night outside the Academy, where she was taking a live-model nude course. I would walk her back, arm in arm, to her place by way of streets selected because they were the least brightly lighted and had the least traffic, and, although we sometimes stopped to kiss, we talked mainly about Phidias and Praxiteles, Rembrandt and Van Gogh, Plato, Villon, Spinoza, and Nietzsche.

Love? Yes, of course, but mainly an intellectual one, in which the flesh eventually played its part, but without frenzy or ecstasy.

She lived with her family in a huge, impressive house, with an entryway dating back to the time of carrriages, a great porte-cochère, old stables at the back of the courtyard, and a broad marble double stairway leading up to the main floor. The family spent most of their time on the second floor, and soon I was going up there every evening, to stay until ten.

A living room with period furniture; a young sister, Tita, with her braids still down her back, who played the piano while her father, who looked like a smug well-to-do bourgeois, turned the pages of the music for her; her mother, small and broad, always on the go; and a little girl as pretty as a Chinese porcelain, who danced all by herself and was to die very soon because she was a mongoloid.

My father-in-law-to-be had almost the same background as the Simenons. Orphaned at an early age, he had made his way as an apprentice cabinetmaker, and a neighboring family, with many children of their own, had adopted him. What was one more when there were already seven or eight and no inheritance to worry about passing on? My mother-in-law-to-be was one of those five or six children, and she fell in love with the boy her family had adopted.

The father was a most extraordinary fellow. Working as laborer or foreman in a boiler factory at Valenciennes, on the French side of the border, he had invented a new system for cleaning boilers, which had been widely adopted. Having thus become an inventor, and being able to live off the royalties of his invention, he had given up active work and spent his days sitting in his armchair, looking serious and pensive. When he was asked what he was thinking about, he would answer, "I'm inventing. . . ."

Unfortunately, he never invented anything more, and the day came when he simply had to get a job to keep the pot boiling. Since he had a fine baritone voice, he became the cantor of the parish church. By a curious coincidence, the father of my second wife, whom I will refer to as D., as I have been doing for the past fifteen years, had also been a church cantor, in Canada, shortly after his marriage.

My Renchon father-in-law, once he got married, went up the scale quickly, and when I knew him, he was the most famous decorator and maker of luxury furniture of his own design in the city. My uncle Henri-de-Tougres, Henri-the-Rich, my mother's brother, had called upon his services, as had so many others, when he furnished his château in Limbourg.

My father-in-law had four children, as I was to have four. He lost one of them, a daughter, as I lost a daughter. But did we lose her? Doesn't the missing child remain the more alive in us? That was what happened to my father-in-law. And what happened to me, my darling little girl.

I was seventeen when I met Tigy. I was eighteen when, after enlisting instead of waiting to be conscripted, I was sent to spend a freezing winter with the occupation troops in the Rote Kaserne (or Red Barracks) in Aix-la-Chapelle, where I saw women going to do their marketing with a wheelbarrow full of hundred-, then thousand-, and eventually million-mark bills, whereas we, my fellow soldiers and I, with our close-shorn heads, could dine in the most expensive restaurants on our daily pay of twenty-five Belgian centimes.

Every day, with frozen fingers, I wrote a long letter to Tigy, sometimes two, and I suppose she kept them. They were a hymn to love, because my heart was running over with it. I later understood that it was a hymn to woman, rather than to one person in particular. I confess that I would enjoy rereading those feverish phrases, probably the most romantic I have ever written in my life.

In order not to remain separated from Tigy, I put in for and got a transfer to Liège, to the Lancers Barracks, less than a quarter of a mile from my mother's home, and every evening, at eight o'clock, I was able to climb the two flights that led to my future in-laws' living room.

My father died while I, in Antwerp on an assignment for the *Gazette*, was making love to a distant cousin of mine in a house of assignation. When I got back, I found Tigy and her father waiting for me at the train, to break the news gently to me.

My father was laid out, fully dressed, with his hands crossed on his chest, and I had to make an effort to bring my lips to his cold brow.

I was nineteen. A few months later, I left Liège for Paris, where I had been promised a job as secretary to a writer, very famous at the time but forgotten today.

I am not forgetting, Marie-Jo, that this is your book, and consequently your brothers' book too. I apologize for having gone so far back into my past. I think it was necessary, even if I have dwelt on a few things I have said before. Even though many years went by before the birth of your eldest brother, Marc, whom you were so often to run to for comfort, I am now at last about to get around to him.

Good night, little girl.

3

A poorly lighted railroad-station platform, at night, in Liège, with fog to make it more dramatic. On the platform, Tigy and her father, whose faces and good-bye waves were a blur to me through the moist, dirty windows. It was December 14, 1922, a date that must seem terribly long ago to you but to me seems very recent.

As day broke, the outskirts of Paris, houses rising like cliffs on either side of the tracks, poor, gray houses, most of which had lights in the windows, in which common people were dressing hurriedly so as to rush toward their day's work. The Gare du Nord, a horrible station, in which I don't know how many trains poured out their human cargo; half asleep and cranky, they headed in droves toward the doors.

It was raining, and before long the icy water had gone through my cotton raincoat and my worn-out soles. My fake-leather suitcase, with all my worldly goods in it, was heavy and made me lean to one side as I walked. "Madame, would you have a room available, not too expensive?" "Full up."

Every place in Paris hotels was filled up in this postwar period.

As I looked around, there were buildings different from the ones I was used to, an astounding amount of traffic—streetcars, hansom cabs, and taxis all intermingled. A long sloping street. Five, six, maybe ten more or less appealing hotels.

"Full up," the answer came each time, dry and impersonal, and the wet cold went through me more and more.

A circular intersection. A boulevard to the left, Rochechouart, whose name I knew from novels. So this was Montmartre! A dirty, gray Montmartre.

A windmill across the boulevard. The Moulin Rouge. Empty, closed cabarets with names like the Dead Rat, and Heaven and Hell . . . Place Pigalle. Place Blanche. I dragged along, my hand getting numb from that suitcase, but I felt happy.

Place Clichy. The Brasserie Weber, where so many painters and, especially, famous writers had sat on the terrace. In December, there was no terrace and, through the rain, you couldn't even see the lights inside.

Boulevard des Batignolles. Bringing back an old refrain heard on the street corners of Liège: "Maria, Maria, the terror of the Batignolles . . ."

A street on the right with a hotel sign. "Excuse me, sir, would you . . ." Yes, there was a free room, up under the eaves, a floor above where the red carpet on the stairs ended.

I put down my load. I rush to the address sent me by the writer whose secretary I was supposed to become. At the end of a cul-de-sac, a small stunted house. The door is wide open. A voice calls down to me from the top of the stairs, "Come on up!"

All gray, all dirty, all dull, like certain government offices open to the public. Two young women, a man with a flushed face and red hair, another, older, better turned out, with a small brown mustache.

He introduces himself. "Captain T. . . ."

"I came for the job of . . ."

"Oh, you're the young Belgian? Do you speak French?"

I was never to be the writer's secretary. One of the two young women with long, madonnalike faces has that job, and what they are looking for now is an office boy. So much for my dreams. I'm happy enough to be in Paris and earning my way, unlike so many of the other young men and girls whom trains from the provinces spew forth every day in the capital's railway stations.

Paris! That is all that matters.

"You'll be paid six hundred francs a month."

"Yes, sir."

"Call me Captain."

In reality I have been hired to work for an extreme right-wing political league, of which my novelist is the president. He lives on the ground floor.

They show me the place. A kitchen table covered by wrapping paper stuck on with thumbtacks. Two hours later, I am admitted into the holy of holies, and a fat man with a hoarse voice, a monocle in his eye, gives me the once-over.

"You the little Belgian?"

"Yes, sir."

"Captain T. will be your boss. I've read your references."

A noble sweep of the hand to show me the door. I would only one more time enter this room, which, for the people upstairs, who now include me, has something sacred about it.

I'm hungry. I'm always going to be hungry; this time not because of war or occupation, but because all I earn is six hundred francs a month and I've promised my mother two hundred and fifty. I get along mostly on bread, Camembert cheese, or tripe *à la mode de Caen*, the greasy gravy of which helps wash down quite a lot of bread.

At the corner of Boulevard des Batignolles, a big food store attracts me like a magnet. A whole windowful of cold dishes, lobster salads, halves of crayfish in aspic or mayonnaise, dishes of assorted cold cuts, and, my face pressed against the windowpane, I salivate the way my horses did, back in the barracks, after an outing.

Someday . . .

I am not ambitious. I never will be during my whole career, which starts off so humbly. I am happy, today, for that more than modest start, which drew me closer to the common people of my hometown neighborhood. I did not detrain at the Gare du Nord "to conquer Paris," as one of my fellow Belgians so proudly told me he had, only to leave France and his great hopes behind two months later. I came because . . . In truth, mainly because Tigy is a painter and wants to immerse herself in the atmosphere of Montparnasse, where, in those days, you rubbed elbows with all the painters in the world.

We met them at the Dôme, at the Jockey, and some of them, Vlaminck, Derain, Kisling, Picasso, were to become friends of ours.

Before that, two months of weighing and stamping letters and packages, carrying them to the post office, addressing envelopes to league members, for use in case of emergency meetings. For instance, to discuss strikes, such as the Métro and streetcar strike, when the military engineering students of the Ecole Polytechnique, in uniforms and white gloves, manned the throttles until the strikers had to come back to work.

My novelist summons me again to the holy of holies.

"How would you like to become private secretary to one of our great friends who has just lost his father? He is the bearer of one of the great names in French history and . . ."

Okay. I ring the bell at his home, an impressive town house on elegant Rue La Boétie. A concierge in livery. A huge vestibule furnished with real period furniture. A sitting room through the door of which I can see a ballroom that can accommodate two hundred people, with gilded chairs and settees all around and chandeliers whose crystal pendants, tarnished by time, begin to tinkle when I take a timid step toward them.

I am no longer in the present, but in a past I had pictured only through Saint-Simon, Stendhal, and Balzac. Everything goes back at least to Louis XIII, and then from Louis to Louis till the one who lost his head. "If monsieur will come with me." A valet, youthful and blond, still with a country smell about him, although decked out in black trousers and a starched white jacket, shows me into another room, which could be an office, where I find a handsome man with an open face, a bit past forty-five, with some white hairs at the temples. It is eleven in the morning, and he is in a silk dressing gown, over lighter silk pajamas, and looking at me rather welcomingly.

"Not married, I suppose?"

"I'll be getting married in March."

His face darkens.

"I travel a great deal, and my secretary has to go with me. I spend parts of each year in one or another of my châteaux."

He is not showing off. To him, that's natural. His family, the de Tracys, has been noble since the thirteenth century. He himself, born a viscount, became a count when his elder brother was killed in the war, and now a marquis at the recent death of his father.

"I wouldn't want to be taking a wife along. . . ."

"My wife-to-be and I are mainly just good friends. She is a painter and has to think of her career."

"In that case, I'll take you on, for a trial period. But you'll have to promise me . . ." I promise.

I buy the secondhand tuxedo of a young fellow from Liège, now in Paris, destined to become a king's prosecutor, then a member of the Belgian Academy, which he will force me to join one day too, and where he will sponsor me.

A very modest wedding ceremony, despite the Renchons' impressive home. Three carriages outside the door. Tigy and her father are in the first, her mother and grandmother in the second, my mother and I in the third. On the way, I have nothing to say to my mother, who is sniffling, and, in order to try to cheer her up, I explain to her how in France they fry potatoes in oil instead of lard.

Church of Sainte-Véronique. No organ march. Just the usual habitués scattered among the pews. The Renchons are atheists and Emile Zola is their god.

Actually, the Renchons' son, Yvan, his wife, and Tita must have been there too, but I don't remember them.

Never having been baptized, Tigy had to take three weeks of private catechism lessons. She was baptized yesterday, and early this morning took her first communion, so now she can have a religious wedding such as my mother demanded. That is why, unbeliever though I am, I made sure, children, that all four of you were baptized.

A crowd at the city hall for the civil ceremony, because here I am Little Sim, the reporter who for three years covered that beat with rather tart reports. My colleagues are all there. A deputy mayor officiates, making a somewhat rambling speech, at times slipping into Walloon, and pronounces us man and wife. My colleagues have chipped in to buy us a big red-and-white cut-glass heart.

Carriages. This time I am with Tigy and not with my mother, who must be in a carriage with some of the members of the enemy clan. She never cared for the Renchons, or for Tigy. "My lord, Georges, how ugly she is!" she exclaimed after I had introduced my fiancée to her.

And as for those people in the fine town house on Rue Louvrex, "they're just *grandiveux*"—a Walloon word that means something like "upstarts." But it wasn't my father-in-law's fault that he had acquired the stature people attribute to the upper bourgeoisie and his profession required him to wear suits made by fine tailors.

Luncheon for ten at most, just the family. My mother's eyes are red, though at times she squeezes out a forced smile. The conversation is full of embarrassing holes.

Fortunately, Tigy and I are taking the afternoon train, and for the first time we get to go into her bedroom to change. Outside the door, we can hear the heavy breathing of my father-in-law, who adores all his children, but Tigy especially.

Unlike me, he dreamed of turning each of his children into an artist, and the strange thing is, he succeeded.

Yvan, who was ten years or so older than I and was an architect, was one of the first, at least in Belgium, to study the structural resistance of reinforced concrete, at a time when other architects were still concerned only with its aesthetic aspects. He pondered the then poorly understood problem of soundproofing, which won him the job of architect to Queen Elisabeth, the wife of King Albert, a great patroness of artists, especially musicians, for she herself was a violinist.

Yvan was the one who erected a huge building with soundproof studios for her foundation. Every year, it took in a batch of promising young musicians, who could study there and give concerts in auditoriums of various sizes without any financial worries.

Yvan lived long enough—he died ten years ago or so—to see his son, whom I was very fond of, also become an architect and, I have been told, a highly regarded one.

For Tigy, eldest of the daughters, there was painting, the Academy of Fine Arts, exhibitions. Does she still paint? I have no idea; she never discusses it in the friendly letters she writes me.

Tita, whom I was secretly in love with, won a first prize at the Conservatory and later gave piano concerts in many cities and on French radio. She married a piano tuner, the son of a police superintendent—O Maigret! She turned to giving lessons as she got older and, once widowed, settled somewhere in Touraine.

The last time we saw one another was in Liège, when I went there with Teresa. Her husband was still alive, which did not keep us from hugging each other tenderly in a café. Teresa and she looked at each other with more than understanding, a kind of complicity, and exchanged affectionate smiles.

My marquis turned out to be a real fairy-tale nobleman, with several châteaux throughout France, vineyards in the Loire country, forests, fields, and tenanted farms (twenty-eight around one of the châteaux), landholdings near Paris, rice fields in Italy, a huge Islamic-style villa in Tunisia, town houses in various cities, and who knows what else.

Until his father died, he had spent most of his time at the Jockey Club, hunting, and attending parties in aristocratic châteaux, since over the centuries his family, through a series of brilliant matches, had become related to all the old nobility of France and other countries.

The death of his father left him with a mass of paperwork and other problems of which he understood nothing. And I, at twenty, was supposed to get him out of the mess.

First stop: Aix-les-Bains, where he took the cure each year and where at great expense he had had set up the kind of bungalow the British Army used in India. Of course, Tigy was along, unknown to him, but I alone went with him to fish for char in the lake.

Then to a château, the oldest, smallest one, surrounded by a famous vineyard, but filled with books piled up over the centuries, which delighted me.

Tigy was there too, in a very good inn, on the opposite bank of the Loire.

Yet I was writing, for I had a need to write, just as I had been writing before I left Paris. But now I was writing to make a living, to earn some food, and what I wrote was not literature but little stories for the risqué weeklies, *Le Rire*, *La Vie parisienne*, *Sourire*, *Sans Gêne*, and eventually for the big daily *Le Matin*, at which I was to meet and become a friend of the great Colette.

"Too literary, my little Sim," she would tell me. "Make it simpler, simpler, and simpler. . . ."

She whose writing was as elegant as the tendrils of a grapevine!

Another château, the one with the twenty-eight sharecropped farms, forests full of game, and ponds that had to be emptied each year to get rid of tons of carp and pike.

Up to me to organize the hunting dinners, to place each person exactly where his rank dictated, because those people are ticklish on that point; and the huge morning buffets, while the beaters waited, the ten game wardens stood at attention at the foot of the porch, and the dogs barked.

Little did I dream that someday I would have my own big-game preserve, in the Orléans forest, that I would be disgusted from the first day, after finishing off a wounded young deer, and that, under the terms of the bill of sale, I had to hold at least one hunt a week for a year, though not necessarily in person, thank God! I was replaced for the occasion by my good pal Maurice Constantin-Weyer.

Phone calls, sometimes at night, to a banker in Paris, London, or elsewhere, with whom the marquis wanted to discuss some financial deal that had just occurred to him.

In this way I learned that a well-born gentleman doesn't pay the bills from Cartier, Van Cleef & Arpels, his tailor, or his wife's couturière before being dunned for a year or two. And also that bills from small suppliers or artisans get paid only after some delay, and then only after crossing out the figures with a red pencil and replacing them with others ten or twenty percent lower. "Those people inflate their prices because of our name. . . ."

I learned that there were, that perhaps there still are, very rare first editions of Pascal and other famous authors in the unexplored libraries handed down from fathers to sons through the centuries.

I learned a great many things in two years, and, although I rather liked my marquis, he would sometimes lapse into a Talleyrand smile, because I remained unshakably the little boy from Outremeuse, that special, separate area across the river from the heart of Liège, and my rebellions were therefore the more violent.

I needed to be in Paris to get on with my little stories, to sell them, to try, perhaps, even to write "dime novels" or "potboilers."

Tigy was always along, incognito, sometimes a dozen miles away, and

I biked over to spend the night with her and was back at the château at eight in the morning. I don't recall that the marquis ever met her.

He and I parted good friends, and I was to see him again several times, on a different level, once even when I went to try to buy one of his châteaux, of course only one of the smallest ones.

Good night, Marie-Jo, and good night, boys.

4

As far as I can go back in my memory, I always find an unsatisfied hunger to know everything about whatever lives or does not live. I wanted to be not just myself, so young and insignificant, but all people, those of the land and of the sea, the blacksmith, the gardener, the bricklayer, and all those to be found on the different rungs of the well-known social ladder.

To learn my trade, which I was just getting into, I forced myself through the apprenticeship everyone must have—virtuosos doing their scales or professional athletes spending years developing their muscles and reflexes. I wonder today, at seventy-seven, whether my whole life was not spent learning and doing scales, both studying in the university of the streets and reading all available books until I was dizzy.

Here, again, I find the joy of expressing myself, although with the same anxiety I experienced for sixty years—no longer by way of a typewriter, or a tape recorder—I find again, I say, in using a pen, that same exaltation, as if life were starting all over again.

Barely a week ago, one of my foreign readers, who told me he had read everything I had written, found himself at odds with his son and asked me to referee, by answering just one question: "Is work a joy or, on the contrary, a punishment inflicted upon us which we accept only with sullen rebellion?"

As against the Bible, which has the God of the Jews and the Christians saying, "Thou shalt earn thy bread by the sweat of thy brow," I answered that work brings us both joy and pride, provided, however, that we had the good sense or good luck to choose work that interests and absorbs us, which, unfortunately, is not given to everyone in our society.

You know something of that, my darling, you who tried so early to adapt to several disciplines, and who, after giving them up at times, still went back to them during your last days.

I told you, at the beginning of these notebooks, that I would speak of you and your environment, especially of your mother and your brothers.

But before getting around to everything you wrote during your short but very full existence, I believe I have to situate you and bring out everything that made you into the exceptional being you were, that you continue to be for me and no doubt for several others. So I need to tell you and your brothers in all frankness what I was, because the image that each of us conceives of his parents is necessarily incomplete.

Some of my confidences are not new. I have often spoken of myself in my books, even through the characters of my novels. More and more people have read everything I've written. Yet their letters prove to me that they did not all conceive the same image of me.

So, what about the others? What about you four?

You, for one, really read and even reread everything, making notes in the margins, and the questions you asked me, your comments, prove to me that you were always trying to understand me. As for your three brothers, I don't know what they may have read, because they are men, and men show a certain resistance toward asking questions and revealing themselves in confidences. They saw me with their children's and adolescents' eyes. They did not choose the images indelibly imprinted on their brains, and now it is more difficult for them to open up before an old man.

Don't be afraid, Marie-Jo darling; I won't go on long talking about myself, however much of a joy it is for me to chat with the four of you without constraint. I will try to give an overview of what you have not known, what you know only partially about my life, not by following the calendar, but providing you with some quick images, some simple sketches of what, to my mind, counted.

I had got as far as my marquis, whom I left to take flight, as I had taken flight from Liège, toward adventure. He taught me a great deal, in a discreetly affectionate way.

Just one more image, which will remind all of you of some of my reactions. For a time, in Liège, mixing with young painters, with art students, I had affected a floppy broad-brimmed black hat, big loose bow tie, also black, and let my then heavy, wavy hair grow long. Wasn't that putting on a kind of uniform, and do I not have an instinctive distrust of all uniforms, as also of all medals, diplomas, titles, and honors?

Now, at the marquis's, I had again let my hair grow long, although only moderately in terms of yesterday's and the day before yesterday's hippies. One evening when he and I were having dinner alone in one of his town houses—we both had a penchant for kippered herrings, which we ordered from his butler more often than was decent—he came close and, with a paternal gesture, slightly raised the blond curls that hung down the back of my neck. I can't say that his gesture was sarcastic or scornful, but I understood that it meant "Really, do you need all that?"

The next day, I went to the barber.

For my part, I also felt something about him that would not have made him happy. He had inherited a newspaper in the former province of Berry. Then, this man of the past, who lived surrounded by his glorious ancestors and dealt only with his peers, decided, at forty-five, that he wanted to become a senator. Why? True, one of his ancestors had been a peer of France, but that was when there was a king. What he was going after was a political position, in a republic more democratic than it is now. And I wrote—for his signature—campaign articles—until he realized that he hadn't the slightest chance of getting elected.

Small weakness of one of us; small weakness of the other.

A tiny hotel room on Rue des Dames, in the populous Batignolles quarter, once again. This time, there were two of us, not exactly to go hungry, but to do without a great many things. Tigy, who had never had to cook, heated, on a window-sill hot plate, dishes we bought precooked, since a sign at the foot of the stairs warned tenants that they were forbidden to do any cooking in their rooms on pain of immediate expulsion.

My stories were becoming more numerous, and, not being able to afford to buy it, I had rented a clickety old typewriter. I increased the number of my pen names as the papers I contributed to grew in number, and we were able quite often to go to Montparnasse to rub elbows with the painters everyone was talking about and to visit the galleries on Rue du Faubourg-Saint-Honoré and Rue La Boétie.

How many pictures I fell in love with and would have liked to buy! Even the cheapest were too much for my purse, and some of them today are to be found only in museums or are worth fortunes.

My time had not yet come. I didn't have a proper calling card. I could not even tell the world I was writing, because I was still an apprentice, writing little stories signed Gom Gut, Plick and Plock, Poum and Zette, or Aramis, which collectors fight over now that I am an old man.

• • •

I worked very fast. I sometimes wrote as many as eight stories in a day, and we were thus able to rent one huge room and a smaller one on the ground floor of one of the magnificent buildings on one-time Place Royale, which, during the French Revolution, was renamed Place des Vosges.

A short vacation by the sea, in Normandy, where we visit a newly made woman friend who has a house there as lovely and naïve as a child's toy. She has no guest room, but she won't let us go and insists that we spend our vacation in her village near Etretat. So we rent an empty room in a farm-house.

We have no furniture and are not about to buy any, not even a bed, for just a few weeks. No matter: I ask the farmer's wife, who spoke old Norman, to let us have two or three bundles of straw, which Tigy and I spread on the bare floor. She lends us a pair of sheets, an unpainted table, a single chair, and there we are, set up for several months, because your mother and I, Marc, are so happy there that we decide to stay on awhile.

The farmers wonder whether we haven't just come out of prison, since we are comfortable sleeping on straw. Our two little windows have no curtains, so the farmer's daughter and her girl friends—including the one who was to become Boule and join our family, of which today she is the center even more than I—come after dark to watch us make love and then watch me wash afterward at a basin just in front of the window.

"What do you think it looks like?" they ask, and think it over.

Then they agree. "Like a mushroom."

Boule, whose name is Henriette, worked for our friend a few hours a day. At thirteen or fourteen, she had left school to work as a nursemaid at the château. Yet she remained quite unaware of the facts of life, apart from the "mushroom," and I soon felt curiosity, affection, and desire for her. When, in the fall, we returned to Place des Vosges, she went with us, and the three of us were to live together in greatest intimacy.

Tigy was uncompromisingly jealous and informed me that the day she found out I was unfaithful to her she would commit suicide. I lived for twenty years with that threat hanging over me.

Boule and I, during those first years, were only half unfaithful to her, then three-quarters, then nine-tenths, for the three of us were living in two rooms.

I have always avoided, and still avoid, in spite of the change of moral standards that has occurred since my adolescence, depriving an innocent girl

20

of what her husband someday might hope to have given to him. As if it were a right, without any counterpart, to be sure.

You must be laughing, my little Pierre, who now stand six foot two and some but who are the youngest of the family, you who have the same need for women as I but who are lucky enough to be living in a time when all those complications have vanished.

I had sex with virgins only three times in my life. The first was Tigy. The second, Boule, in the old château in the Orléans forest where we lived during the thirties. The third was a young girl with firm breasts, with whom I had the most tender of relationships and who today is one of Teresa's and my best friends.

When I explained my reticence to her, despite the unfulfilled sex we had had together, she laughed, with the fine, warm, and witty laugh she has retained through the years, and three or four days later, as we were hugging one another, she triumphantly announced: "Now, you can."

I understood. In order to overcome my scruples, she had gone to the trouble of getting herself deflowered, and I don't even know by whom.

Place des Vosges. Tigy at last had room in which to paint. At that time, on Place Constantin-Pecqueur in Montmartre, they used to hold what was called the "Foire aux Croûtes" (Junk Art Fair), an open-air show in which young artists hung their canvases or drawings from trees or from lines strung between the trees.

To make them attractive to eventual buyers, the works had to be framed, and I used to go to Rue de Bondy to buy framing wood by the meter. Then to the saw, glue, and nails. They weren't always quite right angles, but who cared? For those petty bourgeois who went from painter to painter, wasn't all that mattered the discovery of the future Renoir or Modigliani, who would make a fortune for them?

As for models, we found them in the low-down *bals musette* of Rue de Lappe, not yet a part of the standard Paris-by-Night tour. These, as well as a joint in La Villette, were where the gigolos and gigolettes, as they were called, got together, the real members of "the life," girls, often very young, who, barely arrived in Paris from their provincial homes, had been turned out on the sidewalks of Boulevard Sébastopol, with the nightly reward of being allowed to dance the java with their pimps. We would take them home, the women to pose nude, less often the men, whose faces were those of real toughs, and Tigy would sketch them in charcoal.

• • •

"You look so tense," Tigy said to me once at Place Constantin-Pec-queur. "Go sit down some place in a café, or take a walk. You're scaring the customers away."

I took her advice, sat down on a terrace on Rue Caulaincourt, and wrote my first dime novel, *Le Roman d'une dactylo* (A Stenog's Romance),* not without first having read several that the same publisher had brought out, to find out how they were done.

The publisher Ferenczi accepted it and ordered more from me, of various lengths and types. Because I was still writing at a very rapid clip, I spread my business among the four or five companies in Paris specializing in this type of book.

Each collection had its own taboos. In some, the word "mistress" was forbidden, and in none did couples "make love," but "their lips met," or, if you were very daring, you could picture them in "an embrace."

There were collections especially aimed at the young, and the ency-clopedic *Grand Larousse*, which I had succeeded in buying, told me all I had to know about the flora and fauna of a given area of Africa, Asia, or South America, as well as about the native tribes. *Se Ma Tsien—le Sacrifi-cateur* (Se Ma Tsien, the Sacrificer), *Le Sous-marin dans la forêt* (The Sub-marine in the Forest), and so many, many more titles. The whole world was my oyster, and the universe of *Grand Larousse* was certainly exciting to write about.

Love stories for shopgirls, full of misfortunes. But lots of love and marriage at the end. *La Fiancée aux mains de glace* (The Fiancée with Icy Hands), *Miss Baby*, for I had become the "friend," as those novels put it, of Josephine Baker, whom I would have married had I not, even though still unknown, recoiled from becoming just Mr. Baker. I even went with Tigy to the island of Aix, off La Rochelle, to try to forget her, and we were not to see each other again until thirty years later, in New York, still both as much in love with the other as ever.

Up to eighty typewritten pages of these novels a day, so that we were almost becoming rich, compared with what we had been.

A free apartment on the third floor of our building, and we rent it, while keeping the ground floor to become Tigy's studio.

The 1925 Exposition of Decorative Arts fascinates us, and I order from an avant-garde decorator there the décor and furnishings of our new place.

---

*If a work has not been published in English, a literal translation of the French title is given in roman type (as here); if the work has been published in English, the title under which the work appeared in English is given in italics. —PUBLISHER

Stand-up bar covered with frosted glass that was lighted from below by any number of bulbs, so that having cocktails, when there were a number of us, was like a fireworks display.

Me as bartender, in a white turtleneck sweater, grabbing the bottles one after the other to make the proper mixtures. Some representatives from Montparnasse, from Foujita to Vertès too—but why enumerate them? Sometimes Josephine herself, in all her glory, some Russian ballerinas, the daughter of an Asian ambassador, and at three in the morning a certain number of naked bodies with others stretched out on the black velvet cushions on which they would spend the rest of the night, while at 6:00 A.M. I would settle down to my typewriter for my daily eighty pages . . .

Then Porquerolles, where at the time there were only a few summer people and where we are able to spend several months thanks to Tigy's having sold a large nude to an Armenian art lover for eight hundred francs. And there, for me, going from rock to rock at the edge of the absolutely transparent water, contemplation, the fascination of the life of fishes and other marine animals, always on the alert, always on the lookout.

Multicolored fishes not intended only for bouillabaisse, crabs, morays, congers, and rays, an infinite fauna without a second's respite, eating those smaller than they, or eaten by those larger. A permanent drama, in the water made iridescent by the sun, which always made my head spin.

And me, not getting the promised overdue money order from one or the other of my publishers, spending a week sucking on an empty pipe, for want of the thirty or forty centimes to buy myself some tobacco.

The endless struggle for life, in a word!

Porquerolles, where I was to have my house and my boats, has remained one of the high places of my life. I knew every one of its hundred and thirty inhabitants at the time. I felt at home. I have been told the island has so changed since the war that I don't dare go back.

Touring France by way of its rivers and canals. Tigy, Boule, our dog, Olaf (a Great Dane), and me on board a little boat with a tent to shelter Boule at night, which, come morning, would become my office. My typewriter on a folding table. My backside on a folding chair. And a canoe, dragging behind, holding our mattresses, our supplies, and our cookware.

A page out of my life, but when they're written down, pages have a way of becoming unbearably long.

Good night, little girl. Good night, you three big fellows, my sons.

5

If the sea with its intense life overwhelmed me, it also conquered me, and for a long time I would think only of it. Not of a place on the sand, under the sun, between almost naked bodies shiny with suntan oil, not the sea of the many-colored parasols, the casinos, and the big concrete cubes with their large bay windows, but the primitive and eternal sea from which all life came, with its languors and its furies, its primordial cruelty. The sea!

I who had lived nineteen years on the concrete of an industrial town almost Nordic in character had seen it, or, rather, sensed it, like a postcard, only at Ostend during a brief trip. Now I am filled with a passion for it that has taken hold of all of me, and just as soon as I am back in Paris I decide to have a boat built, a real one, that can stand up to the sea.

This is not to be one of those time-passing playthings the graceful sweep of whose white sails can be watched from afar, even less one of those little affairs with powerful motors, leaving a wake of foam behind, that can turn your head with their speed. Such boats don't caress the sea, but seem to tear it wrathfully apart. What I am dreaming of, what I want, is a robust boat, slightly sprawling, like those of the northern fishermen, big enough for the four of us, Tigy, Boule, Olaf, and me, to live on.

I rush to Fécamp, where, even from the railroad station, you can smell the strong aroma of cod and herring, and where there are still a few sailing Newfoundlanders among the black metal hulls bumping together in the port awaiting the signal to be off. Boule's home village is only a few miles away, atop its white cliff. Her father lived through a score of campaigns into Newfoundland waters on a schooner that made it back to home port only after eight months at sea. Eleven times, following his return home, he left his wife with child before going again, on the shorter herring campaign, which starts to the north of the British coast and follows the fish's annual exodus southward toward Fécamp.

I don't stay at a hotel, but in a café at the port, frequented by sailors, where there are two or three primitive rooms for rent. By day, I am at the shipyard, working out the details of my boat with the builder. It will be made of thick oak, with a rather short mast, so that the heavy cashew-colored sails can be raised by one man alone.

In Paris, without neglecting my stories and dime novels, I bury myself in the *Coastal Captain's Manual* and the tables of logarithms, the usefulness of which escaped me when they were taught in school and I refused to study them. In the almost provincial atmosphere of Place des Vosges at the time, I familiarize myself with the use of the mariner's compass and sextant, the yearbook of tides, logbooks and drift calculations, how to improvise a wheel in case of accident, and, finally and foremost, the handling of sails. Even though my boat is to have an auxiliary motor to facilitate the way in and out of ports.

No white hull, no sails made to look like gulls for the people lying on the beach to admire as they go gracefully by. Heavy, solid stuff, rubberized sails, reddish-brown, to resist the brutal assault of a squall and the onset of deterioration.

Sometimes I go to Fécamp alone, sleeping there for two or three nights, which I devote to my passion for women, as great as my recent love of the sea.

The boat begins to take shape, and, because it has the roughness of our distant ancestor, I baptize it the *Ostrogoth*. It has bunks without springs, a table with a faucet connected to the reservoir of drinking water, a short, stocky coal-burning stove, on which Boule will do the cooking for nearly two years, and only later will I find out that those two years are to change my life.

We bought yellow slickers, half-hip boots with wooden soles, waterproof hats.

We were not playing games, the day we sailed out of port, all flags flying, for the sea has its traditions too.

Le Havre. Up the Seine to Rouen, making our way between freighters that look like mountains to us. The Seine as far as Paris, where we tie up at the tip of Vert-Galant, right in the middle of Pont-Neuf, and get our boat christened, out of respect for tradition, by the curé of Notre-Dame, while a great crowd of gapers and friends looks on. Three days of living it up, drinking and carousing, the boat mobbed from hold to top deck, and never knowing whom you might be sharing your bunk with.

Time to leave. Through the canals, we get to the Meuse, to Belgium, for a short stopover in Liège. Holland. Maestricht. The flat country that Brel sang so well about, but no better than you, Marie-Jo, when, even at your last visit, so near the time when you left for good, sitting on the arm of my chair, you brought tears to my eyes.

The flat country, you see, Belgian and Dutch Limbourg, is where my roots were. On my mother's as well as my father's side. The sky there is immense, for want of any hills. The distance is more distant than anywhere else, what with the white and red spots of the little houses that look like toys so far apart.

Wider and wider canals, and ocean-going boats. Amsterdam, which I was to take the three of you to, for Pierre wasn't born yet. The Zuider Zee, then really a sea, for it had not yet been padlocked behind a colossal dike, to gain more arable land and leave it only a lake. In the middle of the Zuider Zee, we were unable to see land, for the first time, and, sails swelling, we headed for Friesland, for the little port of Staveren, where we were going to spend the winter. Soon, every morning we had to break the ice away with a pike to keep the wood from cracking under its pressure.

We reached Delfzijl, at the estuary of the Ems, and then the great German port of Emden. The city welcomed us cordially, even though we flew a French flag because a boat flies the flag of the country in which it was built.

Wilhelmshaven, already high up in the North Sea, the old war port in which a hundred-odd disarmed German submarines were slowly rusting away. Why not tie up to one of those wrecks, since I didn't find a berth at the wharves? Alas, the port police saw us and severely enjoined us to follow them to another mooring spot. There were students parading by on the quays, and Boule's unmistakably feminine shape inevitably caught their eyes.

I was working. For *Détective*, a magazine published by Gallimard, under the editorship of my two friends the Kessel brothers, Joseph (Jef to his friends) and Georges, I was writing a series of mystery stories for which readers were supposed to guess the solutions. "Thirteen Mysteries," the first series, brought so much mail to the magazine that mailmen had to haul it in by the sackful, and more than forty people had to be hired to check the answers.

Jef asked me for another series of thirteen, which he wanted harder to figure out, so they would have fewer answers to choose among: "Thirteen Enigmas." Followed by the even-harder-to-guess "Thirteen Culprits."

One evening, as Tigy and I were asleep in our bunks, Boule was dancing on deck with I don't know how many students, and a professor who happened to walk by took offense, for World War I had not been over so very long. He ordered them, in a rough sergeant's tone, to leave the boat on the double. Which they did not do. Unfortunately, since we had been planning to go on to Hamburg, and then perhaps to Belgium.

The next morning, a plain-clothes inspector from some police force or other came aboard to interrogate me, for two hours. My typewriter was an especially suspicious-looking object to him. He demanded to be shown what I was writing. I have no idea whether he could read French, but he led me away to a big building with dark walls, where, after a long wait, I was confronted by what seemed a very important functionary.

"Are you French?" he asked.

"No. Belgian."

"Then why are you flying a French flag?"

I explained it to him.

"Why did you come in to Wilhelmshaven? Since the end of the war not a single French boat has put in here."

I kept trying to make sense out of the questions he threw at me, often unexpectedly, since he kept craftily switching the subject.

"And how does it happen that you receive telegrams that are signed 'Detective'?"

This one spoke French well, in spite of his accent. He had probably been part of the occupation forces.

"Are you a detective?"

"No. That's a weekly that publishes crime stories."

"Then, are you a policeman?"

"No, but I write stories about detectives."

"Why?"

"Because I get orders for them."

"In other words, you are carrying out orders?"

This was my first experience of the third degree, and I was sweating abundantly. I remember that he pressed a button, and an employee came rushing in to take down a short text he dictated to him. Was it a warrant for my arrest? Was I going to get locked up in one of those German prisons that French papers so obligingly described in lurid detail? What about my wife? And Boule, and Olaf, and my *Ostrogoth*?

The important character sucked on his cigar in silence, as he eyed me with curiosity, and I kept quiet too. I was not quite twenty-five, and I looked younger. What was he thinking about as he stared at me with his light eyes? The employee came back and handed him several copies of a typed statement. He shoved one of them toward me.

"Sign it."

"But I understand only a little German."

"Where did you learn it?"

"At school, in Liège. But I wasn't very good in German."

"Because you don't like our language?"

Finally, I signed the thing. He then signed it too, and rubber-stamped it two or three times. Another copy to be signed, and then another. He got up and announced to me in a toneless voice, which this time seemed almost kind, that I was under orders to be out of German waters by that evening.

"But, that's impossible! I have to fill up with water and gas and lay in supplies."

"I'll close my eyes until tomorrow noon. I'm advising the port authorities. Tomorrow noon, don't forget!"

And the next day at noon, there I was, waiting for the raising of the huge bridge, which was being crossed by streetcars, autos, trucks, and a cloud of bicycles. The center of the gigantic bridge finally began to rise, and I slipped humbly out among the boats that, like mine, were taking advantage of the tide. Where to go? I was no longer allowed to sail in German waters. I didn't dare to go on the high seas to continue our voyage north; that would have meant going up to Norway through straits that were always rough and often covered with haze.

We headed back to Delfzijl, where I discovered that my boat, which had been built of green wood, instead of the wood several years old I had been promised, now needed recaulking. Which meant that the *Ostrogoth* would be drydocked, and men dressed in white outfits would, for an indeterminate time, be stuffing oakum between the planks of the deck and between the boards of the hull with great blows from their hammers, making our comfortable cabin resound like the inside of a bell, and then spreading burning tar over all the cracks.

Other boats, alongside ours, were undergoing the same sort of noisy treatment, and yet I considered it would be humiliating to go to a hotel. Besides, I needed to write, just as I needed to when I was fifteen and still need to at seventy-seven.

In the evening, calm returned. The caulkers went home, and we could have dinner and sleep in peace, provided we got up early enough in the morning. We were used to doing that.

I found the solution as I wandered around the port. Beyond a dam, I discovered a stagnant-water canal, which was no longer used for anything but to float out from inland the tree trunks that covered almost the whole width of it, and an old abandoned barge at the edge of a green-decked quay spotted with little pink and white houses.

I apologize, children, for having taken so long, but for me, and for you too, these apparently insignificant events are of great importance.

In the half-rotted barge, in which rats merrily swam, I brought together some old crates, set up my typewriter on the highest one, sat on one just below that, and rested my feet on a still lower one, barely above the level of the stagnant water. Two days later, I began a novel, which might be a dime novel like the others, or perhaps something else. It turned out to be *Piotr-le-Letton (Maigret and the Enigmatic Lett)*, in which for the first time there appears one Maigret, who, I didn't know then, was to haunt me for so many years and turn my whole life around.

Two years later, when these novels began to appear on a monthly basis, I would no longer be an apprentice, but a novelist, a full-fledged professional. And two years beyond that, I was to free myself from the detective novel and write the novels that were being born in me: *La Maison du canal (House by the Canal)*, *Les Gens d'en face (The Window Over the Way)*, *L'Ane rouge (The Nightclub)*, *Les Pitard (A Wife at Sea)*, and others.

You were not to be born, as I had had the luck to be, among the common people, which is something I am often sorry about. Willy-nilly, you would inevitably be a daughter and sons to luxury born. At Delfzijl, I didn't know that yet. And that was not what I intended when I created Maigret, whom I would be obliged to call back into harness every time I tried to have him retire.

The money from *Détective* allowed Tigy and me to rush up toward the Arctic Ocean, not on the *Ostrogoth*, but on board a big boat, the deck of which housed cows and pigs as well as barrels of cod, as it lazily navigated, from port to port, up the coast of Norway, taking us beyond North Cape, to Kirkenes. There, beyond a narrow band of Finland, with field glasses we could see Russian soldiers patrolling their border.

To get there, our keel had had to break its way through ice. In sleds drawn by reindeer, we crisscrossed Lapland, from reindeer-hide tent to reindeer-hide tent, across the endless white expanse, and we ourselves were dressed like Lapps, not for local color or to make pretty snapshots, but because otherwise we would have been unable to withstand the below-freezing temperatures.

For years, Tigy and I alternately visited cold regions and torrid ones, crossed the Equator several times in different oceans, got to know every one of the continents. And my typewriter—no longer that old one I had once rented—followed us everywhere, in a specially upholstered box. I wrote everywhere too, in Panama as well as in Tahiti and Australia.

What was our destination? Where were we headed? Everywhere. Nowhere.

In search of what? Not local color, to be sure, but humankind. We didn't "travel," for everywhere we felt at home. Planes did not yet cross continents and oceans. Ocean liners took forty-five days to go from Sydney to London, with innumerable stopovers in Asia, the Near East, and the Mediterranean.

I was writing, not about what I was seeing. Instead, characters I had met in my childhood in Liège, then later in Paris, in the French provinces, where I settled, as if for life, at times in a château, at others in a farmhouse.

When we got back, we found our faithful Boule and good old Olaf, as well as crates full of mail, often asking: "Where the devil are they running to?" We were running almost endlessly, after humankind, after life; we were running in order to learn, and, although I may have stopped running, I never stop learning.

About the four of you, for example. Why not? Aren't you the most important part of what I will leave behind?

I am going to delve back into your childhood, now that you have all gone your separate ways, and you, Marie-Jo, are forever in my little garden, where one day I will join you.

As for the character who ended up being my friend, he still exists, but in bronze now, larger than life-size, at the very spot where he was born fifty years ago, on the bank of a disused canal where the barge that served as his cradle must long since have slowly dissolved in the stagnant water. I owe him a great debt, because it was thanks to him that I ceased being an amateur and became a novelist.

Now, I have ceased being that. I am a father, writing, as I suppose every father writes, to his children. Not at such length, no doubt. Nor perhaps so tenderly.

Good night, you four.

6

All my life I've been curious about everything, not only about man, whom I have watched living at the four corners of the world, about woman, whom I have pursued almost painfully because my need to fuse myself into her often became like a throb within me, but also about the sea and the earth, which I respect as a believer respects and venerates his god, about trees, about the smallest insects, about the least little being, still formless, living in the air or beneath the water.

I have had dogs and cats, like everyone, and horses. With one of these, true bonds of mutual affection were established—an Arabian thoroughbred, bought from a circus, that was white and light gray, ardent, as impatient as I, and we became friends to the point that he would let no one else ride him, not even Tigy. I never tugged at his bit, and needed neither spur nor whip; I spoke to him, in my own voice, with my legs hugging his flanks, and he answered me with movements of his ears.

We were living then at La Richardière, not a château, but an old country estate not far from La Rochelle, with a narrow tower that in olden days was called a "dovecote."

When we came home, sometimes after hours of riding by the sea, over the flat wetlands of the Vendée, which were slashed by canals that had to be leaped over, I unsaddled him and took off his bridle before entering the courtyard, and he would roll voluptuously in the grass. No one disturbed him until he got near the kitchen and knocked a few times at the window with his muzzle to ask Boule for his customary hunks of bread—or sometimes cookies. There were four other horses in the stable and a laughing young red-headed groom to take care of them.

In the big pond, which at high tide got its ration of sea water, swam some five hundred ducks, going in and out of the little green houses on an islet. Behind the vegetable garden, we raised white rabbits with red eyes, which old women from the village regularly came to pluck. About fifty white turkeys walked peacefully around among the geese and chickens. The biggest one, the most impressive, was nicknamed Maigret, because he took over with authority whenever a fight loomed between two males. One might have thought he was in charge of the barnyard police. In the woods, we raised pheasants, which we never slaughtered and which came and ate out of our hands.

From Ankara, we had brought back three young wolves. One of them had a broken paw and could not be saved by the veterinarian. The female, which until then had been very nice, broke out with a kind of eczema all over her body. She refused to allow the prescribed salve to be used on her, became irritable and threatening, and she had to be given a final shot.

That left Sazi, a big muscular male who followed us on a leash when we went walking along a narrow canal leading to the sea. He often spent the evening in the big studio that was both our living room and our office, where he felt comfortable.

For my trotter, I had bought a sulky and delighted in going to La Rochelle to do the marketing with this equipage.

Tigy's workshop, above the studio, for a long time was the habitat of I don't know how many exotic birds, which we had bought by couples on

Malta, in those days the great bird market. With the windows closed, they were free to fly all over the room, and when it had to be aired out, they voluntarily returned to the great birdhouse. Where were we coming from when we acquired those shimmering birds? From Turkey or from Russia and the Black Sea?

I was a great one for picking mushrooms, the ones that grew in the wet fields at dawn and the ones in the forests.

I practiced indoor boxing and, until not long ago, exercised every morning on a punching bag just about every place I ever lived. Later, all three of you boys had your own boxing gloves and a punching bag in your playroom, and I taught you the basics of that art of self-defense.

At seventeen, in Liège, I had ridden the highways of the Ardennes on big American motorcycles. They didn't belong to me, of course, but to the *Gazette*, which got them in exchange for free publicity.

I went in for golf, canoeing, volleyball.

I even— But this is beginning to sound like a litany, the longest of all, the litany of the saints, and I have read the Bible and the Gospels many times over.

I fished with ground bait in the Seine, above Morsang and at the dam at La Citanguette, trolled for pike among the reeds along the canal, and later tried my hand at deep trout and char fishing in the Lake of Geneva, without ever catching any.

I did underwater diving at Porquerolles before Cousteau was ever heard of, then professional fishing with my "lateen" and my sailor, Tado, trawling, seining of all sorts, even for lobster, whole nights through, with drift nets, for which I needed six strong-armed sailor-fishermen.

Tado and I spent entire nights off the Riviera's Levant Islands, and when our faithful companion Olaf died of old age, Tado and I went out there to give him a deep-sea burial. At that time, my own wish too was to be returned, someday as far off as possible, to the living cradle of the sea.

A little farm, during World War II, in the hills of the Vendée. Three cows, which I milked myself, and an immense vegetable garden that I tended with the help of an octogenarian gardener who had never in his life been outside his village, not even to the neighboring small town. He had never been on a train either, and when one passed he watched it with a distrustful, if not hostile, eye. Another gardener, in another place, neither smoked nor chewed tobacco, but always had to have a sprig of violet in his mouth, so I had to keep some growing in the hothouse all year round.

I crisscrossed the Mediterranean in a topsail schooner a hundred feet long, customarily used for the transport of old iron junk, which I rented for a year from an Italian shipowner, complete with its bare-chested crew, who wore handkerchiefs knotted at the four corners on their heads. In each port where we dropped anchor we would issue a challenge to the local *boules* team.

I have worn white tie and tails as often as five times a week when, in Paris, we were living in a very elegant apartment on Boulevard Richard Wallace and following the sheeplike herd of the great of the earth, the successful artists, and the habitués who went from opening night to opening night and to exclusive suppers in very high-toned nightclubs, where you could be admitted only if you had the credentials to get by the liveried doorman.

At that time I drove my Chrysler, which had come straight from America and aroused curiosity wherever we stopped, or my convertible Delage, with its endlessly long hood. I had my own table at Fouquet's and at Maxim's and belonged to I don't know how many gastronomic clubs which held weekly or monthly luncheons in the restaurants of famous chefs.

And yet I was writing novel after novel, I don't know when, I don't know in what state. When I wanted to take my sacrosanct walk, which helped me build up the still-vague idea for a new book, I crossed the bridge, a few steps away, and lost myself in the teeming, lively streets of Puteaux or Billancourt, where, in their habitual cafés, at counters made of real zinc, I clinked glasses with workers from the Renault and other factories, with whom I felt more at home than with my friends.

I spent a lot of time with the human flotsam in the Mouffetard neighborhood, out beyond the Latin Quarter, where the old men slept "on the rope" in flophouses above sordid hole-in-the-wall cafés. A real rope was stretched in front of them, and they rested their heads on it to sleep a few hours after eating (most often out of garbage cans). As soon as the sun was up, the owner would let the ropes fall, row by row, to wake the sleepers, whose heads fell forward on the hard tables.

I knew bankers, newspaper publishers, producers whose names are still bandied about today, and high-flying swindlers, including Oustric, Mme Hanau, and Stavisky, and I was often present at the marked-card games held in fancy hotels at which impeccable gentlemen fleeced rich foreigners or provincial industrialists.

I got my clothes from a famous English tailor and went to London for my hats and to Milan for my neckties.

I intimately knew André, when he was the owner of the casinos at Deauville, Le Touquet, La Baule, and Cannes, where a well-known Greek held the bank all night at table stakes while his yacht kept its steam up in the port so he might get away quickly in case of mischance. He was no adventurer, but a man who had studied extensively, spoke I don't know how many languages, and as each card was faced up he did immediate mental calculations of the probabilities remaining, according to the mathematical formulas of Henri Poincaré.

The nervous tension he was under and the effort he expended facing the two layouts with several million francs' worth of chips on them were such that a time came when he just had to relax. At that point, he would let an assistant take over and disappear through a little door, beyond which a pretty girl, never twice the same, was waiting for him, always kept in readiness by some unseen supplier. Less than ten minutes later, he came back to his place in front of the green baize table, refreshed and alert, as if he had just been bathed in the Fountain of Youth.

The most beautiful women of the demimonde were allowed into the gaming room only if they were wearing very expensive hats bought from the milliner who in private life was married to the manager.

I gambled, sometimes for rather high stakes, but André, who liked me, steered me away from the chemin de fer and roulette tables by pointing to the great crystal chandeliers that lighted the rooms. "You see, Simenon, if the gamblers had any chance of winning, those chandeliers, which have been up there for half a century, would long ago have been sold at auction."

I rarely gambled again. Nor did I smoke opium again, as some good women friends urged me to, because I could see that women reach the heights of sexual excitement under the effect of the drug, whereas men experience exactly opposite effects.

I was a regular backstage and went to supper with playwrights and stars.

I had swimming pools here and there, in America, in France, and in Switzerland, where I had the finest one built on my estate at Epalinges, which I lovingly designed myself, thinking that at last I was settled for all time.

The swimming pool and the house now are empty, and you children, who spent part of your youth there and who brought my grandchildren there to visit, will someday decide the fate of that property. I avoid going by it except from time to time to look at the birches I planted there without hope of ever seeing them grow into robust, proud trees. That, they have become.

Did I have periods of snobbery? Did I try pulling the wool over people's eyes? Did I derive pleasure from playing a certain role and associating with certain circles? I have asked myself those questions and think I can frankly answer no.

I wanted to see everything, try everything. In one of the first interviews

I ever gave, almost fifty years ago, the newspaperman asked me: "How does it happen that there are never any society people or important personages in any of your novels?"

I had to think about that. When I was with my boss the marquis, I had rubbed elbows with the aristocracy and leaders of high finance and had seen them at close range. I nevertheless answered: "I'll never be able to create a banker character until I've shared breakfast boiled eggs with a real banker."

I have done so since, with one of the most famous. I have done so with all kinds of people whose names appear in the papers or who are listed in *Bottin Mondain* or *Annuaire des Châteaux*. I have even been listed in both, myself. I have known ministers and heads of state. Wasn't I obliged to seek men out everywhere, at every level of that well-known scale?

You will find few such people in my novels, children, and Maigret, when he was absolutely forced to do so in carrying out his functions, mixed with them only reluctantly and always felt uncomfortable. But not out of timidity.

That brings me back to my search for man. Did I finally find him? Can I, after so many years, give up my exhausting quest?

The man I prefer is not to be found in drawing rooms, or among those whose pictures appear on billboards; even less in those fortresses that are called "banks." And that goes even more for official government buildings.

Peasants, if there are any left? Workers? Scientists? Intellectuals with sophisticated vocabularies?

My preference, to be perfectly frank, is still for the black, shiny-skinned man I was able to meet in his tribal home in the heart of the bush country or the equatorial forest, who at that time lived far from white people and had no idea of what the word "money" meant.

He was naked, slept in a straw hut that was built in one day by a few people getting together, on everybody's land, and in the morning, shortly before the sun rose, he picked up his little bow and his very pointed little arrows to go off with a lithe but careful step, without the slightest sound, on the qui vive, attentive to the slightest fluttering of the high grass or the leaves of the trees, while his wife or wives, naked as himself and shining in the sun, surrounded by large-eyed children, crushed the millet in mortars hewn by stones out of wood.

In this man, and those women, I discovered a human dignity that I found nowhere else. They could barely be seen or heard as they blended in with nature and lived at its rhythm.

Did they smell bad, as some people claim? They, on the other hand, are made uncomfortable when they meet white people by an odor that reminds them of that of a corpse. They have thick lips, kinky hair. But who established the canon of human beauty? If I were to draw a Venus capable of being put alongside the Venuses of Greece, I would go looking for her in Africa, to the extent that there still may be some in the pure state.

It happens that they eat their fellow man? They are cannibals? Well, weren't we, in some distant past? I have met four sailors, one of them a captain, who had also eaten some, or at least sucked out the still-hot blood to survive. Some three or four years ago, newspapers reported how a group of young men, whose plane had gone down in the Andes, far from any possible help, had eaten the weaker of their comrades. They were what are usually called "young men of good families," with good manners, university students to boot, and all of them fervent Christians.

I have no concern with racial problems. I ignore them. Millions of years ago, I probably would have found along the banks of the Seine, the Rhine, the Po, the Danube, or the Dnieper, the man I have so long sought, who had learned life not between walls but at the so much truer school of nature.

All of us once were naked men, or, in less temperate climates, men dressed in the skins of animals, which we then did not kill without a purpose, not unless we were hungry; not just for the pleasure of killing, in a word, or to reassure ourselves of our own superiority or power. Why are we ashamed of those faraway ancestors? They certainly left deep traces within us, and, in some among us, those ancient reflexes reappear unexpectedly.

What do we do with those people, who nonetheless are like us? We tag them with names, which in each war I have seen dreamed up to humiliate the enemy or to give us good reasons to kill him without remorse; with pride, on the contrary, as our fliers added a star to their planes for every enemy plane they downed, as our foot soldiers cut a notch in the stocks of their rifles every time they killed a man.

As for the naked man, he was satisfied to live at the rhythm of the earth, the sea, and the sky, and when he looked for a god, he selected a star or a familiar animal.

In my drawer I have my silver badge as a superintendent of the Police Judiciaire, in the name of my friend Maigret, it is true, with the number 0000 on it; the prefect of police has number 0001. In Arizona, I was given a deputy sheriff's star and I always carried a long-barreled Colt in the glove compartment of my car. I never fired a shot.

If I have pursued some of my fellow humans, they were all women, since I have ever been on the lookout for love, for physical love and tenderness.

That is the most exhausting and also the most discouraging hunt there is, because, in the society we have elaborated, or, rather, that others who were shrewder or more grasping elaborated for us, little by little, always more constricting century by century, love and tenderness are rarer than diamonds, especially that tenderness we all dream of, the need for which is riveted to our bodies, and which, if we do not achieve it, accounts more and more for a world full of malcontents, unstable characters, robots, and unhappy people.

———

7

———

Toward the middle of the year 1937, living in my luxurious apartment on Boulevard Richard Wallace, I was suddenly seized with revolt against my surroundings, against the puppet role I was playing in the world of puppets I had penetrated in order to get to know it. I was disgusted by the life I was leading, and I still wonder today how, since the days on the *Ostrogoth,* I was able to write six novels a year for Gallimard, in spite of all my travels through Europe and over five continents. Not simply novels that were not detective stories, but what I called "hard" novels, and on top of that the short stories, news reportage, and, several months each year, fishing at Porquerolles, where it was so hot that, beginning at 4:00 A.M. to write a chapter in my minaret, I would end up stark naked by the time I finished it.

One morning, I said to Tigy: "I want to work someplace else, in a small house my own size, far from cities, far from tourists, with the sea close by."

We departed in August or September, in our convertible, leaving Boule behind to take care of the apartment. I can remember that morning very well, the warmth in the air, the slight murmur of the leaves in the Bois de Boulogne, and, in front of our building, the Hispano-Suizas, Rolls-Royces, and Packards of the tenants, all movie stars or producers. I was never again to set foot in that building.

The problem before us was to find a house sufficiently isolated, at the seaside, not too big, where I could hide away and write. Especially, far from crowds and the tourists I had seen year after year invading Porquerolles— for the rush to the seashore had already started then, as the rush to the ski slopes was to start later on.

You will never guess, Marc old man, where we started on our quest for happiness. By the shortest routes we headed straight up to Delfzijl, in northernmost Holland, for the country of our dreams could be anywhere at all. And from there, in leisurely stages, we followed the coastline, going gradually farther and farther south. We wanted none of the beaches, to be sure, with their hotels that all looked alike and their summer mobs. But neither could we build in a desert of dunes from which we would have to go much too far to fetch supplies.

Nothing in Holland, that Holland I love so much—all four of you have some Dutch blood in your veins—or in Belgium, where the entire coast is nothing but one long beach interrupted by three or four seaports.

. . . The Vendée . . . that region of France that is flat, like Limbourg —the section of Belgium, Holland, and Germany from which so many of our ancestors came—and consequently has much more sky than you find anywhere else, the special kind of luminosity that Vermeer so beautifully captured in his paintings . . . I feel I am getting near my goal. From time to time, for want of a coastal road, we have to make an inland detour, only to rejoin the shore some ten or twenty kilometers farther on.

One clear morning (why are my recollections almost always of early morning and sunshine?), we suddenly come out at a cove and see a turreted house we know very well, meadows where once I ran so much, a few white farmhouses: La Richardière appears to us, decrepit and with most of its shutters closed. Tears roll down my cheeks and my chest feels tight.

At last we have found what we are looking for, after six weeks or two months on the prowl.

This is where I want to live, near La Rochelle, where I could go twice a week with Boule to do the marketing.

A phone call to Dr. Bécheval, at Nieul-sur-Mer, whose practice now extends over four or five neighboring villages, and who has remained our good friend. Luncheon at his home. His surprise when we anxiously ask him, long before dessert is served: "Do you know of a house for sale, as isolated as possible?"

La Richardière is occupied by its old owner, who had always refused to sell it to us. He and his wife have set themselves up in two or three rooms and let the rest of it go empty. Bécheval thinks it over, shakes his head.

Of course, there might be Old Man Gauthier's place. A farmer whose daughter worked for us way back when.

"It's five hundred meters from the sea. They say he intends to sell it and move in with one of his children at Lagord. If that's true, it'll take a lot of work to put it in shape."

Your mother and I look at each other, our eyes shining. It's quite a large house, hidden away behind an old wall and a low building. It can barely be seen from the path that leads to the oyster beds and mussel fields. It is built of fine local white stone, and the way in to it is by a tiny little door that leads to a huge mulberry tree in the middle of a nondescript garden.

There is another, larger, garden on the other side of the house, surrounded by walls with fruit trees growing against them—something the Charente people are so proud of, because it shows how mild their climate is—a palm tree, the top of which reaches the roof.

We had to negotiate for a long time, because that's the way it's done in the country. One day Old Man Gauthier was ready to sell; the next day he wasn't so sure anymore. A month later, however, the bill of sale was signed in an arcaded street in La Rochelle. As we came out of the lawyer's office, I remember saying nostalgically to Tigy: "A real grandmother's house, where the grandchildren come for their vacations . . ."

Did those words have any influence on your mother? I can't say.

Feverish months, with old local workmen busying themselves all over the place. Your mother made several trips to Paris to send down to Nieul a lot of furniture.

Tapping the walls with the white-haired bricklayer, we discovered three or four windows that had been walled off long, long before, as people used to do in the last century in the country, because taxes in those days were levied not on income, but on the number of doors and windows one had, and the number of pianos and dogs, except for watchdogs. We also brought to light an immense door surrounded by antique sculptures. As I was later to learn, the house had in olden days been a priory, and in what was to become my office we found wall recesses that had housed statues of saints.

A very old linden tree. A highly promising vegetable garden. A silted-up stream, two or three meters wide, which one crossed by way of a wooden bridge, and apple trees, plus bamboos so close together that Boule dubbed this end of the garden "the Congo."

We traveled a great deal while the work was being done, seeking out furniture fit to go with the house, three or four centuries old. Mostly Louis XIII furniture, heavy and solid. The ground floor was being tiled with those fine hard red bricks of the South called "tommettes."

Your mother, Boule, Olaf, and I set ourselves up for the duration of the work in a typical little villa, called "My Dream" or something, on the outskirts of La Rochelle, and every morning, while the two women went to Nieul on the various errands they had to run, I would write, not novels, which would have required too much concentration, but fifty-page stories, one a day, which later appeared under the titles *Le Petit Docteur (The Little Doctor)*, *Maigret revient (Maigret Returns)*, and *Les Dossiers de l'Agence O (The Files of O Agency)*.

At noon, with my work finished, I would rush to Nieul, where lunch was waiting for me, and spend the afternoon digging, planting, hammering, or whatever else. We were all stimulated and excited. When the sun began to go down, we would all go and have a swim in the nearby ocean.

By knocking out some recently added walls, we had turned the second floor into a huge room dominated by a monumental fireplace made of white stone with delicate moldings. We had to put in a septic tank, clean out the old well, have an impressive kitchen stove built that would also supply us with hot water for a bathroom lighted on three sides by windows. My punching bag, my rowing machine, my dumbbells all fitted in there quite easily (yes, indeed, dumbbells, Marc my boy, which were probably what gave you your taste for muscle development).

The work went on for months, during which we were able to see our first flowers burst into bloom. The trees against the wall were heavy with huge pears and apples, and there was one fine, sunny, sheltered flower bed in the garden that was reserved for all sorts of aromatic herbs, among which Boule delighted in making her selections.

Grandmother's house!

That, it finally was, smart-looking on the outside, bright and comfortable within, and the hallway outside my office had walls covered from floor to ceiling with all our books. There was even a hothouse now, beyond the vegetable garden. To keep the wasps from getting into the fruit, I bagged each piece separately in a small cellophane envelope so they could ripen out of harm's way.

By August, everything was in place, including the fruit storage bin I had put up, with its openwork pull-out shelves, and a laundry in a little building that stood between us and the path to the sea.

The village blacksmith, who was young and full of ideas, had patiently hammered out two fine grillwork gates that we had designed together, to separate the two gardens. While he was at it, over the broad tree-lined walk, he had put up hoops on which vines of various kinds would soon be creeping up.

Again, just like Grandma's.

And it was on an August day (or morning?), when everything was ready, that your mother said to me, quite simply: "Now, I'm ready to have a baby."

She didn't have to tell me that twice. That very day, perhaps within the hour, you were conceived, Marc, in the room on the second floor, where a kind of carved wood communion bench separated our two beds, which by day were couches. Conceived but not yet born, and, before you were to see the light, you would be subjected to many involuntary travels and adventures.

The house at Nieul is still there, the same as always, I presume, and Tigy, who has turned into a very alert grandmother, still lives there. Your two children, Marc, did and still do spend their vacations there. Your brothers and your sister, who were to be born much later, also were and still today are given the warmest of welcomes there, even though they were born of a different mother.

So, as you see, you are not only the son of a man and a woman, but, if I may so express it, also the son of a house, for, without Nieul—as we familiarly refer to it, just as if it were a person—you might never have existed.

How much hunting we had to do, from Delfzijl to La Rochelle, to end up with you! And how many other complications besides. That was 1938, and you were born in 1939, dates that are as important to you as they are to history.

8

A dazzling month of August. The sun came into our house through its many windows, and I must have written a novel in my new office, where I felt like a god. What I remember mostly is the garden and the barnyard, which had been set up in the nearest corner and in which we raised only Leghorns, because of their whiteness.

I had a new secretary, youngish, with big merry eyes, a greedy mouth; she was greedy for everything, not only things to eat, but also sun, movement, colors, and I can still see her, one afternoon, bringing from the farm across the way barrowfuls of hot manure, which we spread on the flower beds.

Everyone worked in the garden, Tigy, Boule, the secretary, whose name was Annette, and I. All in overalls under which, because of the heat, we wore nothing else. We were in a hurry to see the garden bloom in time for your birth.

Already, a man with a hoarse and commanding voice had been screaming over the radio in a language none of us understood, probably beating his fist on the lectern. I'm not sure, because there was no television yet. One name was always recognizable in his speeches: Danzig, which Tigy and I had been through when we were going to Latvia, then Poland, Hungary, Romania, and all over Europe. We had not seen the city or its port because the train went through with all doors sealed, curtains down, while uniformed armed men patrolled the corridors, rifles cocked. A narrow band of Poland, that country's only outlet to the sea, cut Germany in two.

We were far from believing that the imprecations of the man who was getting so angry might, so soon after we had settled in, tear us away from our jubilation.

You were minuscule, my big Marc, still close in size to the spermatozoon I had imparted to your mother and which month by month was going to grow bigger inside her. So you probably don't remember your prenatal peregrinations, although today some scientists claim that we unconsciously have a certain memory of that period when we swam like little fishes inside a liquid universe.

Tricolor posters on the walls, at the city hall of our little village of Nieul. France was calling up some of its categories of reservists, and England, which did not have obligatory military service, was enlisting young men to lend a hand to its professional army.

Was this war? Everyone thought so, and a phrase ran from mouth to mouth, usually pronounced with venom: "To die for Danzig!"

Where was this old Danzig that came back more and more often from the lips of the madman with the threatening voice? Was war going to start tomorrow, or the next day? Would a general call-up follow a few days after partial mobilization? If so, I would be called back to Belgium, far from Nieul, and there was a good chance I might not be there to see you born. Worry gave way to panic, and cars became more and more numerous on the roads. Why, as long as it was still possible, shouldn't I drive Tigy to Belgium, where her family would welcome her and welcome you when the time came?

We still had the enormous Chrysler bought back in 1932 or 1933, a heavy, powerful car such as they don't make anymore. We had had a solid steel platform built on its rear end to house the barrels of wine we used to buy in Burgundy, the Loire country, or the Bordeaux area, from small growers. We preferred to carry our wine away in this manner, thus being sure that it would actually be the wine we had tasted at the wineries.

A black trunk that two men could hardly carry when it was full—and how full it was!—was loaded on this rear carrier. The car was filled with everything that might come in handy over what seemed a rather long period ahead. Neither Boule, who really was a member of our little family, nor Annette, nor our Breton charwoman, nor Olaf went with us. At the last minute, I wanted to go and say good-bye to the desk I had hardly used, and I was surprised to see a robin perched on it, not even scared off by my entrance.

We drove all night long, slowly, for there were no expressways in those days and I didn't want to shake your mother up. Once across the Loire, we passed a veritable procession of cars as heavily laden as our own, all going in the opposite direction, south. They looked at us, unable to understand why we were the only ones heading north, where the enemy might be invading any day now. On the roofs of some of the cars, we saw, for the first time, mattresses held down by ropes. Also for the first time, I drove twenty-three hours at a stretch, slowed by denser and denser bottlenecks.

The sea at Calais, then sand dunes and the Belgian border near De Panne. A border guard comes to check on our identities, and gives us a worried once-over. "Where are you going?"

"To Brussels or Liège. I expect to be called up, and my wife's family are all there."

Another border guard rushes into the office to answer a ringing phone. His colleague holding our passports says: "Wait . . ."

I have the feeling something is happening. He goes toward the office, and the minutes go by while Belgian cars waiting to cross into France grow impatient. It was around five in the afternoon, and a red sun shone over the place.

My border guard appears at last at the top of the steps, still holding our passports. He yells delightedly: "Peace!"

Everybody looks at everyone else, incredulous.

"They've just signed a treaty at Munich—Chamberlain, Daladier, Mussolini, Hitler. . . ."

He whispers to me as he holds out the passports: "You can head back home!"

I immediately thought of that robin perched on my desk, and in the little house in Lausanne where I am writing now, we have a redbreast that hops around in the garden and seems to wink at us.

We spent the night at De Panne, where, as was the custom in those days, we were served hot shrimps with fresh bread and butter for breakfast. Then we started back, still against the current, for now we were again passing those cars with the mattresses on top that we had seen before going south.

It seems that at the very moment the customs man was announcing the good news to us, Daladier was getting down from his plane and, hoisted by the mob that had assembled at Le Bourget, being passed from hand to hand overhead to the roar of acclamations. Just a few moments before, he had been trembling with fear of the kind of reception he thought the French might give him.

Our house at last, Boule, Annette, the Breton woman, and Olaf. No robin on my desk or in the garden. I never saw him again. He must have felt his part had been played.

You were growing bigger, and your mother's belly expanded from week to week. Finally it seemed too heavy to carry, but that did not keep Tigy from doing her share in the garden. It was apple-picking time, and we started with the ones on the old tree near the stream, which, although scraggy, gave us fine sweet-smelling pippins, golden yellow with little darker spots on them. They couldn't be picked by hand, because we would have broken the branches off, so I had had clippers attached to the end of a bamboo pole that we worked with cords strung through rings, like those on fishing rods. The fruit fell gently into a bag placed near the clippers and did not get bruised.

Then we went after the trellises on which we grew pears and apples as big and fine as the ones you see in the pages of illustrated magazines.

My fruit storage room would finally be put to use and its many slatted shelves would be filled, labeled with the names of the species they held. Soon, immediately on opening the door one felt invaded by an aroma both sweet and spicy at the same time, an aroma I would never forget. I had to go to the room every two or three days to turn the fruit over and throw out the pieces that were turning rotten.

During the period of the spring tides, at break of day one could hear horses pulling old wagons toward the sea; a man or woman stood in them, holding the reins. These were the mussel farmers, in their rubber boots, on their way, as the water receded, to take care of their mussel fields, and sometimes also of their oyster beds, where the small oysters brought up farther out were left to grow and fatten.

Between La Rochelle and the tip of L'Aiguillon, the farmer is not only a man of the land but also a man of the sea. I liked to go and watch them work. The women, even the old and fat ones, wore wide trousers and heavy sweaters, a bucket on their backs, and brightly colored kerchiefs on their heads. The men, partly sinking into the mud or using a light punt, went to inspect the mussels, which they moved about as they got fatter.

Five or six whitewashed cabins were lined up on the grassy knoll, and I found out one day that by buying the house at Nieul I had acquired the right to build one of these. My old bricklayer with the white hair and constantly red face got to work on it. I wanted a fireplace, bought two weatherworn wooden benches and a table, and on the brick floor spread a pandanus rug brought back long before from Tahiti. A single window looked out on the sea, and I thought that someday I would like to write here, that you would bring your first boat, your pails and shovels here.

Our little cabin was used only once or twice, to change into our bathing suits.

Is my memory impregnated only by sunny days? Yet I can see the snow falling, silently covering ground and trees; that happened that very year, which was colder than usual in the region, so cold that I used to wear the black otter hat I had bought in Norway.

One morning, we saw our quenouille trees covered, not with fruit, but with big brownish motionless birds. A heron, our first heron at Nieul, stood stock still on the frozen stream. It was your mother, I guess, who first went near the birds with the swollen plumage, which were thrushes. Cold-struck, they no longer had the strength to move and were just waiting to die. Was it with some secret hope that they had perched so close to a house, within easy reach, as if asking for help?

We brought them into the kitchen, a few at a time, of course not getting them anywhere near the stove. Although we could still feel their hearts beating weakly beneath the soft chest feathers, they remained stiff and inert.

Tigy and I remembered how we had treated our guinea fowls when we lived at La Richardière. Boule heated up some red wine, which we sweetened and spiced heavily, and we all started putting it into the birds' beaks, drop by drop. After a short time, their eyes began to shine and looked us over with curiosity and without fear. A few more drops and the little bodies were trembling, the claws hanging on to the fingers that held them.

The first to get this treatment began to stand up, still tottering, and we went out and plucked others off the trees, as we might have plucked fruit. Soon, there were no dark spots left on the branches, but thrushes trying out their first steps and their first flutterings all over our kitchen.

Outside, everything was white. Snowflakes were still falling but the air had lost its bite. When the little group of birds seemed up to it, we carried them out, in a washbasket, to the Congo, where they could be sheltered by the bamboos, and on the way we caused a woodcock to take flight.

I don't remember, my Marc, that we ever told you that ordinary story. You were not yet officially born, not supposed to see or hear anything. How many times, later on and even now, were you not to save injured animals, not only birds but also small and large mammals and even snakes!

I was thirty-five at this time. Your mother was thirty-eight. She had never had any babies, and sometimes I worried that her delivery might be difficult, even dangerous. Privately, I confided this to our friend Dr. Bécheval and asked him if there was a good private hospital in La Rochelle, for at that time public hospitals were used almost exclusively for charity cases. Now, there's a term I heard a great deal in my childhood but which has almost disappeared from current usage.

Bécheval shook his head. "I would feel better about it if Tigy were in Paris or somewhere else."

He was rather outspoken where his fellow doctors were concerned. I understood what the shaking of his head and his comment meant.

"Your friend Pautrier, whom you introduced to me and who is a professor at Strasbourg, would be able to give you better advice than I can," he went on.

The Strasbourg hospital was not a hospital for charity cases, nor even an ordinary kind of hospital. I was quite familiar with it. I had given a talk there and met a number of the professors. There was a huge park on the St. Nicholas Canal, practically in the center of town. Small buildings spaced far apart, some amphitheaters, and, for each professor, two or three private rooms in his own personal pavilion.

I was enthusiastic about the idea and discussed it with Tigy, who was no less relieved by it than I. That very evening, we phoned Strasbourg, and Pautrier approved highly of our plan.

"You'll be surrounded by all kinds of friends, and the gynecologist-obstetrician, Professor Keller, is world famous. I'll talk to him about it, and I'm sure he'll be delighted to take care of Tigy."

We expected you to be born in April but, for fear of early labor and urged on by our impatience, we set out at the beginning of March and spent quite a little time, on all sorts of local roads, trying to find the château of Scharrachbergheim, which Pautrier had rented for us.

We had lived in other châteaux, and, in the Orléans forest, in a Cistercian abbey, where in the park one could still see the skeleton of the ancient

46

church. Yet this château now before us left us speechless. It stood, all red stone set off against the greenery below and about it, in the middle of a moat of bluish-green water, which one crossed by a drawbridge that actually worked.

Once inside, more wonderment. The walls were so thick that within the opening of a window I was able to set up a table for my typewriter, my chair, as well as a small file cabinet. And all the windows were like this, their little greenish panes lighting rooms so huge that the old furniture looked like children's playthings.

So you were to be born in Strasbourg and spend your first weeks in this feudal château. The next day, a short, round, pink, graying man, after examining your mother, reassured us with a kind smile. He was Professor Keller. The man, one might say, who invented the idea of a saltless diet during the last months of pregnancy. Tigy was already following that regimen, for Pautrier had phoned us and told her about it.

Tigy was strong; I never knew her to be sick, except perhaps for a few days of discomfort, especially during the worst heat spells at Porquerolles.

We went into Strasbourg, for prenatal examinations, once a week. I had sent for Annette, whom I missed, and the Breton woman remained alone to take care of our house. We didn't read the papers, especially here, where most of them were printed in German, or, more precisely, in Alsatian. I might add that we didn't really read the papers at Nieul either. We didn't have time for them, and we were not much concerned about Danzig or the Sudetenland, another pet subject of the gentleman who yelled so loud.

I was still writing my novels, which Gallimard brought out at the rate of six a year. Even in the commotion of Parisian life, I always found time —I don't know how—to fulfill the terms of the contract signed in 1934, which we extended every year.

At Nieul, even while I was busy with apples and thrushes, with the seedlings in the small hothouse, and the cabin by the sea, I wrote *Chez Krull* and *Le Bourgmestre de Furnes (Burgomaster of Furnes)* first, both of which, coincidentally, were set in Belgium. In January, when your arrival was getting near, I wrote a book about fatherhood, *Les Inconnus dans la maison (Strangers in the House)*. Here, surrounded by the moat beyond which there was an extensive park full of old trees, I began to write *Malempin (The Family Lie)*, the story of a father and his son.

Add to that listing a Maigret here and there, to keep my hand in, but I can't be sure of that; at the time, I didn't yet put dates on my manuscripts.

Here, I must admit, the sky was often gray and I lost count of the rainy days.

. . .

I am hesitant about taking a small break here, Marc, to make a confession to you. I hope it won't hurt you, the way D.'s book hurt Marie-Jo and drove her to despair.

Why did I expect that the baby would be a girl, when most men dream only of having a son? Who planted that idea in my subconscious? My love for women, for woman, which goes back to my childhood? The wish to be able to select dresses for a little girl? I rather think it was a presentiment, and a presentiment that misled me, a fact that was to make me extremely happy.

The days went by at Scharrachbergheim quietly, with me a little bit nervous. Then one afternoon, between March 10 and 15—I don't remember exactly—our friend Pautrier arrives unexpectedly at the château, with a long face and not smiling, as he usually was.

"I've just had lunch with the local prefect," he says. "He knows about your presence here. He knows you are expecting a child. . . ."

I feel a pinch of anxiety in my chest.

"He wants you to leave as soon as possible. . . ."

I stare at him wide-eyed, as if I have just been accused of having done something wrong.

"Confidentially," he goes on, "last week he opened envelope number two."

Pautrier explains to me that every prefect has in his safe several sealed envelopes, which he is to open only on orders of the government. Because of the Danzig Corridor, which the Treaty of Versailles, after the 1914–1918 war, cut out of the German Empire for the benefit of Poland, and because of the Sudetenland, that is, the one-time German territories incorporated into Czechoslovakia, the gentleman who is no longer shouting has, unusually, deployed some troops and dangerous weaponry, which threaten several frontiers.

"Envelope number two, now opened, is just a prelude to number one, detailing extraordinary precautions to be taken."

"And what about number one, which the prefect expects to get the order to open shortly?"

"That one means general mobilization."

Pautrier stops for a moment, and then says in a hollow voice: "And the organized removal of all inhabitants in the border area. The prefect doesn't want to be caught with an about-to-be-delivered woman on his hands."

Pautrier, your mother, and I talk in low voices for a long time.

"When do you advise us to leave?"

"This very night. The child might come any day."

"Where to?"

"Belgium is still neutral. So it won't be bound by the treaties that bind England and France."

"It was invaded in 1914, and I was there, with my parents, in the cellar, listening to the hoofbeats of the uhlans' horses in the streets and the shelling of the forts of Liège."

"At the highest levels, they expect, if war breaks out, that there will be a frontal attack on the Maginot Line."

"What does Professor Keller say?"

"One of his former students and assistants, whom he trusts as much as he does himself, is practicing in Brussels and on the staff of the best hospital in Europe, the Edith Cavell Clinic. Since there is no way of telling whether Tigy won't have her first pains on the way, his best nurse will go along with you, taking full equipment for emergencies."

Tigy and I look at each other. She does not flinch, does not even pale at the idea of possibly giving birth in a car—which would present some difficulties—more likely at the roadside. We both go into Strasbourg, while Boule finishes packing at the château and Annette is busy phoning to get herself a train reservation.

Keller is satisfied with his examination. "You have nothing to fear. The midwife who will go with you has my fullest confidence."

A woman dressed in white, slightly bulging in all directions, with light hair, blue eyes, and a happy smile on her lips. I have forgotten her name. I buy road maps. We have to take the shortest route. Good old Marc, now where will you finally see the light of day?

We leave at nightfall, and I drive carefully. Your mother is next to me, her belly looking as though it were about to burst. We pass several armored trucks, but there are not many of them yet.

Belgian border. Soon there are forests as far as the eye can see. For how many miles? Tigy is holding the map on her belly as if it were a lectern. "First road to the right," she says.

The sky is finally growing pale, and then yellowish, and at last we start seeing big patches of blue. Just as we get into the suburbs of Brussels, the sun lights up the brick houses. I easily find my way to the Gare du Nord, which I am familiar with, and the Palace Hotel, where we have reserved a suite. All four of us have breakfast together, or, rather, all five, counting you, and then the nurse, who won't hear of going to bed for a rest, as I suggest she should, heads for the station. I phone the doctor, who sounds nice and gives us an appointment for that afternoon. Boule is emptying the trunk and the suitcases. This trip has rather upset her.

The doctor is tall, with an open face. He takes Tigy into his examining room and, when he comes out, is very reassuring. "Your wife and the baby are none the worse for the trip, and it may be a week yet before she is ready to deliver."

I forgot to mention that, as we came through an almost new section of the city, we stopped off for a moment to see Yvan Renchon, Tigy's brother. The breakfast table was set for five. Only Yvan and his wife were sitting at it, but the three children were soon down, sleepy-eyed, in mussed pajamas, still smelling of warm beds. They kissed their mother and father, and then us.

I looked at them avidly, hoping that someday, perhaps . . . For I felt like a father already.

9

Popular belief has it that a good fairy watches over the birth of every baby. I am not sure I believe in fairies, but one of them certainly helped your mother and me to wait for you and then take back to Nieul the little man-child who had been conceived there and for whom the house had been set up. I am still impatient, like all young people, in spite of my age, and when I want something, I want it right away. When we were in Brussels we had been waiting for you for nine months, and the nervousness I had been trying to hide from Tigy was almost turning into anxiety.

I was pawing the ground. Whereas your mother kept a calmness I have rarely seen her lose, and looked at me with a slightly compassionate, if not mocking, eye. Fortunately, we had made that brief stop at Yvan's. His wife, Yvonne (Yvan and Yvonne, like the words for a song), for the next two weeks was going to take over without ever appearing to.

I had not seen much of her in the elder Renchons' big house in Liège, where the young couple lived quite separately on another floor. My recollection of her was rather vague. Certainly a fine-looking brunette, but one who seemed continuously ill at ease and rarely laughed.

The day after we moved into the Palace, she phoned to ask whether she might come and see us. Now, less furtively than during the family breakfast the day before, I was able to observe her at my leisure.

Yvonne, who is approximately the same age as I, had become a real woman, much surer of herself, and softer at the same time, and her three childbirths, instead of prematurely aging her, had given her a fullness and serenity such as I had rarely come across. A mother by instinct, she carried out her duties without ever grumbling or complaining, and seemed able to juggle her various homemaking tasks, doing everything herself and yet finding time for her own leisure pursuits.

Your weight didn't keep Tigy from still walking briskly, and Yvonne came to pick her up every afternoon to take her to the stores, where, on her advice, your mother bought everything you would need. Yvonne knew the city inside out, and indulged in the local tradition of stopping at one of the tearooms or pastry shops where the young and less young ladies of the city gathered after leaving the department stores loaded down with packages.

What creamy pastries they then consumed! And what laughter could be heard in those sweet-smelling places! They gained weight little by little. They laughed heartily about it, since fashion did not yet call for women thin as a rail.

Yvonne was not fat, and if her silhouette had rounded out a bit, that only made her pleasanter to look at, especially since she had retained her limberness and, since the Liège days, had become much more vivacious. They wanted no part of me on those daily excursions, perhaps because, as back at the Junk Art Fair, my nervousness showed too much.

"Are you familiar with Avenue Louise, Georges?"

Of course I knew Avenue Louise, the most famous street in Brussels.

"On the left, you'll find a store with three display windows that will interest you. . . ."

I went there, all the while wondering whether Tigy's water might not have broken in one of those shops from which they returned with things new to me, light and fluffy kinds of garments that in the end constituted a baby's full layette, to say nothing of the pink cans and jars of talcum powder, creams, and oils, all variously scented.

The store on Avenue Louise appeared at first glance to be the finest in the world, and I do believe that at the time it was the only one of its kind. Later, I never found anything to equal it in Paris, London, or New York.

Three huge floors of things of every kind, from baby carriages and strollers to the most varied kinds of furniture for children's rooms, with toys, bathinettes, and everything else to go with them. I came back from that first visit with my arms full.

I was sorry now that, before leaving Nieul, I had bought in a little shop in La Rochelle what was needed for your future nursery. Here, everything seemed so much finer! I was nevertheless proud when I thought of the surprise in store for you when we got you home, which I had had to order well in advance: a bathtub, a real baby-sized bathtub, solidly attached to the wall, so that your mother would not have to bend over.

I returned there almost every day, always buying things that we might never use but that appealed to me as likely to please you. Tigy and Yvonne had already bought the traditional baptismal gown, made of Brussels lace, naturally. Wasn't that one way for us to feel we were already with you?

One afternoon, as she was coming home with Yvonne, your mother's water broke, without her realizing it, just being surprised at what was happening to her, and I could at last breathe more freely. The breaking of the water, I had been told, was the prelude to confinement, or, rather, to the labor that preceded it.

Phone call to the gynecologist. I was so excited the calm doctor must have thought I had lost my wits.

"Take her to the Cavell Clinic, where they have a room reserved for her. I'll drop by and see her later in the day."

A magnificent, almost new hospital, at the edge of the famous Bois de la Cambre. I admiringly contemplated the main building, but the three of us were shown to a smaller building, surrounded by greenery, for your good fairy was still with us.

Everything was light and cheery, and the nurses and midwives wore charming caps that identified them as part of Cavell. I was to find out that they had a school for nurses and midwives, many of them physicians' daughters, and that while studying there they were required to wear the Cavell uniform even off duty.

To me, they all seemed to be pretty and laughing. There was no hospital or clinic atmosphere, and at times it seemed more like a boarding school. The head nurse of Maternity too, despite the strict discipline they enforced, had a soft voice and a maternal smile.

The sun was setting. During all those days in Brussels, all I can remember is sunshine and blue skies. It may well have rained and the wind may have blown. I guess I didn't notice, or else my memory, as almost always, just refused to record the drabness.

"Madame, do you think I might sleep here, on a folding cot?"

She looked at me as one does at a child. "Do you want to very much?"

I didn't want to be separated from you, my Marc, or to be awakened in my room at the Palace by a voice telling me you were born.

"It can be arranged. Provided you are out of the hospital every morning by six."

"That would not bother me." Hadn't I been getting up since childhood before anyone else in the house, including my parents, and later sat down at my typewriter by six in the morning?

"You'll also have to promise that you'll control yourself. . . ."

I gave her my promise, but I'm not at all sure she thought I could keep it.

"And behave yourself with our girls."

"Good morning, doctor."

They put Yvonne and me out, and we take a walk on the lawn. Tulips are beginning to bud, and tulips are one of my favorite flowers. The doctor comes and joins us a little later.

"Everything's fine. But I do think it may take rather long. . . ."

Well, I have a cot to sleep on, but they don't serve me any meals. So I seek out a little restaurant in the neighborhood, and find one, sparklingly clean, at the corner of a quiet, residential street. In the morning, I drive across town to our hotel, where Boule is impatiently waiting.

"Is he born yet?"

"Not yet."

Boule, who adores children, is rather frightened by babies, maybe because they seem so fragile to her. I take my bath, shave, and go for coffee and shrimp salad by way of breakfast, adding to it a glass of beer as an afterthought.

Babies, I have been told, during the last months usually kick their mothers' bellies. I have had nothing to do with any babies before, except for one Simenon niece to whom I was godfather when I was twelve but whom I saw mainly during the ceremony in church.

For at least two months we have been able to feel you moving around by putting a hand on your mother's belly. It sometimes thrusts up in spots. Not violently. Tigy told me one night that it wasn't painful and that it seemed more like a little greeting. I know you well, my Marc, whom I have often called "my sweet Marc," especially when I saw you watching the sky with dreamy eyes and you seemed to come back from another world when you heard my voice. What were you dreaming of inside your mother's warm womb? One might have thought you liked it there and were trying not to leave it to come out into this big-people's world. I almost believe you were already dreaming.

However that may be, you kept us all with bated breath for several days, days of the same routine. I arrived at ten-thirty. At noon they put me out, and I went to have lunch at the little corner restaurant, which smelled, above all, of beer. It was mainly a neighborhood café, where the local habitués came at their appointed hours to have a game of cards. I would return from there slowly, by way of the affluent, almost empty streets.

Yvonne arrived at two o'clock, always well dressed, with her comforting smile that inspires confidence.

"Go take a walk outside, Georges. I'm staying here till five, which leaves me the time to prepare my supper."

In Belgium, people have "supper" at six or six-thirty in the evening, just as they do here in Switzerland.

I went back to my Paradis des Enfants on Avenue Louise, and the manager informed me that he not only sold ready-made furniture but also manufactured it to order, with the kind of wood and in the style the customer specified. Twenty years later, I was to remember that store while I was awaiting the birth of your brother Pierre, and I designed furniture for the nursery that might serve till the age of six, to be made of cherry, one of my favorite woods, because it is cheerful.

I also walked around the downtown streets, then went to the hotel, where Boule always had the same question for me: "Still nothing?"

It irritated me. Any little thing irritated me, because I was beginning to be worried. But then, hadn't I been for the last nine months? Why wasn't this child moving around more than it was and why hadn't the real labor pains started yet? The doctor kept reassuring me in a routine way, and each time I wondered whether he was telling me the truth.

As I passed by an open door, I caught sight of a woman with white hair, lying in a bed next to a cradle. She looked briefly at me and quickly turned her head away, as if she were ashamed. And the fact was, as one of the young Cavell girls told me, she was, if not ashamed, at least ill at ease with other people and even, it seemed, with her husband.

"She is fifty-two. She already has two grown children, including a married daughter. When this happened to her, she blushed and mumbled, 'At my age, who would have thought it was possible?'"

Good old mother who for years had considered herself an old woman and now looked with such surprise and tenderness at the little thing she had just brought into the world, when her own daughter perhaps was also pregnant!

She and I had a talk that evening.

"It's especially on account of friends, neighbors . . . They must have been laughing behind my back, or thinking I had caught God knows what kind of sickness, when they saw me getting so fat. . . . At the beginning, that's what I thought too. And so did my husband."

I met the husband, a man with short gray hair and pink cheeks who wasn't embarrassed by it at all, but, on the contrary, proud of his feat. "It's really something, isn't it? At our age . . ." And he burst into a hearty Brussels laugh.

Dinner at my little café-restaurant, where the owner used to come over to talk to me.

"When is it due?"

"I don't know. We're waiting."

"Here, we're used to that, you know. You're not our first!"

Should I say she looked good or bad? Your mother was in pain, with her hands crossed over her belly, and little plaintive cries crept in between her moans. I called the nurse on duty, who asked me, as if it were the most obvious thing: "Every how many minutes?"

I was a greenhorn, an apprentice father.

"Her pains?"

"I don't know. Maybe every half hour . . ."

"Then we have lots of time. When she starts yelling every three minutes . . ."

Which the doctor confirmed to me toward the end of the morning, after I got back from the Palace.

"Is this normal, doctor? It's two days now that . . ."

"It happens often with primiparas of her age."

Well, then, what about that old lady next door? How long had her husband had to wait?

"I'll be back again this afternoon. She's in good spirits," the doctor said.

I kept repeating the word "primiparas" to myself, because it was new to me, and made me think it was probably more suited to veterinarians. Good old Marc!

One afternoon, finally, the midwife put me out, telling me that the contractions had started and that she was phoning for the doctor. I went and phoned to your good fairy, who was also mine and your mother's, and who got there after putting her own children to bed.

"Is it due tonight?"

"The doctor is there. We're waiting, but it can't go on much longer."

We walked in the moonlight on the lawn and I stopped to look at the yellow tulips as if I were asking them to be a good omen. Yvonne would leave me from time to time to go into the pavilion, from which, for that night, I was barred. Fortunately during one of the times she was away, I suddenly began throwing up on the grass.

"Is she having a lot of pain, Yvonne?"

"It's a bad time to go through, but afterward you forget all about it."

Husbands were not allowed, in those days, to be present at their wives' confinements, because it was feared that they would need the doctor and nurses more than the woman would. I was still a rookie at it, as they say in the army, but much later, I got my hash mark and was allowed to be present, dressed in hospital gown and mask, at the birth of one of your brothers and your sister. I didn't bother anyone. After all, it's more of a strain to stay in the wings, even if the wings happen to be a fine green lawn dotted with blooming daisies and tulips.

Finally, when I no longer dared look at my watch, Yvonne appeared and joyfully called to me: "Hurry up!"

There was no need to urge me. I rushed toward the room, pushing nurses out of the way, opening the door, just as Yvonne added: "It's a boy."

And, as I looked at Tigy, very pale but smiling nonetheless, then at the little rectangular cradle in which you were waving your arms and legs, I felt like crying as, quite without my will, in my head ran bits of a song I had heard in Paris ten years before: "The little boy was me, that the stork had brought, ought, ought. . . ."

You were not green, as, according to my grandmother Simenon, I had been at birth. You were red and whiny. I took pictures of you, stark naked, lying on the table on which the nurse had placed you, then I asked for permission to pick you up.

You had been born, my son. You weighed, they said, seven pounds and eleven ounces, and your voice was a lot harsher than it is today.

"Are you happy, Georges?"

Didn't it show? I was as if drunk.

"Now, let her rest. Come back early in the afternoon."

"Did everything go all right?"

"You see how it turned out."

"They didn't have to use any . . ."

I didn't dare pronounce the word "forceps," which had haunted me so.

"They didn't need anything except the mother's pushing."

At times, Tigy, exhausted, closed her eyes. I left in my car, with scarcely a thought for our fairy Yvonne, who stayed behind, and as I drove along, I tooted my horn from time to time, while I sang at the top of my lungs: "*J'ai un ploustiquet en brique, En brique, en brique . . .*" Which might be translated: I've a kid who's full of tricks, Made of bricks, made of bricks . . .

I kept repeating those words endlessly. They must have been coming back to me from the depths of my earliest childhood in Liège. In the local patois there, a *ploustiquet* is a little boy, and "made of bricks" of course had to mean he was as solid as the bricks they make the local houses from.

Solid as a brick. I had a child solid as a brick, with two arms, two legs, a big chest, which could be gauged from his yelling power, and a well-formed head, without any trace of those damned forceps I had so worried about. Toot . . . Toot . . . Just like a car with newlyweds in it . . . People turned to look at me, and I didn't give a good goddamn.

I got to the Palace and yelled at the door to our suite: "He's born. It's a boy!"

Boule turned pale with emotion, and no one could then have foreseen that she would be the one to take care of bringing up this son's own son and daughter later on.

It was a great feeling, Marc. Some relief!

But you know it as well as I do, because you've been through it too. You were young then. Your wife too. I was thirty-six and felt that I was already aging. You know what I had been doing for the previous several weeks, if not months? Intensive calisthenics, so that you wouldn't be disappointed when you first set eyes on me.

Now, back to the road. I'm going to have to transport you once again, if only to get back home to Nieul, your real nest. Not right away, to my great regret. At the time that you were born, recently delivered mothers stayed in bed, and then in their rooms, for at least two weeks, and our good doctor advised us not to take you on a trip before you were at least a month old, preferably older.

And to think that the first flowers we had planted in the garden to welcome you had probably already bloomed. You were born on April 18, and the next afternoon I had to go to register you at the city hall of Uccle, the district in which the Edith Cavell Clinic was located.

What did I do in the interim? Where did I eat? I've forgotten. It doesn't matter. I had a son, a little *ploustiquet* made of bricks, the sun was in its heaven lighting the city as if for a feast day, and I—I don't know what. I was as happy as I am today. I think the sun is shining today too. And if it isn't, that's just too bad for it.

10

It's good to find peace of body and mind again after undergoing a long period of nervous tension and sometimes feeling a lurking anxiety deep within oneself. One is enveloped in a kind of savory, beatific lassitude, and everything becomes fine and good. The days now were going by much faster than during that long night of your birth, and your mother and I could wait peacefully, with all our thoughts on your definitive(?) transplantation to your home at Nieul-sur-Mer, furnished with such delight and so brightly awaiting us not far from the sea, which your baby eyes were soon to discover.

Your mother, Marc old man, was able to nurse you at her breast only a few days, which presented no problem because, as the doctor put it, the main thing was that you had sucked her first milk, which contained the cholostrum that a newborn baby needs. One morning, at Cavell, when I returned from my little café, I saw a nurse working hard over an ugly machine that was attached to Tigy's breast, but that mechanical "milker" was no more successful than you, and I was secretly relieved, for otherwise it would have been up to me to work that inhuman contraption, for months perhaps, and I just didn't feel up to it.

The Renchons arrived from Liège, and the first thing your good gray-haired grandmother did was to grab you up in her arms and kiss you. The young father I was interfered, saying that a new baby was supposed to have the least possible contact with people who came in from out of doors. I hurt your grandmother, naturally, for, as the eldest in her family, she had raised several of her sisters and brothers.

I tried to make up for it but was too awkward and uncontrolled about it, and Mother Renchon was to hold it against me for quite a while, forgiving me only when I apologized to her and explained how inexperienced and sorry I was.

You seemed to me such a precious treasure, my Marc, and I had awaited you for almost twenty years! For others to touch you, to handle you, to make you their own treasure, however slightly, seemed sacrilegious to me.

Did my mother come too? I don't remember. She must surely have come by, on tiptoe, fading back as was her custom, and if she said anything, it was only in a timid voice devoid of any great warmth. To this grandmother, at your birth, didn't you belong, after all, to the enemy clan?

As for Boule, it took me a little while to understand her reaction. I expected her to be very enthusiastic. But she remained silent as she looked at you, able to muster only a banal "Yes, he's fine-looking. Really a fine boy . . ."

Poor Boule, almost twenty years before, she had attached herself to a young couple and thus acquired a new family, to whom she had totally devoted herself. She too, in her small fisherman's home atop a Normandy cliff, had seen many younger brothers and younger sisters arrive. The tradition, in her family, was that a girl at six or seven must be ready to help with the latest addition, for the mother alone could never cope with eleven children to raise.

Water had to be drawn from the well, in winter as well as summer, wood had to be cut and the fire kept up in their small house, where a kettle hanging from the end of a chain was the cooking pot for their meals. A new child, in the circumstances, was an ordinary event taken for granted. And here we were, after so many long years, making the birth of a baby an event as solemn as if it had been the birth of an heir to a throne. What place would be left for her now, in the family and in our hearts?

Once you were born, I was no longer allowed to sleep on the cot. So I moved into the Château de Tervueren, all by myself, and that was literally true, for I quickly realized that I was the only lodger there. Have you ever discovered you were all alone in a cathedral?

Everything was too big, the hallways, through which a car could have been driven, the bedrooms, which with a few partitions might each have become a suite. Steps echoed hollowly in the emptiness, beneath ceilings high enough for giants, and the only persons one met, from time to time, were stock figures, maîtres d'hôtel in white tie and tails, waiters in white jackets starched as stiff as coats of armor, which would have seemed more appropriate in this place, room valets in yellow-and-black vests and red hair (maybe they didn't all have red hair, but that's how I remember them), chambermaids in their white caps and lace aprons over their black uniforms, and a giant doorman in gold-braided livery, wearing a high hat with a cockade. What the devil did he have to do, at the foot of the outside steps, in fair weather and foul? He was standing guard, obviously. But over what?

A dining room that . . . But I'm tired of trying to find comparisons. At any rate, there were at least forty tables laid with immaculate tablecloths, fine porcelain plates, and solid silver utensils.

At breakfast I selected a corner near the door, for, although I feel lost in a crowd and always a little frightened of so many people, I discovered that one can be even more ill at ease in an empty place, under the gaze of four or five statuelike captains and waiters. I was formally handed a leather-bound menu, which I didn't even look at, and I ordered in an almost controlled voice: "Two rollmops, some rolls, and two glasses of beer."

The wax dummy showed no surprise and walked off with dignity. Ten minutes went by, a quarter of an hour, and Tigy must have been expecting me at the hospital, although not you, because you were still unaware of the bondage to time. Finally, I was solemnly brought some fillets of herring, decorated with hard-boiled eggs, olives, something red, and some cute spirals of mayonnaise, as well as two potbellied steins of beer.

"Don't you have any regular rollmops?"

I must tell you, Marc, that in Belgium rollmops are the national specialty, to be found in large bowls in every grocery store and on the table of every "fry shop." They are raw fillets of herring, rolled around a fat gherkin, slices of onion, some herbs, and I don't know what else, which have been steeped at length in a marinade of herring milt and vinegar. Had I been deliberately moved, out of cussedness, to order this plebeian dish in the austere, silent château? Maybe in part. But the fact is, I really liked rollmops for breakfast.

I ate my high-class herrings without further complaint and then went to see your mother and you. I told her the story, and Tigy laughed. "What are you going to do about it?"

"Going to a grocery to buy the biggest bowl of rollmops I can find and tomorrow morning bring the whole thing down to the dining room."

The next morning, as I had told your mother I would, I placed a huge glass bowl on the embroidered tablecloth of my breakfast table. The maître d'hôtel barely batted an eyelash. "How many of them shall I serve you, sir?"

"Two, with two glasses of beer."

I acknowledged the portion with a nod, and five or six of them stood around watching me eat. Their mouths may have been watering, after all, for in spite of their acquired dignity, they had not been born to the purple any more than I.

Your mother arrived, with Yvonne and no doubt Boule. You were the most precious load our old Chrysler had ever carried. Consequently, I had driven slowly, avoiding bumps, my pipe in my pocket, for I never lit it in your presence. Wasn't a newborn babe fragile, after all?

One day, I was allowed to give you your bottle, and, although I felt very clumsy about it, I was also filled with terrific joy.

How long did we stay at Tervueren? Maybe two weeks? Maybe a little longer? The doctor came to see you every couple of days and was satisfied with his examinations of your mother. Her belly had disappeared and she could wear the new dresses she and Yvonne had bought to surprise me.

In the afternoon, your aunt was always there by two o'clock and we would take you out for a stroll in your temporary pram; you had a shiny English perambulator awaiting you back home. The woods, the lakes and ponds, the river were all as stiff and set as the staff of the château, but we were all smiles in the sunshine, from which we protected your fragile skin.

"Now, you're ready to go. By train, of course."

Our first separation, Marc, short as it was, was very upsetting to me just the same. I had reserved a full compartment for your party, lest you be exposed to any contamination.

The fact is, I still wonder whether I believed that your presence was real! I drove you to the Gare du Nord and saw you leave, with a twinge in my heart, then I took to the road, no longer singing and blowing the horn to the tune of the *ploustiquet*, but watching the milestones at the side of the road and counting how much distance I had left.

I was the first to arrive in our new flat country with its red-roofed white farmhouses, and the sea for background. I wonder whether you and your mother didn't make a stopover in Paris so you could both get some rest. Probably, because there was no way to make the trip without changing trains. Do you know how I spent that night? Hard-waxing the floor of the second story, the way professional waxers do it, not all by myself, of course, but with the help of Boule and the Breton woman.

The wax was hard to crush, even harder to spread, but it smelled good, and you would be breathing that odor of beeswax, which I liked above all others.

How, at what time, did you make your entrance into your new domain? Strange as it may seem, after a long wait and all the unexpected complications, I find no trace of a recollection of that. At any rate, there you were, home at last, in your home, our home, in the lace of your own cradle, then in your baby carriage, which reflected the sunshine in our garden. To my mind, that sunshine was not the same as sunshine anywhere else.

Your good fairy left, shedding a few tears, and we were not to see her again for a very long time.

There were now three of us, four counting Boule, who watched over her "frog" with a loving smile. It would not have been hard to imagine you were her child instead of ours, and she would not allow the Breton woman to lay a finger on you.

Peaceful weeks, a warm summer, the household getting bigger. There were no washing machines then, and the idea of letting an electric motor do our laundry, your laundry, would have made our hair stand on end. But we did have a Frigidaire, which we had been among the first to get back on Boulevard Richard Wallace. I say Frigidaire rather than refrigerator because no one used the latter word at the time and, as best I can recall, Frigidaire was the only brand then exported to Europe. Boule, who, like me, had grown up by oil lamps, felt distrust toward electrical contrivances, and I was always bringing newfangled gadgets back from La Rochelle.

We had at first hired a laundress, and then, since she soon could not handle all the washing and ironing, her fifteen-year-old daughter, beautiful and with eyes as candid as those of an Italian Renaissance angel.

From the garden, you were taken on out to the sea path, and you smiled at the immensity before you. You smiled often, with a light, dreamy smile, which you still have at forty. People called it an internal smile.

I was writing novels, in my office; your mother got up before me, to prepare your bottles, dressed in her painter's smock. She once more had all the energy that you still find in her. On the advice of Dr. Bécheval, whom among ourselves we referred to as "the little doctor," we tried ass's milk. It wasn't easy to find, and I had to drive over into the Vendée to get it at a small farmhouse. But the experiment failed. You preferred your Brussels formula.

The big event, for a while, was your christening. It was, for us, just a chance to show you off to our best friends, and I wanted it to be a worthy celebration.

We invited all the people we really liked, some forty men and women. Professor Pautrier was your godfather and, because Vlaminck and his wife were Protestant, their eldest daughter was your godmother. I had made arrangements with a delightful priest and with two local violinists, who played a Bach sonata for two violins that had always moved me, and still does.

The little church at Nieul was full of flowers, and full of people, for all the villagers were there, overflowing onto the church steps and into the yard. The curé had suggested that we follow a very old tradition, which consisted of the godmother placing the child for a moment on the high altar, and at that moment the music of the violins flooded the church.

Another tradition was throwing Jordan almonds, pink for a girl, white for a boy, and I asked the local confectioner to make up small bags of them.

Boule, between supervisory looks at the oven, was there, of course, and weeping with joy. You didn't cry, didn't even make a face when they put a bit of salt between your lips, or when they poured the holy water over your head. You looked at everything going on around you as if in a dream.

Some neighboring farm women came in to help Boule prepare the meal for forty. I had ordered several cases of champagne, and I must have been seeing too big, as they say in my country, and as seems to be my habit, because we still had some of it left two years later.

Was our little doctor called away for an emergency delivery? That happened to him all the time, especially at night, mainly in March, a month during which he was called for such cases as many as twenty times. He was a count, and his name had had a "de" in front of it, which he did not use on his letterhead; I only found out about it by the greatest of chance. He was a happy, witty fellow, very open with his patients. "You're gonna kick the bucket, old man. I give you another month, if you go on downing eight bottles of wine a day."

He was also the one who, twinklingly, asked me: "Do you know why so much hot water is needed during a confinement?"

"Well, because . . . because . . ."

"Not at all! Just to keep the women in the family busy, especially the grandmothers, and keep them from coming into the bedroom and bothering the doctor with their advice."

Vlaminck, a sort of Gargantua in jodhpurs and boots, with a red kerchief around his neck, made himself heard from one end of the garden to the other with his stentorian voice and his categorical affirmations. But you must have slept through it all, and your mother busied herself with one group after another.

Then peace in the house, the daily chores in the garden, the fruit bins, the smell of ironing from the room that served as laundry, which always had its door open. You began to crawl around on a goatskin rug and turned over, puffed with pride, looking at your mother or me as if to say, "See what I can do!"

You got fat and your color showed that you were out in the country and near the sea.

During that time, far from our peaceful little circle, the man with the raucous voice was hardly ever raising it anymore but he was shoving his brown- or gray-clad troops, like chessmen, toward the borders of his country. There was conjecture in the chancelleries of Europe and elsewhere. Discreet measures were taken without the good people being told about them. Life had to go on, didn't it? It was not a year yet since that agreement had been signed at Munich by the gentleman and his Italian sidekick, by Daladier and Chamberlain, who were no longer being borne triumphantly on upstretched arms when they arrived home at their respective airports. There were more and more airplanes with the tricolored cockade in the summer skies above us, and then, all of a sudden, wham!

The Germans invaded Poland.

On September 3, at ten in the morning, I went with my young secretary to La Rochelle on some business or other. I do not remember the sky ever having been so pure, the air so caressing. We went into a café, and suddenly the tango that was being played on the radio was interrupted. There was static, crackling, and then a grave voice announcing: "In keeping with the treaties that bind them to Poland, the governments of Great Britain and France this morning declared war upon the German Reich."

Around us, people looked at one another, trying to understand. One fisherman, still wearing his rubber boots, shouted: "So, they're going to send us to get slaughtered for Danzig?" And, downing his drink in one gulp, "Shit!"

No one replied. Annette's little hand was trembling in mine. We went out without a word, and the car got us back to Nieul in one jump. The radio was rarely turned on there. No one had heard. Tigy in her white smock was sterilizing bottles.

I tried to find words. And finally, quickly, without introduction, I blurted it out, as if to get rid of it: "It's war!"

"Are you sure, Georges?" And then, after a bit, "Do you think you'll be called up?"

"Not yet. Not for a while. Belgium is neutral."

As it had been in 1914, when it was the first to be invaded by the Kaiser's troops.

She was worried. So was I. In order to chase away the dark ideas, I got some of the bottles of champagne left over from your christening, and we clinked glasses, not the way you do when you're celebrating, but in order to give ourselves the courage to face the future. I had to go after another bottle, because Boule and the other members of the household had to be told, and as we drank we all had tears in our eyes.

Except you, my little Marc, in your carriage, in the shade of the linden tree; you just watched the shimmering of the leaves above your head. What new peregrinations might be in store for us? You didn't know any more about it than we did as we leaned over you and did our best to smile.

When would they leave us in peace, for God's sake?

11

Well, it was war! The next day, I wouldn't say we were resigned to it. There had been stupefaction at first, indignation, sometimes fits of rage and a few clenched fists; faces had hardened among the country folk as well as the city dwellers.

Each one, nonetheless, had to go about his daily chores, take care of the animals, lead them out to pasture; in La Rochelle, go to their offices, or studios, or shops on time, and the market was still held twice a week in the public square and along the arcaded streets. Boats still set out to sea with the tide, came back, their brown sails taut, to unload the catch in front of the fish market.

For several months, I should have been perceiving advance warnings from such things as long lines of big, heavy trucks coming from the north and east to unload on the plain their pieces of pylons and metal plates, which at first seemed mysterious, between Nieul, the nearby village of Laleu, and the port of La Pallice, twin to the port of La Rochelle, where now the long jetty that went out as far as deep water had at last been completed.

It had been talked about for twenty years. People had discussed it in the café and at the communal councils. And now here it was finished, with its rail line and its powerful cranes capable of loading and unloading the largest ships, even transatlantic liners. And right alongside, the drydock for ship repairs.

I had paid no attention. Yet I often went to Nieul's only café to play cards with the farmers, the deputy mayor, and the butcher. Sometimes they talked about it in hushed tones, but I barely listened. To tell the truth, I was no longer interested, since I had become a father, in anything but our white house, its garden, and the little circle living there, with you at its center.

The center of my attention especially, because now I was at last in a position to observe a little man-child, who, after nine months as a prisoner, was breathing free air, to watch his reactions to his surroundings, a universe of shadow and sunshine, the leaves of a big tree that murmured and was full of bird song, the proud crow of the cock, the faces that bent over you.

Indoors, your first attention went to the flies, which you followed with your eyes, looking grave and curious. And, should one of them happen to light on the lace of your cradle, you reached out your pudgy little hand, slowly, in a very gentle gesture, as if you already understood that living beings, especially the smallest of them, take fright easily.

I believed that, when the fly flew just as your hand got near, I could see disappointment and incomprehension written on your pink face. Why did that dark wisp of a thing fly away when you intended it no harm, but, on the contrary, just wanted to get acquainted with it?

Our electrician in La Rochelle, who had worked for us at La Richar-dière, sent us an apprentice after I phoned him about some minor job to be done. I was surprised. "Couldn't your boss make it?"

"He left yesterday. He's a soldier in the reserve, and has to guard a bridge over near Charron."

There were beginning to be empty chairs in the café on the square. The blacksmith informed us that he was mobilized in place. In the Charentes, at least, although people might have heard of tractors, they had never yet seen any. Young farmers were mobilized in place and assigned to stay for the plowing and sowing. Afterward, they would be off to the front, like every-one else. The old men and youths could then take over.

You were growing under our very eyes and becoming pudgy. It was fascinating, moving, to see those very light eyes of yours, much lighter than Tigy's and mine, concentrate on the tiniest object, on the most insignificant living thing.

I often saw you, in your playpen, which we set up under the linden tree, where I had planted daisies, my favorite flowers, intensely contemplating a bee gathering nectar. You were just as patient as the bee, and when it finally flew away, sated, toward its hive, you were disappointed, on the point of tears.

You rarely cried. Nor did you yell, even when you woke up at night and waited patiently for your mother to come and change your diaper. Just a discreet little call, as if you knew that someone would come.

The war was on in earnest in Poland. The papers told of populations massacred and villages burning. Would that sound and fury reach our peaceful village? Reason made us reply that anything was possible, but the life instinct, our attachment to our dear ones, to our garden, our house, made us deaf, and we egotistically fell back on the small human nucleus the group of us formed.

I knew well enough that Belgium would not remain forever neutral, that no quasi-heavenly border guard would appear on the steps of his little station, as had happened at De Panne, to shout triumphantly to us, "Peace!"

I would have to go someday or other, but, since I was now among the oldest men still eligible, since I had never wanted any kind of NCO rating, since the army no longer used horses and riding them was all I had ever been taught in my military service, the chances were I would be among the very last called up.

Do you know what people then were talking about in the café on the square, and laughing over? A well-to-do farmer from Marsilly who lured little boys to a run-down cabin at the seashore. Most of the kids ran away. One day, they got together and decided to get even with him. One of them, the shrewdest one, followed the farmer to the cabin, while the others hid in the darkness, ready to act when needed.

"You're a nice little fellow. Take down your pants."

"Only after you take off your trousers and shirt."

The man did, and when he was practically naked, the gang of kids came rushing in. A few minutes later, the big lout of a farmer was stretched on the ground, panting from the fight he had put up, and they daubed his backside with hot tar. After which, his yelling notwithstanding, they shoved some chicken feathers up his anus. The kids merged into the landscape like so many starlings, leaving behind the naked character, covered with tar and trailing feathers behind. He was in great pain and had to go home that way, phone the little doctor, who, to the great anger of the farmer's wife, melted the tar off with a whole loaf of butter and pulled the feathers out. Our friend Bécheval told me it had actually happened, without mentioning the man by name, but in the café on the square, everyone knew who it was.

The Germans didn't seem in a hurry to come into France or Belgium, as they had in 1914. From the Siegfried Line to the Maginot Line, the Führer's troops and the French could see each other without field glasses. No one was firing, though. The only assaults were being made by loudspeakers set up on either side of the frontier.

As the prefect had announced, in Alsace, villages and cities had been evacuated, including mayors, priests, and pastors, and some had already resettled some thirty miles from La Rochelle.

German loudspeakers, to the strains of "Lili Marleen," were calling on the French to lay down their arms. The English humorously played the same tune back to the opposing soldiers, with different words. The French were still singing the old "Madelon" of the previous war.

. . .

It was the phony war, as history was to call it. A standstill war, fought with slogans, while huge gasoline storage tanks surrounded us, one not much more than a hundred yards from our stream.

I remembered the 1914 war, the years during which I had continually felt the pinch of hunger, the long lines outside the schools, which had been turned into food distribution centers, and others the courtyards of which had been turned into soup kitchens, with soup poured into any containers the people brought, my father helping out in the school I went to.

Standing in line! My mother and I took turns at it, and at home the kilogram loaf of black bread was cut into quarters. We even weighed each ration. And it didn't matter that my father, who stood almost six foot three and worked all day long, walking half an hour four times a day to get to and from his office, needed more calories than we. He was the one who insisted on this share and share alike.

Because of these memories, one morning I started tearing up the flowers in the garden, row by row. We filled big baskets with them, and Boule, Annette, and the young girl with the angelic face deposited them at the village church. Not for religion's sake. Or to get from the Virgin or some saint special favors for the future. Simply because we didn't know what to do with them and had no family graves in the cemetery to put them on. You looked at us from your little playpen and must have wondered about that colorful, odorful massacre of all the living world around you, which we had in fact originally planted with you in mind.

It was war, and the very next day we were all plowing, raking, sowing vegetable seeds that I had bought in the same shop where I had gotten the flower seeds. Peas, green beans, potatoes, on both sides of the hoops up which the grapevines were beginning to climb. Turnips, but also melons and strawberries. Tigy had her nose buried in gardening books and circulated among us with advice.

One morning, when we least expected it, something happened that was to be of prime importance to you. We were all in your room, where we had just bathed you, and, naked, pink, and plump, you started moving on the goatskin rug toward a goal you appeared to have chosen.

This was so consoling a picture of innocence and freshness that I went to get my Leica. Your mother, sitting in an armchair, followed you with her eyes, for you had never before moved your little body with such strength or such determination.

What you were going toward was a long, low piece of furniture, with rounded corners and with three dull-gold bands around it (made of paint, of course, not of the metal that today has people all over the world running after it). Its nine drawers, wide and deep, contained all of your baby clothes. Unbelievable how many clothes so small a being can require.

You finally got where you wanted and sat up to catch your breath. This was when we began to understand what you had decided to perform for us. Kneeling, you first grabbed hold of the lowest gold band, then paused, and turned toward us as if to ask, "Isn't this something, though?" We must have smiled, not without some apprehension, since we were afraid you were heading for a disappointment.

One of your hands reached out, got hold of the second band. You were moving slowly and cautiously. At each step, you paused for breath. One further effort and, holding on to the protruding gold bands so hard that your knuckles were turning white, you were almost standing. Yes, you were standing, and looked around at us now in triumph.

What inspiration made us not rush over to you to kiss you? You were no longer looking at us. All of your attention was concentrated on this dresser, which was well over two yards long. Now you were putting forward one unsure foot, then raising the other, your hands still solidly gripping, and you were taking your first step. It was happening as in a slow-motion movie; you seemed in no hurry at all, but as if bent on having all the odds on your side. One foot. The other. Once again you looked at us.

A long pause, a third step. Another stop and a fourth step. They were little, hesitant, careful steps. I didn't count them, but my Leica kept clicking away. You must have those pictures, Marc old man, the pictures of your first steps in life. When you got to the end of the dresser, you took one more look, then slowly let yourself slip down, and there you were again on your rug.

Shortly after that, you were walking in the garden grass, held up by a harness.

"Did you see my little frog, my fine young gentleman?"

That was what Boule called me, Boule, who was bound to me by very close ties but in whose heart you were beginning to take up more and more space. When you in turn had a "frog," your son Serge, who is now eighteen, she asked permission to go and be with you near Paris.

It was war and there were beginning to be lines at the food stores. Like everyone else, I stocked up on sugar, flour, coffee, peas, dried beans, and pasta. The war was supposed to be a lightning affair, to last no more than a few months at most. I had heard this when I was a boy, and that war had gone on for four years. I was therefore all the more determined to put in ample supplies.

There was nothing more I could do, so I decided to write a novel, with a title taken from a sweet pastoral song, which, though written during the French Revolution, is still sung today as a children's nursery rhyme: "Il pleut, il pleut, bergère . . ." It goes something like this:

It's raining, little shepherdess,
Look after your white sheep.
Let's hurry inside, shepherdess,
To the hut where you sleep.
I can hear in the treetops
The noise the raindrops make,
For the storm is now upon us,
The lightning makes us quake. . . .

I just kept the first line of it for my title, *Il pleut, bergère (Black Rain)*, and my thoughts went back to the author of the song, a comrade of Robespierre's who had nevertheless been sent to prison and later to the scaffold by Robespierre himself. The author composed the song while he was waiting to be guillotined.

My main character was to be a little boy, not so small as you then were, Marc, but still a boy. In that way, for ten days or so, bent over my typewriter, my mind filled only with that boy, I could get my thoughts away from the war, which was not to remain phony very long.

The winter was going by, and we heard that German troops, in a lightning attack on a peaceful and virtually unarmed Norway, had entered Narvik, in the far north.

I found time to write another novel, *Oncle Charles s'est enfermé* (Uncle Charles Locked Himself In), before finding out that Belgium, justifiably worried, had begun to call up its specialists. Some weeks later, it mobilized the younger reservists, while tens of thousands of soldiers still stood marking time, without firing a shot, some on the Maginot Line, others on the Siegfried Line.

You had become a little boy, a still very young boy, whom we nevertheless used to take bathing with us in the Atlantic from the little beach at La Rochelle. Your first contact with salt water did not make you cry, but you clung desperately to your mother's hand.

The sun was bright, the weather warm, on May 10, when the radio announced that Holland had been attacked and that, in order to gain some time, it had flooded part of the country by opening the dikes that separated it from the sea. The same day, German tanks entered Belgium, which delayed them as best it could, and this time called for general mobilization of all manpower. My turn had come.

12

I was expecting a shock, a violent emotion, or I'm not sure what, but anything except the calm, the serenity, which was the same as every other day, anything except a noontime meal during which no mention was made of imminent departure, even though the whole household was aware of it.

Millions of men had more or less recently left their homes, all over Europe, not knowing when they would see them again, or whether they would. Was their reaction the same as mine? It is true that I had been expecting this for a long time, without its having changed anything in my state of mind. My concerns had remained exclusively material, such as transforming our flower garden into a vegetable garden and stocking up on supplies.

The afternoon also was calm, except for half an hour during which we searched through closets, file cabinets, and even old boxes, looking for my military identification papers, which I couldn't remember having seen after leaving Liège. We finally found them in the most unexpected place. Yellowed and not very clean, with a bad ID picture of a ghost, a pale young man, skinny and tense, whom I didn't recognize.

In theory, I was supposed to check in, wearing the uniform that had been issued to me long ago, at some barracks in Brussels I had never before heard of. We found my fatigue cap, with its little pompon that swung back and forth on my forehead. We laughed when I tried it on. As for the uniform, long since moth-eaten, it had disappeared during one of our many moves. Nor would it have been of any use, since my build and my waist were no longer those of the adolescent of those days, and I would have had a hard time getting into the blouse or buttoning the trousers. No trace of my belt, either.

We even smiled as we packed the only suitcase I was taking; henceforth the Belgian Army would assume responsibility for me.

You were peacefully asleep under the linden tree and looked handsomer than ever to me. Only the Breton woman kept endlessly weeping and wiping her nose. She wept at any pretext, as if on command, and even sometimes wept with laughter.

Boule was silent, her forehead knit, furious that her "fine young gentleman" was being taken from her, and Annette kept looking hard at me, as if she were trying to make sure she would remember what I looked like. We didn't drink any champagne, because this afternoon had to remain just like any other. And your mother, who was not demonstrative, had her everyday look on her face as well.

Maybe I went just a little more often than usual to sneak a peek at you. Was that how all the others had gone off, and still were going off?

I set the alarm, because I had to take a very early train at La Rochelle, and had phoned for a cab to come from there to fetch me. Your mother had always refused to learn to drive, and would only do it much, much later.

I slept. The alarm tore me out of bed. Boule, as she did every morning, brought me my huge mug of coffee, which she often said looked more like a chamber pot. I slipped into my fancy tailored riding breeches, my soft leather boots, a tan shirt, a tan jacket too, all of which, except for the jacket, might well have passed for being quite military, especially with the regulation fatigue cap.

I looked at you at greater length than other mornings, without thinking anything special. I picked you up and my lips lightly grazed your skin, which was as delicate as ever.

"*Au revoir*, Tigy."

"*Au revoir*, Georges."

No visible emotion, just as if I were off to do the marketing at La Rochelle or on my way to Paris for a meeting with some movie producer.

The taxi was waiting. A quick look back at the house, the garden, and the whole little household, gathered to see me off. At the station, I was checked in by the military, and was much surprised to find myself in a virtually empty train.

What did I think of during that trip? Nothing special, certainly not about the future. Little farmhouses went by, grouped into villages or hamlets, sometimes isolated in the greenery that was spotted with the white and brown of cows in one place, white and black farther on, and sometimes only plain brown or black. Innocent steeples pointed up toward the pastel blue sky.

It was all very pretty, very pure. I could sometimes visualize old paintings, Dutch, Flemish, French, with their precise lines, and sometimes Impressionist pictures in which the contrasting spots created an intense, luminous life.

Why not think about children's toys, about the little painted wood animals we had recently bought you, their little farmhouse surrounded by chickens no bigger than a bean? We often had to get down on the floor to locate them under some piece of furniture.

Little towns, at times, a sudden application of brakes, and the train chugging as if it were about to rear. People getting on in a hurry or running. Hankies being waved here and there in the countryside; sometimes a tiny man behind a pair of oxen or heavy horses, alone in the middle of the vastness. It did something to me. My eyes were glued to that earth rushing by and on which all the humans appeared so innocent.

The suburbs at last, not yet with today's medium-income housing projects, but spotted with little red-and-white homes surrounded by that dream bit of garden. Montparnasse. Was it actually the Gare Montparnasse, or the Gare d'Austerlitz? I just can't remember. I had never taken this train, and all I can recall is a mass of people hurrying, a huge hall with ticket windows along one side, shiny steel tracks leading somewhere, anywhere. One had to use elbows to get a taxi, because they were few in number and as much in demand as a winning ticket in the national lottery.

A few curious looks at my getup, but there were so many soldiers of all kinds that no one was too surprised anymore.

"To the Belgian Embassy, Rue de Surène!"

The only embassy I had ever been to was the old one, on Rue de Berry, but I recognized Rue de Surène, rather short, affluent, and quiet, so close to the Madeleine, with its outmoded upper-middle-class and aristocratic town houses. The taxi stopped at the corner of Rue Boissy-d'Anglas, where a dense crowd was overflowing from Rue de Surène. Some Belgian uniforms, though not too many, for almost everyone was at least my age and there were potbellies aplenty.

No one was in a hurry; they just stood there, pressed one against the other, faces expressionless, all eyes on the gray stone embassy building, in which one at times caught sight of a fleeting silhouette.

At the station, I had seen a sign reading: "Belgians called to the colors are requested not to return to their country without first going to the embassy." No doubt another visa to get, or marching orders, I thought.

"Have you been waiting long?"

"Some have spent part of the night here."

I slipped discreetly forward, apologizing a thousand times. I finally got to the threshold of the embassy, which was guarded by an impressive display of police.

It just happened that I had met the counselor of the embassy, mainly because his father had long been an important politician from Liège and, having interviewed him several times for the *Gazette* back in those days, I had met the son.

"Our orders are not to let anyone in."

I did not insist, but wrote a short note and asked that it kindly be delivered to the counselor. A few minutes later, the sawhorses barring the way were opened, and I was led up to the second floor. There was feverish agitation, with clerks and stenographers coming and going in all directions. A door finally opened on a large quiet office, only one person in it, elegantly dressed and well mannered, very much the man of the world, and on the telephone. "Have a seat, Simenon . . ."

I was more impressed by the silence of the place than by the excitement outside.

"Yes . . . Yes . . . At what time?" and he listened as he made notes on a pad while looking at me. "What about the minister?"

I had of course not heard the answer to that, and he had barely hung up when another phone rang. He sighed. "It's been like this since yesterday, and it didn't stop all night. . . ."

His features looked drawn and his somewhat reddened eyelids bespoke a sleepless night.

"No. I just got a promise that . . ." He shook his head as he listened. "I don't want to keep them down in the street any longer. I was told three o'clock. . . ."

When he hung up, he gave a long sigh, and came over to shake my hand.

"I'm glad you came up to see me. Over there, it's an absolute madhouse. . . . All I get is orders and counterorders. . . . You'd think everyone in Brussels must have lost his mind. . . . First, the minister orders that everybody be allowed to take the train, and a little later GHQ begs us not to send along any more personnel. It seems the rail line has been cut already, and two trains have been unable to get through. . . . Yet, the minister . . ."

He wiped his brow with his handkerchief.

"I can't send men out under such conditions. . . . Listen, the best thing you can do is go and have lunch with some friends. . . . You must have a lot of them in Paris. Come back to see me about three this afternoon, because I got a promise that I'd have some meaningful word by then. . . ."

Telephone. Handshake, and me on my way out on tiptoe, closing the door behind me, and slipping as quietly as I could through the crowd, which was getting denser and denser.

• • •

On Rue des Saussaies I knew of a little restaurant with very good cuisine, which I had found in the old days, when I went to police headquarters, then called the Sûreté-générale.

I didn't want to impose on anyone for lunch, and yet I did wish I could kill the waiting time with some friend. There was one woman whom we often visited in La Rochelle and who just as often came to see us. She and I happened to have been born on the same day of the same year, so that we were more or less twins, a subject we often joked about. I knew she had an apartment in Paris, and in the phone booth I looked her name up in the directory.

She was free. I made a date to see her at her place right after her breakfast. She was a tall brunette, fashionably dressed and beautiful. Her husband, a very handsome man, was to disappear during the war into that mysterious fortress known as Nacht und Nebel, from which no one ever came back alive. She had a very feminine, tasteful apartment near the Quai d'Orsay, with big bay windows looking out on the Seine.

Wasn't I a ridiculous picture in my pomponned fatigue cap? I could have put it in my pocket, but in those days men did not walk around bareheaded.

We kissed on the cheeks, as usual. I gazed at her and recorded the picture in my mind so as to have it there, in case. . . . There was a true friendly feeling between us, and, on my part at least, there was more than a little warm tenderness in it.

I filled her in on what was happening and gave her news of Tigy, spoke to her a great deal about you. She was wearing a dress the simplicity combined with elegance of which delighted me, and I could not take my eyes off her long silky legs. I did not feel sexual desire for her. Yet her legs, at that moment when my fate hung in the balance, seemed to me the image of woman that I most preciously wanted to keep with me.

Finally, I told her frankly that, before leaving, I would love merely to caress those legs, and I felt she understood, because she smiled and motioned to me to come closer. If I were to claim that touching her was a purely chaste gesture, I would not be believed. Yet, that is what it was. My hand stopped just where her naked skin began, and hurried back down as if it felt it was doing something wrong.

I got up, satisfied, perhaps a little red in the face, and, at the door, we again exchanged kisses on the cheeks.

Rue de Surène. The police had been reinforced, but this time they let me in right away, and it seemed to me the second floor had become quieter. Some electricians were busy setting up a huge loudspeaker on the balcony and cables were stretched across the hall. I was asked to wait a few minutes.

"This time, I have an answer, but I didn't finally get it until ten minutes before you got here. Are they beginning to get angry out there?"

"They're impatient."

"Same as I was. GHQ was right. German tanks are all over the country and taking their toll. Our troops resisted as much as they could, but the enemy is surging forward in ever greater numbers toward the French border."

Despite the closed door, we could hear a strange voice, distorted by the loudspeaker.

"They're being told not to try to go any farther, to stay in and around Paris until new orders come through, in the barracks the French Ministry of War has put at our disposal."

And then, jumping from one subject to another: "Do you get along well with the authorities at La Rochelle?"

The bugling metallic voice had stopped, and there was heavy silence in the street, where men must have been looking at one another, without saying a word.

"Yes. I am well acquainted with the prefect, who came to dinner with us just last Sunday."

"How about the mayor?"

"We're on the best of terms. Just a few years ago he had a tethering-ring installed under the arcades across from the Café de la Paix because he had several times seen my horse standing out there, with a boy holding his bridle, while I played cards inside." I even knew his whole family, including some of his grandchildren. "Why are you asking?"

"Because, by agreement with the French government, the two Charentes have been designated as relocation areas for Belgian refugees. We have no one on the spot there, except a vice-consul who is French."

"Yes, he's my insurance agent."

"But we do have a quartermaster general and half a hundred men in uniform."

"I know. The general used to repair my clocks and jewelry in Paris."

I was amazed by these coincidences, without seeing how I fitted into the picture.

"I am going to phone Mandel," he said, referring to the then French minister of the Interior, who had once been Georges Clemenceau's closest aide. "I'm sure he'll be agreeable to having me appoint you high commissioner for Belgian refugees. You must be familiar with the region, which extends all the way to Bordeaux. I know that thousands of Belgians are already heading south, and they will all be directed toward La Rochelle.

Your job will be to get them relocated. You have carte blanche, and you will have power of requisition. Leave this very evening, and tomorrow get in touch with the prefect and the mayor, who will have been notified."

And he closed with a bitter smile, for the news of the day was not such as to inspire happiness or merriment: "Those are orders, Private Simenon."

I took the night train, disconcerted and a little frightened by my sudden responsibilities, though I could not foresee that more than three hundred thousand of my fellow countrymen would be looking to me to house them, feed them, find them work. I especially could not foresee the trainfuls, machine-gunned en route, that would arrive with dead and wounded aboard, women who had given birth in their carriages and then, the track being cut by the enemy, had to go miles, sometimes on a stretcher, before getting to another train.

At daybreak, I was back home at Nieul, where Boule eyed me with amazement. Everyone else in the house was still asleep. On your mother's night table, I was surprised to see a big picture of me, as if I were already dead. While we kissed, I looked at you over her shoulder, and your eyelids began to flicker, your eyes to open. I picked you up once more, as I had done two days before, and for you another sunny day was about to begin.

"I have to change my clothes and go right over to the prefecture."

The phone rang a little later.

"Simenon?" It was the prefect, already aware of my functions. "We have four big Belgian trawlers that went right through the barriers of French boats and came on into the harbor, and now they won't leave. They talk Flemish, and nobody can understand them."

"I'll be right down."

Only when I got into the city did I realize, on seeing how empty the streets were, that it was Sunday.

The prefect repeated to me the things I was supposed to do, and, getting to first things first, I headed for the port, where four big white trawlers, from Ostend, were almost blocking the narrow passage between the two towers on either side of its mouth.

I had studied Flemish, as all Walloons did, in elementary school, but I remembered only bits of it. It was very hot. The shimmering of the water hurt the eyes. I hailed one of the boats, on the deck of which could be made out a mirrored wardrobe, some tables, a sewing machine, and I was to discover later that other furniture was stored in the hold. These sailors had loaded their wives and children and, while enemy airplanes strafed them, had sailed down to La Rochelle, from which they were determined not to budge.

The palaver, as long as those with African tribes, went on until noon, interrupted by phone calls from a little bistro on the wharf to the prefect and then to the mayor of Charron, a small port north of La Rochelle.

Finally, I didn't have to yell, using my hands as a megaphone, to make myself heard across a dozen yards of water. They came for me in a dinghy. A big man with white hair and a red face received me in a dignified manner; the other masters had spontaneously made him their spokesman. In a mixture of two languages, I explained to him that they would be able to drop anchor in the small port of Charron, where there would be living quarters for them and from which they could go out to fish. Did he understand? Or didn't he? He nodded and repeated a phrase I in turn did not get. He pointed to my car, standing on the wharf, and then touched his chest and mine with his finger.

He wanted to go and see before making a decision, and I nodded agreement. He explained to the others what was going on. Twenty minutes later, we were at Charron, where he had no interest in going to see the mayor, but headed directly for the tiny harbor. He examined it closely, shaking his head. Then the mayor showed him a few houses, after which he had a friendly smile and put his hand on my shoulder.

Peace was signed. At night, the Ostend trawlers left the waters of La Rochelle, and the prefect, next morning, sighed with relief. A week later, when three or four hundred refugees had already been settled in portable sheds, facing the railroad station, the big white-haired captain, helped by his sailors, brought me three huge baskets of fish, which ended up in the big soup kettles.

Some trainloads, shunted from station to station, had taken three weeks to get down from Belgium, and the occupants looked at our wooden sheds and their bunks unbelievingly. The mayor had lent me a green-painted cabin, at the entrance to the camp, as we called it, which served as my office and that of the women working with me, and we had a telephone.

I had many volunteer helpers, men and women, French and Belgian. Some girls from the city and one girl scout took care of the office, others took charge of relocating the refugees. One nurse, a model of devotion, efficiency, and good humor, helped to unload the trains, dress wounds, wash babies and children, take care of the women who had had their babies en route, for the hospital was already overcrowded and the doctors overwhelmed with work.

I had been given a square-tipped key that opened and closed train doors from the outside, and some trains, those in good shape, were sent on. We separated the good trains from those that had been too long on the road and had been machine-gunned.

Some Belgians came by car, and I issued gasoline ration tickets to them so they could reach their destinations. Others came loaded in trucks, buses, and even one hearse arrived, carrying a whole live family.

Some boy scouts from Ostend, aged fifteen to eighteen, volunteered to keep order, and they were wonderful. A "high society" lady of La Rochelle asked me whether she might help me by peeling potatoes, say, in the small circus tent we had found already set up. For entire days, she peeled, and scrubbed carrots, which the market women freely gave to the boy scouts.

One morning a small truck stopped briefly in front of the camp, deposited five corpses of old men in gray outfits on the sidewalk, and pulled quickly away before we could come out. The old men had died on the way, of natural causes, and had no identification papers on them. They probably came from some Belgian old people's home, but we were never able to identify them.

Some of the men went to work in the nearby airplane factory. They were surprised by their rate of pay, and brought me part of it spontaneously, to be shared among the needy. In the suburbs, some local women had created centers to which I was able to send elderly people who needed special care and comfort. Sometimes planes flew over the city and dropped bombs, and we had to make everybody lie down until the alert was over.

One night, on my way back to Nieul, where I spent very little time, because I often slept on a bench in the railroad station between train arrivals, I saw a fire burning near our house. One of the gasoline tanks was on fire, and small flames made the road hazardous. I sped through unharmed. The women were standing in our garden, watching the show, and you, Marc, were peacefully sleeping through it all.

The fire did not reach our place, but three nights later, Tigy roused me from too short a rest. I heard bombs exploding, fragments hitting our shutters.

"We can't stay here. We have to find shelter."

There was no cellar to the house and no other means of shelter than the ditch beside the road, to which your mother carried you, wrapped in a blanket, while I stayed asleep in bed. All of this may seem very dramatic to you, and we did go through many dramatic moments. We were no longer aware of them, any more than we were of our lack of sleep.

· · ·

The city needed wood for the bakers' ovens. By a happy coincidence, a train just then came in from the Ardennes. I asked all the lumbermen on it—for they are numerous in that province—to stand to one side of the arrival area. That very day, some Belgian trucks we had requisitioned took them to a forest about ten miles away; the next day, the bakers had wood again.

Then there were . . . But these were really just the fringes of war, without comparison to what people elsewhere were suffering. Little by little, Frenchmen from the north started mixing in with the Belgians, and before it was over La Rochelle was an invaded camp: Normans, then Parisians. I found among them some old friends and associates, both Belgian and French. An order from the Ministry of the Interior informed me that the city of Royan was to be reserved for the Antwerp diamond merchants, who organized their own community.

At last, all roads and all of the countryside were swamped, and it was disorder, a hopeless mess. The end.

La Rochelle, with a normal population of fifty thousand, now housed two hundred thousand people, and the same was true of all the towns and villages of the two Charentes.

I didn't listen to the radio but I heard the clamor of the inhabitants of the camp, hugging one another and weeping for joy: "There's an armistice!"

I thought that my job was over, but, once the Germans arrived, I had to discuss with them how we could repatriate all these people, who all wanted to get back to their own homes. So many trains, so many doctors, so many stations for their departures, so much bread, butter, ham, coffee, sugar, so many baby bottles . . .

When I finally returned home for good and rejoined your mother, Boule, and the others, I was not very steady on my feet, and now it was English planes that were bombarding the nearby port of La Pallice while German searchlights tried to pick them up in the sky. There was nothing more for me to do. We all left together, to try to find a place to stay in the forest of Vouvant, in the nearby Vendée. There we located a small farmhouse to rent.

You were still traveling, my poor Marc. And this was just the beginning. As for me, I was unaware, when we left Nieul, that I would never again return to our home there.

13

A real forest! Years before, probably at the time of La Richardière, I had driven beside it for a long spell, starting from a little town named La Châtaigneraie. Tigy and I, traveling in our open car, on the country road, had stopped in a small café to have a refreshing glass of the minor local white wine.

This forest had enchanted me. Unlike the forest of Orléans, from which I had fled because of the silence and dullness of its pine trees, lined up in regular rows like one of Napoleon's armies, this one was alive and colorful, with trees of all species and a few white birches that made them look even merrier. My recollection of it was rather vague, but by looking at the map I found our forest just where it was supposed to be, a little beyond Fontenay-le-Comte, at the other end of La Châtaigneraie.

There were four of us, your mother and you, Boule, me at the wheel, heading nowhere in particular. We wanted calm and rest, if possible hidden away from anything active and the war.

As for the little farmhouse in which we were about to spend several months, we must have heard about it at the inn in Vouvant, a village deep in the middle of the forest.

This was really a very little farm, a farm for impoverished farmers, less than a mile from Vouvant. The husband, one of the first to be called up, had disappeared. His young wife and his son, blonder even than you, had moved into just one room, then into the stable, and that very evening the farm was ours, that is, we were able to live in it.

It was in a declivity surrounded on all sides by forest, and only four or five cows grazed in the fields. The owner was thin, distraught over the fate of her husband, and she did all the farmwork herself.

August, the end of August, if memory serves. The trees were already taking on color under a hot, heavy sun. You had become a little boy. A big kitchen, without running water. We had to go get it from the well. No toilets: a wooden outhouse, which we shared with the farm woman and her son, who soon was your friend. You already needed friends, the first little boy or little girl you met as well as a dog, a cat, a snail, or an ant that you tenderly held.

I think that Boule slept in a space near the kitchen, we in the so-called mansard rooms, which were really a garret, for there were no proper stories to the house. The beds were very high, with two or three feather mattresses, into which we sank, and by way of covers, an eiderdown, also stuffed with feathers.

I remember now and then spending whole afternoons making all kinds of little cookies for you, some with finely grated lemon peel in them, others with orange peel decorated with a piece of angelica, still others spiced with different flavors, nutmeg, cinnamon, and something else I can't remember that was like the "speculas" of my childhood. We stored them in tin cans, in which they could be kept a month or more, and you asked for three or four every day, thinking very seriously before selecting the color you wanted.

The whole little house then smelled good, of fruit, sugar, and flour, and with cookie cutters I formed the dough into various shapes. Pinked circles, hearts, outlines of animals laid out on buttered paper, and I had to work fast, because once the oven was red hot, it took just a few instants to bake them. You watched me with your grave, curious eyes, and didn't miss a single one of my gestures.

I would also go up to sit at the table in our garret-bedroom, where wasps nested between the tiles and rafters, to do some typing, and this was where I wrote *La Vérité sur Bébé Donge (I Take This Woman)*, a novel in which there was no war, no commotion, albeit some dramatic action, full of sunshine and harmonious gardens.

War, like life, is a lottery, and one has to follow his fate without protest. Some fight determinedly or undergo the anxiety of bombings. From one end of Europe to the other, people are killing and torturing one another, whereas, for no apparent reason, some islets of idyllic peace subsist. It seems almost shameful to be in the calm of one of these, to be making little cookies, to go each morning up a path crossing the fields to do the marketing in Vouvant.

The woman who runs the inn has a husband from whom she has heard nothing, but will soon learn that he is a prisoner in Germany. The Luftwaffe attacks London every day, and the sirens there instruct the inhabitants to go to shelters in the Underground. Houses crumble in every neighborhood.

You follow along the path that takes us to Vouvant, your little hand in mine, and you ask few questions. It would seem that you are bent on figuring out the answers for yourself. You would like to go over and pet the cows, the donkey looking at you with its great dreamy eyes. You want to pet everything that is alive; you dream of a world in which everything would be friendly.

One day, when we are in the woods, you ask me to trim a stick for you, and I choose a branch, which I strip of its twigs, using my big knife. I take off the bark, round off one tip. My knife slips, and your cane-to-be hits me violently in the chest. I try not to make a face, although it is very painful, but your eyes show anxiety.

"Hurt?"

"No, son."

I rarely called you Marc. I preferred "son," a word that seemed so fine to me. I used it for your brothers later, as my father had applied it to me.

I tried to smile. I wondered whether I had fractured a rib, and Tigy daubed me with some kind of unguent. I spent a bad night. By morning, the pain was duller but more worrisome.

"I'm going to Fontenay-le-Comte for an X-ray."

There was no doctor in Vouvant. Your mother wanted to go with me, but she had enough to do taking care of the house with you and Boule, not to mention your young friend, whose pink face could be seen at any time peering in through one of the small windowpanes.

Walking eased the pain. I took almost two hours to get to Fontenay-le-Comte, where I was surprised to find that, without getting exhausted, I had covered almost seven miles along the edge of the forest.

I was directed to the radiologist's affluent home. I told him with a smile, as if to apologize, that I must have cracked a rib. He was young, but serious, sure of himself, not a bit pompous.

"Take off your shirt and place yourself here."

Chest bared, I had to slip behind a smoked glass that pressed me against a hard partition.

"Don't move . . . Breathe . . ." He was sitting on the other side of the plate, which spread a vague kind of glow into the darkness, and was giving me brief commands. "Breathe . . . Hold it . . . Inhale . . . Turn a little to the right . . ."

With a worried brow, he went to fetch a sheet of transparent paper, which he placed against the plate and started sketching what he saw inside my body with a squeaky pencil. I kept watching his ghostly face, and it seemed to me to be growing more and more concerned. This lasted at least a quarter of an hour.

Holding the large sheet of paper, he showed me into a huge office full of scorching sunshine. "Sit down."

His gestures were slow and measured. The forest, our little farmhouse, even the street, silent beyond his windows, all seemed far away, in another world. He was still penciling; then, using a flat ruler, he traced mysterious lines on the picture he had made and wrote figures in the margin.

"Is your father still living?"

"No."

"At what age did he die?"

"Forty-five."

"Of what?"

"Angina."

A small smile, as if that delighted him.

"Are my ribs . . . ?" I began.

"There's nothing wrong with your ribs at all. It is much more serious than that. Look at this . . ." His ruler was at an angle, over the image of one of my organs.

"Your heart is . . ." I don't remember how many centimeters he said it was at its widest point. A figure that was far too great, at least so he solemnly told me. "An enlarged heart, you see. What is commonly referred to as athlete's heart. And this . . ." A kind of swelling about the heart. Another bad sign!

"Do you smoke?"

"A pipe."

"You'll have to stop smoking. Do you drink?"

"Wine."

"No more. As of today."

"Do you work a great deal?"

"I usually write six novels a year."

"Ah! You write novels?"

I was almost ashamed of my profession.

"You'll have to stop writing."

"What will I do?"

"Rest. And, especially, no sexual activity."

"Just what is wrong with me?"

"You have the heart of an old man."

I was thirty-seven and had just done almost seven miles on foot without even feeling the need to stop for breath. I also had a son, a *ploustiquet en brique*, whom I was just getting to know.

"Am I in great danger?"

"I give you two more years, provided you follow all my instructions."

He "gave" me two years. And he wasn't the kind of man you could bargain with. I almost felt like begging him on bended knee, "Please, let me have five." It was two years. Period.

"No straining yourself physically, either. Walk slowly."

This solemn, categorical man, who was playing God the Father, had cast a spell on me. His office was impressive, his face, his clothes; his even voice allowed no contradiction.

"That will be two hundred francs."

He saw me to the door of his fine house, and I walked mechanically, putting back into my pocket the pipe I had unthinkingly taken out of it. Under a noonday sun that burned the nape of my neck, I walked the seven miles that separated me from our temporary home, as temporary as all of our homes. This time, I stopped several times, as if my heart, which I felt with my hand, were beating too hard.

All of this had the same character as the declaration of war, my departure for Paris, Rue de Surène. Nothing dramatic about it, but as if I were anesthetized. I simply accepted things. Two years . . . I might have been killed a little while back during one of those bombardments of La Rochelle. . . . It never occurred to me to go looking for a second opinion. Wouldn't another doctor have told me the same thing as his pontificating confrere?

I stopped for a moment at the only café I came across, and, at the point of ordering a glass of white wine, I switched to a glass of mineral water.

Not to smoke anymore. Not to write anymore. Not to make love anymore. Not to . . . But at least I would be alive! For two years . . .

And you, son, would never know of your father's youth. You would know nothing, later, about your grandparents, Liège, your aunts, your uncles, and your cousins by the dozens. . . .

As I walked, a still-vague project was taking shape. Dogs, horses, even bulls have pedigrees. And you would know about yours only on your mother's side. About the Simenons, nothing! Your father would probably become an out-of-focus figure on some yellowing snapshots, in some novels you might someday read but in which you would find nothing of me.

That solemn gentleman had forbidden me to write because I had confessed to him that I was a novelist. But what about, little by little, writing down my memories, in a notebook that I could will to you? By the time I got to our farmhouse, I was satisfied with the solution I had found, and even a bit proud. With two years, I had plenty of time, even if I wrote only a quarter of an hour a day.

Tigy was waiting for me, with a smile on her face. She had felt all my ribs the night before, and although she agreed to my going to Fontenay, it was only to set my mind at ease.

"My ribs are all right."

"I knew it."

"Only . . ."

"Are you sick?"

"Yes."

"Your lungs?"

"No. My heart. It seems I have an athlete's heart."

She could hardly keep from smiling. "Well? That's good, isn't it?"

"It means my heart is enlarged."

"Is that serious? Can it be cured?"

"It seems there's no cure for it."

This time, she started to get upset, and turned white. "Do you feel ill?"

"No. I went to Fontenay and back on foot."

"Tell me the truth, Georges. Don't go beating around the bush . . ."

And then I blurted it out, with relief, as if she had the right to know, and anyway she would quickly have caught on.

"Like my father, more or less . . . I have two years left to live. . . ."

She became rigid, her way of showing she was moved. "Are you sure?"

"And that is only if . . ."

I told her about my pipe, the wine, the light meals, for he had also said to eat light meals, which I forgot to mention. About abstinence, chastity, and the avoidance of all effort . . .

"We can't stay on here, where there isn't a single doctor and we are far from everything."

We confessed to Boule only part of the truth, and she fell into my arms in tears.

A week went by, maybe two, in the peacefulness of our mini-valley, and you and I played together in the shadows of the forest. How alive you were, so straight on your sturdy legs! How handsome you were, my Marc, with your sharply defined face, your eyes full of dreams!

Did you wonder why I no longer carried you at arm's length and no longer tossed you up to straddle my shoulders? I had been ordered to avoid all strenuous effort, and I was obeying. I didn't protest. After all, I've obeyed all my life, obeyed the stupidest orders and regulations, even when I was inwardly rebelling.

I have driven cars for over fifty years on all the continents, with their wide variety of regulations, and never got a ticket. So how could I disobey destiny? Two years? Millions of men did not have two years of life before them, some not even a day, not an hour, and they had done nothing to deserve that, they had been as obedient as I. It was just—or maybe I should say unjust?—because they had indeed obeyed that . . .

Tigy was the one who went to Fontenay-le-Comte and found a small house for rent there, with a garden, on the river called the Vendée. That house . . . But no need to describe it to you, because I told you all about it in the notebooks I started writing for you to have when you grew up.

On the first page, I had drawn a robust tree, and each branch carried the name of one of your Simenon ancestors. The title was written in India ink, to look more imposing:

PEDIGREE
OF
MARC SIMENON
with a portrait of his father, his grandfathers
and grandmothers, his uncles, aunts, and cousins

All I wrote, in notebooks much like the ones I am blackening at the moment, was two or three pages a day, and I missed smoking my pipe. I spoke directly to you, and I called you Mahn, which was what you called yourself before you could pronounce an *r*. At that time, you always talked about yourself in the third person: "Mahn is hungry. . . ." "Mahn has to make pipi. . . ."

I went to a G.P., and he examined me, phoned his confrere the radiologist, and then suggested I consult a famous cardiologist in Paris. Fine! But it was wartime, and we were in a coastal area. We were Belgians, therefore aliens, therefore suspect, and as such in theory I was supposed to go to the police station every day to sign a register. We did not technically even have the right to leave the very charming city in which we were living.

I went eeling, outside our house, and you watched me, with great amazement, the day I pulled a huge eel up out of the river.

The doctor did say it was all right, when you were tired, for me to push your little folding stroller. And even to do some of the work in our garden, where, in spring, you were so filled with wonder at seeing our first vegetables grow.

Annette had gone to La Roche-sur-Yon, to be with her father. When the railroad station of which he was stationmaster was bombed by the English, he had had both legs shattered, and they had had to be amputated. Today, at eighty-five, he still walks about on his artificial limbs, and was driving his car just two years ago.

Two years! Exactly the time left to me to live, of which I didn't want to lose the slightest crumb. I practically never left your side. Wherever I went, I led you by the hand and pointed out to you everything that there was to see: the reflections in the river, the inverted image the water sent back of the old stone bridge, and then the first lilacs.

"They smell good, Marc."

"Smell good."

You were still mine, understand? And all that I was writing in my notebooks was so that later on a little bit of me might remain with you.

The publisher Claude Gallimard came to see me. He had a pass to get into the Unoccupied Zone and was on his way to meet my friend André Gide on the Riviera. Gide had asked him in a letter what I was writing and whether he could bring him some of it to see. So Claude took along a photocopy of my pages.

Someone informed us that the Château de Terreneuve, which dominated the hill above, was for rent, a fact that was only partly true. Half the château was for rent, the other half remaining occupied by the owners. We moved once again. Why not leave fine images in your memory as long as I still had the means to?

"Another château?" you might say. I wasn't doing it on purpose. Here, you had your own immense park, with bodies of water, and dense woods in which, after a rain, we would go to "pluck" snails off the tree trunks and leaves. You were always the first to spot them, as you did the mushrooms.

"There, Dad, another one . . . a big one."

Now I had only a year and a half left before me. Your mother, Boule, and I never mentioned it, and I, for one, never thought about it.

Gide sent me word, through Gallimard, that I ought not to go on with my notebooks in the first person but, because I was a novelist, should type them directly, as I did my novels. I followed his advice. Don't I always obey? And so I got back to my typewriter, started over from the beginning, in the third person, using fictitious names.

One day I was watching you as you sat on one of the steps of the porch and had your eyes riveted on the sky, which seemed to fascinate you. I wondered what you could be thinking about, what hypnotized you up in the immense blue expanse. I quietly got nearer to you, and only a great deal later did you turn toward me, sighing, disappointedly: "It's gone away, the cloud. . . ."

You had a hard time pronouncing the words, and were still looking overhead for the little pink-and-white cirrus that you had kept your eyes on until it disappeared.

As I . . . But no! I had no time to think about that.

14

We spent about two years of calm, uneventful life in this calm, uneventful subprefecture, which had the same discreet charm as most subprefectures. There is a legend about subprefects often being poets, and ours, whom we used to see going by each day, young and very blond, with a faraway look, must have been one of those poets who somehow got lost in an administrative job. This was when we lived in our narrow little house on the banks of the Vendée, and the subprefecture building was a hundred yards down the same quay.

Two years! Those two years grudgingly allotted by the pretentious doctor who enunciated his diagnoses as if they were eternal truths. Little by little, I was forgetting that those two years were to be my last. In the end I believed it while not believing it, or, more precisely, I lived each day for itself by taking maximum advantage of every passing hour.

I worked little; I might say I didn't work anymore at all, for writing my childhood memories alongside my own child, who was getting bigger, was more of a pleasant pastime, and I now think that watching you sharpened my memory and brought up the freshest images.

From the very first days, your governess, a young and merry woman, stole you away from me a bit, because it was she who took you to the park and the woods of the château. When I heard that she had a little girl of her own scarcely older than you, whom out of discretion she had not mentioned to me, I asked her whether she would like to bring her along, and at first sight you and the little girl became best friends. I've forgotten her first name, because you've had so many other friends since then, girls and boys, of all descriptions! She was pudgy, merry as her mother, with very curly hair. I ordered a load or two of sand, which was dumped at the far end of the park to make a sandbox. Little beach pails, painted red and decorated with primitive images. Children's shovels and rakes . . .

I had had an impoverished childhood, but had received a "proper upbringing," in which I learned to hold out the "correct hand," not the left one, in greeting, to say "Thanks" and "Sorry," which I still do, as if by instinct, at my age, even when someone else bumps into me or steps on my foot.

My horizon had been a quiet street inhabited by minor clerks, petty government employees, and modest pensioners. The hazards of war had willed that you live in a château overlooking the city where once upon a time the French poets of the Pléïade had met, and even Rabelais had visited, as attested by his name on Rue Rabelais.

Often, getting you away from your governess, your mother, Boule, or the Breton woman, who was back with us again, I would take you down the steep little stony path, with hovels from times gone by crazily leaning against one another on either side, and we would go and watch the various kinds of horse-drawn vehicles that brought the peasants in to the market-place.

The horses, the smell of their manure, and the activity of the market fascinated you as they had fascinated me at your age, and you opened wide eyes to absorb everything, the colors of the foods displayed on Place Viète, the shadows of the trees, and I am sure that you intently listened to the cackling of the chickens and the crowing of the roosters in their openwork crates, the powerful voices of the men, the sharp ones of the women calling out for customers.

But the biggest fun of all, for you as for me, was the monthly horse and stock fair, on the other side of the river, with hundreds of creatures tethered to the iron bars that went all around the enclosure. You would have liked to pet every one of them, including the pink pigs, and I can still see the longing in your face as you watched a sow surrounded by a dozen piglets fighting each other to get at her teats.

You would have liked to have everything, Marc, everything that came out of the earth, from trees to flowers, the earth itself. Those images, those sounds, those odors—I was delighted to see you fill up on them, because later that would keep you from ever being surly, cranky, or unhappy.

I didn't miss a single market day or fair. I never have missed any, wherever I was in the world, even though I overlooked the "picturesque" sights, the historical monuments or museums. You must know today, since you have been through it yourself, the warm exaltation a father feels when he takes his dazzled little boy walking through the colorful crowd of a marketplace, as well as crossing a still-dewy field or a wood in which a thousand barely perceptible sounds reveal an intense although invisible life.

Subprefecture towns are usually bourgeois by nature, and our life in ours was bourgeois and sheltered. Fontenay-le-Comte at the time had a little over five thousand inhabitants, and, as time went by, almost all the faces became familiar. For me, that began at the town's biggest café, the Café du Pont. It was the typical café of small French towns, at the time, with mirrors on all sides, marble tables with fancy ironwork legs, and, near the inevitable columns, a shiny metal ball, which the white-aproned waiters opened for an instant to take out or put back the cloths they used to wipe off the tables.

Almost every afternoon, I met there with some of the local bigwigs, a lawyer, a physician (not the one who had foretold my happy, or, rather, unhappy, ending!), sometimes the subprefect, and a retired police commander. Always seated at the same table, we played a very serious game of bridge, which lasted until dinnertime.

That did not keep me from also being an habitué of another café, almost across the street but farther down, which was noisier, more working-class, and resounded with bright laughter. I sometimes even ventured, as if about to commit a sin, to order, in a voice full of shame, a small glass of white wine, to spite, or perhaps to challenge, my pedant of a radiologist, who lived in the higher part of town, reserved for the upper bourgeoisie, and never deigned to enter either of the two cafés.

On Saturday mornings, I couldn't resist the marketplace bar, smoky and crowded, where the countryfolk stood elbow to elbow along the zinc counter and talked in loud voices as they downed their drinks.

The main street was Rue Clemenceau, long and broad, so that from the bridge what one saw first, all the way at the far end, beyond a rather long slope, was a small red-and-white railroad station that looked like the work of a Sunday painter. Everything was fine and good. One barely noticed the two or three Germans in uniform standing outside a house like all the others that the occupiers had taken for their Kommandantur. The troops were stationed rather far outside town, on a plateau where they had built an airstrip. We sometimes heard machine-gun fire from there, but paid no attention to it.

I was no longer obliged to go and sign in every day at the police station. The superintendent was a refugee from the Ardennes, from a little village on the Belgian border. He was a charming man and of his own volition suggested to me that, since I lived outside town, I sign in only once a week, putting seven signatures at once into his record book.

When I asked him whether he knew someone to take care of the vegetable garden and the poultry I had on part of the château's land, which was set aside for my use, he introduced me to a strapping reddish-blond husky who had been a slate miner in his hometown and was now living here with his wife and nine children. His name was Victor. He was a fervent, active Communist, which did not bother me but had kept him from finding any employment in Fontenay.

So we had chickens and ducks, vegetables growing in the garden, and Victor did whatever needed to be done, preferring the heavier chores, for, up north in his hometown mines, he had been used to climbing a ladder with blocks of slate weighing well over two hundred pounds on his back.

Because of the first war, I had had experience of how things can drag out, whereas the French still believed this would be a rather short war. Just below us, on the other side of the Vendée, was a bicycle factory. Since I was no longer entitled to use the official medallion the prefect of La Rochelle had given me at the time of the Belgian refugee camp, I felt it would be wise for us to have some other mode of locomotion. I knew that bikes were now to be had only on the black market, and tires were all but nonexistent. Nevertheless, I tried my luck by going to see a cordial and smiling gentleman whom I had glimpsed at the Café du Pont, without knowing who he was.

"I apologize for making a request that you must hear ten times a day. Is it still possible to buy a bicycle?"

"Of course, Monsieur Simenon. Because you *are* the writer, aren't you? I have a couple dozen of your books. My wife and I are among your avid readers. . . ."

All around me in the huge workshop were new spare parts, lined up in orderly fashion.

"Did you want a man's bike?"

"And a woman's too, if possible . . ."

I was getting more daring. He was a nice fellow—not just because he read my books, but by nature.

"What would you say to an exchange?" he asked.

People were gradually getting back to the barter system of olden times. For instance, the barbed wire that farmers needed to fence in their meadows or their fields was no longer bought for money, but for ham or butter. Even nails had become precious and could be traded for merchandise of the greatest usefulness.

"Ten autographed books per bike; what do you say?"

I was a little ashamed of the high value he attributed to my novels, which, truth to tell, were no longer to be found in the bookstores.

"I'll give you thirty for the pair."

"What about your little boy? I saw you in the street with a little boy. . . ."

"He may need one someday, but he's still too young."

"I'll give you an extra-small bike, anyway, for the autographs."

He looked at me with a mischievous, friendly eye. "Is that all? Nothing else you need?"

"Well, there's Boule—that is, our cook. . . ."

"Fine, then, one men's bike, one child's, and two women's . . ."

He led me to the back of his large glass-domed workshop and showed me a sparkling new small black motorcycle.

"Would you like it? You have quite a climb to get up to the château. I could let you have it at cost." Which was a ridiculous figure at a time when everything was selling for astronomical prices.

"In that case, I'll give you a set of my complete works, in the de luxe edition."

The works at that time ran to some fifty volumes, and I had two full de luxe sets.

Two days later, he had put together the bikes, and I was teaching Tigy to ride hers on the big public square where the stock fair took place and where she was in no danger of running into a pedestrian or a wall. Henceforth, I went down to town on my little "two-stroke" motorcycle, which reminded me of the days I rode one to cover stories for the *Gazette de Liège*.

And that wasn't all. There was a horse trader who rode around town in a sulky drawn by an adorable little horse and—yes, that's right. I went to a cartwright and had a light chaise, or cart, made, with two big wheels painted yellow, the way one sees them in English prints. The cartwright, delighted to get a change from the heavy country carts he usually had to make, devoted his best efforts to it.

All I had to do now was find a double pony. The German Army had requisitioned all horses, but not ponies or double ponies. The horse trader brought them up somehow from the Pyrenees and sold them as having been bred at Tarbes. As I was later to learn, they actually came from Spain, where they had been used a lot during the civil war.

I bought one, perhaps a little too lively for my taste. His light coat was so handsome and he was so affectionate to me that I kept him just the same, aware that I would have to keep a close watch on him. Ponies are less predictable than horses, even thoroughbreds, and in the country they have a reputation for often being vicious, a word I have never used about a horse or any other animal, or a human being.

After a few days, I had control of him, and you, Marc, held by your mother, took your place on the single bench. Henceforth we could discover the surrounding countryside, the dirt paths, the farmhouses hidden away.

Our doctor, the one I played bridge with, thought you were looking sallow and suggested that I take you away for a month or two at the seashore. Foreigners were not allowed on the coast, whoever they were. The interpreter at the Kommandantur, armed with a certificate from my doctor friend, nonetheless got us an *Ausweis* that allowed us to spend two months at L'Aiguillon.

Titine, the woman who sold us fish and used to go to the coast to get her stock from the fishermen, found us a tiny cottage, far from the village, sparsely furnished but surrounded by dunes. You probably don't remember it, Marc. The sea washed up less than a hundred yards from us, and in the kitchen, by hand, I wrote the pages of *Pedigree,* which I would type the next day in a little office at the rear of the port's inn.

It was sunny. And hot. I went swimming every morning. Since the sea was cold, all I swam was a few strokes, and a new secretary, who had come with us, waited for me at the water's edge with my robe and gave my back a vigorous rubdown.

You followed me along the dunes, where you could always spy before me, as you did with mushrooms, light-green wild asparagus, which we all ate with relish. We also went to watch the fishermen returning to port, and their still-wriggling catch fascinated you.

A two-month intermission in our life at the château. You now had your full color back again. The days went by without our noticing. I worked on *Pedigree,* which became a long book, though I had it published only very much later, for fear that the picture I drew in it of my mother might hurt her.

Being prudent, and knowing that anything might happen, I had four or five copies made of it. I sent one to my bank at La Roche-sur-Yon, to be put in their vault, another to Gallimard, to whom I was not selling the rights but, as a friend, was asking him to put it in a safe place for me. The others were similarly dispersed, and I had come to the end of the two fateful years, as healthy as ever, if not more so, and still as hungry for life as I had been for food, first as child, then as adolescent.

Then there was, back at Fontenay, a visit from a cold and slightly sinister man who was a Vichy commissioner, in the service of one Monsieur Darquier de Pellepoix, in charge of "Jewish Affairs," that is, charged with ferreting out all who were hiding, men, women, and children, and turning them over to the occupying forces, who, in turn, would send them to the German camps, from which mighty few came back.

He looked at me with his somber eyes, and literally spat at me: "You're a Jew, aren't you?"

"We have been Christians from father to son, and for several generations we have all had the name of Christian among our given names."

"Simenon derives from Simon."

"Oh?"

"And Simon is a Jewish name."

"I can swear to you . . ."

"I don't give a fig for your swearing. I need proof."

"I can show you that I'm not circumcised."

"Some nonreligious Jews don't get circumcised either."

I would not have been ashamed to be Jewish, any more than had I been a Negro, Chinese, or Iroquois. But I am not, and I felt that my fate and that of my family depended on this man with the heavy shoulders and even heavier look in his eyes.

"Are you trafficking on the black market?"

"I have never sold anything except my author's rights."

"Ham? . . . Butter? . . ."

"I've bought some for home consumption, but never sold any "

"You're a Jew!"

I was sweating, because it seemed nothing could change this man's mind.

"I never make a mistake. I can smell a Jew ten paces away. . . ."

I was unaware that I was giving out any odor, unless it was that of my perspiration.

"You have one month in which to get me the birth certificates of your parents, your grandparents, and your great-grandparents."

"My grandparents are long since dead, as well as my father, and the only great-grandfather I ever knew was a former miner in Liège, who died blind at the age of almost a hundred."

"Just the same, get me all those papers within a month."

The town down below us was so peaceful, so smiling, and one could see smoke rising from a few chimneys, passers-by like ants in the streets, the red-and-white railroad station in the distance.

Tigy had been sent rudely out of the room. "What I have to say to your husband does not concern you. Too bad for you if you married a Jew."

She must have been behind the door, livid and rigid, listening to it all.

"I haven't the right to travel."

"Your mother lives in Belgium."

"She is very old, and all of her family, as well as my father's, came from the Limbourg country. I can't see her, at her age, going from village to village, from church to city hall to . . ."

"That's your bad luck. I said a month. And don't try to run away. We're keeping our eye on you."

He had never taken his hat off, so he had no need to put it back on. A last threatening look at me, the most threatening of all. "In one month, I shall return."

Poor Mother! I mean mine, not yours. She was a nervous, emotional little creature, who prayed every morning with all the strength left to her in front of the statue of the Holy Mother in St. Nicholas Church.

I could not avoid writing her, though I toned down the threats of the commissioner for Jewish Affairs. She went courageously out on the road, using what transportation I have no idea, through a countryside where farmhouses are very far apart and villages even more so. Fortunately, she and her sisters had continued speaking the Flemish of their childhood, or, rather, a dialect of it that isn't taught in school.

How much she must have begged, trembled, entreated, insisted, so that uninterested church sacristans and municipal employees would dig through old records stored who knows where. Three weeks later, I had copies of baptismal certificates and excerpts of birth certificates covered with rubber stamps and showing no names that were anything but Flemish.

My bogeyman showed up promptly, relishing his triumph in advance. I held the papers out to him; more precisely, he grabbed them from my hands, adjusted his thick-lensed glasses, sat back in his armchair, and lit a foul-smelling cigar.

"What language is this?"

"Flemish. The province of Limbourg is Flemish-speaking, and my maternal grandmother was born in Dutch Limburg."

"Dutch, hah?"

Was that an aggravating circumstance? Were the Dutch more Jewish than the Belgians?

He kept reading, taciturn and weightier than ever in his armchair, like some phony Maigret, the very antithesis of my own good old Maigret.

"Is that all?" he finally asked, regretfully.

"You asked me to go back three generations. My mother was able to do it, though I don't know how or in what state."

I almost expected, in the ferocity of his disappointment, that he would pull an automatic out of his pocket to give me one last scare.

He shoved the papers in his pocket. I protested.

"I might need those again sometime."

"That's no concern of mine."

"I will soon be leaving Fontenay-le-Comte, and I can give you a new address . . ."

"Why are you moving? Isn't this château fancy enough for you?"

"Fontenay is right on the edge of the Vendée marshes. It is very humid here, and suffocating in summer, so the doctor advised, for the sake of my son's health, that we move somewhere in the Bocage, at some altitude, where the air is drier."

"And where in the Bocage are you going?"

"To Saint-Mesmin-le-Vieux, near Pouzauges, where a mover in Fontenay has a villa he has agreed to rent me till the war is over."

"Why don't you go back home, to Nieul?"

The so-and-so was well informed, but not well enough.

"Because there are German officers occupying my house."

"Don't you like German officers?"

"I don't know them. The deputy mayor of Nieul let me know that my house had been requisitioned a year ago."

"Saint-Mesmin-le-Vieux . . ."

He enunciated the words as if looking for some other reason to get at me.

"Just a small village like so many others."

"Like the ones the maquis hide out in?"

"I have no idea. I've never set foot there yet."

He didn't say another word. Teeth clamped on his cigar, hands thrust deep in his pockets, he left the living room, and I saw him one last time as he walked by the four high windows, toward which he did not deign to look.

I never saw him again. It was true, my poor old Marc, that you were about to move again, to leave your curly-headed little girl friend, but there you were to find many new friends, Victor's children. My mover had also rented an empty house for them, close to ours.

You would not be wanting for friends, or animals, or mushrooms, which I didn't yet know, because, as usual, we were going off into the unknown. A new period of your young life was about to start, in different settings, with different people around you and a different governess, whom you were candidly going to dub "Madame Nouvelle."

As for me, I was hardly surprised, but quite satisfied, still to be alive, despite the deadline that pompous radiologist had set. I was alive! And I was going to add: more intensely than ever. And *Pedigree* was completed. And you weren't sick. And our little group of humans . . .

Let's get going, son! Don't be afraid. Once we get there, the truck will bring me back here to Fontenay so I can get the cart and the pony, who by now has also become your friend.

15

Scientists, people who are so referred to with respect and often with veneration, as if they were supermen or oracles, even though the most illustrious among them, those who have made the most significant discoveries, humbly confess that the more they learn the less they know, these scientists, in all disciplines, are divided into two camps. Some claim, for instance, that the life of the fetus remains imprinted on him and speak of an "intrauterine memory"; others deny this with just as much energy and good faith.

I tend to believe in some kind of memory in the embryo, and that, after birth, we retain only a confused recollection of it, which grows continually dimmer during our first years, although the grown man will unconsciously retain some traces of it. Is this one of the reasons I so passionately observed you, especially your instinctive reactions?

At Saint-Mesmin-le-Vieux, you were going to be four, and you had lived so much already, covered so many miles since our first flight to Belgium, which the border guards stopped and headed us back to the calm of Nieul-sur-Mer, our cocoon.

At Saint-Mesmin, you were soon discovering a different world, a new countryside around you, the Bocage, or Upper Vendée, as it is also called, with its deceptive lanes in which the armies of the French Revolution had once been massacred by the resisting peasants known as Chouans. The Germans must have known that aspect of French history, for here they were nowhere to be seen. At most, very occasionally, a car bearing the swastika would speed by on the road. These peasants were unlike any others, hospitable but tough, taciturn. All the lanes, surrounded by thick hedges, held no secrets from them.

I no longer had to sign in at the police station, since there was none in this village that might have been unknown, or at the city hall, which I don't recall ever having seen. If there was one, it was a gray house in no way different from the others on the only street, which led down to a tiny railroad station. The only authority in town was the rural policeman, actually a tinner by trade, who beat his drum on Sundays near the church and announced the news in a thundering voice. He and I became friends. You were fascinated by his drum and his uniform.

This was almost forty years ago. It might just as well have been a hundred, or even two hundred or more. Did we have food ration cards there, as they did everywhere else in France and the other countries at war? No one paid attention to them. I wonder whether somewhere an idle bureaucrat sat waiting for a local inhabitant to come and claim his.

During all the time we lived there, I did not read a newspaper and I never saw anyone read one. We were like an enclave protected from the hubbub of the world by its hedges and its deep lanes. Everyone more or less lived on what they themselves produced. The farmsteads were not big, and one had to look hard to find them in some declivity hidden from the road.

Our villa was neither large nor grand, something built by some city person at the turn of the century on the outskirts of the village, on the road to Pouzauges. That road was lined by chestnut trees, the fruit of which was free to anyone to pick. We had a pretentious, outsize porch. On the ground floor, to the left, a living room and a dining room, which we used only rarely, when we had guests. A hallway that was too narrow, the toilet at the end of it; on the right, a room that adjoined the kitchen, in which we all ate. A cellar where I went for the wine, and to which Boule, who was afraid of the dark, would not go down without you, as if the little boy that you were could protect her. From what? She would answer simply: "The dark."

Upstairs, four little bedrooms. I shared one with your mother. Across from it, I had set up my office. Next to that, your room and the governess's, who insisted on keeping your door open all night so that she might hear you in case you needed her, and which you all the more determinedly insisted on shutting, for you were not afraid of either the dark or being alone. Boule slept up in a mansard room, in front of which there was an attic with my crates of books stored in it.

As soon as we were moved in, Tigy used the truck we had rented to go to Nieul, where our house, which in my mind has always been your house, was occupied by German officers. They were polite to her, letting her come in and take out the ebony bookcases I had designed years before for our apartment on Boulevard Richard Wallace.

Your mother brought back I don't know how many of my books, which Victor, without seeming effort, loaded onto his shoulders and carried up the steep narrow stairs to the attic.

We had hired an old gardener, so old that he walked bent in two, as if he were trying to get closer to the earth, and in his whole life he had left his village only one day, when he had had to go to Pouzauges and register at the city hall for military service, from which he was exempted. His whole world consisted of the village, the meadows, and the woods around; he had no curiosity about what might go on beyond those limits.

We had a stable and a barn, near an unoccupied annex that we turned into our grain silo and where I could sneak away to get a quiet snooze in the loft. I bought a cow, since, along with the house, I had rented two meadows big enough for her to graze in.

The cow was not our first animal. One day, you saw an old donkey which was finishing out its days on a little plot of ground, from which it was led to feed off the leaves of the hedges.

"I would so like to have a donkey, Dad!"

So you got it, along with a worn saddle and rusty spurs. Victor shined up the saddle and spurs, and you were put up on the donkey's back. To everyone's terror, the next day you rode right out of the garden and, very upright and very proud, without ever looking back, you headed for the village, while I watched you at a distance.

So a cow, of Poitou stock, I believe, a fine red, which I milked every morning at five before breakfasting on thick soup and sometimes a steak, as the neighboring farmers did. That cow was a nightmare to Victor, who never learned to milk her.

"The lousy animal don't want to," he would grumble as the cow kept kicking at him.

He was afraid of our pony too; but he finally learned to harness it, unharness it, and lead it back to the stable for currying.

One of Victor's sons, a little bruiser of a fellow with a crew cut and a northern accent that sounded like the one in the Belgian Ardennes, had become your pal, from whom you were inseparable. Except when I took you out exploring the neighboring roads in our smart little cart and we stopped at farmhouses or alongside the river.

I was surprised to discover how much I had been able to write since getting the verdict from the radiologist in Fontenay. First, the book intended for you, which had appeared under the title *Je me souviens* (I Remember). Then the story of my own childhood and adolescence, *Pedigree*.

While still at Fontenay, I had, moreover, completed seven novels, almost all of which were set in a small provincial town. Here, in spite of my cows—for we finally had three in the barn—my pony, my vegetable garden, in which I did a good share of the work, I was to write several more.

My friends in Paris, who were short of everything, asked me for butter, which I sent them by mail in cracker cans enclosed in sackcloth sewed together with string. The only condition I set for sending such packages was that they return the empty wrappings to me, because I could not replace them. We were not rationed on meat either, and soon I was sending meat as well as butter, or, rather, Tigy was, for she had taken over this chore.

In order to feed my kine, I needed rape, Jerusalem artichokes, and oats, and corn for the chickens, ducks, and turkeys. You were interested in everything, with your little friend and often other children, from the village. His family too, like ours, needed butter and milk, and I supplied it.

I was fond of Victor. And, as strongly, I detested your governess. She was one-hundred-percent bourgeois, almost a living caricature of the petty bourgeoisie petrified in its own dignity. She had been married, and widowed, and run a glove and umbrella shop, and all her life long she had known nothing but misfortune. Long and skinny as a plucked bird, always dressed in black, she nagged you constantly with admonitions that were orders.

"Don't say . . ." Because your vocabulary was not always exactly *comme il faut*. "A good little boy doesn't do . . ."

I would break in, politely but firmly, because I wanted you to be free, although at the same time I could find no one else to take care of you.

We had had to dig a trench near the road, by order of the German authorities at La Roche-sur-Yon. The best thing to do was to obey. The ground was clayey, and rain water stagnated in the bottom of the ditch. One day when I was working rather far down in the garden I heard the sharp voice of your governess, whom I found, despite her habitual pallor, crimson with anger.

"Just look at him, monsieur!"

She was panting with indignation as she pointed to you happily wading around, fully dressed, in the bottom of the ditch.

"So?"

"But to get filthy like that on purpose, can that be allowed? More like a little wild animal . . ."

"I can't see any harm in it."

"And who'll clean him up then?"

You seemed to have understood and came back up to us, muddy to the roots of your hair.

I put you up on my shoulder and, going through the sweet-smelling kitchen, carried you to the only bathroom we had, up the stairs.

"No, son, don't get out of your clothes."

I turned on both faucets, and the tub quickly filled. I set you delicately down in the water, which was almost shoulder high, and it turned brown as your governess stood by inwardly churning. To put a child into the tub fully dressed! A child from a good family! She must have wondered what kind of creature I was, she whose father had been a doctor or a lawyer. I poured pitcherfuls of water over your head and face, had you stand up, and little by little got your soaking clothes off. A few more pitcherfuls on your pudgy body and you were as clean as any "well-mannered" child. I opened the drain and let the water run out over your clothes and underclothes.

"Earth, madame, is never 'dirty.' Moreover, I don't ever want to hear you using that word."

I was rubbing you, drying you, putting clean clothes on you. And that was that. It hadn't taken fifteen minutes. Your eyes were shining with joy and pride. I guess you never loved me quite so much as at that moment.

"He can go back into the ditch as often as he likes, and his friends with him."

By chance, to replace your donkey, you got a Shetland pony, scarcely taller than you, who had free run of the place and came begging for pieces of bread at the kitchen. You never rode the little pony, but played with it as if it were a dog. It especially liked nudging you in the back, whereas with Victor it had a tendency to try to bite.

You found a blindworm in the garden and showed it to me triumphantly.

You kept it in your pocket hours on end, and put it down wherever there was greenery and slugs, and it did not run away. The two of you got along well together, so well that, before coming in in the evening, you put it down on the kitchen steps. To my surprise, it was waiting for you there the next morning, and you put it back in your pocket.

We had a black tom turkey taller than the others which you used to pick up without its trying to get away. When I had a caller, which was not often, you showed off your blindworm as if it were a precious gem, then, crossing the garden, you got the turkey, which you had trouble carrying, and some of them took pictures of you doing that. I would swear that animals, whatever they might be, understood you, perhaps because you treated them all with the same affection you felt for humans.

One morning, a mad bull sowed panic in the region. Knocking over fences and barbed wire, foaming at the mouth, it charged at anything that moved. Someone, perhaps the rural policeman, phoned Pouzauges, because no one in the village had a firearm. This brought a German vehicle to town. Two soldiers, with rifles cocked, tramped through the countryside looking for the bull, and Boule came to tell me there were two officers at the door. I told her to let them in. One of them spoke excellent French and explained to me that he could not make head or tail out of the information the locals were giving him. The bull was said to have been seen everywhere, and yet there was no trace of him. He wondered whether it was a hoax.

"I saw it go by too," I told him.

They were sitting in the living room when you came in. You looked their uniforms over, wide-eyed, and disappeared up the stairs to join your mother and tell her the Germans had come to arrest me. I answered their questions as well as I could, showing them which way the bull had gone, and they left after saluting me politely.

The war was raging in Africa, where decisive battles were being waged. Rommel was holding on, but the English were making headway in the desert sands. When Narvik had been taken by the Germans, in their first advance against the West, up near the Arctic Ocean, I had assured my friends in La Rochelle that the outcome of the war would probably be decided in Africa. Was I just joking? I can't remember. But now I could see no reason why that should not come true.

The French were beginning to have a glimmer of hope, and the occupiers were getting nervous.

Soon one boy, and then another, was coasting down the slope in boxes with skate wheels, and I got one for you, Marc old man, despite the admonitions and reproaches of Madame Nouvelle. You were a little man, weren't you? There wasn't one automobile a day going by on the road, so there was nothing to fear. And I taught you, as well as your mother, how to ride a bicycle, but you insisted on keeping the training wheels that kept it from tipping over.

Vlaminck's daughter, your godmother, came to see us, to see you. You wanted to show off for her on your bicycle, and she pretended to be disappointed. "When you take off those training wheels, you'll be a real boy."

She was as tall and as solid as her father, and had become the mayor of her town. You looked at her, much impressed, both ashamed and undecided. Then she took off the training wheels.

"Now, go ahead. Ride around the house."

No one could hold out against Edwige, and you took off, zigzagging at first, but then straightening up, proud of your feat.

I got a letter from Paris saying an undernourished young girl would be happy to come to the country as a mother's helper. I sent for her. She was very merry and replaced Madame Nouvelle, whom I could no longer bear to see either sitting across from me at the dinner table or off in the distance, long and dark, as she watched you and your friends at play with an equally dark eye. She made me think of a crow, although I really have nothing against crows.

I think your new little governess—I should really say playmate—was named Yvonne. In a month, she had gotten her fat back and her open face was the picture of health. She adopted all of your playmates, boys and girls, whom you brought to our meadow, where a huge cherry tree threw a shadow as big as itself. We never tasted any cherries from it, because it was so old and so tall that even with a ladder one could not have gotten up to pick them. Victor, who was afraid of nothing except cows, insisted that he could climb up into the cherry tree, but because he had a houseful of children I didn't want him to take such a chance.

That was how life went along at Saint-Mesmin-le-Vieux, during the war, of which we knew nothing, and I would go over and drink my split of wine with the villagers and farmers, especially on market day. I felt as though I were a part of the village, as I believe I was part of Fontenay, Nieul, and so many other places I have lived. I never felt alien anywhere, in the African bush country or the South Sea islands, in Australia or India.

There is an American term that expresses what I mean: "to belong." In any American town, "you have to belong." To the community.

I think that I don't belong only to one country, one continent, our little ball of earth, but to the universe. I hoped it would be the same for you, someday, Marc of mine, and I believe I got my wish.

16

My friends, including some very important specialists, are surprised at my memory. I must admit that, except for dates and chronology, I have quite a precise memory, that I have retained a surprising number of pictures of the past, colored, moving pictures, as if a color film ran off at will inside my brain, with the added advantage over a film that they are accompanied by odors and the cold, heat, or warmth of the air. I forget my novels as soon as they are written. Yet, if someone reminds me of them, I can see the décor that was around me, a few of the scenes, without my being able to put a date or place on them.

I knew that at Fontenay-le-Comte, in a little house beside the water, I wrote a novel near a window. Only by consulting the chronological list of my books did I find out that it was *Le Voyageur de la Toussaint (Strange Inheritance),* and that it was followed by three Maigrets, *Signé Picpus (To Any Lengths), L'Inspecteur cadavre (Maigret's Rival),* and *Félicie est là (Maigret and the Toy Village),* all four during the summer, then, the following spring, *La Fenêtre des Rouet (Across the Street).*

During the long period in which I conscientiously played at being a farmer at Saint-Mesmin-le-Vieux, I can hardly believe that, in addition to revising *Pedigree,* I was able to write *Le Bilan Malétras (The Reckoning), L'Aîné des Ferchaux (Magnet of Doom), Les Noces de Poitiers* (The Wedding at Poitiers), *La Fuite de Monsieur Monde (Monsieur Monde Vanishes),* and *Le Cercle des Mahé* (The Mahés' Circle), the characters of which, with their problems and surroundings, were in such contrast to our occupations and the ambience around us at the time, especially since I still was, theoretically, under sentence of death by that pedantic radiologist.

Even more than at Fontenay, we had become part of the local life, and on market days I could call the women by their names, most of the men by their first names. As for the tragic events taking place in the world, I knew so little about them that, in order to write these memoirs, I had to have a list made up for me of the dates that have become important in history.

One of our neighbors was a jolly physician, country-bred, who used to take you and me down to the lower meadows to go net-fishing in a pure little stream that I could jump into. We netted as many as two hundred and fifty crawfish in less than two hours, especially beneath the old willows with their roots under water. What wonder in your eyes at all that teeming life, and what tenderness when you picked up a crawfish that tried to bite your still fragile fingers!

Frenchmen are reputed to be born hunters and, in this faraway village where all rifles had been requisitioned at the beginning of the war, the farmers still hunted at night, in the meadows and fields, using the same kind of nets, held open by two long sticks, that are used for fishing for shrimp in the sea.

What did they hunt this way? Partridge. You and I never went with them, but they would send me dozens of partridges, as gifts, while Boule raised her arms, exclaiming, "Now what am I going to do with all these critters?"

We sent some on to friends in Paris. What didn't we send in addition to the weekly butter and meat!

I remembered that in my childhood, despite our near-poverty, my mother had had my shoes made to order, for she had had a great deal of foot trouble in her life. I also remembered a bootmaker in Paris, near the Madeleine, who specialized in children's shoes. Your mother sent him outlines of your feet, and your exact measurements, and a month later we received some shoes that were not likely to twist your feet out of shape. The bootmaker preferred being paid in butter, so you really owed your shoes to our cows.

Your first mackinaw was made in Paris too, to measure, from sheepskins from our own flock.

Some Parisians would come all the way into the Vendée region in search of supplies, and it was painful to see their almost tragic surprise at the bountiful area we lived in.

I asked the rural policeman to point out a village woman whose husband was a prisoner and who was finding it hard to raise her children. She did all the dirtiest work available. Her son was about your age. I went to call on her, and asked her permission to give him, as well as his sister, the same gifts, the same treats I gave you at Christmas, Easter, saints' days, and birthdays. They didn't go hungry—no one went hungry in the region—but children need something more than just food.

Do you remember the communal bake oven? It was still in use, for thereabouts they believed in kneading their own bread. One day each week, the person in charge lighted the oven, and groups of three or four customers came, with their dough wrapped in good white cloth, at their appointed hour. It was located at the corner of a little road we often followed in our cart, because it led to the river, on the other side of which we went hunting for flap mushrooms. There again, you were first to spot them, fine golden brown things among the dead leaves.

As for bread, we ate traditional country bread, made of whole wheat, round and rather flat, each loaf weighing almost seven pounds. We used to go to the oven once a week. We also had beehives, like everyone else. Since I didn't know much about apiculture and was afraid of getting stung, I used to call on one of the neighboring farmers to harvest the honey for me.

Your mother was in charge of the supplies, and periodically, as my mother before her had done with eggs, she would candle macaroni, noodles, and spaghetti to make sure they had not been infested with tiny white worms.

Everyone had plenty to do, my little Marc, especially you, since you wanted to be in on everything, and that was why I didn't remember that I had written so many novels during that period.

We of course had electricity, but there was talk of blackouts, ordered by the occupying forces. I bought some lamps and a large can of kerosene for the storm lanterns we used in the stable and barn. I got a workbench, various tools, a whole crate of nails and hooks, which had become scarce and could be had only in exchange for ham.

We raised one or two pigs a year, fat pigs which weighed as much as two hundred and twenty pounds and which the village sausage maker came and butchered after we took you off somewhere else. He was also the one who, in a huge cast-iron pot, cooked them up.

I so far have not mentioned to you the most important character in the place, since I didn't get to know him for several months. He was a sixtyish man, broad and short, potbellied, impressive, with skin that was always pale although he spent most of his time out of doors. He was to become our friend, and he told me that he had angina pectoris, the kind from which my father had died much younger.

Since then medicine had progressed, and when he felt an attack coming on, he took a small box from his pocket and swallowed a nitroglycerin pill. He was able to live that way for a very long time and carry on an exhaustively active life. He was the one, in fact, who bought up, even from great distances around, all the farmers' wheat, oats, barley, and corn, and a private railroad spur ran from his warehouses to the railway station. His overseer was something like the one at Paray-le-Frésil whom I used in part in creating the character of Maigret.

He lived in a large, harmonious house, luxuriously furnished, but his greatest pride was his vegetable garden, which was kept up by the best gardener he had been able to find.

I had only glimpsed him at a distance, but one afternoon I saw him come into my garden, cordially but slightly timidly, in spite of the important place he held in the area.

"I apologize for disturbing you, Monsieur Simenon."

He was looking my vegetable garden over even as he introduced himself.

"I was told you had succeeded in growing some very fine eggplants. Neither the climate nor the soil here is especially suited to them, and my gardener has never been able to."

His garden, ruled off by narrow passageways, could have been used to illustrate a seed company's catalogue. He felt our big eggplants, with glints of gold in their purple, and could not believe his eyes. "How do you do it?"

"I just followed the instructions in a gardening manual." I had read not just one of those, but half a dozen.

"Now, you'll have to come and have a look at my garden. Why, you even have asparagus!"

The latter don't give full yield until the third year. I never got to eat any of ours, nor did your mother or Boule, since we had not planted them early enough. But as soon as the sun was up, when they were in season, you would go out to inspect the row of them, which stood higher than the other rows, and one day you spied three tiny purplish heads peeking through, which I probably would not even have been able to see.

"Quick! The knife, Dad . . ."

The asparagus knife, with its little horizontal blade at the end that cut the asparagus off at the base. You carried three stalks of asparagus in to Boule, asking her to cook them for you, and you continued that way every morning during the season, bringing your trophies to the kitchen, sometimes five, or eight, or nine, and even ten stalks, but not enough to make a meal for us, so they were yours alone.

The local grain merchant made me think of the "rich man" of your grandmother Brüll's family, who lived in a château and also sold fertilizer and other things. He invited us to dinner one Saturday. He had a beautiful daughter, who was the mother of a little girl, and her husband, a professor of neurology at the University of Nantes, got down here only on weekends.

Little by little, we turned into a friendly group, having dinner or lunch at one another's houses, often with a bridge game. The merry doctor also was part of our group.

One day I got my nerve up and spoke to the neurologist husband about the medical examination I had had at Fontenay and the verdict the radiologist had pronounced.

"Did he give you the X-rays?"

"To my knowledge, he didn't take any. I just remember that he 'radioscoped' me for a long session, during which I sweated as much as I had all the rest of my life."

He looked at me for a moment. "Of course, this is not my specialty. I can understand that you would like to clear the matter up. In Paris, there are two famous radiologists, who, incidentally, don't always agree with each other. If I had to choose . . ."

"As a foreigner living in a coastal zone, I have no right to travel to Paris or anywhere else."

"You might give it a try. I can give you a certificate, which the Germans might just be willing to honor."

Suddenly I was frightened by the idea of setting off on such an adventure, all by myself. What if my heart were to act up on the way? I knew that trains were few and far between, always mobbed on arrival and then overcrowded, and that on account of the bombed bridges it was often necessary to make difficult changes.

"Would you like me to go with you?" he asked.

I dared not say yes, but it brought tears to my eyes. He was my age, but more stylish, with very light hair and blue eyes.

"You'll have to choose between the two professors."

"You know more about that than I do."

He mentioned a name to me that I had many times heard on the lips of my friends in Strasbourg.

"You won't be afraid of the fact that he's very old, will you?"

He wrote to Paris, made an appointment, and organized the trip. He also worked things out with his university. I don't remember anything about the trip, which was without incident; no English or American planes bombed us. Bombs were not what I was afraid of, anyway, but the verdict I was soon going to hear. I didn't smoke on the way and all I drank was mineral water.

The George V and the Claridge, where I was accustomed to staying, had been requisitioned by the Kommandantur and were reserved for German officers, as were most of the first-class hotels. We stayed at the Bristol, on Rue du Faubourg-Saint-Honoré, across from the British Embassy. The first people I bumped into in the big lobby were two of my best friends, Marcel Pagnol and Jean Cocteau.

We fell into one another's arms.

"Where are you coming from? Where were you? I thought you must be either dead or in America. . . ."

Marcel was the one who was so surprised, because before the war I had told him that I wanted to settle in the United States for a few years if I had a child. I had known since Tigy and I made a trip there that I would like my son or daughter to have an American as well as a European education. When the war came, I had almost gone, as so many others had, but I knew that one had to wait a long time, sometimes months, in Spain or Portugal before being able to board a ship for America. You were too young then for me to drag you into that kind of adventure.

"What brings you to Paris?"

I explained to both of them, and their faces clouded over.

"When are you seeing the great man?"

"In an hour."

"We'll be waiting for you here."

I went by bicycle-taxi (something I had never before even heard of) to a quiet patrician street not far from the Chamber of Deputies.

A silent, rather dark apartment, deep-carpeted, with velvet-upholstered armchairs and venerable furniture that smelled of good waxing. A tall, white-haired old man, very thin, with gentle eyes, soon came out of his office and held a bony hand out to me.

"Seems they've been giving you a hard time, eh? . . . You have a young son, I've been told. . . . Things must be all right in the Vendée, in times like these. . . ."

He was putting me at my ease, and little by little my worry was lessening. What a difference from the man who . . . that . . . the only man, I do believe, that I've ever really hated!

This one, world-famous and often called in to take care of heads of state and other great personages, smiled while putting electrodes to my wrists, ankles, chest, and I was surprised to see that he wasn't assisted by a helper or nurse. I relaxed, trustfully, not asking any questions.

He examined me at length, then had me walk through the apartment, including the dining room, to another room, where there was a man almost as old as he, with long white hair like a maestro.

"A fellow here who seems to have bumped into a jackass," he told him. Then he said to me: "The best radiologist in Paris, and he doesn't practice anymore except when I call him in on one of my infrequent cases. I'll leave you in his hands."

This time I wasn't put behind a screen but, first standing, then lying down on a moleskin-covered table, on my belly, on my back, the roentgenologist with the mischievous eyes took X-rays.

"You can get dressed. Go out for half an hour's walk and then come back to my friend's office."

This was so unlike medicine as I had known it that I felt I was in a dream. I went out into the quiet streets of Faubourg Saint-Germain and looked at my watch a score of times.

The old professor was waiting for me, alone, in the middle of his living room.

"Do you have a pipe in your pocket?"

I blushed. "Yes."

"Fill it and light it."

His kindly eyes were full of gaiety.

"Do you have friends in Paris?"

"Yes, two very good ones who are waiting for me right now at the hotel."

"Go on back to them and treat them to a good meal, in the best restaurant—they probably know one. Order a fine old wine, and . . ."

I almost yelled, or thought that I yelled: "Isn't there anything wrong with my heart?"

"Your heart is perfectly normal and in the best of shape. Are you enjoying the pipe?"

I was filled with joy such as I had rarely known, if ever.

"What about athlete's heart?"

"I've heard that term before. Your radiologist is a clown, and he had no right even to examine you, since you hadn't been referred to him by a physician. Think no more about it. You and your friends just have a good dinner, and don't forget to take along my young colleague who brought you to me."

Jean and Marcel were waiting for me, so concerned that I felt ashamed. When they saw me, they understood at once, and Marcel pointed to the pipe. "Doctor's orders?"

A huge dinner, with the best of wines, all on the black market, obviously. I couldn't phone Tigy, because of that damned "coastal zone," in which the Germans were feverishly putting up their Atlantic Wall. Did I get drunk? I've no idea. I think we all did, more or less, and the beds at the Bristol were more than welcome.

I had no heart disease; do you hear, sonny? I was perfectly healthy and was on my way back to Saint-Mesmin, with a suitcase full of coarse pipe tobacco, such as couldn't be found anymore in the Vendée, but only in Paris, on the black market.

Down there, I had put in two hundred tobacco plants, illegally, for only professional growers are supposed to raise tobacco, and the inspectors from the government monopoly regularly come by to count the leaves. I had improvised a drying shed and asked the tinner-policeman to build me a sort of drum, with a handle, so I could "cure" it the way the manual recommended.

I had hired five or six girls from the village to roll the browned leaves into cigar shapes. The local carpenter had built me a tiny guillotine, and the girls put the undried tobacco into it to cut it into thin slices. Dried, they swelled and turned into tobacco more or less like that put out by the monopoly.

Was all that incongruous work going through my mind on the train? To think that I had spent so many hours, so many weeks and months, to write *Pedigree* for you, which I would now have ample time to tell you about in person.

I saw the group of you at a distance on the platform of the little station. I felt light enough to jump off the train while it was still moving, but I was afraid that would be setting you a bad example. I almost squeezed you to death, and your mother too, and after I thanked our neurologist friend with all the vigor I could muster and made a date with him to have dinner with us soon, we walked up the sloping street, you between us, one hand in mine, the other in Tigy's.

What I do remember is the jellied calf's head, a Belgian dish from my childhood, which I loved, and you did too.

"Bring one of the finest bottles of Bordeaux up from the cellar, my little Boule."

Did we laugh? Did we cry? You looked at us with surprise, because, not having understood our secret ordeal, you must have been wondering why we suddenly talked so volubly and burst out laughing from time to time like a couple of kids. Yes, my Marc, big people remain children until one day they turn into old children.

17

Get up, my Marc! We're off again. This time on a short quasi-pleasure trip. Parents as old as Tigy and I are more frightened by their child's slightest ailments, especially if they have only one, than younger parents. You had a sore throat, which is not necessarily serious, and we called in our neighbor and friend Dr. Eriau, who covers the countryside on a big racket-making motorcycle that always fills you with wonder as it goes by. Eriau is a happy devil, with candid eyes that warm the heart, and he was born in a farmhouse just like the ones he now makes his calls at. Just a country doctor; nevertheless, to the amazement of his city confreres, he was able to save a woman with first-degree burns over almost all of her body.

"What do we have to do to get him back on his feet as quickly as possible?" Tigy asked, pointing to your pallid face.

"I know a garageman not far from here who has installed a charcoal burner on an old jalopy and who could drive you to La Bourboule. It's a children's spa in the Puy-de-Dôme that specializes in respiratory infections. Taking the cure there, at that altitude, can only do him good."

And one morning, bright and early, a strange-looking car stops outside our door. It's a crate so old it wasn't worth requisitioning, and on its side there is a broad, high, black metal cylinder that looks like the stove in a railroad station. I had been warned it would be wise to take along some chickens, and we packed them, alive and cackling, into the trunk of the car. At each stop we would use them to buy the charcoal required, in place of nonexistent gasoline, by this wartime gazogene. Money is no longer acceptable here in the country.

We stop every six or eight miles to refill the water tank that is heated by the charcoal. Our car looks like the railroad locomotive some very young child might have designed. Our doctor friend gave us a certificate to produce on demand, but no one stops us except for one French policeman at the entrance to La Bourboule. He insists that, even before going to the hotel, where we have two rooms reserved, I go and explain it all to the police superintendent.

People are wary of everything these days. So I explain our case to the police. A quarter of an hour later, we are at the hotel, and bright and early the next morning you and I are over at the baths. At times with what they call "adhesive splints," at others, in another room, for inhalations and I don't know what else, you're being treated with the miraculous water that flows nice and warm out of the volcanic soil. Since you want me to go with you every day for all these treatments, I decide that, because I'm a heavy smoker, it won't do me any harm to take the treatments too. They brought you right back to top shape, but only gave me a painful case of sinusitis. At first, they thought I had an abscessed tooth, and the local dentist, after a thorough examination of my jaw, decided to remove my only bridge and make me a new one.

Our hotel was located at the top of a very steep incline, which we went up and down by means of an old hydraulic funicular. My dates with the dentist were at eight in the evening, and at that hour there was nobody handling the funicular. I was instructed in how to operate it and, although terrified of high places, I had to run this dizzying contraption every night in the dark.

I also had to have one of Tigy's small jewels melted down, because the dentist needed the gold in order to make the new bridge, nowhere near as good as the old one. In reality, there was nothing wrong with my jaw, and they discovered too late that the trouble was in my sinuses.

There were mushrooms there in profusion, including one pinkish-white one that looked just like a penis in erection.

I'm not recalling all these things for my own amusement, but because they show that even during wars life goes on just the same.

Nevertheless, after our return we found something changed in the atmosphere at Saint-Mesmin. Rommel had lost the battle of the desert just when he thought he had it won. The Americans, in the war since Pearl Harbor was bombed, were landing in North Africa, Sicily was invaded, and then Italy.

People talked about it in whispers at the little corner café run by the bicycle dealer, and they were now looking sarcastically at the posters the Germans had put up on the walls of French towns and villages. These showed Allied tanks in the shape of snails inching along, at the pace of those animals you liked so much, across Italy.

We began hearing more planes in the distance, and one day, when the explosions had seemed nearer, we learned that there had been a British air raid on Nantes, where, having missed their target, they had destroyed the biggest department store in the city, causing over a hundred and fifty casualties. The BBC was urgently imploring all coastal Frenchmen, from the Spanish border to the Belgian, to get clear of that region. A landing was being prepared, but no one could guess where along those hundreds of miles of coastline it would be.

Biarritz, Arcachon, Bordeaux, La Rochelle, Les Sables-d'Olonne, Nantes, and on up northward through all of Brittany, Normandy, Le Havre, Fécamp, Dieppe, Calais—were all of these places going to be abandoned by their inhabitants, including the tiny ports, the villages, and would we be seeing another one of those heartbreaking flights on the roads? The news reports were contradictory, and people became skeptical. After every aerial engagement, each side claimed to have brought down a hundred or two hundred planes, while at the same time each side also admitted that five or six of "our aircraft are missing."

For a long time, the war had been a faraway happening, but now we could feel it closing in on our Bocage. The trenches we had been ordered to dig alongside the roads were beginning to have real meaning. In case of an Allied landing, they would be useful to the Germans as prepared positions to fall back on. Even our cheerful little garden! Might we too not one day have to flee?

Our pony and cart would be useless to us. I had given my little motorcycle to the butcher in Fontenay the day posters appeared instructing all motorcycle owners to register with the Kommandantur. Since I didn't trust them, I thought it better to get rid of mine and make someone happy at the same time.

Hidden under the straw in the barn, I still had the canary-yellow car I had bought a few months before the war. It had a powerful motor, and in the days when I was in charge of the Belgian refugees it had carried as many as a dozen people at a time, some on the roof or the hood. When I was no longer entitled to the official medallion from the La Rochelle prefecture, or my outdated pass, I had taken a chance and hidden it under the straw intended for our stable. I had also managed later on, in exchange for precious food supplies, to get a large drum of gasoline, which I had carefully hidden. But what good would a car be if the occupying forces quickly saw and confiscated it?

The springtime was getting more and more radiant, and my friend the bicycle dealer, whom I saw every morning in the café, where, along with the others, I tossed down my daily split of wine, made for me a little aluminum cart, a comfortable kind of body with a nice soft seat and even a little windshield. On a smaller scale, it looked something like those bicycle-taxis I had seen in Paris. This trailer could be solidly attached behind my bike.

You were so crazy about it, felt so comfortable in it, that wherever I went, you were there behind me.

One Sunday when the sky was clear and blue we were able to discern some planes flying very high in a tight formation. A first wave, then a little later a second, a third, a fourth. We counted them, and then there came even more, making the air quiver like the skin of a drum.

These planes, as we were later to learn, were American, and what they were bombing, in wave after wave, from so high up that the antiaircraft fire could not reach them, was the charming little town of Royan, where the middle classes of Bordeaux a few years before had been accustomed to spend their summers. Why Royan, which was neither a naval nor a military base? By mistake? Were they in fact aiming for the port of La Pallice, almost forty miles north?

Yet you were living in a cocoon of calm and joy with your little playmates. Sundays, I took you to church, not for Mass, but so that, when it let out, you could delight yourself with the sight of a white-clothed table covered with tarts, cakes, goodies of every sort that each farm wife of Saint-Mesmin devoutly did her best to concoct according to old family recipes.

Your friend the rural policeman, in formal uniform, beat his drum and auctioned off these cakes, all profits going to help the prisoners of war. There was always one that had been baked in our oven under the ministrations of

Boule. I let you have your pick, and naturally you went after the biggest one. I then had to bid on it. It was a happy Sunday game, because everyone knew I would top any other bid and they kept on bidding to see how high I would go.

This reminds me that I don't have a single manuscript left of any of the books I wrote before that time, because there were charity sales of this kind in every city, every village, and from all kinds of places I got requests for a manuscript to auction off. What became of them? Bought up by horse traders, butchers, or grocers, they probably were used as wrapping for meat or other merchandise.

One morning, when I went down to Pouzauges, I saw a small flatcar going along the rails, with a single man on it, no doubt checking the roadbed. A small angry-sounding plane, with a split tail, came very low out of the sky, a machine gun crackled, and the man collapsed. The car, jumping under the impact, left the rails.

The war was getting ever closer, although life followed its course at home, where everyone tried not to look worried. Big red arrows appeared, on trees and telegraph poles, on the roads, the lanes, and even the woods. Everyone wondered what they might be for. Then newly posted notices— brought in from far away and given to our friend the rural policeman to put up—informed us that those arrows indicated the road all able-bodied men were to take whenever the order was given.

To go where? Did the Germans plan to translocate all of the French population into their country, or were these marching crowds intended to be used by them as shields?

A domestic incident, which I would prefer not to tell about, but which had so great an influence on all our lives after that, happened just then.

I was in the habit of taking a nap in the loft of the small annex near the stable. At three o'clock, Boule would come to wake me and bring me some coffee. Since she had joined our household, almost twenty years before, she and I had had a close relationship, both affectionate and sexual. But such relations were, to be sure, furtive, considering how jealous your mother was and that she had often told me that if I was unfaithful to her, she would not hesitate to commit suicide.

Yet, during our life together, I was "unfaithful" to her almost every day, sometimes several times a day, not only with Boule but with hundreds of women. Did she suspect? I liked Tigy a lot. We enjoyed a very solid friendship, as we still do today, but there was little demonstrativeness be-tween us.

One unfortunate afternoon, the door of the little room where I took my nap and where Boule now lay with me suddenly opened, and there was Tigy before us, straight and stiff in the doorway. We didn't dare move, but she spoke, perhaps painfully, in a voice I didn't recognize.

"Once you have your clothes on, come down to the garden to talk with me."

Was she frigid, as many of our friends suspected? I don't believe so. It was just that she was in such control of herself that she succeeded in never letting her emotions show. I went down a little later, leaving a petrified Boule behind me, and found your mother pacing back and forth in front of the stable. Her expressionless voice pronounced words in an incisive, jerky way: "You will please oblige me by throwing that tramp out of the house right away."

What upset me most at the moment was the use of "that tramp" to designate a person who was so totally devoted to us, and involuntarily I could see in my mind's eye the great stone house in which the Renchons had lived. They had been poor too. They had worked hard without ever getting rich as a result, and that big house, which gave a rich, upper-bourgeois impression, was only a façade needed for their endeavors.

"That tramp . . ."

I didn't like bourgeois people, to begin with, and those words in that context seemed to me to stink of the bourgeoisie. I answered harshly, in revolt: "No!"

"Choose between her and me. If she stays, I go."

With you, Marc of mine? Could she be thinking of tearing you away from me at the very time when we all ought to be closing ranks around you? She went back into the house, and I returned to reassure a trembling Boule that everything would work itself out. You went and sat in the kitchen, as I had suggested you should. We had dinner as on other days, but there was little animation—even artificial—around the table. Your mother was solemn, but more normal now, and I was sure that she had spoken under the influence of the shock she had just had and probably did not even remember the words she had so harshly pronounced.

I told you a story, to get you to fall asleep, the story of a little Chinese boy named Li who, day after day, was the hero of amazing adventures, which I had started making up when you were less than two years old. I went back down after I had closed your door, and Tigy and I were alone together again in the garden.

"Neither you nor I can be separated from our son." And then I added: "You know what those red arrows mean. I may be forced to go away at any time. Two women together won't be too many to handle the developments one can anticipate. . . . Outside of yourself, you have no one but Boule to depend on. . . ."

"Yes, I know. And they might come for me one day too."

And then, in order to turn her bitterness away from Boule, I made one sweeping confession: "There have been so many others, including some of your closest friends!"

"And to think that I was never even aware of it."

We had a very long talk, as between two friends making up after a recent quarrel, that went on along the garden walks while night fell. The fact was, I had perhaps never so fully appreciated what a solid and faithful helpmeet she had been to me for so long a time.

"Now you know that, even if it was hidden, I always retained a certain degree of freedom. Obviously, you have the same freedom. Officially, we will remain husband and wife, but in reality just good friends, and neither one of us will have to give up Marc."

Did she smile slightly in the dark? She alone could tell you. At any rate, we shook hands before going in. We had just one bed at the time, and for quite a while we went on sleeping in it side by side, without ever even grazing one another.

There was perhaps another reason your mother accepted that peace treaty. Our bicycle friend had taken me aside a few days before and informed me that he was in contact with the maquis, and that those young fellows, not much more than boys, couldn't get any wine to drink.

"I could spare two barrels for them. But how would I get it to them?"

"Leave it to me. I'll let them know and find a truck."

He drove me and the two barrels to a small wood I knew well, just a few miles away, but where I had never suspected the presence of any human beings.

At first I saw only their leader, a dark, handsome fellow in a bright-red shirt. He whistled, and a few men appeared to unload the barrels. From our arrival in the Vendée, I had never heard a word about any maquis, or any Resistance groups in the region.

"Are there a lot of you?"

"Enough."

"You can speak freely," my friend told him.

"Something over a hundred."

Yet there was absolute silence in the little wood.

"Is there anything else you need?"

"We're always in need of something."

"Butter, for instance? Poultry?"

"Anything like that will be welcome."

"In that case, I'll be back."

"No. My friends and I will come to your place. We know where you live."

And they did indeed come, five or six of them, in a broken-down old auto, and the man in the red shirt would stand guard on our porch, his submachine gun trained on the road, while his comrades stocked up on poultry, butter, eggs, sugar, and other items. I never saw them again. The whole village knew about it, but nobody mentioned it. Yet, wouldn't someone talk, if only out of carelessness? In that case, Tigy and I would be taken away God knows where. What about you? Was that what she was thinking about when we concluded our peace pact? Could be. To me, it's the likeliest hypothesis.

But we were soon to be running other risks. One day, our bicycle friend, who looked so innocent but always knew more than anyone else in the village, asked me: "Do you still have your car?"

"Well hidden under the straw, yes."

"Would you consider lending it?"

"To whom?"

"To some English paratroopers. There are several of them in the region and they need a fast car to carry out their mission."

I didn't expect them to arrive the very next night, while the doctor was at our house playing cards. Some men came in, in RAF uniform, and held their hands out to us, each introducing himself as he did. They spoke unaccented French, which was not surprising, since they were Frenchmen who had joined the British forces. In order to be more comfortable, they put their weapons on the table, submachine guns, large-caliber automatic pistols, grenades, and when we headed out to the barn to get the car, I saw that two armed men were standing guard outside.

"Did you make your jump long ago?"

"A few days ago."

They spoke in the vaguest terms, which I could well understand, and only after their second or third visit did I find out that they were wearing uniforms only so that if they were caught they might be treated as prisoners of war and not shot out of hand.

"Are you familiar with this area?" their chief asked me.

"Fairly, but the doctor is much more familiar with it than I am."

"See you tomorrow night."

They were enchanted with our big yellow car, as well as with the large drum of gasoline, which they did not take with them. They disappeared, and reappeared the next evening, armed, unflustered, and my friend and I were informed that their job was to blow up the railroad lines, especially at junctions, to stop, or at least impede, the comings and goings of the German trains, which were always so mysterious to us.

A great many of these had been coming by recently. Sometimes we caught sight of the long necks of coast artillery guns on them. Some came from the interior and were headed toward the sea, whereas others, full of uniformed men, headed in the opposite direction, which was hard to understand.

Little by little, we and the paratroopers were getting more familiar with one another. The doctor would show them on the map the places where one could get closest to the tracks without being seen.

"That's my job," said the youngest one, smiling.

He would put a priest's cassock on over his uniform, a priest's hat on his head, and, his nose in his breviary, in broad daylight innocently walk to a predetermined spot to stick blocks of plastic explosive that he carried in his pockets on the rails and attach detonators to them. One of his pals told us he had been a lieutenant in the spahis in North Africa and that his *nom de guerre* hid a real name that had historical significance.

The second evening, my car was no longer yellow, but green, and in the rear they had made two camouflaged openings, through which they could aim machine guns.

We saw trains held up on the tracks, and people in the area talked about plastic-explosive attacks. One night, a German automobile was machine-gunned just two miles outside Saint-Mesmin, and three bodies, one that of a colonel, were found in it.

The next day, the nearby village of La Chapelle, on the other side of the river, was one mass of flames. The Germans had gone there in strength, at break of day, routed the inhabitants from their houses, many of them from their beds, and, without letting them take any of their belongings, herded them to a neighboring village. After that they had set fire to all the houses, and all night the village had burned, while the inhabitants of Saint-Mesmin watched the flames, so close by.

That was the price for killing a German colonel. A short time later, I met one of the inhabitants of the destroyed village, a refugee from the north, a man well past his prime, who had thought he would be safe here. He was a one-time art dealer. He confessed to me with tears in his eyes that among the ashes of his house were those of several Renoirs, some Légers, Derains, and other canvases he had been able to save when he had had to flee.

· · ·

The road past our house was no longer deserted. Troops kept parading by, in columns, convoys, and cars marked with swastikas.

One afternoon, around four o'clock, as I was working deep in the vegetable garden, a terrified Boule came running out to me. A blonde lady accompanied by a German officer had come asking for me, and Boule had had the presence of mind to answer them most innocently that I was away.

"When will he be back?"

"In an hour or two. He'll be home for dinner. We have dinner at six."

I darted into the field separated from our garden by a rather high hedge, after instructing Boule to see to it that the bicycle dealer was informed of what had happened and was told that I had to get away in a hurry. Meantime, Boule was to bring me the heavy knapsack that your mother had had ready for me for the past several weeks, for just such an emergency.

In it were underwear, food, and even a little box with some morphine ampoules, in case of too painful a wound. Tigy had packed only half of those, so that there would be some left at home. Our friend the doctor had supplied the morphine and the needles, because country doctors still had to act as druggists, considering how few pharmacies there were around.

Tigy came out to say *au revoir* to me. We kissed each other warmly on both cheeks. I saw you at a distance, in the garden, with one of Victor's sons, and could only say a silent good-bye to you. The bicycle dealer quietly appeared at my side, led me through the fields toward a motorcycle that was ready by a hidden path, and a half hour later let me off at the farm of a friend of his.

"You'll be safe only in the garage. I'm afraid you'll just have to sleep on straw. I'll go and get you a couple of blankets and some soup."

I slept there only two nights, but I must confess I slept very well. It reminded me of my tours of guard duty in the stables when I had done my military service.

My friend brings me news. The German blonde came back with an officer, just like the first time. Then she came back again still later, but, probably having to catch up with the long convoy that had disappeared, she finally left and now was gone. From the descriptions Boule gave us, we decided she might well have been the famous spy Mademoiselle Docteur, who had been talked about in the papers and had made herself so useful to the German secret service in a lot of places, including the Vendée.

By a strange coincidence, one of the villagers, who lived a couple of hundred yards from us and had a very bad reputation, disappeared the same day.

. . .

"There are still groups of soldiers, officers' cars, and even civilian cars going by. Do you know a farmer named Maurice?"

He was the one I got my partridges from!

"You know where his farm is?"

"I've taken every one of my cows there."

"Sure. I forgot that he had a stud. Your family is no longer safe. . . ."

"In that case, neither is the doctor's, because he was there when . . . "

"Yes, I know. I'll warn him too. They're going to come and join us in one of Maurice's meadows, which is almost impossible to find, and I'll bring a cart over with as many mattresses and blankets as may be needed."

The meadow, on a slight incline, was surrounded by high hedges, as is the manner in the Vendée. We put the mattresses down one next to the other, along with the blankets, against one hedge. Food was not in short supply, or drink. There were a dozen of us, including Dr. Eriau, his wife and daughters, sleeping side by side on this huge improvised bed.

We felt we were so safe that we forgot all our worries. During the day, you played with the doctor's youngest daughter while the adults told one another stories. A big plow horse in the meadow was not the least bit bothered by our presence. You were able to pet him without his flinching. He was soon your friend. Late one afternoon, perhaps trying to impress you, I jumped on his back, the way I had learned to do in the army, without saddle, bridle, or stirrups, and had him go around the meadow at a walk, then at a trot, finally at a heavy gallop, directing him with my thighs and calves. When I stopped, the horse was bathed in sweat. I was too. Soaked through. I went to freshen up at the stream that ran at the bottom of the meadow.

We slept as we had the previous nights. Two days later, our bicycle friend told us the last Germans had come through and that the village was calm. We walked back all the way, across fields and meadows, and reached our house and our garden, to which you returned as if all this had just been part of some new game. A little later, we got our mattresses and blankets, our pots and dishes back.

I found out that the boys in our maquis had attacked the troops occupying La Rochelle and a third of them had been killed. No one knew where the survivors had gone.

I was in pain all night with stitches in my side, and when the doctor got there, I was burning up. He said, "I think it's pleurisy." I had had a case of that at Nieul.

It was the beginning of another period. After it, we would be on our way once more.

18

During my whole life, which might well be termed nomadic, I was never without impatience and even sorrow in periods of transition, for they are also periods of waiting. At Saint-Mesmin, as elsewhere, I had fixed up our house, the animals, the vegetable garden, our crops and our meadows spread around the countryside, and organized the life of our little tribe as if it were forever.

Certainly, deep within me, I knew that all of this was only temporary and that, for us, Saint-Mesmin would last only as long as the war. You had turned into a real boy here, strong, curious about everything, attentive, and familiar with everything around you, and now one day sooner or later we would be leaving again.

It was at Saint-Mesmin that, one morning before you were dressed, I got down on my back, bare feet high in the air, and hoisted you up on my feet, without your losing your balance or being afraid. You looked fine that way, delight written all over your face. I bent my legs, and you came down with them, then back up again.

"More!"

Then I slightly bent first one knee, then the other, and your body, remaining perfectly straight, swung with the movement. Finally, for a worried Tigy, who held her arms out to you, you sat down and then lay down on top of my two feet. I didn't revolve you the way they do in the circus, and you just lay still. How proud you were of yourself, my little Marc!

You often asked me to repeat this game, until the day when I had to confess to you that you had become too heavy for my legs.

That was Saint-Mesmin; and it was so many other things too! A whole segment of life was about to disappear forever, and we were already beginning to take it down, the way they strike sets in the theater.

I was never a participant in that dismantling, which made my chest tighten; I always selfishly left the details of it to your mother, who had become expert at them. Usually, I was gone before the dismantling, off alone to prepare our new "home," where little by little our familiar furniture and other belongings would begin to arrive.

Perhaps the pleurisy that forced me to stay in bed, between four walls which in my memory are yellow but which may not have been, was a stroke of luck.

The fever was making a hodgepodge of ideas and images inside my head, which seemed empty to me. The window opened to the south and, first in August and then in an early autumn that was unusually hot, my room was a sweatbox in which I was so drenched that my skin stuck to the sheets, and my worst pain came from the little pimples on my skin and the itching. From who knows where, they were able to get me one of those round inflated cushions with a hole in the center, like children use today to float on top of the shallow wavelets of the sea.

The sea—of course, but it isn't time yet to mention that. Then, as soon as possible, America; for years I had been dreaming of taking a child there, because what I had seen of it left me with an image of a children's paradise. In the meantime, I remained patiently within my four walls, my body bathed in talcum powder.

In the morning, Boule brought me my coffee and breakfast and looked at me with pitying eyes. I didn't look at all like her "fine young gentleman," for, whereas my body was visibly getting skinnier, my feverish face seemed to me to be swollen when she held the mirror up so I could shave.

Then it was Tigy, in her white painter's smock, which always made her look like a nurse, and she was just as efficient as one. She knew I was short of breath and had trouble speaking, so she asked few questions. She could also guess that I didn't want to hear about what she was doing. She proceeded to give me a bath, as one would a child or a very sick hospital patient, soaping, rinsing, and drying before covering me with the talcum powder the way pastrycooks in their kitchens dust their tarts with sugar.

The latest events had happened so fast I forgot that we had with us, in the meadow where we had hidden, the daughter of a friend at La Rochelle. She was about fifteen, had later gone off, I don't know where, and her place with us had been taken by her brother, a student of barely seventeen who was mad about jazz. He was nice but nevertheless put me through tortures as, hours on end, he played my records at top volume, so loud that the floor shook under me. I am crazy about New Orleans jazz, and my record library was well stocked. But, with an empty head and a panting chest, music that loud can be torture.

My friend Eriau came to see me every morning and gave me news of the outside world. The Allies were making rapid headway in Italy and, along with French troops brought up from darkest Africa, were heading north, toward Strasbourg, according to reports.

Paris had been liberated, but the war was not over, and the furious fighting known as the Battle of the Bulge was about to take place in the colorful Belgian Ardennes, which I know so well.

"Incidentally, I phoned a doctor I was a student with who is now a lung specialist at the hospital in La Roche-sur-Yon. Unfortunately, he can't come for a consultation; there is too great a shortage of doctors everywhere. But he suggests that it might not be a bad idea if I tapped your lungs. . . ." Then, almost shame-faced, he confessed, "I've never done that before, but he explained to me exactly how to do it. Is it all right with you if I do it tomorrow morning at this time?"

The genial, potbellied giant was visibly uncomfortable. "I'll bring along a doctor from Pouzauges who's a little more experienced at this than I am."

I was not afraid. The main thing was to remain where we were until we could realize our secret plan.

I had heard our cows being led away, but I had not asked whom they had been sold to, or the pony. Accustomed as I was to the slightest noises in the house and outside, I knew more or less, in spite of myself, everything that Tigy was up to. My job had always been to build for a time a small family universe; hers, to demolish it when the time came.

Several times a day, the door would open a bit without my having heard any steps on the stairs, and I would see a pink face appear, more serious-looking than usual, and tenderer. "Are you all right, Dad?"

It was you, Marc, and I have no idea what explanation you had been given about my unaccustomed remaining in bed. They must also have advised you not to kiss me, or to come too close, without mentioning to you that it was for fear of possible contagion. Penicillin, which would have had me up and about in a few days, at the time was available only in England and the United States. There was some to be found in Paris, sold on the black market by American soldiers, but that was far from us. The soldiers there sold everything, the bike dealer told me, including their rifles and their military rations.

"Is your little girl friend downstairs?"

"She's so funny-looking, with her front teeth missing."

The doctor's youngest daughter, whom you had already taken over, as you did any children within your reach, had become your playmate.

You tiptoed out again after blowing me a kiss, and then I would hear your voice in the garden.

I had no idea whether rail connections with Paris had been restored, but knew that many important bridges had been blown up. No matter. I had time. First I had to get well.

Our barnyard wasn't bare yet, for I still heard the cocks crow. I knew that Boule went out to pick vegetables, because I could hear her voice when she was doing that.

The music, seeming to come from right below my bed, sharp and obsessive. The lung tap by the two doctors, our own and the one from Pouzauges, dry and serious, sure of himself. I did not anticipate a syringe that looked like one of those old-fashioned enema injectors, nor, especially, a needle as thick as a nail.

Lying on my belly, I heard the two men whispering, feeling the bottom of my spinal column with their fingers. They seemed unsure. A first unsuccessful try made me cry out. More whispering, more fingers digging in my flesh, another outcry.

"Don't move. We're almost done."

It seemed to me that they were slowly, painfully, pumping out the vital essence of my body.

"That's it. All over."

An odor of disinfectant, moist applications, a bandage stuck to the base of my spine.

"Everything seems shipshape. We'll have confirmation of that in two or three days."

Despite what I had expected, I was not impatient. Just eager to get away, to leave this haven at Saint-Mesmin I had enjoyed so much, but now, for me, already a thing of the past. Did I even say *au revoir* to my friends in the village, whom I was never to see again, just as I never again saw the house at Nieul that was so dear to my heart?

In the past few days, I had had many callers. My paratroopers, scattered now, on more or less distant assignments, came to see me, and each one asked for the same thing: an autographed book. Some of those boys from the maquis, who had so daringly attacked the Germans at La Rochelle, came to see me too, and for each one I signed a book.

I began to walk. I looked through the window at a setting that had become alien to me. I was thin and my legs wobbled.

Knowing that we were leaving soon, Victor had taken a job as a road maintenance man, which the local municipality had offered him. His family and children were still entitled to stay for another year in the house I had rented for them.

· · ·

A big car, a real one, no longer the kind of locomotive that had taken us to La Bourboule. There was room for all four of us, your mother and me, you and Boule, and we were not going very far, just to Les Sables-d'Olonne, a place I was familiar with, where you would once again see the sea, much bigger than at Nieul, a beach a hundred times wider and longer than at La Rochelle, with a promenade all around the bay called the Remblai, for in reality it was a dike that kept the water at high tide from flooding the lower areas.

You peered "with all your eyes," as my mother used to say, at the ocean I was in such a hurry to take you across to a new "home."

A small hotel, Les Roches Noires, at the very end of the promenade, on the edge of a pine wood. Roly-poly patron and patronne, with good welcoming smiles. A young niece with a well-endowed bosom whose pink face reminded me of the bonbons of my childhood. Another daughter with dark hair who helped with everything. Because of the war, we were the only guests at the hotel, aside from the few people, never more than four or five, who came in for meals.

Two rooms, one for you, because you didn't want to sleep with anyone, another for Boule and me. Your mother was going back to Saint-Mesmin in the car that had brought us.

One of the Resistance fellows who had come to see me had gotten as far as Nieul, recognized our house, which I had described to him, and been inside. There were no Germans left in it. It was empty and in a mess, the garden gone to seed.

It seemed perfectly natural to you for Boule and me to sleep in the same room. As for her, she shone with delight at the idea that at last she'd have you all to herself to take care of.

The hotel owners, finding that I was deplorably skinny, served us steaks as big as the plates. They put themselves out in every way to take care of us, and from the fishermen got thick soles, which they cooked for our evening meal.

We would walk slowly on the Remblai and on the beach, where you lovingly sank your hands into the sand, as if you knew it was alive. Only the pine wood, so tempting and so close by, was off limits to you. The Germans had sown it with land mines before leaving, and four or five children had already been blown to bits.

The house next to the hotel was occupied by a brunette, a school-teacher, some forty-odd years old whose hair had been shaved off after the Germans left. What she had done was no business of ours. Her hair was growing back; this would not have been the case for her breasts, which were almost cut off but which she had miraculously saved. She was nonetheless serene, without hatred for anyone. She agreed to give you private lessons, in her house, taught you to read, and started to teach you to write.

You had not had, as most children do, picture books with bright colors, because there were none to be had at Saint-Mesmin. Your last "Mademoiselle," as you called her, had scarcely had the time to teach you to recognize big block capital letters; once the country had restored her to health, she had fled back to Paris.

By chance, I ran into a man I had known many years before, who had turned into a kindly skeleton of an old man. After having studied law, he had lived it up, as they used to say in those days, hungering after everything, especially women, gourmet meals, and fine wines, which had forced him, once he ran through all his money, to sell the manor house and estate where he had been born. He had been given a sinecure as justice of the peace in Les Sables-d'Olonne, for he was a local fellow and everyone knew his story.

Now retired, he lived as best he could, pinching pennies, and playing bridge in a café on the Remblai with friends. He was one of the most cultured men I had ever met and was soon to play an important part in my life.

Just as a pipe, a simple pipe, and three or four cans of tobacco were to have unpredictable consequences.

The first letter I received from Paris was on the letterhead of a book shipping company I had never heard of and signed by a Danish name that was even less familiar to me. It informed me that the writer was sending along the proofs of a book by a young Norwegian he wished me to read and, if I thought it deserved it, to write a preface for.

The proofs arrived; I read them and, enthusiastic about them, wrote a rather long piece. The owner of this Messageries du Livre, who was about to become a publisher, was named Sven Nielsen. He asked me how much he owed me, and I innocently replied that one didn't expect payment for a preface. In this I was all wrong, because the most famous writers, members of the academies, get a pretty penny for dashing off a few laudatory lines.

Sven Nielsen and I continued our correspondence, and as soon as I was able to get out of my contracts with Gallimard, he became my exclusive French publisher. Today, his son, in whom I have equal confidence, has taken over for him.

The owner of the hotel let me use an empty room, in an annex, and, feeling completely well again, I wrote a few tales, which Sven eventually published, under the title *La Rue aux Trois Poussins* (The Street of the Three Chicks), for there were many children in those little stories.

. . .

One day when you were out for a walk with Boule, a mongrel dog, ugly to look at, smelled you and followed you home. He had adopted you, and you had already adopted him too. I do believe that was the first tragedy of your life.

As you were coming up the hotel steps with "your" dog, the owner, usually so agreeable, glimpsed the animal. "No dirty creature like that around here . . ."

He didn't know of your passion for animals, your love for everything that is alive, and he drove the dog away with a vicious kick. This came as such a shock to you that the patron was ashamed of what he had done, tried to make it up to you, and finally went inside to get a superb old Louis XIV or XV pistol, beautifully carved and silver-incrusted. You didn't want to take the thing in your hands, and it looked as if you were going to refuse the gift.

You did take it, though, but without saying thanks. You had just learned that men, even the best of them, can sometimes be cruel. You had also just discovered your own fascination with firearms.

The desire to see you play in the sand by the ocean had made me commit an infraction of a basic medical rule. It is true that, early in this century, doctors committed it too, by sending tubercular patients down to the Riviera.

I was not tubercular, I hoped, but the coating of my lungs had nonetheless been damaged. So I should have spent my convalescence in a dry climate, preferably in the mountains, but surely not breathing humid air at the seashore. I had a relapse, so serious that the doctor at the hospital, an understanding and excellent practitioner, suggested calling in a famous lung specialist.

I had met one coming home from Bombay, whom a rich local merchant had summoned, at a time when people didn't make such trips by plane, but by ocean liner. The doctor was diabetic, and all the way back home he had to weigh at the table all the food he ate, something he did on a small folding scale he always carried with him, along with one or two lumps of sugar. This did not keep him from being merry, optimistic, and unafraid of seasickness, which in his condition might have had serious consequences.

Knowing that he was a passionate bridge player, I organized daily games with some English people, and our games would go on for hours and hours on days when the sea was rough. Always and everywhere I have had friends who were doctors; the best of them feel the same curiosity about and attraction to human beings as I do. In Paris, where he lived, we used to have lunches followed by bridge games before the war, sometimes at one person's house, sometimes at another's, and in that way I got to know a great many leading medical professors.

My Sables-d'Olonne doctor phoned him. Dr. Coulaud, who ran the tuberculosis hospital in Paris, took the trouble to come and see me under very precarious conditions. He did not hide from me the fact that pleurisy rarely fails to damage the lungs seriously, if not giving a start to tuberculosis.

Another session in the single glow of a phosphorescent screen, behind which my teeth were chattering with cold as I awaited the verdict with more confidence than I had had at that solemn idiot's office in Fontenay-le-Comte. He turned the light back on, and I saw a fine confident smile.

"No lesion. Not the slightest spot. But you nevertheless have to take very good care of yourself."

Just in case, he had brought along a few shots of the oh-so-precious penicillin, which he had been able to buy from a butcher in Paris. Butchers, with their refrigerators, were the ones who dealt in this medicine, which had to be kept cold in order not to spoil.

Coulaud went back to Paris, taking along some fine thick juicy soles I had been able to get from the patron of the hotel. The penicillin made me feel better quickly, but I still had to stay in bed for a long time, and then in my room.

My friend the onetime justice of the peace, to amuse me, brought me old bound volumes of yellowing paper, collections of the court reports of the second half of the last century. I delved into them with delight and thus got to know all the famous cases adjudicated back then in the courtrooms of Paris.

Afternoons, he would come to my bedroom with three or four of his friends, and we whiled away the time in endless games of bridge. The owner of the hotel was feeding me a very rich diet, and brought up from his cellar the finest of wines for me and my visitors.

You went on taking lessons next door with the teacher who had almost lost her breasts. You went out a great deal with Boule, whatever the weather, and you were getting along splendidly, while I was slowly recovering.

Good red meat was still hard to find, so your mother would send us packages of it from Saint-Mesmin, from where she commuted to Nieul. You came to spend longer periods with me, since there was no longer any danger of contagion.

I don't know when it was that I took my first steps out of doors with you, but the sun was surely shining.

Tigy, who was piling up at Nieul everything that was needed there, came to see us now and then. I rented an apartment toward the middle of the Remblai, where we were close to the heart of this picturesque town and its fish market.

Finally, your mother came back to be with us, and had her own bedroom. Boule was happy to be back with her pots and pans and prepared the most delicious dishes for us.

I had to hire a secretary, because correspondence was getting heavy, not only from France, but also from some of the places in which I had been translated, among them England, the United States, Spain, and South America.

She was a gorgeous girl of twenty, whose name I've forgotten, so I'll call her Odette. Her hair was golden blond, her face ever radiant, and her body so tempting that men turned to stare as she went by.

I was trying to buy a car, which was hard, if not impossible, at that time, and I finally located a very old little Peugeot with a rectangle in the roof that could be slid open. The tires were smooth, but there were no others to be had at Les Sables-d'Olonne. A charming police superintendent got me a permit for the car, although I had to wait over a month before the prefecture and the French military authorities approved it.

I went out scouting, leaving you in the hands of your mother and Boule, who by now were getting along together just fine.

Spring came early. My secretary and I went out in the rickety little car, well aware, after the promising looks we had so long been exchanging, of what lay ahead.

A blowout forced us to stop in a tiny town. It was a cheerful, bright town, showing no trace of the war, and our tire had decided to breathe its last in front of a small hotel. A nearby garageman said he could let us have a tire, or maybe two, used but not nearly so bald as ours, of course at black-market prices.

We took one room for the two of us, and it was simple but clean. Since it had no bathroom, but an old-fashioned washstand with a marble top and a bowl and porcelain water jug with pink flowers painted on it, we had to make do with rather summary ablutions.

The next day, we stopped twice more to pick up, with much difficulty, additional secondhand tires. We slept not far from Paris, and by noon, at last, we pulled up in front of the Claridge.

In the lobby, I bumped into Jean Gabin, whose hair had been dyed blond by Hollywood. He was with Marlene Dietrich, who held on to his arm possessively. Kisses all around. Lots of uniforms of the different Allied armies, lots of officers' insignia, even on the uniform of a lawyer I knew from Fouquet's, whom I was surprised to find rigged out as a colonel.

The first night, we slept in a de luxe suite in which, when I first arrived in Paris in 1922, I had interviewed a Belgian prime minister who was friendly to my paper.

19

Before you were conceived, I had traveled around the world, driven by an irresistible need to meet men from everywhere and nowhere, so that I had had a great number of more or less passing nests. Later, over a period of more than five years, things had been different; then, it was events that forced me to move about. At each place, we patiently rebuilt around you another nest, another home of our own.

Now, we found ourselves facing a new situation. It was as if we were in a vacuum, anticipating the New World, which I had had only a glimpse of and where I wanted you to set down roots for some years, if not forever.

What month it was when I got to the Claridge, from which I was to set out to find for you and our little tribe a shelter that I imagined to be very temporary, I cannot say. At any rate, spring was in the air. March or April, the famous springtime in Paris so many songs have been written about?

I had only the phone to connect me to you, and sometimes it took hours to get through. Tigy wasn't always there, because she had a great deal to do to close out Saint-Mesmin, to fill myriad crates, number them, and list in notebooks the contents of each. Just books alone filled some forty crates, and we had no idea how much we would be able to take with us overseas.

I felt alone—with a beautiful girl, to be sure, who was merry and ardent, but who was only an interlude.

The Paris I now found upset me by its frantic activity and the quantities of rules I knew nothing about. The day after our arrival, the hotel manager, whom I knew well, called me into his office.

"You have to fill out a form this very day or I won't be able to keep you here. I apologize for this, but the authorities are very finicky. I've drawn up a letter for you that you may find useful."

He told me that in order to get a hotel room one had to apply to some office for a "lodging ticket." The hotels were broken down into categories, as were the applicants for rooms, and the most favored ones, the ones vying for a "coupon" entitling them to a de luxe hotel, were high-ranking officers, diplomats, officials of friendly governments, big wheels of all kinds, with only the rarest of exceptions for plain ordinary people.

Not being a big wheel, I fell into that last category. In a very expensive apartment that had been turned into improvised offices, I found myself facing unknown civilian and military characters, on whose decisions I depended. I stood in line, for lines were everywhere, especially in front of places where you could get some kind of rubber stamp.

A military character read the letter from the Claridge. "How long have you been there?"

"Since yesterday."

"Do you intend to stay long?"

"I can't say. That depends on what I have to do to get my visas."

"What visas?"

Before the war, it had been so easy!

"You know that the Claridge is one of the first-class hotels most in demand? . . . Well, stay there for the time being, but you may be bumped out of there from one day to the next, depending on how many people qualifying for it turn up."

I went back to the hotel. The lobby and bar were as ever overflowing with people in uniform, chests full of medals, gold-braid caps, and occasional civilians. I gave my room number to the concierge, the same one who had been there before the war. He gave me a different key, and I looked at the number on it in surprise.

"I forgot to tell you that we had to switch your room. Some Russian generals got in this morning and we had to vacate several suites for them."

You needed a peaceful haven, and I could tell it would not be easy to find. That afternoon, at the Belgian Embassy, where I no longer knew a soul but where they were very amiable just the same, they first told me that my passport had expired and that they would get me a new one in three days.

"What's your address?"

"The Claridge."

"You're lucky. A member of the Belgian Chamber of Deputies last week was sent to some old hotel out in the Fourteenth Arrondissement. . . ."

"I'm expecting a visa for the U.S.A."

"That's difficult. It'll take months. Thousands of people with the same idea are besieging the embassy. . . ."

It was reassuring to hear your little voice on the telephone, which you were learning to use. "When are we going to come and be with you, Dad? Will we take a train?"

What made me think of Place des Vosges, where I had lived for so long and which, until 1930, had been my home base?

When I left there, I had turned my lease over to a friend from my early days in Paris, Ziza, the most faithful, most devoted one, who wanted that apartment less to live in than as a base to return to, where he would find an environment that for him, as for me, held so many memories.

He had been assistant manager in the branch bank where I opened my first account, which was really skinny. He had followed my slow rise in the field of the dime novel and had seen me paint, in green, on my door the nom de plume that I used at the time: SIM. He liked me a lot. When he left the bank, it was to go into business for himself, and, the last I heard, he was the head of a big outfit on the Mediterranean coast.

At Place des Vosges, I found the same concierge, an old lady now, who had known Tigy and Boule and me, and had always been very sweet to us,

"Monsieur Sim! You here! What about Boule? And your wife?"

"We now have a son too."

"Are you going to live up there again? Monsieur Ziza told me that you might be coming back someday and that you should feel right at home. He left the key with me for you. . . ."

Was this, finally, a solution? Of course, before the war, my friend had often extended such an invitation to me. Was he still down south? I had a lot of trouble getting through to him by phone.

"Sim! Where are you?"

"In Paris."

"With Tigy and Boule?"

"I have a son. They're down in the Vendée waiting for me to find a temporary place for us to live."

"You know that your old studio is yours for the asking. You'll find some good old bottles there. Drink them to my health!"

"Do you really mean that?"

Effusive reassurances. We really were very fond of each other.

"Did you know that I'm married? I'll have to get you to meet my wife someday."

He did, much later. In the meantime, I had found a pleasant temporary nest for us, and for you, Marc, Place des Vosges, where all the children from the neighborhood came to play.

I finally was able to reach Tigy on the phone.

"That's all well and good, but is food to be had readily in Paris? Do people still need ration cards?"

I had no idea.

"Do you think you'll get the visa very soon?"

I had no idea about that either.

"Maybe we'd better wait a little longer. The climate here at Sables agrees with Marc, and we have everything we need. I'm kind of scared of Paris with him. . . ."

She was right. The day before, coming out of the concierge's at Place des Vosges, I had gone into a tiny café–tobacco shop where I had once gone often. Lots of people there too, some local shopkeepers and all the ordinary folk of the Marais neighborhood.

"Monsieur Sim!"

The faces were more serious than at the Claridge, and I didn't hear the same happy voices as in the old days. I could feel that these people who earned their bread with difficulty were full of mistrust, if not antagonism. They had gone hungry. They had thought that the end of the war would bring a new kind of life to them. They had seen rich people get richer on the black market and through the worst kind of collaboration. Yet now, for some of those there was wealth, celebration, pomp, while the little people still had to wait in line to get their ration cards stamped.

On the Champs-Elysées, very little had changed since before the war. At Fouquet's, I saw the same faces, a few friends, but also a few empty places that no one mentioned. In neighborhood restaurants, the waiter would negligently ask, "Do you have your bread coupons?" He smiled to make it clear he was just asking to cover the obligation.

I saw Marcel Pagnol again, and he told me he was about to get married and apply for membership in the French Academy. "We'll all be members —you too, and Cocteau, Achard, the whole younger generation—and we'll raise holy hell there. . . ."

I saw Raimu again, who hadn't changed at all. "You put one over on me, didn't you?" he grumbled in his usual way.

"How's that?"

"You had a son and you got a different godfather. You promised me, you know. . . ."

Yes. I had promised, one day when I had drunk a bit, that if I ever had a son, Raimu would be his godfather, and he would be named Jules; if I had a daughter, his wife would be godmother, and she would be named Esther, after her.

"Don't hold it against me, Jules. We were so far away. . . ."

"You were far away plenty of times! Anyway, is he good and strong, the littl'un?"

We had dinner together in one of the little black-market restaurants, the addresses of which circulated by word of mouth.

I don't remember how many times Odette and I had our room changed, and we didn't dare mix with the noisy crowd at the bar, full of American noncoms who went after every woman they saw, even if she was with her husband. Most of them had recently risked their lives in an infernal landing. Wasn't it only normal for them to let themselves go?

That was the way it was, especially at night, in the bars just off the Champs-Elysées, on Rue La Boétie and Rue Washington. Pretty women were not hard to find. Sometimes one might see a couple making love in a doorway, with no regard for the passers-by.

This was a Paris I didn't know and in which I felt a stranger. My old pal Jean Rigaux, the topical songwriter, had opened a nightspot just a stone's throw off Avenue George-V. Hugs and kisses, as at each reunion with old friends.

"You've got to come tonight. It'll be fun. . . ."

It was fun mainly because Rigaux, who was very sensitive, hid his rages and indignations by making fun of everything with a petulance that made even his victims burst out laughing. In the small space, there was nothing but the real upper crust, plus a few American officers who spoke French like natives, because they knew France and Paris from way back when.

Rigaux introduced me to one of them, slim and lively, leaning against the bar next to me.

"Colonel Justin O'Brien. Just think, in civilian life, he's a professor of French literature at Columbia University. Now here he is a colonel in the secret service. Shh! But he's a great guy, anyway."

I was to see proof of it that same night. Now and then, American enlisted men, some of them with black skins, would peek in the door, see the insignia inside, and, without further ado, go quietly on their way.

But one group of Marines decided they'd brazen it out. They were all drunk. When O'Brien patiently explained to them that they were out of bounds here, one of them let him have a punch in the jaw so hard that the colonel fell off his bar stool.

The others just stood there, worried, surprised, not knowing what to do, while O'Brien got up, without showing any reaction. Rigaux and I expected to hear him bark out orders at them and call for the M.P.s, as would have been the case if he had been a French colonel.

But that wasn't the kind of man he was. After brushing the blood from his lip, he simply said, in English, to the awe-struck men, "Have a quick drink and get to bed. It's on me."

I saw a great deal of him, and he played a big part in my life. He was a highly lettered man, and his wife, who was no less so, did me the honor, sometime later, of translating one of my books.

From that period of transition, I retain so many disparate images that I have to select from among them without any order, because at that time everything was happening very fast.

We often had dinner with Raimu and Esther, with Pagnol and his young wife, whom I had met when she had the lead in a play that was on tour—in Fontenay-le-Comte, of all places.

Tigy would send by freight packages of meat, which the Claridge kept in its refrigerator for me.

"My father is in Paris," Odette said to me one day, with great emotion.

"Did you see him? What did you tell him?"

He was a French major who had just been repatriated from a German prison.

"They can't be seen for two days. They're kept in a kind of barn, where they go around naked while their clothes get disinfected. They all have to have very thorough medical examinations. It takes two or three days."

Her father wanted her to return to Les Sables-d'Olonne with him. The day she left, I swear, I suddenly found myself face to face with the girl scout who had helped me so efficiently at the Belgian refugee camp. She was no longer in uniform and didn't seem like such a little girl anymore.

"Are you alone in Paris?" she asked.

"For the time being." I told her that my secretary had just had to leave.

"Would you like me to replace her?"

"When?"

"Right away. Just long enough to go get my things."

It was as simple as that, perhaps because of the war. Those days, we happened to have a suite. So they were luxurious days. But we were soon moved to a maid's room, narrow, with an iron bed, and the toilet at the end of the hall. The girl scout could put up with anything. Me too.

Who else? What else?

You, my little Marc, whom I went to the station to welcome, along with Tigy and Boule. Oof! What a relief! I moved the three of you in, on Place des Vosges, and since there was no room there for me, I went on back to the Claridge.

Short trip to London, just between planes, after my girl scout spent ten hours standing in line to get me my visa. A movie contract to be signed. I was reunited with Julien Duvivier, who had directed *La Tête d'un homme (A Battle of Nerves)*, based on my novel, and Charles Spaak, my fellow Belgian, who had written, among other scenarios, the one for Jean Renoir's *Grand Illusion*. Alexander Korda, who had become one of the leading British producers, invited us to dinner in his suite at Claridge's, a majestic-looking, somber hotel, where black marble was dominant, frequented mainly by lords and ladies.

"Where is Jean?" Renoir was my best friend, and I didn't know what had happened to him.

"He's in Hollywood. He's become an American citizen."

Wouldn't I be getting a chance to embrace him soon?

I was commuting daily between Place des Vosges and the Claridge. When your mother went off to Nieul or elsewhere—it was no longer my business—I would sleep in the big studio with Boule. You yourself asked me to! "Why don't you sleep in the big bed with Boule? Then we'll all be together."

I had finally found out what the system was. In order to get an American visa, a person had to be sent on official business for an Allied government.

A one-time newspaperman on *Le Journal*, whom I had once known quite well, had become minister of Information or something of the sort, and had offices in a great private home on Avenue Friedland. I went to see him. He was cordial and apparently amazed at holding so important a position.

"Are you naturalized French?"

"No. I still travel on a Belgian passport."

That made him hesitate a moment. Fortunately, he didn't have a bureaucratic turn of mind. "Bah! We can fix that up! Do you have any connections in the States?"

"My publishers."

"Have your books been translated there?"

"Over twenty of them."

"What would you say to carrying out a survey of American and Canadian publishers? The Canadians are important, because French is spoken in Québec."

"I'm published there too."

"Well, I'll have travel orders made out for you."

"On what kind of business?"

"Whatever you say. To lecture on French literature. Or nothing at all, if you like that better."

A big official document, "in the name of the French Republic."

"Thanks. But I didn't mention I'm taking my wife and son. . . ."

"Then get a Canadian visa for them. It's not as hard to get, and the ambassador is the most charming of men."

Everything is difficult. Lines to stand in. Mistrust everywhere and vague promises. Then, suddenly, by chance, it all becomes easy, almost too easy.

At the United States Embassy everything goes as smoothly as can be. "Come back in two weeks. It'll be ready. We have to make an investigation of every individual, but since you're going on government business . . ."

I am exulting. What month is it? It's hot. Patton has long since invaded Germany, and the Russians are crossing it from the east. Patton wants to reach Berlin first, and could. He's furious when he gets orders from the high command to let the Russians be first into the German capital, where they all meet after Hitler's suicide.

Finally, Hiroshima, of which nobody is too proud, and the Parade of Peace down the Champs-Elysées, to which some people come with ladders and others climb to the tops of trees.

"Peace!"

This time, for real, it seems, and all of us, you, your mother, and I, are in front box seats to watch the parade. At the Claridge, I have a room without a balcony. More Russian generals have come in, including one, with an artificial leg and a jolly face beneath his white hair, who goes up in the elevator night after night with two or three pretty girls with him. He's not in any maid's room, and doesn't have to sleep with his girl friends on a narrow iron bed, the way my girl scout and I have to!

Flags everywhere, at the windows, on the roofs, up above the crowd, so dense that it is just one howling colorful mass.

The balcony we are on is that of a movie producer I met many, many years ago, at winter sports. His wife, very ordinary-looking, like a quiet housewife good at turning out tasty dishes, was dropped a score of times from British planes, and each time, returning to London from improvised airfields lighted by candles in simple clearings in the woods, she brought back British fliers who had escaped from German prison camps.

On her simple little jacket, she has more ribbons than I can count. She has no idea what happened to her Jewish husband. Will she ever find out?

. . .

Your mother will not hear of our taking Boule along to the United States, threatens to stay in France and keep you with her, and of course I have to give in. Not without promising Boule that I'll bring her over a little later.

We are taking along a mountain of luggage and crates, which only Tigy knows the contents of.

I saw Pierre Lazareff, the newspaper editor, back from Hollywood and New York, where he spent the war years. He has left Jean Prouvost, with whom he used to run *Paris-Soir*, and is now at the head of a new paper, *France-Soir*, in which he wants to publish my next novel.

The Parisian newspapers have changed names, owners, staffs. *Le Petit Parisien* is now called *Le Parisien libéré*. All the papers are liberated, as everything has been liberated, especially by the English, the Americans, and the Canadians. By a few French regiments too, but many people will never forgive the foreigners for the fact that they owe their liberty to them. It is true that they too had their heroes.

London. We have to go by way of London to get to America. All shipping has been pooled, meaning that it is under the orders of a committee, located in London, including the different Allied general staffs.

We stay at the Savoy, where your mother and I have often stayed and where we know almost everybody, from the doormen resplendent in their uniforms to the manager.

We wait. We are on the list. What list, I have no idea. We are advised not to stray too far from our hotel, because the order might arrive from one hour to the next for us to go down to Southampton, or some other port, after quickly picking up our tickets at the steamship office, probably that of the Cunard Line.

No! No way to get tickets ahead of time, and we will have to wait a month like this. I see my publishers, who went on publishing my novels during the war. They owe me a rather large sum, which I ask a Canadian bank to transfer to Canada for me. Your mother and I have decided to settle first in Québec, which is bilingual, so as to learn English. Now that she and I have each regained our liberty, I will make rather long trips to New York, where I have a lot of business to attend to.

You spend the better part of your days in front of the hotel with two giant doormen who have befriended you. When a guest comes out, one of them blows a whistle several times to call one of the taxis parked down the dead-end street. You earned a quick promotion, Marc, because they gave you a real whistle one day, after they discovered that you could make the same shrill sound by putting your fingers into your mouth, the way the bad boys do in Montmartre and around the Bastille.

In Paris, I had bought you an accordion. A truck was parked outside a little café not far from where we lived, and some Foreign Legionnaires, back from Germany, were offering for sale all kinds of musical instruments, radios, cameras, whatever they had been able to pick up along the way. Around the truck, it was like a grab bag. A person called out a price. One of the Legionnaires answered yes or no. I offered fifty francs for the accordion and brought it back to Place des Vosges to you. So it must have been somewhere in our luggage.

I took you over toward Westminster, the tolling bells of which fascinated you, to a little steamboat that crossed all of London, takings its passengers as far as the famous Tower of London by weaving in and out among the freighters and liners that formed a real procession on the river. That spectacle, the docks, was fascinating to you. Everything fascinated you. You didn't have eyes enough to take it all in. We went up and down the Thames at least twenty times like that, and you never tired of it.

Almost every night, I went out to try my luck, and I discovered that Englishwomen are not the flat, cold things they are reputed to be.

The phone call finally came. We were to be, next morning, on I can't remember what quay at Southampton to embark. I let Tigy know and rushed to the nearby Cunard office, got at the end of the line in front of the ticket window. When I finally reached the window, the clerk was being served tea and cookies from a little cart.

I held out my papers in vain. He didn't look at me. While I boiled, he drank his tea in small greedy sips and savored his cookies. How long did that last? To me, an eternity. What if we were to miss the boat?

Finally, the man filled in the blanks on several printed sheets, slowly, deliberately. Then he told me how much I owed him. After I paid, I made a beeline for the bank to withdraw the balance of the money I had on deposit there.

When I got back to the Savoy in a sweat, Tigy had already sent on their way to Southampton the crates, trunks, accordion, and all the rest. Now we just had to take the train. The two doormen came to shake your hand through the lowered window of the taxi that was taking us away.

Lord! How little our ship was! A Swedish freighter, with only a few passenger cabins. You had a two-bunk cabin with your mother, and I another two-bunk cabin with a strange man.

We leave in the middle of the night, ten hours later, with the tide.

. . .

The freighter was deadheading it, and that meant that it tipped to the slightest swell, the least breeze. On it, I met a Frenchman, with his mistress. He was a total stranger to me, yet he confided one day as we sat on deck that he was taking with him two liters of attar of roses, enough to make thousands of liters of perfume, which was his entire grubstake.

He asked his pretty red-headed companion to show me her bracelet, which was a wide, heavy leather thing. Underneath, when she moved it away after making sure no one could see us, was another bracelet, made of diamonds.

"I'm planning to organize auto races over there," this recently met friend confided.

Friend? Well, the way people get to be on a ship that has only a dozen passengers, and knowing they will never see one another again once the crossing is over. Every time I chanced to pass an American prison later on, I used to wonder whether my man with the attar of roses wasn't behind its walls.

In the small dining room, you were able to give vent to your greediness at a buffet that offered a variety of *smörebröd*, canapés of red caviar, herring, shrimps, various kinds of sausages, ham, and all sorts of other tempting things you couldn't resist. You had not yet understood that after stuffing this way, one sat down to two or three different hot dishes, followed by pastries filled with thick cream.

Right in the middle of the Atlantic, a storm blew up that quickly reached force 10. Our little boat, empty and too light, nose-dived into the waves, which broke over the deck, reared, and jumped around every which way.

The decks were off limits, the doors hermetically sealed, but you insisted on going out just as you did on other days. I talked to an old Norse sailor, and explained to him in some kind of bastardized language that all he would have to do would be to tie you to the end of a rope and keep a good hold on it. . . . Almost everybody else stuck to their cabins, felled by seasickness. But you were allowed to venture out on deck, at the end of your tether, and you made your way back without falling once, but not without getting soaked from head to toe. Your mother didn't approve of my initiative. But then, she was seasick.

After a couple of days, the sea calmed down. It took us twelve days and twelve nights to reach the Statue of Liberty. Little motor tugs came out toward us, boarded us, dropping off first a pilot, then the health inspector, Immigration, and finally a handful of newspapermen and photographers.

There was somebody else with them, in a colonel's uniform: my friend Justin O'Brien.

"I'm out of the service," he told me. "I put on the uniform just to make things easier. I've found you rooms in a hotel run by a Belgian who served in the same branch as I did. The longshoremen are on strike, taxis are mobbed, but with my rank we'll make out."

You stared at the buildings, skyscrapers that stood nine hundred feet high and more. That night you were going to sleep on Park Avenue in one of those very skyscraper hotels.

Welcome, boy! [In English.]

At last!

20

Another transition period, to be sure, but this one without impatience, without nervousness. The other times, I had been going where events pushed me, at least during the past few years. This time, I was at last reaching a goal I had set myself years before and, contrary to what so often happens, was feeling no disappointment. Instead, a deep satisfaction, as when one finally gets back home and voluptuously relaxes. Joy too.

As for you, my little six-year-old Marc, your eyes did not reflect any amazement and you weren't even impressed by the fact that our hotel room was on the fortieth or forty-fifth floor. Through the friendship of Colonel O'Brien, now Professor O'Brien once more, and the cordiality of the hotel's manager, we had a large suite with two bedrooms, one for you and your mother, the other for me, and between them a large English-style sitting room.

The newspapers had announced my arrival, published the first interviews made on board ship. The very first evening, I got a friendly phone call from a famous French writer who had spent all of the war years in the United States and who invited me to dinner in a restaurant the next day.

More newspapermen. Photographers. A press conference in our room. You couldn't go and get your blindworm or your turkey to show them, but the first picture of you shows you playing(?) your accordion.

You were calm. You accepted, as if they were the most ordinary of things, the images that rushed by you at accelerated speed. And the view of the city from the roof of Rockefeller Center must have left you with no other impression than that of the flocks of birds flying practically on top of our heads.

You weren't interested in landscapes. What interested you were the little things, even pebbles, everything that was alive, blades of grass, birds, insects, which you could always spot at a glance.

How long were the three of us in New York? Ten days? Two weeks? I saw my publishers and drew up new contracts. I met other French "refugees," a boulevard playwright, a painter, my old friend Kisling, known to everyone in Montparnasse as Kiki, who, during the war years, had painted portraits of the women of café society, soon to become the jet set. I met . . .

It would take too long to enumerate them all. What struck me was how they all invited me to eat in French restaurants and how eager they were to get back to their native land. None had adapted to American life, which already seemed familiar to me.

We took the train to Montreal, in a club car with movable large, deep armchairs, which could be set up around equally movable tables for a bridge or poker game.

You barely looked at the passing countryside, the little white churches with their red or black tile roofs, the Hudson, with real freighters on it, the few towns in which we stopped.

What intrigued you the most in Montreal was the glass door of the railroad station that opened automatically as a person approached it and closed noiselessly. Electric eyes were not yet in use in Europe, and you walked back and forth to try to get to the bottom of the mystery. The fact is, I must confess, I was as much impressed by them as you were!

It was October and everything was covered with snow. Another hotel. Another suite. More reporters. After two or three days, one of them asked me: "What are you looking for in Montreal?"

"A car and a secretary."

"The car may be hard to find. They haven't built any new ones since the war began. Secondhand cars fetch astronomical prices, as do tires. . . ."

I was familiar with that! To my great surprise, I got about a hundred and eighty letters from would-be secretaries, and decided that the easiest thing would be to have them all in on the same afternoon. The hotel management let me use a small sitting room, and there was plenty of space in the lobby for those who were waiting their turn.

Most of them were young. I questioned them, sometimes took their names and addresses. A person can't work with a secretary with whom he has no empathy.

One of them was escorted by her father, an upstanding middle-class type. "My daughter is only nineteen," he said, "but . . ." and went on to enumerate her qualities. Good stenography, bilingual, as the others were, as almost everyone in Montreal is, the main newspaper there, the *Star*, being in English. She was pretty and had nice, honest eyes.

I probably would have hired her if the father had not gone on to say, "I am well aware, Mr. Simenon, of everything that may be expected of a private secretary. . . ." He especially stressed that word "private," and although I wrote down her name and address, I had already decided to drop her from my list.

In the end, I did not hire any of those applicants.

Once I was able to buy a car, I drove into the Laurentians, some twenty-five miles north of Montreal, where there were houses and cottages for rent.

The snow was piled in high drifts on either side of the icy road, to act as a soft cushion in case the car went into a skid.

Sainte-Marguerite-du-Lac-Masson. A village, or, more properly, a hamlet, and, around a great frozen lake, log cabins like the ones in the song "Ma cabane au Canada." Three bedrooms, living room, bathroom, of course, and all modern appliances. But where would I have worked? The overseer showed me, across from these cabins "with one foot right in the water," an ordinary little cottage of some grayish stone, and I rented it at the same time, to be my office and house my future secretary.

A sixteen-year-old local girl applied for a job, and there was room for her too in the cottage. She was charming and sang all day long.

My plan, my treasured plan, had been, once you were all settled in, to commute to New York, and now that your mother and I were truly free of any obligation to one another, to meet a few pretty women there.

But first, my commutation was mostly to Montreal, usually alone, for three- or four-day stays. Many of my books had been published there in French, and I was not at all satisfied with the terms I was being offered, considerably under what I was getting in France. I finally, after a struggle, got what I wanted.

A young publisher offered me a dazzling contract, which, fortunately, I didn't accept, for he went broke two years later. But at least he filled me in on where and how to meet willing feminine playmates, and it wasn't long before I realized that they were even more numerous and more available than in Paris.

A second publisher I saw had a sort of partner or right-hand man, a very agreeable humpback, who asked me at our first meeting: "Have you found a secretary yet?"

"Not yet. I haven't been able to make up my mind."

"Don't worry. I have one for you. But you'll have to wait for me to contact her; she's in Philadelphia at the moment."

I had to buy skis for all of us, and very warm clothing, for I was told that in December the temperature would go down to twenty, if not forty, degrees below zero.

A month went by, and you adapted to our new life style just as you had adapted to everything. You were recording everything, as you were to prove much later when you took your wife and children to visit every one of the houses we had lived in on the other side of the Atlantic. There were to be a lot of them, some for a short time, some for several years, in the north, south, east, and west.

I don't remember who it was who sent us a rather young, patient schoolmarm, who lived in the cabin with you and who, when she wasn't busy teaching you or your mother English, played her guitar and sang sentimental songs.

We also ran into a young woman I had first met at the same time as Boule. She was the daughter of friends with whom we had eaten and played croquet that time when your mother and I were sleeping on the straw at the farm. She was married but childless. Her husband, a Frenchman, had founded in Montreal a factory in which women turned out fancy boxes for jewelers, perfumers, and candy companies. They were both nice people, and we often ate with them.

One day, on the path leading to the village, you gave me a strong squeeze on the arm and whispered, "Look!"

Two black bear cubs were rolling in the snow as their mother stood watching them. You gravely shushed me, and we were able to get within a dozen yards of them, which Mama Bear must have decided was close enough, for she then unhurriedly led her offspring back into the underbrush.

Alone in New York once again. Publishers. Discussions. Contrary to what most people in Europe believe, such agreements are very slowly arrived at.

I meet a russet-gold-haired model whom I take to dinner in a small

Italian restaurant. I am much attracted to her, not just for a one-night stand, but for a meaningful and perhaps lasting relationship.

After dinner, we go dancing, as is customary here, and then I invite her up to my hotel room for a nightcap. She accepts, and we behave ourselves, merely kissing and necking a little. I had been warned that it wasn't wise to try to "make" an American girl on the first date, but to wait for the second one before trying to score. We set a date to have dinner again three or four days later.

Then, the next day, I am awakened with a start by the telephone and am only to find out later how important that phone call was to be in my life, yours, and that of your brothers and sister still to be born.

At the other end of the wire was the Montreal humpback. "I saw the secretary. She'll be in New York tomorrow and has agreed to meet with you."

I had already forgotten about the humpback and the girl from Philadelphia. I was, of course, getting a lot of mail, but this wasn't the first time that I was answering it myself.

I was half-asleep. "What day is it anyway?" I grumbled.

"Monday. I know where I can reach her. Where do you wish to meet her?"

I didn't *wish* to meet her at all, for I was thinking only of the beautiful redhead, who called me, so amusingly, as I was to become used to in the United States, "George," with those hard English *g*'s.

I suggested, unconvincingly, "How about the Brussels?"

I had lunch there almost every day when I was in New York, and you had eaten there with Tigy too. The owner was an Italian who had long run one of the best-known restaurants in Brussels. Now, in New York, he had an establishment with a distinguished clientele. I never failed to order as an appetizer a Belgian specialty I especially liked: *anguilles au vert* (eels in wild-nettle sauce).

The same day, another phone call informed me that my old friend Kisling was ill and bedridden. I promised to go and see him the next morning.

As in Paris, he had a large studio, facing Central Park, with one or two bedrooms, bathroom, and kitchenette.

It was difficult to picture Kiki bedridden. I had always known him bursting with life, health, appetite, especially for women, of whom a small court always surrounded him even when he was painting. I had never seen anyone more frankly joyful or more noisily so than he. The next morning at ten I was at his place, where three or four friends were keeping him company.

Paler than usual, he still had his sense of humor and did a very funny imitation of the American doctor who had prescribed absolute rest for him.

A young woman of uncertain nationality, whose position in my friend's life was equally uncertain, served us some wine. We gabbed about this and that. We raked up old memories of Montparnasse. Time went by very quickly. I suddenly saw on my watch that it was half past twelve. That was the time at which I was supposed to be meeting the humpback's protégée. I hate to be kept waiting; I feel that, when I am, my time is being stolen from me. And I equally hate stealing other people's time.

I embraced Kiki, shook hands with his friends, and once outside raised my arm to try to hail a taxi. There was none to be had. I finally decided to walk to the Brussels, which I was sure was not too far away. But it took me no less than half an hour to get there, and when I did, I was winded. The hatcheck girl, a tiny little thing I liked and with whom I often chatted, told me with a mischievous smile: "There is a pretty lady waiting for you at your table."

Pretty or not, at the moment I could not have cared less. If I was here at all, if I had left my friends so abruptly, it was purely and simply so as not to offend that humpback.

Waiting for me, there was indeed a rather pretty woman, petite, dressed in a blue suit with a white ruff or something of the sort.

"You're impatiently awaited," the owner told me.

And she, looking quite put out: "I've been waiting for you for half an hour. I'm not used to that sort of thing. If I had had anything in my pocketbook other than a check, I would have left long ago. But they served me one drink, and then another, and I didn't have any cash on me to pay the bill."

But she held her hand out to me just the same. She was wearing a little white hat and she explained that her skirt and jacket were so short because of wartime restrictions.

"I am not sure I can take the job with you. I have an appointment at three-thirty, at the Waldorf-Astoria, with the Canadian head of Air Liquide. He's looking for a secretary. . . ."

I really didn't care yet. I say "yet" because, once we had eaten, seeing that she still had a little time before her appointment, she suggested that we take a short walk over to Central Park. What did we talk about? I can't remember. We spent some time watching a duck and her ducklings begging for bread.

"Do you like animals?"

"Very much."

"Me too."

148

Although born in Québec, she had later lived in Ottawa, where English is spoken, and she had no accent in either language.

She wore a lot of make-up, extremely high heels, and her little hat just reached the level of my face. A brunette with slight hints of red, dark-brown eyes that constantly changed from one expression to another.

I left her in time for her appointment with Air Liquide, went back to my suite, and had a bottle of Saint-Emilion sent up. Not to drink by myself, but to share with her when she came back . . .

If she came back. She had told me that if she made a deal with the man at the Waldorf, I wouldn't see her again.

"Wait for me until four-thirty. If I'm not at your hotel, it'll mean I've gone to work for Air Liquide."

I watched the hands of the clock go around in my sitting room furnished with late eighteenth-century English furniture. Now I was getting impatient. I tried unsuccessfully to make myself believe what I was thinking: "She's wasting my time."

And I tried to get my mind back on the red-headed model, who had such a wonderful body. Fashion had not yet turned to flat women who live on a grapefruit diet.

Four-thirty-five. The desk called to say a young lady wished to see me. I said to send her up.

"So?" I was surprised at the anxiety I heard in my own voice.

"The green lights were in your favor."

"Green lights?"

"Yes. When I left the Waldorf, I walked along Park Avenue and decided that if I had green lights all the way, I'd come up to see you."

"Otherwise?"

"Otherwise, I would have taken the other job."

Traffic lights in New York are synchronized, so that if you go on one green light and keep a regular pace, you are likely to get green lights at every block.

"A miracle!" she said. "Fate decided it."

I opened the old Saint-Emilion; she had mentioned how much she liked French wines, and especially Bordeaux. We finished the bottle and then, by mutual agreement, went out. We walked slowly over to Rockefeller Center and then turned toward Times Square. On the way, she bought me a tie from a street vendor.

Small and thin, darkish, quite the opposite of my beautiful redhead, whose long silky legs I had caressed with so much pleasure. But had her eyes been as expressive as those of the woman who was with me now? I had a date with her for the next day, but I already knew I would break it.

A first bar. She ordered an Old Fashioned. Second bar, with a wall covered by a huge photograph of Churchill and Eisenhower.

We had dinner in some little restaurant, by the light of candles, while a piano played, and she softly sang along with the music: "Kiss me once, And kiss me twice . . ."

For the first time I was about to experience what people call "passion," a real fever, which some, including psychologists and doctors, consider to be a sickness.

The evening was only beginning and already I was feeling the first symptoms. I couldn't believe it. I defended myself against it as best I could, but she would look at me, with eyes that reflected all the nostalgia in the world.

I had never believed in love at first sight, and that very morning had been laughing my head off at Kisling's bedside as he told us of his wild affairs.

Everything was in the balance. My life, yours, your future brothers' and sister's were about to be decided for a long time to come, for years and years.

She is the one I now refer to as D., the initial of her first name, and you, my children, all four of you, have the right to know everything, the more so because D. herself wrote a book, filled with more inaccuracies than truths, which hurt Marie-Jo so deeply, and still hurts all three of you, my boys.

I am not complaining. I shall speak without hatred, without acrimony. I have held my peace until now, but there are some truths that you must know.

Till tomorrow, you four. And excuse me if I still have a bitter taste in my mouth.

21

That evening, we weren't yet really drunk, in spite of all that we had had to drink since our meeting at the Brussels, but we were a little high. D. had a deep voice, which came from way down in her throat, the kind you hear in nightclubs and cabarets, and that voice got to me.

At one point we had held hands, then taken each other's arms, and after dinner she said, "How about going dancing at Café Society?"

At that time, the same man owned two different Café Societys: Uptown, which was very elegant and attracted the affluent, the gold diggers, and Broadway types, and the original one, Downtown, in the heart of Greenwich Village, attended mainly by artists, bohemians, eccentrics, a more motley crowd, plus the rich upper classes who went there "slumming."

The latter was the one D. selected. In the taxi taking us there, we sat very close together, in fact, hugged rather intimately. She said to me: "It seems you're quite a well-known French novelist."

"Up to now, I've only written about sixty novels."

"I think I read one of them that my father had on his bookshelves. I forget the title. It took place somewhere at the seashore. I skimmed through it on a train ride. In general, I only read English books, because my mother still keeps close tabs on what I read, and since her English isn't that good . . ."

To tell the truth, she was familiar with few writers, English or French, and had never heard of the Russians. The only name of an American author she could bring to mind was Henry James.

"How come you're not translated into English?" she asked.

"I have been for over ten years."

"In the United States?"

"Yes, about thirty books."

"Even though I was raised in Ottawa, I'm French at heart. I hardly have any friends other than French."

"I'm Belgian."

"The hunchback didn't tell me that."

Was she disappointed? I've no idea. Maybe drink, instead of making my mind fuzzy, was making me see things more clearly.

"All my ancestors were French. My mother's family goes back to the conquest of Canada. . . ."

"What about your father's?"

"His grandfather was one of the most famous prime ministers of Canada, around 1850."

I wasn't laughing. I wasn't smiling. I was looking at her stupidly, passionately, in the half-light of the taxi.

Then suddenly the heat, noise, crowd of Café Society, where a black pianist was playing the blues. The customers were squeezed in one against the other, and it took some doing for us to find room on a rather hard banquette.

We danced, and her brown hair tickled my chin. She was thin and lithe, and the more we danced and the more whiskeys we drank, the closer she pressed against me.

The pianist took a break. He was a handsome black with a big smile and fine laughing eyes.

"Wait for me a minute." She went up to the dais, addressed the pianist, who motioned her to a stool alongside him. Was I jealous? I believe I was. She took a notebook or pad out of her purse, spoke to him animatedly, with the same ecstatic air as when we were dancing.

Sometimes the black man answered, briefly, then laughed. I was sitting there like a wallflower, as they say at proms. The pianist's fingers were tickling the keys, he was humming a bit of a tune. D.'s eyes shone brightly.

Finally, after he finished his glass of beer, he had to go back to work, and she returned to me, delighted to have all eyes upon her.

"He's a very famous pianist," she told me as she sat down.

"Did you know him?"

"By name only. I've heard some of his records."

"What were you writing on your pad?"

"Any old thing. I told him I was a newspaperwoman and wanted to interview him. My father was a newspaperman a long time ago, a music critic, and when I was a little girl, he used to take me to concerts with him."

As we danced, and drank, we became more and more animated. I put my hand on her knees. I heard some square characters sitting near us whispering to one another as they looked at us.

"What are they saying?" I asked her.

"That people should be ashamed to carry on the way we're doing."

"What else?"

"That it's obvious that we're French . . ."

I think we were both looking at those squares defiantly. We were very proud of ourselves.

"I know a nice little nightspot you'll like. I used to live in this neighborhood and share a room with a girl friend."

"In Philadelphia too?"

"Yes. I have a roommate there too."

We walked down the almost deserted street, and on another one we saw an unobtrusive little sign. Inside, the light was so dim that it was like seeing people through fog or through smoked glasses.

A large bar. Comfortable seats, sofas. Another room, as well padded as the first, and a few couples hugging. Soft, nostalgic music. We drank some more. It was almost two in the morning.

"Do you like walking?" I asked her, because walking is one of my favorite pastimes.

"I adore it!"

I had no desire to go to sleep, but I needed fresh air. On one end of the counter there were some wooden or porcelain souvenirs, among which I noted a mother duck with four little ducklings, all white except the last one, which was black. I bought them for her as a memento of the ducks in Central Park. I suggested, since she liked walking, that we walk back to the hotel.

"It's over fifty blocks," she said.

"Well, then, let's have a bite to eat first."

She pointed to an open-air stand that served hot dogs, bacon and eggs, ham and eggs, and the like. She got a hot dog, which she ate as we walked along, looking like a young society girl out slumming.

"I love to eat hot dogs and ice-cream cones on the street."

At first, she kept pace well, up on her high heels, and we stopped every so often to kiss.

"My mother comes from a very rich family. When she was fifteen, she had her own riding horse. My grandfather owned a whole street in Montreal. He spent his nights at his club, the most exclusive one in the city, where he gambled for high stakes, and lost everything. He was in metals."

"Blast furnaces?"

"No. He sold metals wholesale."

I almost said, "A junkman?" But would she have gotten angry at that?

"My father's father . . ."

"The prime minister's son?"

"No, his son-in-law. He was a gentleman farmer and rode all over the countryside on horseback. A dreamer. His tenants robbed him blind and he didn't care."

"Until the day he lost everything too?"

"How did you know? All he left my father was a country house about twenty miles outside Montreal, where, when I was a child, I used to spend all my vacations, with my two grandfathers and the whole family. One grandfather died. The other one always had candies in his pockets for me, like a surprise. . . ."

She broke off. We were well up Fifth Avenue, and she pointed to a light on a side street. "That must be a bar." She was thirsty.

Maybe I was thirsty too, but as we got to the door, a shirt-sleeved waiter told us, "We're closing up. . . ."

"Just five minutes. Time for one drink?"

"Sorry. Impossible."

Disappointed, she set out again and stopped—not talking, and she was a voluble talker—but to point out a little church to me.

"Maybe the door is open," she said.

"You want to go in?"

"Yes. One day, when I was leaving a friend's room . . ."

"A boy friend's?"

"A lover's. I dragged him into a church like this so we could both go to confession."

"Are you Catholic?"

"My parents used to be very devout. Especially my mother, and she still is. But my father went to Mass regularly every Sunday. After he got married, he even was a cantor in church. . . . They lived in Montreal. He had a very fine baritone voice and he was often asked to sing at charity affairs. Poor old Dad . . . He was a handsome man, very tall, very erect, and I was his favorite. He adored music and he . . ."

I knew; he took her to concerts with him. But I was still obsessed with desire, with a mad urge to merge into her.

"I was raised in a convent by the nuns. Most of the girls, who came from the finest families in Québec, were boarding pupils; the convent took only a few day girls. The sisters were very strict, terrible prudes. You know what they called a backside? A 'dignity.' I was a boarder for a while."

It made me think of the Ursuline Convent on the heights above Liège, where my aunt was a nun.

"I was one of their prize students, maybe best of all."

"Until what age?"

I don't remember the figure she gave. Sixteen, if I'm not mistaken. Maybe seventeen?

"My dream was to be an actress. I had acted in amateur plays."

Well, one play, anyway. She had the second lead, and I read the notes in the margins that the director had given her.

"Didn't you ever want to write for the stage?"

"I'm just a novelist."

"That may be. But some novelists have written plays, haven't they?"

"Some."

I interrupted her with kisses, and by now we were both pretty excited.

"At eighteen, I founded a girls' club in Ottawa. We used to give dances. I'm still the president. . . ."

And I, big fool that I am, was swallowing it whole, swallowing all that stuff that I hated. I loved blonde, plump women. She was skinny and dark.

I loved simple women, and here I had on my hands the most complicated one I'd ever met.

"I have three brothers and one sister, who's the oldest."

"How old is she?"

"Almost forty. She never got married, because she never met the right man."

"What about your brothers?"

"The oldest is a lawyer in Montreal, married, with two kids. He's a terrific lawyer, and his wife is the daughter of . . ." I can't remember whom. Someone brilliant, anyway.

"My second brother has an important job with Radio Canada. During the war, he followed the troops all over the front, and his broadcasts were famous."

"Married?"

"His wife is the daughter of the biggest shoe manufacturer in Canada. He made the shoes for all our soldiers. They have two kids too. My young sister-in-law is a doll. My third brother wasn't so lucky. He was sick for several years, starting when he was seventeen. I was the one who stayed with him most of the time. . . .

"When war broke out, I enlisted in the Red Cross and worked in a hospital in Ottawa. My father had become the head interpreter in Parliament. He's the one who translates the laws from one language to the other, and he holds the rank of minister. . . ."

I wasn't even smiling. All of it was more or less true, just barely touched up, as I was able to check out later on, for I got to know the whole family, the house in Ottawa, and the country one near Montreal left by the grandfather.

A typical bourgeois, ultrabourgeois, family, in which everybody ended up being a bureaucrat. The lawyer, whom I was fond of, left the bar to become a judge and has had a fine career. The sister was secretary to a senator. She spoke with a pronounced Québec accent and had a great sense of humor. The second brother, the Radio Canada reporter in Québec, became head of programing in Ottawa. And the third one, in spite of his handicap, followed in his father's footsteps and, before retiring, was something like second-in-command of the interpreting section of the Canadian Parliament.

"Do you mind if I take my shoes off?" she asked. "They're really hurting me and we still have ten blocks to walk. I was supposed to take the train tonight, but you've made me miss it, and there's no finding a hotel room at this time of night."

Maybe we didn't say it all that night, for there were a great many more

155

nights, but walking along in her stocking feet, she went right on talking.

"The English wanted me to run a department for them in their Philadelphia consulate. My father died suddenly, on the street, from a heart attack. He was taken into a drugstore. He was the man I loved most in the whole world."

My father too had been felled that way, alone in his office on Rue Sohet.

"I'm in charge of distributing British propaganda films, war films, to as many American movie houses as possible. Now that the war is over, they wanted to send me down to Texas. I said I wasn't interested, and I'm finishing at the consulate at the end of the year."

"And then coming to work for me?"

"Maybe. That's not certain yet."

At last, my hotel, where the night clerk pretended not to see that there was a woman with me. America was still puritanical. I had a room with twin beds, and D. said: "Promise me that nothing's going to happen. Can you lend me a pair of pajamas?"

She went into the bathroom, and came out in my pajamas, of course much too big and too long for her.

"You really promise? I don't have anything to worry about?"

I promised again and went and got undressed. Before getting into bed, however, I did pet her more intimately than we had done at Café Society Downtown.

I had an appointment at ten in the morning to see one of the leading American publishers, about bringing out an American edition of some of my books—in French. I wanted a pretty hefty advance, which was agreed to, but there were some other clauses of the contract that had to be ironed out.

What time was it? After 4:00 A.M. I left a call for eight-thirty.

For quite a while, we were both silent, in our respective beds. Finally, I sighed. "Are you asleep?"

"No."

"Aren't we being awfully silly?"

"Maybe. But you promised."

"You could let me out of my promise."

She didn't answer, but threw the cover off and didn't kick when I took her (my) pajamas off her. Naked, she was skinnier even than I had thought. She had a little girl's breasts and her belly was crossed by a wide almost-bright-red scar.

I threw myself on her, and was barely inside when she started moaning and trembling. Her moan turned into a cry that must have been audible in the next room. Finally, as her whole body was shaken by a spasm, her eyes rolled up, and I was almost frightened at seeing nothing but the whites.

I had known a great many women, but I had never seen one experience an orgasm of this kind. For a moment, I wondered whether it could be on the level, and I was not wrong; it was not until six months later that she had a real orgasm for the first time.

"At twenty-one, I was a virgin," she told me. "I had to ask a friend who worked at the French Embassy to sleep with me. I went up to his hotel room and demanded that he show me everything I wanted to know. I can still see him spreading the bath towel over the sheet. . . ."

Well, none of this turned me off, and we went at it again, and then again, with her eyes getting glassy each time, cries, trembling, but no real inward sign of fulfillment. Her friend from the French Embassy hadn't been much of a teacher. Nor had her other lovers. She had had others, twenty-seven, if I remember correctly; she enumerated them all to me, as if to see whether I could take it. No, not "as if." Plain and simple, to see whether I could take it.

"When I got to New York yesterday, it was really with the idea that I was going to commit suicide. The idea has been haunting me for a long time. You see . . ." She began to cry, to sob, and yet went right on talking. "I know that my whole life has been a failure, that I'm good for nothing, that men treat me as if I were a plaything. I tied all the letters from my lovers up in a pretty ribbon and bought a nice box to lock them in. Don't laugh . . ."

I wasn't laughing. I had a feeling that I was beginning to catch on.

"Do you know Karsh?" she asked.

"The photographer?"

"Yes. He's supposed to be one of the greatest in the world. Churchill came to his studio in Ottawa for that portrait of him that you see every place. He has photographed all the world celebrities. I went to see him. I wanted to leave behind my portrait done by him. He charged over two hundred dollars. He let me pay it off in installments. That, with the letters, would be all I left behind, because all my clothes are bought secondhand. That way, my nieces and nephews would know that their aunt wasn't some homely old maid, and that men appreciated her. . . ."

She was weeping, and smiling. And I was moved, because I knew that this distress was real, even though, from the first moment at the Brussels until now, she had been putting on an act for me, switching roles from one moment to the next, but with each one having some semblance of truth in it.

"What kind of operation did you have? When?"

"A month ago. Salpingitis. One of my ovaries was affected, and it had to be removed. I probably won't ever be good for childbearing anymore." And she laughed. "I don't know which one among all those officers of the French ship anchored at Philadelphia was responsible. . . ."

"How many were there?"

"I went with five of them. I also went with an English lord who has a magnificent estate near Philadelphia, and is very rich."

"Married?"

"Of course. You know what he gave me as a memento? Pass me my bag."

She took a silver dollar out of it. It had been hollowed out so that it contained a tiny blade.

"The funniest part was what he told me about it. 'It was a gift I gave to my wife, but I swiped it from her so I could give it to you.' " She was proud of it. And laughing.

"Is this what you intend to commit suicide with?"

"Idiot! I have my own ideas about that. And I've never told anyone. That'll remain my secret."

I was looking at her the way a Saint Bernard must look at the tourist it finds lost in the high snows.

"Maybe you won't commit suicide."

"You the one who's going to keep me from it?"

I don't remember anymore whether she was laughing or crying when she fell asleep. At eight-thirty, she was very calm, very much the Ottawa girls' club president. She ordered coffee, and bacon and eggs, and ate hungrily.

"My train leaves in an hour. Could you lend me a little money?"

I gave her two hundred dollars, and asked, "Am I going to see you soon again?"

"I don't know. Maybe next weekend. Maybe never."

"Promise me . . ."

"I won't promise anything. I have to think it over. Phone me one evening during the week. Sometimes I'm home; most of the time, I'm out at a party. . . ."

She left, in her little blue suit, wearing her tiny white hat. I shaved, showered, dressed, deliberately, trying to sort things out in my head. All I know is that I was determined that I was going to see her again at any cost, whatever might happen after that.

I had a hangover that made me feel slightly groggy when I went to the appointment with my publisher, an old gentleman with a white beard, surely puritanical and finicky. I signed the contract, one of the best I ever had, with a hand that was shaky.

At noon, Marc, I phoned you and tried to sound as happy as possible.

"When are you coming back, Dad?"

"I don't know."

And the truth was I didn't know. Not a thing about a thing. Except that the whole course of my life had changed.

22

I took the night train that very evening, because having heard your voice gave me an irresistible need to see you, with your fine bright eyes, to hold you in my arms, to see the snow all about again, on the paths, the trees on the hill, the frozen lake, to breathe the cold air in which our human breath created a light transparent cloud.

I felt at home at Sainte-Marguerite and was surprised to find that nothing there had changed, not your mother, who smiled as she shook my hand, or our little maid, with the tiny breasts under her black smock, who spoke French with such a local peasant accent that we often barely understood her.

You were bursting with health and happiness in that scintillating universe and you were always outside, in your great boots, your jacket, and the red-checked cap that came down over your ears.

"You look tired, Georges."

"I am."

I worked the first day at answering the mail that had piled up for me in my new office with the great log fire in the fireplace.

That evening, I couldn't keep from saying to Tigy, casually: "This time I think I'm really in love."

"With a girl from New York?"

I answered yes, rather desultorily. I did not want to spill the whole thing, as if out of superstition, but I couldn't get D. out of my mind. It was on Thursday evening, I think, that, no longer able to hold off, I phoned her, and the phone rang and rang before she answered.

"Who's this?"

"Me."

"Georges?"

"Yes."

Her contralto voice seemed to move me even more on the telephone.

"You're lucky. I'm just washing my hair. That's why I couldn't go out."

On the phone she spoke more formally, and this suddenly made her seem more distant.

"Am I disturbing you?"

"No."

"Are you free this weekend?"

"I believe so. . . . Yes. I can work it out. . . ."

Who might she otherwise be seeing on Saturday and Sunday? Her French naval officers? Her English lord? Others she hadn't mentioned to me?

"I won't keep you on the phone any longer. I imagine your hair is wet."

"Yes."

"Just sing me, 'Kiss me once . . .' "

Already that had become "our song," the one she had sung to me in the bar and then in our hotel room.

I listened, surprised to realize what it did to me.

"You love me a little?"

"I'm not sure yet."

"I'm at Sainte-Marguerite."

"Is your wife all right? And your son?"

I was disappointed. She was farther and farther away.

"Saturday, then, for sure?"

"I'll be on the train that gets into Pennsylvania Station at about eleven o'clock."

"I'll be there."

You and I played together a lot and walked hand in hand in the snow, which was so high we had to lift our knees way up. Seeing you, one might have thought you had been there for months, if not years. I also was wearing a heavy wool jacket, with red and black checks, and a matching hunting cap. I had bought a pair of huge sheepskin boots, smooth on the outside, but lined with raw wool, which I slipped on over my shoes.

"You going to stay here long?"

"I'm leaving Friday night and I'll probably be back Monday."

Mornings, Tigy and I would go to the post office together to pick up the mail.

"How do you find Marc?"

"Fine. I hope his teacher isn't too tough on him."

"She's a fine girl, in spite of what she looks like."

She slept alone in the cottage, and was very scared. Almost daily, she asked Tigy, "When will your husband's secretary be moving into the other bedroom?"

"I think he's still trying to find one. He is rather hard to please, where secretaries are concerned. He usually gets rather young ones, so he can train them, because he hates it if they have habits they acquired elsewhere."

Night train, in a comfortable single roomette. A bath at the hotel and a change of clothes. I put on the tie she gave me, which I don't like. I've always been very picky about ties and own dozens of them.

Pennsylvania Station seems bigger to me than Grand Central, where it's easy to find one's way around. There are iron stairways that bother me. Tracks and platforms everywhere, and I'm worried that I'll be in the wrong place, ask ten times whether this is right. D. told me she'd be in a little after eleven. The colorless clock overhead says eleven o'clock, and I watch the big hand jerking forward, second by second.

What if she didn't come? If she was teasing me? If . . . Had I not sensed in her certain ambiguous attitudes and phrases? At certain moments, I had felt I understood her. At others, I had had my doubts, imagined the worst. But all that I knew now was that I needed her, with a throbbing need, whatever she might be.

Eleven-twenty, twenty-two, twenty-three . . . Trains everywhere. Masses of humans in movement toward almost every platform. Finally, hers, a black noisy monster that didn't seem to want to stop. I searched feverishly for a little white hat among the crowd of travelers and finally discovered her, standing in the blue suit she had worn before in front of a stand where they sold something or other.

I hugged her as if I had not seen her for years, and she pushed me away both sweetly and firmly, as she laughed.

"In America, that's not considered proper. . . ."

We had to wait for a taxi. I wanted to put my arm around her shoulders, and kiss her voraciously.

"Not here . . ."

Had she changed since that wild night we had had? Finally, the hotel. She is carrying a large hatbox, which intrigues me. Suddenly bashful, I don't dare ask her what's in it. A bellboy tries to take it from her but she refuses to let go.

Up in our room, she bursts out laughing, as if she had just played a good joke. On me?

"You know why I wouldn't let him carry my hatbox?"

"No."

"Pick it up."

I take it by the string, and almost drop it, it's so heavy.

"Hotels here are very strict; this one more than others. I knew it by reputation. . . ."

"By reputation only?" I'm already jealous.

"Yes. It's supposed to have the swankiest guests, some down from Boston, others up from the South. They don't take Jews, and so, unless they know you, they won't accept reservations by mail. Lots of Jews have English-sounding names. So they want to see what they look like."

I'm listening, feeling that she might very well look Jewish, but I had expected something else. She seems much more distant than on Monday, and is talking, talking. . . .

"If I had had my overnight bag, they might not have let me come up."

"Overnight bag?"

"Yes. That's what they call the little bag women carry when they're sleeping over with a fellow."

"Do you have one?"

"Sure; everybody does."

She's defying me, making fun of my confusion. After all, I'm just a weekend date like the others, and if she didn't bring that "overnight bag" —the whole idea shocks me, saddens me—it's only because the hotel might not approve.

She is brushing her short curly hair, putting on her lipstick, daubing blue pencil on her eyelids.

"I'm sleepy," she says. "Got up very early. I almost missed the train."

What would I have done if she had?

"Did you go to bed so late?"

"I don't remember. Maybe two o'clock. I was at a party."

I've heard what those parties are like, everybody drinking a lot and eating canapés or sandwiches, and people pressed close together "copping a feel" wherever they can, when they don't pair off to go and make out in the bathroom.

"Do you go partying a lot?"

"Sometimes to two the same night."

"After dinner?"

"No. They take the place of dinner." Another throaty laugh. "That reminds me of a big estate, a few miles outside Philadelphia. Very rich people. Politicians, businessmen, beautiful women. After about an hour, I'm bored and I go out in the dark, over to the swimming pool that the host showed me when I first got there. All around, trees and bushes. I feel like swimming; I've always been a nut about swimming. I even won a silver cup in Ottawa. No bathing suit, but there's no one around, so I strip. I dive in, swim, having a wonderful time, when all of a sudden floodlights go on at the four corners of the pool. Everybody is standing around, watching me, so I go on swimming, because I don't want to get out of the water in the buff in front of all of them. They finally get the idea and go back inside. . . ."

She *has* to be doing this on purpose. I feel like slapping her, but hold back.

"Where are we having lunch?" she asks.

"Why not here? The bar and the dining room are very nice."

"What's wrong with you? Are you jealous?"

"Yes."

"Already? Well, I'm not and never will be. Do men really have to keep reassuring themselves by making what they call 'conquests'?"

What about women? What about her? I give her a hard, almost mean, kiss, squeezing her against me, so thin, so frail.

"Stop that! You're going to make me redo my whole make-up."

We go down to the virtually empty bar. This time she orders a dry Martini. The lighting is discreet, the bartender generous. After she finishes her drink, she says: "I forgot to tell him to put a little white onion in it."

I order two more, with onions, and the bartender informs me that in that case they're Gibsons.

"Double?" he asks.

I say yes, why not, and she doesn't complain. They're very strong, strong enough to make our cheeks burn, and I see the light in her eyes that was there the other night in Greenwich Village.

"What would you like to eat?"

"Any old thing. I'm hungry. At lunch, I usually just have spaghetti. Do you like Chinese food?"

I shake my head. I ate some in Cannes at the home of a Chinese philosopher, and his wife spent two days preparing the meal, which was a treat. Later, I had tried a highly regarded Chinese restaurant, and swore I'd never be caught in such a place again. Incidentally, the wife of the philosopher, who, after having lived in the United States, London, and Paris, was on his way back to his country, which was in revolution, loved to cook and she reminded me of Mme Maigret, for she had the same kind of curves and the same confident smile.

What did we eat, in the dimly lighted, elegant hotel dining room? Lobster, for one thing, washed down with an old Pouilly-Fumé from the vineyards of my onetime boss the marquis. Then a rather sophisticated dish, in a creamy sauce, which must have been very good, for D. ate it heartily, although it was a little too rich for me. Some old Burgundy. Coffee. A so-called Napoleon cognac, out of a dusty bottle and served in big snifters.

"How about going upstairs?"

She suddenly didn't seem to feel sleepy anymore. "I've upset you," she said.

I assured her she hadn't. But not too convincingly. Elevator, vestibule, living room, bedroom, where she started to undress like a striptease artist, watching me out of the corner of her eye.

I plunged into her as if I were trying to come out on the other side, and her eyes began to turn up into her head, showing all white, just as they had the first night. This time, she not only sighed and moaned: she was crying out, really crying out, and between cries she called me "her love": "*Mon amourrr* . . ."—rolling her r's the way people from Burgundy do, the way the great Colette does.

Did she love me even a little? She seemed to lose all control, and the second time around she yelled louder than ever.

We were sealed in an enclosed world. Nothing existed outside these four walls—within which the telephone had now been insistently ringing.

"Are you expecting any calls?"

"No."

"Me either. Nobody knows I'm here. Don't answer."

"But what if my son . . ." And my throat caught.

"Mister Simenon? This is the desk. It seems there's something wrong with the radiators in your suite. The repairman is on his way up to check them. Sorry to disturb you like this."

She sullenly slipped into my robe, which dragged around her feet, while I put on a pair of pajamas. There was a knock at the door. A man in blue overalls explained something that I didn't understand. He first checked the living-room radiator, tapping on it here and there, then the one in the bedroom, where he seemed embarrassed at seeing the bed in such a dreadful state.

"What's he saying?" I asked, my English still being rather elementary, and the man muttering between his teeth.

"He says everything's okay. It must be another suite."

She burst out laughing as soon as the door was shut. "Don't you get it?"

I didn't, so she went on: "A neighbor must have heard us yelling."

Heard her yelling, that is, because I hadn't yelled.

"They wondered whether maybe you weren't murdering me, so they used the excuse of the plumber, to come and see."

I laughed too. But my laugh must have sounded hollow.

"I love you, Georges."

There were times when I wondered whether I loved or hated her as I looked at her, naked again and so fragile, with that scar that seemed bloody across her belly.

"Back to bed?"

"Whatever you say."

"I'm not sleepy anymore. I'd like to get some fresh air."

When we went by the desk, the clerk gave us a funny look.

"See? What did I tell you?"

I learned much later, from her sister and brothers, that when she was still very little, they all called her the Diva. But that Saturday, I didn't go that far yet; I was just feeling my way.

We walked around the lake in Central Park again, holding each other by the arm, and perhaps we were both trying to recapture the newness of our first walk together.

"What did you do with the little ducks?"

"I set them out on my shelf, in order of size. I adore the last little one, that's almost all black. . . ."

More bars. Streets. Avenues. She no longer claimed to be a great walker, and needed frequent breaks. In bars. Where else? In one of them, the bartender greeted her familiarly: "Well, how are you, Miss D.?"

Dinner at a steakhouse, where the steaks are hung in a refrigerator with a glass door, and you pick out the one you want. As in all restaurants of this kind, they just about covered the whole plate. Wine.

We were not far from Times Square, and I remembered a bar I had been taken to in 1935. Most of the faces in the place were rather dangerous-looking, and the friend who was with me had said: "This isn't the kind of place to come to after midnight. The Irish especially love to pick a fight over any old thing. And if one of them has had a few and offers you a drink, never turn it down, because he'll be terribly insulted."

I told D. about it and said I'd like to see some joints of that kind again. She just said, "Come on."

She took me to some dark, miserable streets, very far, it seemed to me, from the big lighted avenues. She didn't hesitate at all, but walked right down a few stone steps, pushed open a door, and we entered a universe made up of smoke, alcohol fumes, sour beer, and voices.

"Aren't you afraid?" I asked her.

The men whistled at her, and it seemed to me that she was used to it. Some called out some slang words to her, and she went right on toward the bar without missing a beat.

"What are they saying?"

"Things too vulgar for me to translate."

Three, four, maybe five bars. Beer or whiskey.

"Be sure to finish your drink. Otherwise, they'll think we just came in here slumming."

Sometimes we went up a few steps, sometimes down. One place was full of Marines, who all undressed her with their eyes; another, full of soldiers just back from Europe or the Philippines, who were no less aggressive.

"Have you been to these places often?"

I had seen that kind of smoke-filled bar in Antwerp, Hamburg, Stavanger. Later in Bombay, Port Said, Cairo, and elsewhere. The atmosphere was nothing new to me. What surprised me was how much at home she felt in it.

"Occasionally . . ."

"Who with?"

She kind of waved. "Still jealous? Now can you understand why I was ready to end it all? I still am. I don't know. . . ." And her eyes as she looked at me seemed to be saying "Help!"

"After all, I'm nothing but a whore. That's what you think, isn't it?"

"No. I just think you're a scared young lady."

"Scared of whom?"

"Of herself."

All at once, she was no longer the little lady in blue at the Brussels, and without her excessive make-up she might easily have passed for a youngster who was afraid to look life in the face.

Didn't she need to be reassured, need especially a lot of tenderness she hadn't dared ask for, for fear of being taken for a schoolgirl, and which no man had spontaneously offered her?

I was feeling sorry for her, and held her around the waist on the way back.

"I'm not worth very much," she was saying. "I know you're trying to understand, but there's really nothing to understand. I'm just a . . ."

"Don't ever say that word again, please."

"Don't you believe it?" There were tears on her lashes.

"I'm certain that you're not."

"Hold me tight." And she whispered, half in tears, "Kiss me once, and kiss me twice . . ."

I couldn't keep from kissing her, tenderly, under a lamppost, right on brightly lighted Fifth Avenue.

"The other night, you kissed me under a lamppost too."

So, she remembered?

In one last nightspot, a fancy one, a Mexican girl was singing, "*Bésame, Bésame mucho* . . ." and I could see D.'s lips move with the words of the song.

"I'll be spending the holidays in Ottawa."

"At your parents'?"

"At a big ball given by the girls' club that I'm still president of. The whole French colony will be there."

"Including your first lover?"

"I don't know."

"But if he is, will you . . ."

Before I could finish this sentence, she cut me off with "Maybe."

My hand was faster than my thought and landed solidly on her cheek. She was not at all surprised. I'd swear that she was delighted with it, that in her eyes this constituted a victory.

Sunday was quiet and lazy until I took her back to the station.

We met again, at the hotel, every weekend, and in between I went to refresh myself at your side, my little Marc. Once, I brought you a fine, tiny green-colored turtle, which you petted before putting it in a glass dish filled with water.

Then there was the purchase of toys in a store with three or four floors entirely filled with electric trains, canoes, and even motorboats, electric cars, anything one can imagine. Of course I had brought you a cowboy outfit, because you had devoured the pictures in books full of heroic cowboy-and-Indian tales. I think you also had an Indian outfit. You piled up the weekly comic books, especially *Little Lulu* and *Dennis the Menace*.

You devoured everything, life, pictures, snow, and you skied down a little hill to the frozen lake, where the slope ended. You often fell down, and when you got up you would proudly announce: "I don't hurt."

At Sainte-Marguerite, I avoided liquor, for fear it would heighten the desire I was never without. Each Monday, when I got back to you, I felt guilty. Which did not keep me from phoning Philadelphia and opening with, "Sing . . ."

And she sang the two songs that had become "our" songs.

"Do you love me?"

"Maybe. When I know, I'll tell you."

"Same time Saturday?"

"Yes, if I'm free."

Unlike love—the word we used because we didn't seem to have any other for it—passion also feeds on violence. By now I was sure that she was purposely trying my patience, to get me to brutalize her. And I did brutalize her, at that period, when we needed drink to keep our inside fire burning. Often, when she didn't succeed in provoking me, she would slap me. I didn't flinch, and she would say: "You see how it throws you when someone stands up to you? There's nothing I don't know about men, you know, and you're no different from the rest."

It was untrue. The "rest," whose names I was learning by heart, had all stopped seeing her after three nights, a week, or a month, even if they had sent her flaming letters that she tied up in a ribbon to keep for her nephews and nieces in a pretty box.

I, on the other hand, was convinced that I loved her, ferociously, violently, that I really wanted to make her happy, to drive from her mind all the things she was ashamed of, was afraid of, her fits of pride too, and her tears.

The girl we had known so long before near Etretat had now become Tigy's and my friend. She used to come often to see us with her husband. They had no children and looked at you with a spot of envy in their eyes. Tigy and she went to New York several times together, and I have every reason to believe that they had a very good time there.

Last weekend before the holidays. Lighted trees everywhere in New York, the traditional gigantic Christmas tree at Rockefeller Center, Santa Clauses everywhere, on the sidewalks and in the stores. Loudspeakers blaring "Jingle bells." Others across the way answering with "Santa Claus is coming to town. . . ."

New York at fever pitch. Me too. D. too perhaps? This time, she had left Philadelphia for good, and her luggage, which she was taking back to Canada with her, gave our hotel living room a look I had never seen in it before, somehow temporary. Well, wasn't everything about us temporary?

We made wild love, as if to tear each other apart, and there was always that moment when her outcries and her turned-up white eyes made me uncomfortable. Had she learned this from "the rest," in order to impress them? I often felt like saying to her, "You don't have to put on an act. I know. . . ."

What would I have set off if I had? Sobs or slaps, or else would I then see the last of the "pretty lady," as the hatcheck girl at the Brussels had described her?

She was too unpredictable, and I couldn't do without her. I took her, luggage and all, to the train at Grand Central.

"When will you come to Sainte-Marguerite?"

"Probably in January. I haven't made my mind up yet. Maybe the fourth or fifth of January. Unless I have to stay longer with my mother and brothers."

"Maybe never?"

She didn't answer and, as the train was pulling out, our lips grazed furtively. That night, I phoned a call girl, out of frustration or just to relax. It gave me no pleasure.

"Did *she* run out on you?" she asked me.

Had D. actually taken the job with Air Liquide and just used me to while the time away?

At Sainte-Marguerite, Christmas was a happy time. Our friends had brought you a grocery counter almost five feet long, made of plywood, with a cash register and shelves with all sorts of jars and little packages. I opened several bottles of champagne and didn't take a single sip, despite all your mother's teasing.

"He's mooning over his great love in New York," Tigy said, with a protective smile, as if she felt sorry for me.

And people should indeed have felt sorry for me. Until the phone rang at midnight. I ran to answer. Everyone watched me in silence. A hoarse voice I was very familiar with: "Kiss me once, and kiss me twice . . ."

Fool that I was! I felt that I was going to break down and cry in front of everyone.

"*Bésame, bésame mucho . . .*"

I opened my mouth to say words that wouldn't come out. Then I heard a dry click at the other end of the line.

"Oh, does she sing too?" your mother asked.

Merry Christmas!

23

It was a morning like any other and the snow that covered everything glistened in the ice-cold air. My bedroom and bath were on a balcony roofed by a terrace.

I had gone to work early in my office and, shortly before noon, went back to change, since it was almost lunchtime. I felt nervous, with a yearning. Then I heard your steps on the stairs and you were knocking at my door. You seemed excited.

"She's downstairs," you joyfully proclaimed. "I showed her into the living room. Your new secretary."

You went down with me. It was true. I can't remember now whether it was January 3 or 4, but there she was, in boots and a big civet coat, a fur hat on her head, looking lost in the outfit.

"Surprised?" she asked me, beaming. "Your son," she went on more formally, "welcomed me like a gallant gentleman and held a chair out for me."

The cold of the Laurentians had brightened her complexion, lighted up the glints in her brown eyes. I was dying to take her in my arms, but I had to hold back for more than an hour.

I took her fur coat and hat. "Sit down, do sit down."

I wasn't quite ready to let Tigy know that this was the young woman I had told her about. To her and to Marc, D. was just the secretary a Montreal friend had found for me. The rest had to remain a secret for a while between D. and me, and we thought that was good fun.

I called Tigy and introduced the women to one another. I did not open a bottle of champagne but asked each of them what they would like to drink. The table was all set, and our young maid would shortly be serving lunch.

"What would you like?"

"A small glass of sherry, or vermouth, if you have any."

"How about you, Tigy?"

Your mother smiled as she carefully looked her over. She was usually very observant. This time, she was wrong. It was as if sweet peace had finally returned; everything that day was fun and happiness.

There were five of us at the table, Tigy sitting across from me, you, Marc, next to me, by your tutor, and D. on the other side.

Did we have wine? I can still hear your mother explaining: "It's strange. Since we have been in America, we don't drink wine with our meals the way we used to in France."

I was amazed to see D. so calm, so relaxed, so natural, and I could have sworn she wasn't just acting. She watched you, especially watched Tigy, just as closely as the latter was watching her. Yet, to an outsider, we would have looked exactly like a family peacefully at dinner.

I was relaxing, persuaded that the stormy times were over, and that the weeks were going to roll along almost calm and serene. Of course, there were still a few storms, if not hurricanes, ahead, a few rebirths of violence and confrontation, but on the whole our life fitted in with the white setting, the almost perpetually blue sky, the brisk, regenerating air.

We had to wait until I led her over to the cottage, where logs burned all day in the fireplace, for me to take her in my arms, and then, as our lips touched, they gave off an electric spark, which made her laugh.

"This always happens up here in the north. You may also see an aurora borealis."

"You're here!"

"Does your wife know? Don't you think she guessed?"

I was feeling her. I wanted to absorb her. She was wearing a simple black wool dress which, had she not been wearing make-up, would have made her look like a schoolgirl.

How far away the New York D. seemed! Wasn't I finally discovering the real D., whom I had so long searched for?

We made love, in her bedroom, without getting undressed, and she had enough presence of mind to ask, "Is the door locked?"

"No, but no one will come in. Marc knows this is where I do my work."

"How about Tigy?"

She already called her that, quite naturally. Our embrace was brief. She didn't cry out. Her eyes did not roll up into her head.

"You mentioned make-up," she said. "Don't you approve of mine?"

I admitted to her that I never liked make-up to hide the real personality of a woman, because that turned her into something that looked just like everybody else.

"Did you have a good time in Ottawa?"

"I spent most of my time thinking of you. Surprised?"

I briefly showed her around.

"This your office?"

"Yes, and yours."

Through a large bay window, one could see the lake, the path leading to the village, and the wooded hill, on which every tree looked like a Christmas tree.

"That's a handsome son you have."

"He's healthy, and happy here."

Tigy had gone back to painting. I went to your room only in the evening, to tell you your story and tuck you in, my little Marc.

From the first day, you appeared to adopt D., whom you promptly called by her first name and asked to come and play with you.

D. and I did not sleep in the same room. She spent the night in the cottage, with the hired girl, and I in my bedroom. I simply walked D. back every evening at ten or so, which was a far cry from our wild and sometimes violent New York nights. For you especially, even more than for your mother, I wanted everything to come gradually.

Our friend from Etretat would sometimes come to see us, by herself, for several days, staying at the nearby hotel, and she would pose in the nude for Tigy.

Tigy wanted to continue going to the post office with me, around ten in the morning, to pick up the mail. Was it to make the point that, although we were separated, she was still Madame Simenon? I felt bad about it, because I knew that D. could see us as we went by with our long strides and that her eyes would follow us.

When Tigy had finished the nude of our friend, she asked D. whether she would mind posing for her, and D. said she would not. She posed in the nude, as I learned on the first evening. And I found out from our friend that after the first session of posing, Tigy had told her, "For a while I thought she was *the one.* . . ."

"But now I know that's not possible," Tigy had gone on. "Georges would never sleep with a woman who has a scar that's still red on her belly."

Our friend winked as she told me that, since she was in on our secret. At sixteen, she had been in love with me, but once, when I had furtively caressed her breast, I had gotten a good slap and let it go at that. Considering her age, I would not have gone any farther anyway.

I reminded her of that incident.

"What an idiot you were! I was just dying to!"

"Then why the slap?"

"Don't you understand anything about women?"

All that winter, this friend, whose first name was something like Nina, shared D.'s and my confidences, while continuing to see a great deal of your mother.

The scar business went back more than twenty years, to our beginnings on Place des Vosges, when Tigy was doing a lot of painting and used to ask me to go to Montparnasse and find models for her. One day I found a blonde with porcelain-blue eyes, like a doll, and a limber body delicately molded in the manner of Botticelli.

I watched her pose. I saw that she had a fresh scar. Just by exchanged glances, the girl and I had come to an understanding, and when she was dressed again and I saw her to the door, she slipped a piece of paper into my hand, with her address on it, and three words, hastily scribbled: "In an hour."

Your mother asked me, with knitted brow: "What were the two of you up to behind the door?"

"I was paying her for posing."

"Is that all?"

Tigy was the jealous one, in those days, the days when I still had to hide what I was doing.

"Didn't you see her scar?" I answered. "I could never make love to a woman who has a scar on her belly. . . ."

So D. remained just the secretary referred to me by a Montreal publisher.

Not for long. You, D., and I went for long outings on our skis. Sometimes you didn't come along, and then the two of us were alone together. The thermometer must have been down around five degrees below zero, which was most invigorating. We didn't dare kiss out of doors, not only because of the electric sparks, which were not bothersome, but because D. assured me that our lips might very well freeze together.

One day when we were on foot, D. wearing her furs, me in a ski outfit with a mackinaw over it, she pointed to a pile of snow along the roadside.

"It would be fun to make love in the snow."

"Have you ever?"

"No."

By now, I believed everything she told me. For she had given up her make-up, and her face was that of an anemic gamine.

"Should we try?" she suggested.

Her civet coat protected her from the snow. There wasn't a soul for a mile around, and we made love, proud as Punch.

That was probably the day I contracted laryngitis. At any rate, my temperature quickly shot up and I had to stay in bed. Tigy wanted to take care of me. But I said no.

"You see, we're not a real couple anymore. We don't sleep together. Taking care of me would mean cleaning me up, sleeping in my room."

"Would you rather I called in a nurse?"

She was a little pale.

"No."

This time, she caught on.

"Is she the one?"

"Yes, and she'll be the one to take care of me. . . ."

From that night forward, D. never went back to her bedroom in the cottage, and you, my good little Marc, didn't seem the least bit taken aback. It was as if you too were in on our little plot, especially since D. was always ready to play with you.

My temperature kept rising, and there was a great snowstorm coming. The closest doctor lived in a village some six or eight miles the other side of the hill. He didn't come by the road, but skied through the woods. He carried his satchel in his rucksack and from it he got the medication I needed, probably some antibiotic.

D. brought my herb tea and meals up to me, slept alongside me, and during the five or six days I was sick we were virtually never apart. Tigy came to see me now and then, acting as though our intimacy were perfectly natural. You had been forbidden to come into the room for fear of contagion, so you would peek through the door, the way you used to do at Saint-Mesmin.

"Hello, Dad. How do you feel?"

You were the picture of health, and your pink face was getting tanned, making your features stand out even more.

When I was back on my feet, D. and I continued sharing the balcony bedroom.

I worked. In order to get back into the swim, I wrote *Maigret à New York (Inspector Maigret in New York's Underworld)*, as if I had lived there all my life, and when an American translation was published, no critic pointed out any factual mistake.

Since D. was also my secretary, I had explained to her my filing system, worked out long before and about which I had strong feelings. I had been translated in many countries with which, during the war, there had been no communication. So correspondence kept pouring in from everywhere. Each country had its own correspondence file. Contracts were in separate folders, which I was later to put into a bank vault, keeping a copy for reference. Even if, as in France, England, and the United States, I had several publishers in the same country, they were all to be filed together under the country's name and the subhead *Publishers.* Another file covered movies, still another newspaper and magazine reprints, and so on.

While I was typing my Maigret book, D. was filing everything that had accumulated. Once the novel was finished, I was surprised to find that my filing system had been turned upside down.

"That's the way I've been used to doing it," she said. "You'll see; it's much more practical this way. . . ."

Alphabetizing everything, she mixed up countries, movies, radio, and eventually television. I was disappointed and might have thrown a fit, but there she was before me, so innocent-looking, so proud of herself. . . .

I didn't suspect that this was just a first step that would lead to many others. Hadn't she displayed her good will and perhaps even love by giving up make-up? She was also letting her dark hair grow long, as I had shyly asked her to.

Too bad about my filing system! Too bad about me!

Our friend Nina asked Tigy whether she wouldn't like to go to New York with her for a few days, and I encouraged the idea. You were by now a big boy of almost seven and didn't need constant supervision. By leaving the door open, we could hear if you called.

And the very first evening, D. announced: "We'll sleep upstairs."

I frowned. Upstairs, there was only one free bed, Tigy's. I was no puritan, nor was I narrow-minded, but for the two of us to sleep in Tigy's bed, for us to make love in it every night while you slept right next door, seemed shocking to me.

Once more, I kept still and went along, and to my great surprise you found the whole thing very natural, just as you found it natural when I slept with Boule in the same room with you on Place des Vosges.

I wrote often to Boule, from the very moment we landed. She could not answer, because Tigy went to the post office with me, and I didn't want anything to happen to delay Boule's coming over.

One evening, during one of those trips to New York from which your mother and Nina came back loaded down with packages, D. and I were watching the first aurora borealis of the winter. At midnight, the sun seemed to be rising on the horizon, and the atmosphere was charged with even more electricity than usual.

"How about celebrating this in style?" D. suggested.

"What do you mean?"

"Do you have evening clothes here?"

"Yes."

"Champagne?"

"I think there's some left."

"Phone the restaurant to send over two or three bottles."

I objected that it was too late, but she countered, "They'll come. They're used to it."

My chest tightened. How would she know that?

"I'm going to give you a surprise. Let me make the phone call, and you go and dress. Don't worry about a thing."

She kissed me sweetly, and I went into our bedroom, a bit perplexed. We didn't have the excuse of having drunk anything. To dress in evening clothes, here, practically in the wilderness . . .

I had some trouble with the stiff shirt and collar. She had asked me to wait. So I waited, not knowing quite what to expect. Until the door opened and a very elegant young woman, in a 1900-style gown, came through and curtsied to me.

She was wearing the Bovary dress your mother had ordered from Jeanne Lanvin before the war.

"If you would be so kind as to escort me," she said, holding out her arm.

I found the living room lighted with candles, a bottle of champagne in its pail, glasses, and, putting her finger to the record player, she started some muted music. "Kiss me once, and kiss me twice . . ."

Her arms opened for me to dance with her, and we whisked around, her gown making a corolla around her body and her small breasts appearing above the deep décolletage of the bodice.

It reminded me of our society days, when we lived on Boulevard Richard Wallace. I remembered the occasion for which that gown had been ordered: the big annual gala at the Théâtre Marigny given by the Motor Yacht Club de France, to which I belonged. Maurice Chevalier was on the bill, and after his turn he said to me, in his dressing room, "They never stopped chattering while I was on. These society people think they have to put on a show of being blasé, and they would be ashamed to pay attention to the entertainment."

I took a quick drink.

"Is Marc alone upstairs?" I asked.

"I asked the tutor to stay with him for one night."

D. pointed out to me how the sky turned pink, blue, violet as the aurora borealis made the stars fade out.

"To our love," she purred, in her Colettesque tone.

I didn't get into the swing of it until we had downed the first bottle. Did we really drink three?

"Close your eyes, and promise me you won't peek."

She changed records, putting on "*Bésame mucho*," and when she told me to open my eyes, she was stark naked, improvising a wild dance to the muted music. I didn't laugh. She came and threw herself into my arms, still naked, her body wracked by tremors.

It must have been five in the morning when, dressed again, she preceded me upstairs.

I took pictures of D. a few days later, and when she saw the prints, she made a disappointed face.

"Is that what I look like?"

"Yes, the real you."

A little girl, who was hardly even pretty, slightly worried and somewhat pouty.

"I'm awful-looking. Promise me you'll tear them all up."

I didn't actually tear them up until fifteen or sixteen years later, because that was the way I would have liked her always to look.

A short but violent storm in Montreal, where we had gone to the opening night of a friend's play. No big crowd. Polite applause. After the show, groups of people lingering on the sidewalk, and a man about my age leaves one of them to come toward us, hand outstretched, delight on his face.

"D.! It's been such a long time!"

"I'd like you to meet my boss, Simenon."

He shakes my hand and gives me a knowing wink. Knowing what? I greet him coldly.

"How are you, my pretty pet? You look kind of pale."

He had probably never seen her without make-up. Only with messed-up make-up.

I lead D. away and squeeze her arm viciously.

"Another one to add to the list?"

"Just once. He's the French consul, and we're very good friends."

"Why only once?"

"I don't know."

"Are there many only-onces? Like that, on the fly, just between friends?"

"That's my business, and nobody else's."

"Excuse me. By now, it's mine too."

We walk through streets I don't know and reach an empty square.

"It would be better for you to draw up a new list for me. The list of those you didn't sleep with."

I feel the slap coming. I don't duck. But my hand in turn wallops her cheek, once, twice, one side, then the other. It is true that we had been drinking. Whiskey, as in New York.

Some young fellows on the other side of the square are slowly moving closer, and she drags me away.

"Those boys are likely to take a crack at you. Around here, they don't like to see women get beaten up."

"They just fuck them and leave them."

Teeth clamped, she remains silent, and we walk on in silence long enough to calm down. Somewhere, we go into a bar. I had been expecting it. She orders two double Scotches, takes a gulp of hers, and looks at our reflections in the mirror, among the bottles. Then her hand seeks mine.

"I'm sorry, Georges. I didn't know it was that bad. I could really have lied to you." She looks at me with almost candid eyes. "Does it make you very unhappy?"

"Very."

"Do you want me to go?"

"No."

"Smile at me."

I try. The storm is over, but we are each hurting.

Sainte-Marguerite. Our cabin and your welcome, Marc, your warm, joyful welcome. Tigy looks closely at D.'s cheek. Does it show?

"Was my husband the one who asked you not to wear make-up any-more and to let your hair grow?"

She stresses the "my husband," since legally she is of course still my wife. And D. comes right out with "I love him."

"That's your affair. I'm just warning you that you won't be the only one for long. . . ."

"I'm not the jealous type."

Is the little war beginning already? However, at the table, with the whole household together, the two of them chatter as if nothing had happened.

The young hired girl sleeps in a small room near the kitchen. One evening, when we come home from the movies, we see her door is open, and she is lying completely nude on her bed. She pretends not to see us; her hand is down between her legs, playing with herself.

"Did you see that?"

"Yes."

"Don't you want to go down to her?"

"No."

D. is excited by what she saw and makes love the way she did in New York, her eyes up in her head, but without crying out, because here that's not allowed, on account of you, Marc.

Three months later, the little maid will come and confess to us that she's pregnant. Not by me, that's for sure. By a lad back home who jilted her.

Tigy and Nina, more and more friendly, go to New York together more and more often. What they do there is none of my business. What is my business now is D. I saw the little box in her bedroom, and each time I turn my eyes away. It's snowing. We are alone in the cottage, where the only sound is the crackling of the logs.

"Would you like me to burn them?" she asks.

How does she know I'm thinking of those letters?

She goes and gets the little box, opens it with a tiny key, and reveals several packs of letters, bound with colored ribbons.

"I bet you'd like to read them, wouldn't you?" ·

"I don't know."

"Maybe you'd understand me better."

She takes the ribbon off one pack. "Here. I'll get you a drink."

"What about you?"

"I'll have one too, of course."

I started reading, despite myself, unable to resist.

> My darling little D——,
> It is eight o'clock in the morning, I have just gotten back aboard ship and my body is still bathed in your aroma. . . .

How stupid a man can be!

> . . . I love all of your body, and especially the smell of you when you come, when your eyes can't see anything but . . .

Poor idiot. There are only three letters from him. His last letter is not a farewell note.

"Why did it end?"

"How should I know? Just like that. We would see each other again when I went on board the ship, and it would be as if there had never been anything between us. He was handsome. He looked wonderful in a uniform."

I throw that pack into the flames, and, without watching it burn, she finishes her drink.

I pick up the next pack.

Last night with you was an unforgettable night. You are the most passionate woman I have ever known. I hope you'll be waiting when I get back on leave and . . .

Into the fire!

A third, a fourth pack, all tied in ribbons, like goodies at a christening. Five letters and a picture of a man with a pompadour who would look very ordinary if not for his officer's uniform. With a cigarette dangling from his lips, he is leaning against one of the ship's air vents.

You see, my darling, if I weren't married and didn't have two children . . .

Into the fire! I feel like laughing and crying at the same time.

Two letters in English, which I am still not up to understanding. Beginning with "Darling" and ending with "Love," before an illegible signature.

"This the lord?"

"Yes."

"He didn't use the letterhead with his coat of arms and he signed so you can't read his name. Cautious fellow, wasn't he?"

"You think I could have blackmailed him?"

Next!

I am heartbroken to hear what happened to you. You know that I was very careful. However, as long as you are having it taken care of, I'm enclosing the money for the . . .

"Were you pregnant?"

"No."

"Was he the reason you had to have the operation?"

"No, not that either. Surely not him. He just thought that . . ."

"You led him down a garden path."

"I was totally broke. I was in debt. Now can you understand why I wanted to commit suicide, why I was so ashamed of myself?"

She is silently weeping.

"I told you about the picture Karsh took of me. I'll go and get it for you."

She disappears into her room, and I hear her opening a suitcase.

"I wanted to be remembered the way you see me there."

A white satin evening gown. She is sitting on a tapestry-covered chair. She has obviously just come from the hairdresser's. One arm is nonchalantly placed on the arm of the chair, and her hand seems to be holding her cheek up while she gazes at something with dreamy eyes. In the background, a grand piano. Typical picture of the "young girl of good family," as I used to describe them in my early dime novels.

"Is that what you think you look like?"

"That's what I used to look like. Before. Don't forget that I didn't start in till I was twenty . . ."

"What was there before?"

"I was a mystic. I had a secret notebook in which I described my moods and my flights of fancy."

"About God?"

"Don't laugh. I was deeply religious. I had a father confessor I saw every week."

"In a confessional?"

"In his little office. He was a Dominican."

"In a white robe? Young and handsome?"

"Young enough. Nothing ever happened between us."

"You did let him read your secret notebook, though?"

"Of course. He was the only one . . ."

"Do you really want to keep that picture?"

"I didn't order it for myself. It's for . . ."

"I know. Your nephews and nieces."

"Georges, you're being nasty."

I throw the picture into the fire and watch the face on it grow gradually darker. I also throw in the other letters without reading them. There are none from her family, which I would not have burned.

"If my father had only known . . . The fact is, he was the only one I ever loved, and only after his death did I accept that appointment in Philadelphia."

"Which didn't keep you, back in Montreal, from . . ."

She kneels down in front of me, pathetic. I raise her up and take her in my arms. She has a good long cry, and when it's over, one of her hands strokes my cheek.

"Did all this hurt you very much?" she asks.

"Yes."

"How could you expect that, at twenty-five, I should be . . ."

"I admit it was wrong of me. But I can't help it. Your past keeps haunting me."

"What can I do to wipe it out?"

"Destroy everything that reminds me of it."

"Haven't I done enough?" She points to the fireplace, in which the burnt paper makes ugly black spots on the logs and seems to be snuffing them out.

"There is still this." I touch her black woolen dress, then point to the coat hanging on the wall. "Everything you wore when you met those men."

She smiles a sad little smile. "You want me to go naked?" A little throaty laugh of hers.

"We'll go to New York tomorrow and get you a whole new wardrobe."

"And burn all of my old clothes too?"

"All of them. Even your suitcase. And your overnight bag."

I heave a sigh of relief. She hasn't kicked!

"It'll take a long time to burn."

"The little maid is just your size. We'll give it all to her, the suitcase included, provided she doesn't wear any of it around here."

We went the next day, to one of New York's most elegant stores.

On the women's clothing floor, I said to her, "Take your pick."

"You pick for me."

From the racks, I selected some dresses, two coats, a suit. We went around to the different departments, and at lingerie I said to her: "Here, you'll have to decide."

We bought shoes and two suitcases. At last there was nothing left to remind me continually of the other men. Mores were not what they are today, nor were morals, and I guess neither were the dreams of a man in the toils of passion.

"You're going to break yourself," she teased.

We drove back to Sainte-Marguerite with the car loaded down with packages. I was relieved.

Then my eyes caught sight of the gold chain she always wore. I touched it.

"It was present too at all your . . ."

I was going to say "lays," cruelly. Passion can be cruel, and D. knew how to be cruel also at times.

"It was my father's watch chain. My eldest brother inherited the watch."

"Why shouldn't he have the chain to go with it?"

"Is that what you want?"

I didn't say anything, because I was ashamed of myself. Hadn't I too, at eighteen, parted with the watch of a father I adored, for one night with a black woman I ardently wished to possess?

That's all. The next day, she spent the morning in the cottage and when she came to lunch, she had a new dress on. In the evening, the little maid was much happier than she had recently been, unable to grasp the idea that she had come into such a lot of gifts.

I never saw the chain again. I bought her another.

I was not proud of myself. I confess, however, that I was relieved of a great weight. She was too, it seemed to me.

24

An almost quiet winter. Much skiing with you, big Marc, and it was a delight to see you flailing around in the snow. You liked D. a lot, because she was always ready to play different games the two of you made up, which was more than could be said for your tutor, who preferred spending her spare time knitting or singing, accompanying herself on the guitar, near the big fireplace.

Tigy, as far as I know, never did play, and I have sometimes wondered whether she ever was actually a child. She had a passion for reading, painting, discussing art and philosophy, which was just what had brought us together.

You respected the cottage, reserved for work, but, as soon as I came out of it, you'd call: "D.! Come and play with me?"

She was ready, smiling a happy smile I had not known her to have in New York. If she had been pale and almost pitiful in the first days she went without make-up, now her skin was coming to life again, taking on color in the lively air and sun, and her eyes shone with brilliance that owed nothing to any artifice.

Every evening, before going to sleep, you demanded "your" story, the story of the young Chinese Li, who, according to my inspiration of the moment, got involved in the wildest adventures, never brutal, but always dramatic, which I tried hard to entertain you with, sometimes even planning them before dinner.

Li was happy, carefree, like you, and, as with you, his best friends were always animals; like you too he traveled a lot, doing his best to make himself understood in the greatest variety of countries.

D. and I drank a little, at the one bar there was, at the end of the road.

One morning, I got an invitation to a white-tie dinner from the French ambassador at Ottawa. The same mail also brought an invitation for D. I was soon to understand that our relationship was known, in both Montreal and Ottawa, and tacitly approved of.

So we went to Ottawa by train, a day ahead, because D. had to buy an evening gown.

At the Château-Laurier, the concierge greeted her by name. The floor waiter also addressed her like a frequent visitor: "How are you, Mademoiselle D.?"

I was well aware of everything that had gone on here when D. decided to start living a free life, and she showed me the room in which she had had her first sexual experiences. This time, I did not flinch, and if for a moment it did something to me, I did my best not to show it. The sky, as far as we were concerned, was now a constant blue.

The French Embassy in Canada at that time was one of the most modern and largest, all white, built on simple lines, and dinner was served in a pleasant room that seated some forty guests. We arrived together, to no surprise on the part of the ambassador or his wife, who were greeting the guests. He was an Hauteclocque, a brother of the Comte de Hauteclocque, who since World War II has been better known as General Leclerc.

He must have been my age or slightly older, and our meeting was cordial, with none of the stand-offish politeness of most career diplomats.

His wife, a daughter and granddaughter of French ambassadors, had been born in Peking, and from embassy to embassy had lived in all the most important capitals of the world.

I was seated almost directly across from her husband, and at the end of dinner, he called happily to me: "Here, you may smoke your pipe, Simenon." And, as if to encourage me, he took a well-caked clay pipe out of his pocket, filled and lighted it. So I did likewise.

"I know that it's not customary to smoke a pipe in the foreign service, but I can't do without one after a meal. I bet you feel the same as I about it."

"That's true."

"Here, people have got used to it, and no longer take offense."

He had a light-colored mustache and a face as frank as his frank manner of speaking. Later, after we had left the table, he told me quite naturally: "I knew D.'s father very well. I used to see her when she was just a very young girl. Her father was a great music lover, and he and I shared the same tastes."

It seemed to me as if we were in cahoots, and that, in this huge country, news spread as fast as it does in a small French provincial city.

So, even in Ottawa, people knew of our relationship, and did not disapprove of it, at most perhaps smiling a little.

I was to have another proof of that the same evening. We were ushered into a huge room where we joined a crowd of hundreds of other guests. Only at rare intervals was I able to find D. in all that mob, but I was with her when spotlights took the place of the chandeliers and, from the top of a monumental staircase, down came a score of dancers in cancan costumes, gracefully moving to the sounds of an invisible orchestra, for all the world like Toulouse-Lautrec's Moulin-Rouge chorus girls.

It was the ambassador's wife in person who was the lead dancer, and D. informed me that the other dancers, raising their legs in the devilish wild rhythm, pirouetting, falling on their hands, and finishing with a split, were none other than the ladies of the diplomatic corps. They had rehearsed for months, and everyone applauded them wildly, including the prissiest old ladies and gentlemen.

Then the guests danced, less acrobatically and in more sober attire. I danced several times with D., and no one could have guessed that she was wearing no make-up.

A large white homespun robe among the black suits. I knew that this must be D.'s Dominican, her father confessor, the sole reader of her girlish notebooks. He was young and handsome in his monastic habit. I went over to him, and he smiled at my approach.

"Simenon," I said.

"I know."

He had a hearty handshake. He added, letting me know that he too was aware of the situation: "I saw D. a little while ago. I found her changed."

"For the worse?"

"For the better."

We looked like two plotters.

"She's a rather complicated young lady, isn't she?"

Now it was my turn to smile, a smile as ambiguous as his remark had been. "Very."

"I got the impression that she's happy."

"I'd like to think so."

While we did not say much, every word was pregnant with meaning, and he eyed me with an indulgent kind of curiosity.

"It hasn't been too arduous a task, has it?"

"Not any longer. At least, I hope not."

"I'm happy for her," he said, and hugged me as if to give us his blessing. I understood from this initial contact that he knew D. much better than I did.

I was comforted by this, not just because of his ecclesiastical garb. Dominicans have the reputation of being the most tolerant of all religious orders. I had known some in the past and had always gotten along well with them, despite my agnosticism, which didn't bother them. They never tried to bring me back to the Catholic faith of my childhood.

Never in my life had I had the idea of playing Pygmalion to any woman, because I have much too much respect for human personality.

Very early, however, I had seen so many lives go wrong, end in tragedy, that I used to wonder why there weren't people to treat those who were temporarily defenseless, counterparts of doctors who treat people's illnesses.

I had not then read Freud, whom I discovered only when I was twenty-five. Later I read all of his works and those of his disciples, but I was leery of psychoanalysis, despite the great place it earned for itself.

I was thinking of something else, something rather obscure and complex, men who would play the part in society of "menders of destinies." To stop a young girl on a bridge who is planning to jump into the river on Christmas or New Year's Eve. To bring back to good humor a man who is pursued by depressing ideas.

It was all very vague. I dared not speak of it, for fear of being laughed at. Later, the great amount of time I spent with the Paris homicide squad and the things its inspectors told me showed me that some of them, a small minority, consciously or not, thanks to their experience of the miseries of humankind, did play a role much like the one I had thought of.

In one of my Maigret books, I think, I finally used the term "mender of destinies," giving my inspector character the same confused aim I had had.

Is that what, from my very first meeting with D., brought forth within me that passion I had never before encountered, which now was getting the better of me?

I believed I sensed that she was weak, defenseless, without any solid support, torn between contradictory aspirations, which might explain the successive roles she played, sometimes switching them from one hour to the next. I didn't want to change her. I was convinced that I was just helping her to discover the real D., who felt obliged to hide behind different masks.

Was I right? Was I wrong? At any rate, I was sincere, and the term "mender of destinies" did not fit. More modestly, I was trying to get her to find her true identity, the one that too many one-night men, too many more or less "wild" parties, too many whiskeys had hidden away.

This evening, hadn't she been radiant? I spent the whole night in euphoria, and didn't ask her whom she had danced with. No doubt, in that crowd, she must have met some of the men who . . .

I refused to think of it. We slept late, and the next day returned by train to our cabin and cottage buried in snow. You greeted us. You looked fine. You were sturdy. Your smile was that of a little man in harmony with nature, with all that surrounded you. You and the universe had mysterious links that you alone knew about, which gave you this smile, which was a bit like the famous smile of the Mona Lisa.

Often, when you were a child, I used to ask you what you were thinking about at that moment, and you would answer, as if suddenly brought back from a dream: "I was watching the logs. . . ." Or the sky. Or a tree more heavily laden with snow than the rest. You absorbed, and today I still wonder what memories, what images, what sensations, what "treasures"—as you used to say back at the château in Fontenay when you buried everything you found, whether an ant or a beetle—you were storing up within yourself.

At forty-one, your smile hasn't changed.

During a quick trip to Montreal, we made a date to meet D.'s oldest brother in the bar of our hotel, and I saw coming toward me a big strapping athlete of a fellow, with a ruddy face, forthright and rugged, as one imagines Canadians to be.

"Well, now, little sister . . ."

He kissed her, held her at arm's length the better to observe her, then turned toward me with curiosity.

"Are you the one who did this? Are you the one who scrubbed her face clean with a wire brush? Now she looks like a real country girl."

His handshake was firm and sincere. "What are you drinking?"

"Beer," I said.

"I'll have a double Scotch."

I felt we were already friends.

"Still at Sainte-Marguerite? My little sister hates to write letters, and we hear about her only by chance."

We were to meet again often, even in Arizona, where, with no more surprise than today, he was to find her pregnant.

That may have been the day he exclaimed to me: "She's a strange girl, not easy to understand. She dreamed of going on the stage and, even when she was little, was always playacting. We used to call her the Diva. Didn't we, D.?"

She smiled as she turned toward me. Had she not told me that of her own accord?

I saw him later with his wife, a pretty woman, more conventional than he, in their house on the hill that at that time was Montreal's "better" neighborhood. I met their three children. I met her sister, a big lanky thing who was very outspoken, with a strong French-Canadian accent and a great sense of humor.

During another stay in Montreal, D. asked me to return a hat she had borrowed long before to her other sister-in-law. D. was in bed at the hotel, running a temperature. It was in the evening. I happened into a modern apartment where a party was going on. Everyone was cheerful and, though they didn't know me, greeted me nicely. Her second brother wasn't as tall as the other, and his features were sharper, but he was just as cordial.

"How is my little sister doing?"

To all of them she was "little sister," the baby of the family, as my mother had been, which had been such a trial to her. Had it been a trial to D. as well? Had she felt crushed under the weight of all those older siblings?

I spent only a short time at the party, since I was anxious to get back to the hotel. D.'s temperature had gone up, and she was having trouble breathing. But she wouldn't let me call a doctor.

What worried me the most was that D. was no longer perspiring. Her skin was completely dry.

I gave her two sulfanilamide tablets I had managed to get, then I lay down, naked, next to her; she was naked as well, for that was the way we were used to sleeping.

"You have to perspire."

"It's not my fault, Jo."

She had started calling me Jo, pronounced with a soft *j*, through my own fault. The man she had had her longest and most passionate affair with, almost two whole months, one of those Philadelphia sailors, was named Georges too, and I had read his letters. Since then, if she called me by my own name during one of her passionate embraces, I wondered whether she didn't mean that other Georges, and it hurt me.

When I told this to her, she said, "Well, what do you want me to call you?"

"Anything except Georges."

She called me Jo, which I detest, because it isn't even an abbreviation of Georges, but, rather, of Joseph. I didn't object, though, and I was to be called that, fortunately only by her, for many long years.

I massaged her. I tried to pump a little life into her, and suddenly the idea came to me to take her in my arms, hold her tighter than I ever had. Until I finally felt a little sweat beginning to crop out on her skin. Until, more properly, she pushed me roughly away and ran into the bathroom.

I could hear her hiccuping, then vomiting abundantly. This went on for quite a while, but I didn't get impatient. She had often vomited, in New York, on nights when we had overdone the bar-hopping, but never like this.

When, much later, she came back into the bedroom, tears were running down her face, but she was smiling.

"Funny, isn't it?"

"What's funny?"

"Making people well by making love to them."

She fell asleep almost immediately, and the next morning her temperature was subnormal. We took the train to New York, where I signed a contract, not with my usual publisher, whose terms I had turned down, but with another, just as well known.

Winter finally died away, the snow melted, and, by agreement with Tigy, we all piled into my old car to go to the seashore.

Another stage, Marc. A rather important stage. Our luggage was following by train. By way of roads that were often washed out, through a landscape in which white splotches still bespoke the recent winter, we crossed much of the Province of New Brunswick, and reached the Bay of Fundy and a rather select resort called Saint Andrews.

As so often, friends had found us a likely place to stay. A lady of Montreal's "high society" had a house there, almost on the beach, and since she was spending this summer's vacation in Europe, she was happy to rent it to us for three or four months.

I was forgetting to say that, at Sainte-Marguerite, which we now left behind us forever, I had written, in between two short trips and around our afternoons of skiing, a novel that was not a Maigret, in which I treated passion for the first time: *Trois Chambres à Manhattan (Three Beds in Manhattan)*.

D. claims that I wrote *Inspector Maigret in New York's Underworld* with a bottle of whiskey next to my typewriter, and that all of my novels until this one smelled of alcohol. Yet, she had read only one of them, by chance, on a train. I sometimes wrote "on white wine," though not to excess, and later "on Bordeaux"; I never wrote with the help of whiskey, but much more often with coffee or tea, which I kept at the right temperature on a hot plate.

What is true is that, since we did not have a hot plate at the time and I have always done my writing alone in my office, she did undertake to keep some tea hot for me while I was typing, and as soon as my cup was empty I would open the door a crack and take the fresh cup she had ready for me.

So, to Saint Andrews.

Our house is roomy and comfortable, except for the dark, almost lugubrious, living room. Yet that is where, in ancient and venerable armchairs, D. and I were to spend our evenings. The big upstairs bedrooms that get all the sun are reserved, one for your mother, Marc, the other for you. At the end of the hallway, two small bedrooms and a bathroom, for the help. Your tutor sleeps in one of those. D. and I share the other, which has only a single bed, but, with much laughter, we make do.

Someone found us an excellent cook, who comes in early each morning and in the evening goes back home to a neighboring village. She is a pastry specialist, which delights you from the very first day, because she bakes cakes that neither you nor we have ever eaten before and is very proud of them.

The port is small and picturesque, with lobster pots stacked all around and white boats trimmed in bright colors. What most impresses you is a kind of pool covered by a shed, in reality a lobster bed in which the shellfish can be seen moving about clumsily.

One of your favorite haunts will be a coastal research center where two seals, brimming with health, live in an enclosed space, diving, surfacing, working their way onto the ground, and coming close to you as they get to know you.

Saint Andrews is where you will learn to swim, but not from me; from a swimming instructor. When I was your age, you know, there was no such thing as the crawl; people first mastered the breaststroke, then the sidestroke, backstroke, trudgen stroke, which is something like the crawl, only slower, because it is a long-distance stroke. So the swimming instructor holds you out at the end of a kind of fishing rod, and you learn very quickly, even though you always come out of the eternally cold water looking pretty blue.

You fish, we fish together, in an inlet where we mostly catch plaice, for there are no real soles on this side of the Atlantic, and also devilfish, with their huge mouths and spine-covered bodies. They aren't edible, and we throw them back into the water, after I get them off your hook for you.

I give D. driving lessons, in our creaky old car, and in no time she gets her license. Then your mother takes lessons from D., because she doesn't feel I have the patience to teach her. A garageman in Montreal promised me he would find me a secondhand car, if possible one in good shape, because there are still no new cars to be had.

I write a novel or two, in our little bedroom, while D. tans herself in the spring sun in the garden. She is finally putting on some weight, laughingly claiming that I am stuffing her so she'll look like Mme Maigret. The truth of the matter is that she's quite a big eater.

No more whiskey. Only beer. We go together to Calais, Maine, across the International Bridge from Saint Stephen, New Brunswick. The town has only one street, but on it one can find anything, even Dunhill tobacco, which I have been used to for over fifteen years.

A few miles from Calais we discover a small airfield where young people, some even children, are taking flying lessons.

You watch those small two-seaters flying around above. I can guess what's on your mind. No one except the pilot can go with you, because there is no room for anyone else and there is a weight limit.

"Won't you be frightened?"

"No."

You fly off, and your mother, D., and I follow you with our eyes, slightly concerned. When, after half an hour, you are brought back to earth, you're flushed with excitement and find it hard to express yourself in words.

"It's won . . . just wonderful!"

Later, you'll confess to me that you were rather scared.

Pierre Lazareff cables me to ask for several articles about Canada. He also wants to know what I may have heard about an atomic explosion that is scheduled soon to take place at Bikini, an atoll in the Pacific.

Pierre is now the editor of *France-Soir*, the biggest evening paper in Paris. He is better informed than I, for we don't see any newspapers.

I write two pieces on what little I know about Canada. Then a phone call informs me that the garageman in Montreal has a car for me. I make a date with him and reserve two seats on a plane leaving from Saint John, an important city up the bay.

While at Saint John, D. and I hear that the Bikini bomb is to be set off the day we fly, while we are up in the air. There is some talk of possible catastrophes, tidal waves that might reach the shores of America, terrible turbulence in the atmosphere, and I don't know what else. At any rate, we are practically the only ones adventurous enough to take that plane.

The time of the atomic test comes and goes, and our flight continues peacefully. It is true, of course, that it would take some time for any fallout to reach Canada.

The garage, where we are full of admiration for an Oldsmobile much younger and in much better shape than my car. We decide to give it a test by touring the Gaspé Peninsula and Nova Scotia in short stages. It is summer. Everything looks fine, especially in the Gaspé, which, with its white fishermen's villages, looks like Brittany. Coves. Small hotels. Rocky roads often on the very edges of cliffs.

You are not along, and I am in a hurry to get back home and give your mother her new car, which we have had simonized and checked over in Saint John.

My English has improved greatly. You are beginning to speak it and learning to write it.

Autumn looms, and with our two cars we decide we will go down to Florida. Your mother, who doesn't feel too confident at the wheel, will go in one car with your guitar-playing tutor. You will be in the other with D. and me.

Another departure, my poor little Marc, for a very long trip this time, which will take us all the way down the coast from Saint Andrews to Miami. I have my typewriter with me, my files, suitcases, trunks. The car is so overloaded that the shock absorbers groan.

Almost like an adventure, isn't it? Going from the snow to the orange trees and coconut palms. But you take it in your stride. And go on dreaming.

25

Before getting around to the recollections of our long, slow trip, which, with many detours, was to take us as far as the Gulf of Mexico, I want to recall a few more images that come back to me from our life in Canada.

For instance, my meeting with D.'s mother, in their family home, during my second or third visit to Ottawa.

A spacious wooden house, such as are still abundantly found up north, as well as in the Deep South. Standing halfway up a hill, among similar houses redolent of a proud and self-assured bourgeoisie, it had a peaceful, familial feeling.

I was received in a large living room with old family furniture, dating back to the grandparents' days, if not the great-grandparents'. Through a large opening I could see into an equally quiet and reassuring dining room.

What should I say of the woman who welcomed me in this somewhat underlighted room?

"Maman, I want to introduce my new boss to you."

"Delighted, monsieur. Please sit down."

I eyed her with some surprise. She was rather tall, as broad as her eldest son, whose size had impressed me in Montreal, heavier, more massive than he. Yet she did not strike me as being big, but, on the contrary, as if her solid mass, supported by columnlike legs, had been cut out of granite.

Her face too, sculpted with broad hammer strokes, rather than molded. Her hair was silver gray, and everything about her seemed gray, immutable. She was a living statue, the true "matron," not in the sense given to that word today, but as it was used in ancient Rome, with its cult of the mother, guardian of the hearth and the traditions of the race.

At first glance, her aspect was that of a severe, proud lady of the upper bourgeoisie. Nevertheless, when I looked into her eyes, so light a blue, and saw her thin mouth imperceptibly fluttering, I thought I detected signs of a kind of vulnerability, perhaps a bashfulness she was trying to hide.

Did she too know, as her sons did, and as most of the people I had recently met did? She did not let on. We had a formal, difficult interview. The little maid, whom D. had mentioned to me and who was the only help in the house, was very tiny indeed, frail-looking, and almost distorted.

Yet these two so very different women had been able to cope with everything that had to be done in the house at a time when five children had been born there one after the other, and had grown up there, first a girl, then three boys, and finally D., the last of the lot.

I pictured the whole family, when the father was alive, sitting around the table I could see in the dining room, having to be fed and cared for.

I had no idea how many rooms they had upstairs. D. had told me that she had shared a bedroom with her sister, which had grieved her, for a very unexpected reason. Her sister loved the color green. She insisted on having the whole room painted green, even the furniture, and all this green had finally so gotten on D.'s nerves that she could no longer stand anything green.

Isn't green the dominant color in nature all around us?

I also knew that there was only one bathroom, as in most of those old houses, and the family had to share it, each one having a turn, a specified time, each also obliged to make sure it was left clean after use.

I was full of wonder at the heavy silverware, which brought a smile to those thin lips.

"All that has been in the family for over a century."

Today, there were only the three women left in the house, the mother, the elder sister, unmarried and somewhat bohemian, and that ageless, almost humpbacked little maid, who seemed to go on forever.

What did we talk about? Even as I was leaving, I would not have been able to say. I brought out a sentence only tentatively, awe-struck and perhaps bristling a little at this monolithic woman, who in turn let words slip from her barely parted lips only out of convention.

I left behind this past with the feeling that it had led to the little lost young girl I had one day met at the Brussels and who had then become my mate after so many rough reversals for her as well as for me.

Yet I was still far from thinking that one day she would be my wife. I had told her that I never intended to marry her.

"I wouldn't want you to, either," she had shot back.

But still, in a closer and closer future, that monolith would become my mother-in-law and there would grow up a kind of affection between us.

"Oh, come now, D.," she would often say, later on. "Will you go on making things up forever?"

How many times had I not asked myself, and was I not to ask myself for years to come, whether I was not the dupe of a skillful bit of playacting!

Well, I accepted such a possibility when suspicions overcame me, and either gritted my teeth or threw a fit of temper, something I had never done before meeting D.

That, son, is what is known as passion. It is not wrong to say that it is a sickness not easy to get over, when, indeed, it is not fatal, as it almost was in my case.

This was the time when, as had happened to me at the same age, you were given to sleepwalking. You would get up, looking haggard and unaware of the darkness, and call for D. as one calls for help.

Your mother tried everything possible to calm you down and get you back to bed. Finally, giving up, she would take a few steps out into the hall and call D. herself.

D. quickly got into a robe and went to you.

"I'm dead, D. Can't you see that I'm dead?"

Was her contralto voice what got to you, as it did to me?

"Come, Marc."

She took you by the hand and led you into the bathroom, up to the toilet, and in a moment you were making your pipi and your features began to relax.

You would look at her in surprise. "Is that you, D.? Where am I?"

"In your own bathroom."

You recognized the familiar décor and the walls.

Then you would head toward your bed and go back to sleep. The next day, you had no recollection of it. You never did sleepwalk, if my memory is correct, after you got to be fourteen or fifteen years old. I still did until I was past forty. My parents once found me outside at the corner of Rue Puits-en-Sock, in my long flannel nightgown. Even at Epalinges, when I was over sixty-five, I sometimes had short fits of it.

Wasn't your son, in his turn, a sleepwalker? But that takes us far away from America, the frontier of which we were about to cross in our rickety car, with its bald tires and its tired springs, because the car bought in Montreal was your mother's.

We are going to drive through Maine and, as we go along prudently and very slowly, I explain things to you, as if you were in school.

"Maine's forests and lakes still bear the names given them by the Indians who once lived here."

We will see Indians. On the very first day, we go by a reservation, where the members of some tribe or other are segregated. They are supposed to sleep in their traditional tepees, which we can see clustered together; in reality, behind a thick curtain of trees, they have little whitewashed houses with corrugated-metal roofs.

I buy you a tomahawk made of very light wood, a war drum painted with colors that run in no time. But I make sure not to puncture your dreams by letting on that in a little while, when the visitors have gone, the Indians will get out of their fringed native garb and into jeans and checkered shirts and go on home to their houses.

We follow the coastline as much as possible, though that is not always easy. The roads in Maine are not all blacktopped, and sometimes we go astray because road signs are somewhat sparse. Are you dreaming? Are you watching? What did you see and think during this trip of ours?

How many pee breaks we took along the way! When you call out "Dad!" in a certain tone, I know why it's time to stop, in the wilderness, and on occasion I'm the one who calls for the stop for the same reason. As much as we can, we bypass big cities. We are often along the seashore: noisy, animated beaches, many of them flanked by a kind of country-fair midway, with merry-go-rounds, Dodgems, shrill music, the smells of hot dogs, doughnuts, cooking oil and fat, and the body oil that bathers, both male and female, rub on themselves.

The Dodgem cars make me dizzy, and D. goes on them with you. After a while, you each have a separate one, and you do your best to bump D.'s, while she laughs heartily.

By the second or third day, we are in Massachusetts, where roads get wider, but then the cars line up bumper to bumper.

We get to Boston. In an impoverished, somewhat scary suburb, we blow a tire. And we hear noises in the engine, right in front of a small garage. The man who runs it, who looks just like a movie gangster, promises us the car will be in good running order by the next evening.

Since you were born, I have never ceased observing you, trying to figure you out, as I would do later with your brothers and sister. The "profession of father," to use a term I will often repeat, is fascinating to me; I feel myself to be a father in every fiber of my being; I feel bound to you by invisible threads.

I watched you grow as if I had never seen a child before. You are, of course, the first one that I conceived, but I would observe the following ones with just as much fascination, for each individual is different, and I am to discover that the individual is already there, full and complete, in each little boy or girl from their earliest years.

I go as far as feeling jealous of your mother, as if she were depriving me of part of something that is mine, which, of course, I know is ridiculous. It was one of your brothers who one day informed me: "When I'm thirty, I'd like to have a child." Then added, after thinking it over, "If only I could have one without being bothered with a wife."

I observe you as always, two days later, when we are on our way again. The repair job turned out, they claim, to be much more complicated than at first estimated, and I am forced to pay what I consider an exorbitant amount. Once on our way, I discover they have stolen from the car the Leica that I had dragged all around the world with me and was deeply attached to.

We decide to make a swing around Cape Cod. There is a small museum, which you visit and which seems to fascinate you. There's a model of the Mayflower, Pilgrim costumes, and under glass an old volume, which you point a finger at as I tell you the story of those men and women who in search of religious freedom left their homeland and came here.

"Look! The Pilgrims' telephone directory!"

That precious old tome is none other than the venerable Bible from which their pastor daily read them a few verses to help them weather the storms.

For you—as for me perhaps—time does not seem to exist. Why should the telephone have been invented only recently? Why not a few centuries earlier? After all, the Chinese invented gunpowder long before the Roman Empire came into existence, but they didn't use it to kill people, only for fireworks displays such as the ones you are so fond of.

Next we go through Connecticut and spend the night at a charming inn with delicious food. No more whiskey for D. or me. She seems serene, very attentive to you. You are not what is commonly referred to as a difficult child. You're rather too easy to please, and Tigy was even worried about that for a while.

"He almost never cries, never has a temper tantrum. It seems he doesn't let himself go the way other children do, that he holds everything back inside himself."

I feel that you live in your own little world, which you like very much, and keep it jealously to yourself, as if it were your most precious possession. You would know best about that, Marc old man, because I don't think you've changed a great deal with the years.

Each of us has his or her own inner universe, and yours is filled with sunshine, streams rippling through meadows and woods, animals visible or not whose songs or cries are sometimes heard in the night, a unique universe in harmony with nature.

Even though I don't much care for that overused word, you are a poet, and I foresee that you'll remain one all your life.

Do you know that, back in tribal times, poets were revered, and their songs in the eyes of primitive peoples represented the voices of the gods?

We skip New York, and spend the night in a questionable-looking hotel in New Jersey, the only one not full that we could find. Two beds. At least that. A bathroom with a dirty yellowish bathtub. A radio that only works when you slip a coin into a slot. We prefer not to wonder who last slept between the sheets and lie down with resignation.

I think of Boule, who still hasn't gotten a visa and now, in Paris, hardly dares hope she ever will, on account of the quota. I have been told that she would have a better chance of getting a permanent-entry visa if she were already at some town just across the American border.

We are heading south, in the direction of Mexico, and, as soon as we know where we are permanently settled, she is planning to go to that country. "Permanently"? Well, let it go. Haven't each of our successive places been permanent?

We're on the road again. We feel dirty, because rather than use the questionable towels in the room, we dried ourselves on yesterday's underwear.

We cross an endless iron bridge, and if we follow the highway, we will have to go through Philadelphia, a prospect that makes me heartsick. Fortunately, luck is with us. Just before we get to that smoke-covered city, there are signs announcing a detour, and we find ourselves going through rich pastureland around affluent farmhouses that remind me of Holland.

A little later, we are across the Mason-Dixon line, which divided the North and the South when they battled so fiercely in times gone by. Then Virginia, the Carolinas.

We see tobacco plantations, and blacks seem to outnumber whites. We stop at a large hotel in some city or other. They have a floor show that starts at eight, while dinner is being served, and another show goes on at midnight.

You get all dressed up. So do we. We are going to have a sort of party. I explain to you: "From here on, Marc, don't ever use the French word 'nègre.' "

"Why not?"

"Because people may misunderstand it as an offensive English word. If you have to say something, say 'noirs.' "

"Isn't that the same thing?"

"Not in the South."

We have a table for three in a large ballroom with true Southern charm. The staff are all black-skinned, so their white uniforms gleam the more by contrast.

We are given a very impressive menu. The band is playing a nostalgic waltz.

"What would you like, Marc?"

We read off names of dishes you never heard of before, but you nevertheless gravely select from among them. Then, just as the smiling captain is about to turn away, you change your mind.

"D.," you say to her in French, "would you ask the nè . . . the nè . . ." You start to blush, and blurt out, "Ask the white man please to give me a glass of water."

The captain speaks French. He is not the least bit offended, but looks at you with a smile full of comprehension and replies: "*Oui, monsieur.*"

While we are having dinner and the chorus girls are doing their numbers, I wonder where Tigy and your tutor might be. Have they gotten farther than we or lagged behind? Did they make as many detours?

Tigy had not specified what route she would follow, feeling she'd rather take it as the spirit moved her, and saying only that she'd spend at least one day in New York.

But then, aren't we taking it as the spirit moves us too, without knowing just where we're going, except that we are to rendezvous with your mother in Miami? But not to stay there. Just for a more or less long stopover on our way to—where?

I have always set out for "someplace," and now all of us together are on our way to "someplace," a someplace we have no idea of, which may turn out to be permanent, or may be only temporary.

Out of politeness, you applaud the red-headed songstress. Almost every American floor show had a red-headed singer, always a contralto, slightly throaty, like D. Some people call such a voice "sexy," or, as we say in French, *vaginale.*

D. is on her best behavior, and all through this long trip there is not the slightest lack of understanding between us.

Will I finally believe this state of things is here to stay?

26

Saint Augustine, by early morning, a delightful old white-and-red Florida city, its peaceful streets lined with trees bearing great bright-red flowers, which I long ago got to know in Tahiti, where they were called "flamboyants." No ostentatious wealth, or any signs of poverty either: a kind of general well-being beneath the numbing sun. I would like to stay on here and make a vow to return someday, but I have a surprise in store for Marc a few miles farther on.

A high, broad structure, with one foot in the ocean. A long corridor. I have Marc walk in front of us, and he suddenly stops, bedazzled. Behind a giant glass partition, the underwater world has been re-created, and Marc's eyes dart this way and that, taking in rocks, living corals, sand, and living algae too, which sway softly back and forth.

Crabs, crayfish, lobsters move about or remain motionless, on the alert, while fishes of all colors and sizes swim on in their endless pursuit of survival. A huge black shadow goes quickly by: a hammerhead shark.

This is not a museum. It is Marineland, which I learned about from a brochure. I understand other places like it have been created since then, but this one is the first. The natural living conditions of the deep sea have been rigorously respected.

"But, Dad," you say to me, as you see a shark gobble up a fairly large fish, "the sharks will eat up all the rest of the fishes."

"You see that there are still quite a few."

Indeed, the little fishes, silver, pink, or striped, right before our eyes, are doing real aquatic-ballet maneuvers, disappearing within the moving algae or slipping inside the corals.

"Are you sure, Dad, that . . ."

You are as affected by this as I was when, from a rock at Porquerolles, I was so upset to see the bitter struggles that went on endlessly within the limpid waters. But I was twenty-two at the time. You are only seven, and I am not about to let you know that here in Marineland the species that get devoured are replaced by a new supply fished from the sea.

The big ones eat the little ones, a truth for fish as it is for all animal species. It is a truth for humans too, and, to make sure that there is always a sufficient supply of little ones, some countries give incentive bonuses to parents of large families.

You'll find all that out soon enough, my bedazzled Marc. Now, you go from one discovery to the next. We go up a gentle incline, the gigantic aquarium still before our eyes, and at each level we find more species, as in the ocean itself.

"An octopus, Dad! And what's that—a snake?"

"A moray eel."

A seal dives under and seems to be watching you with curiosity through the glass. You can't get the words out, you are so greatly excited.

"But, Dad, how did they do it?"

I am as much at a loss as you and D., who is silent in her surprise. The bottom now is well below us, but we can still see it.

Congers, clouds of tiny shiny fishes followed by a few cod. A thousand, ten thousand species? I have no idea. A swordfish with its threatening blade. A sawfish . . .

You think you're dreaming. Your wonder gets ever greater, and you are bright red with excitement. That will reach its height when the dolphins rub against the thick glass, as curious about us as we are about them.

The sky over our heads. The surface of this miniature sea, in which the dolphins now jump high into the air.

A bell. A sailor in summer whites comes forward on the diving board, holding a basket full of fish, and every time he throws one, high over the water, the dolphins leap straight up at it.

The sailor calls them by their names, which they seem to know, for they don't try to get ahead of one another, but wait their turns. Another basketful, and then another.

Through the clear water, one can still see the dark furtive shadows of the sharks, which remain below.

The dolphins' lunch is over, and a young woman in a bathing suit comes out on the diving board. The dolphins look as though they have been expecting her, and when she dives in, they go into a real dance act with her.

You stammer, "But, what if a shark . . ."

But none does, and the girl, whose blond hair floats like aquatic plants, pets her dolphin friends, who make a show of their joy and affection.

We went back down, and you wanted to go back up the gentle incline once more.

"Can we come back this afternoon?"

"Yes, son."

It is very hot. The air is humid, and our shirts are soaked with perspiration. We have a very good lunch and then go back to Marineland again. At four o'clock, we head on south, toward another motel.

From here on, the main road remains almost constantly at the edge of the water. Big white clouds in a dark-blue sky. Sometimes a black cloud, which will burst somewhere, occasionally on our car, refreshing us for a moment.

The tourist traps along the road become more and more numerous. In New England, they were all so-called antique shops, displaying oil lamps and chamber pots with red or blue flowers.

Everything that is a surprise to you here, including motels and drive-ins, you will find springing up someday in France.

We cross a muddy river, and your eye, attentive to everything that moves, calls my attention to a kind of floating log.

"It opened its mouth, Dad. It's a . . . a . . ."

"An alligator. All the rivers in the South have them, wherever there are marshes."

"And crocodiles?"

"They are found mainly in Africa."

However, we will see some later in another tourist trap along the roadside, where, for half a dollar, one can see the saurians apparently sleeping in a ditch—just as I had seen so many of them in the Congo.

"Antique Weapons." You want to see everything, and we stop often. Muskets, Civil War rifles, old-time cowboy revolvers, the ones they used when the first trains in the West were attacked. Indian bows and arrows.

You swallow it all, avidly, and I now know that you will be this way all your life.

The big Indian and Harley-Davidson motorcycles of the road cops swish past us noisily, and you are no less fascinated by them.

I wired Tigy that we are spending several days at Miami Beach, that you're in great shape, and that our trip had been without a hitch. I have no idea what roads she took. In spite of her fear of driving, she arrived ahead of us, probably making fewer stops.

We bathe in the high waves, which break foamily over us, and we dry out on the sand. We have dinner at a restaurant, the other side of a bridge. A big concrete tub filled with sea water, on the sidewalk, has big live tortoises in it, such as I used to see and eat in Tahiti.

"Do you want to taste them, Marc?"

"Can they be eaten?"

"Yes, of course."

"In the shell?"

"No."

We have a tortoise prepared in some kind of sauce.

"They taste like veal. Where do they come from?"

"They're local. The sea is full of them."

The third day, while I am dictating some letters, we hear the sound of our shutters closing, even though there is very little wind. We investigate. The manager is nailing the shutters tight.

"There's a hurricane on its way north. We're used to them. It may not hit us." Then, pointing to the set that comes with the room, "You'll be kept informed by radio every hour on the hour."

We go to a local grocery store to get some supplies. Three days' worth, as the radio advised, especially at Miami Beach, a sort of island that can sometimes be cut off from the mainland.

This recalls old memories. Before the war, in a Pathé newsreel, I saw a hurricane devastating Florida, Miami in particular: little boats washed up on land, roofs blown off, wooden houses blown down, and trees torn up with part of their roots.

We go to bed. Toward the middle of the night, we hear coconuts hitting the ground, the wind whizzing by, the waves breaking loudly a hundred feet from where we are.

The radio announcer reads an official bulletin asking doctors, nurses, firemen, and other such types of people to go as quickly as possible to their designated assembly points.

He also says that hundreds of cars are streaming northward out of the city.

"They are wrong," he quietly comments. "No one knows where the hurricane will hit. It is still over two hundred miles away and may just as well turn out to sea as toward the mainland. Now, a little musical interlude, before our next newscast."

The next day, the storm is still far away and moving at only forty miles an hour. One plane has gotten to the eye of the hurricane, where the winds are swirling at over a hundred and fifty miles an hour.

"Up here," the pilot broadcasts, "you don't feel as if you're moving at all. It's like sitting in the middle of a merry-go-round. More later."

Music. Another bulletin.

"Listeners are advised to start using batteries if they have them, because the electric power may be cut off at any moment. Phone in your requests, and we will try to play them."

The whole thing is as well organized as a military review. Night comes. You go to sleep. D. and I, in the living room, keep the radio on.

The hurricane is now only a hundred miles away. The pilot in the eye of it comes back on. There's a certain amount of static. His voice is not too clear. He's bored, staying there in his hurricane.

"This crazy storm doesn't seem to know where it wants to go. Sometimes it seems to be going east, out into the middle of the Atlantic. Then it makes a U turn. It's a good thing I have plenty to eat and drink with me. I'm sorry I didn't bring something along to read. It's so noisy here, I can't even hear the radio."

How can one be frightened when people act like that?

The announcer is joking too. "Now that I've played all of your requests, I'll indulge myself and play my own favorite." And through the noise of the storm, we hear Saint-Saëns's *Danse macabre*.

We have something to eat, drink some cold beer. D. makes up games for you the next day that I've never heard of.

The hurricane passes, just grazing us, instead of hitting us full force. Some small boats sink, some trees are broken, some roofs are blown off nearby houses, and one bridge is out, but not one of those leading to the city proper. On the other hand, before dying out, the hurricane will do some serious damage in some towns.

We consult the map to see where your mother is, in Sarasota. We have to cross the most humid part of the region, a huge marshland called "the Everglades," in which the sea has carved out something like fjords. It is full of alligators, to say nothing of mosquitoes. The air is suffocating, and you frequently tell me, "I'm thirsty, Dad."

I am too, but there aren't many houses, and even fewer restaurants. We drive on through it the whole day and finally come to a group of houses with a hotel at the middle of them. We didn't meet many cars on the road and what we saw mainly was long lines of pine trees.

The next day, in a few hours, we are out of this suffocating density and can once again see the blue sky, solid ground, the Gulf of Mexico, and finally the little town of Sarasota.

Your mother is not at the hotel; she has already found a small house. You are excited to be back with her and would like to tell her everything, but you don't know where to start.

She takes me aside. "I would prefer, Georges, that while we are here we live separately. Marc will stay with me. His tutor has left. He can go to school, and you can come for him every weekend."

I agree half-heartedly, because it hurts me that you and I will no longer be living together. Just weekends. The fact is, I will often come by to see you during the week, and weekends begin on Friday night.

D. and I are looking for a place to live, because we know we will be staying here for some time. About fifteen miles away, we discover an island connected to the mainland by a long bridge, Anna Maria Key, offshore from a little town called Bradenton.

The key is practically deserted, and its coast, on the gulf side, is just a beach with a few dozen houses, a hotel, a barbershop, a grocery, and a souvenir-and-shell shop.

There is a real-estate office, to which we go, and from there we are driven to the end of the key. A wooden cottage, all white, crisp, and clean.

In front, a beach almost a mile long with not a soul on it. The nearest neighbors are about three hundred yards away.

We rent it, and unload our old car. We have been told of a grocery, not far away, that sells everything, meat, fresh eggs, delicatessen. A pine counter separates our kitchen from our living room. Two bedrooms, not too large, but almost new. You will sleep in one of them even more often than I had hoped, because your mother decides she has to take a trip to Europe, where she has some business to attend to and wants to make sure everything is as it should be at Nieul.

One morning, the sea looks strange to us. It is flat, and a strange pink color that doesn't come from the sun. And that evening, almost bright red.

The next morning, the beach is littered with dead fish, and we are told that this is the "red tide," which happens only every fifteen or twenty years. Swimming is out of the question, fishing even more so. We are full of consternation; the dead fish, soon piled three feet high, have to be removed by bulldozers.

The smell in the house becomes so unbearable that we go to Bradenton and rent three rooms at the hotel. By morning, my face is broken out and I can't shave. The doctor shakes his head over it and suggests that I may get some relief from a viscous salve, which smells bad too. My beard grows out, and I don't want to be seen in public looking this way.

So you usually go to the lunch counter downstairs and order toasted ham-and-cheese sandwiches. The street is very quiet. I watch you from the window, and in no time see you surrounded by a gang of little friends.

"Dad, can I have some money to go to the movies with them?"

I give you some money. I suspect you're paying for more than just your own ticket, but don't say anything about it to you.

"Can I go bowling?"

The bowling alley is next door to the movie house. Two lanes are reserved for ladies, who use smaller balls than the men. And now you have a new passion! From time to time, you come back, looking animated.

"Can I have a little more money, Dad?"

Bowling is expensive, but that doesn't matter. First thing in the morning, your little friends come calling for you, and I'm not sure you don't treat them to sandwiches.

My skin irritation starts getting better. Christmas is coming. Your mother has returned from Paris and wants you back.

I begin to feel that we won't be here very long, but right after the holidays will be on our way again. The same question as always: Where to?

I have no idea. A long time ago, in a *National Geographic Magazine*, I saw pictures of a state where the grass was blue and rivers snaked through it. I also remembered a river lined by great trees and, especially, horses freely grazing. It was some place in the South or the West.

Open spaces. Horses . . .

Was that the goal of my long quest? Or would there be many more stages still? However that might be, D. and I were to go off, while your mother waited until we found something.

Something undefinable, which perhaps didn't even exist.

27

It was June 1947, and, practically overnight, we left Florida to go west, like the pioneers in their Conestoga wagons with their one-shot rifles.

As luck would have it, we didn't have to set out in our old prewar jalopy, which seemed ready to give up the ghost at every mile. One afternoon while we were in Bradenton, probably to get some fishing tackle, for we were always looking for better and more up-to-date reels, rods that were more flexible but stronger, we stopped short in front of a store window displaying what to us was our dream car.

It was the first ultramodern car manufactured after the war. It was long, oh, so long, and low-slung, in a sky-blue color that was both soft and cheerful. The inside, upholstered in red leather, was even more attractive, indeed breath-taking. It not only had a fully automatic shift, but also a set of metal buttons controlled the automatic opening and shutting of all the windows, together or separately. Another button released the light-tan top, which rose to a vertical position and then came slowly into place on top of the windshield. Finally, another button supplied heat or cool, almost icy, air.

We fell in love with it and wanted to take immediate possession, but the salesman said he had to keep it on display five or six days more. Too scared it might get away from us, we bought it then and there, paying cash, to the surprise of the dealer, who was of course used to selling all his cars on time.

I think he gave us a forty- or fifty-dollar trade-in on our noisy old crate, which had carried us through the United States from the northern border to the southern tip, through a dozen states or more.

For the moment, we are again in a state of suspension. We expect to be leaving any day, so I sit back and try to take stock.

In October 1945, New York, and that skyscraper hotel, and then Montreal, my frequent trips to the U.S., and that same month, defying all expectations, my meeting with D., throwing all my plans into a cocked hat, the almost insane passion that for a long time to come will indeed throw all of my life into a cocked hat.

What a difference between that artificial young woman with the endless, unpredictable roles she played, at times cruel, at others tender, and the D. at Anna Maria Key! I can scarcely recognize the one in the other. The transition was slow, sometimes stormy.

I have already told you about how she arrived at the lakeside on January 3, and you were the one who so gallantly welcomed her. And now I discover it was in that same month of January, while war and peace were alternating between her and me, that I wrote my first novel on American soil, *Three Beds in Manhattan,* with New York, in the final analysis, as the principal character.

Her new long hair got hard to handle, so I bought her a lock of natural hair. I had sailed for several years, though only as an amateur, and as a result was rather adept at knots. The motions needed to connect her own hair with the lock were the same as the ones used to join the two ends of a halyard or a painter. She could then wind a thick braid around the top of her head, making her look not unlike a woman of the Caucasus.

Was it this, with the lack of make-up, that wrought a change in her mood? Sometimes, I wondered whether this change was real or whether it might not just be one more role being played by the Diva of her childhood.

In March, I had written *Inspector Maigret in New York's Underworld.* And at Saint Andrews, I'm surprised to find today that I wrote a lot: *Au bout du rouleau* (The End of the Line) in May, then *Le Clan des Ostendais (The Ostenders)* and *Maigret et l'inspecteur malgracieux* (Maigret and the Ungracious Inspector).

Here in the intense heat of the cottage, sitting naked at my machine, with handkerchiefs tied around my wrists so that the sweat coming out of all my pores would not soil the typewritten pages, I wrote *Lettre à mon juge (Act of Passion), Le Destin des Malou (The Fate of the Malous), Les Petits Cochons sans queue* (The Little Tailless Pigs), and *Le Passager clandestin (The Stowaway),* or some nine volumes in approximately one year.

• • •

A fortuitous meeting with an agent of the Immigration and Naturalization Service is to delay our departure for a month and send us all off under an unexpected sky. I was a little bit concerned about the fact that my passport described me as a "Government Official." I was wondering whether in spite of that I might be considered a resident of the United States, and the Immigration man confirmed my concern.

It turned out I had technically been authorized to reside in the United States "until fulfillment of government mission." But that mission had merely been a contrivance, and the Immigration man advised that I would be better off going into a neighboring country and reentering the U.S. on a permanent visa.

"Why not go to Havana?" he suggested. "It's just a short hop by plane from Miami. In two days there, you'll have your entry visa."

So, off we went, all four of us. I can still see our hotel in downtown Havana. You and your mother have a fine suite with a view on the street. D. and I from our windows can see only some rather crumbling houses and some housewives, chattering away all day long with strident voices, washing or ironing their laundry on a terrace.

It is twice as hot here as in Florida, and sleep at night is not very restful. By day one can't sleep on account of the women talking and singing outdoors.

The American ambassador receives us graciously. "You'll have your visa in two days."

The city is noisy. The streetcars have bunches of humans hanging to them, and one expects to see them fall off any minute; the automobiles, very old, crisscross one another in every direction, climb up on sidewalks, and bawl one another out at the tops of their horns. The din is deafening.

Evenings, on the Prado, groups of young girls, most of them beautiful, walk about while groups of boys in white shirts call out to them teasingly and provoke merry bursts of laughter.

We discover an excellent, very clean restaurant. Batista is still in power; but the real power is actually in the hands of the American Syndicate, in other words, the Mafia. They own the ultramodern and very elegant hotel in the best neighborhood in town, as well as the one we are staying at, the casino, the bars, the nightclubs.

At Anna Maria, D. and I had drunk only a little beer, or some California sherry. Here, when the heat takes one's breath away, there are air-conditioned bars where one can consume a daiquiri or two. Bah! It's only for two days!

・　・　・

Back to the ambassador, as gracious as ever, but concerned. "You didn't tell me you had come over on a diplomatic mission."

"I thought that was evident from my passport."

"I hadn't noticed it."

"The mission was so general . . ."

He smiles mischievously. "I know the kind. You're not the only one. But unfortunately I can't issue you a permanent resident's visa until the government that sent you advises us that your mission has been completed. We would be accused of 'raiding' foreign diplomats for our own purposes."

"But I'm not a diplomat."

"I know that. Cable Paris. The department that issued those orders to you can simply reply: 'Mission accomplished.' As soon as I have such a document, I can issue you your visa."

I feel even hotter than outside, notwithstanding the air conditioning. I can hardly remember what minister or undersecretary issued that mission to me. His name is never mentioned anymore in the French papers that I happen to see.

I send cable after cable to Paris. No one there remembers the mission, which at the time seemed so miraculous to me. We have to wait almost a month, writing, cabling, asking the help of the French ambassador, who becomes our friend. He is a bachelor, and a cultivated gourmet. We have lunch at his home several times, and he lets us in on a secret: his cook is an escaped convict.

There are many such in Cuba, who come up to you the minute they hear you speaking French. There are also a lot of "houses" in the same class as the two or three famous Paris "houses," which have nothing but beautiful girls. They are elegant, discreet, private town houses, and the owner of our hotel is only too glad to give us their addresses. He is one of the Syndicate's best gamblers, the kind of professional player who is sent around to casinos in Europe or South America, with a big bankroll, to play for big stakes and sometimes break the bank.

In Havana, there are fortunes as big as the ones in Texas: the five or six top cigar makers, for instance, and the sugar-cane plantation owners. The daughter of the manufacturer of the world's most famous brand of cigars gets married while we are there. For the occasion, the two best-known "big bands" in the U.S. are brought in. The cost for the event in flowers alone is said to exceed fifty thousand dollars. The whole affair costs over a million.

We keep cabling. The French ambassador cables.

One afternoon, D. and I decide to visit one of those famous houses of assignation. Did we drink a few daiquiris? Maybe. D. is completely at ease in the place, looks admiringly at a tall girl, with the finest black skin, whose naked body is flawless.

"Why don't you sleep with her?"

"Why not?" I answer, unaware that D. plans to watch, and not merely watch.

A few days later, she mentions another house to me, which Americans especially like and our hotel owner has recommended. We go there. It is less elegant than the first one, but more lively, more animated, with couples drinking and chatting out on a patio.

We select two young women, a blonde and a beautiful, lascivious mulatto girl. On the patio, they have some drinks with us, then take us to a room where we spend almost two hours with them. D. enjoys it so much that we go back twice, three times, even more, and the blonde will blushingly give us a large-size photograph of herself, in the altogether, which she inscribes to both of us.

While waiting, you, Marc, D., and I go off by taxi to a beach the ambassador has recommended to us, about twenty miles from town.

We drive through villages so impoverished that in spite of ourselves we have to contrast them with that million-dollar wedding. A few rich people, too rich, with private planes and fleets of yachts. Maybe three or four hundred semirich? And millions of poor, who are terribly, terribly poor.

At the beach hotel, you meet some friends your age with whom you can bowl. They come in all colors, and you are not the least concerned, not seeming to notice it, which delights me.

The ocean is warm, the beach nice, and we swim several times a day. I write letters by hand, with a carbon underneath, for almost all of them are to my European publishers. For years, I have made it a habit to write in French to publishers of all countries, asking them please to answer me in my own language, which they all do, even my very British English publisher of that time, who complies only after first grousing about it.

I now speak English—or should I say American?—rather fluently, but not enough, for example, to carry on an important business transaction by phone. So D. takes all the calls, but I dictate the letters to her, and all she has to do is translate them. Hasn't she been trying little by little to assume a larger place in my business life than I want to give her? I recall those first days at Sainte-Marguerite, when she upset my whole filing system.

One evening, a storm. Not in the sky or on earth, but over our two heads. One night, rather. I have no recollection of what brought on the crisis. I can still see her walking out of the bedroom, dressed in a short chemise. At a distance, I keep my eye on her. She leaves the hotel, crosses the beach, walks straight ahead out into the deep water, and then I go in after her. She is an excellent swimmer and gets farther and farther out, while I keep begging her to turn back.

I finally catch up with her. She fights me off, but I force her to come along, while she keeps repeating in a toneless voice that all she wants to do is die. She will not calm down until after I get her back into bed and she falls prey to another frenzy, which reminds me of those turned-up eyes of hers on our first nights of love together.

She discovers she has lost the wristwatch I gave her for Christmas. She cries. We finally fall asleep. This is just a warning signal, to be sure, but it worries me nonetheless. She seems not to be completely cured. The next day, however, she has resumed her lovingly peaceful look, and we go back to Havana.

It seems the French ambassador will soon have the document releasing me from my mission. The casino, much like those in Las Vegas, one evening, in the company of the ambassador, who will drive us to the airport.

As the American ambassador has promised us, the formalities are done in a single day. I'm almost ashamed, as I see the long line of people outside the embassy, half of them having spent the night there and perhaps planning to spend another.

A last daiquiri. Warm farewells to our friend. Miami. Our beautiful Buick there waiting for us, to take us through the alligator- and mosquito-filled Everglades.

Now we have permanent residency in the United States, the next thing to being citizens. And we are about to undertake the long trek west, toward a place the name of which I don't know, that place with the wide-open spaces, the blue grass, and the horses running wild.

You are used to taking off, aren't you? It doesn't seem to bother you. All three of us sit on the front seat, because it is a wide car, and we put the top up only when the sun becomes too scorching. To distract you from your mysterious daydreams, we sing.

We cross Alabama, Mississippi, Louisiana almost without realizing it. We stop frequently, for lunch, dinner, a night's sleep, and sometimes we only do three or four hundred miles at a stretch, so as not to wear you out.

When we stop at a gas station, people gather around to look at our car as if it were something from outer space. They lean over to see all those shiny buttons, which intrigue them. If by chance we leave the car unattended, children get in and press the buttons haphazardly, delighted to see the windows go up and down at their command.

Which will turn out to be a dirty trick on you, my poor Marc. One morning, after we've been on the road for an hour, you complain about the heat.

"It's no hotter than yesterday."

"Yes, it is. It's burning . . ."

You complain that way for a couple of hours, even when we let you switch seats, even after I put the top up.

"Where is it burning?"

"Every place. But mainly—especially on my behind."

I stop, sit where you were sitting, and find the spot is burning-hot indeed. I'm not fully acquainted with all the magic buttons yet. I check them one after the other, and discover that the heater was left on by some of those kids this morning or last night.

Texas. Dallas. A gorgeous, ultramodern hotel. In the morning, you and I decide to go get a haircut. Red-faced, well-fed men talking in loud voices, sure of themselves, sure that they are the most important people in the state that is the most important and richest in the world.

I notice that, while they are having their hair cut or getting shaved, their big white hats are turned over to girls who give them a quick blocking in the next room.

I decide to get one of those Stetsons. Once, a long time ago, I traveled on a ship with Mrs. Stetson, the heiress to the hat company, who kept us in the saloon playing bridge so long that we barely got to see the Panama Canal.

Not a white Stetson. I select a more discreet, tan one. You have been wearing a cowboy hat of that shade since we were in New York.

We spend a day and a night in Dallas and are surprised at how pretty all the women are, even the cafeteria waitresses. I ask a restaurant captain about it.

"Yes, sir, that's right. Here in Texas, in both Dallas and Houston, we get the prettiest girls in the world. Hollywood has nothing on us on that score. In Hollywood, they're all trying to be discovered by a talent scout so they can get a part in a picture. Here, the men are richer than any place else in the world, and that means more in the long run than a screen test."

Plains as far as the eye can see, prairies, cattle grazing peacefully among the oil derricks. Everywhere, the stink of oil, which is not a stink to everybody.

How many days have we been on the road? We can no longer count them. The countryside goes by. Wide-open spaces, yes, but still not the ones I've been dreaming of ever since I saw that picture in the magazine.

Soon we are at the practically waterless Rio Grande, of cowboy-song and Western-movie fame. We spend an afternoon at El Paso, on the Mexican border, where we go across the bridge that separates the two countries, and have dinner in a Mexican restaurant.

Sand now takes the place of grass. Indians appear as well as blacks. We are in New Mexico. The sand is red, and the hills above the plain are almost red as well.

Then we get into Arizona, where the wide-open spaces seem to me to be wider and more open than anywhere else. There are herds of thousands of cattle. Cowboys on horseback who make your eyes bug out, Marc, because, with their silver-studded boots and saddles, they are just like those in the movies and comic books.

At two o'clock, we are in a city, to my eyes like no other in the world, so firmly set in the desert that in some of the streets sand creaks under our shoes on the sidewalk. The streets are wide. Horsemen ride in among the cars.

Tucson! A turn-of-the-century, solid, roomy hotel, the Pioneer. We go in. Everyone is dressed in open cowboy shirts, high-heeled boots, black or tan sombreros, just like mine.

We go up to our spacious, very airy suite. Although it is as hot here as in Florida, the air is dry and seems to retain a desert tang. In my mind's eye, there has to be blue grass around here.

After dinner, I sit down with a sigh of satisfaction, and declare, "Well, here we are."

"What does that mean, Jo?"

"That we're staying here."

You clap your hands, Marc you devil, because you feel as much at home as I in this setting.

"For a long time? Are you going to send for Tigy?"

We haven't even visited the city yet!

"I'm going down to wire her right now."

And you add, "Me too."

I repeat, in the elevator, "Well, here we are."

"For good?"

"Yes, for good."

"Yeow!"

A new period is beginning. A capital period, children, for you as well as me. For all of us.

It was a Sunday.

28

Tell me, Marc old man—because right now I am not speaking to the child you were, but to the man who is going to be forty-one years old next week—why do you think that that particular Sunday, after having crossed part of Arizona and stopping on the outskirts of Tucson, I was able to say with virtual certainty, "Here we are"?

D. could not understand my sudden decision. We had crossed wide-open spaces in Alabama, Louisiana, and New Mexico, not to mention Texas, as famous for its cowboys as for its oil wells and its multimillionaires.

Before that, Maine might have appealed to us, with its forests, its lakes, and nearby ocean. Had I not always felt that I could live only near the sea, which was why I had selected Nieul after such exhaustive searching? We might have settled near Saint Augustine, where you were bemused by the marine fauna. We might also have gone on to nearby California.

You were a boy who expressed himself little by words or broad gestures, but I am convinced, through my habit of observing your eyes, that that Sunday you knew we had reached our destination, and that neither you nor I was wrong, since it was here in Arizona, and soon right out in the desert, that your personality was truly going to blossom.

Instinct? An almost animal prescience? I believe in instinct, especially that of animals, which, through the centuries, have not become as sclerotic as men.

Perhaps, had it not been for events that depended on neither you nor me, we might today still be in those vast stretches of sand, where a few houses had been put up back in the days of the pioneers. I would regret that, as far as I am concerned, because, without that imponderable, I would not in my late years have attained the goal of my endless search. How about you?

A small incident occurred during our first dinner at the Pioneer, in the dining room, which, though austere, was full of human warmth. We had been served tomato juice, and alongside each glass was half a lemon.

How did it happen? Was my attention distracted by the setting and the people? At any rate, my half-lemon got away from me as I was squeezing it and, after describing a long parabola, landed in the glass of an elegantly dressed young woman.

She too had tomato juice, and it spattered into her face, making large red spots on her blouse and skirt. I thought we would hear recriminations, if not worse. Men in the South and West are reputed to be not very patient, especially where their womenfolk are concerned.

To my great surprise, she smiled at me as she wiped the spots off with her napkin, while I was blushing in embarrassment. I rose awkwardly, went over toward her table, and mumbled something in my English hobbled by a strong French accent.

The men at her table also smiled. You must have been dying of fear. I was too.

"Are you French?" she asked.

"Belgian."

"Please don't worry about my dress. Have you been in Tucson long?"

"This is our first day."

"Are you planning to stay?"

"As long as possible."

"Well, let's hope this little accident will bring you luck."

The very next morning, we went up to the hotel manager, who was standing in the lobby. D. probably did most of the talking, as she usually did. I understood the language less well than she, especially the way it was spoken locally.

"Is there a real estate agency hereabouts?"

"To buy a house?"

"To rent one."

He was cordial, and smiling with amusement.

"Would you be happy with a big hacienda?"

The way I looked at D. told him of my enthusiasm.

He led us into his office, which was furnished in true pioneer style.

"This house is not usually for rent, and no agency has it listed. It belongs to a very rich old lady, somewhat eccentric, who most of the time lives there by herself. Sometimes, when she wants to get away from her lonely existence, she spends several months at the home of a friend of hers, whose house is just as large but who has much more help.

"The lady I have in mind is the widow of quite a well-known painter, and sometimes, if she likes the people, she will rent her house to them."

I was already excited.

"The best time to go and see her is late in the morning. Afternoons, she plays bridge with friends."

We dash over there. We find a very quiet neighborhood, with empty streets. Patrician houses, well spaced, hidden behind thick, semitropical greenery.

We ring the doorbell, our hearts thumping. We had been told that the lady came from an old Virginia family. That scared me a little, because old Virginia families consider themselves, as much as, if not more than, those of New England, the aristocracy of the United States.

A very lively old lady, with even livelier eyes, finally answers the doorbell and looks us over curiously. Over a simple cotton frock, she was wearing a cleaning woman's apron, made of heavy blue denim, and had a big rag in her hand, which fitted in with the pail of soapy water we saw standing in the large tiled hallway.

"Excuse us for disturbing you at such an hour. But we were told . . ."

"By whom?"

"By the manager of the Pioneer. He said the best time to find you in was late morning."

"Yes. Because that's when I do my cleaning."

She smiles, noting that our eyes are irresistibly attracted to her bony hands. On them are three or four rings with huge diamonds that hardly seem to go with the cleaning rag and the blue denim apron. She understands everything at a glance, and smiles again, mischievously.

"Well, if Ben sent you, you must be looking to rent. Come in."

She closes the door behind us, and at the end of the hallway we go into a room of unexpected size, three walls of which are lined with books from floor to ceiling.

"How long do you expect to stay in Tucson?"

"For a long time."

"I only rent for specific periods, because I am very fond of this house. My husband and I were very happy here."

She points to an oil painting of a fiftyish man, with light hair and blue eyes like yours, Marc.

"Are you wondering about my diamonds? I never wear them when I go out, even in evening dress. I like them for themselves and only wear them in the morning, while I clean. That's just an old lady's idea of how to do things, I guess."

We are seated. Her sharp eyes seem to be seeing right through us.

"Are you married?" she asks.

Ouch! This is puritanical America!

"No. We live together."

"How about this boy's mother?"

"She'll join us here in a few days."

216

This amuses her. She seems really to relish the unconventionality of our situation.

"You see, I'm a nonconformist," she says. "I love to shock certain people of my acquaintance. Some people just call me a crazy old lady, and . . ."

She showed us through the hacienda, all on one floor but no less huge for that. To the right of the living room, a spacious bedroom, which will become Tigy's and yours, Marc. It has another bedroom adjoining, smaller, for D. and me, opening onto a patio. Each of the rooms has its own bath.

An outside stair leads to a terrace that is something like the bridge of a ship, and there is a small white structure there, with another bedroom and bath.

Outside, everything is white. In the back, a garden full of cactus, pebbles, sand, and palm trees.

The kitchen, in size, is reminiscent of a kitchen in a château, and on the walls copper pans shine softly.

Another bedroom, in the other wing, which is Mrs. K.'s own, another patio with white walls and green plants. A dining room.

"You can see it's all rather large for a woman alone."

Everything is unexpectedly sparkling clean, considering that she does all the work herself, without help.

"Would you take it for six months?" she asks.

"Longer, if possible."

"I can't commit myself beyond six months. It may be that later on I will decide to go and visit my cousins in Virginia, of whom I have dozens. . . ."

She is not laughing, but her smile is a silent laugh, a little like yours, Marc.

"Did Ben mention a price to you?"

"No."

"It will probably seem high to you. Eight hundred dollars a month. The house as is, with the furniture, accessories, books, silverware, and dishes."

I had indeed not anticipated so high a figure.

"The garden will not be your responsibility. I have an Indian who takes care of it. He goes back to the reservation every evening, about ten miles out of town. He's a Navajo chief, and the Navajos are nice, peaceful people."

We can see him, his round face, his obliging air, dabbing paint on the grillwork that leads to a dead end at the rear of the garden.

"Is it too expensive?" She looks at us regretfully, and not because she won't be making the money, which she doesn't need. She likes us. I like her even more, and I don't want to haggle.

"All right. When can we move in?"

"Give me a week to straighten things out."

When Tigy arrives, we are all moved in to the hacienda, a real, honest-to-goodness hacienda, almost a hundred years old.

She likes the house. And naturally she takes over the master bedroom and gives orders to our local cook, pending the arrival of Boule, whom I am still trying to get into the United States. She will soon be at Nogales, just across the Mexican border.

The first days, I drive you to school in the convertible, because the early morning sun is not too hot. You have lunch at school and take an outdoor nap there. Your first real school, an elementary school, and I go to pick you up in the afternoon. After three or four days, you refer to the other boys and girls as if you had all been friends for months.

Your mother and D. appear to get along together. We discover an unpaved street, with a bare sand roadway, which is called Broadway. As if by irony, it is the narrowest street in Tucson, and along it there are pretty houses and gardens. One of the houses belongs to a French couple who have lived here since before the war. I had been well acquainted with the woman's father in Paris, and in no time we are friends, frequently visiting each other.

Your mother has her own friends. We will not mix ours and hers until several months later, when we give a party for some hundred guests, to which we also invite Alexandre de Manziarly, the French consul general in Los Angeles, whose jurisdiction includes Arizona. Two professors at a local university have come with their prettiest girl students, and there is a lot of merriment in the two patios, the gardens, the living room, and on that terrace like a ship's bridge.

The Immigration inspector from Nogales is there too, and, in a private chat, he promises me that when the time comes he will help Boule get her visas.

That is still rather far away, although getting closer. I have told Tigy of the plan, and she agrees that Boule come back and be part of our family, as she has always been.

I work. In a basement, at the same level as one of the gardens, there is a big room decorated with larger-than-lifesize stone statues. Almost a museum. This was the studio of Mrs. K.'s painter husband.

We now have our landlady in for bridge, one afternoon a week, with some of her lady friends. During one of these games, she explains to us seriously, but not without a sneaky smile:

"Before, I didn't want to become an old woman, and I did everything to keep young. How crazy I was! I noticed that, on the day I decided I would really be an old lady.

"Since then, I am continually delighted that I did. There is nothing nicer than being an old lady, because you can get away with anything, your hats, your dresses, no matter how eccentric they may be, and especially your behavior and your language. I have got used to saying everything I think, and nobody holds it against me. On the contrary, they look at me with an approving smile, and I know they're thinking, 'Well, she's an old lady.'

"What a delight to be one at last, and not have to go on cheating!"

Her closest friend, who is about the same age, nods agreement. She has inherited a moving-van and storage company in Tucson, and also owns the only large fashionable women's store in town, but she never mentions it. The manager of the warehouse, an unflappable character, is our fourth at bridge, and we have tea and cookies.

Never at any of these get-togethers, at our house or elsewhere, did I ever see Mrs. K. wear her diamonds. She never wore any jewelry, except when she was cleaning house. Wasn't that her right? Wasn't she "an old lady"?

That basement room, from which I could see one of the gardens and one of the gates, had become my office, and I worked a lot in it. A school bus stopped at seven-thirty in the morning at our corner, and you rushed into it with two or three of your schoolmates who lived nearby.

At Christmas, walking down the decorated streets, D. and I discovered a very young kitten, which rubbed against our legs and meowed like a lost baby. We brought it home, and naturally it was called "Christmas."

It was really more like a puppy, because when we went walking, it would walk along with us, jumping into a garden from time to time and then running back.

Do you know, Marc, you are the only person who has ever seen me at work on one of my novels? In spite of the DO NOT DISTURB sign on the doorknob, you were allowed to come into my basement, where I had been typing since 6:00 A.M. You came in so softly that I never heard you enter. All of a sudden, I would feel your lips on my cheek, and by the time I turned around you were already scampering across the garden.

My first Tucson novel was set in what I then saw around me, something that has rarely happened to me. I had called it "La Rue des Vieilles Dames" (Old Ladies' Street). Sven Nielsen, didn't, however, consider that a good selling title, and I accepted, instead, *La Jument perdue* (The Lost Mare).

I would take a half hour's walk by myself after dinner, through the neighborhood, and when I got back I would put down the first four or five sentences of the next day's chapter.

After that book, I did *Les Vacances de Maigret* (*No Vacation for Maigret*) and *Maigret et son Mort* (*Maigret's Special Murder*), one after the other.

Christmas was already following me on my evening walk when I wrote the next one, *La Neige était sale* (*The Snow Was Black*), which in my mind did not take place in the north of France, as the critics supposed it did, but in a small Austrian town I am well acquainted with.

By then, on my return, I no longer merely put down a few lines in pencil on my yellow pad, but wrote almost the entire chapter, which I would then type, with many changes, the next morning. This habit was the one I would follow for several years, except for the Maigrets, which I always typed directly.

Near the desert, there was a sort of corral that rented horses and had real cowboys for riding instructors. You would go with me, to take lessons. I, on the other hand, went riding with one of the university professors, out among the cactus and those tall green plants that look like candelabra and are covered with spikes.

I had my English saddle, my boots from back at La Richardière, and I now ponder a question to which your mother alone might know the answer. Where did they come from? Where did they and my bridles and riding gloves come from? I knew that in France Tigy had filled crates and more crates with disparate articles. How had they followed us in our meanderings? And how had they now ended up, with hundreds of books, in Mrs. K.'s friend's warehouse?

De Gaulle used to say, "Supply will follow." That being the case, your mother would have made a great quartermaster general, because everything followed, and, when needed, appeared like a rabbit out of a magician's top hat.

I suspect that her trips to France, which she made time and again, were no longer merely business or pleasure trips. That was why I was not surprised to find, when we eventually got back to Europe, that the furnishings and various other things from our successive homes had all ended up at Nieul, carefully catalogued by her.

I stuck to my determination to ride English style, which amazed the locals. Of course you rode Western style, and looked born to the saddle.

29

I don't know which novel I was busy writing when the incident occurred, but I know that to my mind that novel was quite important and difficult. Perhaps *The Snow Was Black*? My memory is precise for images, odors, sounds, including words spoken and the faces of my partners. It is less so for chronology, except where I have reference points, and sometimes I may put some minor event before another.

This one night, then, I heard your plaintive voice coming from the next room, and you were never one to complain. I could hear your mother coming and going, and whispering to you. The next day, she told us your throat was irritated and sore, and that must have been what was bothering you.

All my children have apparently inherited from me a certain susceptibility to throat trouble, and I can remember how my father, when he came home from work, would wrap a moist compress around his neck. In those days, a sore throat, or grippe, for that matter, was not acceptable as a reason to miss school or work, and I can to this day hear, among the noises in my classroom, where I was in charge of keeping the charcoal fire burning in the big black stove, coughs, nose blowings, throat clearings, all as habitual as the scratching of the chalk on the blackboard.

By evening, you were running a little temperature, and your eyes were shiny. Early in the night, Tigy came into our room, in her nightgown and robe. She said to D.: "Listen! You have my husband, why don't you come and take my son too?"

It was just a passing bad mood, of course, which today I can understand. What noises, after all, did she not have to put up with from us?

Did we call a doctor? I doubt it, because I think I would have retained a picture of him. I went on with my novel. Three days later, you were back on your feet, but for some time thereafter your bed stayed in our room, to the great delight of D., for to her it was a kind of symbol of her official recognition.

. . .

About this time, I got a letter from Boule, telling me that she was finally in Nogales.

I rushed there, relieved of a great weight. Boule had occupied and still occupies an important place in my life, as in yours, Marc. D. had never seen her, but I had often spoken to her about our Boule, and she was well aware of the bonds that united us. I don't think she liked the prospect of her coming to join us.

As for Tigy, she had long since been prepared for this arrival and become resigned to it, pretending that it did not matter to her. Or perhaps in fact it did not? Wasn't she, after all, Mme Georges Simenon? When we sent out the invitations to that big party of ours, she had insisted that the invitations read as follows: "Mr. and Mrs. Georges Simenon / and Miss D. [followed by D.'s full name] / request the pleasure of your company at . . ."

That was somewhat ambiguous. But D. was certainly my accepted companion, and Tigy knew almost none of the people we were inviting. She nevertheless remained the titular woman of the house and wanted to retain that prerogative. I never held that against her, and can understand her. Had she not shared my life, for better and for worse, for over twenty years?

This irritated D., I know. So did Boule's arrival, since Boule shared memories with me almost as old as Tigy's.

She preferred playing the good sport and letting me go to Nogales by myself. We had often driven that wide and almost untraveled road together, sometimes going all the way without seeing more than one or two other cars. It was not yet an expressway, but was perhaps the only road in the United States where there was no speed limit.

This morning I sped down it as fast as my powerful car would go, which was not my usual way of driving. It was two years, if not more, since I had last seen Boule, from whom I had had only infrequent letters with never any very specific news.

Nogales is not an ordinary border town, because the border in fact runs through the middle of it, cutting it in two by a very high fence with a gate as well guarded as the Berlin Wall.

On one side, a small middle-class town, with shops in which everything you want is available. On the other, a typical Mexican village, poor, teeming, many beggars, vegetables, fruit, and meat in uncovered displays swarming with flies. A few larger houses, nonetheless, a lot of unappealing cafés, and, beyond that, a ghetto.

Going from the U.S. into Mexico, cars merely slow down, and the people wave to the policemen and Immigration agents, who wave back.

Going in the other direction, they may be searched in a small building flying the Star-Spangled Banner, they have to have proper identification, and they may have to fill out all sorts of questionnaires.

Boule is on the other side of the fence. I look for the address she gave me in her letter, and find, on a rather well-to-do street, a small Spanish house with an inviting exterior. It is a boardinghouse, with only three or four boarders, all of whom, I suspect, are here awaiting visas, just as Boule is.

A fat, clean-looking Mexican woman with gray hair greets me at the door, and I barely have time to say who I am when Boule, whose room is on the ground floor, comes bursting out. No need to say that we fall into one another's arms, our eyes full of tears.

Alone in the bedroom, behind the closed door, Boule is still crying, with joy, and I find out that her stay in France was worse than I had imagined. The friend—but then, in Paris, people tend to refer to each other as "dear friend" from the very first time they meet—the friend whom I trusted and whom I had instructed to pay a sizable monthly allowance to Boule never did it.

Once Boule had exhausted the sum I had left her for the first period, she lived with kindly Mme Foncrier, the concierge at Place des Vosges, who, on retiring from her position, had rented a small room with kitchen in the neighborhood. The two of them supported themselves by sewing, which Boule had never mentioned to me in her letters, and even now she is letting me learn the truth only reluctantly.

I hold her tenderly, then in a more intimate embrace, on a very clean bed.

"Will it still take long, my fine young gentleman?"

"Did you give the American consul your passport?"

"Yes. He told me to wait."

We go to see him together, a charming, still-young man, who greets us most cordially. Luckily for me, he has read some of my books and wants to know whether I am comfortably settled in Tucson. We talk over a glass of beer. He looks curiously at Boule. I tell him how many years she has been living with our family, how attached my son is to her, and I don't know what else. I must have made myself pretty clear, because I could read the laughter in his eyes.

"Listen, Mr. Simenon, I can understand her impatience and yours, as well as your son's. Administrative routine exists in America as well as in France, and you know how strict our quota system is. Miss Liberge is now third on our list."

"How long should that take?"

"It depends on Washington. Not more than a month."

After two years of waiting, a month now suddenly seems too long to us. However, I don't insist, because government officials don't anywhere like to be hurried.

"Could I drop by again next week?"

"It would be my pleasure."

We have lunch, perhaps at the Grotto. I take her back to her room and cross the fence in the other direction.

I come back three or four days later, for I have sensed that Boule is near the end of her rope. I come back yet again, each time renewing the pleasure of our intimacy, and I see the consul again.

"Maybe in two weeks, Mr. Simenon."

We chat as we drink our cold beer. The temperature here is hotter than in Tucson, perhaps because of the red mountains that surround the city. Good silver mines have been discovered here, and the shops display crafted silver pieces. The pesos are silver too. One of the pioneers who discovered those mines was a Belgian engineer from Liège who had one day gone off seeking adventure in Indian territory.

When he returned to Europe, immensely wealthy, he bought himself an island in the Mediterranean, where I met him with his wife and children. He also owned—for today he is dead—one of the biggest apartments on Paris's Avenue du Bois de Boulogne, now Avenue Foch.

The silver mines are almost exhausted, but copper was discovered practically at the surface of the soil, which explains the reddish coloring of the mesas.

You, my Marc, now burned as red as an Indian, are impatiently awaiting Boule. I think that your mother is eager for her to come too, because she doesn't get along well with our cook. Tigy has trouble learning English, and I have every reason to believe she dislikes having to call D. in to help her.

The latter is probably not unaware that my meetings with Boule are anything but platonic. But she does not mention the matter to me. At the start of our affair, she told me she was not the jealous type, and even today I try to believe that she never was. Our "lays," as she will later call them, do not affect her. Did she ever indeed attach any importance to physical sex? Even with me?

No storm, however, not even when I triumphantly bring Boule, all her papers in order, to our hacienda.

You are excited about it, Marc. You devour her with your eyes, but your joy does not get translated into words.

"My frog!" she says to you. "How you have changed!"

Boule can't take her eyes off you, or stop being amazed by the house, the patios, the garden, but she stops short on seeing the Mexican cook.

I reassure her: "In a week she'll be gone."

She visits the bedrooms, and does not see any for her. "Where will I sleep?"

I lead her up the outside stairs, and on the terrace she finds the little white house, with her own room and her own bath.

"All this for me?"

I am probably the most feverish of the lot, having three women on my hands to harmonize, to get living together in peace. D. and I take Boule on a trip around the city, and I know that she is wondering what her relationship will be with this young woman with black braids, whom she knows only through my letters, and who will be sleeping in my bed.

There is no warmth, only curiosity, in the looks the two of them exchange. Will war break out, or will it be only a cold war?

An invitation comes from Hollywood, signed by Alexandre de Manziarly, consul general of France. A dinner is to be held in the city's most famous restaurant, Romanoff's, run by one Mike Romanoff, who has nothing whatever to do with the family of the czars. The place is often mentioned in the papers. It is frequented by stars, directors, and famous producers, and one has to be known to be welcome there.

A good chance for us to let Tigy and Boule have time to get acquainted again. The invitation is for me and D. No mention of Tigy. Nor does it specify whether it is "white tie" or "black tie." So, because it is not an official affair and the dinner is to be in a restaurant, we take only street clothes with us.

Getting to Los Angeles in the evening, after driving across the desert, we stop at the Beverly Hills, a mind-boggling luxury hotel.

The party is for the next night. I phone Manziarly. We exchange pleasantries. He is a refined man of the world, at ease with the great. He is popular in Hollywood and well liked by the stars, because, instead of making them come down to the consulate, he sends one of his staff out to stamp their passports.

He and we will be following parallel roads for a number of years. I will come across him again as high commissioner of French tourism in New York, then in Switzerland as consul general at Geneva. He will invite me to dinner with former crowned heads, putting me on guard to speak to them as often as possible in the third person, and from time to time to drop in a "Sire" or "Your Majesty."

Now, he says, "Did you bring a tuxedo?"

"No. From your invitation, I didn't think . . ."

"I do apologize. I did, actually, plan to have just an informal dinner. At the last minute, I had to invite some additional people. After dinner, we'll be going elsewhere, and evening dress will be required. I am sorry. Do you have time, by tomorrow . . ."

"Don't give it a second thought. We'll work it out."

"I apologize again. If you find a minute, in spite of all that, drop in to the consulate to say hello. Your companion is with you, isn't she?"

"Yes. You invited her too."

"Will she be able to work things out as well?"

Exhausted, we nonetheless have a fine dinner while watching the beautiful girls swimming, for here as in Texas all the girls are gorgeous. We make love furiously in a setting that is new to us, and go to sleep. Naturally, using only one of the beds in our suite.

Early in the morning, we ask at the desk where the best stores are to find a tuxedo, an evening gown, and everything to go with them. Fortunately, the United States is ten, if not twenty, years ahead of Europe. "Ready-to-wear" can be found here, with the finest labels, and most of the stores are bunched together in two or three blocks.

What worries me the most is the tuxedo. Since my dime-novel days, I have never worn suits off the rack, and I can't imagine what I'll look like in a ready-made tux. As it turns out, clothes here are made in several different sizes, according to width of shoulders, length of arms, legs, and so on. I find one that fits me without alterations and, in the same store, shirts and silk socks as well as patent-leather shoes that don't hurt my feet too much. Plus a black tie, naturally.

For D., it's a little harder. We go from shop to boutique, and from boutique to store, where she tries on I don't know how many long dresses.

"We could have it ready by tomorrow."

"I need it for tonight."

Finally, a black dress that fits. And she looks good in black. We carry the packages to our car.

She still needs an evening coat, or cape, or something to cover her shoulders and her deep décolletage. It is five in the afternoon by the time we discover a light silk white cape that will do.

Shoes, stockings, bag. We go through the same block ten times, and at six o'clock drive back to the hotel. No jewels.

• • •

A dry Martini at the bar. A bellboy takes our boxes and packages through the lobby and up to our suite. We haven't had time to drop in at the consulate. Did we have time for lunch? Probably a hot dog in one of the many cafeterias.

Ready. We smile at each other, and D.'s eyes have never been brighter. Her hands, gloved to the elbows, hold a small gilded bag, which will take the place of jewels.

They tell us at the desk how to get to Romanoff's, and D. tells me which streets to take. There is already a crowd in the big dining room, where almost all the faces look familiar, because we have seen them on the screen.

Manziarly comes to greet us, leads us to a huge bar, where we find even better-known faces. Charlie Chaplin is there, and we are introduced first to him, then to another Charles, Boyer, who, like Chaplin, will become a good friend of mine.

"Jean!"

My old friend Renoir is a little like a brother to me, and his warm old expression hasn't changed. We embrace one another, and we will have occasion to see each other often again in his adorable little home in Beverly Hills, with his second wife, a sweet and cultured Brazilian, with a singing accent, who will be for Jean, until his death, what Teresa has been for me for the last nearly twenty years now. No artifice whatever. Eyes that hide nothing, because they have nothing to hide.

"Well, Georges, old man?"

Jean-Pierre Aumont, whom I met when he was very young, back in the twenties, and who visited me at Porquerolles. Also his brother, later to become a director. Everybody is happy, and a fresh icy glass is constantly being slipped into one's hand.

"Georges!"

"Georges!"

For we are both named Georges. This one is Georges Kessel, whom I used to see a lot of when he and his brother Jef ran the magazine *Détective* for Gallimard. Georges is the best-looking one in the family and could have made a fortune as a gigolo.

I introduce D., and everyone greets her warmly. A few American stars, men and women, who know Paris and speak French. People switch from one language to the other. A captain shows us to a long table, at which I am separated from D., whom I only get a glimpse of from time to time. I think we all had a lot to drink at the bar, without realizing it. Mike Romanoff comes by and shakes hands with all the guests, kissing the hands of the ladies.

He is a small, skinny, stunted man, who nevertheless lords it over all the celebrities in the room.

If I remember eating a lobster mousse, I've forgotten all the rest of the menu. Charles Boyer is sitting next to me, and invites me to visit the Boyer Foundation, in which American film makers can find documentation about everything relevant to France. He also invites me to his home. He has a son your age, Marc, and you will soon meet him in Arizona, where I will give him a collection of local minerals, which are his hobby.

Where do we go after that? To Manziarly's, I think. There is a grand piano in the living room. Chaplin sits down to it and for almost an hour entertains us with wonderful old English ballads.

Some of the guests are sitting on cushions, others right on the rug, informally. Manziarly, who lost a leg in the war, has a wooden one. The scion of a noble old Polish family, he has broad cheekbones, and the light-blue and tender eyes of his compatriots.

A great friend to women, he has much success with them, for they find him "exquisite." That is the right word. Sitting on the floor, he plays a guitar and in a nice voice sings nostalgic songs.

My eyes look for D. and find her in a corner with three or four people. Her face is red with anger, and she is crying as she tries to get up. When I get over to her, worried, she tells me between sobs: "I want to leave right away. You stay, if you feel like it!"

This is the old D. of New York days and the early times at Sainte-Marguerite. She is sitting between Aumont's brother and Georges Kessel, who are trying to calm her down, especially Aumont's brother, who, naïve and timid, it seems to me, has put his hand affectionately on her shoulder.

"What did they do to you?" I ask.

"I won't stand for being insulted and treated with scorn."

The two men look at me, as much as to say nothing of the sort has happened.

"There are people here I will never again set eyes on, even if they are friends of yours."

Kessel winks at me. "We were kidding a little," he says. "We didn't say anything offensive."

I know Georges, a deadpan practical joker, with a terrific sense of humor.

"He's a cad!" D. yells quite loudly, standing, and still crying.

The guests pretend not to notice anything; Manziarly goes right on singing. They applaud. The guitar is softer for another song.

"And aren't you going to do anything about it? Aren't you going to say a thing?"

Am I supposed to come to blows with one of my old friends? From D.'s look I can tell that Georges is the guilty party.

"I just made a play on words, on Canadian. I was referring to the sheepskin coats that are called that." (A mackinaw in French is *une canadienne*, a Canadian, in the feminine.)

"You implied that . . ."

"For the tenth time, I assure you I meant no aspersion on you." Turning toward me, he explains. "I said something like 'In winter, when it's cold, it's good to have a nice warm Canadian, to keep the chill away. . . .' "

"And I repeat that you're nothing but a cad."

I see her again as she was during the most violent storms of our first days together. Only, here we are guests, and all around us, while appearing not to notice, no one is missing a bit of the scene she is making.

Aumont's brother takes her by the arm, leads her toward the door; I follow in confusion. "Do you still want to go?" he asks.

"Yes, even if I have to walk. Walking doesn't scare me."

This reminds me of the only time she really did walk, carrying her shoes, from Greenwich Village way up to Midtown.

Aumont is heartbroken. He had done his best to smooth things over. One can tell he's just the kind who would.

"You don't have to come with me," she says.

She has found her little white silk cape, and we are finally both outside. She stumbles on the sidewalk, and I keep her from falling. I don't hold it against her that she has been drinking. I have been drinking too. I don't hold it against her that she's drunk. I've been drunk in my time too.

I don't really hold anything against her. I only regret having brought her here too soon. The fact is, she is still convalescing, and I realize it will take longer than I had thought for her to . . .

For her to what? To become the real D. again? But what D. is that? I feel torn between my passion and a sort of despair as we get into the car and go back to the hotel.

Once we are there, once she is undressed, she asks, almost innocently: "What will your friends ever think of me? Are you angry with me?"

"No."

"It was that fellow with the dark curly hair."

"I know. Georges. He loves to tease women."

She weeps softly, and we make love with a fury, as we did in the early days.

I am sad. My passion has not gone out. Tomorrow, we will have to act as if nothing had happened, as we take to the road again to return to Tucson.

30

There you are, my Marc, with three women around you, three women vying with one another in showering you with signs of affection and tender, loving care. You are a big eight-year-old, a schoolboy, and history starts for you with Christopher Columbus, the way for French children—even the young French-speaking blacks of the colonies in Africa and Asia—it all starts with their ancestors the Gauls, Vercingetorix, Clovis, and Charlemagne.

Three women in every way different. One of them your mother, who certainly loves you but maintains a kind of stiffness, as she did when I first met her, because of her difficulty with being demonstrative. Did she ever play with a child? She decided to have one only when she was nearing her forties, and as a result she would always feel awkward about it.

Boule, on the other hand, from your earliest days more or less adopted you when she dubbed you her "frog." In her very large family, a girl at five or six took charge of a younger child, who became her "slug," because their mother could not cope with all of them. If she didn't call you a "slug," it was out of a kind of instinctive reserve. While she was waiting in Paris, and then in Mexico for the right to get through the fence that kept her out of the United States, she missed you as much as she did me, and in every letter she mentioned her "frog."

Did Tigy ever forgive her for the shock she got at Saint-Mesmin-le-Vieux, the picture she had before her eyes, the confession I made to her that I had been having intimate relations with Boule since Bénouville?

Tigy was my wife for more than twenty years. During the three years of our engagement, however, our relationship was no different from what it was after the wedding. Since I became engaged at the age of seventeen, she certainly has seniority, and, moreover, she alone became my legal spouse.

At Tucson, she never allowed any animosity toward Boule to show, and Boule did not seem to hold against her the two years she had had to spend in Paris because of your mother's ukase.

Boule is used to children, instinctively understands them, knows how to talk to them, to entertain them.

As for the third woman, she is and will remain to the other two the newcomer, the stranger, the usurper. She, of course, is D., who shares my bed and goes practically everywhere I go.

D. is full of attention for you, full of indulgence too; she is the one who helps you with your homework and drills you in your lessons, because Tigy, for all her good will, will never feel quite at home in the English language, and in that regard Boule, going entirely by instinct, will quickly become more adept than she.

What are you thinking, my big boy, as these three women's faces smile at you?

And of your father, who always observes them with a sneaking sense of disquiet, for fear the peace that he knows to be so fragile might come apart?

From the very first evening, I made sure things were clear to D. In my pajamas and robe, I announced to her: "I'm going up to be with Boule for a little while. She must feel very lonely up there."

D. didn't flinch. Had she not assured me, from our earliest meetings, that she was not jealous? Had it been otherwise, I probably would have had courage enough to break off with her.

By the outside patio stairs, I went up to what I called the bridge, and we spent an hour in hot intimacy.

When I got back to our bedroom, D. said nothing, but cuddled tenderly up to me. After a long silence, she sighed and asked, hesitatingly: "Did you make love?"

"Yes."

Then she insisted on having her turn.

I felt for Tigy, as I still do today, a friendship that was colored by all our shared memories, in addition to a perhaps naïve faithfulness to the vow taken by a very young man, hardly more than a boy.

Other links, both carnal and tender, bound me to Boule, more of a woman than your mother.

As for D., I remained under the spell of a passion that had seized me during our first nights together in New York and clung to my skin. Yet I was lucid about it. If I kept trying to get her to return to the simplicity she had so badly been lacking, the Hollywood incident had just proved to me how far I was from my goal.

Which was the real D.? A first contact with some of my friends, in a milieu where I was at ease but to which she had never before had access, was enough to make her revolt. Did she feel inferior? To whom? To what? To me, the individual alone is what counts, whoever he or she may be, and I have never accepted one person's superiority over another because of the social class in which they had artificially been placed.

I wanted to instill self-confidence in her, and I was going to get an opportunity to. A major Hollywood studio had made an offer for the movie rights to one of my short stories, "Sept petites Croix dans un carnet" ("Seven Little Crosses in a Notebook").

So we went back to the world's most artificial city, where a person is worth only as much as the salary he gets, and has to live, whether he likes it or not, up to the standard of that salary.

In Hollywood, this time, where one gets into a studio only if authorized and an armed guard phones from the gate to find out whether one is really the person the boss is expecting, I decided to let D. have her head. My English, good enough for everyday use, was not up to negotiating specific contract terms.

I could have taken an interpreter along, as statesmen do when they go abroad. I have always handled my negotiations in person, for book rights, films, and radio, without using a lawyer or, what is worse, an agent. And D. is to find herself up against not only the important principal, but also a specialized lawyer as well. I give her my instructions, and I am surprised at how well she handles the matter, so I am able to sign the contract.

Was I wrong? Was I right to give her this satisfaction and thus the sense of self-confidence?

By one of those paradoxes of the American studios, the film, which was to take place in Paris, would be shot, not in the U.S., but in Mexico.

We had a good time going to dinner at the home of good old Jean Renoir, who, in the unassuming house he had built, had included a baker's oven, in which he could make his own French bread.

Around Jean and Dido, his wife, the atmosphere is always friendly and relaxed. With his sort of babyish face, his eyes that might be taken for naïve yet see through to all the human truths, he knows how to make everyone feel comfortable, even D., whom he more or less took under his wing.

A bit of a joker, that evening he pulled a trick on his guests. He solemnly uncorked bottles of fine French wines, saying, "What do you think of this Château-Latour?" His guests, all being "wine connoisseurs," find it wonderful. Then, "How about this Châteauneuf-du-Pape?" And they all applaud, and almost religiously sip it.

At the end of the meal, Jean mischievously informs them, "Well, children, what you drank tonight are California wines. Not the ones you can buy at the supermarket, but the kind that can be reserved at small vineyards."

He goes and gets the original bottles, from which he had decanted the wine into the ones with the authentic French labels.

I could go on about Jean and Dido for hours, just as he can talk endlessly about the people he likes.

D. and I visit the movie studios. We go to see the homes of the stars, not in one of those tourist buses, but at random in our own car, which here doesn't attract any attention at all.

Back to Tucson, which we will soon be leaving, for the year we finally were allowed is up and the delightful Mrs. K. wants to move back home and do her housecleaning with all her diamonds on.

On the road from Tucson to Nogales, there was in 1948 a village, or, more correctly, a hamlet of a few houses, called Tumacacori. During the year, D. and I had had a chance to crisscross Arizona in all directions. With you, Marc, we had been to the village of the Papagos. I call it a village because nothing in it looks like a reservation. It is truly a village, with nice little houses, surrounding a mission church, all white, dating back to the Spanish period.

The Indians here cultivate their own little plots of ground, own horses and cows, dress in blue jeans and white shirts, the women in cotton print dresses. They are cordial and hospitable. The same day, by contrast, we also went to a ghost town, like so many others in the desert. They were built, in times gone by, by gold or silver prospectors. The rudimentary houses are made of clay and red sand, and one can still see the signs of the cafés, the gambling dens, and the whorehouses. The mine once exhausted, everyone moved on, leaving what had been a village or town to go to seed.

"But nothing has fallen apart here, Dad."

"That's because this one is a fake ghost town, built for movie-location purposes. The film makers might have selected any one of a number of real ghost towns, some in California, others in Nevada. They preferred to build a new one, to suit their needs, and then leave it as is."

You think that's funny. You record it mentally, without saying much.

This time we don't leave Tucson to go on farther, toward some unspecified goal, as we have so often done before. We came here looking for wide-open spaces, and Tucson, built in the middle of the desert, won our hearts.

What would you say now to living right in the desert itself, to riding freely in the sand among the cactus and the few twisted, stunted bushes, to going with the cowboys as they take their herds from one point to another? That is what lies ahead of us, son, at Tumacacori, less than a half hour by car from Nogales and Mexico, fifty minutes from Tucson.

A few houses scattered around a store where they sell just about every kind of thing, among others over twenty different brandies, some thirty whiskeys, not to mention French, Italian, and California wines, liqueurs, spices, and what all! The post office? It is in one corner of the general store. The school? Founded by the local ranchers for their ranch hands' children, and some of them send their own children to it too.

You will have schoolmates who are Mexican or Indian. In this school, the students feel really at home. To the point that, when we come for you, you will often ask, "Can't I stay another quarter of an hour, Dad?"

You dress like the others and, thank God, you make no difference among the races, between the daughter of a wealthy rancher and the daughter of a Mexican cowboy.

We move, and this time Tigy, who has always had to handle it, is helped by Boule. The house is not far from the ranch gate, a modest house that was once a schoolhouse. Dining room. Three bedrooms. Bathrooms. Sand and cactus all around.

The home of the rancher on whose land we are living is three or four hundred yards away, all white, with a big colonnaded patio. The W.s are nice people and hospitable. How much land do they own? We never got to the ends of it, and it is not fenced in.

There not being enough room for us, D. and I occupy a strange building on the other side of an arroyo. It is very low, with the kind of split stable doors that one can open the top or the bottom of, or both halves at once. A large room with barred windows, and in its middle a tree growing right up through the roof and beyond.

It is not really a house, but is called "the stud barn," because it was the place mares were brought to be covered.

The veranda, of slightly rotting wood, has the refrigerator on it. The very small bedroom must have been used by the stallion's keeper. A butane heater in a corner, two or three armchairs, a long table in front of one of the windows, which I will use as a desk.

W. is young, very tall, dark, dressed in jeans and a white shirt, just like his cowhands. He is married to one of the prettiest Mexican women I have ever seen, and one of the most charming and spontaneous. She is passionately interested in art, literature, and music. Especially music. In the large living room, thousands of records are stacked, facing as many books.

They have a little girl younger than you, who is just as attractive as her mother, and whom you will awkwardly play big brother to.

That's not all, Marc. They are building a wooden stable near the stud barn. We are going to buy some horses. The first one is a real cowboy horse, fiery in temperament and rust-colored, which you will dub "Red." D., not being as experienced as you, will have a gentler one, and mine will be a golden palomino, with white mane and tail, which I will name "Sunday." Isn't it as good-looking as a horse decked out in its Sunday best? Your mother did not want to have a horse.

Sometimes it is Tigy, sometimes we who take you to school, when you don't go there with some of your school chums. How many different little chums you will have had during your childhood!

The space between our two houses is nothing but sand, and there is only one house to be seen, far off to the left. On the advice of W., with whom I am soon on friendly terms, I buy a .38-caliber pistol, such as the movie cowboys use. They sell them here the way they sell chewing gum, no permits or explanations needed.

I always keep that impressive, loaded gun in the glove compartment of the car, or close at hand when I am indoors. At the stud barn, we are completely isolated, and we are told that prisoners sometimes escape from the closely guarded penitentiary at Yuma and make a desperate dash for the Mexican border. The sheriff gives almost anyone a deputy's badge, because when one of those prison breaks occurs, he calls on all hands to help him form a posse.

Aren't you living in a dream? To be sure, there are a lot of rattlesnakes, not perhaps around your house, but around the stud barn.

One day, Boule sees some black spiders, not very large ones, with red marks, and when she goes after them, they take refuge in the air shaft of your bedroom. She tells us about it at noon. Neither she nor Tigy has ever heard of these beasties, but D. and I turn pale. They are black widows, and their sting is mortal.

Boule is repelled equally by snakes and spiders. Very cautiously, using a broom handle, we drive a whole bunch of black widows out of the air shaft, and the next week we have an exterminator in from Nogales, to fumigate the old schoolhouse as well as the stud barn.

When you come over to visit us, you come on horseback. There are two gates to go through, and you jump off your mount to open them and then close them. One would have thought you had been born here. On your first vacation, you will go with the cowhands as they round up the herds. Naturally, they have all become your friends, and one day I see you, alone on Red, bringing back some stray cattle.

You had acquired a Southern accent. Here you start sounding Mexican, just like your pals.

I have bought a typewriter for D., because the keyboard of an American machine is different from the French keyboard of the one I have dragged with me everywhere and which I am very much attached to.

At the W.s', where we often stop off to drink a refreshing mint julep, the true Southern and Southwestern drink, we met what were called the "neighboring" ranchers, which meant people living anywhere from forty to eighty miles away.

The scale of distances here is not what it is in the rest of the United States, and even less what it is in Europe.

We all visit one another, if only for a mint julep. Or for dinner. We drink. We finally decide to finish the evening at another ranch, where the group gets bigger, and then at still another one. These parties may go on for two days and two nights, if not three.

I write my first novel about the real desert, and Hollywood will make it into a film: *Le Fond de la bouteille (The Bottom of the Bottle)*.

I sometimes leave the stud barn alone to go and pick you up or go riding with you. In that case, D. keeps the impressive revolver alongside her typewriter. In the beginning, she is very much afraid of the Mexicans who come by every so often on their way to California.

They are the poorest ones, some of them part Indian. How did they get across so well guarded a border without any papers? I still wonder. They keep off the roads, walk endlessly through the desert, thirsty and hungry.

By chance, the stud barn is on their way. When they see us, they come forward hesitantly, and we give them some bread, two or three cans of sardines, and some cans of beer. They don't speak English. They go on off toward some big field or orange grove or apple orchard where they will be hired at very low wages because they are illegals. Their arms are needed in the "agribusiness." Legal residence papers are hard to come by, and those who have them demand better wages.

When D. and I are both out, we leave the veranda open and on it enough sardines, bread, and beer for some of these wanderers, whom we rarely see, but who discreetly help themselves.

One day when two or three men had gone by in this way, and we had fed them, the sheriff rides up with a uniformed posse.

"Did you see any Mexicans go by?"

We don't say yes or no. We are foreigners here too, and the laws are strict.

"Which way did they go?"

I look toward D., who can lie much better than I while keeping a straight face.

"I can't say for sure. I heard some voices, in the distance."

"Didn't you see them?"

"Just outlines, through the window."

"Which way were they headed?"

"I can't say for sure, but I guess that way. . . ."

She points to the faraway mesas. The sheriff and his posse trot off in the wrong direction. Good Lord, how well she lies! For once, I appreciate it. I would have answered the way she did, but not as convincingly, and would probably not have been believed.

Your mother takes another trip to Europe, and since Boule is afraid to stay in the house alone with you, we have to go over there to sleep. And I have to get up early every morning to go and look after the horses, feed them, and clean up their stalls. Sometimes all three of us, with W. and his wife, ride over to the mesas, and on the way we often see the blanched bones of a cow devoured by coyotes.

At the stud barn, we hear them all around us, maybe a hundred yards away, at night. In the light of the moon, there may be as many as fifty of them baying at it. They are so smart that they keep out of all the traps set for them. They are our friends, even though we would rather they let us sleep.

The days go by peacefully. D. gnaws away little by little at what I consider to be my prerogatives, and hands me letters to sign that I never dictated. She needs two pages to say what I would have said in half a page, but I don't dare discourage her. Yet I know I am wrong to be giving her so much rope. She would also, I am aware, like to be handling my European correspondence, but since all my publishers over there are friends, especially Sven Nielsen, I remain firm on that point.

Your mother must have stayed away a month, and all she has to tell me when she gets back is that on board a French ship she met a famous crooner, with whom she got along swimmingly. I don't ask any further questions about that.

I have bought a Winchester, and you practice shooting next door to the old schoolhouse, at a wooden panel on which I hang targets. You soon show as much aptitude with the rifle as you did on horseback.

"Dad! Couldn't you teach me to shoot a revolver too?"

You are red-hot with a long-suppressed desire. Why not, after all? In these open spaces, no danger of your hitting anyone.

"Do you realize that there will be a very strong recoil?"

"I don't care."

I take the revolver out of the glove compartment and put up another target.

"You hold it like this, and raise your arm slowly, until . . ."

"I know. I've seen how it's done."

Three shots go wild. The fourth is on target, as well as one of the next two. You don't ask me to reload the gun, and I know that your arm hurts all the way up to the shoulder.

While at the stud barn, I write *La Première Enquête de Maigret (Maigret's First Case)*, *Les Fantômes du chapelier (The Hatter's Ghost)*, and *Mon ami Maigret (My Friend Maigret)*.

D. and I went all sorts of places, but this is not intended to be a tourist guide. You often went with us, Marc, curious, but as impassive as a cowboy.

One day I suggested to D. and you that we have some riding lessons in a corner of the desert that seemed suited to it. You didn't have anything to learn, but D. could not control her mount with the required assurance.

Standing alongside the ring, which our horses had marked out in the sand, I played drill sergeant and shouted my commands, as long ago in Liège at the barracks riding school.

It didn't go too badly for a while. The sun was as scorching as ever, but didn't affect us.

"A lighter hand, D. . . . Don't stick your feet out . . . Trot . . . Gallop . . ."

D. probably held the reins too tightly. Her horse reared its head, and she was thrown off. There was only one pile of stones beside the ring, but that was what she fell on.

I was farther from her than you, Marc, and I saw you rush by, at full tilt, hop from your saddle alongside her, and bend down. When I got to you, she was moaning, not moving, her face covered with sand and red earth, blood on her cheek and hands.

"Go get help from the ranch, Marc."

You took off again on horseback while I tried to comfort D., who kept looking at me with supplicating eyes. I didn't want to turn her over, because that can be dangerous.

Some cowboys came with my car. Her spine did not appear to be affected. I knew that the doctor in Nogales, who was the closest one, could not leave his large practice to come out here. I took a risk, I realize. We stretched D. out on the back seat, and I drove away slowly. One of the cowhands had given me half a bottle of whiskey.

Very imprudent of me. I was wild with fear, because she was moaning more and more, so I put the bottle to her lips and, after taking a swig, she seemed calmer.

Halfway to Nogales, she murmured, "Give me another drink, Jo. If you only knew how I hurt . . ."

"Where?"

"In the head, the arm, the ribs, everywhere."

I gave her the bottle again and then took a drink myself in the hope of calming down. I knew where there was a small hospital that looked like a convent, run by some sisters.

As if in a nightmare, I mechanically answered the questions of the Mother Superior.

"Can I see her?"

"After the doctor gets here, if he says so."

I went to have dinner at the Grotto and came back to the hospital, where I waited a long time in a bare, silent room.

The doctor came to speak to me.

"I don't think it's very serious. But we'll have to keep her for observation a few days. Now, she's asleep and won't wake up all night. I'll be back tomorrow morning."

"Can't I see her?"

"It would be to no purpose. Now, tell me just how it happened."

Explained in so many words, my behavior sounded so silly that I was embarrassed.

"Tomorrow morning, about nine . . ."

What would I do in the meantime? I first had to reassure Marc, and tell Boule and Tigy what was happening.

I didn't know that a new legend was about to be born: one about a snake coiled around the horse's right leg, which had caused her mount to bolt.

A bad night. And all because I had wanted to play drill sergeant!

31

I spent a very agitated night, alone such a long time, in the bed of a very adequate hotel in Nogales. I kept seeing, and would keep on seeing, the pathetic picture of D. covered with sand, dirt, and blood, as if disjointed and almost unrecognizable on the pile of stones. The doctor's words had not completely reassured me, and I was upset at not having been allowed to stay with her.

Despite my surface assurance, I am rather a worrier, especially where people I love are concerned, and I have a tendency always to feel responsible for whatever happens to them. The thought of having hurt anyone, even a stranger, is enough to make me feel remorse.

Hadn't it all been my fault? Because her mother had had a horse when she was young, D. had fancied herself an expert horsewoman right away. I had selected the oldest, least excitable horse for her. But she tried to keep up with us. I should have calmed her down, explained to her that before World War I the army took five years to train a cavalryman.

At the hospital, I waited in the little white room where a crucifix on the wall was the only decoration. The doctor finally came in. I had only vaguely recognized him the day before. He was the one we had once called to Tumacacori to take care of me, at ten in the morning, because of chest pains and heart palpitations. I was still, in spite of everything, in spite of the reassurances of the old cardiologist in Paris, thinking of my father's fatal angina, which, as child and then adolescent, I had seen develop in its various phases.

That was not the first time I had had such distress, and I had learned from the doctor that nothing resembles angina pains as much as those brought on by aerophagia.

"Well, doctor?"

"I've looked at her X-rays. No fracture of any kind, either skull or any of the limbs. However, your young lady has multiple contusions, all over her body. Her left leg got the most, and I'm concerned about possible phlebitis."

"She won't have a cerebral thrombosis, will she?"

"When there's a clot, thrombosis is always a danger if it is not dissolved in time. I have given her some anticoagulants. In my opinion, there is nothing for you to worry about."

"Do you think I should wire her mother or her brothers? As you know, she and I are in a somewhat delicate situation."

"Yes, I know. But I wouldn't do that. If any complications should arise, I would be the first to suggest that you keep her family advised. Incidentally, what's this business about a snake having wound itself around the horse's right leg, causing it to bolt?"

"Is that what she told you?"

"Yes. She's lucid, and quite voluble. What kind of snake was it? Did you see it?"

"Neither my son nor I saw any snake. And she was never out of our sight."

He smiled. "In my whole professional life, I never before heard of a snake doing that."

"When can I see her?"

"In a little while. I suggest that you not stay with her too long, because talking gets her excited. Come and see her if you wish two or three times a day, but for the time being keep your visits short. She has an excellent nurse looking after her. This is a private religious hospital, and I am only a consultant here. I'll be back this afternoon, when I get done with my other patients."

"Will she have to stay in the hospital long?"

"As long as that phlebitis hasn't been eliminated." He smiled at me optimistically.

I go to her along the veranda that runs around the patio. A merry young nun shows me the way, saying, "Don't tire her out."

She opens a door, and I see D. in bed, her eyes open, looking very pale. Her eyes are shinier, tenderer than ever, and I also feel tender toward her, a tenderness that I don't know how to put into words.

"Did I give you a lot of worry, Jo? Did you go back to the ranch to sleep? How is Marc? He was just wonderful. He was the one I was most worried about when I saw that horse rear. . . ."

"I slept at the hotel. How do you feel?"

"I ache all over, especially in the head. What did the doctor tell you? I hope you didn't phone my family."

"I almost did. When I asked the doctor, he told me not to, and swore you weren't in any kind of danger."

I would like to kiss her, but don't dare, because of how weak she looks.

Her body, beneath the sheet, seems to have lost weight, to be almost lifeless, and yet, as I had been told, she talks most animatedly.

"Are they going to keep me here a whole week? Are you sure they have to? To think that that snake . . ."

I do not flinch, even look as if I am agreeing with her, but for years and years I am going to go on hearing about that nonexistent reptile. At the moment, it does not upset me. On the contrary, I feel slightly moved by her need to make up a spectacular truth for herself. For, to her, it is already a truth, and nothing will ever get her to change her mind about it.

I was wrong. As I had been wrong to plunge her without warning into a world she was not familiar with, to let her see all my friends warmly gathered around me. It was much too soon. Her running afoul of them, what she considered to be her humiliation, had to be translated into something dramatic.

I love her. I convince myself of it there by her hospital bed, and if anyone told me this was passion and not love, I would be the one to get angry. I also have the image of her, in pain, moaning, on the back seat of the car, gluing her lips to the bottle in the hope of easing her pain. Incidentally, I forgot to say before that the doctor scolded me for that.

"You made a serious mistake in letting her have a drink of liquor, Mr. Simenon. If she had sustained injuries that required surgery, I would not have been able to give her an anesthetic."

Now I remember what I answered. It's all been happening so fast since yesterday afternoon!

"Your colleagues, before the second half of the last century, operated without anesthetics. They merely knocked the patient out, sometimes with punches, or else had him drink a pint or more of rum, even when, because of gangrene, they had to amputate his leg."

I don't mention any of that to D. I would love to hug her, to squeeze her to death with my tenderness, and her eyes look tenderly at me too.

She says: "I just remembered that, when I was twenty, I had a friend who was an insurance man. He practically forced me to take out an accident policy. I kept the payments up, out of superstition. You'll find my last receipt and the address in my drawer."

The little nun with the pink cheeks and innocent eyes knocks at the door and says I should let D. rest now. Besides, it's time for her "to be taken care of," a phrase I detest. Am I reassured now? Or, to the contrary, even more worried?

There is nothing for me to do for hours, and in the heat walking in the almost empty streets is out of the question. Nor can I stay locked in my too-characterless hotel room. I don't feel like reading. I go through the gate, have lunch at the Grotto.

In the afternoon, D. seems less pale to me. When I mention the Grotto to her, she asks: "Did you request *'Bésame mucho'*? I knew you would."

With her, I wait for the doctor, who then asks me to step outside, and he seems to me to be taking a very long time. I imagine him examining D.'s naked body. I confess that I am jealous, just as, in some hidden little corner of myself, I remain jealous of her past.

The doctor is reassuring. She does have a bit of phlebitis, but it doesn't seem serious. Not enough anyway, he says, to warrant anticoagulants any stronger than the ones he's been giving her.

"When do you think that . . ."

"Are you in a hurry to get her back to the ranch? I can understand that. It depends somewhat on you."

"On me? How?"

"If everything goes as I expect, she could go back there in about ten days, on one condition. You would have to rent a hospital bed for her, which is easy. And then, I could find you a private nurse, who would stay with you and whom I could give the necessary instructions."

"Is that really possible?" It seems wonderful to me.

"You'll have to rent a folding bed for the nurse, too. And since she'll be with you around the clock, you'll have to feed her as well. That reminds me. Your friend just told me that she carries accident insurance. You should inform the insurance company. Let the Mother Superior know about it."

The latter, when she sees me, smiles encouragingly at me. "The doctor has just told me that our patient is insured. I must make a note of the name and address of the company. We religious have paperwork to do too, you know."

Nogales to Tumacacori is only a matter of eighteen miles, on a fairly deserted road. I talk to myself as I drive. In the old schoolhouse, I find Marc, still worrying, Boule, and Tigy, to whom I give the reassuring news. You ask permission to come to the stud barn with me.

"She's not going to die, is she, Dad?"

"No, of course not, son."

I make a joke of it. To a question you ask me, I answer that she is not allowed visitors.

"What about you?"

"That's not the same thing."

You answer solemnly, "I understand."

In the old stable, there is the little maid we hired when we first took over the stud barn, the pure-blooded young Indian girl, whose father has a brickmaking shop and lives in one of the hamlet's houses. She has a round face, with prominent cheekbones, but she is pretty and always smiling.

"How is the missus?"

I reassure her and burrow through the drawer I have never opened before, which has nothing in it but letters from her family. I discover the insurance policy and the receipt for the last eighty-dollar premium. The two typewriters, on the desk, about three feet apart, have their covers on, and that gives me a strange feeling.

"When will you both be back, Dad?"

"In about ten days."

I go to see the owner of the ranch and ask him to have one of his hands look after the horses while we are away. He treats me to the customary mint julep.

Our young Indian girl will go on cleaning the place, because the desert sand gets in everywhere, as do the cockroaches, so prevalent in the South and the Southwest, which even, no one knows how, often get into the refrigerator.

"I can ride Red while you're away, can't I?"

This is December 1948, and you're a big strong nine-year-old, afraid of nothing, and yet always careful. I trust you.

Remember the date, because it will have a great bearing on our future, even though neither of us suspects it.

Back to Nogales, the Grotto, the hotel, and my lonely bed. I feel suspended in time, in a vacuum.

D. seems more alive. The head of her bed has been raised, not very much, but enough to make her look better.

"You must feel bored, eh, Jo?"

"What about you? You're the one . . ."

"Sister Julia is very nice. There's only one thing I can't stand: the food. Just seeing it takes my appetite away."

"What are you allowed?"

"Anything I want. The doctor wants me to eat so as to get some strength back. I can order things from outside."

"What, for instance?"

"Steaks, vegetables, fruit."

"I'll see to it. You know that soon you'll be able to . . ."

"With a hospital bed and private nurse. I know. You won't have to stay up with me. The doctor knows a very nice one."

In a hardware store, I get three small saucepans that fit one into the other. Henceforth, each noon and evening I'll have them filled with a whole meal and carry fruit in a plastic bag. It keeps us busy, planning meals, which is fine, because there isn't all that much else to talk about. Conversation is not easy when one person is lying down and the other, standing or sitting, knows he should not bring up too many outside matters.

"Do you miss me very much?"

"You know I do."

"I mean . . ." and her eloquent smile tells me what she doesn't put into words. "Why don't you go and see our girl friends, up on the hill?" Now she is smiling like a secret sharer, which is what she is. "It would make me happy if you did."

I did go, not that evening, but the next one. The Grotto was where we had first heard about that rather strange house to which D. and I had often gone. Halfway up the hill, a rather large building of red adobe, like the hill itself. Inside, a bar as long as the one at the ghost town of Tombstone. Fifty feet long? I'm afraid I may be exaggerating, but the longest bar I've ever seen.

A cool room, big electric fans with wooden blades lazily turning at the ceiling. Around one of the tables, six or eight girls babbling in a language we don't recognize, neither Spanish, nor English, nor Indian. A little of each. Some of them are sewing or knitting. All are young and pretty.

We spent many an evening there, and D. became a great favorite of the girls, whose language she was soon able to handle. After a while, she would say to me: "Well, Jo? Why not have Marina? She's dying for it."

So was I. And it excited D. to see me go off with Marina or one of the others. While I was making love, she held court in the middle of a friendly, respectful little circle.

The atmosphere was very relaxed, with nothing prurient about it, as if this were a place without sin or shame, even though it's a very Catholic area.

She talks to a young girl. "She says she's thirteen years old, but that she's been nubile for a long time already. After all, I was at nine."

She will often mention that when she was nine she had her first period, but without ever getting me to believe it.

The girl has huge black eyes that attentively gaze at me, and I have the feeling I'm reading a prayer in them that I fully understand. The point is for her not to lose face in front of her older, more developed companions, who are looking at her and smiling.

I go off with her unenthusiastically. I have never been attracted to very young girls, nor indeed to virgins. I go with the little Indian girl, who carries herself with great dignity, like the black women of the African bush country, only so as not to hurt her.

In the whitewashed room, with a crucifix in the place of honor and on the dresser a Virgin Mary under glass, she drops her red cotton dress, under which there is nothing but her bare little body, well-shaped breasts, pubis already shadowed by a slight black down.

She talks to me, and I don't know what she's saying. She motions to me to get undressed too, and when I don't, she comes over, both forthright and proud, and frees my penis, which she warmly caresses. Embarrassed, furious at myself, I am unable to keep from getting an erection. Then, triumphantly, she lies down on the bed, spreads her legs, and with her delicate brown fingers spreads the lips of her vagina.

I shake my head, and she begins to pout. Then I make an effort to caress her, and am surprised to find how womanly her reactions are. She is not pretending, for very shortly my hand is wet and she tautens in a paroxysm of orgasm. I am not proud of what I've done, motion to her to get up, and hand her her dress. She gives me a quick little kiss on the lips before closing the door behind her, then walks proudly toward the circle of her coequals, and resumes her place among them.

That red hill is where D. is sending me now, and I confess that I'm not unhappy to be going there. At almost every one of our visits, there are one or two new girls, and they are usually the ones I go with. They are nothing like the women one meets in similarly hospitable houses in Paris, even the fanciest ones, where bourgeois housewives come and earn enough in an hour to beef up their wardrobes unbeknownst to their husbands.

Nothing sneaky here, no pretense, nothing to hide, no fake dignity. No playacting, either. Is it because of the local climate, the mixture of races, the proximity of the border? Almost all the customers are Americans, with fancy cars like mine, and sometimes they come from far away.

The girls are surprised to see me alone. I explain to them to the best of my ability that D. has had an accident, but that it isn't serious.

"Poor thing!" they say, or at least that's what I understand them to. The little Indian girl stares intently at me, and, in order not to let her down, I make sure to take her with me, along with another girl, who has utterly splendid breasts.

"Well?" D. wants to know the next morning. "Did you go? Weren't they surprised not to see me?"

"I told them about you, and they were happy that it wasn't serious."

She wants to hear all about it in detail. "What about the little Indian girl?"

I talk and talk, and can feel that she is being turned on. Her hand is at her crotch. I can tell from the folds of the sheet.

The next day, her bed has been rolled out on the patio, in the shade.

"I wanted to surprise you," she says. "They promised yesterday that they would."

I have rented the hospital bed, along with the folding cot. The nurse, in her thirties, is well built, seems to know her business, and will make a phone report to the doctor every evening.

I drive up alone, slowly, ahead of the ambulance. The hospital bed is in our bedroom, from which our own bed has been removed. D. is beaming. We can now kiss each other several times a day, and I am allowed to fondle her breasts.

Each morning, I go for supplies at the grocery–post office. I help our Indian maid prepare meals. She is happy; she is engaged to an Indian boy, is to be married in a few weeks, and we are invited to the wedding. D. will be up and about by then.

Her bed now has a kind of trapeze over it, for her to pull herself up on, because the doctor wants her to start getting some exercise, gradually.

January 1949. Always important dates, my big Marc. For, now, soon, you will not be the only one I am talking to in this. For a while, you won't be the main character anymore.

The days go by without incident. D.'s color has come back. Boule comes to see us from time to time, and I often stop at the onetime schoolhouse when you are there. Tigy is friendly.

The almost constant presence of the nurse, nice and merry though she is, is beginning to get on our nerves. When she finally does leave, the two of us are alone together in our tiny house, from five in the afternoon on, that is, as soon as our Indian maid goes home for the night.

We lost no time in taking advantage of the fact, prudently at first, in a superficial way. D. is still bedridden, and I am the one now who takes care of her. She has never been so relaxed. She has the smile of a convalescent and wants to know everything that goes on outside, where I am now sleeping on the folding cot.

I take time to answer the most urgent mail, and she is anxious to read the incoming letters.

One evening, when I am getting her ready for the night, and she is naked, without any black-and-blue marks left, I ask her softly, "Do you think I might . . . ?"

She understands. She is radiant. "Of course, you idiot! The bed is strong enough to hold us both."

I possess her cautiously, feeling that she is too fragile. Her body barely responds to mine, as if it were numb. Her orgasm and mine are both without paroxysms, without shudderings.

Since the third month back in Sainte-Marguerite, I had not taken any precautions. Didn't that mean I was ready to accept responsibility for whatever might happen? That is now three years behind us, three years that have gone by without the slightest suggestion of any pregnancy.

During the next ten or fifteen days, we make love every evening, always with the same sweetness.

And now, you, Johnny, are the one I have to start telling this to, for there is every reason in the world to believe that it was on that hospital bed, but in our own bedroom, that you were conceived. In a stud barn, of all places. And do you know that the relationship between a stallion and a mare is very tender, that they caress each other at length before there is any insertion?

Because of D.'s accident and her convalescence, our relations were cloudless, stormless, and it was in that atmosphere of peace and loving care that you were given life, my boy.

We didn't know it yet for a while. We also did not know that your birth would change the course of our lives, Marc's, Boule's, Tigy's, as well as those of beings whom we didn't know and who would for a while still remain in limbo.

Greetings! My Johnny to be! In a month, I will be advised of your existence and begin impatiently waiting for your arrival.

32

It is said that convalescence brings us a renewal. And it's true, as I have been able to see several times during my long life. The sky is blue, the air warm and dry, the nights voluptuously refreshing and lulled by the coyotes. One gets used to anything, and by now we look upon them as friends serenading us.

D. has lost weight, and when the nights are too cool I light some logs on the hearth, wake up later on to add more. They smell good. After the first steps indoors, first steps outside, in the sand that is all around us, and soon the car will again take us at noon and in the evening to the old schoolhouse for our family meals.

You exist, Johnny, but we will not know it for a week. We don't go horseback riding, but I've begun again to groom our horses morning and night. Marc comes to get Red on his days off from school, and the ranch's cowhands now take him along as a matter of course.

He has learned that when passing near grazing cattle one has to slow to a walk so as not to frighten them. I learned that myself, in Charente and in the Vendée, and as a result the outspoken Westerners pay me a compliment that most of the rich tenderfeet would give a great deal to get. To begin with, they are amazed to see how I ride on so short and narrow a saddle, without a pommel. When they saw me bring Sunday to a walk as we got near the cattle they said to me: "Well, Mr. Simenon, anyone can see you're no dude!"

Neither are you, Marc.

Five weeks later, D. and I go to Tucson to see the man recommended to us as the city's best gynecologist. I had first asked whether there wasn't a female gynecologist thereabouts, for I do not appreciate the intrusion of a man into an intimacy I would like for myself alone.

I sit in the waiting room. Anxiously? When D. comes back to me, she says the doctor still can't say for sure and that we'll have to return at three in the afternoon.

Lunch at the Pioneer. We are calm, full of smiles, but keep checking our watches more often than usual. We hardly dare talk, and certainly not about you. At last, 3:00 P.M. The doctor good-naturedly greets us with "Guilty! Very, very guilty!"

I can still remember his hearty trencherman's laugh and his joy at seeing our joy radiate from us.

The guilty gag is one that he must use for every patient, every couple that comes in hanging on his words. He gets up and congratulates us with a handshake so overly hearty that it makes our knuckles ache.

"Come back and see me in a month. Then every month after that, till the sixth or seventh, after which I'll want to see you every week. And each time you come in, bring a urine specimen." Then he adds, "Get plenty of exercise, but no horseback riding."

Your mother must have mentioned that to him.

"I also suggest that you don't smoke, don't eat very spicy or fatty foods. As little salt as possible."

Then I ask him, "What about sex?"

"Until the third month—that is, two months more. After that, my dear sir, you'll just have to do without, I'm afraid."

We laugh at his jokes. He sees us out, and we immediately head for a small hotel with a reputation for tolerance. They give us the key to a room, and we fall into each other's arms, very moved, panting slightly. In no time, we will be naked and take advantage till we're breathless of the merry gynecologist's prescription. It's practically our way of greeting you, my Johnny! We are happy on the way back to Tumacacori. D. asks, "Are you going to tell them, Jo?"

"Tomorrow or the day after. After all, they're entitled to know."

You, Marc, will be the first to hear, from me, that you are going to have a little brother or a little sister. Several times, you had said to D. in the past: "Why don't you give me a little brother, D.?"

Well, now it's done, and D. is dead certain about it: "It'll be a boy. I feel it."

It doesn't matter to me if she is wrong. But our cowboy Marc would like it to be a boy, because he can already envision himself riding through the desert with him.

I take Boule aside, and confide in her: "My little Boule, we're going to have a baby."

Her eyes get big and tears dart from them. From the heart, she cries out, "What about me?"

I understand all the contradictory feelings in those words. The same thing happened when Marc was born. She wondered then whether she would still have the same place in our lives, in my life.

She adores children. She wonders how Tigy is going to take it, and I don't know myself yet. I'm optimistic, and won't let anything get in the way of my happiness.

"I have great news to tell you, Tigy."

She pales, as though she knew what was coming, as if she expected it.

"D. is going to have a baby."

"Oh? When?"

"In the fall."

I hadn't counted the months and just tossed that off.

"What have you decided to do about it?" she asks seriously.

"What is there to decide? We'll just go on as we are."

"Haven't you thought of getting a divorce?"

I say no, unthinkingly. I haven't thought of it. Aren't we all fine just as we are?

"Is that a promise?" she asks.

I answer yes, without taking time to think it over. The fact is, I have never much believed in marriage and have often said, even later on television, that it's insane for people of twenty or twenty-five, or even older couples, to go before a justice of the peace, or judge, or priest, and make a commitment to love each other all their lives.

How can one know at the start how each will develop? Twenty years later, the cells are no longer the same; a different woman and a different man will be facing one another, chained by the promise they made back then. When we came together, Tigy didn't believe in such commitments either, whatever they might be. We got married only because our parents would never otherwise have allowed us to live together.

Wasn't her dream in Paris that we should live apart, each in his or her own place, making dates with each other by phone?

For the past five years now, we have been living freely separated, without feeling that we need some official to give us permission to do so.

I fill D. in on my triple announcement and the reactions.

"Do you really believe she will gladly accept living with us and our child?" she asks.

"Marc is all excited about it. Boule will get used to it."

Days and weeks go by. I remember what D. exclaimed when we came out of the gynecologist's: "He'll be handsome, Jo! Children conceived in love are supposed to be the best-looking."

I think of our house in Nieul, "Grandma's house," the afternoon on which Marc was conceived. I am happy, but nonetheless start asking myself questions. I remember, for example, that in France, as in Belgium, a man cannot be punished for adultery, unlike a woman, but that he may be found guilty if he "keeps a concubine under the conjugal roof."

What is the law in the United States? Don't they make me take two rooms instead of one when I register at a hotel with D.? This is still a puritan country. And what would you be, my Johnny, under such conditions?

Yet, perhaps by atavism or on account of my upbringing, I feel bound by my word, even if grudgingly given, even if only a legal formality. My mind is all mixed up, and I am hesitant about making a decision that, whatever it be, will displease me. Did D. influence me in this? I can't say for sure.

Finally, a few days later, looking more solemn than I would like, I confess in private to Tigy: "I'm afraid we're going to have to get a divorce. Otherwise, we might be deported to Europe for moral turpitude. Don't forget, we are aliens here."

"I understand."

"Of course, I will assume all the blame for it. I'll write my lawyer in New York to explain the situation to him, and get his advice."

That lawyer, who specialized in international law, is a Belgian, like me, the son of an Antwerp diamond cutter.

I write him at length, holding nothing back, and just then Jean Renoir lets me know he's coming to see me. We spend an unforgettable day with him and Dido. From my first days in Paris, at the time of the avant-garde cinema, I have been one of his greatest fans. I knew his first wife, Catherine Hessling, who was so overwhelming in *The Little Matchgirl,* one of Jean's first masterpieces. They were both our guests at Place des Vosges, before Jean came to visit us aboard the *Ostrogoth* when he wanted to buy the film rights to my novel *La Nuit du carrefour (Maigret at the Crossroads).*

We did the screen treatment of that together, in a rented villa at Cap d'Antibes, and I met his two brothers, Pierre, who was the first actor to play Maigret, and the adorable Claude, with the round baby cheeks. I also visited Les Colettes, their father's home, hidden among centuries-old olive trees.

During the war, we were separated. Jean, after shooting a film in Rome, took the first ship out to the United States. He was not subject to military call-up, because, during World War I, he had received shrapnel wounds in the leg, and they had not been able to remove all of the pieces, which accounted for his unusual gait.

How many things he and I now had to tell one another! He was the same Jean as ever, with that almost childlike, seemingly naïve face. Yet so knowledgeable of men and things!

In Hollywood, he had been received with open arms, for he was considered one of the film pioneers, and perhaps the most talented one. However, problems in making pictures would arise if he retained his French nationality. That seemed as unimportant to him as it does to me, and he became a naturalized American, just as he became a married man, and as I became a married man. We are much alike, the two of us, except that he's a genius!

We have dinner at Tigy's. He has known Boule for a long time, and she outdoes herself in the kitchen in his honor. I was able to get some old French wines at our general store.

Later, he and Dido, whom he married in America and whom I adopted from the first time we met, come over to our place. They likewise both adopt D., whose belly is sticking out more and more.

"Listen, Georges. Promise me that, if it's a boy, you'll let me be the godfather. If it's a girl, Dido will be delighted to be godmother," Jean says.

We promise and are happy over this additional bond between us. Jean continually gets up to pace back and forth; like me, he doesn't like to carry on a conversation sitting quietly in a chair.

He is wearing very low-waisted American trousers, which don't squeeze his belly but have a tendency to slide down. And when they do, Dido softly calls, "Jean, you're losing your pants again."

They speak to each other in the formal second person plural, a Brazilian custom. Jean has problems too: his films are being shown everywhere, and he would like to go to Paris from time to time, but his first wife, from whom he never got divorced, has pressed charges against him for bigamy. She is a rather unpredictable girl, whose career came to an end after she separated from him.

"You understand, old man," he tells me. "It's so easy to get married here, in a few minutes, that I never took the trouble to go back to Europe and get a divorce. Catherine and I had been living apart for so many years! My lawyers now are trying to straighten it out. In the meantime, if I set foot in France, they'll have to put me in jail. Recently, I had to go to Berlin. The normal flight goes by way of Paris, with a stop there. I had to take a complicated detour to get to Berlin and get back."

He laughs. He is able to laugh at everything in life. He tells me about a novel by an Englishwoman I haven't heard of that he wants to make into a movie, *The River*, which takes place in India, not far from Calcutta.

"Those stupid damned producers don't want any part of it. They're still a little scared of me. But I'll get to make it sooner or later. . . ."

One day? Two days? I no longer know. A fountain of youth and brotherhood, because I consider Jean my brother, and we are to continue to correspond regularly until his last day.

My lawyer writes that indeed I will have to get a divorce if I intend to stay in the United States. But we have to find grounds for divorce recognized by the laws of the United States, Belgium, France, and other countries where I may want to settle. He is looking into the matter, which is both complicated and thorny, because of course he has to find grounds that do honor to both Tigy and me. He says he will be in touch again soon.

D. in the meantime writes to her brother Roger, whom I already know, to invite him to come and visit us.

"Did you tell him why?"

"He'll see as soon as he gets here," she says with a mischievous smile and a pat on her belly.

She has given up smoking, drinking, has become amazingly sweet and loving. I fill Tigy in on the lawyer's letter. Moved, which is not like her, she simply comments: "Georges, someday you'll come asking me for consolation."

At that moment, I hold that sentence against her but keep from replying. I'll often have occasion to remember it.

The big brother drops in on us without warning, bubbling with life, as always. One look at his sister is enough.

"Well, sis, so that's it, eh? Are you two happy about it?" he asks. He wasn't upset, or surprised.

We take him to dinner at the schoolhouse, and he meets Marc, Tigy, and Boule. His noisy good humor and his Québec accent appeal to all of them.

We haven't mentioned the divorce to him. Isn't he going to ask us about it? Isn't he by now, as eldest son, the head of the family, which means a lot in Canada? Besides, he is a Catholic, and a lawyer.

The next day, there is to be a religious festival in Nogales, Mexico, with local costumes and local color, bringing out people of all races and attracting spectators from far and wide.

We have dinner at the Grotto, and he does justice to the food and drink. From a kid going from table to table, he buys a big Mexican straw hat, which he wears. He is several sheets to the wind, but that's nothing to a Canadian.

The sounds of a brass band. Songs. It's a torchlight parade moving slowly through the colorful crowd. Some floats go by, with people in brilliant costumes, while others are dressed in black and wear death masks. The various pieces of music merge into one another, happy or sad, and men wearing often-grotesque masks dance frenziedly.

Roger is very enthusiastic about the whole thing, and takes off his outsized hat and waves it over his head, yelling *"Olé! Olé!"* in his powerful voice.

The bystanders look at him reprovingly, but he cares not a whit. He seems intoxicated by this folk festival, by the crowd, which he takes to be deliriously happy.

D. whispers in his ear: "Roger, this is a religious festival for these people."

He bursts out laughing. "With those masks and those dances? That's what you say!" And gives out with more *"Olé! Olé!"* He claps his hands and makes big gestures.

I notice some people stirring in the crowd. It's all D. and I can do to drag the huge fellow through the dense rows of spectators, whose faces have become threatening.

We get to our car and drive toward the American border, beyond which we will be safe.

He's not the kind of man one can hold things against. I can understand the mistake he is making. He has just fallen from the blue, almost literally, into a country where the religious traditions are as sacred as those of Québec. And you can imagine what would happen up there if, as a plaster Virgin

Mary or a girl playing the part of the Holy Mother went by, some madman were frantically to wave his hat and shout "*Olé! Olé!*" at the top of his lungs.

The next day, a little before noon, we knock at his door. No voice answers. The door is not locked, and we find him asleep, his face sweating but serene. He wakes up, runs a wet towel over his face, and once again he's as fit as a child, without the slightest trace of a hangover. We go over to Tigy's to lunch.

"Did you have a good time, Roger?" she asks.

"Some crazy people, down there!" he says. "Seems they don't know how to take a joke, and I made an ass of myself."

You, Marc, look at his hefty shoulders with admiration. You take a chance and ask: "Do you ride?"

"I never tried. Don't care too much for that kind of animal."

"I have a horse named Red. Dad has a golden palomino, and D. has a horse too."

"That threw her to the ground!"

Yet, he is about to get to know the equine species more deeply than he expected. In the afternoon, there are half a dozen mares tied up at one of the ranch fences. They've been brought to stud. Our friend the rancher is going to supervise the operation.

To Roger's amazement, they put a huge plastic condom over the stallion's member before he covers the mare that is brought to him. All the cowhands stand by, ready to play their parts. The coupling takes only a few instants, and immediately the almost full contraceptive is taken off the stallion, which is led away by two boys. The sperm is gathered into capsules and, with sleeves rolled up, these are inserted as far as possible into the mare's womb.

That takes longer than the first part did. Roger alone, among these Westerners, is wearing a coat, and the rancher asks him: "Would you like to try one?"

He hands him one of the capsules, and the lawyer, getting into the spirit of it, takes off his coat, rolls up his sleeve, and is about to show them that a Canadian will try anything once. He is obviously apprehensive of the mare. She is being held tight and her pink vulva opens spasmodically. Then, he courageously shoves his arm in up to the elbow as he has just seen the others do, and his face turns red.

"How was that?" he asks.

"Very good. Now let's go have a drink."

The usual mint julep. W.'s wife is, as ever, the most hospitable of hostesses. The place is cool. We stay around. And joke.

"How do you like what's happened to my little sister?"

W. blushes, but retorts wittily: "After all, she *is* living in the stud barn."

Dinner at Tigy's is a merry affair too. Out of the blue, Roger asks her: "Do you have a car?"

"Yes."

"Then how about taking me out for a ride tonight through this wonderful country? I'd like to get to know the desert a little better, and it seems my sister is no longer supposed to take bumpy rides."

D. doesn't seem happy, but rather worried, and the future, the all-too-near future, will show that she is right. Roger is no longer the same man when we go to wake him the next morning.

"You bitch!" he yells at her as we walk in. "Aren't you ashamed of yourself? Here was a family living nice and peacefully. You want to lay the husband, that's one thing. But to drive him to get a divorce . . ."

D. is livid, and her eyes can't tear themselves away from her brother's purple face.

"It's not her fault . . ."

"Georges, you keep out of this. I know my sister better than you do. . . ."

He had never used such a tone to me before.

"You're making him get a divorce so he can marry you, right? That's just like you, all right. You know what I, your brother, told Tigy last night? That I'm ready to come back from Québec to represent her. You're just too much of a shame to us, to me and to the whole family. I'm still wondering how I'll tell Maman what's going on."

"I'm expecting a child."

"Tigy has a child too."

He means it all, and after he gets back to Canada he writes her a long letter that is just as violent, and writes to Tigy at the same time.

We did not go over to the old schoolhouse for lunch or dinner for the next few days. D. wept constantly. I did my best to console her, and it was only after her brother left that I was finally more or less able to. This was not the moment to subject her to violent emotions, so I took her to dinner at the Grotto, where they sang *"Bésame mucho"* to her. The meal was not quite over when an Indian burst wildly into the restaurant and several times shouted an incomprehensible word, as he pointed out toward the mountain.

"What's he saying?"

"I don't know. I'll go and find out."

Some American tourists were surprised to see their bill handed to them when, like us, they weren't finished eating yet. D. came back, nervous.

"We have to get out right away. The red mountain has a hat on, as they put it. That means that at any minute huge amounts of water are going to start pouring down, accompanied by violent winds."

I pay, and quickly put the top up on the car.

What they told us is true. In a few minutes, a wall of water will be barreling down the arroyo, carrying everything before it, and there is no bridge between here and Tucson.

I speed up. The sky has gotten darker. Sometimes, we can see the arroyo, which already has a little water in it. There is a first ford, halfway to our place, but it's too late when we get there: it is completely flooded.

"That's what happens every year. It can rain for two or three weeks, and the waters just get higher and higher."

"And will we be isolated?"

We say nothing more. I'm giving it all the gas I can. We absolutely have to be at Tumacacori before the wall of water.

Our arroyo, which we have never seen anything but dry, now has almost two feet of dirty brown water in it. We barely get across. In half an hour, or maybe less, the torrent will be over six feet deep, maybe deeper. The annual deluge surrounds our little house, which does not keep us from hearing the coyotes howling all night long.

Once sheltered from the rain, we feel like laughing over our adventure. Isn't that sort of thing just what life out West is supposed to be like? Haven't we seen it in all kinds of movies, without completely believing it? The rainy season this year is late, but it has finally arrived. We lie close in each other's arms, chastely by now, like sweethearts in a Western, following the doctor's recommendations.

Pointing to her belly, I make a joke: "I just hope he's not too scared, in there."

You, Johnny, won't have many such experiences of desert life, because fate, like the wall of water has just done, will wash us on farther, always farther and farther.

Good night, my two sons.

33

The wall of water went by. During the flood, our rancher friend had a wire cable stretched across the arroyo, with a pulley, a hauling line, and a rope hanging down with a "sitting knot" at the end, just as on a boat; I am familiar with the whole arrangement. In the morning, I send the seat over to the other side, our little Indian maid sits on it, and I slowly bring her back to our side. At five in the afternoon, we do the opposite maneuver. The first times, she quakes with fear. Later, crossing the raging arroyo is fun for her, and her brothers and sisters, even her parents, come down to watch it.

It is already almost a thing of the past. The water is going down. I can now cross it on horseback. Then, D. and I are able to walk across it at night, holding our clothes up over our heads, and, naked as Adam and Eve, we cross the mile and a half or so of desert where no one can see us.

When the sunshine and heat come back, right on schedule, I am reminded of my good old tweed outfits. Neither here nor in Tucson have we ever had occasion to wear wool, and I am beginning to long for the countries where one can enjoy four seasons and Christmas brings snow. But it is only a brief longing, for I am fond of our desert, our horseback riding, the life in the West.

We go on living that life, at such a pace that I have only a few images of it left, a few important events.

D. and I one morning attend the wedding of our maid in a nearby Catholic church, white and red as a toy, off to the side of the road. Apart from us, all the others are Indians, properly attired in black, with white shirts and dark ties, as in any European village.

They don't seem to notice that we are Anglos. The ceremony, the censer, the genuflections all remind me of that time long ago when I used to serve at Mass, and after the rings are exchanged, the sacramental words spoken, we take our places in the line to congratulate the bride and groom, who are impressed and radiant.

To the doctor's in Tucson. He now anticipates the birth for August and is concerned that we are so far away.

"A month from now, I would be happier if you stayed in Tucson. Even though there is nothing to worry about, I have to think of all contingencies. If anything untoward should happen, I would have to send a helicopter out into the desert."

A quick trip to Los Angeles. An independent producer wants to acquire the rights to my novel *La Tête d'un homme* (*A Battle of Nerves*), which was filmed thirty years ago with Harry Baur as Maigret. Now, they tell me that they want Maigret played by that unforgettable actor of *Mutiny on the Bounty* and *The Private Life of Henry VIII*, Charles Laughton. He is introduced to me. He is a huge smiling hulk of a man who moves with the grace of a ballerina. We immediately get on a friendly footing.

In France, producers or directors came to see the writer. In Hollywood, it would be impossible to imagine one of the movie magnates, flanked by his bodyguards, calling on a Faulkner or a Steinbeck. I sign the contract. We go back.

Tigy in her turn goes to California, to meet with a famous divorce lawyer whose name someone gave her.

At meals, we speak less and less, and poor Boule, who wonders where all of this is going to leave her, is visibly worried. No matter how often I tell her to have faith in me, she still cries, "What about my poor frog?"

"Everything will work itself out, Boule. I'll see to it, you can be sure."

Something happens earlier than expected.

"It's moving, Jo!"

And indeed you are moving, in your mother's belly, you devil, Johnny. Soon, you'll make yourself felt so vigorously it will be visible to the naked eye.

Marc puts his hand on D.'s belly, excited. It seems as if your brother were about to talk to you. A few days later, when the schoolchildren have a day off, he brings some of his pals to the stud barn, some Mexicans, some Indians, and one white.

"Touch it," he tells them.

They each touch D., and Marc is very proud.

The lawyers' letters keep coming, mine to them more and more urgent, because I am becoming impatient. I have never known how to wait, or how to live in suspense, as we are now doing.

To calm myself, I type my third novel at Tumacacori, *Mon ami Maigret* (*My Friend Maigret*), almost like a postcard from Porquerolles, where the story takes place and where I did so much fishing on my "lateen" and played *boules* so much with my Genoese and Neapolitan friends. I ended up talking a mixture of the dialects of northern and southern Italy.

According to my lawyer friend in New York, who berates me for being so impatient, the differences between the laws of the various states of the United States and the various countries of Europe make the problem of our divorce almost inextricable, for the specific grounds, while numerous, are almost all dishonorable for one or the other of the parties.

Neither one of us deserted the other. Quite the contrary, there is the matter of "maintaining of a concubine under the conjugal roof," which would lay D. and me, and you too, Johnny, open to being deported. These laws, in 1949, are not what they are today, and none of them allow for divorce on mere grounds of incompatibility, even less by mutual consent.

One bit of good news, however. I get an extract from the laws of Arizona concerning the legitimacy of children. I am of course concerned about this, not for myself, but for you, whose character and eventual views on the subject I have no way of knowing. While all such legal formalities are repugnant to me, I want you to have every advantage on your side, whatever may happen, whatever you may become.

The Arizona law, like that of Sweden, which is even more sweeping on the subject, provides in essence that any child born to a man and woman is a legitimate child, even though one of its natural parents, or both, may be married to a different spouse.

At that time, only two other states had adopted such a profoundly human law, and I jumped for joy over it. Thus, you are my legitimate son, with all the rights pertaining to that condition.

You start moving about so much that you remind us of a young wild animal shaking the bars of its cage. You seem to be angry that it is taking so long for you to gain your freedom.

Following the gynecologist's advice, we look for a small house in Tucson. In the Southwest, because of the scorching-hot summers, university vacations are longer than in the north. One of the university professors is off to Europe, and his house is for rent until September.

It is clean, comfortable, in a neighborhood, halfway between downtown and desert, that is inhabited by middle-class people and a lot of intellectuals. It is furnished like any American middle-class home: lots of light-colored chintz, comfortable armchairs, bedrooms in light colors too, in the Anglo-American style. We strike a deal and are to move in at the end of June.

D. carries her bulging belly, so disproportionate to her small size, proudly in front of her, almost like a challenge, and Tigy makes a point of avoiding looking at it. Has she forgotten that she only agreed "to give me a child" when she was thirty-nine and I almost thirty-six, after insisting until then that I take all sorts of unpleasant precautions? That was before the pill, the IUD, and when French students snake-danced to a song that went: "Rubber, rubber, you're not my mother, / Rubber, rubber, no way at all . . ."

I write to my friends a great deal, to Jean Renoir and Dido, and to André Gide, among others, and he also writes me often. One day, he lets me know he is coming to visit me in Arizona, "provided his stay in the United States can be incognito." I wonder where I will receive him and whether his presence can really go unnoticed; then another letter informs me that his doctor has forbidden him to take so long a trip.

I had spoken to him of my passionate attachment to D., which distressed him greatly. He assures me that double harness is unfavorable to artistic creation and might dry it up entirely. He asks me a lot of questions about you, Marc, envying you your life as a fair-haired, free-living young husky.

Another trip by Tigy, a mysterious one. On her return, I tell her that I am thinking of eventually moving to San Francisco, which is said to be the most beautiful city in the United States. It is still just a fairly vague idea. But we will have to settle some place, once again. Marc is ten and needs a different kind of school from the one in Tumacacori. Why not San Francisco?

Tigy leaves again. I have made no secret of the fact that under no circumstances will I accept being separated from Marc. That further complicates the work of my New York lawyer. I also want my marriage to be under the rule of separate maintenance, for I have seen too many community-property arrangements lead to dreadful complications.

The lawyer advises me to get my divorce and get married in Reno. The marriage license does not make any mention of property arrangements, but a separate legal document can be attached specifying these conditions.

D. says, "I would never agree to marry you under a community-property agreement. I brought nothing with me when I came to you. Everything that I own belongs to you, since you gave it to me. As for your novels, you wrote them all by yourself."

Despite impatience, a feeling of some euphoria. Tigy tells me, in June, that she is going to California with Boule and will leave Marc with me until she settles somewhere.

She never did like to drive. Like most people who learn how late in life, she does not feel sure enough of herself, and I approve her decision not to risk having Marc along. She has packed everything, sent it all to the Tucson warehouse. Alas, Marc, you won't stay long with us. As for Boule, for a few days she had the lost look of a dog which sees its familiar universe crumbling around it, piece by piece.

Our rancher will try to sell our three horses for us, including your Red, which you liked as much as he liked you. Now you also are going to leave. A letter from Tigy, at Carmel-by-the-Sea, tells me she has found a house there near the seashore, with a fine bedroom for you, and that you can be enrolled in a school attended by the sons of Bing Crosby and I don't know what other celebrities.

She specifies the number of the train you are to take from Tucson to Los Angeles. It's a luxury train, all private compartments, in which passengers can have their meals served to them.

"Give the porter a good tip and make sure he takes care of Marc."

So you too will be leaving us, my big Marc, and my heart tightens at the thought. I reserve your compartment for you. We drive you to the train, and neither one of us cries; we both want to put a brave face on it. One more trip, alone this time, like the big boy you now are. Your mother will be waiting for you in Los Angeles, and from there you'll take another train to Carmel. I looked at a map to see where it is located. It is a very small town, but well known, as our friend W. confirms to me.

"It's supposed to be a very quiet place. No industry. No businesses or anything like that. Is that where you're going to live?"

I don't know. As during the war, events are leading me this way and that.

Our new six-foot-wide bed, with its smooth oxhide headboard, is taken apart and sent to storage. We take with us the typewriters, our clothes, my files.

And we move into the professor's house, separated by lawns from the neighbors. No walls, no fences, no barriers. An invisible line separates the gardens, and the houses, which in Europe would be called "villas," are all new and modern, breathing cleanliness.

"Come and look at this, Jo!"

D. is standing, dumbfounded, in front of an open closet. It is full of men's and women's clothes. And the drawers are full of underwear.

I had been told about this American custom of leaving one's things when renting one's house during vacations or other absences. Here, people do not have a sense of privacy. When we drive about in the evening, we see all kinds of open windows, curtains pulled back, and can look right into people's private lives.

The very day we put Marc on the train, to be watched over by a reassuring, smiling black porter, I type a letter to him, in English, the first letter I ever wrote in that language, which I am beginning to speak fluently. I didn't learn it from books, or in school, but, the way children do, I picked it up by speaking it, without fear of making ridiculous mistakes. I never cracked an English grammar, but read three American newspapers daily, as well as the weekly magazines. Yet I noticed, as I wrote to Marc, that I made few mistakes in spelling.

Every day while we were separated I wrote a letter to him, never saying how much I missed him or anything else that might depress him. If I typed the letter, it was because I was afraid he might not be able to read my handwriting. I didn't write to him as to a child, but as to an adolescent, and refrained from offering any advice.

Recently, he had become excited about baseball, and played it often with his friends, preferring to be the catcher. At Nogales, I had bought him a real catcher's mitt. Now I commented on the latest results, especially on the Dodgers' games, his favorite team. Sometimes I pasted to my letter some cartoon I had cut out of a paper or told him a short funny story I had read.

He answered me in English, of course, because he had never set foot in a French school.

A gardener came every week to tend our lawn and the semitropical flower beds. The professor had told me he would. I was intrigued by that gardener. He was very tall, very thin, and I knew that, with his pickup truck full of tools, he also tended the gardens of a number of other houses. But even in blue overalls he had something elegant about him that was surprising, and a popular novelist would certainly have described his face as being aristocratic.

I asked him in to have a beer or a glass of white wine. I found out then, not only that he was French, but that he bore the title of an illustrious noble family.

The Comte de R. (he went by plain R., without the title) was a direct descendant of the Duc de Saint-Simon, the author of those extraordinary classical *Mémoires*. He had been born and had lived in an impressive old château, with all the domestic staff that went with it, from the liveried butler whom his ancestors would have called their "chamberlain," to the stable boys and dog handlers.

He had been rich then, idle, intensely interested in riding, history, and literature. While still young, he had married under a community-property arrangement, which had turned out to be his undoing. There had been virtually no intimacy between him and his wife, and in his forties R. had fallen in love with a woman his own age, divorced from an important colonial official in Hanoi, where she too had known a life of idleness, surrounded by some fifteen native "boys" always at her beck and call.

It had been true love, and R. had asked for a divorce. But he ran into the stubbornness of a woman more determined than he, who made every possible demand in order to thwart his plan.

At the end of the war, R., out of patience, said farewell to his château and his fortune and came to America with his new love, whom he married. The embassy might probably have found him some employment worthy of his rank. But he did not even ask. For months, in New York, he decanted wine into bottles in a cellar, while his wife took in sewing. They were happy.

They quickly became our friends and in order to help us while away the time, since they understood how impatient we were, they would come in and play bridge with us several evenings a week.

You had become so feisty, you little devil of a Johnny, that on at least two occasions your violent somersaults knocked your mother's cards right out of her hand.

Mme de R. was a fine cook and made your mother English pound cakes, of which D. allowed herself to eat a slice or two a day.

She made fun of herself. "I'm going to look like my mother; I always said that someday I would look like her."

She laughed. But I suspected it was to cover up a little fear.

August was getting near. Every week we went to the gynecologist's.

"As far as I can tell, it'll be toward the end of the month."

D. waddled; her legs had become too heavy. Toward the end of August, you were still not showing signs of coming out for air, despite all your acrobatics.

"Aren't you missing it too much, my poor Jo?"

"It" had a specific meaning between us. I had, from my youth, been used to making love every day, often two or three times. At Tumacacori, the house on the hill had been an outlet for me. There was nothing like that in Tucson. I had, actually, peeked into a certain bar I had been told about, near the outskirts of the city, but I had quickly turned away. The women were pretty and attractive enough, but the questionable atmosphere made me feel cautious, and the men inside didn't look like the kind to tangle with.

I went swimming every day, and D., who was no longer allowed to, watched over me like a mother hen.

She was not having any troubles, did not have the "mask," as they say about some pregnant women whose features become set. Nor did she have any sudden yen for pickles, anchovies, or anything else.

The doctor was still convinced the baby would come in August, and I was equally sure it would not be here till September.

In the meantime, we had to move again. In this comfortable house, where the sister of our little Indian bride had come to work for us, I had written two novels, in a nook I had made for myself among the professor's trunks in the garage: *Les Quatre Jours du pauvre homme* (*Four Days in a Lifetime*) and *Maigret chez le coroner* (*Maigret at the Coroner's*).

The latter book was practically reportage. At the local courthouse, we had been fascinated spectators at a trial which particularly interested us, because it involved the tragic death of a girl at a certain place we were well acquainted with, between Tumacacori and Tucson.

The courtroom was small, and the audience sat on plain benches. No sooner was the judge seated than he took off his jacket, and the district attorney and defense lawyers were also in shirt sleeves. Four soldiers were involved. They were seated on a bench in front, without any police to guard them. The boys admitted having been dead drunk the night they had gone out with the girl in question. Were they, then, responsible for her having met her death under the wheels of the little train at that spot near the Tucson-Nogales road?

The judge, prosecutor, and defense lawyers talked calmly to one another, as if among old friends, which very likely they were. An expert, sent by the railroad, drew maps on a blackboard standing on an easel.

The red-faced coroner, also in shirt sleeves, told of the inquest.

In the courtroom, people conversed, betting one way or the other on the GIs' guilt. From time to time, the judge gaveled for silence.

"Twenty-minute recess."

Everyone rushed to get a beer or a Coca-Cola or lined up to get into the toilets.

I could just imagine Maigret, so ill at ease whenever he was called to testify in a case in Paris, watching this procedure, so full of good-fellowship, even though the death of a young woman was involved.

"Which one of you slept with her?"

The soldiers eyed one another.

"I did," one of them timidly said.

"Where?"

"At the edge of the road."

"Where were the others, during this time?"

"In the car."

When it all came out, they had all slept with her, and the girl, who had gone across the border with them at Nogales, where they had all had a party, was then as naked as they.

265

Why and how, then, had the girl been decapitated by the train a hundred yards away? It was really none of my business. I just wanted good old Maigret to get acquainted with Western-style justice, and that was why I wrote this novel, which was not much more than a report of the trial.

But that wasn't enough to make the time pass more quickly. We had been told by the doctor, and I remembered from Marc's birth, that we would have to stay close by for a month after D.'s confinement. We had found a place, where the town meets the desert, which was neither motel nor hotel. Three rows of well-furnished bedrooms, most of them with living rooms, all with bath and kitchen, were available for monthly rental. Our suite was the one closest to the gate, its walls of bare brick, one room with a skylight.

We ate our meals at a drive-in that featured mostly fried chicken and steaks. One day, we wandered into a Hungarian restaurant, where we feasted on an appetizing goulash served by girls in Hungarian costumes. It was very nice and very intimate.

The days went by, we were into September, and almost all of that month went by without any alert.

We went to look over a lying-in hospital, which had been recommended as the best one. This was another convent, even quieter and fancier than the one in Nogales. The floor of the reception room was made of black marble. While the sister in charge of the reception desk did her endless best to try to reassure a worried father, we read the black-bordered notice on the wall. It informed expectant mothers that, by order of the head physician and the mother superior, in case of serious complications, the life of the child would be considered ahead of that of the mother.

That gave us a chill, and we tiptoed out. There remained only the Tucson hospital, brand new, with pink-brick pavilions and a sandy garden.

That, Johnny, is where you were born, without my being allowed to be there. But I stayed with your mother until the nurse decided it was time to take her to the delivery room.

It was September 29. I waited for almost two hours in the corridor. The obstetrician finally came merrily out to tell me everything had gone just fine and you were a boy. Almost a wonder boy, because you weighed over eleven pounds and were the biggest baby ever born there.

I would have liked to see you and your mother right away. But I was thrown out and, not knowing what to do at that time of night, I went over to our friends the R.s to tell them the good news and have a cold beer with them. Then, at the station, I sent off triumphal wires to Marc, Tigy, my New York lawyer, your future godfather Jean Renoir, after whom you were named, and I don't know who else.

Jean-Denis-Chrétien Simenon was born!

I had to wait a long time for the florist's to open, and then sent D. I don't know how many roses. A lot. Too many, the head nurse was to tell me when she saw me. "Newly delivered mothers' bedrooms are not flower gardens."

At three o'clock I was able to go to your mother's room; she looked fine and wore a radiant smile. You weren't there. I was not allowed to breathe the same air as you until your eighth or tenth day.

I wrote to Marc, and then went to sleep, which I had not done for the past two nights.

At seven o'clock, I joined the other fathers and grandparents in the slow parade before a window, and at last I found your name on one of the labels.

A big whopper of a boy, with dark hair and big brown eyes, who calmly gazed back at the people watching him. Because everyone there was watching you. You looked like a colossus among midgets. I heard people whispering, "He looks more like a month-old baby."

I went to see your mother, who looked at me closely. "Did you see him?"

"Yes. He's magnificent. Now I know why he kicked so vigorously."

"You really think he's handsome, Jo? Are you happy?"

I was, Johnny, and proud of my new son.

As for you, my Marc, you now had your "little" brother.

34

A funny month, Johnny dear, for you who just opened your eyes on the world, for your mother and me, because once again we are in suspense. It is the end of September, but since there are no seasons in this wonderful world of Arizona, I can't call it fall, and we know that in a month, as soon as you can "take the trip," we are to be going to California, to settle there for a more or less long time.

So, in our lives, this is an interlude, and the first week or ten days, while you were still at the hospital, were for your mother and me full of deep joy and almost painful impatience.

I had had a month of waiting after Marc's birth, but at least I had been able to sleep on a folding cot alongside his mother's bed, hold him in my arms, see him at any hour of the day. You cannot imagine how painful it was for me not to have any contact with you, except through a window.

Your mother had milk for you and was very proud of it. Six times every twenty-four hours, I think, you were brought to her; but you weren't left with her long, and if I was feeling frustrated, she felt just as much so.

I believe I told you, even before you were born—for you had already been alive for quite some time—that we were then living in a strange place that was not exactly a motel, but a huge patio set up in the sand which was actually part of the desert. It was very cheerful, thanks to the glass skylight and the bay window on the shady side, but it wasn't that way for me during the days I had to stay there alone. This strange building was the idea of a cultivated, fiftyish man, a professor, doctor, or lawyer up north, who had fallen in love with Arizona and given up everything to come down here to run a hotel. In France, he would have been considered crazy. But not in the U.S., where, at the time we were living there, a banker late in life discovered that his real vocation was being a clown, and switched to a roving circus to fulfill his dream.

Why does this come back to me now? Because that period was such a mixed-up one for us, and the slightest cloud assumed great importance.

D. felt as I did that the rules in the city hospital were unfair, not allowing her to have you stay with her more than a few moments a day and restricting my visits to twice a day. She complained to the nurses, but they couldn't change the rules for her. She complained, perhaps vehemently, to the head nurse, an old maid who was three months away from retirement and who as a result was stricter than ever.

Supposedly, she told D.: "You should consider yourself lucky, an unwed mother like you. . . ."

The second night, D. was crying, feeling she was being victimized by the old nurse. To console her, I made a date with her, at curfew time, at her window.

The hospital buildings were widely separated by sandy stretches. They were also at the edge of the desert, and there was no fence. So I waited until the day shift had left, then for the lights to be out, and I went over to the window I knew was D.'s, taking along one of the iron chairs that stood all around the place, and making no noise.

Your mother opened the window, and we were able to kiss, and to have long talks in the moonlight. Quickly consoled, she told me about you, your voracious appetite, your crying that could be heard all over the building when you were hungry, as you were any number of times every day. Your big brown eyes were both tender and determined.

The days seemed long to me. In the morning, I typed my letter to Marc. That was another, longer wait. I wrote him one hundred thirty-three letters before seeing him again and introducing to him the brother he had for several years been eager for.

He was ten. In Carmel, he had entered junior high school. He had made many friends, with whom he went fishing for abalone and crabs. He raised crabs, he told me in one of his weekly phone calls, just as he "raised" frogs in the garden of the house that Tigy had rented.

I walked a great deal, and one morning I happened by the home of the professor who had rented his house to us for the three months that he was in Europe on vacation. There, falling apart, was the shop, or stand, that Marc had built out of old crates and planks when we were there. With a friend his age, he sold glasses of Coca-Cola to passers-by. At the time, Coke was ten cents a bottle. He sold it at a nickel a paper cup, getting three or four cups out of each bottle. That's called "Americanism" too, Johnny boy!

Sometimes, as I looked at you through the window, I imagined that you recognized me and made little secret signs to me. How could you have recognized me among all those fathers who were waving to their babies? I noted that you were one of the few who never cried during the hour that you were on show. You stared fixedly, almost fiercely, at all those unknown faces pressing against the window, as if defying them. Have you changed much?

Once my housework was done and my letter written, I wandered any old place, making my lunch most often of two or three hot dogs or a few hamburgers. In the evening, before going to see you and your mother, I would go to the Hungarian restaurant we had found while we were still waiting for you to appear.

At least there I had a familiar spot, and each day I ate the goulash that was the house specialty, and they served it to me without even coming to ask for my order.

Finally, I brought you and your mother back to our rooms, and I never drove the big Buick more carefully.

Once there, I found out that you knew how to make yourself heard and didn't like to be kept waiting. You had a deep voice, so loud you could easily have been heard in the farthest seats of an opera house.

In the morning, I would go out to get meat, vegetables, and fruit at a supermarket less than four miles away.

I learned to change your diapers and how to make them snug with a double-sized safety pin. That pin scared me because it was very thick and took some strength to push through the thick fabric, and I was always afraid that the point would go too far and stick into your tender skin.

Why did we have to call a pediatrician? Maybe because you started crying more often, and louder? Maybe because you refused to let go of your mother's breasts?

He examined both of you. "You can't go on nursing him, Mrs. Simenon," he told D. "You don't have enough milk for a child his size with such an appetite."

I listened anxiously, afraid he was going to talk to us about that machine for milking women's breasts that had so scared me before Marc was born.

"I'll give you a formula."

He wrote out a long prescription, and then said to me: "You'll find an all-night drugstore. Buy some bottles too, and a saucepan to sterilize them in and to heat the milk. Just follow my instructions. I'll be back in two or three days."

Six or eight bottles a day? I no longer remember. After he left, I first consoled D., who was heartbroken at not being able to breast-feed you, then teased her.

"It's all your fault. Why did you have to have such a big, fat baby?"

When I finally had her smiling, I went out to find the drugstore. The pharmacist read the prescription and told me: "Come back in about an hour. I'll have it all ready."

"I have to get some bottles too, and a saucepan, and nipples . . ."

"I know. I have the whole business. You're not the first one who ever had a baby."

So I went walking, walking, through the dark streets. I was already worrying that you were going to waste away, that all this would be unwholesome for you. You can't imagine how long a single hour can go on. When I got back to the drugstore, the pharmacist handed me a carton with some white powder in it and explained to me how it was to be used, and also explained that the new kind of bottles he was giving me had a valve in them that kept the baby from swallowing air.

A funny month! And a funny night especially! When I got back, D. and I read the instructions through two or three times, then, on the kitchen gas range, we sterilized those wonderful new bottles, mixed the powder with the proper amount of water, and waited for the milk we had just made to be at the right temperature.

Were you going to drink it or would you reject the rubber nipple that was unlike your mother's breast? You drank it—greedily.

Days went by. They seemed long in spite of the cozy atmosphere in which the three of us were living. I decided I would write a novel, so as not to see the time go by till the end of the month. Impossible to write in our little apartment, where you took up so much space—or at least your lungs did. The owner let me use an empty apartment almost directly across the patio from our own.

I got up at six in the morning, drank my coffee, took a big mug of it with me, and, after giving you a kiss, crossed the courtyard and sat down in the almost empty room where my typewriter waited.

That was how I wrote a rather long novel, *Un nouveau dans la ville* (Someone New in the City). Why that one? Why any other? I have never known the why or wherefore of the theme of any of my novels.

By 9:00 A.M., my chapter would be finished, and I would rush back to you, and then go to the supermarket.

A very sweet month, just the same, without the slightest cloud between your mother and me. Didn't we have a new tie to unite us?

Our departure was getting close. The pediatrician found you in perfect shape and told us we could go. However, he suggested that it would be better for you not to make such a long trip by car. The train would be faster, more comfortable, even though we would have to change trains at Los Angeles and spend a half hour in the station.

What to do with the car? Our friend the gardener-count offered to drive it to Carmel for us, to the hotel we had selected from a brochure as the best place to stay. He would come back to Tucson by train.

The Buick left ahead of us. A taxi took us to the station, happily carrying you in your portable crib. You take everything in with your big shining eyes, and the train is no more than twenty miles out when you noisily let us know you are wet. We didn't figure the distance in miles or kilometers, or even in hours, but in bottles and diaper changes.

When we get to huge, teeming Los Angeles Union Station, your mother has some urgent business to attend to. Your little behind is all red, irritated by the disposable diapers, which were new and probably not yet properly perfected. There must be a drugstore in the station. One finds everything in those big American stations, even softer diapers.

So I am left alone with you, your crib on the floor, in the big waiting room, with hundreds of travelers going back and forth, bumping one another, rushing toward ticket windows, buffets, restaurants, or departure platforms. I try to fence you off, because I am afraid that some of the people in their hurry might bump into your crib. Then, all of a sudden, you begin to yell. To yell so loud that everyone stops to look at the two of us, either smiling, or reprovingly.

I have to change you. I had learned to do it, but it was harder here, kneeling down by your crib and afraid of the surrounding mob. I feel awkward. Especially because you haven't just peed. I also have to clean you off. Fortunately, we carried a bottle of water.

So I display your naked behind to what seems to me like thousands of people, most of whom are shocked at the sight. I wash you off, powder you, and I confess I am relieved to see your mother coming back with a big package of diapers. She finished the job, just in time for us to catch our train.

We were headed for Salinas, some twenty or so miles from Carmel, which is not on any rail line. We are to get there about four in the morning and have told the porter to be sure to wake us at three. We get to sleep very late, because in the next compartment five or six men are drinking and playing cards, telling more or less off-color stories and laughing their heads off.

We finally do sleep, and suddenly we hear someone on the platform calling, "Salinas!"

The stop there is only three minutes, and we have to get you off, as well as our luggage and typewriters. The apologetic porter does his best to help us make it. We must look like acrobats. We are barely off when the train starts on its way to San Francisco. Only a little more time and we might still have been on that train, sound asleep.

It is not yet dawn, but there is one taxi outside the station. Your first trip, Johnny, was a little hectic, wasn't it? As we ride along, the sky lightens, and when, from the top of the hill, we get a glimpse of the ocean and the red roofs of Carmel above the greenery, it is almost daylight.

The hotel is a comfortable one. After a hasty breakfast, I am pacing back and forth in front of a drugstore waiting for it to open. We need a new supply of your formula, which the druggist has to prepare.

At eight o'clock I phone Marc, now beautifully tanned, who rushes over and is ecstatic at seeing you.

"Is he called Jean or Johnny?"

"Johnny."

"Where are you going to live?"

"We don't know yet. I'll look for a house."

"Ours is big enough for everybody."

How can I explain to him that his mother no longer wants to live in the same house with us and that we will soon be divorced? In his innocence, Marc includes everyone around him in his love.

"I have to run so I won't be late. I'll come back this afternoon after school."

Was it that day that, with the help of the hotel manager, we found our house, or the next day, or the one after that?

Carmel-by-the-Sea is unique in California, if not in all the United States. Seen from above, it looks like a fairy village, with its colorful houses surrounded by trees and flowers, set on the side of quite a steep hill. It's more a big hamlet than a town. Two streets run through it from end to end, parallel to the beach, the two main streets, with all the others running down from the hilltop to the sea and crossing them. The houses are mostly one style, Cape Cod, which is surprising on the Pacific seaboard.

Almost no shops. No electric signs. No billboards. All such things are (or were) strictly forbidden, by an equally surprising population. Everyone is rich, or at least comfortable. Most of the people are elderly, old ladies who are widowed or divorced, most of them cultured and interested in the arts. Some of them are musicians, others paint, and some write.

The men are mainly artists of a sort, young and old, among them the greatest American poet of the moment, whose neighbors we are to be, at the very end of town, where it suddenly makes way for cliff and sand.

I am surprised to discover that there is no mail delivery here. Everyone gathers around ten in the morning outside the post office to await the arrival of the truck. Someone explains: "We could have mailmen, but we don't want any. We prefer to have everybody meet at the post office, and that way have a kind of community feeling."

Drivers are as courteous as if they belonged to another century. No one tries to pass anyone else. When two ladies meet, each in her car, they may pull up alongside one another and carry on a long conversation right in the middle of one of the main streets. No one disturbs them. They wait. At the intersections with the perpendicular streets, no traffic lights. People drive slowly. They signal who has the right of way.

The grocery store stocks merchandise from every country in the world, and I find canned snails there with a little bag of very clean shells. And also, of course, frogs' legs. The library is a meeting place, like the post office. To my amazement, there are books in any number of languages, most of them the works of poets.

It seems to me that Marc has grown, broadened, that his voice has gotten deeper.

"Well, Johnny old man? You know that I'm your big brother? Someday, I'll teach you all kinds of games."

Tigy doesn't come to see us. Nor does Boule, who hasn't gotten used to the idea of the new baby.

Our home is rather strange, not New England style, but an entirely new type, created in San Francisco, which in the next few years will reach the whole country, and in ten, or twenty, Europe. It is built of shimmering Oregon pine and has thick windowpanes, which take the place of one wall out of two, so that on all sides the light pours in. Its lines are new, daring, the living room more than spacious, the bedroom as well; the bathroom, fortunately with smoked glass, faces the road. Only months later will I realize that from the outside, when the lights are on, one can clearly make out our naked bodies going back and forth. But then, no one goes by there.

Our bedroom on one side opens onto a fine terrace, on which you, Johnny, will spend the greater part of your days. Flowers everywhere. Greenery. A kitchen that takes my breath away; never have I seen anything so daringly modern. Even today, you don't see anything like it except in the advertisements of fancy shops.

Across from us, woods. In the woods, a strange tower. The house must be at the foot of it, hidden by trees. Beyond, the sea, with its whitecaps breaking against the cliff. It is the home of the poet, a little white-haired man, though still rather young, whom I catch sight of only once, fleetingly, in his garden.

You are in tiptop shape, Johnny boy, and you have the appetite of a giant's child.

We have a black housekeeper. She drives a Studebaker that is almost as long and shiny as my Buick. The garage, across the road, has room for only one car. "What about mine?" she demands. She seems to expect me to let her have the garage. Apart from that, she's very accommodating, always cheerful. She has a bedroom and bath on the ground floor. In the evening, she comes up into the living room and sits in one of the armchairs to watch TV. Our presence does not bother her. She scarcely notices that we are there, and when the program we have on doesn't suit her, she gets up with a sigh and twists the dial until she finds something she likes. This seems natural to her, so natural that we can't hold it against her.

We get organized, that is, we organize everything around you. First, we have to get you a real crib. In a neighboring town, we find one that seems wonderful to us. Made of wood painted white, at the right height so one can kiss you without bending too far over, it has a kind of top that, when you close it, turns the crib into a big box. Of course, the top is made of netting, which shields you from mosquitoes and other insects. We roll it out on the terrace, or, for the night, into our room, or, when we wish, into the living room.

We buy you a carriage, and I take you out every morning, while, through one of the windows of our house, we see your mother, in a nurse's outfit, cap included, preparing your bottles.

It is October 1949, Johnny boy, and there are still a lot of things for you to learn, for us to learn about you, before summer, that is, before our next departure (still another one!) for new horizons.

Good-bye, my boy!

35

I'm going to tell you a secret, Johnny, and hope it won't upset you too much if someday I make it public: You never were a real "baby," an infant-in-arms, like most of the ones who lay around you behind that window in the Tucson hospital.

From your very first day, I have watched you with as much attentive tenderness as I did Marc, and then the two other children I was to have after you. I watched all of you grow with passionate curiosity, and as luck would have it I was almost alone in bringing you up, from the time you were still quite young until, at the end of your adolescence, you each flew from the nest to carry on your activities or studies far away.

In Tucson, you did not cast a vague or indifferent glance on the humans outside, whose features were distorted by the thick glass. You stared right out at them, without blinking, as you examined us in our house on the edge of the desert, then in the train, at the Los Angeles railroad station, and, finally, in our house in Carmel-by-the-Sea, and I'd be willing to swear that anyone looking at you was more intimidated than you ever were.

Your brother Marc as a child smiled at us, smiled his sunshine-filled smile at everything he was gradually discovering of the world. He smiled and dreamed, surprised when his dream was interrupted.

Psychologists—many of whom these days study human children—may make fun of me if I assert that you did not dream, but were attentive to everything you discovered, and then thought about it. Why the devil should what we call "a baby" not think about things, not come to his own conclusions about them?

Later, you saw in our home, in our many "homes," young, familiar animals. From the moment they came in, didn't they set out to reconnoiter the place, smell it out, select their corners in it? While we thought we were training them, wasn't it they, very often, who recognized our characters and our weaknesses and took advantage of them to train us?

One recollection comes back to me. When he was only a few months old, in our big studio at Nieul, where the light poured in through six windows, I would pick Marc up and hold him against me, his head up over my shoulder, and he knew what was going to happen. With my free hand, I would press the button of the phonograph, which always had the same record on it, a song that Arletty and Michel Simon had sung in a then-recent movie called *Circonstances atténuantes* (Mitigating Circumstances). It was a waltz, and I would hum the words along with them as I swung about with him to the rhythm of the music. It was called "Comme de bien entendu" (Sure Enough). And I danced and sang with you too, in our Carmel living room, to the tune of another record, this one by the Gershwins, "Looking for a Boy."

You did not meet my eyes furtively, or dreamily, or thoughtlessly; you *confronted* them, and I could have sworn that you were drawing conclusions from what you were seeing.

As with a young animal, it took you only a few days to "smell out" the farthest corners of the house, to pass judgment in every way on the behavior of those around you, and to know their comings and goings as they conformed to the clock. For example, you never waited until you were hungry to call for your bottle, as if you understood that there would be a wait for it to be properly warmed up. You called ahead of time, consciously or not, for you were already as intolerant as I of being kept waiting. In order to stop your crying quickly, we rushed to the kitchen, and you smiled with satisfaction, as if once more you knew you had won.

Because you drank so greedily, the Tucson pediatrician had told us to take the bottle away from you once or twice during each feeding, so that you would not spit up, as you had at the beginning. Your mother and I vied with each other to do this agreeable chore, and we did our best to get the nipple out of your mouth when you were half-done, but your little body stiffened so and your eyes became so demanding that we didn't have the courage to go through with it.

Medical fashion at that time dictated that when the bottle was finished, you be held over a shoulder until you burped once or twice. That position, that warm, affectionate contact, appealed to you, and I am sure that you held the burps back as long as possible in order to prolong the pleasure before returning to your bed.

Whenever Marc burst in, noisy, his sandy clothes smelling of the sea, you were immediately awake and devouring him with your eyes, as if you admired and envied him his liberty.

Marc at the time was in his finest shape, ruddy and full of boundless energy. He kissed you and looked at you with laughing eyes brimming with tenderness. He was supposed to be living with his mother and Boule, but he came running to us whenever he had a free moment and, if our lunch or dinner appealed to him, sat down to eat with us. Like you, he had an unbelievable appetite.

He didn't tell us much about school, except to say that he had a whole lot of friends, including Bing Crosby's boys. He sometimes brought along two or three of the chums with whom he went fishing after school.

"Is there enough ice cream, D.?"

I had been over to see his mother, in her house right near the water, which was much larger than ours. I won't say our relations were cold, but, considering the circumstances, they were necessarily somewhat strained. While we felt no antagonism toward one another, we had nonetheless become, by way of our attorneys, adversaries.

Tigy was well aware of how close Marc and I were to each other, yet it was she who would soon have legal custody of him. Was she going to separate me from one of my sons? She knew I would never stand for that. And yet she was free to do it, or would be as soon as the divorce was final.

We did not mention it to one another. We spoke mostly about Marc, whose irresistible attraction to fishing and outdoor sports concerned her. Was I right or wrong to place more importance on his health, his physical development, and his balance than on his marks in school?

I tried to set her mind at ease, and Boule listened to us in silence, visibly worried. Without meaning to, I had brought about a delicate situation, and I tried to get out of it as best I could, not for my own sake, but for that of my two sons, who had already recognized that they were brothers in the full sense of that word.

As long as D. had not been pregnant, it had remained possible, as in Canada and Tucson, for all of us to coexist under the same roof. Tigy remained my legal wife, at least in name, and she accepted more or less willingly that my secretary-mistress should live with us, even leaving Marc in our care when she went off to New York or Europe. In a word, she retained the position she had earned through twenty years of marriage, and she was the one who appeared magnanimous, allowing the strange woman to usurp part of her place.

When D. became pregnant, she still thought things might remain the same, and I thoughtlessly hoped so, until the day I mentioned divorce.

When your birth, Johnny mine, was impending, the situation changed, and Tigy decided to move to Carmel with Marc and Boule. That left me for one hundred and three days without Marc, but I can't hold that against his mother.

As I can't hold it against D. that, once she became a mother, she was no longer satisfied to remain in her equivocal position. Was it not up to me to take upon myself all the sins of Israel?

At Carmel-by-the-Sea, the two women did not see each other. I met Tigy several times, once even with you, Johnny, when I was wheeling your carriage. She leaned over to look at you, and merely said, "A fine boy."

And what about Boule in all this mix-up? Wasn't her position the hardest of all to define? For twenty-five years, she and I had had close ties, of affection as well as sex. In the house at Carmel, Marc, it was to you that Boule remained faithful, and when she looked at me, her eyes were sad and forever on the point of bursting into tears.

Faithful Boule, the most faithful of the three, had, in reality, adopted Marc only a month after his birth. Wasn't it that she instinctively feared her own place in my life might be reduced by his presence?

The same applied to you, Johnny mine. I would have liked to take her in my arms, to reassure her, make her understand that nothing had changed between us, but I was a guest then in a strange house, and all we could do was exchange looks, hers weepy and as if ashamed, mine full of warm tenderness.

She came to see you, Johnny, only once or twice, on the fly. She too thought you were amazingly hefty, but she remained somewhat aloof. Only when I was seeing her out, at the bottom of the stairs, did I kiss her, before sending her on her way, still confused but at least reassured.

While I was passionately poring over your young existence, taking you out walking, often giving you your bottle, burping you on my shoulder, singing you one of my favorite tunes, the lawyers of the party of the first part and the party of the second part, as they say, were writing to each other and to us, one to Tigy, the other to me, and no week went by without new questions coming up, new problems, not to say new antagonisms.

For my part, the one and only consideration was that I keep my two sons, and I trusted my friend in New York to make sure of that. Tigy on the other hand had been to San Francisco several times and put her interests in the hands of the best divorce lawyer in California. He specialized mostly in society divorces, the kind that involved famous names and great fortunes, which meant, of course, that he was very expensive. (And I was paying his fees!)

Knowing all the ins and outs of American and California laws, he had told Tigy she should simply have me jailed, which, it seemed, she could do under the laws of California. She had informed me of this, immediately adding: "Naturally, I said no."

You weren't aware of any of this, impetuous Johnny. I admit that I wasn't concerning myself too much about it. One day, I heard that one of my short stories, "Seven Little Crosses in a Notebook," which had appeared in a New York magazine, had won me an Edgar, one of the awards given each year to outstanding works in the mystery field. I had never heard of this prize, which carried a two-thousand-dollar stipend.

Two years later, I was to get another such award, equally unexpected, from the Mystery Writers of America, for the best detective novel of the year. This prize was not a cash award, but an early-nineteenth-century revolver, from the real old Wild West, mounted on wood with a gilt plaque that had my name on it and an inscription. You were to ask me for it many years later, and perhaps you still have that "trophy," to use the hunters' term for it.

In Tucson, while your mother was in the hospital, I was visited by a New York publisher, with whom I spent the whole day discussing business —in English!—before deciding I would switch publishers and let this visitor bring out my books in the U.S.

But no matter. What was important, to you as well as to D. and me, was, for example, taking you over to look at the island with the sea lions. Between Carmel and Monterey, the neighboring city, there is a peninsula with magnificent trees, to cross which one has to follow rigid rules. The road, along the seashore, is called "Seventeen-Mile Drive" and is justly famous for its scenic beauty. How many times you were to go along it, Johnny, attentive to everything, your eyes taking it all in!

Barely a hundred yards from the coast, there was a huge rock, an islet with nothing growing on it, on which huge sea lions lived freely. The males, with tawny manes, watched over the females and the young. We could see them dive, sometimes from high up, swim, and disappear, only to surface again far away and then look back at us, impassively.

The most moving part was to see the females slip down to the water with their young, and push them into it, following close behind, as if they were giving them swimming lessons.

I must admit, Johnny, that we were as fascinated as you. There was one young sea lion which we decided looked something like you. From the moment we got there, we tried to locate him and were as concerned with what he was doing as if he were part of the family. When he went a little too far, we felt like calling out to his mother: "Don't let him get so far away!"

Here, there were seasons, although less definitely marked than in Europe. From December on, skies became gray, sometimes rainy. I was finally able to wear the tweed I dreamed about under Arizona's scorching sun.

D. used to wear a cape I had had made for myself. Handwoven in Ireland out of brown wool, it just would not wear out. Adjusted to fit D.'s waist and shoulders, it went along with us on all our walks. You had a folding stroller, and when we went to Seventeen-Mile Drive, we would put it in the trunk, with you on your mother's lap and me at the wheel. Once opposite the sea lion rock, we would unfold the stroller to take you for a walk under the giant trees.

We went to Monterey once a month to see a rather young, shy, and courteous pediatrician, who gave you very good care. One would have thought, from the way you looked at him, that the two of you were pals. At every visit your weight had taken another jump.

We took you for walks in Monterey, a fairly large fishing port, where seals, porpoises, and dolphins swam about unabashedly, grabbing the fish that the local cannery rejected.

At the end of the peninsula, a clean-looking, rosy house from the beginning of the last century. A plaque on it informed us that it was once a hotel at which the English writer Robert Louis Stevenson stayed for several weeks before sailing to the South Seas, where he was to spend the rest of his days.

From childhood, I had been a fervent admirer of his works, and in 1935, in a lagoon in the Pacific, I had discovered another souvenir of him: a silver cup with his name and a date on it that he had given to a Protestant chapel out in the wilderness.

On one side of the port is a pier and on either side of that wooden shacks, shops, and restaurants that serve seafood and fish. Including Marc's abalones. Shells larger than scallops, black and smooth, that are hard to get off the underwater rocks. Boule has had to learn how to cook them, and your brother keeps bringing her more and more of them!

As you look at the sea, the animals, and the things about you, your eyes are neither vague nor dreamy. You stare at a set point, looking thoughtful, trying to understand. I know every one of your expressions, all your tics, the shadings of your voice. I too am trying to understand, what is going on behind your wide, high forehead, as I did with Marc and will do later with my other two. Did I succeed? Maybe. It was ambitious of me to answer yes, and yet the future was to prove me most often right.

From December on, I got to work. Not to write to my lawyers or my various publishers, but to write novels. Since I have never been able to stand having anyone in the room in which I type my daily chapter so early in the morning, you stay with your mother in the bedroom or out on the terrace while the maid gets impatient in the kitchen or on the ground floor.

That December, two novels: *Maigret et la Vieille Dame (Maigret and the Old Lady)* and *L'Amie de Madame Maigret (Madame Maigret's Friend)*. None of which keeps me from wheeling your carriage around the house at 10:00 A.M. while your mother prepares your bottles. In the afternoon, we go "downtown," usually on foot, with you in your carriage. As long as the road is flat, your mother wheels it. As soon as there is an incline to go up, I take charge, as I do while D. goes into the grocery store, the butcher shop, or other places.

Time goes quietly by and the weather is pleasant.

In January 1950, another novel, just one this time, *Les Volets verts (The Heart of a Man)*. In February, when the air is not so damp and the sky is often sunny, *L'Enterrement de M. Bouvet (The Burial of Monsieur Bouvet)*. In May, when we can go swimming in a sheltered cove about a hundred yards from our house, my last California novel, *Un Noël de Maigret* (A Maigret Christmas).

Long since, we bought you a playpen with varnished bars, in which you studiously make your way about. When you complain, I know what you are calling for, and I put on a record, always New Orleans jazz, which I have been familiar with ever since my first days in Paris. But I have to be sure to put on the right record. You put up with Louis Armstrong, his trumpet and his hoarse voice, but only for a while. I know that I have to change records and which ones you want, the Benny Goodmans. Eventually, he is the only musician you want to hear, and I get almost all the records he ever made.

How is it that, when only a few months old, and not even walking yet, you can tell one piece of music from another, and end up settling on only one type? That has always been a mystery to me, and I suppose to you too. As soon as you knit your brows, and begin to go into one of your tantrums, all I have to do is put Benny Goodman on the record player and you calm down.

You are no longer getting along on milk alone. From the age of three months, you have been eating out of a spoon, on the advice of the Monterey pediatrician, first a mixture of calf's liver and vegetables, and then beef with other vegetables.

Marc watches you eat enviously. If you leave the slightest bit, he's always ready to clean up after you, and from time to time we let him pick out one of your jars for himself and eat along with you. The two of you get along famously, and Johnny looks at you with admiration, showing off proudly for you how he gets up on his knees holding on to the bars of his playpen.

At times like that, Marc has a satisfied and somewhat proud smile, as if he were the father.

I can remember his birthday lunch in April, which he celebrated with us. We know what he likes and how much he can eat. To get going, there are snails, and he devours three dozen without flinching. He loves squab and, just in case, we have gotten half a dozen. And a good thing, too, because he eats three of them by himself, washed down with glasses of milk.

The birthday cake is also huge, and he does right by it, after which he happily belches, on his own, for I would certainly no longer be able to hold him up against my chest the way I do you.

He sometimes brings us one or more fish he has caught, abalones, which we probably cook all wrong, because they always come out rubbery.

The divorce is supposed to go through in June in Reno. Tigy is willing to go there alone six weeks earlier, to establish residence. It is enough for her alone to appear in court in Reno, accompanied by a local attorney selected by her San Francisco lawyer.

I of course take all the blame for the case. My New York lawyer has finally found grounds that cast no aspersions on either of us: "Refusal for three years to perform conjugal duties." This, of course, is no fiction, for I have had no sex with Tigy in five years. She will have custody of the child, but on that score there are certain ways of making it more flexible, which our lawyers are looking into.

These negotiations have been going on for almost a year, and I am beginning to become weary of them, if not disgusted. I wish the lawyers could handle it alone, without involving me.

Happy the couples of today who, more and more frequently, get along perfectly well living together without benefit of clergy or justice of the peace!

From the age of twenty or so, I have always been against all these legal formalities, which don't mean a thing and only complicate our lives. During my own life, I will see many of my youthful dreams, which I never expected to see accepted, come true.

I've had it up to the neck. Fortunately, I've got you with me, Johnny mine, to give me something else to think about. Fortunately too, I can escape into my novels. And, come what may, I have made my mind up that I won't be separated from Marc. I don't care about alimony. I never considered money to have any importance. What I do know, Johnny, is that I'm going to make sure you go on having a big brother.

The volcanic, tumultuous passion I felt in New York, in Sainte-Marguerite, has subsided. There are no longer the outbreaks between D. and me that there used to be. She no longer provokes me. She no longer seems to be playing a part. She no longer takes to the warpath wearing a mask of artful make-up.

Her complexion has become fresh and pink out in the open, and she dresses more soberly. She is more and more a simple, loving woman. Even though, once in a while, I am haunted by a doubt, which I quickly banish from my mind. She has taken to smoking again, but no longer with those affected gestures of stage or screen.

I am comfortable inside what I call my happiness, though not yet serenity. I am still in love with her.

At worst, perhaps I am a little miffed at seeing her infringe more and more on my prerogatives, that is, the running of my business affairs. As far as European publishers and producers are concerned, she does not insist too much, but as soon as it is a question of English or American rights, she too often acts on her own. By now, I am capable of carrying on negotiations in English by correspondence. In the beginning, she would translate the letters I had dictated to her in French, then she insisted on writing them herself, and answering by telephone at length. I don't have the courage to protest, to bring about more confrontations with her. I want to feel I am happy. I want to feel everyone around me is happy.

One day, shortly before June, my lawyer lets me know he is coming from New York; there are details he wants to iron out with me in person before the divorce and marriage. I am happy to see him again, because I like and trust him. But the idea of going back over all those questions that have been hashed and rehashed for months . . . Bah! We're almost there. His visit is a prelude to the beginning of the end.

I will welcome him almost gleefully to our house. He told me he will be staying in Carmel only a day. What, after all, is one day of paperwork?

Afterward, very soon, I'll be through with it, and will be able to take off for new horizons, whatever they may be.

36

A glorious month of May, Marc and Johnny mine. In certain climes, it is considered the finest of the year, despite storms and showers. Here, along the Pacific, at Carmel particularly, it seemed to me more enchanting than anywhere else, even though this exaltation did not come from contrast with the rigors of winter.

For Marc, it meant a warmer sea, into which he marched valiantly, and more abundant catches. Were you already aware of the playing of light, the warmth of the sun on your skin, which was getting tanned, the most varied and penetrating odors?

The old ladies who were the bulk of the Carmel population now put on straw hats, slightly too ornate and colorful. I had sometimes smiled over their artistic pretensions. Yet they all shared a vivid passion, which seems to be characteristic of Anglo-Saxon women, especially after a certain age: love of flowers.

All the perky little houses, in which the color rose predominated, were surrounded by gardens, without walls or hedges or enclosures, and from the top to the bottom of the hill one could see a veritable explosion of flowers of all kinds, which they tended with love and pride. I have never known the names of more than a few flowers, a few trees and bushes. These ladies knew them all and talked about them like experts.

The whole hillside bloomed under a sun that had become very hot, and the colors blended together like the instruments in a symphony. It was beautiful. The sea lions were merrier than in the wintertime, the tawny manes of the males even more copper-colored, the females more attentive to the daring games of their young, who came up as far as the shore.

As for Monterey, where the houses were not lined up in rows but, except for the few business streets, spread out among trees and gardens, it was an orgy of sound, light, and aroma, for fishing was in full swing.

I, my children, went to pick up my lawyer at the airport and was delighted to see him again. I was proud to show you off to him, Johnny, in our strange glass-and-rare-wood house.

Alas, with an attaché case chock-a-block with papers, he had come to work, and we got down to it almost right away. First, he read the draft agreement covering our divorce, and in that moment Tigy, who had so long been my wife, became the legal adversary.

I did not consider myself an adversary. Nor did she, in all likelihood. Her lawyer spoke in her name. At fifty, she had never earned her living. Yet it was thanks to the sale of one of her paintings that we had discovered the earthly paradise of Porquerolles in 1925. She had lived with me through a difficult start in Paris, when sometimes cashing in a few bottles for the deposit on them was all that stood between us and missing a meal or two. Boule had also known that period of our lives.

Tigy was, to be sure, asking a lot. I mean her lawyer was making great demands. Just about everything I owned, beginning with the house at Nieul I had so lovingly furnished for my future children and from which the German officers had driven me.

The stocks I owned became her property, the three sets of furniture stored in the outbuildings at Nieul, the paintings I had bought in days of affluence from most of my painter friends. A single Utrillo, from the white period, two or three oils by my dear Vlaminck, two Kislings, that other Montparnasse pal, whom I had found again in New York and on account of whom I almost didn't keep my appointment with an unknown secretary.

But you, Johnny mine, and you, my big Marc, weren't you worth a lot more than all that in my eyes?

The alimony was high, about as much in dollars as a top executive made at that time, a bit under the salary of a United States ambassador.

At every figure, D. burst out, "It's shameful! She's taking everything."

My lawyer tried to calm her down. "You overlook the unhoped-for concession she finally made on the subject of Marc. According to California law, she should have total custody of him, except for one weekly 'visit,' and part of the summer vacation."

"That makes me mad!" D. retorted. "If a man left me, even after twenty years of life together, I'd go off without asking anything of him, without wanting to keep anything of his, and I'd get by by taking whatever work there was."

Those words, children, still ring in my ears with cruel clarity.

"She's fifty years old," my friend put in.

"A woman ought to have enough pride not to accept anything from a man who no longer loves her."

I hung on to my chair, because I would much rather have been out on the sunlit terrace with you.

"This draft has the crucial clause, and it took me a long time to get my adversary to agree to it. Madame Simenon . . ."

"I'll be Madame Simenon," D. cut in.

The lawyer was used to this and remained calm. "Excuse me, madame," he replied clearly and precisely, "but at the time of the divorce, you will still be the concubine."

"We're getting married the next day, aren't we?"

"The next day is not the same as the day before."

He was finally allowed to go on.

"Custody of the infant Marc Simenon will be awarded to his mother only for so long as she agrees to live within six miles of the home of his father, wherever that may be. Failing that, the roles will be reversed and the child will live with his father, the mother then being entitled only to weekly visits and a part of the summer vacation. . . . There remains the question of insurance. . . ."

That was normal. Anything might happen to me, meaning, more crudely, that I might die, and Tigy would have been left without resources.

The amount provided was high for those days, so high that I was going to have to be examined by two or three specialists selected by the insurers. The annual premium was the equivalent of an average American's yearly income. So? I was thinking of you, of Marc, the sun, the flowers, the sea lions, your fine appetites.

Then began the inventory of what was left to me.

"One typewriter, two metal file cabinets, and the office furniture. The personal wardrobe of the said Simenon . . . the . . ."

The two of them were drinking whiskey, while I drank beer. D. had gone back to whiskey little by little.

"Excuse me," I said. "The two of you continue. I no longer have the heart for it."

I was suffocating in that smoky, booze-smelling room, where, between the huge sums and D.'s feverish protests, they were settling my fate, and especially that of my children.

I went out to be with you, Johnny. On the terrace, when you made your noisy signal, I gave you spoonfuls of puréed meat and vegetables, until it was time for your bottle. It would have been so nice to go out on Seventeen-Mile Drive and watch the sea lions with you, to breathe in the good smell of the ocean as it blended with that of those great trees.

I had to stay where I was, just in case. After all, my lawyer had crossed from the Atlantic to the Pacific to complete the last legal documents.

It lasted a couple of hours. We made a meal of sandwiches. I still had to read the separate-maintenance marriage contract. That was simpler, because D. had no possessions of her own.

At ten that night, I went to bed, while D., in the living room, typed up the documents that had finally been agreed on, and my friend lay down on the sofa, fully dressed.

From my bed, I could hear the clicking of the typewriter, then not another thing until dawn, when that clicking was supplanted by the chirping of the birds.

It was all over. All I had to do was reread the documents, which would become official as soon as the San Francisco lawyer approved them.

"Your wife, whom I represent legally," he said, "will now go to Reno for six weeks' residence."

"Yes, she has agreed to that."

"And after that? Where do you propose to live?"

The fact was, I didn't know. For a while, we had considered settling in San Francisco. D. and I had gone there during the preceding summer.

The city was admirable, with its gigantic harbor, the Golden Gate Bridge crossing it higher than the mast of the tallest ships, its steep white hills with the humpbacked little cable cars going up and down them, people hopping on while they were in motion. I more or less fell in love with it at first sight and was much taken with the piers, similar to those at Monterey, but much more numerous and busier.

We had visited a charming small house backed up against others like it, which in turn back up against others, and so on. It was truly comfortable, and the neighborhood was quiet, although not far from downtown. Behind each house was its own small garden, reminding me of Rue de la Loi and Rue de l'Enseignement of my childhood.

I said no without even having to think about it. The real estate agent kept trying.

No to it all. No to San Francisco, despite the St. Francis, with the extraordinary restaurant in which we had lunch, despite the wonderful hotel way up on top of a hill where we had dinner in the rooftop dining room, which looked out on the lights of the city.

Elsewhere! Not here! Perhaps because the house we had been shown, although new and never previously occupied, modern and cheery, reminded me of the house of my childhood.

I wanted open space for you, Johnny, for Marc, and for myself, who had now become used to it.

Tigy would have liked us to spend some time in Europe. If I say "us," it is because, once all the formalities were duly taken care of, we were to remain linked by an invisible chain, that six-mile clause covering the proximity of our two households.

Why not Europe? If I don't say "France," it is because, like the Americans, I had become used to thinking of Europe as a whole: the other shore of the Atlantic, in a word, and from here one could not tell Frenchmen, Englishmen, Germans, Dutchmen, Greeks, and Spaniards, even Poles and Czechs, apart.

In looking for names for the characters of my novels, I later bought some sixty U.S. telephone directories, which I used to leaf through at my leisure. There were almost no French names, but in every city, especially in the East, a plethora of Italian and Irish ones. In Chicago, German, Russian, and Polish names, and in the Middle West a predominance of Dutch and German among the foreign-sounding ones, whereas in the South Scottish names competed with Hispanic.

Europe? . . . Well, why not? But not for good.

And why not one of those Southern states, where there is such a soft, singing accent and so many blacks? I am thinking mainly of the two Carolinas, North and South, which we lazily went through with Marc and for which I developed a longing.

I don't know. I am no longer able to make a choice. This divorce business has taken a lot out of me, much too much, so that I sometimes feel as if I were not involved, as if in the whole nasty affair I were just a pawn that others were moving around as they pleased.

Yet, I fill out the proper forms. For instance, the Belgian consul has already entered you as a Belgian citizen, but we will soon be getting your American passport, so that you have double nationality. You will be able to choose, Johnny of mine, at the time—that seems so far away to me—you become twenty-one.

Not only are you a Belgian citizen with a passport to show it, but I have had you entered on the Simenon page in the office of vital statistics of the city of Liège.

Jean-Denis-Chrétien thus appears on the same page as my grandfather Chrétien Simenon, as myself, and your brother Marc, and among your given names you all have the name of that old Chrétien and so many other Chrétien, or Christian, Simenons who came before him. All your cousins on the paternal side are also on the same page, and all of them too have the name Chrétien before their family name.

A family of farmers, artisans, common people, in a word, except for one bishop, of whom I am no prouder than I am of the others; quite the contrary.

You see, I've never forgotten Outremeuse, where I spent my youth and adolescence, the big red zinc high hat that towered above my grandfather's shop, and the glassed-in kitchen, on the other side of the courtyard, where the Simenon children and grandchildren got together on Sundays, and my blind great-grandfather, the miner who died after reaching a hundred, bounced us up and down on his knee.

It is precisely because experience has taught me how our childhood influences us for the rest of our lives that I pay so much attention to yours and do my best to fill your heads with happy memories. For the same reason today, at seventy-seven, I have set out to tell you each about your own childhood, all four of you, to tell you about details you yourselves have probably forgotten.

Everything counts in the life of a child, a human child, every hour, every ray of sunshine and the quiet drumming of the rain on the window-panes, all those pictures among which, unbeknownst to us, our young brain selects a few.

It's over! Our lawyer has left. Before driving you out to Seventeen-Mile Drive and the sea lion rock, I rush over to Tigy's. She is aware of the terms agreed to and, as soon as she has seen her lawyer, is prepared to leave for Reno, where she will settle in one of those furnished houses used by the hundreds of about-to-be divorcees who come through Reno.

Marc will remain in Carmel with Boule until she gets back, and we will see him at our house daily. At eleven, he is aware of what is going on, but to him it is an unimportant incident compared to his diving for abalones, fishing, his games with his friends.

I often see Boule, who is upset, like a tabby during a household move. Whom will she end up with? Tigy forced her into two years of loneliness in France but she nevertheless has spent many years with her and me.

She is not yet used to D., whom she treats with a certain amount of distrust. As for you, she comes to see you often, Johnny mine, now that Tigy is away, and she is amazed at your strength and size. "He could be a year old. He'll be walking any day now. And look at how curiously he's looking me over."

She weeps and laughs all at the same time, finally picks you up and holds you in her arms. You don't smile. But you don't cry either. Your eyes try to meet mine, and then your mother's.

I go to see her by myself at their house, and we "get together" again.

"What's going to become of us, my fine young gentleman?"

For twenty years now, she has been referring to me that way. I reassure her, and our intimacy is reestablished.

We take you out a great deal. Before we in turn go to Reno, which we are to do on June 20, we will have to send ahead everything we can't take on the plane with us. I also have to sell our Buick, because it is out of the question to drive across the United States with you, especially since Reno is in the middle of a more scorchingly hot desert than the one in Arizona and after that we would have to cross the snow-capped Rockies.

Changing cars, or even houses, is a minor concern to Americans, and we have somewhat acquired that mentality. As we are about to take to the air for Reno, all I will have to do is drop the car off at the dealership that has already bought it. I will also, at her request and for her account, sell Tigy's car.

I spend hours carefully wrapping up hundreds of books and packing them for the mover to take.

None of all this confusion bothers you. Yet one would swear that you are supervising everything we do. You cry less and less, perhaps because your appetite is better satisfied by your varied menu. You try to say some words, after having observed our lip movements. I keep out for last the phonograph and the Benny Goodman records, which we are taking along.

No more reason for impatience. At least in my case. After a few days of bitterness, I believe that I have understood some of D.'s attitude during the interview with our lawyer. I don't hold it against her. I succeed in burying deep in my memory some of the words, some of the opinions, some of the looks. We return to our earlier relationship and are once again a couple watching over you. I also watch over Marc, and Boule, whom I have to see often in order to keep her spirits up. I believe that I understand all three of the women, but sometimes I feel that some little spring inside me has broken.

D. and I are still in love, or at least lovers. From the very first days, weren't we, above all else, if not exclusively, lovers? I try to keep from asking myself too many questions, try to keep enjoying until the end the charms of Carmel, the varicolored attractiveness of Monterey. To keep enjoying especially my fatherhood, which throughout all my life will remain my great source of joy and my main concern.

The great day comes. A yellow van has carried off all of our belongings, except for our hand baggage. I drive the Buick to Monterey for the last time, and we leave it there and head for the airport.

This is your first air travel, and you don't seem to notice that we are up midway between sky and earth. Flights are not yet in the stratosphere, or at ten-mile altitudes, and one can see landscapes below that keep constantly changing. Trees replace fields dotted with cows. Then the desert, sand as far as the eye can see, a straight road that seems shiny black and cars riding on it that look as small as the miniatures you will one day collect.

When we are right in the middle of the desert, the plane starts descending. Through the window, I finally catch sight of some trees, and finally four or five buildings of an indeterminate number of stories with toy houses around them.

We are taxiing. The plane brakes, stops, and porters in cowboy hats and Mexican boots are helping us. We have a suite reserved at a hotel that has been recommended to us; it turns out to be a skyscraper of a de luxe hotel.

The day after tomorrow, I will be divorced from Tigy, but I don't have to be there. The next day, D. and I will be married by a justice of the peace.

You are almost too big for your portable crib, and you weigh a ton—I know, because I carry you! While your mother settles us, I see about finding a nurse to take care of you, because we can't decently have you along when we get married.

The next day, a very young girl with a round pink face and big, light, innocent eyes turns up. She is used to handling babies, and you make no fuss when she picks you up and holds you.

At ten o'clock, Tigy is getting her divorce, in the same government building in which tomorrow we will be married. We will not see her in Reno. We will be informed of the divorce by our local attorney when we go to see him. He has us sign some documents, gives me his bill, and tells us not to worry about anything else, just be there at ten tomorrow. He whispers to me that, after what can hardly be called "the ceremony," I might discreetly slip a five-dollar bill into the hand of the justice of the peace when he gives us his congratulations and best wishes.

We return to the hotel. I go right out again, leaving you with your mother and the nursemaid, to get some tobacco and I don't know what else. My change is given me in big silver dollars, and I understand why as I go out. Next to the door, there is a slot machine that is made to take only silver dollars.

I get back to the hotel to find it dark, with only a few candles lighting the place. There is a blackout, and suddenly I remember—since the elevators are not working—that we are on the forty-second floor.

"You think it will last long?"

The man at the desk answers by a shrug. "Maybe an hour. Maybe longer."

"Maybe all night?"

Fatalistically, he throws his arms up.

"In that case, I'd better take some food up with me. Anything. Hamburgers, hot dogs, for three, and a platter of cold cuts."

"In a few minutes, sir."

Behind me, I hear the clicks of a slot machine, which an old gentleman is anxiously watching. There are three or four more slot machines in the lobby. I put a coin in one, and get four back. Another coin: I get two. Still another, and six come out. My neighbor, who keeps losing, looks at me as if he thought I were cheating.

They bring me a big silver platter, with cold cuts. And the hot dogs and hamburgers.

"Would you like someone to bring it up for you?"

I grandstand it. The silver coins are jingling in my pocket, and, taking my tray, I start up the stairs, which are lighted by a candle at every floor.

The little nursemaid has left, until eight-thirty in the morning. There are just the two of us, lighted by candles, sitting down to this mess of food that could feed six people.

I am not hungry. I pick at things while D. eats heartily, and you, Johnny mine, are asleep.

37

As we are finishing dinner, all the lights go on in our suite, paling the yellow light of our candles.

I get up, hesitantly, then suddenly decide I will do as I have always done, with Tigy and with D., when we get to some new place. I experience a need to go out alone, to get a whiff of the new air, to make contact with the atmosphere that is still new to me. Perhaps, also, on the eve of the final formality, I am trying to avoid a long tête-à-tête, which I fear might be sentimental or passionate.

"Excuse me, but I have to go out."

"I know," she says simply.

I kiss her. I touch your sleeping brow, Johnny, for fear of awakening you, and I go out to wait for the elevator.

From my first steps outside the hotel, I find myself grabbed by a dazzling world, of all possible colors. This is New York's Times Square, but more brilliant, more concentrated. Music comes from any number of places. Casinos are bunched in a rather small space in the middle of the Nevada desert, with flashing electric signs everywhere, bars, stores that seem never to close, a superexcited crowd rushing into the gaping maws of the casinos.

A carnival atmosphere, that of a sad carnival. The police are dressed like cowboys, with a tin star on their chests; the tourists, mostly gamblers from all corners of the world, are more or less disguised as well. Many of them are women, dressed less garishly; few young ones; most of them fiftyish or over. The same set stare in their eyes, a stare that is reminiscent of that of drug addicts, the drug they are getting their fix on here being gambling.

I follow the crowd into the first casino, a hundred yards or so from the hotel, the one that has the most lights from sidewalk to roof, and am suddenly swallowed up in an unimaginable world, a universe that seems limitless. Where are the walls?

Many partitions, over which one can see what is taking place on the other side, serve as divisions for endless rows of slot machines, most of them in use. The man or woman holds his or her arm out mechanically, like a robot, slips a coin into the slot, then pulls down the rather heavy handle until the rolling drums show some cherries, plums, or apricots, or the little black labels of a well-known brand of chewing gum appear. In the cup below, nothing comes out unless the right number of cherries or other fruit shows up, and everyone hopes for the row of black gum labels that means they have hit the jackpot.

It doesn't take even half a minute, just a few seconds, and all up and down the rows the arms go up again, without respite, slipping the coin in and pulling down the heavy handle.

Some of the machines take only silver dollars; others take half-dollars, quarters, or even dimes.

The fixedness of the stares, the automatism of the movements have something almost inhuman about them. Farther on, I find the big green baccarat tables, at which, in casinos the world over, heavy gambling goes on, with chips of varied colors, some of which may represent a hundred or a thousand dollars.

The dealers rake in the chips, shove some out toward the winner, whom all the others look at with envy; and the same thing goes on at the roulette tables, at which men and women players are bunched three or four deep.

There are also tables for shooting craps, an American dice game that was not to appear in Europe until much later, first at Monte Carlo, then at other casinos. I can't make out the very complicated rules and merely stand

and watch the dice roll out of the black plastic shakers, and the faces of winners and losers, scarcely recognizable as human.

My childhood, by a miracle, is about to come back to me, in a peaceful oasis of this noisy marketplace in which voices are drowned out by music from loudspeakers.

Seated one at each little table, youthful-looking girls in cowgirl outfits wait for players, card deck in hand. They play one-on-one twenty-one, a game that some Russian students taught me as a boy. I used to play it with my schoolmates, for cherry pits, which had been carefully cleaned and shined. In those days, I was a shark at it. I seek out the most attractive of the young ladies, sit down opposite her, and put a dollar on the table.

"Nineteen," I call.

"Twenty-one," says my blonde vis-à-vis with the cold blue eyes as she scoops up my dollar.

I double, but just as unsuccessfully, then double the bet again, and lose once more. Almost all the cartwheels I won in the hotel lobby are gone.

I am not a gambler. Money doesn't count for me, but what else can one do here, except imitate the others? I find a free slot machine in a dollar row, and at the first try come up with cherries. I mechanically scoop up the coins in the cup, and soon my coat pockets are weighing me down so much that I decide to go back to the hotel to empty them.

I find D. there, changing your diaper, and I get a chance to put you back in your crib, which is a bit short for you.

I toss the silver dollars into a drawer, keeping only a few with me as I go out to return to the same casino. D. calls to me, "See, it's your lucky day!"

The day of my divorce! Where is Tigy at this time? Still in this city? Or has the plane already dropped her back into that peaceful, flowery Carmel I left only yesterday?

I don't gloat over my luck. I have been too knocked about by events. I have remained lucid, of course, and nothing that is happening or will happen tomorrow morning is or will be done against my will. I have acted to the best of my ability, but with a confused heart. Before going back to my slot machine I stop off at a huge bar to down a quick Martini.

Serious gentlemen in tuxedos, on the alert, whose tough biceps can be made out through their sleeves, come and go, and one can see the shape of their holsters under their well-tailored suits. Could it be otherwise in this circus where every night hundreds of thousands of dollars change hands? And now I hear a neighbor saying that these casinos operate on a twenty-

four-hour basis, the cleaning up being done, almost unnoticeably, one section at a time.

To my utter amazement, I win some more. I had found my same dollar
slot machine, my gray-haired, red-faced neighbor to the left, a fat lady
tightly ensconced in black silk to the right. Both of them look at me with
envy.

All of a sudden, after less than half an hour, my slot machine starts to
rumble in its entrails, a siren goes off, and, as the silver dollars start bounding
out of the overfilled cup and raining down on the floor, a spotlight shines
on me bending down to pick up my booty.

Two house photographers snap shots of me, and a house cowboy holds
out a wicker basket. He picks up my coins for me, and a potbellied gentleman with a bald head, over which lie four or five hairs that seem to have been
put there with India ink, holds out his pudgy hand to me and, as the
photographers snap away, solemnly makes me an award of—a tiny stainless-
steel slot machine, which, he explains, works "just like the big ones."

The basket by now is almost full. A small crowd has formed, and for
a while I am a kind of hero, because a jackpot doesn't come up every night
in the week.

It is all very well organized. When I try to stuff the pile of coins into
my pockets, I am amiably told, "You can keep the basket too."

What to do? Gamble some more? I have no desire to. Only one thing
is on my mind: to get out of this whirlwind, back to the shelter of our hotel
room. But I have to take a glass of French champagne and drink a toast with
the big boss.

Once I am alone among those rows of slot machines, half-dazed, I start
toward the exit. One of the bouncers with the holsters asks me, "What hotel
are you at? It's not safe for you to go over there by yourself." He nods
toward my overflowing basket of cartwheels.

I don't remember whether he went with me. In our room, D. can't
believe her eyes when she sees me start to unload my harvest of silver dollars
into one of the dresser drawers.

"What did I tell you? It's your lucky day, the day you got . . ."

I stop her short. My divorce; I know. She spends a long time counting
the silver dollars before telling me that they total six hundred forty-five, or
fifty.

"What are you going to do with them?"

"Keep a few for the children . . ." And turn the others in at the bank,
because I can't see myself getting on the plane to New York weighted down
with this load, of which I am anything but proud.

I don't believe we made love that night. I was tense, not as a result of the gambling, but because of certain thoughts that were pestering me and a kind of sense of guilt that pursued me even into sleep.

You wake us twice, sweet Johnny mine, not able to stand being wet and letting out your war whoop.

I shower, shave, dress as on other mornings, and remember my first wedding, my mother alone with me in the carriage, blowing her nose and wiping her eyes, me explaining to her that in France potatoes are fried in boiling oil, whereas in Belgium people use a mixture of beef fat and lard. "It's much lighter than the fat, Mother. You have to try it."

"A person doesn't change her tastes at my age."

She was forty-three, I was twenty. Now, at forty-seven, I wasn't taking any carriage to go and get married, nor to church, but to a justice of the peace close by. Since Reno, at that time, was nothing but a little spot on the desert, and one might well wonder how so many people, so much light, so many passions ever got piled up there.

Wasn't it passion that brought me here too?

Our young baby nurse arrives at eight. At nine, D. and I leave the hotel, to stretch our legs and breathe in the morning air. The sun is as hot as in Arizona, and the sand gets in everywhere.

As we go by the desk, we are asked, "Don't you want a religious service?"

"No. Why?"

"Because we have a nonsectarian chapel here in the hotel, where you can have a Protestant, Catholic, Jewish, Orthodox, or Mormon ceremony performed."

They have thought of everything. This little pile of concrete in the desert is a divorce machine, a wedding machine, a gambling machine, and maybe a machine for satisfying other needs as well. Rumor has it that the Syndicate runs the whole thing like clockwork. I never try to find out.

We go into a drugstore for some purchase or other. Not much, since it came to less than two dollars. I give them a ten-dollar bill and get silver dollars as change.

There is a slot machine near the counter, and D. insists that I try it. It doesn't tire my arm, because in less than three minutes it has swallowed up my eight dollars.

"Strange, isn't it?" she exclaims, smiling, seemingly delighted. "I think that's a very good sign. The day you get divorced, you win money. The day you get married, you win happiness. . . ."

I answer yes, without conviction. We take a walk in a garden that has palms, avocados, and other pretty green trees.

A little before ten, we go up the steps of the courthouse, which looks like the courthouse in any other American small town. Our local attorney is waiting for us, gives me several papers, directs us through white corridors toward an empty and quite unimpressive room.

"Do you want me to stay?"

"I wouldn't want to waste your time. You must be very busy."

"Yes, very."

He's a machine too, a divorce-and-marriage-contract machine.

We remain alone until exactly ten o'clock. Here too everything goes like clockwork. A very tall man, with white hair, wearing a white Stetson and a tan silk suit, comes in, followed by a rather young lady, who takes her place beside him behind the desk.

With a full face and blue eyes, the justice of the peace looks like a noble father on the stage or a judge in a Western movie, full of well-meaning authority.

The secretary passes papers to him, and he reads from them without the need of glasses.

"Are you Mr. Georges-Joseph-Christian Simenon?"

"Yes."

He turns to D.

"And you are Miss ——"

"Yes."

There are empty benches behind us, made of light wood. No decoration other than an American flag and a bronze eagle.

"I presume you do not have any witnesses with you."

"No. Should we have?"

The secretary presses a white button. A short wait. Silence. Two huge middle-aged cowboys come in and sit down near us, as if they were going through a routine long since become second nature.

The justice introduces us all, then reads some official texts to us while I am utterly fascinated by his hat, which he must get cleaned and blocked every morning, the way the Dallas millionaires do.

He reads our marriage contract with conviction, finally signals to us to stand up, gets up himself, looking even more impressive and playing his part more convincingly than the best of actors.

"Do you take . . ."

"Yes."

Then, to D.

"Do you take . . ."

"Yes."

"Do you have the rings?"

I take them out of my pocket. We bought them in Monterey, and in another pocket I have my old wedding ring, which I just took off this morning.

I put one ring on D.'s hand, the other on my own ring finger.

"In the name of the state of Nevada, I now declare you married for better and for worse."

Well, that's it! For better and for . . .

Looking moved, he shakes our hands, and his secretary is so zealous about her work that she even sheds two or three tears. I didn't dare slip a five-dollar bill in the judge's hand. Maybe on account of his white Stetson, his silk suit, his dignified manner. From my pocket, I dig out a ten, which he takes without batting an eye.

He wants us to kiss each other, which we do. I pay the two witnesses. We go outside, and the hot sun hits us in the face. D. takes my arm as we walk toward the shade of a small park.

"Well, what effect did it have on you?"

I have trouble knowing what to answer. Mostly, at the moment, I'm hot and would like a glass of beer.

"Do you realize that now I am Madame Georges Simenon?"

"Yes."

"The only Madame Georges Simenon."

"No. I have a nephew named after me. He is of marriageable age, and his wife will be Madame Georges Simenon too. Some of my other Simenon cousins might also . . ."

That reminded me of a painful argument, in Carmel, when my lawyer was there. Tigy, who for twenty years has had my name and is known by it to all our friends, asked to have the right to continue using it. I naturally agreed. It is a common thing for a divorced woman to go on using her ex-husband's name.

D., obviously displeased, commented: "Simenon, if absolutely necessary. Provided it isn't 'Madame Georges Simenon.' "

I accepted that wording. So did Tigy. The lawyer winked at me in amusement.

We sit down on a bench. D. points to a tiny body of water in the middle of the semitropical growth.

"Do you know what I heard? It's the custom, in Reno, when people get married again, to throw their old wedding rings into that fountain, which is supposed to be very deep."

She is waiting for my reaction. I don't react; in my pocket, I am fingering my twenty-year-old wedding ring.

She is expecting some gesture, I know. I get up. So does she. We go over to the greenish water. I can feel that D. is tense, and quickly I take the ring from my pocket and toss it into the pond, after which I walk toward the street, with D. hanging on my arm. She seems to have been relieved of a great weight. Squeezing my arm hard, she says in a warm, slightly throaty voice: "Thank you, Jo! Thanks for what you just did for me. Now, there can never again be anything standing between us."

In an air-conditioned bar, she asks, while the bartender waits for us to order: "Do you mind if I have a whiskey?"

Why should I? I order beer. Two whiskeys, two beers. Because, you see, my Marc, and you see, Johnny mine, I never did work "on whiskey," as D. was to tell it later on and state to newspapermen. No one ever saw a bottle of whiskey on my desk, or anywhere near my typewriter. As a child and adolescent, I had never seen wine on my parents' dinner table; a friend on the *Gazette* staff gave me my first taste of English beer when I was seventeen.

In Paris, when for about a month I had my lunches at the cut-rate Dîners de Paris, where for three francs fifty inclusive one got an appetizer, plat du jour, cheese, and dessert, they also served each person a split of red wine.

When, later on, I was writing eighty pages a day of dime novels, I fortified myself, wherever I might be, with the local white wine.

The drink changed, as in Maigret's case, according to the region or climate. At Porquerolles it was rosé that got me through to the end of my pages. Later on, I drank Bordeaux, on advice of my old friend Pautrier. "Two bottles of Bordeaux a day, no more, not too new, or too old."

At La Richardière, there were farmers around me who drank up to ten bottles of local wine a day, and everyone felt it was perfectly natural.

When I wrote my hard novels, I worked on black coffee or tea, which did not keep me from having a glass or two of beer afterward. I later gave up beer when I was "with novel," but that again did not keep me from celebrating the completion of one of them by rewarding myself with a bottle of champagne.

In France, I don't remember ever drinking whiskey, either at Fouquet's or anywhere else, and certainly not at home. When friends and I drank a toast, I opted for cognac with water.

It was in New York, to keep D. company, that I drank whiskey, sometimes to excess, though less than she did. At Sainte-Marguerite too, except when I was "with novel."

I am not trying to defend myself. Many legends have been created about me, and I have found out how hard legends are to put to rest. If I let myself wander off into this parenthesis, children, you two and the other two, who are to be born later, it is because that legend, which was started and kept going by D., has been most hurtful to you.

I was thinking of that that morning, right after we got married, as I drank my beer, and that's why I have spoken about it here.

We have lunch, take you out for a stroll. Only that evening do we "celebrate" what happened in the morning, with a champagne dinner.

Our hotel has a rooftop restaurant. It is also a nightclub, and on the bill is one number the name of which I remember: The Arnivelds.

A devilishly active troupe comes on stage, doing pirouettes and cartwheels at a faster and faster pace. Five men and a woman, acrobats all, all loose-jointed. With expressive mimicry and unexpected gags, they dance, sing, sometimes upside down, and play the most unexpected instruments.

Sometimes they call to one another, as circus performers do, and I can still hear myself exclaiming: "Why, they're Belgians!" No mistaking their accent. Not only Belgians, but Walloons, perhaps from Liège.

"Does that make you happy, Jo?"

"Yes."

It is the happiest recollection of my wedding in Reno. I later came across the name of the Arnivelds in other towns, other countries. I don't know what kind of reserve kept me from going backstage that night to shake their hands. I have always been afraid of imposing on people.

When the elevator takes us down to our floor at last, two or three men, maybe four, are waiting for us.

"Sorry to disturb you, Mr. and Mrs. Simenon. I'm from *Time* magazine."

Another holds his hand out, saying, "New York *Daily News.*"

"Los Angeles *Examiner*. We didn't want to break in on you earlier. We know that you got divorced yesterday, Mr. Simenon, and were married again this morning."

"That's correct."

A few obvious questions tossed at D. and me.

"You're his secretary, aren't you? Canadian, if I'm not mistaken."

We are standing on the red carpet in the hall, and I am waiting for the main question, which finally comes.

"Is it true that you have a baby?"

"Yes, Johnny Simenon."

"Is he here with you?"

"Right behind that door. I didn't want to wake him, and that's why I didn't invite you in. I have another son, Marc, by my first wife."

"We found that out. Here, nothing is secret. Reno is just a big little hick town."

"Who's taking care of the baby?"

"A very nice young lady who was sent in by the hotel."

They smile, and one of them cracks, "Here, the hotels send in anything."

"Reno is certainly well organized."

We're on a joking basis now.

"When are you leaving?"

"Tomorrow afternoon."

"Which way? Back to Carmel?"

They've certainly done their homework.

"New York."

"To stay?"

"Surely not. I can't work in a big city."

"Well, then? Europe?"

"Maybe. But if so, only temporarily. Or we may decide on one of the Southern states we've been through."

"In other words, you're just going off blindly."

"The way I always have."

"Why? Aren't you satisfied anywhere?"

"On the contrary. I might very well have stayed on in Arizona or California. Only, there's always someplace else."

"Is that what gives you the material for your novels?"

"I don't have to look for it. It takes hold of me."

"Do you like traveling too, Mrs. Simenon?"

It's strange to hear her addressed that way.

"I will go wherever my husband goes."

"Will you remain his secretary as well as being his wife?"

"I should hope so."

"Are you that much in love with him?"

"If I weren't, I wouldn't be here."

We shake their hands and go inside.

"Did I answer them all right, Jo?"

"Very well, indeed."

I am no martyr. I am living through a real passion with her, with all its bursts of feeling and storms. If at times I feel concerned, it is in spite of myself, and I quickly shake it off. I want her to be happy, simply happy, without artificial exaltation, without putting on any acts, and she has made measurable strides in that dirction, hasn't she?

That night, we make love, and she is tenderer than ever.

Tomorrow, off again—toward the unknown!

Your little nursemaid had left us, Johnny mine, after kissing all three of us, congratulating us.

On what?

38

I had often traveled by plane, in Europe on short hops from capital to capital and to cross Africa from north to south. At the time, it was in small craft, with one or two propellers, even one that for four solid days carried us over the Nile, the desert, virgin forests and brush. The plane flew only at some seven thousand feet of altitude. No pressurization. Twenty passengers in all, in a narrow compartment; portholes that were opened to allow fresh air in.

This time, we were getting on a plane that appeared gigantic to us and carried at least fifty people. It was not yet a jet, and was to make several refueling stops on the way.

You slept at times in your mother's arms, at others in mine, lulled by the purring of the engines. When you weren't using my chest as a pillow, I slept sitting up as calmly and deeply as in my own bed.

So I was asleep toward the middle of the night when your mother shook my arm vigorously.

"Jo, don't you notice anything?"

She looked worried, and a violent thunderclap illustrated her words. Then the inside of the plane was illuminated by a ghostly light, like the arc lamps of my childhood. The thunder and lightning seemed to be shaking the plane, which rolled now to the right, now to the left, and sometimes seemed to be falling straight down, like an elevator.

"A storm," I calmly told her.

"Look behind you."

In the aisle, stewards and stewardesses were getting life belts and inflatable life rafts out of a closet and piling them up near an emergency exit.

"We surely can't be over the ocean," I commented.

"We're approaching Lake Michigan, which is as big as a sea. The hostess just told me."

Most of the passengers, of both sexes, were vomiting, pale, greenish. One fat man snored in his seat.

As time went by, the bumps became worse, like it was in Africa when we flew over an "air hole." The sky had as many streaks of light in it as during the war when there were air raids on La Pallice.

Through the windows, one could make out the beams of strong searchlights, not far from the lights of a great city: Chicago, toward which we were descending in the middle of a whirlwind. You, Johnny mine, were sleeping more deeply than ever. The plane hit the ground roughly, bounced two or three times, and finally came to rest in a brilliantly lighted space.

The stewardess announced a half-hour stopover. Passengers could get out and have refreshments at the buffet.

I went down the ladder with you in my arms. Only then did I feel some retrospective anxiety. On the tarmac, ambulances were lined up and, even more threatening, fire engines.

Had all these impressive preparations been made on our account? Had we been in such great danger? D. inquired of one person after another on her way to the airport building, while the thunder and lightning kept merrily on. Here, on earth, it was of course nothing but a heavy storm. Once inside the buffet, I asked D., "What's going on?"

"Just as we were beginning our descent, up over the lake, another plane, heading for Los Angeles, crashed into the lake, with some fifty passengers."

The ambulances and fire engines were speeding away in a dreadful parade, and foghorns could be heard wailing on the Lake Michigan boats.

"Wait for me a minute. I have to get a drink." She went into the bar.

I stayed on the bench of what must have been a waiting room. Everything seemed strange, the dramatic, almost hallucinated looks, and our soaked clothes. This was all I was ever to know of Chicago, to which I never returned.

"Your turn. Let me have the baby. I have a change of clothes for him."

I can't remember what I drank, maybe whiskey, this time, because now I was scared, and the storm had in no way abated.

We were supposed to make only a half-hour stopover. From time to time, the loudspeaker kept us informed.

"Coast Guard cutters are searching the lake. Departure for New York has been delayed by fifteen minutes."

Then another fifteen.

"Up to now, no trace has been found of the plane or its passengers. The waters of the lake are very choppy, with waves ten feet high, and the search is very difficult."

Another quarter hour's delay. How many such were there? I didn't count. Finally, the storm, with its violent squalls, seemed to diminish.

"Passengers for New York are requested to return to their seats on the plane."

The takeoff was just about normal, and we gained altitude and reached cruising speed. I held you in my arms while D. slept at last, and I waited for her to wake up fully before turning you over to her.

It seemed as if the storm was following us, less violent now, but still with sharp squalls and lightning. Or, rather, because of the quiet spots between, it seemed as if we were going from one storm to the next, going through a whole chain of storms.

At dawn, the captain came back to explain to us in person that because of the air turbulence over a large part of the country, he had had to veer south, and we had just flown over Washington, D.C. As a result, he was sorry to say we would arrive in New York two hours late.

Silence. Silence everywhere, almost eerie after all that noise. The plane slipped through the air without bumps, and the noise of the engines was just an even purr.

"On Lake Michigan, the search goes on, although all hope has been given up of finding the plane or any survivors. Some pieces of a wing have been spotted."

That was it, Johnny! That was your second flight. As far as I can remember, you took it very well, little man, and we landed without further ado. Anxious relatives of some of the passengers were waiting, because the first news bulletins had not made clear which of the two planes passing each other over the lake had been literally lightning-struck and fallen hook, line, and sinker into the watery depths.

Our suite was at the same hotel where on a certain night my fate as well as your mother's had been sealed, and consequently yours too.

This time D. no longer had to sneak in with a hatbox in hand. We settled in. A nice little oak bed had been set up for you. It was broad daylight, and the bright June sun showed no traces of the previous night's furies. I left it to D. to unpack and put our things away, as in the past with Tigy.

We had left your folding stroller in Carmel, expecting to find a finer and better one in New York. No luck. I finally found a stroller in navy-blue sailcloth, and had to make do with that. However, at the same time, I discovered a safety seat for infants, to be attached to the car seat and guaranteed foolproof. I didn't have a car anymore, but I bought it just the same.

I had it all sent to the hotel, as well as some flowers and an opulent basket of fruit, in the middle of which was a pound cake just like the ones your future godmother in Tucson had baked for your mother.

When I say future godmother, it is because at the age of nine months you still weren't baptized. Jean Renoir, who was so intent on being your godfather, had cabled me that in Calcutta, where he was shooting *The River* on the banks of the Ganges, he had been unable to get enough electric power to light his indoor sets. He was sure he would find a way to overcome this, but in the meantime it was delaying him by a year.

Tigy, back in Carmel with Marc and Boule, was waiting for a decision I had not yet made.

Where to go? Tigy had become more or less adjusted to American life, but was handicapped by the language, which she had trouble learning. Your mother, of course, was like a fish in water. But her childhood dream, like that of many French-speaking Canadian boys and girls, was to go and see France. Boule felt quite at home with the American way of life and, paradoxically, got along much better in English than Tigy. The question before her was: "Whom will I now be living with?"

I could not answer that question any more than the previous one. I had been too shaken up these last few months not to wish for peace of mind and heart in some heartwarming place especially suitable for children.

New York was sweltering. I wanted greenery, open spaces. Why not spend a few months back at La Rochelle, one of the cities I like the most in all the world? Tigy and Marc could go back to the house at Nieul, so lovingly set up but no longer belonging to me. As for your mother, you, and me, we could find some little whitewashed house around there, surrounded by great pasturelands, not too far from the sea.

Even though I had not made up my mind, I went to the Belgian consulate to make sure our papers were in proper shape for a long trip.

"Are you really planning to go to Europe with a baby, Simenon?"

"He's big enough to stand the crossing. He's already crossed the United States from west to east under worse conditions than any ocean liner might have to overcome."

"Don't you read the papers? Don't you listen to the radio?"

"Not recently. I've had other things on my mind."

"Haven't you heard of Korea?"

"I only know that North Korea is fighting South Korea. That's the other side of the world, isn't it?"

"Listen to what I have to say. The Americans are fighting on the side of the South Koreans. The North Koreans are being supported by the Russians. There is a certain amount of panic in Europe, and many Frenchmen, who got burned in the last war, have been applying for visas for the United States. I can't say any more than that, but if I were you . . ."

I understood. My mind was made up. No trip to Europe.

"I imagine you're now not planning to settle in Europe with your family?"

"Certainly not. I'm going to find some very quiet country place, a village or small town, where the children can play safely."

"Do you know Connecticut?"

"I came through it on my way from Canada. Too many cities, too much traffic on the roads to suit me."

"But do you know the northwestern part of it, the foothills of the Berkshires?"

I had heard a great deal about those mountains, valleys, lakes, and the concerts that each summer brought classical-music enthusiasts to the region.

On my return to the hotel, I find you sitting in your stroller on the sidewalk, near the door, where a huge doorman in livery is looking after you with a smile. You're smiling too, Johnny, at him, at the passers-by, at the sun, the blue sky, life itself. . . .

The older you grow, the more you smile, a totally unmysterious smile that simply expresses your contentment. You are not yet aware that your fate has just been decided, your fate for quite a long while, this time.

Walking back from the consulate, I had bought a road map of Connecticut. I announce the news to D., who seems delighted at the prospect. I write Tigy and Marc to tell them that in a few days I will be able to inform them about our future. A short sweet note to Boule as well. I discuss the matter with the manager of the hotel, who has become a good friend, and he gives it his endorsement.

"Do you know that in the fall, during what is called 'Indian summer,' New Yorkers go off, bumper to bumper, to see the changing of the leaves in Connecticut, where the colors go from gold to dark russet by way of all the shades of the spectrum? Go and see for yourself. Take the side roads, rather than the parkway, that is, after the first fifty miles or so . . ."

I go to buy some dresses for D., who can no longer wear her maternity dresses, since little by little her figure has returned to normal.

At D.'s request I go to the impressive store, moving from rack to rack, feeling the materials, looking for bright colors, simple lines. Finally, I've made up my mind for five or six summer and spring dresses, and the chief saleslady comes over.

"Give me your name and your room number at the hotel. I'll send one of my fitters over in the morning to make whatever alterations are required."

Fine with me, of course. While I'm at it, I go over to Broadway to a Chrysler agency. I remember my good old Chrysler of the past that remained faithful to me for eight years, until one of my friends in La Rochelle, a farmer, to whom I had given it, turned it into a pickup truck.

I did not buy a Chrysler proper, but a DeSoto, of a new type called "town-and-country."

"Do you intend to pay cash for it?"

"Of course."

"You're making a mistake. You lose a lot of money that way."

"I don't understand."

"Paying in installments allows you to deduct all the interest and carrying charges from your income tax. Even our wealthiest customers never do it any other way."

I had never bought anything on credit, except once in my life, when I was very young and Tigy and I had bought some of the household goods we needed for Place des Vosges that way.

"If you say so," I acquiesced.

"This will just take a minute."

One of the mechanics has already come over to my car, to polish it up and check the engine.

"Everything is fine," the salesman comes back to say. "You are not blacklisted."

"Blacklisted?"

"By our credit bureau, I mean."

I give him a check to cover the down payment. I feel as though I'm dreaming. Things are so easy in this country!

I go off, slightly alarmed at driving for the first time in Manhattan, but get to the hotel without misadventure.

"Tomorrow morning," I tell D., "there'll be someone here with the dresses I bought to try them on you."

I take you in my arms, Johnny mine. Your eyes brighten. You now say several words, and soon you'll be walking.

"Follow me."

D. does as I say, surprised, almost worried. "Where to?"

"Downstairs."

I point out the light-tan car at the curb to her. "Ours. I just bought it."

"Should we try it out?"

"Get in. Hold Johnny on your lap."

And off we go for a tour of Central Park.

. . .

Two days later, D. in a dress I had chosen for her, you seated between us in your safety seat, the search for a home in Connecticut begins. D. studies the map on her lap.

"A few miles from here, we'll have to turn right if we want to go through country."

The landscape is irresistible. We go randomly, and the villages become smaller and less frequent. Rivers, streams, trees, lakes.

By 1:00 P.M. we are all hungry. Across from a fairly large lake, we stop at a restaurant that is all white outside and in. It is quiet; the owner is pleasant. We are happy, and the steaks are succulent.

"Where are we?"

"The little church you may have seen at the bottom of the hill is Lakeville. The lake is called 'Wononscopomuc.'"

"I beg your pardon?"

He repeats it, laughing, syllable by syllable, and adds, "An Indian name that has been kept. It seems it means 'Milk of the Beloved Woman.'"

"Did you hear that, Jo?"

"Another lake, to the left, is called 'Indian Lake.' The path through the woods, halfway up the hill, is called the 'Indian Track,' the path the Indians followed when they went down to sell their furs in New York when it was still Nieuw Amsterdam."

He would make a fine tourist guide, and we feel something like tourists, even though we are looking for a more or less permanent home.

"The village school is called 'Indian Mountain School.' And the building you can see through the trees, on the left of the lake, is one of the two most famous prep schools in the country, the Hotchkiss School."

"Same as the automobiles?"

"The automobiles were only a sideline. At the end of the last century, there were two brothers in Lakeville who had a bike shop. They were very energetic, ingenious fellows, and they perfected something called a 'machine gun,' and the very first one had their name on it. They offered the patent to the United States. But Washington turned it down, because Americans at that time were sure they would never have to go to war.

"The two brothers went to Europe with their patent, and built their factory in France. Making guns has off-seasons, so they decided to build cars, in order to keep their workmen busy."

He was still smiling. As if he had guessed. We were taken with the place, no doubt about it.

"Do you know whether there are any houses for rent?"

"For rent, I'm afraid not. For sale, could be. But they're hard to find.

Better try the real-estate man C. B., in Salisbury, three miles from here. And I think it may take a little while."

"Is there a hotel here?"

"Down in Lakeville. But, with the baby, you'd be better off taking one of the cottages along the lake. Go back the way you came, and turn to the right."

We followed his advice, found a hotel, with restaurant, that had wooden cottages around it with nice shady verandas. They were cool and comfortable, the furnishings rustic but serviceable. We rented one on the spot. As we were about to leave, I figured I could fix Tigy up by renting a second one, not too close to the first.

You may have been surprised, Johnny mine, to hear us sing on the way back.

The decision has been made. All that's lacking is the house, or, rather, two houses, because there has to be one for Tigy and Marc, and maybe Boule, not more than six miles from ours.

I remain optimistic.

39

Going along the lake, one comes to the road with nothing but the little one-story white restaurant on it. A couple of hundred yards farther, there is a gently sloping road; we go by the little slate-roofed Catholic church, in which you will be baptized, Johnny, when your burly old godfather gets done shooting one of his masterpieces in India, on the banks of the sacred Ganges. This little church, more like a chapel, rises on a grassy knoll spotted with wild flowers. To the right, a narrow road, with a few unassuming houses, leading I don't know where.

Immediately afterward, leaving the lake on our left, we get to the heart of Lakeville. On the left, a reddish building, made of baked and rebaked bricks, looks abandoned; its dusty windows are paneless. I find out later that during the War of Independence arms were manufactured in it.

Can Lakeville really be called a village? More like a hamlet, its Main Street not being more than three or four hundred yards long.

D., you, and I discover all of this together, sometimes in our car, where you lord it in your safety seat, sometimes on foot, with you in your blue cloth stroller.

You no longer so often wet your diapers, now hidden under blue-and-white-striped pants and a matching shirt. Your shiny black hair is growing, and your eyes are more and more curious about everything around you.

To the left a pharmacy, a real one, not an American drugstore. A real old-fashioned apothecary's shop, with the traditional large glass jars in the front window, one filled with a yellow liquid, the other with a green. An old gentleman, said to be "eccentric," lives there by himself, in slow motion, grumbling barely intelligible comments when he looks for remedies on his blackened shelves and weighs out powders on a small copper scale.

Almost immediately across from it, the local inn, built of red-painted wood, with a bar in the cellar. It dates back to 1748, and is said to serve excellent food, which people come from far away to enjoy.

That's all on this side of the village. Nothing but the road, which in France would be called a departmental or communal road, leading to Millerton, in New York State. Barely six miles away.

That road, on the right side, becomes the heart of Lakeville. At the corner, a red store, large enough but growing old-fashioned, belonging to the Great Atlantic and Pacific Tea Company, the A. & P. chain, which at one time spanned the country.

Two small houses, then the post office, with its white-columned portico and its Grecian front. Soon you will be going there often with me. Across from it, a shop that sells newspapers, books, comics, records, and just about anything to be found in what are here called "candy stores." It is kept by a Mr. Hugo, no relation to the great French poet, playwright, and novelist. He came here when very young from some faraway Baltic country. He is short and round, jovial, and in no time you will become his best customer.

Next to that, a pink-and-white house is where the only local lawyer, Sam Beckett, has his office, in which he handles trusts, insurance, real estate. He and his family live in another house, across the road, right up against the hill. The shop of a recently immigrated Italian barber, who in a few months will give you your first haircut. And that's almost all for Main Street. Everything here is hills and valleys, lakes, pastureland, and forests.

Salisbury, the business center, is three miles away: a drugstore that sells everything, including hot dogs, Coca-Cola, Seven-Up, and, especially, ice cream of all flavors, toys, pocketknives, household articles.

Across from that, a smallish supermarket, with two aisles along which canned goods, flour, and jars of baby food are lined up; in the back the butcher shop and fish department, run by the boss, a happy-go-lucky young Italian with a big mustache.

A few houses. A larger church than the one in Lakeville.

By way of backdrop, a rather dark mountain, underbrush without any real road through it, crowned by a cone on which there is no vegetation, and it is therefore called "Baldy."

Farther on . . . But we don't go farther on. That will come later. We are satisfied for the nonce with having discovered the nucleus of the little world in which we are going to live.

I phone Tigy, still in Carmel. I fill her in on the international news and the threats of war, since she doesn't read newspapers. I describe Lakeville and the surroundings to her with overflowing, almost lyrical, enthusiasm. Not missing a thing, the hills, the lakes, the woods, the houses spread through the countryside. That kind of enthusiasm, when I was a very young man, used to be terribly amusing to Tita, Tigy's younger sister, when I went to see my "fiancée" on Rue Louvrex. She would discover at first glance that I was wearing a new pair of trousers, or hat, or jacket, or shoes. Shoving her elbow into her sister's ribs, she would say: "Now, he going to 'make his pitch'!"

Well, yes, Johnny, I was so happy with my new purchase that it seemed to me to have all the virtues, even if the pants were to shrink in the first rain or the shoes to ship water.

Had I been wrong when I stopped in Tucson, one Sunday noon, after a long trip, and fell in love with the desert? It was to give Marc and us three exhilarating years, which your arrival crowned with beauty.

The charm of Carmel-by-the-Sea, which I had not been the one to select, immediately appealed to me, as did that of Monterey.

Today, I am sure that I love this calm, green countryside, its lakes and streams. My enthusiasm is deep and sincere, and I trust my instinct.

"Should I keep the cottage I reserved for you? I won't sign anything before you agree."

She tells me she will come by train, in a week.

"Wire me the day and time of your arrival in New York, and I'll come and pick you up by car."

"Have you already bought a car?"

"Big enough for all three of you, plus the luggage."

Now, Marc's turn: "Where are you, Dad?"

"In a place called 'Lakeville,' where the school is named Indian Mountain School. There are six or seven lakes in the neighborhood."

"With fishing?"

"Not only in the lakes, but in streams full of trout."

"Swell!"

Poor, big old Marc! Before I left, he had asked me, confused: "Tell me, Dad. When will I stop changing schools and chums?"

It must have taken a big effort for him to ask me that question, because he is even shyer, more reserved than I.

"Soon."

The future will show him I wasn't talking through my hat.

I ring the bell of an attractive, comfortable middle-class house in Salisbury, where I meet the local real-estate man. C. B. is tall and blond, of Scottish extraction.

He listens to me, then asks me questions. How many of us are there? Do I need an office, bedrooms for help? I can't recall what else.

"Give me a week to find a house for you to look at."

"I especially want to have some space around me."

"I understand."

He did indeed understand. He takes us on a tour of the area in his car, and I realize that Lakeville is a much larger community than I had thought. All around Main Street, hidden by trees and hills, there are isolated properties, some of them luxurious estates.

"Many for sale?"

"Practically none."

"Well?"

"Leave that to me."

I go by myself in the DeSoto to pick up Marc, Tigy, and Boule at Grand Central Station. The trunk of the car is chock full of trunks and suitcases.

Marc and I had rushed into each other's arms, and Boule kissed me too, somewhat reassured about her fate.

"Is it in the country?" Marc asks.

"Not country like any other you've ever seen. Deer and rattlesnakes live in the forests a few hundred meters from the houses. And up on Baldy there are even some white savages. . . ."

"No Indians?"

I tell him what C. B. told me. A century ago, a small religious sect, with very ascetic rules, refused to pay taxes and, when the authorities came after them, took refuge up on Baldy. Several times, the police tried to rout them, but never could. At the foot of the mountain there is almost impenetrable underbrush, and when the forces of law and order find a campfire there, even still smoking, the people who made it have already disappeared.

These "savages" are now into the third generation, and no one knows how many of them there are now. What do they live on? Mostly wild game, berries, and roots. About once a month, a ragged man carrying empty sacks on his shoulder appears like a phantom in Salisbury. He has long hair and a long beard, and walks nimbly, like an Indian. He goes into the supermarket, points to canned goods, flour, salt, dried peas and beans, which he stows into his sacks and pays for with old silver dollars, not seen thereabouts in a long time.

He looks harmless, and no one would think of calling the police. He soon disappears again into the underbrush.

We will go there together, my sons. We will see none of these white savages, but we will hear rustling in the bushes, meaning that we are being watched. We will also ford, halfway up the hill, a trout stream that must be a precious resource for the strange colony.

Ten days. Twelve days. Our real-estate man doesn't show up, and we take advantage of it to crisscross the region. Tigy and D. make sure they don't bump into one another. Each of our little groups lives in its comfortable cottage. Marc shuttles between.

Tigy goes to New York, by train, for there is a little line running from Millerton to the Big City. It's an old, outdated, and delightful train, which we will often ride. She comes back by car, in a very little Renault that is reassuring to her because of its size, for she is still afraid of automobiles.

"How do you like the place, Marc?"

"Okay! Especially the lake. And the woods. I went over to see my school. They have a football field and a baseball diamond. Will you let me play football?"

You are a soft type, my Marc, a timid type, and yet the toughest and most violent games appeal to you. Like American football, so much rougher than European rugby.

The real-estate man finally shows up and, with a mysterious smile, says with assurance: "I've found just what you need and I don't think we have to look any farther. Come on."

D. and I, plus you, Johnny, get into his car. To my surprise, we don't go far. At the foot of the little white church, we take the narrow road with the four or five houses along it. After a couple of hundred yards, an old wooden bridge, barely wide enough for a car to go across and without any railing, crossing a rapidly running stream.

"This is where the property starts."

There is a sign that says: "Private Road. No Admittance."

On the left, all I can see are some fallow fields and a broken-down barn. Another hundred yards or so, an enormous rock, from which some bushes and a tree emerge.

A little farther on, a white house with green shutters and tiny-paned windows. I can't tell how many stories there are, since they aren't called the same here as in Europe, so I will speak of levels, which is the fashionable way today in Europe. This pert little house is on two levels.

"It dates back to 1748, like the hotel, which you already know. You can see that, even though it is built of wood, it is good and solid. Besides, the wood is double thick, separated by beams."

He takes a key from his pocket and, more mysterious than ever, opens the door, which has a heavy wrought-iron knocker on it.

A very large room, with a polished floor, a ceiling with old beams showing. A rough stone fireplace big enough to roast a calf in. On one side there is a heavy iron plate.

"What's that?"

"The baking oven. That fireplace is what is called a 'Dutch oven.' You can see, under the oven, a big space for logs."

A so-called scenic bow window.

"The windowpanes are thick and double, and between them there is a gas that keeps out noise, cold, and heat."

That is new at the time. It still is in 1962 in Switzerland, when I install the same kind of storm windows in our house at Epalinges.

"Why is he selling?"

"You have surely heard of him: Ralph Ingersoll, the well-known newspaperman who founded *PM* in New York. Before that, he was one of the top executives at Time Inc. His wife died, and he doesn't want to go on living in the place where he was happy with her."

A dream dining room, its walls entirely covered by soft-veined maple. An old fireplace, also faced with wood. Two windows opening on the garden and a large bow window framed by recesses outlined in carved wood. "For knickknacks or silverware," says the guide, who is in no hurry.

We go back to the big room with the stone fireplace. He opens a door. "The library."

It too is wood-paneled, with shelving from floor to ceiling. Fortunately, some thirty cartons of books are stored in Tucson, and others in Carmel.

Here too, a fireplace. And a bay window, the large center pane flanked by smaller ones, and beneath them a window seat running all around.

Another door, a long corridor, a universe one would not expect to find, from the outside. Many friends are to get lost in this house, with its innumerable corridors. Built flush against the hillside, it has four different levels looking south.

I see a stairway going down. Where to?

But first I find the kitchen, with its protruding beams, as in all the old part of the house. One side, lighted by two windows, is filled with all the modern kitchen appliances. Elsewhere, cabinets, shelves, in profusion, a back room that is used as a laundry room, and, beyond the glass-paned door, a garden, not a house garden, but an endless stretch of trees and wild growth.

"Now, this is your bedroom." C. B. makes that decision in a calm voice, sure of himself.

A counter and more white closets. A white door opening onto dazzlement: sunshine floods from all sides into the square master bedroom, which also has a bay window.

Another corridor. More closets. The bathroom, with its window opening onto grass and on a wing I have not yet seen.

"That'll be for your little boy."

We return to the bedroom. He opens a door I had not noticed. A broad terrace with a white fence around it. From here, one can see the stream flowing by at the bottom of the hill. A birch, my favorite tree, shines in the light less than fifty yards away. I look to the right: a swimming pool carved out of the rock.

"It is all built on rock. You'll see the cellar; it looks like a cave. Whatever you can see from here, in all four directions, is part of the estate. It has two trout streams, a marsh, around twenty thousand trees, and sheer rock on the other side of the stream. That was once a water mill, and half of a big toothed wheel can still be seen sticking up over the water. During the Revolution, they made small cannon here, and you'll see one that blew up and lodged in the trunk of a tree."

This is too much! Still more bedrooms. Luminously white. Nothing solemn, or garish. The house as it now stands has been slowly accumulated, bit by bit, starting with the original, the simplicity and style of which have been respected.

"And last, behind the fir trees, the small house in which Mrs. Ingersoll painted her pictures."

Around seventy-five acres of lawns, forests, and swamps. All going up and down, just like the house.

C. B. insists on showing me all of it. The red-painted barn, so typically American, which also has a boiler, a creamer, and I don't know what else.

A two-car garage; beneath that, a cellar, hewn from the rock, where Marc one day will be able to raise snakes and water turtles.

• • •

It's just too fine. It's a dream. I am waiting to hear the price, and when he names it, I am ready to collapse. It's expensive, of course, far beyond my means at a time when I have just made over to Tigy everything I own. I fill him in on that.

"I'm sure they'll be able to work something out."

"How about a house for my first wife?"

"She phoned me about it, and I'm going to show her a small house in a delightful spot, Salmon Creek, which doesn't have any more salmon since a dam was built twenty miles downstream."

"Is it for sale?"

"For rent. It was built by an old Polish bricklayer, little by little, year after year, along with another smaller one he's keeping for himself."

"Is it far?"

"Four miles from here."

A flea's jump. Good old Tigy, who seems to be working things out on her own.

My office and D.'s would be above our bedroom, separated from the swimming pool by a glass door. Farther down, we would have a room for files, which the real-estate man calls "your archives." All of that, if . . .

D. and I are in a sweat until the next morning. There is a bank in Lakeville, the kind of small bank that is always held up in Westerns, and I've already opened an account in it.

The next morning, Boule agrees to take care of you while we go to see Beckett, who is to become and remain one of my good friends. He is a man of my own age, empathetic and open, like most of the Americans I have met up to now. He listens, thinks about it, scribbles some figures on a pad.

"The local bank won't be able to handle the deal. We'll have to go to Torrington to see the president of the bank I do most of my business with. It's less than an hour away."

In the end, D. will be the one to go there. I have too much of a tendency, when I get enthusiastic, to say yes to anything. Besides, the lawyer pointed out to us that a woman might more easily grab the brass ring. It would seem he already knows D.!

I stay alone with you, Johnny mine, trying not to appear impatient or nervous. When she gets back, I hear the deal has been made. I just have to sign a large number of notes and make a down payment, which I can still afford, and the house will be mine.

In three days, the bill of sale will be ready, and Ingersoll, who happens to be in New York, will come to sign it.

He is a huge man, with broad shoulders, eyes as gray as his hair, and he is unable to hold back his emotions while signing the deed. He apologizes:

"It reminds me too much of my first wife and the years of happiness that . . ."

I suggest that we all go and have a champagne toast at the hotel's cellar bar. Boule keeps you again, Johnny mine, along with Marc, who has nothing but tenderness in his eyes for you. I don't forget that he was the first one you smiled at.

The innkeeper in person serves us our champagne, then another bottle. I have just made some very serious commitments, of course, but am thinking mainly of what a fine present I have gotten for the two of you. For D. and me too, naturally, but to a lesser degree. Your children's eyes are more precious than our own.

When I get back to the cottage, slightly tipsy, because we polished off a third bottle and separated in a spirit of quite some exuberance, I hug Marc. And then you.

"When can I see it?" Marc asks.

I take the big old front-door key to the original little house out of my pocket. There are four or five other doors to the house, but around here, at that time, no one locked up at night, not since the days when Indian raids came to an end. And that was so long ago.

Well, now I've bought a house. It's mine. But the house is empty, except for bow windows and shelves. And also except, in the barn near the bridge, for a boiler to cook up maple syrup, a quantity of dry wood that will keep us supplied for years, and a few hundred quart cans to hold the syrup. And how you love tin cans, Marc! You'll even have a pool for swimming, in the same spring water that supplies the house.

What month is it? I get lost in dates. I even forget my wedding date. In the last months, things have been happening so fast that, having reached my goal, I'm dizzy.

We are in a hurry to move into this dream house, which is still without a bed or a saucepan. Luck is with us, because a whole household is to be put up for sale in a few days.

The auction is not held in a building, or in front of the house, but right in the middle of a big field with lots of high weeds. The auctioneer is in shirt sleeves, with his collar unbuttoned. It is very hot.

The furniture on display, though outdated, can do for us temporarily. Most of the people, in small groups, are just there out of curiosity, and they gape at us, newcomers to Lakeville.

Contrary to what I expected, there is no spirited bidding. I pick up for a song an outlandish bedroom set, painted green, with flowers and arabesques in all sorts of colors, such as might be found in the Tyrol or

Switzerland. D. says the furniture is blue, so I don't argue; I know I am color-blind. Rocking chairs reminiscent of the Deep South or Old West, two or three tables, some other chairs, "to tide us over." My intuition tells me that won't be for too long.

I want your bed, Johnny, to be new, and we will go to Millerton to get it, as well as some other things. I don't want secondhand pots and pans either.

Millerton has a big general store, and there we get our china and Swedish stainless-steel utensils. My own silverware, as well as two sets of dishes, one ordered long ago from a craftsman at Nieul, the other gotten at the time of Boulevard Richard Wallace, the work of a famous china maker on Rue Royale in Paris, both marked with the single initial *S*, are now Tigy's property, and I have no idea where they are.

Tigy settles into her furnished house at Salmon Creek, with Marc and Boule.

D. and I start cleaning up Shadow Rock Farm.

She first wants to scrape off the varnish that has darkened the beams. We have bought a ladder and the necessary tools. The three of us sleep for the first time in the big bedroom with the bay window and terrace.

We scrape, we steel-wool, using some kind of acid. D. sticks with it three days and then collapses. Not being able to handle it all by myself, I call on Boule for help, and she comes running, dazzled by our supermodern kitchen, the cabinets, the shelves, the view that extends beyond each window and, thus framed by them, makes a radiant picture.

It is August, around mid-August, if I am not mistaken. I get a TV set. You mostly like to hear your records, especially your favorite Benny Goodmans. Soon you'll be listening to others with just as much pleasure. Mr. Hugo sells, among other things, small records of old children's rhymes, English, Irish, and American. They sell for a quarter apiece, the same price as a magazine, and you point to the pile of them whenever we go in there together to pick up the papers.

Hugo also sells me a simple phonograph, easy to handle, and at the age of a year, already standing up, you'll be able to start your own records. They all have the same green labels. Yet, to my surprise, by looking carefully at them you will be able to pick out the ones you like best. Even though you weighed in at eleven pounds, nobody's going to convince me that you know how to read. So? This remains a mystery to me.

Once the house is scraped, polished, washed and rewashed, Boule leaves us, upset and more at loose ends than ever, to go to Salmon Creek.

I guess I already have a desk by this time, with piles of paper and carbons, because I see today that in September of that same year, about a month after we acquired the property, I wrote two novels, *Tante Jeanne (Aunt Jeanne)* and *Les Mémoires de Maigret (Maigret's Memoirs)*.

The latter of these, under peculiar circumstances, for peculiar reasons as well.

40

In retrospect I am surprised that by September 1950 Shadow Rock Farm, empty a month and a half before, should have been presentable and comfortable enough for D., with my agreement, to invite her mother to visit.

Following my divorce, I was all but broke. But now, not only did our big oxhide-trimmed bed arrive, along with other odds and ends, by moving van, but my crates and cartons of books came too, from Tucson and Carmel-by-the-Sea. Even your bed and your playpen, Johnny, which were set up in your nursery, at the end of the long hall with all the closets.

Since you wake up two or three times a night, as soon as you are wet, we have had the electrician, who lives in the first house beyond our bridge, put in an intercom that connects you to our bedroom, the kitchen, the two offices, and the library, so that, wherever we may be, we can hear everything, even your breathing, and every time you turn over. We are also connected in this way to Marc's room, when he stays with us, since he still has rather frequent fits of sleepwalking.

The dining room has somewhat overdecorated Italian furniture. In the living room, a long heavy table, made of maple, with two farm benches. The books, not yet sorted, are pell-mell on the shelves of this room and the library, the door to which is always open.

There are curtains everywhere. We have been two or three times to Poughkeepsie, some thirty-five miles away, to buy copper lamps, which our friend the electrician has put up all over the place. The house is alive. While everything in it is not yet finished, it already looks quite hospitable and cheerful.

By what miracle? you may ask, Marc and Johnny.

By the same miracle that occurred ten, twenty other times in my life. When I was bored and marking time, having just arrived in Paris at the age of nineteen, in the dark, depressing atmosphere of the political league, where I was simply the office boy, the marquis took me on as his private secretary.

Two years later, as I was tagging along with him from château to château, my little stories started selling well enough to the newspapers and weeklies so that I could go off on my own.

Selling one of Tigy's canvases for eight hundred francs allowed us to discover the island of Porquerolles, and later my dime novels were to allow me to have the *Ostrogoth* built at Fécamp.

Jef Kessel's order for three series of stories financed our trip up to the Arctic Ocean and a long journey through Lapland.

From the first Maigrets on, it was mainly the movies that acted as good fairies. Jean Renoir, first of all, came to buy from me the movie rights to *La Nuit du carrefour (The Crossroad Murder;* in England, *Maigret at the Crossroads).* The next week, Jean Tarride bought those of *Le Chien jaune (A Face for a Clue),* to be followed by the sale of *La Tête d'un homme (A Battle of Nerves),* and then so many other novels, which paid for my Chrysler, a stay in the most beautiful villa at Cap d'Antibes, the setting up of La Richardière, and the purchase of three horses, and finally a trotter and sulky.

Sometimes I went two or three years without selling any movie rights —or, more precisely, leasing them, for one language only, for a period of seven, eight, or at most ten years.

Some of the novels have been filmed as many as three times, either in the same country or elsewhere. For instance, just before your birth, my Marc, *Monsieur la Souris (The Mouse),* already shot in French by my friend Raimu, was remade across the Channel by the best English comedian.

My divorce was barely final when I sold the French rights to *La Marie du port* (The Girl in the Port) and *La Vérité sur Bébé Donge (I Take This Woman),* both played by Jean Gabin, with Danielle Darrieux for his partner in one, and maybe in the other one too.

That produced enough fully to outfit Shadow Rock Farm and to hire two people.

The first was a long, thin young girl, with a long face, and a somewhat reserved smile, who was just out of high school. You immediately took a shine to her, and she returned the feeling generously.

Her mother, affable and somewhat noisily cheerful, who had come at a young age from the West Indies, became our cook. They lived on the other side of the hill, in a narrow little valley such as there are so many of around Lakeville. The father, who was almost black, was incapacitated by a work accident and lived in seclusion in a nice, very clean house.

So it was all right for my new mother-in-law to come, and we went to meet her plane at La Guardia.

I had seen her only once. At that time, I was only her daughter's employer. Had she suspected there was more than that between us?

She slept in one of the small rooms on the same floor, far from our own, and D., knowing she might be afraid, had had our neighbor put a bell in so that she could call us at any hour of the night.

I can still see her at the dinner table, in the library, especially in one of the white armchairs in the shade of a tree.

At first, she was surprised, almost shocked, at my calling her Mother, as I had my first mother-in-law. It came quite naturally to me, since I had always addressed my own parents as Mother and Father. In Canada, it seems, a son-in-law was supposed to address his parents-in-law as Sir and Madam.

But how, from her impassive face, could one guess what she was thinking?

She was not used to going to bed before one in the morning, whereas I have always been an early retirer. That upset my schedule somewhat, because she did not read, did not like to be left alone, and could talk on for hours about her friends and acquaintances in Montreal and Ottawa.

I could not spend my days and long evenings listening to her and politely nodding. Nor could I write a demanding novel, which required a well-observed schedule and strict discipline. I was looking for an easy subject, without dream or mystery, and that was when I got the idea of writing *Maigret's Memoirs*. To me, it was something like writing a letter to a friend, and therefore entertaining.

Marc still kept bouncing in with a gang of friends and raiding the refrigerator, pending his starting at Indian Mountain School.

We would set your playpen out on the lawn, facing the house, Johnny, and you were starting to stand, your face contracted by the effort, then your eyes shining in triumph.

D., my mother-in-law, and I carried on many conversations together, and I remember one in particular that later was to loom as most important.

We were talking about D.'s grandfather, about whom she had told me a very strange story. After he died, he had been laid out for the wake in a casket richly ornamented with silver. This casket, the way D. told it, had one unusual peculiarity: at face level, there was a sort of trap door that could be lifted when visitors were there, and under it a fine mosquito netting.

I innocently mentioned this detail to my mother-in-law. The three of us were sitting under the linden tree, in the garden chairs, and it was very warm. For once, the granite woman registered great surprise, and turned to her daughter.

"Did you tell him that?"

"Yes, Maman. It's true, isn't it?"

"I can assure you that that trap door never existed anywhere but in your imagination. It's true that yours is very inventive. When you were still just a little girl, you were always playing different parts. . . ."

"I swear . . ."

"Don't swear, D. No one ever conceived of such a casket."

"Just the same . . ."

"Call up your brothers. They're older than you and a lot more sensible."

D.'s face clouded over. Was she going to burst into sobs? We had been having peace between us for quite some time, and I tried to come to her rescue.

"Sometimes, Mother, childhood memories are more accurate than those of big people."

This is sometimes true; in this case, I didn't really believe it.

"Oh, come now, Georges."

My mother-in-law was truly angry, with a repressed anger, at the idea that her father might have been exposed and then buried with a mosquito-netting opening in his casket.

"Anyway, there were never any flies in the house. I saw to that!"

"There can be flies even in the cleanest of houses."

"Come now!"

I was often to hear that "Come now!" of hers.

If D. spoke of some woman friend of her parents', her mother would say, in her always even voice, without moving a single feature of her face, "Oh, come now!" And sometimes add, "You know that you were always one for inventing things. That woman was nothing like the caricature you are describing."

That reminded me of the little bells that for almost five years had rung inside my head at one or another of D.'s poses. I was finally getting to like my mother-in-law and beginning to feel that, beneath her huge, rigid carapace, there was a shy woman who had learned, from childhood on, to hide her feelings.

I long wondered and in fact still wonder whether there weren't a few drops of Indian blood in her, as in so many French-Canadian families. Had not the women, precariously shielded by a palisade of pointed sticks, often been attacked by the feathered Iroquois? And wasn't it rumored that some of them had broken that barrier of their own accord?

Shhh! That is a subject one dares not mention in Canada, any more than in the Deep South one alludes to the few drops of black blood that experts alone claim to be able to detect by the formation of the fingernails.

Early each morning I was enjoying writing a chapter of what was not a novel, but a sort of self-criticism. Through the pen of Maigret, I was ridiculing the "little Sim" of long ago to a fare-thee-well, while at the same time depicting a young Maigret bashfully in love in the opulent home of his future parents-in-law. I gave him a father very much like my own, a childhood that resembled mine, and already the desire, or, rather, the dream, someday to become a sort of "mender of destinies."

Had I not been trying, for the past five years, to turn one soul away from its own tragic destiny?

On with it! The restored old mill is so fine and cheerful in the heavy September sunshine.

"Coming swimming in the lake, Dad?"

Marc and I go down there, or else dive into our pool, which is deep and always icy. Marc goes fishing too, in both our streams, but not with rod and reel.

Our fishing contraptions are hung on one of the walls of our living room, which looked like the communal room in which owners and servants used to eat at the same clothless table. Near the fishing rods of various sizes hung my Winchester .22 carbine and the big .38-caliber revolver I had bought in Nogales. The two weapons were never loaded, and you always looked at them with secret desire, Marc.

You went fishing with your bare hands, moving ahead in the deep water as cautiously as an Indian on the warpath. One would have thought you simply had to smile at the fish and they let you catch them, because you picked them up, petted them, spoke to them, and carefully put them back into the limpid water.

One afternoon, when it is very hot, we see a brown animal resting on the lawn between our bedroom and the nursery. It is a beaver, which lives in one of our streams. Its curious eyes display no fear. Perhaps he has just come there to sniff out the new inhabitants. He reappears several days in a row, and, in your mother's arms or mine, Johnny, you observe him at length, protesting whenever you are taken away from the window.

Marc's bedroom is not far from yours, two others are ready for eventual occupancy, and a third has been turned into a linen closet.

I soon get a metal desk, with the typewriter built right into it. All I have to do is pull a handle for my typewriter to jut out, on my left, slightly below the desk top, and then I can just swivel around to use it.

Geographies, histories, dictionaries, and encyclopedias fill the broad shelves in my office and, below them, my numerous telephone directories of Europe and the United States.

I am able to take my naps here, lying in my bay window, covered by a thick yellow cloth.

We sometimes swim in the pool three times a day, for even in northern Connecticut the heat is at times hard to put up with, and the next summer we will have to have air conditioning put into our bedroom, which is exposed on the south, east, and west, so that the sun pours into it from dawn to dark.

In New York, D. takes her mother to a dress shop and gets her two or three dresses that are less forbidding than what she generally wears. Old ladies of times gone by, "proper" old ladies, after all, had to wear nothing but black, or gray, with occasional touches of mauve.

My good old mother-in-law feels strange wearing light colors, but her eyes show that she enjoys it all the same, as if she had just discovered that she was a different woman.

"Do you think I can wear these dresses in Ottawa? What will people think? They'll imagine I've become emancipated."

In that way, from time to time, the little girl appears through the dignity of the old lady. In the presence of an old person, I always feel inclined to look for a trace of the little boy or little girl they had been, for don't all of us keep with us throughout our lives a little of our childhood?

We see my mother-in-law off at the airport, and I kiss her as naturally as can be.

In December, I am invited to give a lecture at Yale, and am excited about it, since this is my first contact with American youth. A great writer, Thornton Wilder, who is to become one of my good friends, introduces me. Then, according to custom, I speak for a little more than a quarter-hour. There are at least a thousand students and professors present. What should I speak about? I know only one subject: the novel.

Traditionally, after my preamble, everyone is free to ask questions, whether instructor or student, and I delight so in this give-and-take that much later I will use the same formula in England, France, Italy, on television.

The questioners here, unlike those in France, don't try to show off by tripping the speaker up. I feel they really want to learn. They are neither familiar nor distant; they are natural, as they are in dealing with their teachers. I find in them a thirst for knowledge that I am rarely to discover elsewhere, except in Holland and a few Italian universities.

In the United States, students and instructors meet almost as equals. I realize this when, after more than two hours of questions, the lecture comes to an end. We are taken to another campus building, where a professor and his wife are giving a reception, which some thirty students also attend. Whiskey and beer are generously served, which does not keep the discussion begun in the amphitheater from going right on.

The tone gets freer and freer, the cordiality more demonstrative, so that we are still gloriously at it when dawn appears.

After about three months, Boule comes home to us, despite Tigy's insistence that she stay, and we welcome her like a prodigal child. Our house is filling out, so to speak. We have gone through the necessary formalities to get an English chambermaid; she will have one of the upstairs bedrooms. Boule takes possession of her own, and her place in the kitchen. As for Maria, our cook from Martinique, she will remain part of the staff, substituting for each of the others in turn.

In Lakeville, after all, there is little in the way of entertainment. The staff members feel that, instead of weekly days off, they would rather have a week each month to themselves, to go wherever they wish, usually to New York. And soon D. and I are able to go and spend a week in New York or Boston each month as well. On the prescription of our physician, Dr. Harry Wieler, who has an office at the Hotchkiss School. He is on the staff there, as well as carrying on his private practice.

Dr. Wieler, like most of the doctors throughout my life, becomes a friend, sometimes comes to dinner with his wife, and we in turn are invited to his delightful home.

He is tall, slim, elegant, with gray hair and a slight smile on his lips. At Hotchkiss, he treats the sons of some of the most important families in the United States, and he was not selected at random. He took care of you, Marc, and you too, Johnny, as well as me.

Mainly, he had to take care of D., who rather often complained of different aches and pains, in her head, throat, chest, or wherever. He would unflappably take a bottle of pills from his satchel and put a few of them into a small envelope, maybe the same kind, or different ones, or even placebos; I have no idea.

"Take one of these morning, noon, and night, with a little water."

One day, he took me aside and advised, without having to give any explanation: "Why don't you take her to a big city every month, to New York, or Boston, anywhere, and spend a week there, just the two of you, without any children? Go out a great deal."

His gray eyes are expressive enough for me to understand, and I follow his advice to the letter. D. needs "vacations" too, and also needs "city lights," exciting nights and lazy mornings.

In New York, we go to the Plaza, right on Central Park, which has a number of restaurants and bars, where one can come across celebrities from Hollywood, London, Berlin, Paris.

In an elevator, I bump into Fernandel, who has just completed a film in Paris based on one of my books, of which the title has been changed: *Lettre à mon juge (Act of Passion)*. The name of the main character has been changed too, because Alavoine in French might be taken to mean Oateater, which would be a bad joke on the star's well-known "horsy" profile. So what name did the producers come up with? Cassegrain, which means Grainbreaker!

One morning I have to go to Canaan to buy some sweaters and warmer clothing. Indian summer, with its dazzling colors, is over and the air is turning cold. I have already acquired a Jeep, with deep-treaded tires and four-wheel drive, which I have been told I'll need in winter.

I've finished my shopping and am back on the road, with about twenty miles to go over some rather steep hills, when snow starts coming down, hard, thick, obscuring my windshield, which I have to scrape clean every five minutes.

Except perhaps in Canada, I have never seen such a blizzard, and from the very first hill I pass several stranded cars, right out on the highway. On descents, I prudently let the good old Jeep zigzag as it sees fit, slowly taking it out of its skids when necessary, as I learned to do in the Laurentians.

When I get to our little wooden bridge, it has over a foot and a half of snow on it, and since there are no railings, I leave the Jeep on the road and proceed with difficulty on foot, knee-deep at each step.

Since school started, you have been going there from a quarter of eight in the morning to five in the afternoon, and you are satisfied with the food they serve, my ever-hungry Marc, and especially with the afternoons free of classes.

All afternoons are devoted to sports, according to the seasons, baseball, then football, then winter sports. At four o'clock, shower. Finally, a three-quarters-of-an-hour "study" period that leaves you without homework or other obligations.

The principal was a big, broad, muscular man, slightly fat, with a square face that might augur strict discipline if his smile did not contradict the rest of his appearance.

"Our students are free. They do the serving at mealtime. Sports are obligatory every afternoon. Soccer is reserved for those whom the doctors judge unfit for more violent games. Of course, there are some who are not up to the athletics, so they botanize in the fields and woods and keep up our little botanical and zoological collections."

You fitted into that program as if you had been made for it. You already know the basics of baseball and wear the uniform.

The first month, your mother took you to school and went to pick you up. But once the snow starts, she phones me. "Listen, Georges. I have all the housework to do. I just don't have time to make the long trip, taking Marc to school and picking him up."

That's no imposition on me; quite the contrary. In the morning at seven-thirty I am in your yard, giving a little blow of my horn that brings you to the top of the steps. In the afternoon, I wait for you to get out of school and drive you back to Salmon Creek. Saturdays, Sundays, and holidays, you spend at Lakeville, where you have your own room and friends, and in no time the walls of your room are decorated with the pennants of big colleges and sports teams. Your room is lined with cork and, so it wouldn't be too uniform, there are vertical slats. On the cork, you can put up all the pennants you want with simple thumbtacks.

I bought you an oak bookcase, with glass doors, in which you have put mainly comic books and the shells you began collecting in Florida, and added to in Carmel, including the cheery abalone shells.

No doubt about it, you are an outdoor boy, made for rough sports, wide-open spaces, and unexpressed dreams.

You are very tender with your "little brother," and you show him off proudly to every new friend you make.

For winter sports, soon to begin, you don't have far to go. You might even indulge in them on our road, which is going to have a snow surface until spring.

Facing Salisbury's bald mountain, there is another, more suited to skiing, where in February international ski-jumping meets are held. You start in with four-meter jumps, then six, and you are excited about it.

In November, D. has to take my place at the wheel of the Jeep to pick you up at Salmon Creek and take you back there. For nine days, the time that it now takes me to write a novel, I was writing *Le Temps d'Anaïs (The Girl in His Past)*.

Then, in December, the radio has Bing Crosby continually telling us that "Santa Claus Is Coming to Town."

For you, Johnny mine, who love to play around in the snow, more often sitting or lying down than on your feet, we have bought a waterproof brown outfit with a hood lined with fur so thick that you look like a bear cub.

D. and I spend three days in holiday-crazy New York. All the store windows are lighted up, and some have lines waiting. We buy all kinds of toys, Indian sets, a sled, gifts for Boule, for your wonderful nursemaid, for Maria, for the English maid. We took the train, leaving the Jeep parked across from the little railroad station. We hide all our bulky packages way downstairs.

For Marc, I bought a complicated electric train, with all sorts of commands, and freight cars that open by themselves and let out miniature cattle, which come down a ramp. Our electrician neighbor sets it up, because beneath the big plywood base there are so many different-colored wires that I can't make head or tail of them.

We put a Christmas tree up in the dining room, in front of the big bay window, and another outside, just as fully lighted, so that it looks like the reflection of the one in the window. Garlands at every window. A wreath of holly hanging on the door, the American way.

We have a whole nursery of Christmas trees covering a couple of acres, and I now find out why they were planted. Fir-tree nurseries are considered a preserve for young game, and in this hilly region they have the advantage of holding back the runoff of rain water. Thanks to this planting, done by the previous owner, I am entitled to a reduction in my property taxes.

All the local people, from my lawyer to the barber and including all the categories of inhabitants in between, are entitled to come and pick out a tree for the holidays, cut it down by saw or ax, and take it away. For several days, it's a delight to see the men coming there, most often with one or more children, who very solemnly select their tree and then go off again through the snow.

The big day is getting near. D. is busy making up little packages with gold, silver, red, or blue paper, decorated with ribbons of just as many colors. In the big room, I am busy testing the electric train, which doesn't seem to want to work. It is one in the morning when, at wit's end, I phone the electrician with a desperate SOS.

He must be busy too, because he has two or three small children of his own. But he comes over just the same, covered with snow, gets out of his mackinaw, and starts examining the sick or stubborn train. Sitting on the floor, he crosses and uncrosses wires, and after half an hour or more the train is finally running, goes up a hill and disappears into a tunnel before stopping at the freight station to unload its cattle and barrels.

In the middle and all around the circuit, houses light up on command, and the train whistles and even puffs steam.

"Thanks. Thanks a lot. And a very Merry Christmas to you and yours!"

Oops! That was a near thing, Marc.

We get to bed around three o'clock, or maybe four, and you, Johnny you devil, you sound the alarm at six. We are just a little haggard.

Merry Christmas, my children!

Your first Noël at our home, Shadow Rock Farm.

41

At our home! We are finally at our home. I had in fact many times in my life felt that I had reached my destination, always imagining I was settling in for good. I felt equally elated in 1931 when I discovered La Richardière, standing alone with its dovecote at the end of the fields and meadows, its woods alive with birds, and the sea right there.

Yet I was to leave it four or five years later for new adventures, return to it, find it old and decrepit, but then, just two kilometers away, come across the house at Nieul, where I was to engender my first son, you, my Marc, who never dreamed you were going to become an American boy.

Then . . . Canada; the journey the full width of the Atlantic states, north to south; Florida; Arizona at last discovered, Tucson and Tumacacori, the state where Johnny mine would be born, just as determined as he is today. Carmel was merely an interlude, darkened by unhappy preoccupations.

Here, in our old house at Shadow Rock Farm, I am under a spell, persuaded that I am here for life. I fit naturally into the life of this place and, for the first time perhaps, I have the illusion I really belong.

A warm, intimate atmosphere, which we all fit into. I can't get over admiring it, especially in winter, when the setting around us, framed by each of the windows, looks like a painting by Grandma Moses.

I love our streams under their crust of ice, our wild woods, so wild that I will never get to know more than part of them, the winter snow and cold, as I will love the heavy summer heat and the gold, red, and russet leaves of fall.

I feel happy here; I want both of you to be happy, Marc and Johnny, whose movements and looks I never tire of watching. I know you are satisfied, as is Boule, who has happily taken in hand her new domain, and all those around us who make up our small human nucleus. I want everyone to be happy, including Tigy, whom I sometimes call on in her house at Salmon Creek when I bring Marc back home after school and find her making French fries for him or big helpings of spaghetti and meatballs.

I am persuaded that I love D., now that the stormy fires of passion have calmed down, and I do everything in my power to assure her being happy, just simply happy, at last. In a word, I am mired in my happiness, the happiness I want all of you to share.

Sometime between the ages of sixteen and nineteen, I wrote, in one of my columns for the *Gazette de Liège*, a sentence that has often been repeated during my interviews: "If each person were able to make just one other human being happy, the whole world would experience happiness."

I still think that today, at seventy-seven, even though I have found out it's sometimes difficult, if not impossible.

My days are filled with joys that follow one after another, and I recall so many of those joys that I don't know which to select, so I have to grab them at random like old snapshots pulled from a pile.

The walk, for example, that goes from our front door, the one of the old mill, down to our private road. It is made of uneven stones as old as the house itself.

When I was looking at that red barn with lawyer Beckett—as red as every other barn around and the ones in Grandma Moses's paintings—I pointed to what looked like some kind of rails stacked up along the wall, twenty-foot-long beams connected by planks with a good inch between, and asked, "What are those for?"

"To cover your walk in winter, because when there's snow and ice, you wouldn't be able to walk on it otherwise."

After shoveling off the first snow, Marc and I put out those beams, end to end, and for five months, each morning I was to go out and clear the snow from them.

I know that snowplows go over the roads. But what about my private one, from the house to the wooden bridge?

"Ask your mechanic or your service station about it."

Two brothers, huge fellows with muscles that bulge out of their coveralls. We make an arrangement: for a monthly fee, after every snowfall they'll come over and dig us out.

Everything is easy. D. and I investigate the environs. At Torrington, a well-stocked little town, we find a complete set of dishes, in English porcelain, with a cheery floral design.

D. tells me she needs a sewing machine. We get it.

She is suddenly ecstatic. "Look, Jo! That's just what I've wanted for so long"—she points to a miniature vacuum cleaner—"to clean drawers and closets when we go to hotels."

Before we got the little portable vacuum cleaner, our arrival at the Plaza called for an unvarying ritual. D. began by taking all her clothes off and then disinfected everything in the bathroom with a bottle of disinfectant she carried. After that, all the phone mouthpieces had to be sterilized, while I held down the hook so that the switchboard would not light up. Finally she got around to drawers, shelves, and closets. She disposed of all the paper lining them and replaced it with fresh paper of her own, which we carried along in rolls.

All because one time, because of a convention, we had had to stay at a third-class hotel, where she had had the misfortune of getting body lice.

But hasn't she made immense strides since our first meetings in New York and our dramatically passionate nights?

I am determined to see this thing through. I love her and don't even want to hear that little bell go off in my head because of some action or sentence of hers that scares me.

Now our nights in New York are largely spent in the exclusive places frequented by the jet set. The Stork Club, New York's most select nightclub, or the Copacabana, not quite so exclusive, and the Latin Quarter, where dinner is served at eight, during the first show, and supper at midnight for the second.

To D., this is something like inhaling oxygen. Her eyes shine. She speaks animatedly, smiles at me with radiant tenderness.

We still have dinner at the Brussels, where the little hatcheck girl looks at us in surprise. "Didn't I tell you, Monsieur Simenon? The pretty little lady you kept waiting—and now here you are . . ."

We also like Sardi's, where one can see the stage and screen stars whose pictures adorn the walls. And "21," where the maître d' knows in advance what we are going to be ordering and the sommelier doesn't have to ask what wines we want.

D. wears a wild mink, which she got in a curious way. A small independent producer wanted to acquire the movie rights to one of my novels.

"I won't make the payment to you in money, but better than that. One of my friends is one of the best furriers in New York. Go and pick out the finest mink he has, and I'll pick up the tab for it by way of payment."

I had never before had so unusual an offer. Almost for fun, and especially because I knew how D.'s eyes would light up, I accepted. The coat is so unusual that people turn to look at D., even on Fifth Avenue, where minks are not so uncommon.

Only—yes, there was a catch! It wasn't the "producer" who paid for it, but me. If I recall correctly, he had to drop the deal because he couldn't get the right cast. Is that just a trick? Or a "scam," as they say here? He worked in cahoots with the furrier? I find it amusing. I find everything amusing. As I said, I'm happy, and intend to stay happy, no matter the cost.

At a charity bazaar out in the country, Johnny, we found you a patchwork oval rug, made mostly of blue and red scraps by farm women during long winter days, and it's a pleasure for me to see you sitting on it in the library, listening so seriously to the phonograph playing you old children's rounds.

This is where you took your first real steps, without holding on to the furniture or walls, bravely crossing the room, and then giving us a triumphant look. Then you start to talk. In English, because that's your only language.

Another pleasure is seeing the logs burning in all the fireplaces, because when the thermometer gets below zero, the central heating isn't enough. Outside, we wear thick, heavy clothes, and fur-lined caps that cover our ears.

One night, we hear some noise outside the kitchen, where we keep the garbage cans. Boule gets to her window on the same floor just in time to see "some big animals with horns" scamper away, probably hungry deer. Our woods are full of them, and I order some bales of hay to set out on the lawn. At the same time, I order salt bricks, the way I did in Europe for my cows, and the deer take to them.

As for wild rabbits—the bunnies that are so dear to American children —they come right up to our door, and you throw carrots and lettuce to them.

In November 1950, while we were fixing up the house, I nonetheless wrote *Maigret au Picratt's* (*Maigret in Montmartre*).

In 1951, my production was to be more abundant, in spite of the weeks in Boston or New York, and the errands rather far from home, in Poughkeepsie, Canaan, and Torrington.

Without giving up skiing, Marc, at school you have now taken up the most dangerous and roughest game in America, more of a Canadian specialty: ice hockey. You are handsome and proud in your uniform, with the helmet that almost covers your face, but I must confess that every game makes me shake with fright.

The parents always go to these games, sometimes a hundred miles from

Lakeville. And they are expected, if their cars allow, to take along three or four students whose parents may be unavailable.

I remember one winter night when you were playing some fifty miles from home and the Jeep was filled with boys from your school. It was snowing hard, and I was driving cautiously, aware of my precious cargo. When I finally pulled up in front of the indoor arena, I felt a chill down my back as I saw an ambulance parked not far from the door. That is the legally required precaution, because of frequent injuries, and I anxiously watched you play with all the spirit that's in you.

The professional matches, with audiences of thousands, are so hard-fought, especially when Americans go against Canadians, that the crowd can be heard to yell, "Kill him!" Sometimes, there are indeed fatalities. And aren't the worst brutes the ones that get the most applause?

I no longer look on all this as an outsider. When I first got to Lakeville, I was told, "Here, you have to belong. . . ."

And now I do belong to this America into which I am delving more and more pleasurably. Every month D. and I go to the parent-teacher meetings, charity bazaars, and movies given in the community house at Salisbury.

Jean Renoir, in Hollywood, had explained to me: "You understand, America is a kind of club. You'll see that they'll soon suggest that you get naturalized. Naturalization here doesn't mean quite the same thing as in another country. In a club, you're allowed to come as a guest for a period of time, but then the time comes when you feel ill at ease just being that, and you feel you have to apply for membership and pay your dues."

And he added—correctly, as I knew, because I read a lot of newspapers —"They never talk about me as an American director. They write, 'The French-born director Jean Renoir.'"

The same applies to other naturalized artists whose national origins are openly acknowledged.

Wasn't I now here for good, and weren't my two sons already little Americans? Early in 1951, I seriously considered getting naturalized, so that, even though an American citizen, I would be "the Belgian-born George Simenon." Without an s on my first name. Why not?

I got the books from which I could learn what I had to know to take the qualifying examination. Which led me to read the Constitution attentively, and find that it is probably the one that best respects the freedom of the individual.

One morning, I get a letter from one of the more influential members of the Belgian Royal Academy of the French Language, which embarrasses me. I have always tried not to belong to any organizations whatever, even the French professional guild, the Society of Men of Letters. So I answer very politely that I am flattered at being so honored but that in a few months I will become an American citizen.

The answer throws me: "We don't care whether you become an American citizen *after* being initiated into the Academy, which we foresee taking place in 1952. We are just asking you to delay your naturalization until then."

But I didn't have to delay anything, because once again events made my mind up for me. In February of 1950, one Joseph R. McCarthy, a U.S. senator, had accused the State Department of harboring and being influenced by Communists. This was the beginning of what were called "witch hunts," a period of turmoil known as "McCarthyism." For the next four years various congressional committees carried on much publicized investigations, holding hearings before which a large number of people were called to testify about alleged subversion. McCarthy's own committee acted like a trial court. When some of these hearings were televised, I spent weeks watching my set. What we saw was a vicious judge, assisted by two calculating counsel, reminiscent of the bloodthirsty Fouquier-Tinville during the French Revolution.

During this same period, the House Committee on Un-American Activities was hounding Hollywood directors, world-renowned screenwriters, and actors who only yesterday had been idols, into underground obscurity. Such fear was created that the studios blacklisted those who could not get a clean bill of health from the committee. Those who were the targets were mainly intellectuals and artists who were suspected of having leftist ideas.

We already had many friends in Lakeville, but no one ever mentioned this business, as if everyone was afraid of being compromised by just talking about it. I also kept still, even though all my life I have been apolitical, because that too could have seemed suspect to some people.

I was angry at McCarthy and those like him for sullying "my" America. His wild rages, which were sometimes funny, did not surprise me. What did surprise me was that these witch hunts could take place in free America, whose Constitution I had practically learned by heart, along with Lincoln's Gettysburg Address.

In France, I had seen the violent demonstrations of the fascist Camelots du Roi, their attacks against honorable men who happened not to share their point of view. I had known of the campaigns of Colonel de La Rocque, who wanted to throw into jail all those who didn't belong to the extreme right and were consequently to be considered unpatriotic.

In Belgium, I had seen the name Léon Degrelle painted in huge white letters on highways and walls. I knew that he and his fascist followers had welcomed the Germans into my country.

Hadn't such things happened everywhere?

But how could they happen here?

My love for the country didn't diminish. I still felt content here among my family and friends. But, like most Americans, I watched all this fury powerlessly, and worried about one of my friends, a talented playwright I had met at Renoir's, whose plays were not exactly conformist. Nor were those of the greatest American playwright, Eugene O'Neill, whose daughter was to marry Charlie Chaplin.

The latter's name often came up during these discussions, for in his films he had championed the "little man," so dear to my heart. Some eminent persons had to leave the country. Others went to prison. Still others saw their careers as professors or performers ruined, or at least dampened for a long time.

I continued my little life, trying to make my household happy. But I gave up the idea of becoming a naturalized American, an idea I had probably got from the atmosphere at Shadow Rock Farm and the country around it.

D. spent long hours in the office next to mine, where I stayed only long enough to write my daily chapter and take my nap in the bow window. I had ordered from Washington a huge official map of the United States, very good and clear, which, simply framed, covered one whole wall of my office.

What did she do there, even evenings, while I watched television, which was teaching me more fully the tastes and ways of the country? I especially liked the variety shows. Many of them used slang, which I found forthright, colorful, and to the point. In the beginning, I understood only part of it, but then I began to improve, and unintentionally, almost unwittingly, I began mixing slang words into the English (or American) that I spoke.

After a while, when I heard Americans talking on the streets of New York or elsewhere, I could tell by their accents whether they were from New England, the South, the Middle West, Texas, or California.

But what was D. doing all that time? To tell the truth, I hardly know. Was it just a way for her to be alone? If so, it was her right. She answered my mail, except for what came from Europe and my old publishers in various countries. Her letters were long and laborious.

Another domain I still kept to myself: my contracts, including the ones with American publishers. I always drew up my contracts myself, much shorter than the usual ones, knowing from experience that the more clauses there were in a contract, the more chances of lawsuits. And never in my whole career did I ever have any lawsuits with my publishers or my film, television, or radio producers.

So, D. was working. One day, she announced to me that she had so much to do she would have to have a secretary.

Why not? Wouldn't that give her more self-confidence? And wouldn't it add to her "standing," to use one of her favorite words?

She found a secretary, locally, a lady of forty-odd years, with a beaming face, an Austrian countess by birth who had married an important Hungarian official from a famous family. Mrs. V. spoke half a dozen languages, as do most cultured people from Central Europe. She had led a brilliant life, been a generous hostess, entertaining many important personages of the prewar period. Now divorced, she was living in Lakeville with a seventeen-year-old daughter, who was at school nearby.

The two women spent the whole day in the office, which fell silent whenever I went through it. Two or three times, I caught the secretary drying some tears. Why? None of my business. I can only say again that I was happy, loved D., and wanted her to be happy too.

Many American newspapermen came to interview me. A team from *Life,* then the world's leading picture magazine, spent a whole week with me, from morning to night. There were five of them, including the photographers, following me to the supermarket, to Hugo's with Johnny, trimming the wild bushes with enormous shears, with Marc, mowing the lawn, and anything else that came up or they could think of.

D. popped out often, full of smiles, and came over to kiss me before the cameras, but I never heard them click. I hoped that they would take pictures of her in her office, dictating to her secretary, but I didn't dare ask them, because they seemed to be shooting only what they wanted to.

They must have taken a thousand pictures, and when the story came out in *Life,* they ran just six of them.

The New Yorker, which I read faithfully, because it was the most interesting of all the weeklies, sent one of its principal staff writers to do a lengthy Profile of me, which constituted some kind of official recognition. The writer, a novelist and an excellent one himself, spent four or five days talking to me, and he was to become a friend; with his wife and three or four daughters, he had a country home near Canaan.

Life went on, peacefully, with much sweetness.

You were growing up, children. Marc had passed all his exams successfully, and we went to the Indian Mountain School for the graduation ceremonies.

They didn't take place inside the school but in a grassy garden, on a fine warm summer morning. Parents and children sat on the ground. The principal, after a short speech, announced prize awards and scholarships, and then the children ran to the kitchen, from which they returned with paper plates of hot dogs, cold cuts, rolls, and cups of soft drinks. Almost a family picnic, except that there were more than sixty families there.

We were all in shirt sleeves and had a good time, breaking up into groups, one family joining with another, ours with Beckett's, the lawyer having become one of our close friends and his youngest son your pal.

A wonderful fall. And Christmas, of course, after the mad rushes into New York. Presents, garlands, wreaths on the doors, hundreds of cards to be sent. I selected a card with a reproduction of a Grandma Moses painting on it.

42

Your second Christmas in our Lakeville house, Johnny boy, the third of your life.

Now, you are no longer a baby and your energy amazes me. Stocky and solid in your thick fur outfit, you still look like a wild bear cub.

Near our place, there is a fairly large store with a mezzanine, in the middle of which is a classical bearded, friendly Santa Claus. Dozens of children stand waiting to crawl up into his lap and tell him the list of presents they would like to get, while their parents stand off to one side, your mother and me included.

A few steps from you, a little blonde girl, with waves in her hair and a doll's pink face and blue eyes. How long have you been fascinated by her? At any rate, you rush toward her, take her in your arms, and cover her with kisses. Your rush was so sudden that the two of you rolled over, and you go right on kissing her, lying on top of her, as the lined-up parents look on reprovingly.

Your first female conquest, son. I get you off her only with effort, and then must stay alongside you in the line of waiting children. I have no idea what you are going to ask Father Christmas, as we call him in Europe, to bring you. That little girl? Or a little sister? At any rate, that picture remains etched in my memory. You weren't even two and a half yet, you young brute!

The holidays go by normally, the days and months pass. One after the other, in my office with the great view, I write *Maigret en meublé (Maigret Takes a Room)*, *Une vie comme neuve (A New Lease on Life)*, and, when the snow is melting around us, *Maigret et la grande perche (Maigret and the Burglar's Wife)*.

Around the same time, I feel concerned about the future of your nurse-maid, who is so sweet and nice. She is too smart and too devoted to spend her whole life going from house to house, and I suggest to her that she consider studying nursing. So she leaves us, kisses you a last time, holding back her tears, and a young local girl who has finished high school takes her place. Her name is Rita.

She is a fat girl in full bloom, both affectionate and placid at the same time, who is to stay with us a long time and, later, when married and with children of her own, go on writing us annually at New Year's and sending us pictures of her family.

You get along well with her and her open smile. I suspect that she has a preference for rainy days, because then she can sit in my green lounge chair and watch television while you solemnly play on the patchwork rug. Because you do everything, even your playing, solemnly.

Every night, when you feel wet, you cry shrilly until your mother or I come to you. The intercom at the head of our bed amplifies your voice. You quiet down when you see us, satisfied at having been so quickly obeyed, and you almost smile as we change you and then change your sheets. To get you back to sleep, I have gotten into the habit of carrying you with your head on my shoulder as I walk around singing:

> Wooden horsy, horsy, horsy . . .
> Wooden horsy, horsy, horsy . . .
> Going round and round and round . . .
> Wooden horsy, horsy, horsy . . .
> Wooden horsy, horsy, horsy . . .
> One more time going around . . .

A song learned long ago in the Vendée. I sing it three or four times, each time in tones more hushed, and try to put you back to bed. But you like it, and you protest. I sometimes sing that little chorus as many as a hundred times before you are willing to go back to sleep and I can return to our room.

But almost immediately your loud voice comes over the intercom again.

I can still see your sly smile. You have peed again, and the whole business starts over, changing the sheets, changing your diaper, and another series of wooden horses.

Do you remember your lamp? We found it in Poughkeepsie and are proud of it. On the shade, there is a little train, with all its cars, and as the heat of the bulb increases, the shade and train start turning slowly. I never again saw a lamp of that kind and am sorry we didn't keep it.

On the average, two calls per night. A preliminary one when we put you to bed early, before our dinner. We are barely through our soup when the intercom starts to shrill. You, of course! Are you aware that we are having a peaceful dinner? Are you jealous? It's your way of asserting yourself. I suspect you even guess the time when your mother and I are making love, because you never miss the chance to interfere with all the authority you can muster!

As for you, Marc, you are at the house more and more often, with your friend Peter Beckett, and the two of you have built a house in one of our big trees. You spend entire free afternoons in it, amply supplied with sandwiches and hot dogs, coming down only to get ice cream out of the freezer.

Here, your passionate interest in animals is fulfilled. You find, sometimes right in our swimming pool, snapping turtles so big their jaws are hard and sharp enough to bite through a finger.

You collect them, in the cellar of our garage, which will soon look like a mini-zoo. You also collect snakes of all kinds, which you pet as if they were kittens and which seem to enjoy it. In our woods, there are rattlesnakes, just as in Florida and Arizona. I, for one, never saw any. On the other hand, I often saw pheasants and grouse, which don't run away when we get near them.

Our good little life goes on as we prepare for a June trip to Europe. You can't come with us, my big Marc, because you won't be on vacation yet. But Johnny will, and so will Boule, delighted at the thought of seeing France once again. She will act as your nursemaid.

On Main Street, I have my hair cut in the small barbershop of a voluble, fraternal Italian. This is where I take you too, Johnny, to have some semblance of order periodically made of your thick black mane. One afternoon while I'm there by myself, awaiting my turn, there is a sixtyish customer sitting in the barber's chair. His hair is a beautiful silver. A younger woman, with a kind, serene face, is waiting for him.

The barber very shortly calls to me, "How come you don't know him? You're in the same business, and I often see both your names in the same paper."

339

He gives me the customer's name, which is famous throughout the United States and elsewhere: the silver-haired man is none other than the fine humorist James Thurber. Not only does he write delicious stories, but *The New Yorker* each week publishes several of his cartoons, which I have been enjoying ever since I got to America.

My illustrious confrere turns and looks toward his wife. "Simenon?" he says. "I saw that recent Profile on you, and my wife read me several of your books."

I find out he is practically blind. Yet he has enough sight left to do his drawings, the collections of which are best sellers not only in the U.S., but also in Canada and Great Britain.

We become friends. At his home, I see the problems involved in his doing his work. On the porch, preferably in the sunlight, his wife sets up a blackboard on a big easel. And with thick white chalk he traces lines more than a quarter of an inch thick, which in the weekly will be reduced to small cartoon size. There is no bitterness in him.

We make other friends among those who live near us. So there were three weeks at home, in our family atmosphere, with these friends. And a week of New York life.

In Tahiti, I had had the luck to be able to buy Tigy an opal known not only for the fact that it had belonged to the famous opera singer Nellie Melba, but also because it was called the "Feuer Busch," or fire bush, a name recognized by jewelers everywhere.

D. and I love to window-shop on Fifth and Madison avenues, and one afternoon we see a ring we like in a jewelry window, a three-carat solitaire.

Why not make the same gesture for D. I once made for Tigy? We go in, and find out that the emerald-cut pure diamond has its own story. It happens to have belonged to another opera singer, American, today old and forgotten. It is the first important jewel I have ever bought for D., and I am delighted by her joy in it, the brilliant look she gives me after putting it on her finger.

Another recollection. One afternoon when it was raining and we were in our room at the Plaza with nothing to do, D. suddenly said to me: "Why don't you go and see that call girl whose phone number we were given? It might amuse you."

I agree it might be interesting, and phone. I have to give the password, which is the first name of an imaginary headwaiter. In exchange, I am given the name of her hotel and a room number.

Two hours later, when I come back, I have a mocking smile as I tell D.: "First of all, it turned out she was a Canadian, from Montreal, just like you, with a strong accent to boot. Secondly, she's petite and dark like you. Third, she's built just like you and makes love almost exactly the same way. I might just as well have stayed right here."

I was to come across others, later on.

In June we sail on the *Ile-de-France*, because D. insisted that her first trip to Europe had to be on a French liner. The staff are more attentive than on other transatlantic lines, and more interested too. I think it was on this crossing that I bumped into Charles Boyer, who frequently made it.

We meet several couples, and D. is excited by the brilliant shipboard life she is discovering.

Obligatory evening dress. All day long, the ship's hairdresser was on tenterhooks, not knowing who, among so many important passengers, was supposed to have priority. At the captain's table, there are thirty guests or so, separated according to protocol. My immediate neighbor, a countess, I've heard, is a pretty blonde, on the plump side, somewhat "fast."

"Are you married?" I ask.

"Yes. My husband never leaves the cabin except to sleep on deck in a deck chair. He is much older than I, always grumpy, and sometimes he goes for hours without saying a word."

"Not much fun for you."

"No. I'm quite the other way."

Is he really her husband? Is she really a countess? What matter? Her décolletage is deep and, after a few glasses of champagne, her leg keeps nudging mine insistently.

"Are you married?" she asks in turn.

I point to D.

"Is she jealous?"

"Not in the slightest."

We dance, drink, have a good time, and D. keeps looking approvingly at me whenever we pass on the dance floor.

Later, I say to the little countess, "How would you like to come and join us in our cabin?"

"Do you mean it?"

"Absolutely."

The crowd thins out; D. is back with me.

"Do you have a date with her?"

"No. It seems she has a husband. But I asked whether she wouldn't like to join us in our cabin."

"You think she'll come?"

She does come; in fact, makes a rather sensational entrance. Pirouetting, she lets her dress slip off and there's nothing under it but her pink, plump body.

In no time, I am inside her, and she comes once, and a second time, while D. is undressing. Just as the countess feels that I am about to come in my turn, she pushes me gently away with, "No. That's for her." D. is ready and waiting.

That's all.

The trip continues as merrily as it started. One night, we stop at Plymouth. The purser wakes me to inform me that some French and English reporters have come on board and want me to see them for a moment.

"Later. Tell them I'm asleep."

I go back to sleep. When I go out for breakfast, they are there. The Frenchmen had come ahead in order to score a scoop. The two Englishmen are under less pressure.

I am taken aback by what happens at Le Havre. The ship has barely docked when some thirty journalists rush up the gangplank and drag me into one of the saloons. Questions. And more questions. Which I answer as well as I can. Our luggage has been off-loaded and is probably already on the boat train for Paris. Through the porthole, I see a small crowd on the dock, and hear their voices shouting my name.

"So, madame, you are Canadian?" the reporters ask.

"Yes."

"English Canadian?"

"No, French," she proudly replies.

Finally, she is getting some attention, and I am delighted by it. She beams. The formalities take so long that the purser finally has to come and tell us that the boat train is about to leave.

I find you on deck, Johnny and Boule, wide-eyed at what you see. I am wide-eyed too, because I have trouble making my way through the crowd. We finally get to the compartment reserved for us on the train. The news photographers have not stopped shooting pictures all this time.

A young newspaperman from *Le Figaro,* who is to become famous for his novels, and in the not too distant future I suppose a member of the French Academy, high-handedly leads me into an empty compartment. He is very short, very blond, but his eyes have a glint of intelligence. "I need a long interview," he says. "Several columns." And he starts asking questions while his colleagues peer dispiritedly through the corridor window.

The fellow is not a reporter, but a literary critic, and a highly regarded one, I am later to learn. I haven't really seen a French newspaper or magazine in seven years, and there are few faces here for me to recognize.

The interview goes on until we are on the outskirts of Paris. At the Gare Saint-Lazare, there is a crowd on the platform too, and in the first row I recognize the publishers Gaston Gallimard and Jean Fayard, and of course my own, Sven Nielsen.

I get off the train with you on my shoulders, Johnny. Hugs all around. D. and Boule follow. D. is given some red carnations and exclaims, "My favorite flowers!"

I had never heard her say this before, but this sentence will get repeated and everywhere she will be flooded with red carnations.

We go to the Claridge, because I promised D. she could have breakfast on the balcony of our suite overlooking the Champs-Elysées.

But we haven't gotten to breakfast yet. Sven has a surprise in store for me. He has taken the grand ballroom of the Claridge, sent out over a hundred invitations, and I find all my friends here, from Marcel Pagnol to Pierre Lazareff, Marcel Achard to Jean Cocteau, Fernandel, Michel Simon, Jean Gabin, and many more, men and women, actors, newspapermen, novelists, not to mention the inevitable photographers.

I remember especially a picture taken while Fernandel and I were making faces at each other. Sumptuous buffet, with all the champagne and whiskey anyone could drink. The radio interviewers are here too, from the various stations, sticking their microphones in my face and asking, "Tell our listeners how you feel being back in Paris."

I answer whatever pops into my head. Someone wants to know whether I'm not afraid my wife will ruin me at the famous Paris couturiers'. I answer by an evasion: "I'm not worried about high fashion. I'm more worried about hardware." For I had just thought of that mini-vacuum cleaner that we always carry in our luggage.

Sven has gotten us a huge suite, which, in addition to two bedrooms and two living rooms, has a room for the secretary he is lending me while I'm in Paris.

We do have breakfast on the balcony, but we're both exhausted. We will be throughout this trip, exhausted but happy, going from official dinner to supper with friends, from one broadcasting studio to the next.

By the second day, D. has received invitations from the famous couturiers, and decides to go to Lanvin, because that is where Tigy bought some clothes, perhaps in memory of the Bovary dress she wore that night at Sainte-Marguerite.

Nominally, I am a member of the jury for the French detective-story award, the Prix du Quai des Orfèvres. At a luncheon at Lapérouse, I meet my old friend the barrister Maurice Garçon, as well as Dr. Paul, the coroner, trencherman, gourmet, *bon vivant*, and a delightful storyteller.

He explains to us that he cuts up cadavers barehanded, with a cigarette in his mouth (the best of antiseptics, according to him), and sometimes interrupts the process to have a sandwich. One of his delights at society dinners, where he is a treasured guest, is to describe with gestures his most macabre autopsies. Good old Dr. Paul, who is Maigret's sidekick in so many of my novels!

Maurice Garçon, a brilliant conversationalist, sometimes full of caustic sarcasm when he is pleading a case, shows us his glasses and jokingly says: "I must have a piercing look, because all my glasses end up with a little hole in the middle."

D. looks at the glasses and has the misfortune to remark: "I see that the holes are larger on the outside. Don't you think you make the holes in them by looking at yourself in the mirror so much?"

I tremble. Everyone else at the table is an old Parisian, used to verbal jousting. Garçon is a formidable jouster, and very few are foolhardy enough to take him on.

He does not reply, but that very evening he gets his revenge. The famous poster artist Paul Colin, a frequent guest in the old days at Place des Vosges, has invited us to dinner with some friends at his Montmartre apartment. A small intimate group. A dozen friends who go way back, among them Pagnol, Achard, Lazareff . . . and Garçon.

At the beginning, everything is fine, and D. is delighted to be surrounded by so many celebrities whom she had known only by name. I don't remember what she said, but quickly, very quickly, Garçon contradicts her, with the same firm tone she used to him a few hours before.

Disconcerted and not finding an answer, she bursts into tears, and sobbingly gets up and heads for the first door she sees. Good old Colin, who has seen such things happen before, follows her diplomatically, and we all impatiently await his return. When he does reappear, he is smiling knowingly. "I fixed it all up," he announces.

The conversation freely resumes, and then suddenly the mysterious door, which was that of the bathroom, opens. D. bursts out, striking her mouth with her hand as she lets out hoarse Indian war whoops.

Her braids, normally pinned up, are now hanging down her back, with a chicken, or pigeon, or some bird's feather in them. Draped in a bedspread, she dances around the room two or three times, her eyes shining and blacker than ever, her face daubed with varicolored war paint.

We look at one another quizzically at first. Then, as she is about to dance out the door again, we all politely applaud.

· · ·

At Lanvin's, she orders an evening gown, or, rather, two. After two fittings, she is not satisfied and explains to a woman who must dress a good third of the socialites of Paris: "Here, I think it hasn't been taken in quite enough."

Third fitting, which is supposed to be final.

"The waist is two millimeters tighter on the left side than on the right."

Finally, the fitter says to her: "I'm sorry. Either take it the way it is, or just leave it with us. . . ."

She decides she will order her court gown in Rome, from an Italian couturier she has heard marvels about.

We drink a lot, because people shove drinks at us everywhere, and also perhaps in the senseless hope of combating fatigue and being able to take the pace.

A big official luncheon at the Paris Police Headquarters. Turbot Dugléré and duck *à l'orange*. I like both those dishes, but we are treated to the same menu almost every day, once both at noon and in the evening. The chief commissioner, surrounded by the chief inspectors from the Quai des Orfèvres, solemnly presents me with an inspector's silver badge in the name of Maigret.

A little later, he smilingly whispers to me: "You know that some of my officers will be delighted to see you leave?" And, when I register surprise, he adds, "Your son has to be kept under surveillance wherever he goes, for fear of kidnapping."

See, Johnny? Mornings, Boule usually takes you to the Champs-Elysées, where there are donkeys for rent, and you never get tired of riding them. In the afternoon, Sven's car and chauffeur are at your disposal, and with Boule you go for a ride in the Bois de Boulogne, including an obligatory stop at the zoo. You come and go, and have no idea, poor innocent, that wherever you are the police are on your tail.

You also run around the mezzanine at the Claridge, where one showcase is full of pictures of your father. You ask me to buy you a pipe, and continually have it in your mouth, to the delight of the photographers. "Young Maigret!" It all seems natural to you.

There is a miniature duplication of the Fingerprint Ball that had been held at the Boule Blanche, the Montparnasse Martinique nightclub, for the launching of the Maigrets. At the original one, over five hundred people were packed in. This time, there are some forty of us, including the chief police commissioner, and a magician I know from New York, who succeeds in lifting the chief's watch and wallet.

"I'd be happy to hire you to give my detectives some lessons," his victim tells him.

A lot of pretty women. There are now four dancing girls from Martinique, instead of the twenty there used to be; they are as young, beautiful, and voluptuous as the ones I knew at twenty-six. I go to see them in their dressing room, and happen in while they're changing. That gives me a chance to have sex, not with all four, but with two of them, while the others watch, smiling broadly.

A mad life. I am possessed of a sexual frenzy that D. finds very amusing.

Pagnol has invited us to spend a few days at his place in Monte Carlo on our way to Rome. Even though he now lives in a veritable palace, he is unchanged, affectionate and as full of jokes as ever. One evening, Cocteau comes to join us, making a theatrical entrance wearing a white parka and coming down the stairway like a diva. Achard is there too. We all have dinner one evening on Alexander Korda's yacht, berthed at Antibes, and Pagnol, who is terrified of ships and planes, several times during the meal says, "Alex, we're moving. . . . I swear this boat is under way. . . ."

He says he wants to come and see me in the U.S. But I know he will never dare cross the Atlantic. He gives D. a topaz ring, a small reminder of his first theatrical success. His young wife is very nice, discreet and shy, and very pretty to boot. She adores her big Marcel, whom she can't take her eyes off of, and is very proud of her little girl.

Rome. The Excelsior. D. orders a court gown. I don't want to disillusion her, but I know what the court of Belgium is like, and that a divorced man is not likely to get an invitation to it, any more than to Great Britain's.

More reporters. Photographers (soon to be known as "paparazzi"). And for me, a few beautiful Roman women, by way of compensation.

We come back to you in Paris, Johnny mine, where you stayed with Boule. Sven and his wife take us to the Vincennes Zoo, where you get to see lions, tigers, polar bears. Here again, so that you may see over the heads of the crowd, you straddle my shoulders, as I used to straddle my father's during royal and princely parades in Liège. One day, when I was misbehaving, my mother had said to me, "Watch out for the policeman!" There were a lot of them, with hairy shakos on their heads, holding the crowd back, on horseback. It seems I answered: "Just let him come! I'll bust him in two!"

You, Johnny, threatened to "bust" in four, or ten, the lions, hippopotamuses, and elephants.

And then off to Liège. Without you, unfortunately, because the strain would be too great. I had decided to get there incognito, one day earlier than expected. I wanted to avoid the newsmen and photographers while I showed

D. the Place du Congrès, Rue de la Loi, Hôpital de Bavière, where I had assisted at Mass, the whole setting of my childhood.

Nielsen and his wife take us in their car. I feel a certain emotion as we get to the border and, in imitation of an American custom, I take D. in my arms and carry her across it the way a bridegroom carries his bride across the threshold of the nuptial chamber.

We enter the suburbs of Liège, and I guide Sven through streets that are familiar to me. I have him drop D. and me at Place du Congrès, where I used to play so often with my companions, and make a date to meet at the same place an hour later.

"Come on." I take D.'s arm.

Click! A photographer! It is Daniel Filipacchi, at the time a photojournalist for *Paris-Match*, who is here with his crew. We can forget about our private twosome through my good old neighborhood of Outremeuse. All that I can get Filipacchi to agree to is that he will follow us discreetly, and by himself.

In front of the Hôpital de Bavière, I find a Neapolitan ice vendor, just like the one in my childhood. I would swear that his cart, which has a primitive drawing of the Bay of Naples on one side and Vesuvius on the other, is the very same one as in the old days.

Two young girls turn around, whisper, come over and eat ices facing us, and that same evening the whole family will know that I am here, because these girls are nieces I don't know, even by name.

My little pilgrimage is shot, but that doesn't diminish the nostalgia with which I gaze at the great door of the hospital, toward which, on dark winter mornings, I used to hie me as if toward a haven of safety.

43

I wanted my first call to be on my mother. We were in her neighborhood. It must have been six or seven in the evening, and I asked Sven and Lolette to take D. for a tour and meet me a little later on Place du Congrès.

The reason I preferred not having D. with me for this first contact was that I was afraid of my mother's reactions to this daughter-in-law whom she didn't know and who was not even from our country. My mother was an ardent Catholic who made sure each morning to adorn the altar of the Virgin in St. Nicholas Church. And I was divorced, which at that time meant automatic excommunication.

My mother had remarried, with Old Man André, as she called him, but only several years after my father's death, and Old Man André (that was his family name) was widowed. They were in good standing. I was not.

I do not ring the bell of this house I never lived in, which my mother bought long after I had gone to Paris. I might be making a mistake, because most of the houses on the street look alike. I click the flap of the mail slot the way I used to when I was little. I hear her steps coming from the kitchen at the far end of the hall. The door opens.

"It's you, Georges!"

She is very moved. So am I. I kiss her, and feel she is on the point of tears. She looks at me with the shy, slightly backward smile she has always had. She seems to be apologizing for being there, for the very act of existing, perhaps because she was the thirteenth child, of a German father and a Dutch mother. It seems as though she feels superfluous, as if she is the stranger who, at the age of five, still spoke only a few words of French when her father died and she was left alone with her mother, all her older brothers and sisters being married already.

"Come in. I didn't know you would get here today."

"I'm not expected until tomorrow."

She receives me in her dark little living room, full of heavy oak furniture.

It's now over ten years since I've been here, before Old Man André died. At first, I used to come almost every year, but the war, then my departure for America, separated me from her, although I write her about once a month.

"You're not too tired, are you? I read in the papers about all the things you did in Paris." She hesitates. "Where is your wife?"

"I'll introduce her to you tomorrow. I wanted to see you alone first."

An embarrassed silence. I look around. There used to be only one glass-doored cabinet, going back to my father's time. Now there are two. Everything seems to be double, because Old Man André's furniture has been added to what she already had. My mother confuses them, even confuses this house on Rue de l'Enseignement with the one we lived in, during my adolescence, a little farther down the same street. On the wall, I recognize a charcoal portrait Tigy did when I was nineteen.

"You'll have a glass of wine, won't you?"

I don't feel much like it at this time of day, but I know that a refusal would offend her. She runs down to the cellar.

We don't dare look each other too much in the eye.

"You'll stay for supper with me, won't you? Your mother's good old soup . . ."

"We used to have our soup at noon. You cooked it for two days, with a marrow bone from Godard's."

Godard was our butcher, on Place du Congrès, and his son was my classmate at St. André Institute.

"You haven't changed."

"Neither have you, Mother."

She is as slim, as lively as ever. She can't stay still.

"Aren't you coming back to Liège to live for good? You'd be so comfortable here."

"I know."

"Why don't you sleep upstairs with your wife? I have a fine bedroom and I hoped the two of you would use it."

"It would be very hard, Mother. I have all kinds of appointments." I feel sad, without knowing why.

I stay for half an hour. This atmosphere, my mother, my portrait on the wall . . . There is something both dull and pathetic about the whole thing. If I stayed any longer, I might break down and cry.

"I have to go. I have to meet some people. I'll see you tomorrow, Mother."

"Already?"

She's as relieved as I. She stands on the threshold until I turn the corner into Rue Jean-d'Outremeuse, on which I know every building by heart, and then I am at Sven's car.

"Was it painful?" D. asks.

"Not too. She would have liked us to stay at her place."

I had asked Moremans, one of the old-timers at the *Gazette*, to reserve a suite for me at the Hôtel de Suède. But before we go there, I want to eat some mussels and fried potatoes in a little place on Rue Lulay, the way I used to in the old days, after midnight, with my first bohemian friends.

The place hasn't changed much, but the owner has been replaced by a rather young Italian, and the waiters are Italian as well. Paper tablecloths and napkins. The mussels are brought to us in individual pots, and I eat them in the Liégeoise manner, using one of the shells as tongs to pick up the other mussels. D. does likewise, as finally do Sven and Lolette, who find it amusing. The French fries are crisper, not as greasy as in my day. I revel in them. This is a foray into a past even older than my own.

Moremans is waiting for us at the hotel, as affectionate as ever; he is one of my devotees. He has sent me many a letter about this trip, giving me all the details of the schedule, which got busier from day to day. I am first to have a reception at city hall. The mayor and deputy mayors will then give me a formal luncheon at the Ansembourg Museum, then . . . Good old Moremans reads on and on. Luncheon with the governor. Dinner as the guest of my Liège newspaper colleagues . . .

"Listen, Moremans, you can fill me in on all that as we go along. I'm dog-tired."

"I've worked it out so that between two receptions you get a chance to have a little rest."

"Just make sure they give me time to take a leak!"

I'm joking. Yet, as it turns out, I won't always have time to. The welcome by the city of my birth, including the common people of my own neighborhood, is to be so warm, so loving, that I will go from emotion to emotion without ever feeling how tired I am.

The Hôtel de Suède, which had seemed to me to be the height of luxury when I interviewed French President Raymond Poincaré there, Churchill, a Prince Hirohito as young as I, now seemed faded.

There are five or six reporters waiting for me, new men, young ones, representing the papers on which I used to have so many friends. They are nice and ask me much more discreet questions than I used to ask when I was in their place. I treat them to champagne and, almost without realizing it, start to reminisce for them and ask questions about what ever happened to our old bosses. Most of them are dead.

"How about Demarteau?" The bearded publisher–cum–managing editor who gave me my first job at the *Gazette* when I was sixteen.

"Alive and well, that one. And anxious to see you again."

I want to see him, too, because by now I am aware of all the patience he had with the young rascal I was.

It is after midnight when my colleagues finally let me go. D. had listened, in a straight-backed chair that makes her look rather stiff. She was not asked many questions, and I wonder whether her picture was even taken.

We are shown to the royal suite, on the second floor, of which I had previously never seen anything but the living room. Is memory leading me astray? It all seems quite impressive to me still, but decrepit.

The next day . . . Actually, I have to try to keep my recollections in sequence. City hall. From the top of its steps, I show D. the "Perron liégeois," a bronze fountain representing the freedom of the city, surrounded by the varicolored baskets of flower sellers.

People line the way. Flower sellers hold out red carnations to D., for her Paris quip about those being her favorites has made its way here. Our hotel suite was also decked with red carnations.

The large waiting room, with its black marble floor, its forbidding columns, the great staircase I went up when I got married to Tigy. The reception is held in the wedding room, which is black with people. At the entrance, old Demarteau hugs me to his chest. "My little Sim! . . . I never hoped to . . ."

Both of us are deeply touched. His beard is now white, but he stands just as erect.

The mayor, wearing his sash of office. The deputies. Nothing forced in this welcome, but a warm affection, in the Liège manner. A speech, of course, to which I reply with a few words from my heart.

The notables are introduced to me, a great many people who strike me as too young to hold the positions they do. It seems to me that in "my time" important personages were older. Because I was only an adolescent, obviously, and now I'm forty-nine years old! Come to think of it, I'm the one who's grown old. . . .

Champagne and petits fours, as in the old days.

We are loaded into cockaded cars to go to one of the oldest streets in the city, which carefully preserves some of its very handsome patrician buildings.

The mayor confides to me, "We're going to give you an informal little lunch, at the Hotel and Restaurant School, and the menu will be made up of local specialties. . . ."

Trout from the Amblève, a pretty stream in the nearby Ardennes where I often went fishing. Then the traditional goose *à l'instar de Visé.* The wines are poured generously. People tell jokes, some of them in Walloon; they laugh uproariously. Everybody is very high. So am I.

"Tomorrow," the mayor tells me, "it'll be more formal at the Ansembourg Museum."

I am well acquainted with that magnificent old palace of the counts of Ansembourg, now turned into a museum, with everything remaining exactly as it was three centuries ago.

"The city keeps it up and uses it to receive foreign guests."

"I'm no foreigner."

Everyone laughs. They are laughing at anything and everything. The mayor is a *bon vivant,* as are his deputies, including the one in charge of public education, who is sitting on my left and laughingly confesses to me that he is the first Communist deputy mayor of the city. If all the Communists are like him, they must be a bunch of good fellows.

351

"After lunch, you're supposed to go and place a wreath on the monument to the war dead of Outremeuse, at Place de l'Yser."

Where did I go after that? Unless memory is deceiving me, Demarteau took me with D. and the Nielsens to the *Gazette de Liège*. All the staff writers are there, and I once again meet the youngish guy who took my place when I left, and who today is the father of three or four children. Yet his babyish face has not changed, and I immediately recognize him. The linotypers are standing by their machines. There is a good smell of molten lead and printer's ink, and looking down on the stone, I can still read the upside-down letters hot off the linotypes.

We drink a toast, and I have no idea what I'm drinking. Nor do I know where we have dinner. Everything gets all mixed up in my head.

The next morning, in the main lobby of the Suède, I autograph books my fellow countrymen hold out to me. This is nothing like promotional autographing sessions. No books are on sale, and the ones that the men and women of Liège bring me are sometimes yellowed, dog-eared, and include my first novel, *Au Pont des Arches* (At the Bridge of the Arches), of which I no longer have a single copy. Each one writes his name on a slip of paper, and I recognize a lot of familiar names. On one slip, I read: Sophie Simenon.

"Any relation?"

"Of course." She laughs. "I'm your cousin Pierre's daughter." He's a cousin my mother took care of, when he was a baby, for several months after my aunt died.

I thus make the acquaintance of three Simenons I didn't even know existed.

We are taken by car to the Ansembourg. In a dining room paneled with polished wood, a horseshoe table. In front of each chair, a place card. D. bends over at the head table, and I see her switch the card at my right with the one at my left. The former has my mother's name on it, the latter D.'s. My heart tightens a little. I remember D. telling me, right after we were married, that now there was only one Mrs. Georges Simenon, *she*. My mother calls herself simply Henriette André Simenon, thus combining her two husbands.

The meal is refined, the wines are great ones, and there are no speeches. The violins of the Théâtre Royal, seated in an inconspicuous nook, play Grétry, Mozart, and Bach throughout the meal.

Cars take us to the foot of the bridge, and we go into Outremeuse, where I am dumbfounded to see, all along the sidewalks, schoolchildren all dressed in white waving little Liégeois or Belgian flags as we go by.

Place de l'Yser is the place where we used to explode *campes*, at the start of the procession for the parish feast day. A stone monument I've never seen before. A huge red-and-yellow wreath, those being the colors of the city, is put into my arms, and I go forward awkwardly, alone, to the spot where I have been told I am to place it.

Nothing more, except for the silence, which petrifies me. The officials make way for some people dressed in old-fashioned local costumes, the women in striped skirts and colored blouses, carrying baskets on their backs.

We visit the home of Grétry, the Liège-born composer who became *Kapellmeister* at the court of Louis XV. The house where he was born, on Rue des Récollets, near St. Nicholas Church, is narrow, three stories high; its windows still have the greenish "bottle bottom" panes set in lead. A house like the ones found in the paintings of the Flemish masters, in chiaroscuro, with simple, polished furniture. A house I would have liked to live in . . .

Enough of houses! They're making me homesick for ours in Lakeville. This morning, I phoned Johnny and Boule, whom Fernand Voiture, as Johnny calls Nielsen's chauffeur, is still driving around Paris and the outlying woods, under the watchful eye of a police car.

Rue Puits-en-Sock. Rue Roture, with its little whitewashed houses, where Tchantchet and Nanesse welcome us, the two symbols of Outremeuse. Tchantchet and the young girl Nanesse, dressed like the group around us, are quick with repartee and for centuries have been the symbols of the neighborhood's spirit of irreverence.

This is where the famous puppet theater is. Women in aprons, wearing wooden clogs, come out of their houses to kiss me on both cheeks, "in the homely manner," and a few words of Walloon come back to me, to answer their welcome with. The puppet theater is now the Tchantchet Museum, and there is a long tableful of people awaiting us there, all in costume. Immense "black tarts," which is what they call prune tarts, are served, as well as old local brandy, here called "*péquet.*"

We are obliged to drink some of the péquet and eat the tart, which blackens the lips and fingers. We are presented with puppets representing Tchantchet and Nanesse, and—of course!—D. is given red carnations.

Later, we go by my grandfather's old hat shop, which no longer has the red high hat above the window and which no longer sells hats.

I ask Moremans, "What's next?"

"We're having dinner together at a restaurant you know very well, La Bécasse, which you always said was the best one in town."

An expensive, elegant restaurant I didn't often get to go to, for want of the wherewithal. Kidneys *à la liégeoise* a must.

"What about tomorrow?"

"Big luncheon given by the governor, at the provincial palace."

The palace is sumptuous and historical, meaning that everything about it is huge. I am introduced to the governor. His name reminds me of something.

"Wasn't your father the druggist near Place Saint-Lambert?" I ask him.

"Of course! And he often used to talk about Désiré, who was his classmate at the Collège Saint-Servais."

"My father also often talked about yours, too."

Right away we are friends. Despite the impressive setting, there is nothing stand-offish about the meal, and I am introduced to personalities whose names are familiar to me.

In the evening, Sven's car takes us to Embourg, now full of houses, one more attractive than the other. The press is holding a dinner for me. I am shown to my seat, alongside the hostess, a woman around forty, youthful, pretty, very elegant.

My fellow newsmen present me with a very fine gold-banded pipe. We are served a very tasty ham and excellent cold pâtés, with white Pouilly-Fumé bottled by my marquis at the time I was his secretary.

"I know a great deal about you," our hostess says, smiling flirtatiously at me.

"What, for instance?"

"My grandfather was a great friend of your grandfather."

"My grandfather Simenon?"

"Your mother's father, Henri Brüll. The wood merchant who lived at the old Herstal château and had barges on the canal . . ."

She is doing this on purpose, to intrigue me. I have the feeling she's making fun of me, and she is more and more flirtatious, not to say forward. Under her form-fitting black silk dress, her voluptuous body is easy to make out, and I must say I am all ready to make a pass at her.

"Guess who I am," she says.

I try, in vain.

"My grandfather was at the head of the sanitation department for the local roads."

I feel I am growing pale and clench my fists. It's a good thing my mother isn't here, because she would be at the throat of my appetizing, beautiful neighbor. This woman is none other than the descendant of the man who ruined Grandfather Brüll, to the point that when he died he left his wife and thirteen child poverty-stricken. Is she a sadist? Some hoarse words start coming from my throat.

"Do you know that through your grandfather's doing mine was ruined overnight?"

"That may be. It's open to argument."

"Why did you ask me here?"

"I didn't. Your friends the newspapermen, who are also my friends, invited you."

People around us are laughing, talking, and many of them adjourning to the living room. I have no idea what I am going to do. A scene would be painful to my fellow newsmen, who are my real hosts. I grab the pipe they gave me and slowly fill it, to try to calm down, and take a few puffs on it. Then I make a stiff gesture of thanks, and try to spy D. and the Nielsens somewhere in the living room.

"What's the matter?" D. asks.

"Nothing. I'm just warm." And then, to Sven, "Let's go, if you don't mind."

They realize that something has happened. When I shake hands with Moremans, he is concerned too. "Did something upset you?"

"I'll tell you about it tomorrow. It has nothing to do with you."

"Is the pipe any good?"

"Excellent."

That pipe will have its own story. I set it down some place for a moment, and forget about it. I'm in a hurry to be outside, to be breathing a different kind of air.

"That was a fine pipe they gave you," D. says.

I automatically look for it in my pockets, then remember having put it down before picking up my hat and leaving.

The next day I tell Moremans about the pipe, and he phones our hostess of the night before. She answers that her servants have already cleaned the downstairs thoroughly and that they didn't find any pipe. I have not told Moremans about the old affair with Grandfather Brüll, because he might feel guilty.

He is distressed because all the newsmen pitched in to buy the pipe for me. He goes to Embourg to check on it as if he were Maigret, resembling him even to the broad shoulders. He comes back triumphant and incensed.

"I immediately smelled something about her son, who seemed ill at ease. So I gave him a quizzing he won't soon forget."

I smile, since I can hardly picture Moremans doing that. "How old is the boy?"

"Eighteen. He's a student. He finally confessed to me that he's one of your most fanatical fans. When he saw you put the pipe down, he quickly hid it, hoping to be able to keep it as a souvenir."

"Poor kid! Did this take place in front of his mother?"

"I'm not sure he even told her about it. But then, she's a much better liar than he is."

"What did she say?"

"That she was sorry. I would think you'd feel flattered to have such devoted readers."

The bitch! I cleaned the pipe carefully, and went back to smoking it.

There were other lunches, other dinners too, I guess, but I can't remember them.

Two days later, Sven takes us to Brussels, where we are to spend only three days, because I'm in a hurry to get back to Johnny and Boule, and then to Shadow Rock Farm and my big Marc.

We have suites in an old hotel on Place de Brouckère, where I bump into nine or ten members of the French Academy, including my friends Maurice Garçon, Pierre Benoît, André Maurois, as well as Permanent Secretary Georges Lecomte, who is well beyond his eightieth year. Were they coincidentally invited to Brussels at the same time as I? I don't know. However that may be, my friends and I make a very happy, very intimate little gang.

As I had foreseen, they were received by the king; I was not. Nor D., despite the court gown we have been dragging with us since Rome in an outsize cardboard box.

My formal initiation at the Palace of the Academies. I give a eulogy of my predecessor, a writer from Liège whom I never set eyes on, but whose father's watchmaking store I am familiar with, just off Rue Léopold, where I was born. Queen Elisabeth is present, as well as the French Academy members.

My friend Carlo Bronne—the one whose tuxedo I bought to get married in and who is now a king's prosecutor—then pronounces a speech in tribute to me. It is a large hall, but it is filled, and it is so hot that I feel sorry for the French academicians in their thick green uniforms.

As we go out, photographers' flashes and interviews. D. and I succeed in breaking away and taking a walk on the boulevard; we stop at the terrace of a little family café, where I order a bottle of Geuze-Lambic, the famous Brussels beer that I want D. to taste. It is cooler here than in the Palace of the Academies, where I never again set foot. It's restful to be able peacefully to watch the passers-by. D. makes a face, because the beer is very bitter, and I admit that I am not crazy about it either.

The prime minister is having a dinner for the members of both the Belgian and French Academies, which turns out to be very stiff. The

Frenchmen are in full regalia once again. Strangely, wives are not invited to this official banquet, but only to the evening dance that follows in the grand ballroom.

Speeches? I guess so. I didn't hear them. We finally go into the ballroom, where the women are waiting for us, most of them in gala evening gowns, especially D., who is wearing her court gown, spread from the waist down by hoops that make a crinoline of it.

In that outfit she can't dance anything more than a minuet. Nor can she sit down in any chair or armchair, because the hoops turn up and show more than just her legs. She ought to have a high stool.

Pierre Benoît, always a prankster, comes over to me and whispers: "Three or four of us are ducking out. We'll meet outside."

And there, in uniform, swords at their sides, cocked hats on their heads, are Maurois, Garçon, Pagnol, and the incorrigible Benoît, who drags us off to a bar, which seems to be something like a private club and may well be.

The Frenchmen take off their swords and cocked hats and pile them all on top of one of the tables. We sit around in a circle, and Benoît orders a round of whiskey. We are all relaxed, and try to top one another in storytelling. Garçon, Pagnol, and Benoît are especially adept at this sort of thing.

It is three in the morning when we get back to the hotel. Like kids, we tiptoe in so as not to wake anybody. Brussels and its formalities are over. Tomorrow, in Sven's car, we will head back to Paris, where I will at last be reunited with my Johnny and good old Boule.

Come to think of it, how did the meeting between my mother and D. go? Very well? Well? Not badly? . . . Anyway, my mother promised to come and spend some time in Lakeville in August, and before sailing on the *Ville de Paris*, I reserve a cabin for her on a Dutch ship, on which she will feel more comfortable than on one of the French liners, which are too fancy and formal for the thirteenth child of the Brülls.

Our crossing is uneventful. Formal captain's dinner, gambling on the little horse races and other society games, food that's too rich, and finally the tips to be handed out.

You seem to me to have grown, Johnny mine, and you are more and more self-assured, so that you get along just swimmingly with the sailors who each morning swab the decks and polish the brass.

New York and reporters. Our car, with me at the wheel, taking us back home.

A fine trip. Just a few more miles and I'll be with you, Marc, my boy, as well as with the whole household.

44

How handsome you are, my Marc, and how good it is to see you again! You're more tanned than ever, your hair the color of sand in the sun. It is true that while we were rushing from Paris to Rome and Milan, from Liège to Brussels, you and your mother were spending part of your vacation on Nantucket Island. Remember how you took the Puritans' venerable Bible for a telephone directory there?

You'd no longer make that mistake now. You are thirteen and have graduated creditably from Indian Mountain School. You've become a first-rate skier, fine baseball, football, and ice hockey player, not to mention any number of other sports.

You're full of wonder at Johnny, who now looks like a little man in the new clothes we bought him at Dominique, in Paris, the boys' and girls' equivalent of Dior or Lanvin.

You've always had a paternal feeling toward your little brother, ten years younger than you, and you're the one he is most at ease with and most trusts.

You point to a big, statuesque blonde with a proud bosom, who might well be one of the half-naked showgirls of the Folies-Bergère, and ask, "Who's she, Dad?"

"D.'s new lady's maid."

She came back with us on the ship, where we scarcely saw her because most of the time she stayed in her cabin seasick.

Some of Sven's staff found her for us. She's from Normandy, has a milk-and-roses complexion and, in addition, the gift of always being good-natured, a precious attribute in my eyes. I like to see people smiling around me and am ill at ease when confronted with frowns.

D. now has her own lady's maid and her secretary, whom I would never think of asking to do anything for me. I'm happy about it, because that will give her more self-confidence, which she has always needed, and which explains her fits of aggressiveness, doesn't it? I want D. to be well balanced, satisfied with herself and her life.

Your zoo, my Marc, has grown, and you've discovered some new animals. The woods are full of skunks, for example (an animal which in Europe is known only for its fur). They look like big pointed-nosed cats, sharp-eyed and on the qui vive, with their unusual method of self-defense. You explain to me that that "stink gland" can be removed so that they can become pets.

Then there are the bullfrogs, the big toadlike creatures that all night long croak in trombonelike tones. One becomes accustomed to them in a hurry and finally falls asleep to the tune of their croak, as if it were a lullaby.

You've made new friends, including the son of the undertaker, who lives near the post office. Since many Americans are embalmed, in the cellar the undertaker has a room with marble tables in it where he works at embalming, much like my old friend the Paris coroner Dr. Paul.

Your friend gives parties attended by girls of your age, and on one of those marble tables, at thirteen, or maybe a little younger, at twelve and a half, like me, you have your first taste of what is called "carnal knowledge."

Good for you, my Marc!

So life resumes, with one additional person in the house. If I'm not mistaken, her name is Jeanine.

A few days before my mother is to come and see us . . .

Here, I must repeat myself. I have an almost stereoscopic memory for events in their tiniest details, for facial expressions, gestures, and the spoken word. Yet that memory refuses to conform to any strict chronology.

Since I have never kept a diary to which I might refer, or made any notes, I sometimes make a mistake in the sequence of events. During the years at Place des Vosges, I maintained big cloth-covered ledgers in which I recorded my short stories and dime novels, the dates of writing and the amounts they brought me, which helped me make up my tax return at the end of the year.

I very much wanted to keep these ledgers, souvenirs from my early days, as well as my address book, in which each year I made a cross alongside the names of those who had died. D. burned them all.

I didn't kick. She was not jealous of my female encounters, which she encouraged and sometimes set up. But she was terribly jealous of my past, of everything I had lived through before meeting her. In her mind, my life ought to have started the day we met, and she furiously erased all traces of my earlier existence. She hated Tigy and found Boule hard to put up with, because the latter had so many more memories of me than she did. As for my mother, whom we were expecting . . .

But had I not acted the same way toward her? Wasn't this a natural feeling? With difficulty, I convinced myself of it.

A few days before my mother arrived, I experienced great joy, for the third time in my life.

D. asked one morning: "Haven't you noticed anything in the last few weeks?"

What could I have noticed, in the whirlwind we had been caught up in in Europe?

"I haven't had a period in over a month now."

While I was in the habit of making love to her every day, I never paid attention to the "days with" and "days without," as drinkless and meatless days were called during World War II.

We decided to consult a gynecologist at Sharon, a tiny town not many miles from our house. A darling place, all pink-and-white buildings, with charming cottages. In one of these, a complaisant giant, with the hairy muscular forearms of a butcher.

"I can't say for sure before I get the test results, but I would think the answer is yes."

My chest immediately swelled with the joy I knew before your birth, Marc, and then yours, Johnny. Why was I sure the answer was yes? And why, this time, was I ready to swear the baby would be a girl?

"Are you familiar with our little hospital? That's where I expect you'll be delivered. It's not the ordinary kind of hospital."

The hefty, muscular giant has kind, almost naïve eyes. He exudes the joy of living and empathy.

"It was founded by five of us, each with a different specialty. Not only are we friends, but also we have the highest regard for each other. By chance we all happened to come together here in Connecticut, and we got this idea of starting a hospital of our own that wouldn't be the 'ordinary kind.' "

We are shown through the pink-and-white hospital surrounded by greenery. Not more than forty rooms, private and semiprivate, and very attractive. Sprightly young nurses; everybody on a first-name basis. No head of staff, no "professors" here. Flowers everywhere, and daily visits from volunteer ladies who bring books to the patients.

"We've just been named the best small hospital in America for the second time," he tells us.

I am among the angels, as we say in Liège. I'm eager to have you be born here, Marie-Jo, for you are the one your mother is carrying in her slightly rounded belly. How impatient I am!

All the way back, I sing, while occasionally glancing soulfully at D.'s face.

"You'll see, it'll be a girl. A little girl of my own, whom I'll watch grow up, and will dress in flowered dresses."

Why have I always considered, deep within myself, that my children were mine alone? Male egotism? May be. I rather think I've always had a deep paternal feeling, the need to see my children growing up, to watch their eyes opening up to life, to discover them as they reveal themselves little by little, day by day.

Next day, a phone call. A resounding, happy "Yes."

And D. telling me happily: "You'll like seeing me get fat again."

She remains convinced that I like only women with full-blown shapes, on account of the character of Maigret's wife, created so long ago. To put it more simply, skinny women don't appeal to me, especially when they are not healthy and deprive themselves of food to remain stylishly slim.

I like natural women, without artifices, simple, unmade-up women, who live their lives without trying to be someone else. This is something D. has never been willing to understand. True, few other women do either, and magazines, movies, TV, advertising in all its forms encourage them to keep looking like the prototype created by the merchants who determine fashions.

Oh, well! I had invited my mother to visit, and we go to pick her up from her Dutch ship, the captain of which congratulates me on how nice she is.

"Everybody aboard loves her. She is so simple and so cheerful. I hope she will have a fond memory of this crossing with us."

I am shocked to see mother wearing her oldest clothes. All she brought are two small suitcases, and she seems more retiring than ever.

"I guess it's on account of you, Georges, that everyone was so nice and thoughtful to me. They all talk about you, and seem to have read your books."

Holland happens to be one of the countries where I have had many readers right from the start. It's also one of the countries that most attract me, perhaps because a quarter of the blood in my veins is Dutch.

My mother takes in the skyscrapers without surprise, and then the expressway with four lanes in each direction, mostly bordered by woods. She is not admiring. She is looking. Lakeville at last. Shadow Rock Farm.

"Is this where you live?"

She knows Boule. She has seen Marc only as a baby and never seen Johnny.

She seems smaller and more fragile than in the house on Rue de l'Enseignement. We don't tell her that D. is pregnant; I don't know why.

The activity in the house surprises and intrigues her.

"What do you need all those servants for?"

"Listen, Mother, they aren't called 'servants' over here. They are people who work for us, who help us, part of our family."

"They must cost you a pretty penny."

"They earn their keep. I earn mine too, and without them I'd never be able to get my work done."

That doesn't change her mind. Way back at La Richardière, where she visited us twenty years ago, she had the same attitude. Of reproach? Hostility? I can understand you now, Mother. You're still the little thirteenth child, and you've known what real poverty is. At fourteen, you were the nursemaid to your sister's children, but had to leave there because your brother-in-law was trying to get too intimate with you. Painfully shy and terrified, you applied at Innovation, where you became one of the youngest salesgirls. You were pretty, with a nice body and fluffy blond hair. You admired the posture of big Désiré, whom you married. I was born, followed by Christian, who was too heavy for you and left you with a fallen womb, from which you've suffered the rest of your life. You pinched every penny.

You were poor, and proud of it. Are you unaware that I too was poor and that, for all my big houses, and sometimes châteaux, I've kept the soul of the "common people"? I don't try to impress anybody, like your brother Henri, from Tongres, whom you detest, as you have a perfect right to, who built up his fortune by being hard on everybody, including you.

Doesn't the little room you have, so simple, with flowered wallpaper like that of my childhood, appeal to you? Doesn't it help you to understand?

That evening, when we are alone, D. bitterly comments: "She did it on purpose, coming here dressed like a poor relation."

That may be true, but I can't hold it against my mother.

"We'll have to get her some proper clothes."

She has plenty of proper clothes back in Liège. One of her Brüll cousins, who started out poor too, had the smart idea of getting one of the new knitting machines on the installment plan, and then the daring to go to Paris, to Chanel's, and get the right to reproduce for Belgium Chanel's sweaters, and then her dresses.

She bought two, six, ten machines, hired girls, opened workshops, opened a dress shop, first in Liège, then in Brussels, finally in all the big cities in Belgium.

Anna always had a special soft spot for my mother, who can now go into her stores and pick out anything she wants. I know that my mother says she doesn't need the clothes, just as she says she doesn't need anything that I want to get her.

. . .

We go to New York to get Mother a wardrobe, as we did for D.'s mother. D. has gone through the things in the flowered bedroom and discovered that my mother wears a worn-out, shapeless corset. We get her some new corsets. We buy her everything, including shoes, which hurt her feet, because she has a very painful "onion."

I say "we," although I am not present at these purchases. I don't really think they'll improve things any, but what can I do? Am I a coward? I try not to come between the two women, especially since D. is now carrying the baby I am so ardently eager to see born.

A small drama unfolds in the next days. My mother obstinately continues to wear her old threadbare corset. Then D., without mentioning it to me, swipes it and throws it into the garbage, expecting that in this way she will have the last word. But at night my mother goes downstairs silently, opens the garbage can, and takes her old corset out.

The same thing is repeated two, three times, and finally D. gets her way by throwing the disputed thing into an incinerator.

My mother does not mention it to me. She spends the greater part of her days in one of the garden chairs, her eyes closed, and when I come to sit by her she pretends to be surprised.

"Is that you, Georges? You mustn't put yourself out for me, you know. You have so much to do. Your wife too, always locked in with her secretary."

I suspect that she noticed the switch of the place cards when we had that official luncheon in the Ansembourg Museum.

"You can't imagine how nice people are to me in Liège. They call me Simenon's mother, and they're proud of you. When there is a gala at the theater, they invite me to one of the best seats in the house, and come to pick me up in a fine car. Are you happy, Georges?"

"Of course, Mother."

I am on the point of confiding to her that we are expecting another child. But what good will that do? Life has taught her to mistrust everything and everyone.

At La Richardière, she was to have stayed a month. She insisted on going back home after a week. How long will she stay here now? I fear that she will once again shorten her visit. I take her for rides in the car without D., show her the seven nearby lakes, the hills, the toylike villages.

"Yes, it's all very nice, but it's not home. Why wouldn't you come back to live in Liège, or the surrounding countryside? I've been told you're going to become an American. Is that true?"

I had been tempted to. Am I still? I don't know, but I answer her sincerely: "I'm going to remain a Belgian. My children are registered in the public records at Liège, on the same page as my father and you."

She looks at me, and I know she wonders whether that's true. Only with Boule does she feel at ease and can she have open-hearted woman-to-woman talks. They have known each other for a long time, since the first times my mother came to see us at Place des Vosges.

"What's happening with Tigy?"

I explain to her that I see her often, that we have remained very good friends. She still wonders whether it's true. She will wonder all her life. Especially about me and what I say.

When you talk to her, Johnny mine, you answer her in English, in spite of all our efforts to get you to talk French.

"Can't he talk French?"

"He knows how, but he's more comfortable in English."

My mother decides to leave after ten days, and this time to fly, so as to get back to her little house that much sooner. We take her to the airport.

"Thank you, you know, Georges. Thank you too, you know, D." But she has difficulty getting her name out. She would obviously rather be calling her madame, or perhaps mademoiselle.

To see the doctor with the butcher's arms.

"Everything is just fine. As far as I can tell, you should deliver in February. Probably the first half of February."

That delights me. If only you were to be born on February 13, like me, Marie-Jo!

I've already decided on a name for you, which D. has agreed to. I couldn't name one of my sons Georges, as is customary, because my brother, when he was in the Congo, where he spent twenty years, named his son after me. So there is already—to my regret, since I had not been consulted about it—a Georges Simenon in the new generation. Christian did it because he thought it would make me happy; he adored me.

I couldn't possibly name my daughter Georgette. Then why not Marie-Georges, which in our case would become Marie-Jo? I like that name. I can't tell whether you will or not. I have to take my chances. If it's a boy, your mother has decided he will be named Patrick, and I don't object. But it won't be a boy. I can trust my intuition on that.

I enroll you, Marc, at the Hotchkiss School, after we go there together and are both subjected to a tough quizzing by a very impressive stone-faced headmaster.

The campus, on the shore of Lake Wononskopomuc, looks like that of an American college or university. Here too sports are mandatory. There is even a nine-hole golf course, open to the inhabitants of Lakeville mornings, while the boys are attending classes.

I often play there. It's a hilly course, with the kind of steep rises I like, because I'm better with the irons than the woods.

D. and I have to go up to Harvard, where, as one of a half-dozen novelists, I am invited to take part in a seminar on the novel.

Morning and afternoon, there are discussions. One speaker, according to tradition, acts as devil's advocate, maintaining the opposite of the basic theme. It takes place in a large, airy room.

D. joins me for lunch at a nearby restaurant, with my fellow participants, none of whom has his wife along.

Evenings, in a large auditorium, there is a different kind of session, at which, after a brief lecture by each of us, hundreds of students and professors ask questions. It is very lively and goes on till almost midnight.

I am also invited to a nearby university that is for women only. A veritable enchantment. D. goes with me, and we are welcomed as if we were lifelong friends. The girls, most of them pretty, have us to lunch, show us their rooms, chatting and asking questions. Later there will be my lecture and questions, a game I enjoy and through which I get to know the youth of America. Almost all the questions reveal avid curiosity, a great breadth of mind, and my young lady listeners astound me by their frankness.

Another lecture, at Columbia University in New York City, where my old friend O'Brien is dean. Men and women students. Questions, answers, warm welcome.

We are into September, and in a little town in Connecticut, a play is being staged based on my novel *La neige était sale*, which I wrote in Tucson. It's an avant-garde theater that gives its performances in a reconstructed barn.

I won't attend. I'm bothered by seeing plays or films based on my novels. In Paris, Raymond Rouleau staged a different version of *La neige était sale*, and an Argentinian director named Luis Saslavsky is making it into a film in Paris.

As *The Snow Was Black*, the novel was published in New York, first in hardcover, then in a paperback, which has already had a two-million press run. In England it was called *Stain on the Snow*.

D. handled the negotiations, met with the publishers at Lakeville, preferably without my being around, and I got into it only to write the contract terms. She loves phone conversations, long, very long ones, like the letters she writes. To each his own, after all!

You, Johnny mine, will attend Hotchkiss too, but by the side door, so to speak. Many of the teachers live on campus with their wives and children. The wives got together and decided to organize a nursery school, in a building put at their disposal. They take turns running it, and it is delightful.

Soon, I am taking you there every morning and picking you up at noon. The low building is at the bottom of a sloping meadow. You leave me at the edge of the road and make your way valiantly through the deep snow to the building, where one of the women takes your winter wraps and boots off. You don't cry, even on the first day. You barely turned around once or twice to make sure I was still standing there by the Jeep.

Whenever I think back on the past, I am amazed that a human being can do so much in so little time. In December 1951, I wrote *La Mort de Belle* (*Belle*), the action of which takes place in Lakeville. Which means that, in that year in which I got about so much, there were six novels. In 1952, on the other hand, I wrote only four, one of which is also American: *Le Revolver de Maigret* (*Maigret's Revolver*), *Les Frères Rico* (*The Brothers Rico*), *Maigret et l'homme du banc* (*Maigret and the Man on the Bench*), and *Antoine et Julie* (*The Magician*).

Unbeknownst to me, I am elected president of the Mystery Writers of America, an important writers' association, which for the first time has selected a foreigner as its president. I feel very flattered, but object that I won't be able to attend the monthly committee meetings. Rex Stout and the two cousins who collaborate under the name Ellery Queen come out to inform me of my election, sweep away my objections, and I finally accept, and go to New York for the general meeting, at which, of course, I have to speak.

The three fateful months after which I am no longer supposed to have sex with D. are past. I have barely paid any attention to her maid, whom I have simply admired at a distance. One evening I go down to the kitchen and find her there, stark naked, writing a letter.

I tell D. about it, and she says: "Well, what are you waiting for, to move in? I'm sure she's doing that on purpose."

The next evening, I find her stark naked again, as if it were the most natural thing in the world, writing a letter in the same place. She is more than appetizing, and in no time we are in her room. She proves docile, even enterprising and expert. She certainly loves making love, but I soon suspect that it is less a physical need for her than a diversion. I even wonder whether she isn't frigid, and whether her need for a man isn't purely mental. It takes away a great deal of my pleasure; but I still go to be with her often, which does not interfere with my visits to Boule, who obviously knows about her but doesn't say anything. Good old Boule, who has seen so many others come and go, and yet retains her affection for me, come hell or high water.

What I am most anxiously awaiting, Marie-Jo, is for you to start moving around. Our merry gynecologist, whom I confide this to, asks me: "You do want a girl, don't you?"

"Ardently."

"Usually, they move around less quickly than boys. Besides, their movements are less violent."

"Do I have a chance then?"

"I can't promise anything. . . ."

Christmas. Snow everywhere. Marc comes to see us every weekend, and I am allowed to visit him once a week in his almost Spartan room on campus.

Sometimes he brings home friends, who pick out one or another of my books in English, sit in an armchair and stay there reading for hours.

You, Marc, my boy, are not yet curious about what I write, and I find that quite as it should be. There are so many things to attract you in your young life. I am a novelist, as the father of one of your friends is a famous jazz pianist and the father of another pal is an undertaker. Every man to his trade.

One day, however, you triumphantly announce to me: "Guess what they're having us study this week? One of your short stories. In French class. It's real good, you know."

For Christmas, you no longer ask for electric trains, but for Southern snakes, especially a bullsnake, and you prepare the cages for them with your friends, in your zoo down under the garage. No venomous snakes, but rather rare species that I order from a specialized store in Miami.

The bullsnake is the most frightening of them. As big as a young python, it blows its neck up as if to burst it and gives out with a powerful noise, like the sound of a trombone.

Presents. For you, Johnny, more disguises, which you never get tired of. And other toys too, of course, that I can't remember. You can spend hours listening to your records, which you play by yourself on your wind-up phonograph.

A mellow winter, one of warm intimacy. I am counting the months. You are moving, Marie-Jo, not violently, the way Johnny did, but softly, already cuddly.

45

In the final analysis, I think that in Lakeville I prefer winter to summer, and even to the glorious autumn, with its flamboyant colors. I relish the sight of logs burning in the fireplaces and their good smell. Like a child, I watch the snow falling in thick flakes that bunch together on the window and, when the sky clears, the shimmering of all the crystals covering the ground as far as the eye can see and the branches of the trees. What a pleasure it is to sink one's boots into the white powder and hear it squeak at every stop like a happy song! Even the animals of our woods, hidden in summer under the densest foliage, come fearlessly near the house, where Marc and Johnny put out food for them.

Nature is said to be asleep. I find it more alive than ever, closer than ever, in this muted universe in which animals and humans feel as one.

This is the universe you are to be born into, little girl. For our good giant of a gynecologist, without being categorical, is more and more inclined, from one visit to the next, toward the probability of your being a girl.

Your mother is fastidiously preparing her little personal suitcase. And just as fastidiously an even more impressive and heavier one, to be filled with files.

Johnny, no longer a baby, has moved into the next room, between the nursery and Marc's pennant-decked chamber. The lamp with the little trains on the shade still makes them go softly and quietly around when it is turned on.

As for your cradle, I saw to it that it should be very feminine, with lace and pink ribbons. Is it so ridiculous to prepare a romantic setting for the tiny bit of femininity about to be born?

I am not writing, but keeping busy as best I can. At a sale, we picked up some old wrought-copper andirons and firescreens, which I try to shine, but they are covered by endless layers of varnish that generations of iconoclasts have put on them. At the same sale, I was able to get some pewter plates and platters that were going begging, even though I could tell from the stamps on them that they were British, dating from the Elizabethan period.

I will not succeed in cleaning up those andirons and plates until spring, when I can go out to the barn and use the electric polisher I buy for the job.

As the days go by, my impatience becomes greater and greater and I no longer go to my office for anything but taking a nap.

February 10 goes by, and I still dream that you may be born, like me, on the thirteenth. Wouldn't it be wonderful if we both had the same birthday, fifty years apart?

The thirteenth and fourteenth go by. You are waiting feverlessly inside your mother's belly. She has gotten almost as large as she did with Johnny. She hasn't smoked during her pregnancy, or drunk, at least so far as I know. I don't keep tabs on her, and she still spends most of her time in her own office, where I am unwelcome.

I dance attendance on her, try to foresee her needs, as if she had become a precious, fragile thing. Yet for the second time I am having proof that she is never healthier than when she is pregnant.

Nineteenth, twentieth, twenty-first. Suddenly, on the twenty-second, very early in the morning, on her way from our bedroom to the bathroom, her water breaks.

A few days before, there had been a snowstorm. This morning, the sky is porcelain blue, and, reassuringly, the roads have been swept clean and are bordered by two mountains of snow, which would cushion any bump.

It takes exactly eighteen minutes—we have timed it—to get to the little hospital in Sharon.

She gets dressed without haste, gives instructions to the help and her secretary. I kiss Boule on both cheeks; a birth still scares her, even though she saw so many little brothers and little sisters get born back home. Johnny is in school, Marc someplace on campus.

Trees, frozen streams, houses in the valleys. We don't see a single car on the way. A nurse smilingly leads us to the reserved room, so brightly sunlit that she has to close the cream-colored curtains.

"I'll call the midwife."

A fat, fortyish woman, who probably owes her happy disposition to the fact that she sees so many happy babies and parents. She feels D., helps her undress, ties the hospital gown, slit from top to bottom, at her back. I put the suitcase full of files in one corner, against one of the pale-yellow walls. Isn't yellow my favorite color?

"I'll inform the doctor."

But she is no sooner out than D. starts moaning, and the pains commence. I call the midwife. She tells D. to lie on her stomach and massages her back softly.

"You see that?" she says to me. "You can do that each time she gets another pain. Keep track of the time between them, and when they get down to three minutes apart, you can call me. I'll drop in to check up from time to time."

She, of course, takes it in her stride. But I'm very moved by it, because this is the first time I am allowed to have a part, however small, in the actual birth of one of my children.

The pains are coming at ten-minute intervals when the gynecologist comes in and, with rubber-gloved fingers, probes D.

"The opening is still tiny. It will have to reach three centimeters before we can take your wife into the delivery room."

And, seeing how tense I am, the good, jolly giant adds, "In the meantime, keep massaging her whenever necessary. Until you get exhausted!"

I massage. During the letups that follow each pain, D. turns toward me and smiles affectionately.

The pains become sharper, and I massage vigorously, but delicately at the same time, for fear of hurting you, my little Marie-Jo.

Then around noon, the pains are three minutes apart, and D. is screaming. I run for the midwife, who is close by.

The doctor appears, in green rubber boots, with gloves up to his elbows. He throws me a surgeon's gown and a white cap, just like the one he is wearing.

"You still want to be in on it?"

The delivery room seems to me to be all white, and in it I see two young nurses as well as the midwife. They put D. into a strange kind of armchair. She is in greater and greater pain, and gives a sharp shriek when a nurse has tied down only one of her legs. There is no time for them to secure the other. You literally pop out, my little girl, and the doctor catches you, as it were, on the fly.

You are carried head down, bloody and viscous, like all newborns. You kick a little, not too much, and then you regurgitate as you let out your first cry just when the doctor is tapping on your round little buttocks.

D. catches her breath just as you are taking your first real one.

"A nice straight bellybutton," I say, hardly knowing what I am talking about, "not a corkscrew one like mine."

You are now squiggling around on the cloth-covered table where they put you. You have a fine little body, a fine little face, still a little red, a little wrinkled, like those of all human young when they come into the world.

The doctor examines you, feels you all over, and reassures me. "Everything is just fine. I don't know when I ever saw such a quick delivery."

They put you on a scale. "Seven pounds, eight ounces." What American gynecologists consider the ideal weight.

Less than a quarter of an hour later, D. is back in her room, in her bed, somewhat in pain, but not enough to keep her from talking.

"Where is the baby?"

"They'll bring her in in a minute."

They do bring her in, indeed, now all pink and clean, in the usual cloth cradle set up so your mother can see you.

"She's beautiful, isn't she?"

"Gorgeous."

"Looks like a blonde."

That makes me happy. Her hair, which the nurses have cleaned up, is so blond it is almost white. Hasn't my dream always been to have a blonde little girl?

D. and I look fondly at each other, and to my amazement, she asks: "Do you think they'll let me use the phone?"

"To call whom?"

"My mother. I want to tell her myself."

I ask the surprised midwife, who says, "Why not, if she feels like it?" And D. calls Ottawa.

"Hello, Maman? . . . Yes, I'm in the hospital. . . . No, I'm not expecting. . . . I gave birth less than an hour ago. I'm just fine, I assure you. . . ."

In my mind, I can hear my mother-in-law's skeptical, habitual exclamation: "Oh, come now!"

"I can assure you I'm not exhausted at all. . . . I even brought a suitcase full of work with me. . . . I have lots of work to do, you know. . . ."

I'm stupefied. D. seems to be triumphant. Hasn't she, after all, just performed a feat?

"Yes, Jo is here with me. He watched the whole thing. Just imagine, my daughter will be a blonde, unless she turns out to be a redhead like Daddy."

This is not what I had expected of these minutes, which I had wished would be full of sweetness and tenderness. I can't take my eyes off you, Marie-Jo, sleeping, peacefully breathing. From time to time, your eyelids quiver, open, and probably see only the golden sunshine in the room.

"Let my brothers know. A special greeting to Madeleine. How is she? . . . Tell Roger I'd like him to come to Lakeville with his wife and son. . . ." The lawyer-brother who became so indignant at the idea of Tigy and me divorcing that he was ready to plead Tigy's case for her.

"Yes, Maman . . . Everything is just fine. . . . Don't worry . . . I'll be in touch soon. . . . A big hug to you."

The light shining in her brown eyes has a glow of self-satisfaction.

"Maman didn't want to believe me."

Unlike Brussels, here they won't let me sleep in her room and be free to come and go at all hours of the day. Nor will you, Marie-Jo, be allowed to sleep near your mother.

I go out. I walk in the snow, singing. I don't know what I'm singing, but I know where I'll go after eating two or three hot dogs washed down by a nice cold beer. I don't take the car, because I need the exercise. I feel very light and very cheerful. I have a daughter!

I eat three hot dogs at the next corner. Two glasses of beer. Then I head for a fine place I had noted on our trips to the gynecologist's and our exploration of the neighborhood.

A very "distinguished," very "New England," gray-haired woman greets me in her store, which is not an ordinary store. She carries only unusual things. Nor is the woman an ordinary storekeeper, but someone of the upper middle class who, being widowed, wants to keep busy. There are many such shops hereabouts, in which amateurs sell things they like, without too much concern for earning a living.

You, my good old Marc, are as yet unaware that you have a little sister. I am sure you will take Marie-Jo under your wing, just as you did your little brother. I can still see you looking so tenderly at him, trying to get him to smile. Now you will have two of them to love, as if you were their father. I wonder whether that isn't an innate trait of the Simenons, because my father was like that, and I guess my grandfather too. And don't try to tell me that it is just masculine pride, because you know better today, having two children of your own.

"I would like the two big dolls in your window."

The woman mentions two names that I've forgotten, two characters out of American or British fairy tales or folklore. The little girl is dressed in magnificently embroidered clothes of the Victorian era, and has blond hair coming down in broad curls on either side of her face. She has a big navy-blue hat on and is carrying an old-fashioned purse. The boy is red-headed, also dressed in Victorian style. He is freckle-faced and has light-blue eyes.

The woman looks at me, as if in pain. I could swear she loves those two dolls and her heart aches over having to sell them. "I could show you some others, just as beautiful."

"No, those two are the ones I want."

"How old is your little girl?"

"She was just born."

"Aren't they a bit big for her?"

I shake my head, without letting on that I made my mind up on those two dolls more than a month ago. I didn't buy them then out of superstition. At least three times, I had gone by this strange store to make sure they were still there.

When I get back to her room, your mother is busy on the telephone.

Come to think of it, I had phoned too, from the place I got the hot dogs, to tell Boule the good news, and to announce it to you, Johnny, who give me a real American answer: "Is she okay?"

"Absolutely okay."

"When can I see her?"

"Tomorrow afternoon."

"Okay, Dad."

D. is busy talking publishing, at length, while I look at you, "my daughter," my tiny little daughter.

I know there is nothing pressing to discuss with my American publishers. Actually, I'm switching publishers, because I've had an offer from Doubleday, the biggest house at the moment, and have canceled my contract with the previous one.

What can they be discussing at such length? I stand there, swinging my arms, for over half an hour. They're talking about translation details, which can very well wait, since the contract isn't even signed yet. D. is talking to Doubleday's lawyer, and suddenly she bursts out laughing.

"No, I'm not expecting a baby. I had a little girl about two hours ago. . . . Why should you apologize? . . . I feel just fine, and this is no effort at all. Besides, I have my entire file here with me and I expect to go right on working until they let me go home."

When she hangs up, she's still laughing. "Did you eat?"

"Three hot dogs. How about you?"

"The doctor came. They're waiting for my milk to come up, but he doesn't think I'll be able to nurse her."

"I thought about bringing you a bottle of champagne, but then, on account of the milk, I didn't think I should."

"You know I don't care for champagne."

I am sorry to have to leave you, little girl, and to have to leave your mother too, but Johnny is waiting for me at home, and after six I can reach Marc by phone.

I am happy. With you, Johnny, watching TV.

"Does she have brown hair like me?"

"No. She's a blonde."

"What color are her eyes?"

"Too early to tell yet. Very light. Blue or green."

"Do some people have green eyes?"

"More or less green, yes."

After kissing Boule, who has tears in her eyes, I phone Marc.

"What does she look like?"

"A very pretty little girl."

"Does she look like her mother?"

"She's a blonde with blue eyes like yours."

"Will I be allowed to see her next Saturday?"

"I'll take you."

Good old Marc. Today, everybody is "good old somebody" to me.

The next day I am told, Marie-Jo, that your mother won't be able to nurse you, but that you drank a little of the colostrum, which, it seems, is most important. So we'll be making up bottles again, as we did for Johnny and Marc.

I look intently at you, and your eyes are open. Can you see already? Or do you just make out a vague shape, as through a fog? It seems to me there is something uneven in your eyeballs. You aren't cross-eyed, but have a slight cast that we call a *coquetterie*. I ask the gynecologist about it when he comes to check on both of you.

"Don't worry about that at all. It often happens with babies. The slight disparity in one eye will disappear little by little."

The huge hulk of a man doesn't know how to lie. I trust him. I finally show your mother the dolls.

"You really think she'll play with them?"

"She'll keep them the way Marc kept his teddy bear and Johnny that laughing clown that he still sleeps with and probably will go on sleeping with for a long time."

We chat. She tells me the doctor has said it's all right for me to bring a token bottle of champagne, provided she and her neighbors don't drink more than half a glassful.

"You think they have champagne glasses here?"

She laughs. We laugh over anything and nothing. I go home for lunch

374

and come back with Johnny in his winter outfit that we call his "bear cub" suit. I bring a bottle of champagne and four stem glasses.

Johnny looks at you as if he wanted to hypnotize you, Marie-Jo. This is the first time he's ever seen so young a baby, and I wonder what he's thinking. When he finishes the long contemplation of you, his only comment is "Well!"

Nothing more. You must look very tiny and very fragile to him, since he considers himself a big boy already.

"Can I go and play?"

"Where?"

"There. Outside."

There is a snow-covered incline, a miniature hill toward which we can see you rushing, sometimes stumbling in the deep snow. You don't need any playmates. You are quite self-sufficient and can play by yourself for a long time.

Right now, having gotten to the top, you try to slide down, fall on your face, get back up, start again, snow-covered from head to foot.

When will you be doing that, Marie-Jo? D.'s neighbors graciously accept our invitation, and the three women chatter while I open and pour the champagne. They are delighted.

A week goes by quickly in this almost childishly good-natured atmosphere. The suitcase full of files was never opened, but I know D. did a lot of phoning.

We make a triumphal return home with you, to our home, your home, and we place you in your jewel box of a cradle. Everyone comes in to ooh! and aah! over you, and once again I pour champagne, for the whole household.

"You know what bothers me, Jo? She doesn't seem to cry. Not even when she's wet, which she is much less often than Johnny was."

For the longest time, I have wondered why in olden times girls and even women were referred to, in Parisian argot, as *pisseuses* (pissers). Little girls and women much less often than men feel the urge to empty their bladders, some of them only twice a day, whereas the Romans, and the Parisians after them, set up urinals—for gentlemen only!—every hundred yards or so on the boulevards and heavily trafficked streets.

You almost always sleep the whole night through, and all we hear over the intercom is the slight crinkling of your sheets. Sometimes, toward morning, when it gets close to time for your morning bottle, you let out a discreet call, just one very short one, as if you knew that we would be there before long. No need for me to sing to you about the horsies on the merry-go-round the way I used to for your darned brother. No need, after you finish your bottle, which you drink slowly, with pauses, to hold you at length against my shoulder in order to get you to burp.

"You think it's normal for a baby not to cry?"

"I'm no doctor. Call and ask him. It's time for Wieler to come see her, anyway."

He does come, and finds her perfectly normal and healthy.

"It even seems like she smiles diffidently."

"Well, she's not old enough to laugh out loud yet."

"How about her eyes, doctor?"

"Don't worry. She won't be cross-eyed. In a few months, that little cast will disappear. . . ."

This time, Marie-Jo, in New York I was able to buy a fine English perambulator, ivory colored.

Jean Renoir lets me know he'll be coming to see us with Dido. He has finally gotten back from India, having finished *The River*, and cut it back in Hollywood. Unlike so many other directors, he does not let cutters cut his films without him and conscientiously devotes himself to it weeks on end, to the great irritation of producers.

Now, he is on his way back to France, where his problems with his second marriage are over. He has been promised that he won't be prosecuted for bigamy; so dear Jean won't have to go to prison!

The ceremony of Johnny's baptism takes place in the little white church halfway down the hill. The priest, whom I have met, is young and accommodating. Marc insists on being the one to hold his little sister in his arms during the ceremony. Our friend from Tucson, Mme de R., who made those tasty pound cakes for D. when she was expecting Johnny, has been unable to come, but nonetheless, as we promised her, she will be Johnny's godmother by proxy.

It is funny to see our boy looking so solemn as he leads his big old godfather the length of the church. It is a simple christening. There are just a few of us in the baptismal party, and Johnny doesn't flinch when the holy water is sprinkled on his stiff hair or, later, when a few grains of salt are placed on his tongue.

Renoir, on the other hand, is deeply moved. The one-time atheist, who made fun of "priestlets," as he called them, has become a Catholic again, probably under the influence of his Brazilian wife.

An abundant luncheon awaits us at home, and the day, which is too short, goes by in joyfulness. I feel great regret when I see my almost-lifetime friend leave the next morning at Idlewild Airport. He is expected in Paris for the launching of his new film and the rerelease of *Grand Illusion*. This film has not become dated. How many fervent friends and admirers he will find in France and all over Europe!

Soon, Marie-Jo, it will be your turn to be baptized. Marc insists on being your godfather. As for your godmother, the young and beautiful Jacqueline Pagnol will not be able to come, because her Marcel, whom she never leaves, absolutely refuses to get on a ship or on what he contemptuously calls a "flying machine."

"People today think they're birds" is one of his frequent quips.

So, like Johnny, you will have a godmother by proxy.

The days go by. Johnny is home every day by lunchtime, and is much more turbulent, naturally, than you, needing much more supervision.

"Don't you think, Jo, that we ought to have two nursemaids, one for each of them?"

So we get two nursemaids, both young, both American, and one of them will sleep in the house on the floor where there are two vacant bedrooms.

Your brother and you are even going to have three nursemaids. Like Maria, who replaces all the other household help in turn, a former nurse who lives not far away will come in to replace the nursemaids on their days off. She is fifty or more, has silver hair and unflappable patience.

So many people! And "Marc's gang," as I call it, which drops in every weekend. He has some additional friends now, the Redheads, as they are called throughout the village, where they are considered terrors, just as they are the terror of poor Boule.

Three carrot-haired brothers, faces all freckled, with blue eyes that seem never to blink. They look like their father, who is Irish, and remind one of Dennis the Menace. In less time than it takes Boule to try to shoo them off, they empty the refrigerator and take off with Marc and a few others through the woods to a steep cliff, where they sit, letting their feet dangle over the side.

"You know, Dad," Marc tells me, "they may look like terrors, but in reality they're good boys."

While I have closely watched my children, I have never forbidden them anything. Or ever said, "That's bad" or "That's forbidden." When they do something I don't approve of, I merely ask them, "Well, now, are you proud of yourself?"

One or the other appears to think it over, and then says, "That wasn't very nice."

"If you think you did wrong, give yourself whatever punishment you think you deserve."

Almost always, they will lock themselves in their rooms for a given time, and I have never had any reason to complain of them, whatever others may say about "permissive upbringing."

I don't like big words, or solemn sermons.

Incidentally, Marie-Jo, in March, the month after your birth, I write a novel, *Maigret a peur (Maigret Afraid)*. But I am not Maigret, whatever anyone may say.

In that same year of 1953, I also write: *L'Escalier de fer (The Iron Staircase), Feux rouges (The Hitchhiker), Maigret se trompe (Maigret's Mistake), Crime impuni (The Fugitive),* and *Maigret à l'école (Maigret Goes to School).*

I switch publishers in England, because my earlier one is now specializing mainly in poetry, philosophy, works on art, and "essays." I don't feel at home among all those people, much too intellectual for me. So I sign up with a younger and more eclectic publisher, Hamish Hamilton, whom I know so far only by correspondence.

We are going . . . We are still going to do many, many things this year, my three children. . . . Perhaps too many . . .

Until tomorrow.

46

The days are going by, the first weeks of your life, and I do not weary of observing you. Spring is blossoming in the house and everywhere about; the last patches of snow are gradually fading. You are spending more and more of your hours out of doors, in your ivory carriage, while your placid nursemaid, who always seems wrapped up in some inward dream, knits as she watches over you.

You inherited Johnny's nursemaid, because she has a character better suited to a baby, while the new one, who is more energetic, is better able to cope with the exuberance of an already-big boy she has to follow after through the woods.

As the days slip by, I am amazed at how quickly you are coming awake, more quickly, it seems to me, than your two brothers had. Country women, those fat nursemaids of the Parc Monceau and other fine neighborhoods, I know, claim that girls wake up to life much more precociously than little males. For a long time, people shrugged at the idea, calling it an old wives' tale. Now, pediatricians and psychiatrists have studied the matter and admit that this precociousness is a fact, at least for a certain number of early years.

I am seeing it in action. Most often, your carriage is placed in the shadow of our plane tree, which I call "ours" less because it belongs to us than because it is the only one hereabouts.

The Greek poets claimed that the sweetest shadow was that of the fig trees, and I can recall many savory naps taken in the shade of the fig trees at Porquerolles. Nonetheless, I prefer plane trees, which filter the light so delicately, allowing only a warm, golden dust of it to come through and caress one's skin.

I often join you there, treading carefully so as not to wake you if you are sleeping. I sometimes think you are, but then detect on your face the faintest of smiles. Your eyelids open slightly and you look at me, trustingly, yet with just a touch of hesitancy.

Marc, sweet Marc, was the first to have you smile at him. Johnny, the little tough, entertains you with his shouts and his varied faces, and he before anyone else will get you to laugh.

For my part, I find something almost pathetic in your eyes, a sort of beseeching. In everything about you, you are looking for a sign of affection, of love, so that one would swear you were thirsting for it. I can feel your need for contact, even when you are watching the trembling of the plane tree's leaves. Nature around you is flowering in peace and beauty. The snow, as it is absorbed by the ever-more-golden sunshine, uncovers tender green grass, and the buds open to leaves of a childlike gaiety.

Are you happy, Marie-Jo? You who already have papers that make you officially a member of the human race. I have taken out two passports for you, one American, to which you are entitled for being born on American soil, the other Belgian, in view of your father's nationality.

Sometimes, of an evening, when dozing, I wonder whether I was right to name you Marie-Georges. In English, it becomes a fairly common Mary-Jo. I visualize the names in your passports: "Marie-Georges Simenon" and beneath it, the signature (since you are too young to sign): "her father, Georges Simenon."

Was it selfish of me to give you that name, and will you someday hold it against me? Your picture and those of your two brothers are included in my own passport, with my picture, and, like Marc and Johnny, your name has been entered on the Simenon page of the vital statistics record at Liège.

I dream of more children being added to that page. . . . I dream a lot. . . . I snuggle up in our house, in our love, as in a cocoon. . . .

You don't know it, and it is unimportant, but Jeanine, the personal maid your mother brought back from Europe, has left us, as I expected. Not to become a naked showgirl at the Folies-Bergère, but very nearly.

During one of her days off in New York, she met a Frenchwoman who runs a small bar in Greenwich Village. From what she tells me, I can draw my own conclusions about the kind of bar it is. I had had a hunch that this handsome girl had agreed to work for your mother only to get an American resident alien's visa.

One less in the house. I am writing a novel. I finish my chapter around nine-thirty in the morning, because I get up very early. I drive to the village, where the post office distributes the mail, as in Carmel. Here, however, there is a mailman, but we are the last stop on his route, so that we could never get our mail until the middle of the afternoon.

Your nursemaid is coming back with you from a walk. I drive carefully, because I know I am going to see you near the corner of the road leading to Main Street. As soon as you are in sight, I stop, get out of the car, and run over to kiss you. You smile at me. This is one of the most precious moments of my days, and I am light-hearted as I leave you, waving to you from the car. This has become a ritual, and the nursemaid gets right into it with us, as if she were shielding the secret tryst of two young sweethearts.

One morning, just as I have entered the village road, there is another car coming down this rather narrow road. If I slow down, one or the other of our cars may push your carriage off the road, so I speed up in order to spare you.

Through no fault of my own, this is the first time I have failed to stop and kiss you. You are still a baby; will you even be aware of it? I go to the post office, shove my letters into one of my pockets, and go into a little bar, which I recently discovered, a workingman's islet within our strictly upper-middle-class area.

Here I can happily rub elbows with rough-handed, rough-talking truckdrivers and men who follow other callings. They greet me cordially. I drink my glass of beer in the strong smell of this bar, which reminds me of the workers' cafés in Paris, and go back to my car after getting my newspapers at Hugo's.

Before Johnny was in school, he went with me, and we would often walk, preferably across fallow fields.

I have already forgotten about our broken date this morning, Marie-Jo my darling, and I get a shock when I see Dr. Wieler's car in front of our house. Boule is on the threshold, looking forlorn.

As I tremblingly rush through the living room and the library, she says, "In your bedroom. . . ."

I see you lying inert in your mother's arms. The doctor turns to me, and says, perplexed, "She must have had some bad shock. Take her in your arms."

I obey instinctively. "What happened?"

Did I ask that? Your body is limp, as if lifeless, your face ashen. I am afraid to hug you too tightly, yet do so unwittingly. For minutes? Seconds? I don't know. I don't know anything. I will you to live, to come out of this torpor that seems like . . .

No! No! I won't let you. You'll go on living, little daughter of mine. I'm speaking to you. No matter what I may be saying. You have to hear my voice, have to awaken. And then your eyelashes start to flutter, your lids open slightly, and your eyes stare fixedly at me before closing again. I can swear that I hear your heart beating against my own, which is beating so fast and so violently.

You smiled, Marie-Jo, smiled an enigmatic smile, barely discernible, and now the color is coming back into your skin.

"You see," the doctor is saying to your mother. "That's just what I thought."

Then you look at me squarely, and your fingers grip the rough tweed of my jacket. The slight cast makes your eyes look more pathetic. You aren't talking yet, but there is no need for words, my little girl. You're saying to me, begging of me, "Don't do that again, Dad. . . ."

You had put your trust in me, and here I go passing you by without even noticing you, as if I cared nothing for our daily date.

The doctor feels your pulse and little by little his smile becomes reassuring. The nursemaid told him what happened. My car had scarcely driven by, Marie-Jo, when you turned livid and closed your eyes. You suddenly seemed limp, inert in your carriage, and the usually placid nursemaid almost ran as she brought you back to the house.

Your mother came from her office, took you in her arms, and called to the secretary, "Get Dr. Wieler right away. Tell him it's an emergency."

He is a calm and deliberate man, with long experience of life and people.

"Your little girl is extremely sensitive. I could see that from the very first day. Only your husband . . ."

All my life I will feel sorry for having had that daily glass of beer and having taken the time, as I did every day, to get the papers at Hugo's.

Are you really giving me a knowing wink, Marie-Jo? You don't seem to want to leave my arms. We are standing there, in the sunlit bedroom, with Boule, worried to death, hovering timidly near the door.

"Take her out on the terrace . . ."

You and I go out there, and you are unaware that a wonderful world surrounds us, that the sun is striking our faces, that there are some sudden cooler gusts of air. You're alive! You're moving! Wouldn't you like to be able to talk?

The doctor takes your pulse once more and applies the stethoscope to your chest and then your back. You don't even seem to realize he is there.

"Put her delicately back in the carriage . . ."

I understand him. I'm to put you back where you were, as if nothing had happened, as if that nasty old car had not made me be false to you.

I sit near you under the plane tree, and you fall peacefully asleep, smiling to the angels, as old-time mothers used to say.

D. comes out to join me, and we whisper. "Is that story the nursemaid told about the other car true?"

"Yes. I couldn't possibly stop without . . ."

"She needs you."

"I know."

I've always known, from the very first day, the day I saw you get born and went and bought you the two Victorian dolls now sitting together in an armchair that you can see from your cradle.

Do you remember, Marie-Jo? Does one remember one's earliest baby days? I think so, and that is why, for each one of you children, I tried to create the warmest little nest, the most serene and reassuring setting I could.

Life resumes its enchanted flow, to the accompaniment of the stream, now heavy with new water from the melted snow.

Marc has found himself a new passion. Sometimes, in our woods, we come across a pair of opossums, each hanging head downward with its tail around a branch. They are the most easygoing and lazy animals in the world, which explains their fat, heavy bodies.

Marc plucks them like ripe fruit, pets them, runs his cheek against their gray fur without their kicking. Do all animals know by instinct that this big athletic boy is not dangerous, that, like them, he is part of nature? With his innate tenderness, the big boy returns them to their branches, where they go back to hanging and fall asleep.

Johnny has still never seen the sea, August is very hot at Lakeville, and Marc is at Nantucket with his mother for a month. So why not go vacationing somewhere on Cape Cod?

If it were up to me alone, we would not leave our house, where I am so happy, but I have to try to make the others happy too. D. needs to get away from the office, where she spends so much time closeted with her secretary.

Sometimes, of an afternoon, I take D. out for a drive through this dream countryside, where I am crazy about everything. I think out loud.

"Look at that lake and the little white sailboats making such strange patterns on it."

I talk. I say any old thing. Sometimes I hark back to my early days on Place des Vosges, to Curnonsky, the Prince of Gastronomes, whom I met in the days when we were both writing little risqué tales for the same weeklies. In Paris, D. got to meet him, his eyes brimming with mischief. I remind her of that, tell her about the early days of Môme Moineau, the little flower girl with the guttersnipe vocabulary and the taunting eyes. A few friends, including Pierre Lazareff, and I discovered her and got her to go on the stage, where she made a reputation through her slightly off-color songs and her raspy voice.

She married a millionaire, who decked her in jewels and gave her an ocean-going yacht with a crew of fifty-three. She sails on it from New York to the Bahamas. She's gone to fat.

At this luncheon near the Madeleine, we asked her to sing, and she did, although with memory lapses. Still attractive, she proudly tells us: "People say I never wear underpants. It's true. Time it takes to get them off, you could miss out on a good thing."

"Do you remember, D.?"

But what's the use of talking? She's asleep, next to me. I try in vain to find subjects of conversation that can hold her attention. I guess I never hit the mark, because every time we go out together she falls asleep.

"How about going and having a drink in that nice little bar. You know, the one where we never meet anybody," she murmurs as she opens her eyes.

I know. I am familiar with all those "nice little bars." For myself I order a gin-and-tonic or a dry Martini, or, most often, beer, because I like American beer. Just like millions of other Americans.

Like them too, I now trade in my car every year. The trade-in prices are good, and repairs are so expensive that it is more economical to do it this way. In place of the DeSoto, I have a Chrysler, more powerful and smoother. We leave at the beginning of August. D. is sitting next to me with Marie-Jo on her lap, and Johnny behind with the impassive nursemaid.

You are very good, Marie-Jo; and you've become very active, so lithe that you remind me of a shimmering circus acrobat. You want to say a few words, give it a try for a moment, and then close your eyes.

You still never cry. At home, you don't have to stay behind the bars of a playpen as your brothers did, but can be put right down on the clean white sheet covering the carpet. You sit up a bit, then tumble on your back or tummy, and try again. Johnny teases you. To him, you're a kind of toy he has fun with, and it is fun for you too, even when his gestures are unintentionally a little too rough.

We have taken along everything you need, and after lunch you sleep all the way to Martha's Vineyard, the island we have selected.

Edgartown is at the end of the island. A big hotel, a few houses that are even more New Englandish than those in Lakeville. Two nice cottages, in which we will live, but have all our meals in the hotel dining room.

The harbor is full of white sailboats, not yet made of fiberglass, but of hand-riveted teakwood or mahogany. The village itself is about a quarter of a mile or more away. We all go there each morning, Marie-Jo in her stroller, which Johnny insists on wheeling, with D., the nursemaid, and me watching over you both.

A hundred yards or so before we get there, Johnny stops, turns the stroller over to the nursemaid or me, and I know what he is about to say, because it has quickly become a habit: "May I, Dad?" Meaning, run ahead to the drugstore he spotted the first day, to order an ice-cream cone he pays for with the dimes in the pockets of his short pants. He has become very independent, more self-assured than ever. Anything once given to him he assumes to be a right, and better not to try to go against it. Because he would come back with a loud but unanswerable "Why?" Why not?

He is interested in the boats, their lines, the sails being hoisted. Every Sunday there are big races, Edgartown being a center for devoted yachtsmen. Their club has an excellent restaurant, with dancing in the evenings, and, up above, a balcony where young couples can find some privacy.

When you see your brother with his ice-cream cone, you reach for it, Marie-Jo, with a very understandable gesture, and I send Johnny to get you a cone, but without any ice cream in it. Do you notice the difference? Whether you do or not, you greedily munch it, and look at me with thanks.

We don't go bathing at the big beach, which is too crowded. We have discovered a little tiny one out among the dunes, where several other families also come to get the sun with their children.

Leaving the car on the sandy road, we undress between two dunes. All you wear is a little boy's blue trunks, and when Johnny first goes in bathing, we dip you into the sea water, and you discover the joys of sitting and rolling around in the golden sand.

Do you know that by now you're not "cockeyed" anymore, and if you still have a slight cast, no one who didn't know about it would notice it?

Here we come in contact with another American custom, one that will soon reach Europe, after a ten-year lag. The whole staff of the hotel are young girls and fellows, all of whom, except for the maître d' and the supervising housekeepers, are students on summer vacation. It is bad form (at this time, at least) for students to be playboys, spoiled rich kids, or clotheshorses, and all these young people around us work because working is an honorable thing.

In the off-hours of the afternoon, the waiters, waitresses, and chambermaids are out at the beach, in the pool, playing golf, or at the yacht club. How delighted I am at the idea, and I like to think that someday my own children . . .

Quiet! Doesn't that have to be left up to them?

A letter comes from Hamish Hamilton. For a broad promotion of one of my books, he would like D. and me, this fall, to make a tour of major English cities, where, he says, we will be welcomed with open arms.

I don't like the idea. I have never indulged in this kind of exploitation; the only autograph session I ever took part in was that one at the Boule Blanche for the launching of the first Maigrets.

All that D. has seen of England is that one-night stop at Plymouth on our way to France. And we never left our cabin, so she only heard the noises of a great English port.

I feel that . . .

Let's wait till these happy holidays are finished. Johnny and Marie-Jo have fine suntans, and Marie-Jo's hair has never been blonder.

Everything back home has been made ready for you, Marie-Jo, and everybody at Shadow Rock Farm greets you with delighted squeals at how well you look.

In October, a lot of people come visiting, some to have lunch with us, which does not keep me from writing a novel and playing with you for hours on end.

We are invited to a big publishing-world wedding. A good chance to wear, not the court gown, which might cause smiles here, but one of the Lanvin dresses that D. finally agreed to accept without further alterations.

First, a small Protestant church on Park Avenue, with two or three hundred people somehow squeezed into it. Then a dinner dance in the main ballroom of the Waldorf-Astoria. Everybody is there, publishers, writers, millionaires and multimillionaires. Dinner is served at small tables, and by good fortune D. and I are alone at ours. The caviar is in industrial quantities, as if the publisher manufactured it along with his books.

In two weeks we'll be off to England. As I sit or dance, tortured by my wing collar, I am thinking of you, Marie-Jo my pretty, and of you, Johnny mine, and my big Marc, about our house, in front of which I will be back just in time to lay down the wooden walk and take down the screens to replace them with storm windows.

I am fond of London, where almost every year I used to go with Tigy, always staying in the same suite at the Savoy.

The trip seems to be all fog to me, or at least seems a fog in my memory. The *Queen Mary* on the way over, press and photographers at Southampton. Meeting the utterly British Hamish Hamilton, overflowing with cordiality and attention. His wife, who is Italian, is an exquisite hostess.

As we are about to start the tour, accompanied by a young man who was to be ringmaster for our show, I decide I am going to go on the wagon.

The grand tour starts in Scotland, where every occasion brings out old bottles of Scotch, and I scandalize the locals by drinking water. They must think I have some terrible illness. But what does it matter, since D. is radiant and doing enough talking for both of us?

Edinburgh, Glasgow, Liverpool, Manchester, which reminds me of Liège, only stiffer and rainier. Other cities. Everywhere reporters, critics, photographers, and too-hearty dinners.

All of it by train. And, although I am fond of England, I detest its trains. D. is enthusiastic. I do my best. Isn't my reason for being here to make her happy?

Back in London, it isn't over. I am invited—by myself, because women are never invited to these high places of English culture and aristocracy— to Oxford University one day, and Cambridge the next. Our press agent, who is not included either, keeps D. company.

Luncheon in an austere dining room, with the masters and lecturers of various colleges. I am aware of the honor I am being given, but that doesn't keep my mind from straying far away, across the Atlantic. I give my speech and visit the students' spacious Spartan quarters.

All duplicated at Cambridge.

Finally, a big cocktail party at Hamish's London offices, where I tie on a real lulu after a whole month of strict teetotaling and obedience. It is fun and nice, and I believe I chased a very seductively pretty young woman onto the stairway, where Hamish kept me from creating a small scandal.

Return on the *Queen Elizabeth*. How comforting to see the Statue of

Liberty again. We are almost home. Two hours or so by car and we will be at Lakeville . . .

"Where's my daughter?"

"Asleep."

"How is she?"

"Just fine."

"Has she been . . ."

As if, at your age, you could possibly have been asking about me, Marie-Jo my pretty. I tiptoe into the nursery, hear your even, quiet breathing, catch a glimpse of your relaxed little face, slightly pink cheeks. I don't dare kiss you, for fear of waking you.

In to Johnny, also asleep, but more noisily, groaning when he hears the floor creak.

Tomorrow morning, my boy, I'll be the one to drive you to school, and in the afternoon I'll go to the campus to see Marc.

"Are you happy?" D. asks in a very soft voice.

"Yes."

"It wasn't too hard on you, was it?"

Now that it's over, I can even summon up a smile, to answer, "Not too . . ."

I see our bedroom again, Boule who is waiting for us.

"Marie-Jo didn't feel too lost, did she?"

Boule also succeeds in answering, in a voice of which I know every shading, "Not too . . ."

I know she resents my having left my little girl.

I do too.

47

The year 1954 leaves me with the memory of a year like the others, more peaceful and more enjoyable because few events happened in it, with, in addition to my two boys, a little girl who is growing and already strikes me as a tiny bit of woman.

A white winter, like all those in Lakeville, with logs in the fireplace and Marie-Jo beginning to walk.

Marc turns fifteen and, with his school, goes to dances given by girls' private schools, in a tuxedo. On campus, he wears a sober suit and tie, but on weekends he switches to blue jeans and goes tramping the woods with his friends.

Johnny, five in the fall, has taken on height and lost some of his baby fat.

On February 13, we have a family party for my fifty-first birthday, and I am almost ashamed to be so old with such young children.

As for D., she is not so rapidly losing the weight she put on during her pregnancy and she is again haunted by the prospect of someday looking like her majestic mother. She got a mail-order diary that on each page has the same outline of a woman, showing by dotted lines the ankles, calves, knees, lower and upper thighs, waist, bust at breast height, and neck. Each ideal measurement is printed on the left-hand side. On the right, there is a place to put in one's own weekly measurements.

So, each week, I take these careful measurements and, depending on the results, D. either mopes or cheers up, and I never dream of making fun of her. Isn't it her right, after all, to want to emulate the wire-flat figures of high-fashion models?

She eats a lot of grapefruit and green salads, eschewing the dishes with gravy that Boule is so good at, but not giving up her whiskey. Any more than I give up my beer, or, on occasion, especially in New York, a very chilled dry Martini, in which the gin is now often replaced by vodka.

Marie-Jo's birthday comes after mine, and now she sits up in her high-chair, solemnly gazing at the single candle on her birthday cake. Her brothers are all dressed up, and the whole household joins us for champagne and cake.

Very soon we have our little girl baptized, with her godfather, Marc, holding her, in the absence of her godmother, Jacqueline Pagnol. A very simple christening, just the family, aflame with love, in the church that is so pretty in the snow.

Weekends, Johnny is learning to ski on our property; Marc and I are on skis too. A rather long slope ends down at the frozen stream, where Marc, already huskier than I, stands waiting to catch his brother, while I merely slide alongside Johnny, who is afraid of nothing but does everything with the same thoughtful seriousness. D. applauds from the doorway every time Johnny completes a schuss, and he never gets tired.

A year without important events, which therefore allows me to savor to the full my daily joys. A year that is mainly centered on you, my little girl, for you are at the age when each tiny progress is applauded by the family.

You come and go noiselessly from one room to the next, under the watchful eyes of your good, dull nursemaid, who tries to keep out of sight. You make an effort to talk; your first words are in English, as will be those that follow.

We seem more and more like the families of our friends hereabouts, and I have the feeling that I am quite naturally taking my place within American life.

You are a pretty picture, all wrapped up in white fur, in your stroller, which you sometimes wheel yourself, and nothing stops me anymore when, on the way to the post office, I catch sight of you at the bend of the road.

I write a lot of novels, but one might look in vain, even by "reading between the lines," as some critics do, for any reflection of my current state of mind. For the whole year, five novels, not six, because I spend more and more of my time with you: *Maigret et la jeune morte (Maigret and the Dead Girl)*, *L'Horloger d'Everton (The Watchmaker of Everton)*, *Le Grand Bob (Big Bob)*, *Maigret chez le ministre (Maigret and the Calamé Report)*, and *Les Témoins (The Witnesses)*.

Strangely, I, who never cared for the bourgeoisie, especially the "upper," am now getting deeper and deeper into the more than comfortable bourgeoisie around us. It is true that this middle class does not have the stiffness or the petty ideas of the grand bourgeois I had known in Belgium and France.

My real life, children, revolves around you, especially you, Marie-Jo.

I was not mistaken when you were a baby and I felt that you were hungry for love and tenderness. That is as instinctive in you as in animals. When you see some new person in our house, you follow him or her, like a puppy, I might say. Of course, you don't smell them, but you gaze at them for a long time with indifferent eyes. And then, if you discover some real empathy in the newcomer, your eyes soften, and your lips relax into a still-shy little smile.

Animals are rarely mistaken. Your instinct seems equally sure to me, and I have a tendency to mistrust those to whom you turn a hard or expressionless face.

You are a tender one, and want nothing around you that is not tender. Doesn't tenderness, after all, have to be reciprocated? Isn't it your tenderness and the need to have it returned that make you vulnerable?

I literally spy on you, as if I were afraid that some indifferent person might hurt you unintentionally. And yet, you are so radiant, with your hair reflecting the sunshine, and your long little face, your body so lithe and yet so vigorous!

Soon, we are walking hand in hand, and I am always moved to feel your delicate hand snuggled in mine.

I had observed your two brothers with equally passionate curiosity. But you are a tiny female, a woman of tomorrow, and I would so like to protect you!

This is the first time in my life that I am present at the blossoming of a little girl. When I was a child, I envied those of my playmates lucky enough to have a sister.

I don't treat you like a doll but I want you to be pretty, satisfied to be pretty, and from each of our trips to New York or elsewhere, I bring you a flowered dress or some trinket that I select myself.

Spring goes by in happiness, and your mother's and my life is without shadows or bumps. She is happy, in her office, and happy too in the morning, when, with silver pruning shears, she goes out to cut flowers and arrange them in a flat basket. That picture may seem conventional and somewhat dated; it goes with the décor, with the many jonquils on the lawns, and the irises, the peonies, so many other flowers I don't know by name that bloom beneath our windows.

You are present at an event in nature that is almost solemn. We know the hole in a hillock in which an enormous groundhog hibernates. One morning, as we are walking by hand in hand, it sticks its head out, finds the sun warm enough, and, in spite of our being there, brings its whole body out, while staring at us with its two big eyes.

You have no fear of animals, not even of the majestic beaver which comes to warm itself in the sun under the windows of your nursery. You have no fear of anything, actually, except perhaps of human beings from the moment you discover in them some kind of reticence or a shade of hostility.

I try to discover through mysterious signs the girl, then the young lady, and finally the woman you will someday be, whom I would like to be fully in harmony with the world and nature.

I had the same dream for your brothers. Marc is a potential poet, and everything living is familiar to him. Our little bruiser of a Johnny will know how to fend for himself, and I delight in his sudden fits of violent affection.

As we did last year, we spend our summer vacation at Edgartown. You no longer travel on the lap of your mother or your nursemaid. You have a safety seat in the car, between D. and me, from which you watch the landscape flying by.

At a year and a half, I hold your hand as I walk you to the drugstore, where Johnny has gone before us, and where, without waiting, because they already know you, you are given two cones instead of one, without the ice cream.

Sea water is a natural element to you, and you scarcely blink when a small wave splashes your face.

I love to watch your face spattered with sea foam. I love to watch you gobbling up creamless ice-cream cones. I love to keep an eye on Johnny, who goes haltingly into the sea, which he does not trust.

In the evenings we visit friends from the previous year.

Another peculiarity that attracts me in America: the homes of the lower and upper middle classes, and even the truly rich, are never ostentatious; everyone aims principally at cheerfulness and comfort. Armchairs upholstered in multicolored flowery chintz have a friendly tone, and their soft cushions tend to create intimacy. No dark woodwork, very little leather, unless it is colored, thick carpeting that muffles footsteps.

Nor are there any serious discussions. No one talks politics and no one tries to remake the world. More or less controversial subjects are not mentioned either, for to do so would be impolite. People just chatter. About everything and nothing. About yesterday's boat races or tomorrow's, improvements that could be made at the yacht club, sports or gardening, and nowhere have I ever heard such extensive exchanges of cooking recipes.

A few miles from Lakeville, almost lost in the wilderness, is a bookstore run by a naturalized Hungarian. It has as many books in Spanish, Italian, or French, as in English. What the bookseller shows me with the greatest pride are shelves full of cookbooks. Nowhere have I ever seen so extensive a collection. Books about wine are no less numerous, and I am amazed to count no fewer than twenty-two volumes devoted to cognac.

This transplanted Hungarian appears prosperous. So one must conclude that these works, however specialized, find a market. Could one imagine such a bookstore at Rambouillet or Arles, or even Lyons or Bordeaux?

How far all this is from the United States as it is pictured in Europe!

We return home, and your skin, Marie-Jo, is more suntanned than last year, while Johnny's makes him look like a young mulatto. Marc is just as tanned when he comes back from Nantucket, where he spent part of the vacation with his mother.

Come fall, your mother and I go back to our monthly week away. It is no longer devoted exclusively to cabarets and fashionable nightclubs. We see a lot of our publishers. We now have an additional one, who publishes textbooks and is bringing out a selection of my short stories called *Tournants dangereux* (Dangerous Turns). It is a thick volume, which is put on the reading lists of many universities and will remain there for years.

Why "Dangerous Turns"? Because in many of my novels the characters—family, couple, or isolated individuals—suddenly find themselves facing an event that will change their destinies. Had I not had Maigret dream of a profession that, unfortunately, does not exist, that of "mender of destinies"?

In a way, that is my own dream too. I am pained when I see the lives of human beings suddenly taking a "dangerous turn," as if a pebble made them stumble when they least expected it. I have seen so many lives sink in that way, as if under the spell of some inexplicable curse.

Tigy, as soon as it snows, is unable to manage her little car, which skids down a steep slope and turns upside down. Fortunately, the deep snow cushioned the shock, and Tigy is all right, if somewhat shaken up. But she is more worried than ever when, after two days of repairs, she gets behind the wheel again.

She learned to drive very late, when she was well over forty, and now, at fifty-four, she will never again fully trust any mechanical contrivance. Which will not keep her from driving right up to the time I am writing these pages, when she is eighty.

I go to see her every so often. She has grown used to the country and her house. She too goes out and picks flowers in the morning, but no longer, as back at La Richardière, does she have to feed hundreds of fowl of all varieties, not to mention our wolves, brought back from Asia Minor, our pheasants, our mongoose.

Christmas, as merry as our other Christmases, in our warm Lakeville house garlanded with light. New Year's.

I spend most of my evenings watching television in my rocking chair. Everything fascinates me, because everything takes me deeper into American life. Afternoons, I often attentively follow the soap operas. They remind me of my dime novels of so long ago, which also were meant to be tearjerkers. This is yet another America. With the twelve channels I can watch at Lakeville, I have the feeling of going from one discovery to another.

In January, I write *Maigret et le corps sans tête* (*Maigret and the Headless Corpse*).

Our wooden walk is in place, and Marc is now the one who takes the pickup truck to go and fetch wood from the maple-syrup shed. In spite of his age, he is allowed to drive on our own property, and does so at every opportunity. He was the one who put the storm windows up, and he informs me that our sprawling house has no fewer than fifty-two glass-paned windows and doors.

Hamish Hamilton comes to spend a few days with us. I see him coming up the pathway, dressed in a tight dark overcoat and wearing a black homburg, as if he were on the streets of London.

We spend three very nice days together. He stays in the "mothers' room," upstairs, which, with its flowered wallpaper and curtains, reminds him of the English countryside.

Three fine days, "under the sign" of friendship. When I am busy, he moves about, inside the house or out, always with a book in hand. This intrigues Marc, who asks: "How come you are always reading the same book?"

"It's Shakespeare."

"It's who?"

"One of the greatest authors in the world."

"Greater than my father?" Good old Marc seems disappointed. . . .

"He's been dead a long time," Hamish reassures him.

"Who shot him?"

That question is so typically American that it takes my breath away as well as Hamish's.

This is the same Marc, the TV addict, who said to me two years earlier: "Movie actors must be paid a lot of money," referring mainly to the Westerns he loves.

"Why?"

"Because they always end up getting killed."

One evening, when Hamish and I are alone in the library, he asks me an unexpected question: "What reason do you have, Georges, for staying in America?"

I think about it. I mention my little brood, growing up so harmoniously in this atmosphere. Feeling that I am not convincing him, I bring forth other reasons, schools, friends, the individual's rights . . .

"Those have existed in England for centuries."

I find ten, twenty reasons that seem good to me, without satisfying him. He leaves the next morning.

The day goes by, like the others. Post office in the morning. Newspapers, the twenty-five-cent records at Hugo's. Golden nap in the bow window of my office. In the evening, I watch television alone, since D. is in her office, as usual.

When she comes up, around ten o'clock, I ask her, offhandedly: "How long would it take you to get packed?"

"Depends on how long a trip. Where do you want to go?"

"Far away. With the children."

She looks at me in stupefaction. "For a long time?"

I don't dare come right out and say "For good."

I don't know myself whether that is the case, nor am I aware of what has taken place within me, just as I am unaware how long this idea has been germinating.

"For a long time . . . For years . . ."

"What about Boule?"

"We'll take her with us."

"Where to, Jo?"

"To Europe."

"To France?"

"Not necessarily. We'll stay there for the time being, say, on the Riviera, where there are all the furnished villas for rent that anyone could want. . . . And also excellent doctors." I always think about doctors, because of the children.

"And after that, what?"

"We'll see. Holland, Italy, England, which has such magnificent countryside . . . I don't know. . . ."

"How about our house?"

"We'll keep it."

"Why?"

"Because we've been happy here, we and the children both, and maybe later on . . ."

We are both so moved by these ideas that she comes rushing into my arms, sobbing.

"Are you sad?"

"No. They're tears of joy!"

It has happened several times in my life that I suddenly felt alien to everything around me.

"When do you want to leave?"

"Tomorrow ask your secretary to get a schedule of the earliest boat sailings. . . ."

"A French boat?" She is very excited. "Don't you have to talk it over with Tigy?"

"As soon as I know when we can get comfortable ship accommodations. Don't mention it to the children yet."

I anticipated that she would be happy about this, because, especially since our trip to France, Italy, and Belgium, she has been haunted by

Europe. That night, she makes love with an abandon she had lost, and whispers to me, "Thanks, Jo."

I buy a new car, a huge station wagon that can accommodate eight passengers and all their luggage. I know I won't be able to find anything like it in Europe. It's a Dodge, white, which I like.

The *Ile-de-France* is to sail from New York on March 19.

Tigy, as soon as she is over the first shock caused by my decision, is also satisfied. She has never really found her place in American life.

"You can take Marc with you. I'll stay here until I know you are settled down. I have a lot to do before I can leave."

Marc, like a little American, demands of me: "Will you let me work during vacation in a hotel or at a beach?"

I promise. He is not unhappy to be getting away from the rigid Hotchkiss discipline.

Johnny has dazzling recollections of France and his drives with Fernand Voiture.

As for you, my little girl, it is all way over your head. Just as long as we are all together . . .

You are two, and express yourself in English. Johnny is almost six. Marc is almost sixteen, D. thirty-five, and my fifty-second birthday was on February 13.

The wait seems long to me. I don't like seeing the bookshelves, the drawers, the closets emptying out, or the trunks and crates leaving before us in a huge truck.

Why are we leaving?

I have no idea.

Where to?

I can't say.

It just seems that I am fated always to be off in quest of something. But what?

March 19, 1955, my whole family and I leave Lakeville early in the morning, and I dare not look back. The big Dodge goes along the familiar roads, then the highway, and in the afternoon we are walking up the gangplank of the *Ile-de-France*.

The sun is smiling upon us, and I am holding your little hand very tightly, darling Marie-Jo.

I never again set foot in our house at Nieul. I am never again, either, to see Shadow Rock Farm, which we have just left.

48

Well, children, here I am once more at sea, between two continents, as has happened to me so often that I sometimes mistake the ships of the French Line for those of the Cunard and Grace lines, or the Pacific or South American ones.

I know that this time I am aboard the *Ile-de-France*, and I am reminded of another crossing, effected—I was almost going to say "innocently," which is almost the precise word—ten years earlier, when the war had barely ended, aboard a Swedish freighter that was taking us to the United States.

There were three of us then, or I should say four, since our faithful Boule was to follow us. You were along, Marc old man, just turned six. Tigy, your mother, was with us.

Ten years later, this tiny tribe had been increased as a result of a fortuitous meeting barely a month after we landed.

There were not four of us going back across the Atlantic, but six, with one to follow.

I have often been asked a question that I have, being undecided, answered according to my feelings of the moment. Today I feel the need to ask it of myself again, for my whole life has been haunted by a sense of responsibility. Why did I leave an America into whose landscape and with whose people I had fused, and which had adopted me as one of its own? Why go once more from continent to continent, from one civilization to another, when I was so happy in our home at Lakeville and you, my children, were no less happy there?

Why the sudden departure? Homesickness for France? No. I can frankly answer no. Besides, I had no idea what country I would settle in with my family.

Like most French-speaking Canadian girls, D. was raised to adore France, which she dreamed of in her youthful years. Then, hadn't our 1952 trip gone to her head?

She had of course agreed, after a somewhat stormy period, to settle down to our peaceful life in Connecticut, but remember what our good Dr. Wieler had so tactfully suggested to me: "At least one week a month, take her to New York, or Boston, or some other big city."

"With the children?" I had asked, being still naïve.

"Especially not with the children."

From our very first meeting, I had been aware of her unstable equilibrium. Hadn't she herself confessed to me that several weeks before, she had decided to commit suicide, at twenty-five, and made all the arrangements to go through with it?

Months and years of blind passion, of ups and downs, sobs and insults, which I accepted in the hope that one day I would see her calm down and simply be a woman. I am not passing judgment. I am trying to understand.

I maintained correspondence with some of the more or less famous Parisian friends she had met during our trip. That made her eyes glow. After which, a word, an allusion, a nostalgic sigh. She feels herself made for a brilliant life. But New York, to her, does not have the excitement of Paris, which she got only a glimpse of.

Even the trip to London, with our big suite at the Savoy, our dinners with world-renowned writers, added to her nostalgia. Milan too, and Rome, although we only passed through. In a word, Europe. For in the United States people don't say an Englishman, an Italian, or a Frenchman, but simply a European, and I must admit that to me too, in Manhattan, they sometimes all merged into one.

Was it the hope of finally seeing D. happy and blooming that made me decide, one night as I was watching television, to go back to Europe?

I can't make that claim. It's not definite. Be that as it may, here we are aboard the *Ile-de-France,* sailing toward Le Havre. In D.'s eyes, it was a bit of Paris already.

Still, we just missed not sailing. Ten or twelve days before that date, Johnny got the measles, and his face was all broken out in spots. Shortly before the day we were to sail, Marie-Jo in turn broke out with them.

Will they let us aboard with two contagious children? Had it been an American or English ship, it would have been out of the question. In the confusion of boarding, Johnny and Marie-Jo pass unnoticed, and they have a big three-bunk cabin not far from our own, with Boule taking care of them.

The ship's nurse quickly catches on, for she is intrigued by two children who never leave their cabin. She willingly helps Boule cater to them, and Johnny, his face almost clear of any signs, is the first to try going up on deck. I should say, Johnny mine, that you went up and, with your serious demeanor, took it over. From early in the morning on, you watch the sailors at their work, and once I find you all by yourself, at ten in the morning, sitting at one of the bars drinking Coca-Cola through a straw.

There is a magnificent children's playroom on board, but I can't let you go in there. I come by to see you I don't know how many times a day, and good-natured Boule keeps you from feeling any impatience.

By the time we reach Le Havre, you are well, or practically so. Our station wagon, which is practically a minibus, is offloaded, discreetly, because I have advised no one of our arrival. Only a few brief words with the local reporters assigned to cover all incoming ships.

A bare two days in Paris, incognito, and then to Cannes, where we stay at the Miramar, which I am familiar with. The first night, we hear a baby crying, but have no idea who our neighbors are. The next day, we see you playing with two children your own ages, under the watchful eyes of their nursemaid, who is chatting with Boule.

They are the little Chaplin children, who left America just a day or two before we did. Another nursemaid is taking care of the slightly ailing baby, while Charlie and Oona are spending a week with one of our mutual friends.

Marc has gotten himself a job as a beach boy. He sets up the varicolored beach umbrellas and smilingly brings soft drinks or cocktails to the pretty bathers.

The beach has small sailboats for rent. The rules require that those renting them be accompanied by a sailor if they are not themselves experienced. So, thanks to what you learned in America, my Marc, that's another job for you!

You soon inform me that the women who rent these sailboats do so less for the sailing than for being able, far from the beach, to sunbathe in the altogether. You are handsome. You are athletic. Often the sunbathing leads to more enjoyable pastimes, in which you never refuse to participate.

You even on occasion say to me, in the manner of the pals we have become: "You know, that young Norwegian girl I took out yesterday has read a lot of your books. She's dying to meet you. And it would be worth your while, believe me. . . ."

And a few weeks later, having become acquainted with all the strippers in Cannes, I return the favor.

We don't stay long at the Miramar. A real-estate agency shows us some available villas, and we decide on La Gatounière, at Mougins, which has an exhilarating view of old Cannes, the Esterel mountains, and the sea. It is a white Provençal villa with red tiles and green shutters, on top of a hill covered with pines. It has lots of rooms, but they are rather small.

Some other facts strike me: In January of that year, in the peace of

Shadow Rock Farm, I wrote *Maigret et le Corps sans tête (Maigret and the Headless Corpse)*, without imagining that my next novel would be typed on the same typewriter, three months later, on another continent. In April, at La Gatounière, I write an American novel: *La Boule noire* (The Black Ball).

The villa proves too noisy for me to work there and, besides, it has no office. I set myself up in an empty whitewashed room, and I have to go out of the villa every morning to get to it. Because it has no window, I leave the door open, giving me a panorama of the bay.

D. is pregnant and has already selected the child's name: Patrick. While I am deep in my novel, she experiences pains. The gynecologist advises her to go into a private clinic, a charming villa hidden away in greenery.

I sleep at the clinic, which is run by nuns. Early every morning, I go back to La Gatounière to finish my novel and kiss the children.

We have hired, as a chambermaid, a very young Italian girl, Marioutcha, an orphan raised by nuns, who sews marvelously.

Boule agrees, for a time, to give up her cook's apron and devote herself entirely to looking after Johnny and Marie-Jo. We find a local cook and, willy-nilly, we will have to get used to Provençal dishes.

I am writing all this out of order, but everything at the time was without order; everything was happening so fast.

We are scarcely settled into La Gatounière, for instance, when an American movie director asks whether he can use our garden for a cocktail party in honor of his American star, to be attended by a few glamorous people under the eyes of the movie cameras.

One morning the gynecologist informs me that he is going to operate on D. an hour later.

I wait worriedly in the garden, pacing back and forth until someone calls me. When the doctor finally appears, it is only to show me the petrified remains of a fetus that must be no more than four inches long. That is all that is left of Patrick, about whom D., without any basis, will henceforth talk as if he had been a six-month fetus whom she felt moving around inside her. She spoke to Johnny, and also to Marie-Jo, about him, as being their little brother, who was so cute, whom she lost, and the children, especially Marie-Jo, remain deeply marked by it.

To get D. back on her feet, I take her up to Paris, this time to the George V, where I used to stay before the war. It is June. I find all my old friends again. We go out a lot. We drink a lot too, and I remember one early dawn when, under the eyes of the unimpressed street sweepers, D. and Michel Simon danced on the sidewalk of the Champs-Elysées, humming "*La Seine coule, coule, coule . . .*" (The Seine is flowing, flowing, flowing . . .).

It is D.'s favorite song; when we enter cabarets in Paris and in Cannes, the band welcomes her by striking up that popular tune of the moment.

In the chronology I had drawn up for me, I find: "July 5–12, *Maigret tend un piège (Maigret Sets a Trap)*."

The garage of La Gatounière is situated halfway up a private road that is rather narrow and that I have trouble negotiating. At the foot of the incline, a meadow, which belongs to the property. Boule sitting on the grass while Johnny and Marie-Jo play there and among the pine trees.

On July 26, I am off again with D., not to Paris, but on a kind of reconnaissance through the French provinces. Although we have settled at Cannes, it is only temporary, until we finally set up our home somewhere else, anywhere other than on the Riviera, which has only the advantage of a lot of places for rent and some very good doctors.

Tigy and Marc are in a hotel near town, and I have found two or three teachers, especially for French and history, because Marc is deficient in some elements that are indispensable for getting into a French lycée. Mounted on a spanking new motorcycle, he goes from one teacher to the other, from Tigy's place to ours.

So, a trip through France, in our gigantic Dodge, filled with luggage, by short stages. Marseille, Sète, Bergerac, La Rochelle, Les Sables-d'Olonne, Luçon, Bourges, Burgundy, then Lyons, and finally Porquerolles, where I had lived so long. To me, it is almost a pilgrimage, and I am moved as we go by the house at Nieul, which is unoccupied.

At Porquerolles, I find once more my fellow *boules* players, now old, and children I had known now young adults, some of them even married.

Nowhere does D. appear to be inclined to settle, and I promise her we will look further.

The police superintendent of Nice, meeting me one day in my cumbersome Dodge, advises me to buy a smaller car, because otherwise I will not be able to get through Rue d'Antibes to the seashore. I buy three Renault 4CVs, which are then a novelty, and on the one intended for D. I have all the chrome options possible added, so that it is quite glittering with metal.

I was about to overlook Marie-Jo's first encounter with a pediatrician who was to become, and remains still, one of my best friends. At the time, he was head of pediatric services at the Cannes hospital, which did not keep him from having private office hours in the afternoon and even getting up at night to make house calls as much as fifteen miles away. He is the most devoted, most conscientious doctor I have ever met.

I think I remember that Marie-Jo had tonsillitis and that she was still refusing to speak French.

Very softly, so as not to frighten her, my future friend says to her in an affectionate tone: "Well, little girl, now show me where it hurts you."

I can still see you, Marie-Jo, in a little white dress with a blue border. You are almost harshly staring at this man you've never seen before and who, in order not to overwhelm you, has crouched down before you. You remain silent for a moment, and then, pointing to the door, you say to him, in English, "Go away, you!" Stressing the "you."

The good doctor turns to me and says, "What did she say?"

I think a second, and then translate it as "Get the hell out of here, *you!*"

He flushes, being a very sensitive man, but does not take offense. I don't know how he goes about it, but within ten minutes he has won you over and you are letting him examine your throat.

Incidentally, from the top of the retaining wall of our property, both of you, with your mother and me, were able to watch the bicycle racers of the Tour de France go by right beneath our feet. Another very clear picture in my memory.

In one of Cannes's two strip joints, a spiral staircase leads from the scullery to the mezzanine, where the strippers prepare for their entrances. They are just as friendly with D. as with me, and between numbers come to our table for a drink. D. often says to me: "Aren't you going up?"

I do. And there, matter-of-factly, I make love, at times to one, at times to another. They tell me their life stories, invite me to their homes, which are furnished rooms, and I play with the baby of one of them.

They are not required to have sex with the customers. One of them has a B.A. in literature. Another, a Russian, makes an elegant Russian dinner and asks me please not to go beyond a few intimacies.

I am familiar with a luxurious set of furnished apartments where one can have an assignation with very agreeable ladies. Sometimes, without waiting for one of the clubs to close, I get the owner's permission to take one of the dancers there with me, provided I get her back in time for her next scheduled appearance. The whole business is very simple and relaxed, uninhibited, and my memory of these women remains friendly and often affectionate.

One evening, my friend Henri-Georges Clouzot, who was the actual director of the film made from my novel *Strangers in the House,* is with me, along with his wife, Vera. They live in Vence, but often come to see me, and he always wants me to take him to one of those two cabarets. One day, he says: "Why don't you write me a scenario for a film to be called 'Strip Tease'?"

"Because I don't know how to write scenarios. I can write a novel and you can turn it into a film."

So I write *Strip Tease.* Clouzot's producer buys the rights to it. The screenplay is almost done, some of the players cast, when a very commercial film of the same title is released, so Clouzot has to cancel his project.

In September, I write *Les Complices (The Accomplices)*, still at Mougins, in my windowless retreat.

A month later, we are offered the rental of a magnificent property on the heights above Cannes called "Golden Gate." It has a huge bow window, lighted ponds, and a swimming pool cut right into the rock.

Plenty of space for Johnny and Marie-Jo to play in. My office faces a kind of cloister where I can take a walk if it is raining, before getting down to work.

We hire a chauffeur, a secretary, a second children's nursemaid. Tigy writes me a charming letter to tell me that at the age Marc has reached she can no longer be of any use to him and what he needs is a father. So Marc has a bedroom near ours and will frighten me by diving into the pool from the top of a sheer rock face.

Marie-Jo insists on going to school, because her brother is now a pupil at the elementary lycée of Cannes. The chauffeur takes him there in the morning, but I pick him up after school. A few parents, mostly mothers, are there waiting outside the gate, and thus by chance I make the acquaintance of a sweet, charming woman who turns out to be the wife of Marie-Jo's doctor. We then become even friendlier and keep exchanging dinner invitations in the nicest kind of way.

As for you, Marie-Jo, you are going to give me yet another surprise. I entered you, before the age of three, in the nursery school, one of the newest, finest, and most modern in all of France. The headmistress, with whom I empathize, explains to me that she has three groups, the littlest boys and girls, then the middle ones, and finally the oldest, the kindergarten class, aged five to six. She takes you to the youngest group and leaves you there, before returning to her own classroom. She is amazed, an hour later, to see you sitting in the front row of her biggest children.

She takes you back to your own class. A little later, you are back in front of her again, calm and serene, drawing in a notebook. This goes on for several days. I try to explain the rules of the school to you, but you just shake your head.

Finally, you win. You never interrupt the lessons. You don't disturb anybody. You remain seated across from the teacher and draw, sometimes listening, never asking questions.

When I am not "with novel," I make a point of taking you to school in the morning and picking you up later, before we both go to fetch Johnny from the lycée. You try swimming in our pool; Johnny shows more circumspection, I might even say distrust, than you toward that water spurting right out of the rock.

D. and I make a trip back to Italy, where she has no desire to settle. We are going to try Switzerland, which I have fond remembrances of from the time I used to ski at Saint Moritz before the war.

I was almost going to forget a character who played a big part in your childhood, children. A dog. Before the war, Olaf, a slate-colored Great Dane, was Tigy's, Boule's, and my companion. Shortly before leaving the United States, we bought a very young dog, of a breed then unknown in Europe: a royal standard poodle, of a size rarely reached by poodles, and silvery in color. They were to be had from only one breeder, a woman, in Connecticut, who had succeeded in establishing the breed through great patience and trial and error.

As a puppy, he was already so dignified-looking that we dubbed him Mister, and he became your playmate, letting both of you do anything you wanted with him. He crossed the Atlantic with us and lived at Mougins, where he never strayed from you.

I was thinking so hard of you, as I wrote, that I was forgetting our good old Mister, who in Cannes also went to school. Royal standard poodles, being almost as large as police dogs, have to be trained in the same way, and we take Mister to obedience school. We don't think he will adapt to the trainer, but we are wrong. After a few days, all we have to say is "Mister, time for school." He immediately wags his tail and heads out to the car.

When I refer to the two of you, Johnny and Marie-Jo, I should say the three of you, for Mister is really a member of the family.

When he wins the first prize for police dogs (no less!) in Nice, the newspapers all write about him, giving his name as Mystère, as if we had named him that because of the Maigrets being mystery stories!

In February 1956, a trip to Holland with D. and a return by way of Liège. She doesn't find Holland to her taste as a home either.

On our return, I write *Un échec de Maigret (Maigret's Failure)*, then in April *Le Petit Homme d'Arkhangelsk (The Little Man from Archangel)*, the story of which actually takes place in the wonderful Forville Market of Cannes, where I go almost every morning to do the household shopping. Ever since childhood, I have been bemused by markets, and I still am.

At the beginning of June, another trip, this time to Lausanne.
Finally!

49

Why did we select Cannes as a stopping-off place before finding a more or less permanent location? For practical reasons, as I have said, and also on account of the children. Finally, I admit, because I don't enjoy living in a big city, and perhaps because D. needs a certain amount of activity around her.

I had become aware of this at Shadow Rock Farm, a real paradise for the children and me, in a wonderful setting, yet too peaceful for D.

I am sensitive to small warning signs. Whether with Marc, Johnny, Marie-Jo, or, later, Pierre, I have been on the lookout from their birth for the slightest reactions that might allow me very closely to follow the formation of their characters.

From the day I first met D., I never stopped, during all the years, involuntarily noting those shadings of mood, which today I call "signs." And these signs have never deceived me. From the day I took charge of her, if I may so express it, I set myself the goal of making her happy, which I considered to be my duty, whatever the cost.

In Cannes, along the famous Croisette, between the Carlton and the casino—a bare third of a mile—there is a group of stores that one goes by unthinkingly several times a day. Yet they are the most deceptive lure I know of, even more than the displays on Fifth Avenue, because the temptations here are concentrated in so much shorter a space.

Cartier shows its most glittering ornaments just a few yards from Van Cleef & Arpels. Next door, Jeanne Lanvin, and a little beyond the prestigious Hermès. Everywhere luxurious lingerie, luscious leather goods, furs by Weil, and all the most famous brands of perfume.

In Canada I had gotten D. to give up using make-up. I also got her to let her brown hair, with its mahogany highlights, grow long and wear it coiled around her head. Not only had she willingly agreed, but she was proud of having done it.

I remember one afternoon on the Croisette, window-shopping as

Johnny rides along on a little bicycle; Marie-Jo is swinging in the shady casino garden.

Should I say that I have felt coming for a long time the incident that is about to take place? Maybe. But if so, not consciously. D. stops in front of a beauty parlor with all the products of a famous brand in the window. She doesn't ask or tell me anything. But I understand and, with a slightly heavy heart, I open the door.

I smile at her. Yet to me, this is the first sign of true rebellion. She is dying to have in her hands, as she did before she met me, those golden sticks from which all kinds of red, rose, natural, or green shades emerge, those delicate brushes for the eyelashes, the eyelids, the ever-so-elegant bottles with their great variety of perfumes.

I let her make a selection. From time to time, she gives me a glance that says "May I?"

Of course! She may buy everything, all those creams, those unguents, those so-called beauty products that will make her look not like what she is but like what she would like to be.

For me, this means a renunciation, but had there not been many others? The first goes way back, to when I allowed her to answer part of my mail, to negotiate with my publishers and producers, without, however, ever signing any contract I had not myself drawn up. Later, I went further, telling newspapermen that she is my "businessman," that my only function really is just to write the novels. Sometimes letters piled up for three months without being answered, yet all I did was grit my teeth and wait.

Three or four years ago I dictated a volume entitled *Je suis resté un enfant de chœur* (I Have Remained a Choirboy). In a certain sense, that is true. I keep my promises, however hard that may be, even those I make to myself, and, I repeat, I had promised myself I would make her happy someday.

The make-up is the first step. Cartier next sees us, as do Van Cleef & Arpels, Weil, Lanvin, and Hermès. . . . She has not one but two diamond necklaces. However, I make a point, every time I buy a jewel, to repeat to her that it is an investment, which someday will benefit our children.

I love beautiful things, especially beautiful materials, gold for its warmth, silver for its glints, wrought iron for its nobility, wood for its living veins. Diamonds leave me as cold as they are themselves. Emeralds and so-called precious stones leave me indifferent, but I admire certain raw crystals torn from mountainsides.

I appreciate comfort, not luxury.

My action in going into this shop on the Croisette puts an end to my dream of the early days, or, rather, the early nights, in New York: to succeed in harmonizing D.'s tastes and my own, bringing her to what I consider a woman's most precious possession and in a way her fulfillment: simplicity.

In fact, that day I renounce all resistance.

The famous Cannes Film Festival sharpens D.'s need to be seen, to consider herself important by rubbing elbows with important people. I know Fabre-Lebret and the other organizers. I also know most of the producers, directors, stars, many of whom have been connected with films based on my novels. The members of the jury are friends of mine, some of them intimate friends of twenty and more years' standing.

So, at the bar of the Carlton, D. gets a chance to pamper Jean Cocteau, to bring him a pill of some kind when he complains of having the vapors, wipe his brow, and smile at him with the tenderness of a younger sister. She can address him as Jean (as half of Paris does), tutoyer Pagnol and Achard, entertain at lunch William Wyler, Alexander Korda and his young Canadian wife, and lend outfits to some American stars tempted by the sight of our swimming pool.

The second year at Golden Gate, I even gave a party for a couple of hundred people, that whole film crowd. That year, Fabre-Lebret thought he was a genius because he got six members of the French Academy to serve on his jury, and D. was able to entertain them along with the stars and starlets, including Mylène Demongeot, who was later to become my daughter-in-law. A curious thing: Marc wouldn't come to that party, because film was as yet of no interest to him.

Do you remember, Marc? You enrolled in the lycée at Nice, and I bought you a more powerful motorcycle, on which every evening you went off with some thirty other "leather-jackets," each one with "his girl" behind him. Your girl is quite pretty, youngish, with big brown eyes.

One day I get a phone call from a lady whose name means nothing to me.

"Don't you think, Monsieur Simenon, it might be time for us to meet one another?"

"Why, madame?"

"To discuss our children. You are surely not unaware that for several months Marc has been going out with my daughter?"

"I was indeed unaware that she was your daughter, and I know her only by her first name."

"Well, we have to . . ." The voice and tone of someone who knows what she wants. She invites me to come to her house, and I find it very nice, with everything laid out for a classic tea party.

"I am so happy you came," she says. "My husband will join us very shortly. I must warn you, he is a little hard of hearing. Cream? Sugar?"

The husband, who joins us, pleasant and gentle, a bit absent-minded, is a retired bureaucrat.

"Well, Monsieur Simenon, what are we going to decide about our children?"

I look at her in amazement, a pretty lady with silver hair, and a still-smooth, youthful face.

"What would you expect us to do?" I ask with a smile that is just the least bit ironic.

"It seems to me it is time we made some decision."

You are eighteen, my Marc, just getting ready to take your *baccalauréat* examinations, dissecting meticulously the toads and other little creatures that fall into your hands. Do you remember that at this time you planned to become a biologist or an oceanographer?

A few days before my interview with the silver-haired lady, the police superintendent had asked me to come and see him. With a mocking smile, he put a leaded truncheon on the desk in front of him.

"Do you know where we found this object, the possession of which is just as forbidden as that of an automatic?"

"On my son?"

"Yes, sirree. Your son Marc is a member of a gang of motorcycle nuts who have been giving us trouble. Almost every night, they ride noisily through the city and the environs, and, among other things, they have broken the windows of a newspaper whose opinions they didn't like. We of course had to pick them up, and in Marc's pocket, we found this thing."

He pushed the truncheon toward me.

"Take it along as a souvenir. You can show it to him. Advise him to be more careful about who he pals around with. Apart from that, now that you know what Cannes is like today, do you understand why I advised you to stop riding around in that huge American car? Incidentally, what did you ever do with it?"

"I sold it, but it wasn't easy. All kinds of customs formalities to go through. . . ."

The lady is still sitting across from me, the tea table between us, the husband shaking his fine old head.

"Well, what do you think?" she goes on.

"Nothing."

She flushes, doubtless in anger. "What do you mean, nothing?"

"It's purely a matter between your daughter and my son."

"It seems to me that we ought to make their situation official by announcing an engagement."

"This is the children's business, isn't it?"

"But what about the parents? What about their duties?"

"Madame, I am very sorry. My children, sons and daughter, are free to shape their own lives, and I would not under any circumstances allow myself to interfere."

She gets up, livid now, instead of red. She wants to say something. Her lips move, but she is too indignant to get the words out. The husband, who heard none of this, is still smiling agreeably as I head for the door.

Yet you were indeed to marry Francette, Marc.

Cannes, you can see, played a part in all our lives. And your passion for motorcycling had something to do with your choice of a career.

D. and I go several times to Paris, which is always her dream place, and she is now accompanied by what she calls her "personal chambermaid," Marioutcha, who has traded her orphanage uniform for a black silk dress with a tiny apron and a lace cap, such as soubrettes wear.

As soon as we get to the George V, where we have a suite, I know what is expected of me, and I rush to the pharmacy across the street to get a supply of disinfectant and tissue paper. Would my friend, the manager of long ago, have blushed at hearing that D. and Marioutcha take the paper out of all the drawers and closets and replace it with clean tissue paper, after vacuuming the furniture? D., naked, as in New York, then disinfects bathtubs, washbasins, and toilets in both bathrooms, before going after the four or five telephones.

This is also a sign that I unfortunately understand, as certain specialists will understand it on reading this.

Rather than stick around for all of this to-do and be subjected to a smell that reminds me of hospitals, I hie myself to the locale of some Mme Claude or other. The real one, about whom there was so much talk, was not the only madam in Paris, and I believe I knew all of them, at least all those who occupied private houses in what are called the "fine residential neighborhoods."

By way of answer, incidentally, to certain legends that make me out a sex maniac, I take the liberty of pointing out that I have very normal tastes and am not alone in being driven, from earliest adolescence and still today, by urgent sexual needs.

I have spoken of my taste for fine materials, what I call "noble" materials. Is there any material more splendid than a woman's skin, a woman's flesh? Can there be a more intimate communication between two beings than copulation?

I ferociously sought after "woman," the real one, as nature made her. I was twice mistaken, but each time I lived up to my responsibilities.

With D., I am to live up to them for a long time, for too long a time, since my life was almost swallowed up by them.

We have not reached that point yet, only the stage of forewarning signs.

I decide to take D. to Lausanne, as I said, in the hope of finding a haven of rest there, for her as well as the children. We go to the Lausanne-Palace, which at that time had a residential wing, where, while taking full advantage of the hotel's services if so desired, one can rent an apartment by the month.

Is this finally the miracle I had so hoped for? D. is taken with Lausanne and the region. It is true that some old "high society" women occupy some of these residential apartments and that others, very rich and in the limelight, including the old former queen of Spain and her little court, meet in the afternoon in a ground-floor salon for a very distinguished tea.

All we need now is to discover, outside the city proper, a house big enough to accommodate our brood. We decide that we will shuttle weekly between the Nice airport and the one at Cointrin, half an hour from Lausanne. The flight takes a bare half-hour, twenty minutes in good weather, when they take the most direct route, over Mont Blanc.

In Nice, I arrange to have a small space in one of the hangars, in which to leave one of our little Renaults each time we fly off. Another car, garaged at Cointrin, takes us to Lausanne. We don't use it, however, in our hunt for a place, because we are not sufficiently acquainted with the area. We hire the oldest taxi driver in town, who drives with the kind of caution that lets me relax while he takes us from villas to châteaux within a radius of some thirty miles.

One evening, at the bar, where D. is nursing one of her inevitable double whiskeys, we happen to meet a pretty, smiling young woman who at this time is secretary to the owner of the hotel. A one-time Italian bricklayer, with ambition, he had had a fling at the movie business, coproducing a film made by one of the best directors of the period, which attracted a lot of attention before being recognized as both an artistic masterpiece and a commercial disaster.

The secretary, whose name is Joyce Aitken, mainly handled his motion-picture business, working sometimes in the Paris offices of the producing company, the rest of the time at Lausanne. Born of a Scottish father and a

Swiss mother, she speaks, besides French and English, fluent German and gets by in Italian.

Once the motion-picture company goes into receivership, she has plenty of time on her hands, the more so since her boss, having lost his shirt, is about to give up the hotel.

D. asks her whether she would like to be "her" secretary during the days we spend in Lausanne. While she is dictating, I am supposed to spend my time in the living room or go out for a walk.

On one of our returns to Cannes, Johnny complains of a pain in the belly. Martinon, our pediatrician, advises us immediately to see a famous surgeon who has his office on the Croisette, where he even has an operating room. We go there, Johnny somewhat scared, and D. and I are present while he is examined.

"The best thing would be to operate without delay," the surgeon says. "It's simple appendicitis. Won't take more than an hour."

We are dumbstruck. You, Johnny, are very brave about it, even when they put you on the operating table. We wait in a room adorned with tasteful paintings.

Less than an hour later, the nurse calls us. The operation is over, and Johnny is beginning to come to. He stares at us with worried, almost terrified eyes. When he can finally speak, he asks us, in English: "Why did they give me DDT? Were they trying to kill me?"

No one knows what he means. Then the surgeon hits himself on the forehead.

"When your son was half asleep, I called for the anesthetist to give him ether. . . ."

Ether—which you misinterpreted as DDT, poor Johnny mine, and before dropping off you had visions of insects being killed with DDT. That was probably the only time in your whole childhood when you were scared, because when you were very young you got into the habit of facing up to things.

Soon, it is Marie-Jo's turn to give us a scare, and because I feel you are more fragile, my little girl, I'm the one who gets terrified. Our friend Martinon wants to make sure your kidneys are working normally and has us take you to a radiologist. The only way to make your kidneys show up on the sensitized plate is by injecting iodine into your veins.

You are not yet four. You seem frail, and your smile has something both tense and fragile about it. The radiologist makes a few tests, decides to make a urography, and soon informs us triumphantly that your kidneys are performing perfectly well, the more so since you have three instead of two!

So does D.'s sister, and she is nonetheless full of health and energy. Relief!

Another interlude. D.'s mother comes to see us at Golden Gate, where she feels overwhelmed, although she doesn't show it. It is not her fault. She was raised that way. Never to show her emotions. Never to admire anything. Nor to criticize either.

Oh, yes, there is one thing, though, that surprises her, which I've forgotten to mention. The bedroom D. and I have is huge and bright, with a terrace from which the view looks like a picture postcard.

The next room, which also looks out over the sea, is very big, and I had intended to keep it for Marc, since Johnny and Marie-Jo share a charming suite in a corner of the house that also includes Boule's bedroom and from which they have a dream view.

"I need that room to keep my dresses in," D. had immediately informed me.

"You could put them in the room across the hall."

"I don't feature myself having to cross the hall to go and get a dress."

By now she has an impressive wardrobe and never orders fewer than six pairs of shoes at a time. As for handbags, almost all from Hermès, her collection of them has grown incessantly.

I don't put up a fight, my big Marc. Excuse me for my cowardice. I committed other acts of cowardice toward all three, then all four, of you. I wanted to make her happy, come what might, you understand, to the point of making myself as tiny as possible, for I knew how much she needed to be in first place.

We take a short trip to Paris with her mother. I remember our first lunch, at the Cochon d'Or, then one of the best restaurants in Paris. The patron puts himself out. Everyone is at our beck and call. They serve us a meal worthy of the most demanding of gourmets.

"How did you find the partridges, madame?"

"So-so."

Meaning what? That they were merely adequate? That they were not bad, or awful? So-so! Middling! *Bourgeoisie oblige* . . .

I reserve a box at the Comédie-Française, where Robert Hirsch is dazzling in a Feydeau comedy. Nothing shocking. Not an objectionable word. I know that the actors have been told we are in the audience, as is usual in the theater when a well-known person attends. In that case, they keep their eye on the person or persons in question. Some have even told me that those are the occasions when they try to do their best work.

Applause breaks out continually, laughs merge right into one another.

The very full house responds admirably. Except for my Canadian mother-in-law, who remains the great stone face. Only at the end of each act does she delicately, noiselessly, bring her fingertips together.

I ask her in a whisper: "Don't you think it's funny?"

"Not bad."

And at the end, I dare to ask: "Why didn't you clap?"

"Because it's vulgar, and not the thing to do."

As for Cannes, which we will soon be leaving, D. lives fully there, avidly, in on all the galas, dancing with illustrious persons, such as my friend Picasso, who, I don't know why, winked at me from time to time. Perhaps because he does not belong, either, to that Cannes he walks through with legs and arms bare, hirsute, among a crowd he does not see.

If I still have a fond memory of that period in spite of everything, my children, it is thanks to you, with whom I have extensive contacts, taking you to school, at night telling you an endless story the way I once used to do for Marc.

If I never stuffed you with sweets, out of concern for your health, I did get into the habit, before my nightly tale-telling, of putting three anise candies on each of your night tables.

I can still see you everywhere, in our park, in our pool, behind the school or kindergarten gate, on the beach, and in the playground. A Johnny already serious and sure of himself, who could be fazed by nothing but DDT; Marie-Jo, whose blue eyes express a longing for love that an instinctive reserve keeps her from asking for in so many words.

Did you get any from me at least, my little girl? Your letters, your final phone calls, the songs you composed to sing to me on your guitar tell me you did. Deep within me, however, I fault myself for not having given you even more love, not having given you enough to fill all the voids that others left in you.

We will soon be taking you and your two brothers to a château that, for you at least, will be a fairy-tale castle.

Just time before leaving Cannes to go to Nice and root for your brother Marc, taking the formidable *baccalauréat* exams. After the "written," I wait for him in the courtyard of the lycée and take him out to dinner at an excellent wharfside restaurant. For the "oral," I am up in the gallery, near the door of the room in which he is being examined, and I daresay I have more stage fright than he.

As for you, Johnny, I am invited to have a seat in the tent set up in the middle of the courtyard for the scholastic and municipal authorities. When it is your turn to receive a prize, I will be called on to present it to you. From emotion or heat, I am flushed and sweating. You look me straight in the eye, as unflappable as a guardsman.

Before leaving, I buy, from the surgeon who operated on you, a second-hand custom Mercedes. There are only sixteen of them in existence, and I can't resist the opportunity. A sports model with a powerful, silent motor, it is a convertible. The light-gray body looks white in the sunlight, the blue upholstery is made of real leather, which, like tweed, still smells of its animal origin and not of fuel.

I loved that car for itself, and at the Château d'Echandens, it was kept in the place of honor in our garages, until the day I realized that the climate in Switzerland is not the same as on the Riviera, and that a convertible there just doesn't make any sense.

I did not buy this Château d'Echandens, ten miles out of Lausanne, because it was not for sale. But I did get an indefinitely renewable six-year lease.

Before you got there, my children, D. and I scoured all the antique shops of the town and the area, because modern furniture would have been an anachronism in this sixteenth-century château, which had to be cleaned from top to bottom, the walls repainted, the woodwork scraped and polished, the windows made as nearly as possible wind- and rainproof, new electric wiring installed, sockets put where none existed, cheerful curtains selected, especially for your bedrooms, which have a sunny southern exposure.

It had to be. . . . Fortunately, I am used to it. If I selected a château, it was not because it was a château, or for its turrets, its dungeon, its park with old trees, its lawns, its stone stairway that spiraled from ground floor to attic.

The village, around us, at the time has only some three hundred-odd souls, all vintners or farmers. A sprightly little church stands out by itself on a grassy knoll like the one at Lakeville.

Everything is ready by the time you arrive, and I don't let you know right away that the three recesses measuring about six and a half feet by five, with iron bars across their doors and stone floors, are prison cells, from the days of the Bernese occupation.

You find that out later and hide there when playing games with your little playmates, just as you also use a strange drying room at the end of the courtyard, which is reached by a worm-eaten wooden outside staircase.

In our drawing room, a concert grand piano bought at an auction, which a tuner must often come to keep in shape.

You will be happy here, my children, as you were at Cannes. But how will D. react to it? And, in the final analysis, what will be my position in the house, outside of being the father?

Little signs? There certainly are some, too many, in fact, but I don't want to recognize them. The question that remains open and continues to plague me is always the same: Will she finally be happy?

This is July 1957. During our preparatory comings and goings, I write *Maigret s'amuse (Maigret's Little Joke)*, then *Le Fils (The Son)* and *Le Nègre (The Negro)*. As early as August, when we are barely moved in, I write *Maigret voyage (Maigret and the Millionaires)*, then in October *Le Président (The Premier)* and in December *Les Scrupules de Maigret (Maigret Has Scruples)*.

Aitken is now part of our household. She returns at noon and in the evening to her Lausanne apartment, perched on her Lambretta, which gives me the willies.

I write more than ever, in spite of my many trips. Don't I do it, after all, to fill some vacuum, almost angrily, as I have been doing ever since my first meeting with D.?

A vacuum that always, despite everything, I hope someday to fill, as if D. represented some goal I set for myself, which I am dutybound to reach.

Fortunately—I almost said "miraculously"—you are there. And you will never know the extent to which all of you helped me.

Thanks.

50

Americans, at the time I was living in the United States, and perhaps still today, are, with the Nordic countries, including Holland, the most hospitable people in the world. They literally welcome their guests of a day or a week into their homes, and not just into their dining rooms and living rooms.

I, for one, have always had a passion for homes, whether my own or those of my friends, because one never really knows anyone else except in his own home.

Reproductions have been made of the yellow envelopes, large as file folders, on which, before each of my novels, I put down the names of the characters, their ages, ancestry, the schools they attended, the names of their teachers, a thousand other details, of which maybe only two or three will surface in the story itself. What is less well known is that in addition, on a folder of Bristol board, I make a pen or pencil drawing of the layout of the apartment or house; I have to familiarize myself with the surroundings to the point of being able, with eyes closed, to open a door to the left or the right, as the case may be.

Since the Château d'Echandens holds an important place in my life and yours, my children, I feel a need, as for my novels, to describe it.

A high wrought-iron gate, rather formidable, opens onto a paved court-yard. To the left, the outbuildings, among them the shaky staircase leading to the drying room, and, right next to that, the heavily iron-barred doors of the prison cells.

In the back, some low buildings serve as garages. Next to them, an empty space allowing direct access to the garden.

At the corner of the main building, to the right, a square turret, and very close by, the narrow, low door to the château proper. After entering this door, one goes down a step to face a very wide graystone-floored hallway, the walls of which, also of stone, are painted a dark red lightened by litho-graphs and engravings in narrow gilt frames.

The steep unbanistered spiral stairway leads to the upper floors, and I am so afraid for you children that I have heavy iron rings set in the walls along it, with a hemp rope running through.

First door to the left, or garden, side, as it is called on the French stage, but here literally so, for all the windows open onto the garden, in reality a little park, is to a small room containing a sink, a refrigerator, a coffee machine; it serves as liquor closet.

Then a double door, that of the main drawing room, with pearl-gray wooden walls and three high French windows. Red curtains. Louis XV furniture, heavy with bronze. This is D.'s office, which she took over auto-matically, as her right, and which, I must add, to be truthful, I fully con-curred in.

Adjoining it is a smaller office, lighted by a French window and having a narrow fireplace. For a time, this is my workroom, in which I write several novels, disturbed by D.'s and Aitken's voices.

Finally, still on the garden side, an immense glass-paned room, which must have been a winter garden or conservatory. I covered its only two walls with waxed poplar shelves, which, from floor to ceiling, hold all my novels, in both French and numerous foreign languages. Since the ground-floor rooms have very high ceilings, a double ladder is required to reach the upper shelves.

My most vivid recollection of that office is of a day spent there before a log fire with my old friend Michel Simon. He is telling me of his adventures, in many cases erotic. From time to time, D. opens the door, and immediately Michel, modest, whatever one might think, shuts up.

"Don't you want me to get you something to drink?" she asks.

"We have already helped ourselves."

She leaves, obviously ruffled, and after a wink Michel goes back all the more ardently to his memories, which at the least might be called savory.

I just mentioned winks. My old friends and I exchanged many of them, unbeknownst to D., and I will have occasion to exchange some with Aitken, who has sized up the whole situation but nonetheless goes on fulfilling her role as principal secretary to Mme Georges Simenon, as seriously and nicely as can be.

Soon there will be a second secretary, and then a third, in the two offices opposite mine, on the right or courtyard side.

At the end on the courtyard side, a fine bedroom with modern bath, the largest in the house: Marc's room. It has the advantage of having direct access to the street by a private entrance, so that he may entertain whomever he wishes.

He does not fail to, and I am delighted. He often entertains Francette there, and several times Tigy. Since the divorce, my two wives have refused to meet each other. D. even sets a condition on Marc's mother's calls: that she come in only by his street door and not appear in our hallway.

"Let it be!" I feel like saying, with a sigh.

At the other end of the hall, a huge glass double door, leading to a columned peristyle fit for a real château. To the right of the peristyle, a door, a stone staircase going far down into the earth to reveal a vaulted cellar running the whole length of the château, in which old barrels are lined up.

The central-heating boiler is there too, with a thermostat that quite often goes on the blink, and some winter nights I have to go down into this veritable freezer to get the thing going again.

In the park, to the right, the orangery, without any orange trees but serving as both hothouse and toolshed.

At the end of the sloping lawn, I have a portico set up with swings, rings, trapeze, and knotted rope, for the delight of you children. When the village children watch you enviously over the low wall, I get the municipality to allow me to have the same thing set up in the public square.

Second floor. A door, to the left, leads to a hallway and a strange room with an arched ceiling and unexpected walls, which I soon turn into my office and which will also be my den, for the day is not far off when I will need a den to repair to.

On shelves in the hallway, there will then be my telephone directories, my geographical and road maps, the American, English, French, and Swiss medical magazines to which I subscribe, since medicine remains my hobby and is my main form of diversion.

From the hallway, also stone floored, an austere double door into a huge, rather dark drawing room, in which proudly stands the grand piano I bought in the hope that someday Marie-Jo would take an interest in it, which in fact she will.

Next room, the children's playroom, with a double glass door leading to a terrace as large as the living room, surrounded by a wrought-iron balustrade.

Do you remember that, children? If I am going on about it, it is because this is the setting in which you spend the years during which we most absorb what is around us. Each of you has his or her own file, which contains your photographs from those years as well as your report cards, your doctors' prescriptions, and the little notes you exchanged with your playmates. Also, your first crayon drawings, then your watercolors, and, in the case of Marie-Jo, her first oil painting.

I recently went through the photographs, some of the drawings you gave me, and I must admit that I had moist eyes and a lump in my throat.

The dining room with the red walls, and on them the paintings by Vlaminck, my best friend from so long ago, in their gilt frames.

A long, leafed table, of shiny walnut, a serving buffet, and, opening onto the kitchen, a very long service hatch, the walls being inordinately thick. You play "spies," and don't hesitate to slip into this service hatch, which allows you to hear what is being said both in the dining room and in the kitchen.

A very large kitchen adjoins the scullery. A table at which ten can easily be seated.

Third floor, left (garden) side. Above what is to become my office, which I will at times ironically but not without bitterness refer to as my "prison," the laundry, which also serves as sewing room, with wooden racks on which clothes can be hung to dry. A small stairway leads to a storage room, which will undergo a transformation.

Then, off the hall, two bedrooms, for Marie-Jo and her new nursemaid, Boule here having resumed her place in the kitchen. Which of course does not keep her from paying a lot of attention to you children, whom she considers to be partly hers. In the whole house, moreover, isn't she the most maternal of all the women?

Your bedroom, Marie-Jo, is sunny and, through tall trees, looks down on a flower bed and sloping vines.

Your new nursemaid will also play a part in your childhood. Her name is Nana. She has graduated from the best nursery school in the Valais. The school uniform, which the students continue to wear later on, is becoming and cheerful: a blue-and-white-striped dress, with a white collar, and a little starched white cap. Nana is extremely young, very timid, and will take care of you for a long time.

The finest of the bedrooms, the one with the most sun, because it has both southern and western exposures, is the one that Johnny gets. It has no other room adjoining it, and Marie-Jo is still too young to stay there by herself. That will come later on, poor Johnny mine, when Marie-Jo, somewhat older, makes room for a new little brother, and the attic room at the top of the steep stairway will become your aerie, after we fit it out with a tiny bathroom. At that time, it is true, you will be a big enough boy to accept this without flinching.

As for your mother and me, we make do with something on the courtyard side. A boudoir, across from Johnny's room, rather dark, getting sunlight only in the afternoon. One window opens onto part of the garden, the other onto a narrow road, or country path, and the village.

A narrow hallway leads to our bedroom, even darker, where only in the summer, late in the afternoon, does a ray of sunshine find its way in.

In this hallway, a recess has been fitted with shelves, on which my underwear is piled, and with hangers for my clothes. Old châteaux are full of strange arrangements like this.

D. has a round turret alongside the boudoir, in which she can place her dresses and underthings. As for our bathroom, reached by stooping and going down a step, it is in the opposite turret. The two windows, more like slits in the wall, allow us to see the first rooftops of the village, which make a kind of Vlaminck landscape, and I enjoy looking at it while shaving.

Our bedroom is dominated by the huge bed we ordered from Chicago when we lived at Tumacacori. Battlefield of love. It on occasion served that purpose when I brought to it some pretty woman and D. actively joined in with us, as she had done in Cuba.

It is used less and less often for amorous encounters, even our private ones, for I have become accustomed to going to bed early, at ten, and getting up at six in the morning, whereas D. stays up as late as possible at night and spends a good part of the morning in bed or in her boudoir.

That is where she does her phoning. We have phones everywhere.

She also likes to have Aitken come up while she is attending to her toilette in the boudoir, and dictate more or less necessary letters to her, and I can still see Aitken sitting on the step of the bathroom, unruffled, taking in shorthand what D. dictates to her while, four or five feet away, like Louis XIV, she goes about her various bodily evacuations.

Does D. find pleasure in this? She will do the same thing later, at Epalinges, and my reserve, inherited from the Simenons and my altar-boy past, will always find it offensive.

Our help has necessarily become more numerous. Some of them sleep on the top floor, where there are dormer windows and I have had a tiny bathroom installed.

From the start, there were six, including an Italian gardener whom the owner had had come in for a few hours each week before we got there.

D. likes to run her little staff in a quasi-military manner, and each one is assigned specific tasks to be done at specific times. In the evening, after dinner, she calls them all together around the kitchen table for what she calls "the report." She makes that last as long as possible, questioning each one about her or his activities during the day, setting the schedule for the next day, discussing who will have what days off and who will replace them.

I am left out of these "palavers," as the blacks of Africa call them, but I know they are often the occasion for tears and even attempts at rebellion.

That is what will happen with Evolti, the gardener. Actually, we don't have full-time work for him outside. So he is quite agreeable, on days when we have dinner guests, to waiting on table, dressed in black trousers and white jacket. He even gets to like the idea, and I remember one time when . . .

We had invited some friends from Cannes, the Baron and Baroness Van Zeeland, who came to Basel every month for the meeting of the International Monetary Fund or some such organization headquartered there.

Van Zeeland, a man as charming as his wife is charming and vivacious, has a rather long salt-and-pepper beard, in which the salt predominates over the pepper. We are engaged in lively conversation. Evolti is serving. A moment comes when he is to pass to our guest the duck *à l'orange*. He does it in such a way that the eminent baron's beard sweeps through the platter and gets bathed in the sauce.

He, fortunately, laughs about it. We all laugh, and D. makes haste to repair the damage.

Theoretically, according to D.'s plans, early in the morning Evolti is supposed to vacuum the ground-floor offices. After a few days, D. hears that it is not the gardener who is doing this, but the chambermaid who is supposed to be responsible only for the rooms on the second floor.

Arguments over this. The next day, the maid still does the vacuuming. Evolti promises. Then again . . .

This goes on for quite a while. D. forgets that Evolti is Italian and that an Italian male, especially if he is officially a gardener, is loath to stoop to doing women's work. He finally carries the day, explaining that, according to I don't know what doctor, his lungs are such that he can do only outdoor work. Except, of course, when he is our table waiter.

I believe this is D.'s first defeat, and the whole staff laughs over it, because Evolti is the only man among all those women, and he is very popular with them.

Aitken has a gift for getting along with everyone, even when D. keeps her at the office until seven-thirty or eight in the evening. Not to work. Just to have an excuse for not joining the rest of us at dinner. And to talk; but mainly to polish off two or three glasses of whiskey, before coming up, especially on the days when she hasn't had a chance to have them at one of Lausanne's exclusive bars, particularly the one at the Lausanne-Palace, where the friendly Italian bartender knows his customers and gives her good measure. I can still hear D. looking at her glass and saying to him, "Heavens, you've gone and watered it all down again." After which, he gives me a discreet look and adds a large dollop of Scotch.

I have spoken of these signs I note without showing it, but not without sorrow, for I still hope, I will hope against hope till the end.

I remember one bartender in Paris who confided:

"Do you know why so many women seek out discreet bars, especially at times when there's no one else there?"

I didn't.

"You may say it's because they want to drink, which is true. But it's especially so they can confide things they would blush to tell to someone of their own social level. To them, we aren't men, but just anonymous beings, underlings to whom one can confess anything."

We went together to many bars of that kind, D. and I. And even as early as New York I suspected that at those times I was simply not there. She wasn't talking to me, but to the bartender. She could read their faces, tell right off which ones knew how to listen. I, of course, did not know how to listen, or, rather, the only things she had left to tell me were things I had already heard a hundred times before.

• • •

I get in the habit, at Echandens, of taking her out for a ride in the afternoon, usually to the plateau that stretches to the foot of the Jura range and from which, as far as the eye can see, there are only wheat fields and pastures dotted here and there with white farmhouses.

I speak to her. I always have something to say to her, because I am older than she and have had many varied experiences. I try to get her interested, if only in the brown-and-white splotches the cows make so prettily in the landscape. Then, getting no response, I turn toward her and see she is asleep.

This happened many times in the United States, in breath-taking settings. Here, it becomes the rule, and I end up forgetting about taking her for drives or trying to entertain her.

Shortly before the war, I wrote a novel called *Strangers in the House*, in which Raimu did a fine job on the screen; he later told me he felt it was his best film.

At Echandens, if I am not a stranger in the house, I am at any rate an interloper, except when, locked in my office with a DO NOT DISTURB sign on the doorknob, I am writing my novels. What else am I good for? To make love? She wants that less and less often, no longer pretends ecstasy, but is shaping herself to her new life under the billing of "Mme Georges Simenon." The Madame part is all she cares about. Monsieur has become superfluous and is a bother.

It happens, of a morning, after my chapter is done, that I go up to her boudoir, where I find her chatting with Aitken, or her chambermaid, or Boule, or the sewing maid. She half turns toward me and casually asks: "What do you want?"

"To kiss you."

She holds her cheek out, in resignation. And I, hard as it may be to understand, refuse to resign myself to this.

It also happens that, after my nap, I go down to her office.

"What do you want, Jo?"

"You!"

She sighs, asks Aitken to excuse her, and precedes me into Marc's bedroom, when it is unoccupied, which is most of the time. She takes down her panties and gets in position.

"Hurry up," she says.

Do I still feel physical desire for her? To tell the truth, I don't believe so, but this is all part of a whole that I find hard to delimit.

One day—I think she had gone a little heavy on the whiskey, which has become a more and more frequent occurrence—I go down to the office, where Aitken is standing by a Louis XV piece. The usual dialog:

"What do you want?"

"You!"

That afternoon, she simply lies down on the rug.

"Hurry up. You don't have to leave, Aitken."

She stays, and gives me a wink, so I don't have to walk out on D. and leave her waiting there on the rug.

Marie-Jo and Johnny now both go to school. We have hired an old one-legged chauffeur, the only one in the city, because the rules are very strict about the handicapped. His name is Alphonse, and he lost his leg when, even though Swiss, he fought in the Battle of the Marne under the command of Marshal Joffre. On the strength of a personal letter from the old marshal, the city of Lausanne made an exception for him and gave him a license.

For the children, I bought a solid Land-Rover, which can stand up to any collision. Although I don't drive them to school while I am writing my novels, at least I go and pick them up, as I did at Cannes, and that remains one of the best moments of my days.

The children adore Alphonse, and the city police know him so well that they shut their eyes when he parks where he shouldn't. Alphonse does our marketing, and he is no less popular with the tradesmen.

He is a drinker, and looks it, but he is conscientious and disciplined about it. During the week, only three glasses of white wine, when his day's work is done. On Saturdays, on the other hand, when he finishes at noon, he ties a magnificent snootful on at the village inn, and often has to be carried home, just two doors from the café.

He smokes nothing but cigars. I sent him a box of them each New Year's Day, and went on doing so after he left us. In 1980, I still send him his annual cigars.

In spite of writing five or six novels each year, reading a lot, especially English and American newspapers and magazines, I have plenty of free hours. In order to escape from my cage, I again take up golf.

The Lausanne golf course, at Epalinges, which has a grandiose view, conquers me right off. I play there a lot, sometimes twice the eighteen holes in a row, by myself. I phone the day before to reserve a caddy for eight in the morning.

I am alone with him, absorbed in the problems of the different holes to the point that sometimes at night I wake up wondering what mistake I made on the third or eleventh hole.

I go there when the grass is still covered with dew, as well as when it is raining heavily and when the wind blowing across the plateau carries the balls off course. Once my game is over, I settle down in a corner of the bar to recoup with a cool Dutch beer before lunch.

While we were still in Cannes, Martinon gave me the address of a hotel in Villars-sur-Ollon, a Swiss mountain resort, run by a very nice family. They were able to accommodate us for the month of August, and the children were happier there than they had been almost anywhere else.

A large general room, which had nothing solemn about it, was turned into a dining room at mealtimes, and the numerous children played about it freely.

In the basement, there was a sort of cabaret that stayed open, and usually crowded, until very late, because a social director by the name of Serge, a professional vaudevillian, kept the entertaining atmosphere going, singing, telling funny stories, and coaxing even the least inclined couples to get up and dance.

Of course, D. immediately liked Serge and the cabaret ambience; she always wanted to be in the last group to leave, sometimes at dawn. This brought her back to life, like a plant parched for water. In that upper-bourgeois setting, she seemed like a star, and Serge, as well as the barman, became her pets.

There was a nine-hole golf course not far from the hotel, a hilly course of the kind I like, where sometimes one had to drive the ball over a small train that chugged up the mountainside.

Marc was with us, handsome and built like a Hollywood leading man, in the days when leading men had to be Adonises. One day, he pointed out to me a table at which sat a woman alone, a pretty woman in her thirties, whom I had seen in the company of a little boy.

"You like her, Dad?"

"I wouldn't say no."

"Neither would she . . . I think you ought to talk to her. I spent part of the night with her, and she's really worth it."

I asked her to dance once, twice, then to meet me discreetly a quarter of an hour later in our room, after giving her the number. I tipped D. off, and she just laughed. The lady and I spent a delightful as well as passionate hour together. After which, giving no inkling of what had gone on, we returned to our places in the cabaret. I think that this business excited D., because afterward she acted much more sensual, or at least greedier.

The most wonderful part of this hotel was the children's shows that Serge put on in the cabaret on rainy afternoons. He had a gift for adapting his comic talents to a juvenile level, and, besides, he was a truly talented magician.

Parents were not admitted except to accompany the smallest children. I would observe you two, Johnny and Marie-Jo, through a door that was ajar. I could see Johnny, usually so serious, let himself go in fits of loud laughter. As for you, Marie-Jo, your eyes expressed a kind of ecstasy.

D. asked me to get her a complete golf bag and, as usual, I had it made up with her initial.

A *D* like the one on the little house we had chanced to see, and which I then bought in her name, on the heights of Cagnes-sur-Mer, on a tiny steep street that allowed no vehicular traffic, just a stone's throw from the palace of the Grimaldis.

I wanted it to be a sweet setting for her. A huge room, access to which was by an outside staircase. I ordered from a blacksmith who was in love with his craft, as are most blacksmiths, a banister with the letter *D* wrought into it.

My old friend Marcel Vertès, who had been a faithful member of the wild evenings and nights at Place des Vosges, made, out of tiles set into the wall, a picture over six feet high of a naked girl looking both innocent and receptive.

The furniture was designed, in old Provençal style, by a local cabinet-maker. A long bar filled the far end of the room, which was partly covered by a deep balcony, which had the bed and bathroom on it.

The sterling silverware was, like everything else, made up with the initial *D*.

A string running across the narrow street rang a bell in the restaurant across the way, and we then had our meals in a comfortable corner.

The linen was also initialed *D*. It is still there. It has never been used, nor have the crystal glasses, nor the bed or bathroom. Just once, D. expressed a desire to spend the night in "her" house. It was winter. I phoned the restaurateur across the way to have a fire built in the fireplace. When we got there, in the dark, the firemen had the street roped off. The fire had been built too high, and the fireplace as well as part of the ceiling had been destroyed.

I left instructions to have everything restored. That was done, I am told. I never went back there with D. I have no idea whether, in the sixteen years since we separated, she ever again visited that little house furnished with such love. I doubt it, in spite of all the *D*s.

I am writing all of this for you, my children. You may conclude that your father was a perfect imbecile.

Perhaps just a trusting soul. At any rate, a stubborn one.

And one who suffered a great, great deal, without your knowing it.

51

My children,

It is for the four of you—as much for you, my big Marc, who will soon be leaving us, as for Johnny and Marie-Jo, and for Pierre too, who will be born in 1959—that yesterday I set myself the task of describing the château which, for all of you, played a more or less important role in your lives.

The layout, each one's place within it, was not without influence on the recollections you all have of it. It may also have had just as great an influence on a drama in the making, due to explode one day, which I tried so hard, not always successfully, to keep you out of.

Above all, do not see in the pages I have written or those I will yet write the slightest acrimony toward anyone whatsoever. My motto, if indeed I have one, has been repeated often enough, and I have always tried to live up to it. It is the one I lend to my old Maigret, who in more than one way is like me: "To understand, not to judge."

So, if I am writing these memoirs gropingly, without anger, without hatred, without contempt, it is in an effort better to understand what happened, which at this time I was still only having a presentiment of.

The Château d'Echandens, neither beautiful nor ugly, played a part in all our lives. I had to give it its place.

When we moved in, in July 1957, you, Marc, were eighteen, and your life as a man, as well as your career, would be decided here. You were still thinking, as you wrote to me in a long letter full of lucidity and affection, of specializing in the natural sciences, majoring in them at the University of Lausanne, where you had enrolled.

Even as a young boy, you had been very close to nature. Do you remember the mushrooms at Saint-Mesmin-le-Vieux that you went picking with me in the cold and the dew? Do you remember your blindworm, which you kept in your pocket and which stayed all night on the stone kitchen doorstep waiting for you, the huge turkey, as heavy as you, that you used to try to lift in your arms?

Or your horse in Arizona, the trout you picked up in your hands without scaring them away, as if they understood all you wanted to do was to pet their soft, light-colored bellies before returning them to the current of our streams? The water turtles you collected, including the snappers that might easily have bitten one of your fingers off? The snakes you asked me to get from tropical regions?

You seemed to be directly plugged in to nature, which gave your eyes, so light in your tanned face, an often dreamy expression, as if, as one of your teachers at Hotchkiss put it, you suddenly escaped the classroom to gambol somewhere far away.

The sea attracted you too, and underwater diving, the bottoms you discovered teeming with life among the algae and the rocks. Natural history to you really meant oceanography, the study and discovery of a wonderful world that film and television had not yet made common.

In order to be ready for the university, you applied yourself, at the Ecole Lemania, deep within the verdure of Montbenon Park in Lausanne, to mathematics, physics, and chemistry, which were the *sine qua non* of the course of study you dreamed of following. An austere and forbidding entryway to the place of your dreams you were so eager to enter.

I watched you rush off in the car that was too small for you, at odd hours, to take extra private lessons.

You were enthusiastic by nature, but I saw your brow darken as the weeks and months went by. Your mood was a worry to me, your apathy, the thousand little ailments that bothered you.

I would discuss this with your mother when she stayed at a hotel not far from the château or came to visit you through that side door. Tigy had noticed the same things and was as worried about them as I.

I tried in vain to get you to open up to me, knowing you were always afraid of hurting or disappointing me. Then, in 1959, I discussed it with a neurologist friend.

He suggested I send you to see him, not during his office hours, but in the evening, when he watched soccer games on TV.

You went to see him several times. You chatted over a bottle of beer. Little by little, you confided in him, and one day he called and asked me to spend an evening with him too.

He told me right away: "I finally know what's bothering your son. Math and what he calls 'exact sciences' have become anathema to him. . . ."

I have had some such suspicion for a long time but anxiously await the rest of what he has to say.

"Your son Marc, who is truly devoted to you, does not want anything in the world to make you feel bad. He's gotten it through his head that you are set on his getting a university degree. . . ."

Poor Marc! Haven't you yet understood that I never had any ambition, for myself or, even more, for my children? Had you told me you wanted to become a plumber, I would in no way have been disappointed.

But what followed was still to surprise me, for nothing up to then had pointed me toward the path of truth.

"Marc's dream is to get into films. . . ."

I first thought he meant as an actor, because you are certainly handsome enough to be a leading man.

"He wants to be a director, but doesn't dare tell you!"

You have a poet's soul, a boundless imagination.

"Are you disappointed, Simenon?" the doctor asked.

"Delighted, on the contrary. First thing tomorrow, I'll phone my old friend Renoir, who just happens to be in Paris at the moment." Jean Renoir, a dreamer, a poet himself, who, according to everyone, revolutionized the cinema.

"You're not angry? You don't hold it against me?" you ask.

"I'll call Jean tomorrow morning. He's supposed to be starting a new picture soon. . . ."

And you snap out of being the fellow you had recently been. I phone Paris, get Jean. His good, warm voice reassures me in turn.

"I'll take him on immediately as an interne. In two days, I'm beginning to shoot *Le Déjeuner sur l'herbe* at Les Colettes, my father's property. I'll have to have your son here tomorrow morning, because, even to take on an interne, there are all kinds of goddamned formalities to go through."

"He'll be there."

"Can he ride a motorcycle a little? That may sound like an idiotic question, but there are a lot of cycles in the picture, and my assistants don't know the first thing about them. As for me, can you picture me on a motorcycle?"

Despite which, Renoir had fought as an aviator in World War I and for many years crisscrossed France in a racing Bugatti.

Marc, drunk with joy, packs while Aitken reserves a sleeper for him on the night train.

Two weeks later, Jean phones me from Les Colettes.

"You know that your son is a terrific guy? For one important scene, I needed thirty motorcycle daredevils in leather jackets, each one with his girl hanging on to his shoulders. I thought it would take days to find that many. Marc went down to Cannes and came right back with thirty guys on cycles and just as many girls. . . ."

427

Why not? All your pals and their girl friends, Marc, ready to appear as extras just for the fun of it.

"Another time," Jean goes on, "I needed a strong wind, and of course it was the quietest day you could imagine. You know how, in the cinematograph [Renoir doesn't use the word "cinema," which he finds barbaric], we make storms?"

"With an airplane engine and propeller?"

"Marc took our truck, and in a few hours he was back with an airplane engine that could do the job."

Later, Renoir assured me: "You can have confidence in him. One year as an interne, a few years as third, second, then first assistant, and he'll be ready to do things on his own."

The rest is up to you, my Marc. I just wanted to speak to you about your youth and your first start in the business.

What matters to me is that your little house in the forest of Rambouillet is today a haven for all sorts of animals, often the least expected ones, and that on vacations in Corsica or at your mother's at Nieul, you do expert deep-sea diving.

That you shoot films, with ups and downs, like all film makers today . . .

That you continue dreaming and still have your poet's soul . . .

When we moved into Echandens, where we anticipated staying for a year, we got there as summer began, at the start of summer vacation. That year we didn't go anywhere, and I tried to show you all the countryside. First of all, Johnny and Marie-Jo, by driving you each week to Morges, the closest town, on market days, that is, Wednesdays and Saturdays.

Is it because my mother used to take me to market, as soon as I was big enough to stand on my own feet, that all my life I have retained a passion for seeing the peasant men and women seated behind their baskets of vegetables and fruit? Because of the bright or tender colors of everything that comes from vegetable gardens or fruit orchards, the smells changing at every step, the voices, the sounds of all kinds, and in some marketplaces the cackling of chickens, the crowing of a cock, the oinking of little pink pigs?

Wherever I have gone in the world, whether in the French countryside, the heart of Africa, the Pacific islands, Asia, or the northern countries, I have always eagerly rushed to the marketplaces, which have different colorings, more or less variegated according to the latitude, with other sounds and new kinds of vegetables and fruit.

The market at Morges, concentrated in a very wide street flanked by very old houses, including some of historical interest, delighted me, especially the song of its stone-and-bronze fountain right in the middle.

The three of us go there, or sometimes just one of you with me, in the big Land-Rover loaded down with empty baskets. It is still possible to park right in the middle of the market, and we mingle with the crowd, little by little filling the baskets.

Johnny is a big eater; his appetite is as big as, or bigger than, Marc's at his age. As for Marie-Jo, her almost transparent eyes come to rest on the young or wrinkled faces of the peasant women or truck farmers; she is especially attracted by the multicolored bouquets of flowers, which she will often paint, right up to the end of her young life.

I buy some flowers, the most brightly colored ones, which she prefers, and baskets follow baskets, for there are a lot of us in the house, and flowers bring cheer to all the bedrooms.

The long, odorful grocery store, coffee, spices, bags of rice and dried vegetables lined up near the counter . . .

Finally the Italian shop, its Parma hams, ravioli, sausages, salamis . . .

"Say, Dad, can I buy . . . ?"

Of course! Cakes, and even raisin bread, which D. likes. I have no recollection of her ever having been to a market with us. Wasn't she too busy with business, my business? At none do I visualize her.

And at last, the corner café, no longer in existence, where the peasant women and truck farmers went to have a drink or a bite, the men drinking the local white wine in a *trois décis* (about seven ounces). Everyone talks loudly, calling to one another from table to table, with the slightly dragging local accent that both of you, Johnny and Marie-Jo, take on for quite a while from playing with our young neighbors, Anne and Charlie.

Do you have at least a few recollections of the market at Morges, and, later, the one at Lausanne that covered Place de la Riponne, then flowed into a narrow street as far as the city hall, where it broadened, narrowed again, passed above Rue Centrale to climb the steep grade of Saint-François and, swinging to the left, invaded elegant Rue de Bourg?

The house nearest to our château, almost touching the outbuildings, is the large Moinat farmhouse, the stables and barn of which face our windows.

The boy, Charlie, tall and timid, apparently lazy, but only apparently, is Johnny's age. Anne, livelier and more active, will become Marie-Jo's best friend, inseparable from her. And soon all four of you are carrying on together in the playroom, the garden, the outbuildings.

Marie-Jo is the first unconsciously to copy the piquant Vaudois accent of her playmate.

Between Johnny and Charlie, the bonds are different. I won't make you angry, Johnny mine, by saying that, while deep within you you are and will remain a sensitive fellow, the boy you were then had a certain tendency to want to show his authority. You are the one who most often decides what game you will play. You get your way some of the time. Other times, without saying a word, without putting up a kick, Charlie goes off alone into the playroom and buries his nose in a book.

Marie-Jo likes to be well dressed, and I am even more concerned with what she wears. I often drive her to Rue de Bourg, where there is a shop selling only children's clothes and underwear. I love light-colored dresses, especially white and flowered ones, and at this time you like them too. I let you choose. With a sure instinct, you pick out the dresses that become you. The woman who owns the shop, originally Belgian, is always amazed at the quickness of your decisions and the dependability of your choices.

You, Johnny, refuse to try on any clothes, and we often have to alter at home what we have bought you.

On that same Rue de Bourg there is a store one might without exaggeration call a paradise for children, big and small, with everything from stuffed animals to the most highly perfected electric trains. This is where, before Christmas, we go to pick out your presents and the ones for your friends the Moinat children.

This also is where Marie-Jo discovers her interest in the theater, which will remain with her all her life. It starts by her having Punch-and-Judy-like characters, moved by putting one's hand inside, as into a glove. There are not only men and women, cops and robbers, but also animals of all kinds, which come to life as one moves one's fingers. You keep entertained for hours, Anne and you, my little girl, by making these characters perform as you give them improvised dialogue.

Which gives me the idea, for Christmas, to ask the decorator of the municipal theater to build a plywood Punch and Judy show just like the one on the Champs-Elysées, with its red curtain and three or four different stage sets: a farmhouse room where the farmer and his wife argue, a tropical forest with talking lions, giraffes, elephants, and I don't know what else.

These characters, these animals were stored on the shelves of an *étagère* in the playroom, and the two girls, probably with their brothers' connivance, send us an invitation to "a show to be given at 3 o'clock in the playroom of the Château of Echandens." The Moinat parents and grandparents, extremely nice people, have received the same invitation, as have all of our help.

We hear a lot of noise and commotion that morning, at the end of the second-floor hall. At three, everyone is there, intrigued. At the door, Anne solemnly checks the invitations, which people were instructed to bring.

Marie-Jo, as an usherette, dressed in black cotton, a white cap on her head, seats everyone in rows of chairs assembled from all over the place. "This way, sir. The second seat from the end, please."

Once everyone is seated, the lights go out, and everything is dark because the curtain is closed; Johnny and Charlie are working the switch.

The curtain opens on the farm set, lighted by a spot.

"Ladies and gentlemen," says Marie-Jo's voice from where she is hidden with Anne beneath the stage. "The show we are privileged to present has been staged by Anne Moinat and Marie-Jo Simenon. We will begin with a play entitled *The Farmer and His Wife*."

The characters come in from the wings, husband on one side, wife on the other, and the girls improvise a domestic scene which, fortunately, ends with a kiss.

The show goes on that way for almost an hour, including an intermission during which the two girls go up and down the aisle calling "Lemonade . . . Coca-Cola . . . Five centimes. . . ."

Was that our first or second year at Echandens? No matter. Those are the images that so clearly come back to my mind.

Like the one of that steep little street, between gardens full of trees, where one can barely make out the little private school called "Les Lutins" (The Brownies). Public-education rules vary from country to country, and in some countries change with each new administration. In Switzerland, there are private and public schools for children ages four to ten. At ten, children take an entrance examination for a *collège* (or high school), to allow them to take the next six years, channeled to Latin-Greek or to mathematics. After which, the Gymnasium, if they intend to continue higher studies, for two or three years, to complete their *baccalauréat* and be recognized as federally of age.

Johnny and Marie-Jo spend a few weeks at Les Lutins, and my only reason for taking them out is how difficult it is to park a car on that steep little street to wait for school to let out. So both switch to the Ecole Cadichon, run by a mother and daughter.

Johnny is an attentive, brilliant student, while Marie-Jo just stands up whenever she feels like it, to ask a question or to go and talk to some other pupil. Which does not keep her from getting excellent marks, and her drawings are always featured when the parents visit for the distribution of prizes.

The piano bought by chance at an auction has had the effect I secretly hoped. Marie-Jo soon says: "Dad, I'd like to take piano lessons."

Aitken finds a lady who gives lessons at the pupils' homes. For several months, everything is fine, but, for some reason unknown to me, you, my daughter, apparently took a dislike to her. "I don't want to take any more piano lessons. I don't like that lady."

This reminds me of my own childhood. My parents had bought me a violin my own size and were having me take lessons from a teacher who lived in the upper part of the city, near the cemetery. My violin had no case, and we were not rich. I carried it in a cardboard box that was too short for the bow, so that one end of it stuck out.

All I could make, of course, like all beginning fiddlers, were sounds that were reminiscent of an animal being tortured. As for the fingers of my left hand, they were bloody from pressing down on the strings.

But neither one of these reasons was what prompted my decision. My sickly teacher had such bad breath that it made me very uncomfortable, especially since, like most people with that ailment, he spoke to me eyeball to eyeball.

"I don't want to study the violin anymore, Mother!"

I never told them why. Instead, I took harmony lessons from a very ugly young lady, and stuck with it for a year.

During fishing season, while D. is "working," or, rather, "killing myself with work," as she tells anyone willing to listen, I drive Johnny and Marie-Jo to the port of Morges, where we get some earthworms at a little green shack. We each have a rod and lines. We venture out on the jetty, and all three of us start fishing in the waters of the lake, then still crystal clear.

Johnny is first to bring in a bleak, but won't take it off the hook, any more than he ever baits his own hook. He fishes with sustained attention, the way he does everything, and he is the one who gets the biggest catch.

Marie-Jo gets discouraged at first, but is not long in getting the knack of it, so that we come back with a creel loaded with silvery fish. The children insist on having them for lunch, to the great displeasure of Boule, who has to clean and prepare "all those little animals," as she calls them.

I have a chance to buy a motorboat, and Johnny and I for a time go in heavily for more serious fishing, using lines with four hooks on them. We sometimes bring up as many as three pink-tinted fish at once. In half an hour we can bag more than two pounds of fish, and, coming in shortly before a meal, Johnny insists on having a saffron soup with tiny noodles, such as they make in the Midi.

Each diversion lasts just about one season. Behind the outbuildings, our garden narrows, encroached on by plane trees that remind me of Provence. Part of the ground is strewn with cinders and makes an excellent field for *boules*. I buy boules for the whole family, shiny chrome ones, the ones called "integrals," and we all take a great interest in the game, which even D. sometimes joins in.

I hope, children, that you were happy at Echandens, as happy as I was with you. I hope too that the Christmases gave joy to both of you.

A tall tree would be set up in your playroom, and on Christmas Eve you helped me decorate it with little electric lights, balls of gold, silver, red, and yellow colors, and garlands of make-believe snow.

In my childhood, we didn't celebrate Christmas, but December 6, St. Nicholas's Day, which was the children's celebration. The only festivities on December 25 were great piles of pancakes or crêpes, which we powdered profusely with sugar before gobbling them up.

Alas, Christmas became a nightmare for me. Your mother insisted on wrapping up every present, in the American way, the largest as well as the smallest, a rocking horse as well as a paintbox, in all sorts of colored papers, which she then tied up with ribbons, of which I had to keep ample supplies on hand.

As soon as you are in bed, D. gets to work, but not without first celebrating Christmas with her secretaries over a fair number of glasses of whiskey.

It is not easy to wrap a rocking horse or a carpenter's bench in tissue paper. This is just a personal feeling, but I consider all such wrapping superfluous, and I still like to see the toys or other gifts as they are, lined up beneath the tree.

The hours go by with increasing irritation. D. calms hers with the bottle, and, because she doesn't like to drink alone—"it just isn't the thing to do"—I have to keep her company.

By midnight, we are exchanging increasingly sharp words. How many packages remain to be wrapped? I try to count them; D. gets impatient at my impatience, I at hers, which only makes us drink some more.

It is nearly always four in the morning by the time we get to bed. It sometimes happens that we don't get to bed at all, but take baths, hers hot, mine a cold shower, before donning our robes and going to wake you.

There are little Christmas trees in your bedrooms too, and in the living room and kitchen.

I am overlooking one detail. All of our household help goes to midnight Mass on Christmas Eve, and D. sets out for them on the kitchen table a complete buffet supper, with champagne glasses, the bottle cooling in the refrigerator. The table is decorated, and a sprig of holly hangs from the ceiling.

When they return from church, we go down to the kitchen to drink a toast to Father Christmas. It is sometimes a happy occasion. But only infrequently, if I can trust my own and the memories of those who took part in these "ceremonies."

Then back to the playroom. Golden paper, silver paper, tissue paper, ribbons and strings.

I think that on some of those nights I went up to bed alone without waiting for all the packages to be wrapped. So we are a little pale, a little vague when we finally come and kiss each of you in turn in your beds, from which you hop out in your pajamas to rush to the tree.

"Merry Christmas!"

"Merry Christmas!"

Unfortunately, D. has been drinking more and more, and far be it from me to mention it to her. Doctors have long since recognized that alcoholism is not a vice, but an illness, which has to be treated like any other and has nothing shameful about it.

I used to drink too, in the U.S. and Canada. True, I drank only in fits and starts, because I forced myself to abstinence when I was preparing, writing, or revising a novel. With an average of five or six novels a year, how many weeks did that leave in which I could indulge? Besides, I almost always know when to stop, and to go and sleep it off.

D., unfortunately, can't do that. I remember one evening when we had to put her to bed in a pitiful state, and between fits of vomiting, she kept saying: "It's because Cocteau died. . . ."

I was an old friend of Jean's, and liked him a great deal. His death had affected me, to be sure, but not to the point of driving me to drink.

I have already said that, even in the earliest days in New York, I wanted to cure her. Cure her of herself. Cure her of the need, which went back to her youth, to be someone other than who she was. Cure her of her need to shine, which had led her brothers to nickname her the Diva, and which I could see gradually turning into a need to dominate.

This accounted, on the one hand, for her feverish pursuit of contacts with important people, who made her seem important in her own eyes; and, on the other hand, the opposite, the need to surround herself with those she considered her inferiors.

Need for prestige, need to dominate: she was suffering, I am convinced, from this vicious circle, which enclosed her, and the more she suffered, the more she was tempted to drink.

One evening when I had gone to bed early, because I had had a little too much to drink, she found me snoring, with my mouth open. Her reaction was to go and summon the whole household staff and lead that unwilling parade into our bedroom, where, pointing at me with scorn, she said: "Just look at your boss!"

I suppose that that night, like so many others, she was even drunker than I.

I do not condemn her, children, and you must not condemn her either. Nor me, who so fiercely remained attached to the hope of curing her.

52

It is not by chance that, when I started writing these memoirs, it was in relation to the houses I had lived in that my recollections spontaneously fell into place in my mind, with clear images of their walls, their colors, and their surroundings.

Echandens is as important a stage as New York or Canada, but of a quite different climate, for, as in any human life, there were more or less sunny periods as well as others that were dark and stormy.

What was Echandens to me? In sum, I was leading several kinds of lives there. First, the warm, intimate, exalting one with you, my young children, of which I have comforting, sweet images. Two of them come back, helping to lighten the threatening sky of those years. Both have to do with Johnny.

We used to have dinner at six, and most often D., dragging out as long as possible her afternoons in the office, would not be with us. The three of us were then noisily happy, under the amused eyes of young Yole, who, standing near the service hatch in the black uniform D. had decreed for her staff, watched for the moment to bring on the next course.

Marie-Jo would then go up to her room to do her homework, because she made it a point to be at the head of her class and her bedtime was eight-thirty.

Then, Johnny mine, from eight to eight-thirty, we had our moment of intimacy, for you always wanted to watch the TV news with me.

The screen was built into a monumental old piece of furniture, a church piece decorated with cherubs, which also contained our record player, two loudspeakers, and the records.

Every evening, as you were about to take your seat on a chair next to my armchair, my imperious Johnny, as I sometimes called you, you would hesitate. "Is it okay, Dad? You're not too tired?"

We understood one another. Your favorite spot was on my lap. Often, you would whisper, even more shyly, "Don't you want to smoke a cigar?"

I am exclusively a pipe smoker, but there was always, in my office next door, a box of Havanas for visitors. I always said yes to you, and your pleasure at smelling the cigar smoke more than made up for my distaste at having to smoke them. News of all kinds interested you, including political news, and you would sometimes ask me in a subdued tone: "Just what did De Gaulle mean?"

The first times, I answered. One evening, I explained to you that, while I was answering, we missed some interesting things. "Take a pad and pencil. Make a short note of your questions and ask me after the broadcast."

Which you thereafter did. After all, Johnny, you are sensitive, despite your uncontrolled outbursts. After ten minutes or so, you would say, "I'm afraid I'm too heavy on your lap."

"You can stay."

However, a little later, you slipped furtively onto your chair. Do you remember that, my sweet and violent Johnny? For often, even at the dinner table, you had sudden fits of temper. Then you would get up and run out to pace the hall as you furiously gave vent to your revolt.

You never apologized then. That well-known Simenon reserve in you too! But in my bedroom, well after I had already said good night to you, I would hear a slight scratching of paper. It was you, I knew, slipping a note under my door to apologize with a humility and tenderness no one would have believed you had in you. I kept those precious notes, some of them very moving, which reveal the real Johnny.

Another recollection. You often go and play in the drying room, on the other side of the courtyard. You are all in the habit of hiding there, the two girls, Charlie, and you. One afternoon, I see a slight stream of smoke coming out of the partly opened door. I climb the stair without making too much noise and find Charlie and you hiding lighted cigarettes behind your backs.

That reminds me of Marc and the smoke that came up from a bush at Shadow Rock Farm. Here, I am seized with fear, because what is called "the spreadery" has in it cardboard boxes, wooden crates, and all kinds of other inflammable things.

For all my fear, I take the same attitude and use the same words as I did with Marc. "Don't hide your cigarettes, boys. I won't keep you from smoking, except here, where it's just too dangerous."

I don't think that, as with Marc earlier, you went on smoking for long, because it was no longer a forbidden game. This incident was useful in reminding me of the risk of fires. The château is old, the floors creak underfoot, and it has a lot of woodwork. The only way to get to the upper floors or out of them is by way of the corkscrew stone stairway, which could quickly turn into a dangerous chimney.

And we all slept on the third floor, the help up above. I looked the place over from a new angle. The main floor, very high-ceilinged, has a terrace above that runs all along the west side. Unfortunately, one could not jump from it without breaking some bones on the flagstones of the peristyle. From the third floor, on the other hand, if a mattress were dropped from the terrace, it would not be too dangerous to jump, nor would it be from the help's rooms.

In haste, as if there were imminent danger, I order a rope ladder, with strong hooks on it to catch on the lip of the terrace. This roll-up ladder was thereafter always at hand, doing away with my fears for the household.

I felt my relationship with D. was deteriorating little by little, with unexpected storms, followed by calms, and periods of grayness heavy with impending threat.

I do not feel I have the courage to go into that at the moment, and I would never have discussed this subject were it not to have had such dramatic consequences for all of us, especially for the person who, I confess, is dearest to me, my little Marie-Jo, still then laughing and overflowing with life.

Another aspect of my life was the profession I had selected when still an adolescent, without realizing that, whereas it afforded me the pleasure of writing, it also entailed what I considered to be duties. I never had any ambition to "succeed in a career," and was the first to be amazed by the way the Maigrets took off and, especially, everything that grew out of that.

This success did not go to my head, did not change any of my feelings, or my opinions about people or society. I took advantage of it, because it allowed me to travel around the world and to rub up against the life styles of practically all peoples, with an always more pressing need to discover the human being, without adornment, without masks, what I have called the "naked human being,"as he or she everywhere is by nature.

I am not prideful enough to suggest I found him. I feel that, in the final analysis, if my readers in both Americas, Japan, the Indies, the Near East, not to mention the various ethnic groups of Europe, read me in their own languages, it shows that they must recognize my characters to a greater or lesser extent, otherwise they would not be interested, since my novels rarely tell gripping stories.

The success that has been mine has imposed obligations. I have become, quite unknowingly, a public man, and I consider that I owe my readers certain rights, as do politicians and artists.

I remember my painful disappointments as a newspaperman when some personage I was sent to interview slammed the door in my face. So it is not out of vainglory, but out of humility, that I force myself, sometimes even when I am in need of being alone, to open my door to newspaper reporters, radio and television interviewers, and the numerous students who depend on the theses they have decided to do about me to give them access to their careers.

I never complain of the time they take up, and even though they often infringe on my private life and keep me from traveling as I would wish, even though for forty years and more they have been invading my various homes, I offer them a welcome and sometimes, to their amazement, answer their questions with a sincerity that approaches candor.

I remember one of them, in London, a nice, very cultured fellow, who was interviewing me in my suite at the Savoy and who, at the end of a long taping, seemed, as he was leaving, to be embarrassed.

He was one of the leading writers for the *Daily Express*, which I had read for years, even though far from agreeing with its conservative viewpoint. I learned only much later that Lord Beaverbrook, its owner, was one of my devoted readers.

"I hesitate to ask you a question you may find indelicate . . ."

"I'll answer it as I did the others, just as frankly."

He didn't seem to believe me, but got it out: "Mister Simenon, do you like yourself?"

My brief reply was picked up by the press the world over. I even find it reappearing in some biographies about me. It was: "I hate myself."

He did not dare ask me why, so I will answer that today.

I hate myself because of, or, more precisely, I am a little ashamed of, the life that success has forced me to lead. I got used to luxury hotels and their conveniences. As for the household staff who, more and more numerous, surrounded me for so long, they also were a consequence of my public life, affording me the isolation necessary to my work.

From adolescence, from childhood, I have had a taste for fine materials, since there were never any around me then, but I do not consider cherry or maple a luxury, any more than iron wrought on an anvil, which for a while I fashioned with delight at La Richardière.

I love fine porcelain more than plain, and collected it, until all my old dishes from Nevers, Marans, and elsewhere, were destroyed, in the cesspool in which one of my friends had stored them for safety. And by the only bomb that was dropped on the whole island of Porquerolles!

Echandens did not isolate me, despite its distance from major capitals, any more than had my previous residences. Between novels, reporters came by at a rate often of two or three a week, TV crews, from everywhere, took possession of the château with their cumbersome instruments and their six to ten technicians.

At that time, television still required the very bright lighting of what were called "big tubs," those monstrous spotlights that my visitors rented from a specialized firm in Zurich. Our current was not up to such demands, and on each occasion Aitken had to phone the electric company to send men to install thick cables, which crossed the road and came over the roofs.

Some telecasts didn't take more than a day, but those were the exceptions. The BBC, which is perfectionist, required a whole week to get an hour-and-a-half show.

Johnny and Marie-Jo liked to sit down in a corner, motionless, silent, during the shooting, of which they took in every last detail.

Speaking of the BBC reminds me of an amusing incident. I was talking, answering a question, about things I liked, in my little office in the turret that was like a monk's cell. My desk was an old Spanish-style table, and in a corner there was a heavy medieval table, which I called my workbench, because I typed my novels on it, facing a picture of my father.

So, I am talking about wood. They have me pat my workbench. Then the producer remembers that big piece of furniture with the cherubs in the living room and has his tubs moved in there. Wouldn't the cherubs be more photogenic, more meaningful, as these gentlemen put it, than my unornamented workbench?

I pat it. I speak of wrought iron, and here we are out on the terrace, where I have to go into ecstasies about its balustrade.

And it happens I even mention manure, confessing that sometimes, when out for a walk, I will stop in front of the manure pile alongside a farmhouse. It's true. In memory of the manure I used to pitchfork away when I was doing my military service, of the warm smell of the stables that I owned later on. Isn't manure too a living material, rich in color, glittering under the sun? Well, nothing will do but that I show them, almost a mile away, a farmhouse near a fine manure pile, and we all go over there with bag and baggage, to get a few seconds on film.

I have mentioned the attraction of markets. I had to go walking with a basket on my arm through the one at Morges, followed by a boom from the end of which hung a mike, while the cameraman walked backward in front of me. I bought some vegetables, fruit. And the good old country-women who knew me had a hard time keeping a straight face. Under the eye of the TV camera, I also had to go to the corner café and have a cup of coffee among the truck farmers.

Crews came from France, Germany, Denmark, Holland, Italy. The Italian crew was the most numerous and most joyful. Naturally, on each of these occasions we set out drinks, because the heat of the spotlights had a parching effect on the throat.

D. stayed away from the shooting sessions, and did not come along when we went on location. She was ostensibly at work with her two secretaries. But once the shooting was over, she again became the lady of the house and presided over the farewell libations.

The day the Italians were there, did she only "work"? At any rate, she is exceptionally cheerful and voluble among the exuberant Italians. The cars and trucks are waiting for them out in the courtyard, and time and again they look at their watches. She goes right on refilling the glasses, including her own. When finally we go down, night has fallen, and the courtyard has no other illumination than the two (wrought iron!) lanterns on either side of the doorway.

Then I see her raise her skirt high and, in front of my speechless guests, dance a very devil of a French cancan. Aitken stayed with her, perhaps as a precaution, and she was able tactfully to maneuver D. back into the house.

Incidentally, Canadian TV was there several times too, because they present their own series of Maigrets, with actors from Montreal.

We entertain a great deal at lunch, at dinner, for friends and my publishers from different countries. My old friend and French publisher Sven Nielsen comes to visit once or twice with his charming wife, Lolette. Sven always talks about contracts with me personally. I don't say "irons out," because there was never occasion, during all those years, to iron anything out, even less to take umbrage at anything, between Sven and me. Now that he is dead, his son, who has succeeded him, has my affection and faithfulness just as his father did.

One detail will explain why I never had any complications with my publishers. Many writers consider all publishers to be thieves. I never did. However, while I attach no undue importance to money, I do insist that each one get what he is entitled to, both publisher and author. I often made hard demands, but I made sure that not one of my publishers—and, counting textbooks, book clubs, paperbacks, collected works, there are almost a hundred and fifty of them—ever lost one cent on my account.

When, in 1930, old Arthème Fayard decided to start a collection of Maigret books, I went to the best sources to find out about paper costs and weights, printing, binding, and shipping costs, photographic covers, and even the percentages of returns.

I arrived at a sales price of six francs per volume, which was halfway between the cheap, so-called dime, novels, and the "literary" ones.

"A bad figure," Fayard explained to me. "People don't like to put out a five-franc bill and then have to take out an extra one-franc coin. You need a round figure. Five francs."

He is much taken aback when I pull a piece of paper from my pocket on which I have all the costs totted up.

"At five francs," I say, "you will have to cut quality on the covers, and, even at that, either give me too small a royalty or lose money yourself."

He studies my figures, shakes his head. "I don't know why you figure five hundred francs for covers. A good cover artist will do them for us for a hundred francs, a fair artist for fifty. Besides, I've never yet seen a book with a photographic cover."

"That's just why I decided to use them."

The Maigrets were the first books to appear with a photograph that was not just on the front cover, but reached around the spine and over the back too.

They were the work of a very fine artist, André Vigneau, who had revolutionized department-store displays with his mannequins, which had lines as stylized as Modigliani's women.

My friend Man Ray did one, for *Un Crime en Hollande (A Crime in Holland)*, using a paper boat and windmill.

I dreamed of seeing these photographs varnished. It was tried, but the methods available at the time made the paper too brittle, whereas today all paperback covers are made glossy by excellent processes.

Among our guests at Echandens and later at Epalinges, there was one whom my children, not unjustifiably, called "Santa Claus." He was my good faithful Dutch publisher, Abs Bruna, one of the greatest and most daring publishers in his country. He had published my first Maigrets, as had the Norwegians, right after they came out in France, but until our return from the United States our only contacts had been by letter.

He used to come see us at least once a year, sometimes several times a year, and the greatest joy for this jovial man, overflowing with affection, was giving presents.

Once he brought me a very fine old tobacco jar, in delft ware, which long stood on the top of my bookshelf, and which I still have. He also gave me tiles made of the same earthenware showing old Dutch ships. They have not been manufactured for a long time, and they are of the utmost rarity. The ones Bruna brought had been discovered under a layer of plaster when a house once occupied by a sea captain was being wrecked. Abs had those nine tiles set in a layer of cement so that they make up a whole picture.

As soon as the children saw his black Mercedes in our courtyard, they would shout for joy. The Netherlands Santa Claus was of course bringing heavy boxes full of the chocolate specialties of his country. Do you remember, children? Those crisp dry cookies that had such a good smell of faraway spices, which they were full of? And the Hopjes, those coffee candies that one can suck on for so long?

I was especially fond of the barely smoked Holland sausages, which gave such a special savor to partridges garnished with cabbage or sauerkraut.

We went to visit Abs, and his whole family, in his fine, peaceful house in Utrecht and in his office near the canal.

One evening, we had as guests a whole convention of pediatricians, who were meeting at Geneva. Another evening . . .

Where did I find the time to write? And to travel besides, now to Paris, now to London, Amsterdam, Brussels, and Liège?

Five novels in 1957, despite moving into the château and a trip to Milan to buy toys for Christmas.

Incidentally, at the time of the Cannes Film Festival that year, at which we were devoted members of the audience, Fabre-Lebret had asked me to head up the jury the next year. I answered that I had never in my life sought any prize, nor had I been the member of any prize-awarding jury.

Toward the end of the year, almost under duress, I was to go back on this line of conduct. A Belgian minister announced to me that in 1958, on the occasion of the Brussels World's Fair, a great film festival would be held. Contrary to the custom at Cannes, the jury would be made up exclusively of Belgians. They had looked for a president well known abroad who spoke fluent English, because American participation was of the essence.

"We could find no one but you. The organizers of the exposition, as well as the government, urgently beg you to accept."

I tried to get out of it, repeating what I had said to Fabre-Lebret.

"Yes, but this time it is Belgium, and you're a Belgian, aren't you?"

That year, I gave a lecture in January at Morges. In February, I wrote *Le Passage de la ligne* (Crossing the Line). In May, I hopped over to Paris with Johnny, I don't remember what for.

Finally, D. and I were in Brussels. She had a star's wardrobe with her. Marioutcha was along, and when we came down from our suite on Boulevard Anspach, she followed behind us, more the theater soubrette than ever, crossed the lobby behind us, carried D.'s handbag and helped her into the car.

A festival during which I drank nothing except Coca-Cola, and was dazzled, if not humiliated, from the very first meeting, by the motion-picture erudition of the jury members over whom I was supposed to preside; they had seen everything, dissected everything, having at their fingertips the whole history of the movies, the records of every director as well as the actors.

The great stars were in attendance: Sophia Loren, with her husband, Carlo Ponti, Silvana Mangano, with her husband, Dino de Laurentiis, and the American stars, including Orson Welles, of whom I made a friend.

Since the men were getting together as a jury to select the best film, why should not their wives do likewise? This idea came to fruition in D.'s mind, and she did not give up until she pulled it off. The wives of my colleagues were nice housewives, very simple, who did not wear evening gowns. But wasn't D. up to getting whatever she wanted? She found a spot, near the bar, where they could get together after each showing, while we locked ourselves in a private room.

On one of the last evenings, King Baudouin was seated in the first row, and someone in his retinue, probably an aide-de-camp, came to whisper a message to me: "His Majesty wishes to meet you after the showing in his salon, which you will find at the end of the corridor on the right."

D. was not mentioned. So I went alone, and found the king, who gave me a gracious welcome, as he did a moment later to Sophia Loren (without her husband), accompanied by a big American male star.

Champagne was served. I noted that the king was bashful, sometimes blushed, and that to my great surprise he did not speak English. Sophia Loren had not yet learned French, nor did the American speak it, so I had to translate. I still don't know whether it was for that reason or because I was president of the jury that I was invited.

Later, D., in her gala gown and chinchilla stole, and I stopped in a sort of working-class pizzeria, near our hotel, which offered a choice of all kinds of appetizing delicatessen. This was not the first time we had made one of these sensational entrances there and stood at the counter eating some kind of sandwich.

I am reminded of the way D. welcomed the chinchilla when I brought it to her. She had chosen the skins at an exclusive furrier's. As is the custom, she had been asked to initial each skin, so she might be assured that the ones she had chosen were the ones actually used. One day, the furrier brings me the stole. Excited, I carry it in to D., still in bed.

She opens the package, sees the fur, turns it over, and frowns. "It's lined! How can I tell whether these skins are the ones I signed?"

I must have been in a sarcastic mood that day and full of courage, because I answered her, in the presence of one of her secretaries: "Oh, you! Won't you ever be satisfied? If you were given God Almighty on a silver platter, you'd still complain that he had a pimple on his nose!"

The festival over, we make a swing down through Cannes; probably to go to Baroni's bootery, the only place, according to D., that can make shoes that fit her. She spends hour after hour there, then we have to get matching handbags and gloves, handbags from Hermès, nowhere else.

It was also Chez Hermès, in Paris, on Faubourg Saint-Honoré, where one day we stopped short in front of a crocodile toilet kit on display by itself in the window, as if it were some precious object. And precious it certainly was. It was, the salesman told us, the twin to one ordered by the queen of England. Wide and long, very heavy, the outside crocodile, with vermeil lock and identification tag.

Inside, bottles of cut crystal, each in its own red-leather-lined space and each with a vermeil lid. Ivory for the brushes and combs, also bordered with vermeil.

I bought it, I confess, to my shame. I would have bought the moon if it had been for sale and if I had felt that in this way I might help her to find her balance.

On the bottle tops, on the tag, on the leather piece ornamenting the cover of heavy gray cloth, the initials *D.S.* were engraved. Despite its weight, she will insist on carrying this prestigious kit herself, even if only to cross the sometimes rather large spaces between airport waiting rooms and planes.

We got back to Echandens about June 20. From June 26 to July 3, I write a novel, *Dimanche (Sunday)*, and on July 17 we all leave together, with one additional person, the Lausanne masseuse your mother invited along.

We will stay in Brussels only from July 17 to 24, long enough for you to see the exposition, after which we will board a yacht, rented through Bruna, for a tour of the Netherlands, by way of the Zuyder Zee, Stavoren, the canals and the lakes, the way I had in 1928 and 1929 on board the *Ostrogoth*, with Tigy and Boule.

Marc is along; like you, he is on vacation. I drive you to Place de l'Hôtel-de-Ville, with its old houses roofed with real gold leaf like your mother's bottles. We go there when the flower market is being held, and you vie with one another to see who can eat the most of the famous Brussels waffles that are so light and have whipped cream coming out of every cranny.

What impresses you most at the exposition, after the sputnik at the Russian Pavilion (where you get miniature sputniks made of white metal, which will long remain on your dresser tops), is the village of the Ardennes, specially reconstructed, with real houses into which one can go, real old-time drinking establishments where drinks are served, and villagers in old-time local costumes.

I was not expecting the welcome we received. The village's inhabitants await us at the entrance, the men in high hats, the women in dresses of the last century.

D. and I are shown into a large flowered carriage, you into another, and there are others for the city officials. A costumed brass band walks ahead of us. The village is large, picturesque, and, in the opinion of many, the prize exhibit of the whole exposition.

The villagers throw flowers into our carriages.

I turn around often to see your reactions. Marc is smiling a beatific smile, Johnny is all eyes, and Marie-Jo keeps standing up to clap her hands.

The cortege stops before the old-fashioned city hall, a real city hall, where the mayor and his deputies welcome us with speeches and toasts. Our eyes are all shining, even D.'s; she has been given the red carnations that have become ritual since our trip to Liège six years before.

A fine day, my children, of which I hope that you have a happy recollection. This is my country, your country, welcoming you in this way, cheerfully, in their typical hail-fellow-well-met sort of way.

A pretty Dutch yacht awaits us at Amsterdam. The train takes us there, and I see once again the well-dressed, rich women of a country that in a small way is also mine and whose people I admire as much as I do its landscapes immortalized by Ruysdael.

Before we weigh anchor the next day, Bruna holds a party for us on board the yacht and on the grassy wharf. Weren't you right to call him Santa Claus?

The cruise starts with the crossing of the city by way of the canals, then through the port, where there are hundreds of boats coming and going in all directions.

But how will it end?

53

Our trip, begun by that short stay in Brussels, which was a sort of fireworks and carnival prologue to it, will unfortunately continue in a less colorful and exalting climate, a bitter disappointment to me. Perhaps because I had rejoiced in it too much in advance?

Delighted to be taking you three, my children, as well as D., on this sort of pilgrimage to Friesland, where, from the age of twenty-four to twenty-six, I had spent two of the best years of my life, years that, unbeknownst to me, were to become the springboard of my success, because this was where Maigret was born, without my attaching much importance to the fact at the time.

I had discovered Holland at the helm of my cutter, the *Ostrogoth*, where I played at being a youthful captain, with Tigy and Boule as my crew, doing all the dirty work.

Why is Boule not with us this time and why is D.'s masseuse on board in her stead? There was a time when I still had something to say, when I was almost a real captain. Now, D. is the one who makes the decisions, and I resign myself to them, almost never going against her. Mme B. is, at any rate, a youthful and agreeable quadragenarian, with whom I feel quite at ease.

The entrance to the Zuyder Zee finds us all gathered together under the great white sail, which is swelling beneath a promising sun. The yacht is a *tchalke*, a type of boat made only in Holland, from time immemorial, and seen in the paintings of the oldest Dutch masters. It is shiny, white, with white mainsail and jib, its instruments of highly polished copper. I have forgotten its name, as I have those of the captain and cabin boy, who, in addition to their normal functions, are to prepare our food and make up our cabins.

The breeze sending us along over the small waves will in less than an hour turn into a violent wind, while clouds invade the blue sky and the surface of the water boils up in white swells.

The boat begins to list, to the delight of Marc, who is allowed to take over the wheel, his eyes glued to the compass. The rolling shortly becomes more pronounced, and I can still see a very pale Marie-Jo sitting on her pile of rope, staring straight ahead. D. takes it well, as does Mme B., and Johnny doesn't flinch.

The spray starts spurting up over the bow, and we can no longer see shore. The captain takes the wheel back from the hands of a disappointed Marc.

When we head due north to go toward the tiny port of Stavoren, gateway to Friesland, we are both pitching and rolling, and Marie-Jo, trying to be brave, grits her teeth.

Finally, with a relieved beat of the heart, I see the slim steeple of Stavoren sticking up from the still-gray line of the flat coasts.

I took you to see the wharf guard before whose house the *Ostrogoth* had moored for a whole winter, and we broke the ice around it each morning with a pike. He had two daughters, Aaltje and Beetje, then about Marie-Jo's age, whose picture we find on the mantel, taken with Tigy, Boule, and me. They are both now living in America, married and with children of their own.

Was it a mistake to select this return to a past to which D. was alien? Her mood gets darker as we navigate along the canals where one sometimes sees cows being transported on flatboats from one pasture to another.

We reach Sneek, which, like Venice, has more canals than streets and where the market is held at the edge of the port, alive with craft of all kinds in a smell of oil and a continual hum of motors.

Marc has to leave us here to return to Lausanne, where he has to prepare for exams. I buy fishing rods for everyone, lines with ten or twenty hooks for eeling, to be set at night and pulled up in the morning.

We stay on the canal two or three days, moored to one of the city's wharves, and here you happily take from the water your first Dutch fish. I also bought you sailors' sweaters, for even though it is summer, the temperature here is cool and the showers plentiful.

I have no idea what goes on belowdecks. Sometimes I hear more or less angry voices, but I am too absorbed in the two of you and our fishing to pay much attention. At Echandens too, there are often altercations between your mother and the help.

One day, when we are moored out in the wilderness on the edge of Sneek Lake, I see Mme B. come out, hard put to hold back her tears.

"Monsieur Simenon, I have to leave, and I apologize to you. Madame Simenon asked me along as a guest, not as a maid of all work, which is how it has turned out. I have tried to be patient, but I'm at my wit's end."

As I understand it, the captain refused to clean the cabins and make the beds, or, rather, bunks. Mme B. is not along for that purpose. She is perfectly willing to lend a hand, provided she is not treated as a servant.

I am not King Solomon. It is not up to me to decide. I realize that our fine voyage will be clouded by repeated crises. But I have to let our guest, whom I hold in great esteem, depart. As for the almost daily arguments between your mother and the captain, I try to keep you unaware of them. As if children, even the youngest ones, were not more sensitive than adults to the atmosphere around them! The captain tries to get me to side with him, in an English peppered with words from his own language. D. demands that I hold him to the execution of the services he earlier agreed to.

The captain constantly has a small jug of gin within reach. I don't know what D. drinks, but she is high from early morning on.

I lend her a hand in cleaning up the cabins and bunks, then go back up to fish with you, and I confess that Johnny, who eyes the water as if he were hypnotizing the invisible fish, holds the record for his catch. I can still see the three of us in the pouring rain, sitting in the wet dinghy a rope's length from the yacht, soaked beneath our slickers but persevering in casting our lines.

When we are under way, I take over as tourist guide, pointing out the windmills still operating, the affluent farmhouses behind curtains of poplars to protect them from the winds that blow most of the year. I explain to you that, not here but on board the *Ostrogoth* . . . But my heart isn't in it, not even at Groningen, where the boats line up to pass through the great lock in the heart of the city.

I am drinking too. There are surely some passionate embraces between D. and me in our cabin in the prow, but there are also the angers kept muted because of the presence of the children on the other side of the partition.

Delfzijl has now become a large port, but the city, surrounded by the walls that protect it from the highest tides, is still pink and white, like the toy villages.

I show you children the old abandoned canal in which, on an old barge, I wrote my first Maigret. The statue of Maigret is not yet standing there on the wharf to which that barge had been moored. And later on, when I go back there to unveil it, D. will not be with me.

Some of the people in Delfzijl, mostly old-timers, remember me and my female crew of two in sailor pants, which caused so much talk.

It was at Delfzijl, Johnny mine—don't you remember?—that we caught the most eels, and we finally got tired of eating them. On the return trip, not by way of the Zuyder Zee, but by the Drenthe and the Rhine, we also fished a lot, as if unaware of the daily set-tos between D. and our captain, who was as proud and headstrong as she.

A gray cruise, with many clouds, a few good moments, which we make haste to enjoy. A few swims in lakes with water that was too cold for swimming any length of time. On August 14, we enter the port of Amsterdam, and lose no time in returning to Echandens.

In September, already, I take your mother to Venice, to give her a change of atmosphere. She does not know that city of romantic lovers, which I am familiar with. We come back by way of Cannes, relaxed, and this rather short trip assumes great importance for me, and for you too, my Pierre, who were conceived in one of these two cities, therefore under the sign of joy.

In October, I am due back in Brussels. Another minister has come to see me at Echandens. In the brand-new Palace of Conventions, five or six "messages" are to be launched, if I may use that term, by the representatives of leading countries. Jean Cocteau delivered the French message, a Nobel Prize–winner the one from the U.S.

They insisted that I speak for Belgium, and I finally accepted, without it making me feel that I was the kind of personality who could represent anything. The messages were, in fact, rather solemn lectures, later to be published.

So I wrote what came to be known as *The Novel of Man,* on a serious note. I don't feel very proud, following as I do such illustrious people full of honors.

I have stage fright even though what I am now called on to do is read a prepared text. And one, I add, prepared in one afternoon in my strange little Echandens office with the misshapen ceiling and windows.

I go toward the lectern and read as best I can. I have no sooner been applauded than some officials are dragging me off to a hall where gentlemen and ladies in their finest regalia, including D., are waiting for me to join in a champagne toast. It is true, though, that I myself was wearing the cravat of the Order of the Crown or the Order of Leopold, both of which had been awarded to me.

In New York, the Consul-General of France had made me a chevalier of the Order of the Legion of Honor. I never later wore the insignia of any of these orders, and for that I apologize to those who awarded them to me. I am allergic to decorations and to all titles, whatsoever they may be.

That reminds me of the gala evening at the film festival. An hour before, I had been given a decoration, which I was wearing over my stiff shirt and white tie. It was a cheerful evening, and at my table there were some very pretty stars, with whom I danced. At the end, I lighted my pipe, and a lady of a certain age, and no less certainly stiff-necked, muttered sourly as I went by: "Monsieur Simenon, when one wears the decoration you are wearing, it is not becoming to smoke a pipe."

From June 26 to July 3, between the festival and the Dutch cruise, I typed, as I do all the Maigrets, *Maigret et les Témoins récalcitrants (Maigret and the Reluctant Witnesses)*.

Why the devil, then, in December of that same year, did D. and I go to Florence? We must have known that D. was pregnant. It is true, though, that she did not know that unique city, in which, at every step, one comes across works of the Renaissance, for which it was the cradle. Perhaps out of a desire that, carrying her third child, and my fourth, D. should fill her eyes with dazzling, serene images?

Christmas. Less dramatic than the others, considering that we have the joy of expecting a new baby. Girl or boy? That no longer matters, since I already have a daughter.

In January, I write *La Vieille (The Grandmother)*. In April, *Une confidence de Maigret (Maigret Has Doubts)*, and in July, *Le Veuf (The Widower)*.

The most important event of that half-year, of the whole year, is the birth of Pierre, in the Clinique Montchoisi in Lausanne, under the auspices of our good friend Professor Pierre Dubuis.

The clinic is a pleasant place, with a view of big trees and the lake. My room adjoins D.'s, and I spend all my nights there. The event has been prepared for by a method then new, "childbirth without pain."

For the final three months, D. takes classes given to expectant mothers by one of Dubuis's assistants. A certain number of heavy-bellied women sit in front of a platform, and the obstetrician teaches them to control their breathing, their abdominal muscles, and I don't know what else.

I attend two or three of the classes, as husbands are advised to do, and every evening I supervise as D. does her exercises.

On May 25, Dubuis and I are at D.'s bedside. She, not the least apprehensive about her imminent delivery, tells us Canadian jokes that have us rolling with laughter. She is feeling no pain, even though labor has begun. Dubuis watches its progress, and, toward the middle of the night, can no longer hide some concern. He talks to us about music and painting in his soft, always calm voice. Nevertheless, I can finally feel his nervousness. It is almost two in the morning when he summons the nurses to take D. to the delivery room.

Once again, I get into the white gown and cap and follow the procession.

At times D. trembles, her hands go to her belly, but the doctor is still waiting, which scares me a little. At the birth of each of my children I had the same fear of what they call the "small irons," with which they grasp the child's head to guide it out of the mother's womb. In medical works, I have read too many stories of forceps leaving traces, often irreparable, and I *want* my children to be perfect.

Finally, a sharp cry. D. turns toward Dubuis and starts to say, "I think . . . I think that this time . . ." but she doesn't get to finish. She takes deep breaths and relaxes her muscles as she has practiced doing.

Five minutes later, Pierre of mine, Dubuis is holding you by the feet, head down, like a rabbit, and giving you a little tap on your sticky behind.

It is May 26. I now have four children, three sons ten years apart, and one daughter who shyly slipped in between the last two. You yell. You are perfectly made and for the first time are breathing outside air.

We have a new little car I bought for D., who doesn't like it. I use it for my errands in town, because it is as easy to drive as a bicycle. The black-bodied MG has only two seats, and it is so low one has to bend down to get into it. Once inside, however, it is perfectly comfortable, and incomparably easy to handle.

Are you surprised, Pierre, that I am talking to you about a car when you were just born? That's because I have such a happy memory of my return to Echandens in the very early morning, and the purring of the car.

I go on sleeping at the clinic, and I bring Johnny and Marie-Jo to visit. She is the most impatient to see her "little" brother, because until now she has always been the "little one." She is six. Marc is twenty years older than you, Johnny almost ten. They are as proud as I.

We hire a baby nurse named Suzanne, who is a Belgian. A light Flemish complexion, blue eyes, and remarkable patience and tenderness.

Marie-Jo's first reaction is to want the same kind of striped blue-and-white uniform and the same starched cap as Nana has, and I order them for her.

Your mother cannot nurse you, any more than she could your brother and sister, or Tigy could Marc. Marie-Jo, in her uniform, will be an interested spectator of the sterilization of the bottles and other necessary operations. I can still see her, when you are barely a month old, holding you carefully on her lap and giving you your bottle without taking her attentive eyes off you.

•   •   •

I relax by writing a Maigret, as I do each time that, for one reason or another, I don't feel in a mood to undertake a hard novel. That has been true of all the Maigrets, except the first eighteen, which I wrote at the rate of one per month. I used to write two chapters a day, one in the morning, the other in the afternoon, so that some of those novels were completed in three days.

It was relaxation for me to sit down at my typewriter and renew contact with my good old inspector, knowing no more than he, before the last chapter, how his investigation would turn out.

My five dozen pencils have been talked about, photographed, and filmed, and many is the time I had to put them through my little pencil sharpener for the benefit of the cameras.

A legend did get born, actually based partly on fact, which I now have a chance to clarify. In the United States, at night, on the eve of starting a new novel, I would write the first lines of it, to be my starting point the next morning, at my typewriter. Those few lines, written in pencil on yellow pads, have little by little grown into a page, then two, five, and finally the whole first chapter, in very small handwriting that required extremely sharp points.

This handwritten chapter was thus written in the afternoon or evening, and at six o'clock in the morning I would type it up, often without referring back to the "draft," because when writing directly on the typewriter one has a very different rhythm.

I continued for a long time to use this system. Then I realized that in writing by hand, one is tempted to adorn the phrases, to "make them literary," which goes against my tastes.

Of course, I like to sharpen my pencils, make them very, very sharp; yet, although there are still some left on my desk, as there are near the phone, I have not used them for over fifteen years for anything but to make notes totally unrelated to my novels.

Having said that, let me return to our daily life and our activities. In June, Marc, having finally admitted that films were what he wanted to work at, joined Jean Renoir in Paris and went with him to Cannes. It has a strange effect on me to see his empty bedroom, but it remains his bedroom just the same.

Marie-Jo has begun cautiously wheeling through the pathways of the garden the carriage in which you are sleeping, young Pierre, or gazing at the leaves up above you with eyes that one could take for wonderstruck.

D. has gone back to her Louis XV desk and secretaries and, as in the past, she is always very busy.

. . .

Another parenthesis, like the one for the dozens of pencils. For a long time now, psychologists, psychoanalysts, biographers in different countries, most of whom have never met me, have been trying "to discover the truth" about me through my novels and my characters. But I know myself enough to assert that they have gone wrong, and only one or two of them have reached a half-truth. While I have always gotten inside my characters, as long as I was writing the novel, my characters, if I may say so, have never gotten inside me, or, to put it more exactly, none has ever been a reflection of me.

And it has happened that in painful periods I have written sunny, serene stories, just as in joyful periods I have composed tragic works.

But I have thus been portrayed, quite seriously, in books and university theses which may well survive, which would not be distasteful to me. Is that why now I in turn am trying to find my own "truth" about me?

No matter! A director wanted to make a documentary film on how I went about seeking inspiration and how I wrote. I agreed because it is always hard for me to say no, and in August a crew even larger than those for TV invaded the château. They shoot everywhere, and I follow the directions I am given.

For the introduction, the one-time conservatory, now a library, is turned into a long hallway hung with black drapes upon which are displayed my novels in various languages. D. discovers that the drapes, on which she has seen the hidden silver fringes, were rented from an undertaker's, where they usually deck mortuary chapels. She flies into a rage. The producer bends his head under her indignant protests and hears himself ordered to get those lugubrious draperies out of the house forthwith.

I can understand her rage, but I must confess that to me personally, cloth, wherever it may come from, doesn't affect me one way or the other. They shoot some scenes of me at night, for subtle reasons, on a small road in the canton of Fribourg, where there is a grade crossing past which a train comes around midnight. What I am to do is drive up, stop when the gates come down, use that time to fill my pipe and light it, then watch the train with its lighted compartments and drive on when the gates go back up.

I never ask directors why and obey as passively as a Hollywood extra. Yet that short shot takes no less than two or three hours to set up. Obliging policemen, knowing no more about it than I, undertake to keep other cars out of the shot when the time comes.

There are also shots in a luxurious bathroom of the Beau-Rivage, where my typewriter has been set up, because I have mentioned to some interviewers that when traveling I most often write in the bathroom, the quietest spot in a hotel, where no one will disturb you and there is no telephone.

For the same film, here we are in Milan, in a hotel I always stay at. I have to go to the Piazza del Duomo, nearby, and walk through the glass-paned *galleria* with the marble floors. "In search of inspiration, surreptitiously watching men and women passers-by." Johnny is along and finds it very amusing. We do it over four, five times, all the way from the hotel.

I respect professionals, including the directors who have made films of many of my novels, with actors I admire. But I have seen only two or three of these films.

The reason I see neither films nor TV shows taken from my novels is easy to understand, though no newspaperman—I respect newspapermen too, even those who detest or denigrate me—has understood. When I write a novel, I see my characters and know them down to the slightest detail, including those I never describe. How could a director or an actor reproduce that image, which exists nowhere but inside me? Not through my descriptions, which are always brief and simple, since I want to leave the reader the chance to give free play to his own imagination.

While writing *The Widower*, I do not know there will be a drama that will surprise me. Toward the middle of September, Pierre, a little over three months old, is disquietingly pale and shows few reactions. I can remember one day, in his bedroom, gaily papered with bright fifes and drums, D., with a tragic look, putting him into my arms and saying: "Jo, I beg you, breathe your life into him!"

Did she actually say "your life" or just "some life"? I held the little body tight in my arms, as if I really could bring his vitality back to him. Our pediatrician, worried, calls in some specialists, who spend two hours discussing your case, my Pierre.

I understand what they fear and am ashen listening to them. The hematology professor, the most optimistic of the four or five specialists gathered together, is the only one who does not countenance the possibility of a dread disease.

The Lausanne professor of pediatrics is in San Remo, at a medical convention. We try in vain to reach him. Impossible. So our own pediatrician, bathed in humility, suggests we take you to the pediatric hospital in Geneva.

At dawn, we leave in two cars. Nana is with us in the first one, which I am driving, tremblingly, with D. beside me and Pierre in back on the nurse's lap. Never was precious object handled with such care, my little Pierre. Never did I feel such a sense of responsibility at the wheel. Our pediatrician is following in his car.

Your mother and I are not present when you are examined; again we have to wait.

Professor Fred Bamatter, whom I know well, comes out, his brow wrinkled. He is an open-faced man, who speaks frankly and directly. "Listen," he says, putting his hand on my shoulder, "I can't take your son into my clinic, which is old and poorly equipped and in the process of being remodeled. Besides, I would be infringing on the domain of my colleague in Lausanne . . ."

"But he's away."

"He'll be back tomorrow night. It's a matter of ethics. My advice to you is: go directly to Lyons, where Professor Jeune can call upon a very important hematologist at the Pasteur Institute there. If you agree, I'll phone and ask him to reserve a room for you in an excellent clinic I know there."

I say yes, while trying to hold back sobs. I know what real fear is, my Pierre, the kind that paralyzes you, that leaves you speechless and without reaction. Your mother is no better off than I.

Everything seems to turn to ice inside me, and I ask him in a colorless voice: "Does he have a chance, doctor?"

"Fifty-fifty, *with lots of prayers.*" Those words keep buzzing through my head all the way.

Our Lausanne pediatrician, who had previously treated Johnny and Marie-Jo, insists on coming along. The road from Geneva to Lyons at the time is bad, with lots of turns. I drive like a sleepwalker, and I don't know which of us, your mother or I, suggests that what we ought to do is get a good stiff drink. Good, kind Dr. Roger Walther, pulls up behind us at the door of a country inn. He approves of what we are doing and, even though a teetotaler, takes a drink with us.

We have had no sleep all night. Have we had anything to eat?

I don't remember what time it is when we get to the Carlton, to find a message from Professor Jeune. It gives us an address on the other side of the Rhone.

The mother superior is expecting us and takes us to a completely white room with a crib and a sofa in it. "I will phone the professor."

He gets there a little later, tall and thin, accompanied by an assistant who is none other than the nephew of our friend Martinon. The hematologist joins them shortly. Once again your mother and I have to wait outside.

The three men are a little more optimistic. "It is too soon to make a formal diagnosis. But it seems to us that we can discard the idea of septicemia. We will treat him with cortisone until we get the results of the analyses. In the meantime, there is nothing the two of you can do here. You have to get something to eat. Go on over to your hotel, and come back at six o'clock."

Dr. Walther has lunch with us, a late, silent lunch. He has to head back to Lausanne, where he has patients who need him. Nana has remained at the clinic. Your mother and I, Pierre, hardly dare look at each other. We go up to our suite, where, in each other's arms, standing in the middle of the small sitting room, we are finally able to let our sobs come bursting out.

We were to spend the rest of the month of September, all of October, and part of November in Lyons, very often beside your little hospital crib.

54

My Pierre, yesterday, August 20, 1980, in our little house on Avenue des Figuiers, where, since the beginning of the year, I have been engaged in this work—mysterious to all of you except Teresa—which consists of reconstructing the "film," not so much of my personal life, but of the family and human nucleus that has been formed around me since my dimmest past, yesterday, I say, while I was writing in one of my yellow notebooks, an incident occurred, a phenomenon, rather, that concerns you especially and that I want to tell you about.

You, at the same moment, were busy deep-sea diving, very far from here, almost at the antipodes, in the Seychelles, where you were spending a well-deserved vacation.

The first part of these recollections was written without advance preparation, without chronological outline, since events, international and other, served as reference points, and, besides, the dates in the past were of little importance, my family at the time having been just an embryo.

Later on, I made use of Aitken, who, thanks to the files we keep, including your personal files, children, supplied me with a precise, indisputable chronology, which I consult only as I move forward in my narrative.

For May 1959, I came across a note that elated me: "May 26, birth of Pierre."

Images rushed to my mind, still fresh and clear, expressing my exuberant joy.

Then I went on to Johnny, Marc, Marie-Jo, and other family events. Suddenly, toward the end of the afternoon, I came across a note that made my throat tighten: "End September, October, beginning November, Lyons with Pierre."

And I then went into a nightmare I did not know was so vivid. The barely three-month-old baby, almost inert, whom your mother and I carried all the way to Lyons to save, at any cost.

I not only related that mad trip, I relived it, lived it in the truest sense of the term, to the point that, for an hour at least, sitting before my little desk, I had trouble breathing, and I suffered once again the agonies experienced twenty-one years before. I relived them so sharply that, when I stood up, the last words set down, I was haggard, my face bathed in tears, unable to walk, to talk, until sobs so long held back were finally able to come out.

So, my Pierre, I twice lived through that childhood disease of yours, which you were told about all too often, in alarming terms, and which left painful traces in your memory and caused you worry even recently.

Your medical history, as well as your scholastic file, and the one of your early life, is at your disposal, just as your brothers' and your sister's were made available to them.

So I am resuming today in a different spirit, for now I know the outcome, because it was not long before we were reassured about you.

Your mother and I are in Lyons. Marc is in Paris or "shooting" somewhere in France, and we cannot reach him. Johnny and Marie-Jo are anxiously awaiting our return, and we reassure them the best we can about the health of their "little brother," who already holds such a big place in their lives.

Marie-Jo, although only six, is the one who asks the most questions, being mistrustful, and she is the one it is hardest for us to calm down, since we are only partly calmed ourselves.

The first days, the first week, were the hardest to get through. Morning and evening, your three doctors got together around your little bed, watching for the first favorable signs.

At the very least, that first evening the worst diagnosis, septicemia, had been ruled out; your blood analyses, done in the afternoon, lead to new lines of research. As the Pasteur Institute hematology professor forcefully told us, you are "chock full" of golden staphylococci, which wreak such great ravages in infants. This is of course serious, but hopes of a cure are much better than that terrifying fifty-fifty—with lots of prayers.

Our life in Lyons, where we feel somewhat lost, is getting organized. The clinic, Hôpital Sainte-Eugénie, where you remain with your young nursemaid, is situated at the other end of town, and for a long time we will have to go all the way across it, with all its traffic jams, as many as four times a day.

The sisters at the clinic are registered nurses, and all of them, from start to finish, are as devoted as our doctors.

So, morning and evening, we see your three doctors at the hospital. They prescribe a drastic treatment, which, from the end of the first week, seems to be showing results; you begin to react and your inertia starts to diminish.

What joy once again to see your eyes look at us as if you were trying to give us a message, to announce that little by little you are resuming contact with life!

I am ashamed, at a time when you alone count, to talk to you about myself, my Pierre, about the effects of the shock I experienced. But the day after we arrived, going to a pharmacy nearby, I find that I am walking hesitantly and, suddenly seized by dizziness as I am about to cross an avenue, I remain nailed to the sidewalk, waiting for a crowd to start crossing so that I can slip in among them for protection.

These dizzy spells keep affecting me all the while we stay in Lyons and I will experience them again at Lausanne, until I am sent to Paris, to a big ear specialist, who, after a whole afternoon of complicated experiments, informs me that I am suffering from Ménière's syndrome, a noninfectious internal disease of the ear, in my case the right ear.

If I drag out this parenthesis about myself, Pierre, it is to reassure you, to let you know that you were in no way the cause of this illness, but that the shock I got when your mother put your inert body in my arms and when later I feared so for your life was merely what made it surface.

I will finish this subject off quickly, though I must reassure not only you but also your brothers and your sister about me. At the beginning of our stay in Cannes, in 1955, I had felt a heaviness in my left shoulder and arm, to the point where I could not type, while my throat at the same time seemed to get blocked and I was barely able to speak in a hoarse voice. At first, I thought it was due to a cold. I waited a month before going to see the doctor.

He decided to take me to Nice to consult a neurologist with a good reputation locally. A quarter of an hour later, the neurologist's nurse was placing any number of things in my hair, connected by wires of various colors to an impressive, oversized machine. Half an hour later, my first electroencephalogram was finished.

It took the neurologist a long time to read the many fine lines on the roll of paper that had come out of the machine. He seemed somewhat ill at ease, hesitant, as if he were faced with a problem.

"If I can believe the literature, I think you have what is called 'Coxsackie disease.' I have not yet had occasion to treat a case of it. The best thing would be, if you can get him to see you, for you to consult my professor."

He was able to set up the appointment for me, went to Paris with me, and there, in a delightfully old-fashioned apartment behind the Chamber of Deputies, a little man who seemed almost timid, but who was later to be called in by the Russian government in exceptional circumstances, examined me at length, asked me a great many questions, not in his office, but in a well-furnished living room.

After studying the tape of my EEG and carrying on a muted conversation with his one-time student, he turned to me calmly, reassuring, as if we had come together over a cup of tea, and said: "It's a Coxsackie, all right. It is related to poliomyelitis, but is very mild."

Strangely, in this setting, in front of this simple and reassuring scientist, I felt no concern at all.

"Your symptoms can't be mistaken. I've had occasion, although infrequently, to treat a certain number of cases of it, and recovery has always been total."

"What treatment do I have to follow?" I was afraid I might have to stay in Paris, separated from you children, and was surprised to hear him answer, in a voice as muted as his drawing room: "None at all. Without knowing it, you have come through the critical period, and if you have had no more serious episodes in the past two months, it means that the illness is in regression. So I see no reason to do anything about it."

"Will it last long?"

"A few weeks more, during which your stiffness and your pains, which you tell me have been bearable, will gradually decrease."

"Are there any aftereffects?"

"None that we know of as yet."

I went back to Cannes, where the diagnosis proved correct, for three or four weeks later my voice was practically back to normal and my shoulder no longer hurt.

But enough of my own ailments, about which, my children, you must now be reassured. I have had no more dizzy spells for some years now. They did not keep me from leading a normal if often very agitated life, and writing I don't know how many novels. The dizzy spells went away by themselves when my affected ear almost completely lost its hearing, as I had been told it would.

So, okay, you have a dad who's a bit hard of hearing, which at times can be an advantage. But a dad who, well after his seventy-seventh birthday, still enjoys, except for that darned ear, all of his affective faculties, more actively than ever.

I am alone one night out of two or three, for D. then goes to spell Nana, who needs some rest. What good would I, awkward and anxious, be at the bedside of a sick child? And the nuns have said that the presence of a man on that floor at night would be embarrassing to them, a viewpoint I understand.

Back from vacation, Aitken comes to spend several days each week at Lyons. D. insists on the mail being brought to her, and I read it, making a note of a few words on each letter to sum up the reply.

D. will not go back to Echandens, feeling that she wants to stay with Pierre. We have two other children back there. I trust Boule to take care of them but nevertheless feel a need, in addition to the daily phone calls, to go and see them once a week, traveling by an elderly, lazy train that makes the trip seem endless.

It warms my heart to see you two again, Johnny and Marie-Jo. You are aware of the time when a taxi will bring me from the Lausanne railway station and you watch for me through the little scullery window, waving your arms as soon as the car comes in sight.

Each time, I have better news of your brother for you and don't have to lie or exaggerate his visible improvement day after day. Pierre is reacting more and more vigorously to his treatment.

At Lyons, I go to see him twice a day, and each Sunday I bring the nuns some pastries. As I am not unaware, through my knowledge of convents, that nuns share everything, I make sure there is enough pastry to go around. When I go to Echandens, I always have little presents from Lyons for Johnny and Marie-Jo.

When school starts again, Johnny will be ten, ready for the *collège*. We discuss the matter seriously, as if you were already a man, son.

Since we live in Echandens, you are supposed to attend the district *collège*, the one in Morges. I have had occasion to meet the head and I frankly asked him a delicate question, which he answered with equal frankness.

"It depends on what line of study your young son wants to follow. If he thinks he will opt, at his third year, for the humanities, I would recommend the classical *collège* of Béthusy, in Lausanne, which is more specialized in that than we are. If, on the the other hand . . ."

"He has made his mind up for Latin and Greek."

"In that case, to my great regret, I must honestly recommend Béthusy."

I go to see the head of that school, who has no objection, and that is how it comes about that all three of you—because Pierre will follow the same course as his elder siblings—will study at Béthusy, one after the other, having almost all the same teachers.

For more than two months, my heart is shared between Echandens and Lyons, where we will soon be celebrating, with our three doctors, who by now are our friends, the now-acknowledged certainty of total cure. I select a little restaurant still run by one of the famous old-time "mothers," who "mothered" young French apprentices. A happy dinner, warmed by our friendship, our shared fears, the professional satisfaction of the one group and our gratitude to them.

When Aitken is in Lyons and talking "business" in the sitting room, D. sends me into my bedroom, because my presence bothers her, and I spend long hours there reading and waiting.

The days she is doing duty at the hospital I drive her there in our recently acquired BMW, and, after spending a good bit of time with Pierre, who, if he is not sleeping, now recognizes me and holds his little arms out to me, I return to the hotel, only to go back early in the morning to fetch his mother.

Professor Jeune, knowing of my interest in medicine, invites me to attend one of the practical courses in his teaching amphitheater. There are some thirty of us, sitting on the tiers. A religious silence reigns when a nun wheels in a little eight-year-old girl, covered by a sheet up to her chin.

I can still see her troubled look as she notices those rows of men in white. When the professor asks whether any of the students wishes to hazard a diagnosis, a tall red-headed fellow raises his hand, goes down the steps, uncovers the upper portion of the patient's body, and her eyes reflect panic.

The stomach and belly are a swollen balloon. The student delicately touches several points, thinks, states a diagnosis, and blushingly returns to his place.

Three of them do this, after which the professor himself goes over to the stretcher, touches the same points the students did, then two other spots on the body, and finally articulates a definitive diagnosis, which he goes on to explain at some length.

By now the child's eyes reflect indifference, as if she had become alien to what is going on around her.

I had another experience in Lyons, the memory of which haunts me.

"Have you got the guts to look at my hydrocephalics?" Dr. Béthenod, Jeune's assistant, asks. "I warn you, they're not a pretty sight."

When I say yes, he leads me to a glass partition. Here, there are no beds; a dozen human beings, at least by definition, are spread around the room, some sitting against the wall, others crouching or lying down. They are naked, with huge heads and expressionless eyes, limbs that move awkwardly. Their empty expressions show that these people are closer to vegetables than humans. Yet they are fully alive.

"There is nothing medicine can do. Since no other institution will take them in, we have to keep them, without any hope of curing them or improving their lot. There are homes for the aged, institutions for the handicapped, for abused children, asylums for the incurably insane. But for these, nothing except the room you see here. No one comes to see them. No one cares about them. And the state gives us only a pittance to feed them on. We wait."

No need to ask him, "Wait for what?" Some of them, as far as one can tell, seem to be four or five years old, and stubbornly go on vegetating, unknowingly.

What a relief to see you again, my little Pierre, alive, with your eyes wide open now, your body vigorous once more. Looking at you and your promise, I shiver at the thought of those who, from birth, have been nothing but vegetables in human form, or something like it.

We are filled with joy, the joy of taking you away in the car, far from hospitals, to your room at Echandens, which is a soft, cuddly nest.

You have just gone through an ordeal many children experience. And for some time still, in precaution, our hematologist will take blood samples, to be examined at the Pasteur Institute in Lyons.

Ever-more-reassuring reports come, and soon this painful interlude in our life and yours will be nothing but a memory.

Today you are a big twenty-one-year-old, bursting with health, built like an athlete.

My brood is full again; life resumes its lively rhythm, at times too fast for my taste.

In mid-November, I write *Maigret aux Assises (Maigret in Court)*, my fourth, and last, novel for this year.

In Lyons, I had begun to worry about D., and now am worrying more and more. With each pregnancy, she put on much more weight than most women, and once the child was born, she started to worry about her figure. As long as I have known her, that has been an obsession with her, worrying that she will someday get to be as huge as her mother.

As soon as our minds are put at ease about your health, she begins feverishly running to the fancy shops, trying on dresses, buying or having made I don't know how many of them. She also starts drinking again, although moderately. I keep her company. She is eating less and less and will soon go on a strenuous diet. This involves a powder supposed to be nourishing, which is taken in a glass of warm water. With it, late in the evening, a lettuce-and-tomato sandwich. More than ever, to avoid temptation, she says, she stays downstairs with Aitken, whom she keeps with her as late as possible.

Aitken is engaged to an important lawyer in town, and they are both very fond of theater and music. There are regular concerts, often of the highest caliber, in the auditorium of Beaulieu Palace. They faithfully attend these and subscribe to the Friday-evening performances at the municipal theater.

Normally, Aitken finishes work at six at the latest. At seven, seven-thirty, the two women are still in the office, where D. needs company as she drinks her whiskey. I am not throwing stones at her. I am well acquainted with human weakness. Sometimes the phone rings. Aitken's fiancé is concerned, since she still has to dress and have dinner before going to the theater. In a state of euphoria, D. nonetheless goes right on talking and drinking, without that brick of an Aitken ever showing in any way that she is put out.

The children and I have long since finished dinner, and so has the help, by the time D. comes up, prepares her sandwich and her powdered drink, and rushes into the room where Pierre is already asleep, then the one where Marie-Jo is getting ready for bed, while Johnny and I watch the evening news.

D.'s excitement, in the evening, worries me. She has barely seen the children all day and apologizes to them by saying she is "swamped" with work, that her life is "a real hell." She even sometimes keeps them awake late, too late, especially you, Marie-Jo, to whom she makes speeches that bother me.

Even Johnny will become apprehensive of the picture she gives him of the willful, demanding man I am, it seems, who turns her into a slave.

Much, much later, my tender Johnny, you—who observe us, as do all children, and do not miss the tone of certain shouted scenes—you will confide in me: "There is one thing I can never forgive Maman for, Dad, and that is her having kept me away from a father for several years."

Some of the help, excluding faithful Boule, will fall for this too, for they have to wait in the kitchen for D. to come down for that sacrosanct daily report. Unknown to me, for instance, the huge garden and its many recesses are off limits to those who are in our service, except for Nana, who is allowed to wheel Pierre there, first in his carriage, then in his stroller. It seems the "Master" can't stand having people coming and going on the stony paths while he is pacing in this garden, which D. insists on referring to as "the park." Nothing must be allowed to disturb him, because he is then "thinking," and the sight of another person might break his train of thought.

And when, while I am preparing a novel, I take walks in the city, mixing with the crowd, do the people around me break my train of thought?

True, while I am writing, that is, for three and a half hours at the most, I hang a little sign on my doorknob, dating back to the Plaza Hotel in New York, reading DO NOT DISTURB. And no one is allowed to come in. I was surprised one day to see Johnny tiptoeing up the stairs and turning to his sister with a finger against his lips, to whisper, "Shhh!" I was quite moved by the thought that he was doing this on his own. But I finally discovered the real reason for this precaution was just obedience to a strict order they thought I had given.

There are two reasons for the feverish manner in which D. is at present worrying about her figure and running to shops. Two deadlines, both distasteful to me.

After Cocteau, Pagnol, and Garçon became members of the French Academy, while I was far from Paris, Marcel Achard, as dear to me as the other three, is due to be received into it in December. Despite my dislike for all ceremonies, including weddings and funerals, I cannot refuse Marcel's invitation to attend his installation and the elaborate reception to follow.

The other, even more painful, deadline comes up in May 1960 at Cannes. For Fabre-Lebret had come to see me at Echandens and he is a very charming man. "Do you remember, my dear Simenon, that when I asked you to be president of the jury at the Cannes Festival, you answered that you never had been and never would be on any such jury? Since then, you did preside over the one at the Brussels film festival, didn't you?"

"I couldn't refuse. Belgium is my own country."

"Wasn't France the place where you got your real start and your whole career is centered? Aren't you considered a French writer? Are you going to renounce us now?"

Faced with a friend who is also a diplomat, I am lost. I try to bring up a few reasons I know won't hold water, and finally give in. So D. and I are expected in Cannes in May, and she is getting ready for it.

In Lausanne, there is a fine couturier from Central Europe, who dresses the "cream" of society, and D. has become one of his faithful customers. Almost as finicky as she, this couturier, who has since died, puts in two hours and more at fittings, along with his wife, a darkish woman with features as sharp as her eyes, who helps him. The fittings are all the longer because two or three times during their course D. interrupts them for allegedly urgent phone calls that go on and on. "Please excuse me. But I have such a heavy load of work. . . ."

Sometimes, important customers have to wait outside the curtain that blocks them off from the fitting room.

I was thus able to hear, to my amazement, that according to D. I would be nothing without her, that it was she who made my fortune for me, through the work she does, which exhausts her and is finally making her ill. The darkish wife of the couturier has no reason not to repeat all of these confidences, which spread throughout Lausanne and of course are eventually repeated to me.

If this worries me, it is not on my own account, but because of D., whose balance, I feel, is more and more threatened. Rather than shove her any farther along the hill she is already sliding down too fast to suit me, I take it all in my stride.

As for our passional or simply sexual relations, they now are only intermittent, less and less frequent, more and more mechanical and as if to cover the obligation.

We often go to a strippers' cabaret, at which, as in Cannes, D. encourages me to make contact with the young and almost always beautiful performers. We have our own box there, to which we are automatically shown. Champagne is more or less the obligatory drink, but D. is served her favorite Scotch, while I, depending on the times, order either a half-bottle of Pommery or a Coca-Cola.

"Don't you find that girl attractive?"

I do find a lot of them attractive, but they are under no obligation to reciprocate. After their turns on stage, however, they are supposed to go to the bar in the back of the room and try to get the customers to order more drinks.

I go back there to join now one, now another, and get their phone numbers for dates at times convenient to both them and me.

In the book of phone numbers that D. keeps in the office, there are, among other headings, several pages of numbers and addresses, covering Paris, Cannes, Milan, Brussels, and elsewhere, with just one word written in D.'s hand at the top in big block letters: GIRLS.

When I notice this, I get angry, because I don't like terms that demean women, and the French "*filles,*" while it means "girls," does just that. D. gives in and replaces that word by FRIVOLITIES.

On December 13, my children, we have a big party at the house. It is the very ceremonial christening of our little Pierre, the only one to have had a real Catholic baptism, by a Catholic priest, seconded by the village pastor.

According to the rules—since there is only a Protestant church at Echandens, the nice little white one with the pointed steeple in which I am

465

insistent that my last son be baptized—the ceremony ought to take place in the Catholic church at Morges.

I know a Belgian Benedictine, from Verviers, who, after many years spent teaching Biblical exegesis, is finishing out his days at the end of the lake in a retirement home of his order, where just he and three others live.

When I inform him that the bishopric has said Pierre cannot have a Catholic baptism in the Protestant church at Echandens, he confidently assures me: "Monsignor is sticking his finger in his eye." We go to call on him.

The Benedictine, Father Duesberg, will be the one, my Pierre, to put the salt on your tongue, a few drops of water on your head, under the eyes of the Protestant minister, after which both of them come to lunch at the château, with some forty-odd other guests. The two ground-floor offices on the garden side, which get the sun, are turned into a dining room. Your godfather, Johnny, who insisted on standing up for you as Marc did for him, is very handsome in his blue suit. Your godmother is Juliette Achard, accompanied by her husband, the newly installed Academy member. The young Chaplins, with whom you often play, are there too. If my memory is not mistaken, your friends Charlie and Anne stood on either side of a Marie-Jo who was delighted with her very feminine new dress.

Days of pure joy have now replaced those of sadness and anguish.

I would like to close this first period of our life at Echandens on a radiant picture.

Do you know, my big Pierre, that you wore the same baptismal robe your brothers had worn, Marc, who has come for the ceremony of course, and then Johnny, as well as your sister, Marie-Jo?

So, over a period of twenty years, it was used by all four of my children, and it remains a palpable link among all of you.

55

The second period of our life in Echandens is beginning. If, during the first three years there, the barometer of our life swung between "Fine Weather" and "Variable," apart from the scare that Pierre's illness gave us, it will now more or less slip from "Variable" to "Wind and Rain," and end up, inexorably, at "Storm."

I have no idea what pictures have remained with one or another of you from that period, for, whereas I have passionately been recording the actions of each of you from the very first moments of your lives, you also have been recording, unbeknownst to yourselves and to me, and a reserve with which I am all too familiar will later keep you from confronting your pictures with my own.

Just be aware that I devoted to each of you all the time that I could and that the memories of those hours are the only sunny ones of that part of my existence. That is why, before coming to some darker memories, as I am obligated to do, I want to remind you of my joys, which I hope were also yours.

In 1960, Pierre will be a year old, Marie-Jo seven, Johnny eleven. As for Marc, he has flown from the nest, with my full agreement, and I am soon to see him again in Paris, married and surrounded by new friends.

You, my Pierre who gave us such a scare, I see you again in your carriage, then in your stroller along the walks of our large garden or the paths of the village. Nana is with you, and also Marie-Jo, when she wasn't in school, dressed as a nursemaid, proud of your now-colorful cheeks, your pudgy limbs, your eyes that take in everything—the leaves on the trees, the low buildings, peasants going by—with the intensity of awakening intelligence.

Nana and Marie-Jo are not the only ones who proudly take you out. Gentle Mister is always along, appearing from nowhere, and following you step by step with the serious, watchful look of a bodyguard.

Soon you will be taking your first steps, in your bedroom, then in the garden, and, like your brothers and sister before you, you will look proudly over at us after each exploit.

And you, Marie-Jo, do you remember our walks along the paths, around the pointed steeple, your hand always safely held in mine? You shared those times with Johnny, or, more precisely, you fought over them. I always preferred to have only one of you with me at a time, so you might get the feeling that you had me fully and completely.

You are pretty, darling Marie-Jo, slightly fragile, laughing, not a little girl's laugh, but that of a complete human being, who dreams and thinks, and mainly is all love. For you love instinctively, even though you may first gravely look over any new person who arrives, as if gauging him. Overflowing with love as you are, you are no less eager to receive love in return, as I already perceived when you were only a baby.

I still go with you to Lausanne—you insist that there be just the two of us—to buy you dresses, notebooks, everything you need, and soon you are big enough to hold onto my arm. I buy you little silver trinkets, with light and cheery nonprecious stones in them, and I can remember that afternoon when our jeweler pierced your ears, without your reacting, for you never let your defenses drop. When you do cry, my little girl, it is in secret and silently, and no one in the house ever knew anything about it.

Probably we did go and have some of our escapades on gray, rainy days. In my memory, all I find is sun shining gloriously on the city and turning your hair even more preciously blond.

One afternoon, we were standing in front of the window of a small jewelry shop we had never been into. I saw that your clear eyes were looking for something, which you finally found.

"Dad, I would like you to buy me a ring like that."

I at first thought I had misunderstood, because what you were pointing at were gold wedding rings.

"Wouldn't you rather have one with a stone, maybe a blue one?"

"No, one of those is what I want." And you added, solemnly, "A ring like yours."

I am troubled, hesitant. You were then eight years old, and I wonder whether you understand the meaning that is given to a wedding band.

"I don't think we'll find any small enough for your little fingers."

"You can have it made smaller, can't you?"

We go into the shop. I ask that the smallest of their wedding rings be made smaller. You will prove later that you did understand the meaning of this ornament, which never again left your finger as long as you lived, except when, several times, it had to be enlarged. In one of your last testament letters, you urgently ask me to make sure that you are cremated wearing the wedding ring you got at eight.

But this is still only 1960, my darling, and I can recall only your laughter, your curiosity, your joys, your enthusiasms. I will someday have proof that what you were then living through, you were recording, without missing any of it, with an almost terrifying lucidity.

Do you remember, Johnny, the walks the two of us used to take on the plateau at the edge of the village, along the Moinats' property, where the cows came running toward us? It was the walk I had selected for thinking about my next novel, and you adopted in turn, wanting to share it, with Mister tagging along.

Strange little Johnny, the deliberate loner, hard on himself and others, hiding depths of tenderness. I don't know of your having any friends at the Collège de Béthusy, where you are doing so well. Except for Charlie, you bring no one else to the house, and I wonder whether for a number of years he was not indeed your only friend.

At the end of your second year, you have to make a choice between Greek and Latin humanities and mathematical science. You are one of the few allowed to exercise such a choice, by the deliberate consensus of the teachers.

You ask my advice. I don't give you advice as such. I only tell you how useful it is to have a solid grounding in the foundations of our civilization. You choose Greek-Latin and, three years later, you will draw up, on thirty or more big white cardboard sheets, pasted edge to edge and folding up accordion-style, a complete genealogy of the Greek gods, so complete that your teacher calls me into the faculty room to tell me of his surprise and admiration.

"I wonder where he could have dug up the lineage of some of the more obscure gods, whom I must admit I never even heard of. This work would deserve publication, because I don't know of any that equals it."

You have long since given up your temper tantrums. During one of our walks out on the plateau, you told me point-blank: "Dad, I've made a decision."

I wait, anxiously.

"I'll never lose my temper again."

I look at you, somewhat skeptically, knowing what your temper is like.

"Beginning when?"

"Today, Dad."

And you will keep your word. The only violence you ever express is on the percussion instruments you sometimes sit down to, filling the house with a very rhythmic din, for you have been taught the tympani by a good teacher. On his suggestion, I ordered some jazz records with the percussion section left out. How many times, as obstinate as you are in all things, do you accompany those records on your drums?

And now I have no choice but to speak again of what I call the "signs," which recur throughout these memoirs and which others might call "premonitions."

Didn't I have some the very first day I met D. in 1945 in New York, especially the very first night, when we were walking all the way to the hotel from Café Society Downtown, where she had left me to go and interview the black pianist by pretending to be a newspaperwoman?

That was the first sign, and there were others, more and more revealing. If I make note of them, including even the most intimate ones, it is because they are going to have serious repercussions, not only on my life—which is least important—but on the lives of you children and our entourage. Besides, you could not otherwise understand the gray years, with ever more threatening clouds, that we are about to go through, nor the dramas that will arise from them.

D. and you children are not the only ones I observed almost automatically. That is a need I have had all my life, which, no doubt, made me a novelist. Seeing someone on the street, in a café, anywhere at all, I may say to myself: "What is eating away at that man and giving him that fixed stare?" I look for signs. Does he have an ulcer, intestinal trouble? Is he eaten away by sorrow?

The humiliated are those who most attract my compassion, for I am convinced that humiliation is the harshest penalty a human can pay.

In drawing rooms, I observed other beings, who seemed very sure of themselves, and I tried to find the chink in their armor. How many arrogant people are actually nothing but timid ones trying not to let it show? How many proud ones, among the "great of this world," are undermined by an inferiority complex!

These signs, gathered here, there, and everywhere, are what gave birth to the characters of my novels.

By force of habit, this search for the truth was applied to my kin, and *Pedigree* is proof that it was applied to my parents when I was still a child.

Are we not all concerned with the truth about others, especially those nearest to us?

I am not wallowing today, any more than on other days, in accumulating the often sordid signs, although some will say I am. There are no half-truths; only the truth itself.

In Cannes, when we were living at the Golden Gate, a vast and luxurious property, we were able to get along with three women and a chauffeur, plus a gardener forced on us by the owners and partly paid by them.

The first year at Echandens, there were six in help, apart from Aitken. Eight in 1958. Nine in 1960. Eleven in 1961 and 1962.

None of them is, strictly speaking, working for me, and I am not consulted in their selection. Some board and lodge at the château; others live in the village. Some will just be in and out, to be replaced by other strange faces. Some will stay with us to the end and accompany us to Epalinges.

Such statistics may seem surprising. They scare me. They are indeed the sign of D.'s need to keep reassuring herself more and more strongly of her own importance. Whereas I am barely allowed to speak to these people, she truly dominates them, determining their schedules, down to the quarter of an hour, and each one, whatever his or her duties, will be instructed by her on how they are supposed to be done.

She speaks in my name. All of them are supposed to be protecting me and my work. Many of them are thus convinced that I am some unapproachable character, moving about in a rarefied atmosphere forbidden to ordinary mortals.

She will teach a professional laundress how to iron; she will teach a chambermaid how to use a vacuum cleaner, even though the only one she ever used herself was that mini-vacuum she used to clean drawers in hotel rooms.

She will teach Boule, who has cooked to Tigy's and my satisfaction for many years, how to cook—although she herself never has—and she will be the one to establish the week's menus and determine how each dish will be cooked.

As for Aitken, who had a solid classical education, D. will allow her no initiative, except perhaps that of phoning dentists, doctors, dressmakers, bootmakers, to tell them that "Madame Simenon is delayed by a very important business call from Los Angeles and will be ten minutes late."

She must always be late, and I, who almost always have to drive her, am kept waiting at the wheel of the car with the motor purring.

So, D. not only organizes and commands, but also supervises everyone, which may explain why she is so exhausted at the end of the day.

After Marie-Jo was born, D. was too slow, to suit herself, in losing the weight a woman usually puts on during pregnancy. The same thing happened after the birth of Pierre, as I said. So she eats less and less real food and drags out her time downstairs, with or without Aitken.

In the morning, finding it harder and harder to get going, she stays in bed, complains about how she feels, and more and more often replaces her breakfast by a shot or two of whiskey.

Since she has delicate veins, she claims that only our chemist knows how to give her injections. He is a very understanding man and is quite willing to come each Sunday morning to give D. a shot of Dexedrine to fortify her.

Our general practitioner is one of the best doctors in Lausanne and one of the most humane. One day when D. has stayed in bed, she calls him, saying it is an emergency. Calm, deliberate, conscientious, he examines D. at length, and when he is done, tells her very gently: "You have lost too much weight through lack of proper nourishment. All I can advise is that you eat more and put on some weight. . . ."

Had D. been drinking that day and could the doctor smell her breath? However that may be, she sat up in bed as if she had just been insulted or humiliated. With arm stretched toward the door, she said: "Get out of here, doctor. Please never set foot in the château again."

The same thing was to happen to my tailor, who also had a fine reputation. His son had taken up women's tailoring and, under the father's supervision, was doing very well. D. ordered three or four tailored suits from him. First fitting: a fraction of an inch to take in here, a pleat to be made deeper there. Second fitting: the jacket is a shade longer on the right than on the left. My old tailor winks at me, agrees. At the third fitting there is the same scene as years before at Jeanne Lanvin's in Paris. Always a question of a hair's-breadth. Finally, the old tailor can't take any more of it.

"Listen, madame, these clothes fit perfectly. I forbid my son to make any further alterations. You may take them as they are or leave them with us. I am afraid we can't do any more work for you."

D. took home the clothes. I lost my tailor and had to find another one, and I had to change physicians.

Signs and more signs, and I am relating only the most illuminating ones. A French television producer asks me to do an hour show on the life of Balzac. My reason for accepting is that I was very moved on reading the great novelist's correspondence with the various women who figured in his life, from his mother and sister down to his mistresses, and the woman he one day went to find in Poland, only to die a few months after they were married.

I reread the correspondence, underlining certain passages, and since I cannot make use of Aitken, who is monopolized by D., for a month I hire a secretary, whom I set up in Marc's empty room.

On three large white cardboards, like the ones Johnny used, I make columns, one for each year, from Balzac's birth to his death, inscribing in each one the important events of his life and the novels he wrote during that year.

I do a draft of some two hundred pages, much too long, but it is intended only to serve as a guide. The important thing to me is the letters, the often contradictory confidences made to those he was writing to, and some confessions, such as: "Sometimes, when I am alone in front of my desk, I burst out sobbing without knowing why." And: "I have less and less memory for names, and even for nouns, which is a tragedy for a novelist."

As luck would have it, I had happened on a small book about Balzac's health by a Geneva doctor. In making his diagnosis, he depended mainly on a photograph of Balzac completely naked, showing the hypertrophied neck typical of Hodgkin's disease.

The television crew takes a day setting up in my office, in which, come evening, I light a log fire, since it is wintertime.

Standing before my cardboards, with their fifty-one columns, I improvise, without looking at my draft, but often referring to the items entered in the columns. I do not discuss literary merits, because I do not feel myself qualified to. I concentrate on the man, reading long extracts from his letters, sometimes interrupting myself to straighten out a log in the fire or to light my pipe.

When I get to Balzac's last days, I cannot keep the tears from rolling down my cheeks, and my voice is choked as I speak the final lines.

I believe this was on March 3. From the 8th through the 15th, I write *L'Ours en peluche (Teddy Bear)*, and on April 19, Marc got married in Paris, to the girl he had taken along on so many motorcycle rides in Cannes.

I go to see Marc and Francette in their apartment on Rue Saint-Charles in Paris, shortly before the wedding. It is good to see Marc again, settled down and full of pep and plans. But I must nevertheless tell him I won't be able to attend the ceremony. D. would insist on coming with me. Tigy would be there, and for the two women to meet, on a day like that, would not be advisable.

One evening, Aitken informs D. that she doesn't feel she can take the strain any longer and has found a new job.

With Aitken gone, D. is unable to unscramble the maze of business deals she had allowed to accumulate, while making them as complicated as possible. Besides, with Aitken gone she loses the excuse for tarrying in the office in the evening and having more and more to drink.

Shortly before, we had been visited by the celebrated British writer W. Somerset Maugham, whom we had met during a trip to London. He is a believer in Dr. Niehans, the controversial physician who treats old people in his clinic near Montreux. By injecting fresh lamb cells into them, he claims to extend their lives, as he has allegedly done for the then Pope, and his literature also mentions Charlie Chaplin. The latter protests, sues him, and wins; he had never been treated by Niehans. To my knowledge, the Pope said nothing. As for Maugham, an especially youthful oldster, he makes no bones of having had the Niehans treatment.

I remember a conversation between my illustrious confrere and D., who was drinking in every word, when he said something to this effect: "Since you are the one, Mme Simenon, who takes care of your husband's business, allow me to give you some advice. Publishers and film producers are essentially businessmen, and, like all businessmen, they are out only for their own profit. That means that they tend to cheat and cry poverty. When you are negotiating with them don't be afraid to be tough, pitiless. Don't be afraid to be demanding. You'll never be enough so, because where writers like your husband and me are concerned, I know from experience, they always finally give in."

He comes back to see us several times, and D. is not slow to follow his advice, which turns out to be costly to me, because among producers I soon acquire the reputation of being the most expensive author around and I receive fewer offers, and fewer films are made from my works.

D. translates Maugham's words into a more striking and sweeping formulation: "All publishers, all movie producers are thieves."

She has started to tell them this to their faces, and I came across more than one of my faithful publishers, among them a German publisher with white hair, weeping in the ground-floor office.

D. resorts to her talent for getting around people. She phones Aitken day after day, making herself as sweet as she knows how, and as pitiful too, which she can do when she wants to, and finally soft-hearted Aitken agrees to come and help her out two or three evenings a week. When I see her, her eyes tell me she understands; mine tell her how grateful I am.

A second secretary, called "Blinis" because D. thinks she looks Russian, is hired a week or two later. She is a petite brunette, with a clubfoot, but she always wears the most agreeable of smiles and gets along well with Aitken.

Have I mentioned *"L'Homme à la cervelle d'or"* (The Man with the Golden Brain)? That's the title of a tale by Alphonse Daudet, which D. recently read and which she will refer to, not only in dealing with reluctant publishers and producers, but also with our own staff.

She tells the former: "You know the story of the man with the golden brain? Each one comes to scrape a little of it off, until the day when there isn't a gram of brain left. And all of you keep coming here to get a little of that gold that you make fortunes from, without thinking that someday the source may give out, and I will be left high and dry with my children."

When I hear this, from one of my faithful publishers, I blush with shame, and yet, despite anything I say, this sentimental old story will be rehashed with all the attendant feeling to all my callers.

The same goes for the staff, who are expected to surround with their silent protection the oh, so precious man who is little by little exhausting his talent. I am such a fragile object that they barely dare speak to me or look me in the face. Unfortunately, some of them, both men and women, will believe this, and believe especially, as they are constantly led to believe, that I have laid down these rules.

In May, the Cannes Festival, to which I have to go; as at Brussels, I take my role in it seriously. I leave you again, my children, see your little hands waving at the windows of the scullery.

474

At the Carlton, I have reserved our usual spacious third-floor suite, with windows opening onto the ever-changing passing show of the Croisette and the beach.

Apart from many day and evening gowns, my tails and tuxedo, we have with us the famous Hermès kit and another, new, case, which D. has had made for her jewelry by a Lausanne leather-goods maker. Inside, there are a certain number of containers, each one, carrying a number, made to measure for one kind of jewel or another. There is even a special one for combs.

D. has recently stopped braiding her hair, and now rolls it into a chignon. I have had shell combs of various sizes made for her, some decorated with old-gold-colored pearls, which had to be ordered from India.

I have some good friends on the jury, of which I am president, especially Henry Miller, who will look at only a few films and spend most of his time playing Ping-Pong, which he loves. Simone Renant turns out to be a sweet, simple woman, with dependable taste, who, unlike so many others, will keep out of the limelight.

As at Brussels, I am on Coca-Cola, for I have to attend a large number of lunches, receptions, dinners, given by various delegations and some local personalities, including the Begum, who each evening makes a spectacular entrance into the Palace of Festivals.

Has D.'s dream finally come true? She is invited to everything, everywhere, sees Jean Cocteau again, and many of my friends.

The evening screenings take place at nine-thirty. From seven on, D. is getting ready and eats nothing but a sandwich, which she gobbles down while Claude, the hairdresser to all the ladies, at a premium, does her hair and the manicurist her hands and the make-up woman her face.

I have dinner alone in the sitting room, more abundantly, and get into my tuxedo. I finally timidly suggest, "It's nine-twenty. . . ."

The Palace is only a couple of hundred yards away, but one has to cut through mobs of bystanders who are out there trying to catch a glimpse of the stars, just as later we will have to get through the crowd of invitees and photographers who block the main staircase and the balconies, before we can get to our seats.

It takes me two or three evenings to understand that D. is trying to be the last one. After all, isn't she a star, too?

I meet Federico Fellini and his delightful wife, Giulietta Massina. I often walk back with him. I am very much interested in this hulk of a fellow with the broad shoulders, who is simple, sincere, and tormented, all at the same time.

Along with a number of the members of the jury, I often have a nightcap at the bar of the hotel, and we use the occasion to feel out each other, trying to guess our reactions to the film we have just seen.

Then, D. remembers the jury of jurors' wives she set up in Brussels. Here, there are only four or five. Yet, she gets them together not far from where we are. Alas, not a word about them in the papers!

The Bernard Buffets are here, and we will celebrate their wedding anniversary with them, an occasion on which I buy D. one of his paintings, showing Annabel, rear view, in a red bathing suit. I like the painting very much, as I like everything Buffet does. I call the painting "Woman Peeing," because Annabel is standing in such a way that, against the solid sea, she seems to be peeing against a wall. That is the only painting that is actually D.'s own.

The competition is lively between those jurors who are for Fellini's *La Dolce Vita* and those who favor an Antonioni film, *La Notte.* I am enthusiastic over *La Dolce Vita*, which has created something of a scandal. Thanks to the vote of Henry Miller, who doesn't have an opinion and has decided to vote as I do, and one other juror, *La Dolce Vita* wins, and I go to give the list of awards to Fabre-Lebret, who is waiting out in the hall. He is not alone. A representative of the Ministry of Foreign Affairs is there with him, a learned fellow and great film buff, who was the one who originally had the idea of creating this festival, and I like him very much. But aren't both of them being told what to do by Paris?

Our list of winners does not delight them. At that time, it was the president's job to read off the names of the winners at the gala evening closing the festivities. I am hissed, whistled at with police whistles, while Giulietta waits in the wings and sobs on my shoulder.

I was never again asked to preside over any jury, and that is a relief.

56

This year, 1960, of which I have so far glided over only a small portion, was to be the fullest year of our lives, full of everything, bad and good, sunshine and threatening clouds, haunting anxieties and serene joys. But are not all years and all lives like that? Can there be sunshine without shadows?

A year that had weeks "with" and weeks "without" alcohol. Not only for D., but sometimes, less often, for me, who have the advantage of being able to cut it out at will.

Our relations go through various phases too, including phases reminiscent of our passionate days and nights of earlier times.

Is it on the days with or without that her fits of despair erupt? I don't know and don't want to know. At those times, she appears to become the lost and seemingly naked little girl she once had been. On the least pretext, some minor incident or disappointment, she, with her hair unkempt, her face pathetic, will burst into tears, and splotches of mascara run down her cheeks.

"My Jo, I beg you, love me, help me, look at me the way you once used to look at me! I know I often hurt you, that I've always hurt you, but try to understand that I can't help it, it's not my fault, and I hate myself for it. No one ever helped me, except maybe my father, who died too early. Very early, I knew that I am worthless, and I almost curse that humpbacked publisher who arranged our first appointment in New York, when I was ready to put an end to it all.

"I was just a miserable person trying in vain to find a place for herself in life, whom men kicked back and forth to one another like a football."

Her tear-drenched eyes were begging me. Her voice was getting hoarse and her body trembling. "Keep on loving me, my Jo, who has tried so hard to make me happy."

As she drags out that "loving," I vainly attempt to hold firm, but I begin to melt and no longer to believe in all the signs I have unwillingly noted through so many years.

"You allowed me too much hope. You gave me everything and I wanted more. I realize that now. It's because I love you, Jo, because I admire you and would like to be worthy of you. . . ."

Her hand mechanically twists her long hair. "Jo, my Jo, I am begging you on my knees. . . ."

I pull her up, take her in my arms, with a lump in my throat.

"Don't say any more," I tell her, as I rock her in my arms.

"Promise that you will never leave me. Without you, I'm nothing. You know that; I know that you know it," she goes on.

I did not record her words, but I heard them often enough so that they remain engraved in my memory. I am just boiling them down, because these monologues interrupted by sobs were much longer and repeated themselves like a leitmotif.

"I'm not worth a thing, but I love you, Jo, I love you, hear?"

At times like these, I don't try to know which is the real D., this unkempt, desperate one begging me or the one who greets me with a sharp "What do you want now?" when I come into her office, and when I say, "To kiss you," answers, "Hurry up."

These scenes invariably end up in bed, with wild, almost desperate embraces.

Sometimes for several days, a whole week, we then act like true lovers. These almost delirious demonstrations unfortunately have no follow-up, my children, to whom I then rush as if from you I could get the courage to hold on. At this period, which alternates between being excruciating and being peaceful and almost joyful, I start writing in a plain notebook, without any title on it, confidences that I do not mean for publication. I write just a few lines, a few pages of them, from time to time, according to my mood of the moment, while you are at school, Pierre is in the garden with Nana.

We have nothing that can lock, except in D.'s office and where the secretaries keep the files. I have barely started to confide in this way in my notebook when D. finds it, and is concerned. "Why are you writing behind my back?"

"I am not writing behind your back. I write when I feel bored."

"Promise that you will let me see this notebook as you make your entries in it. We are a couple, aren't we? And I read your novels chapter by chapter."

That is true. Because she knows that I used to let Tigy read them that way, and she doesn't want to be any less favored. I also know what she is looking for in those freshly typed pages. Will she find herself portrayed in one female character or another? She is convinced she will, and does her best to recognize telltale details. She is wrong every time, as have been all those who thought they recognized themselves in the characters of my novels, for I am not a portrait painter.

Nevertheless, because I have to let D. read whatever I write, my entries are now distorted. Some of them, of course, put her on her guard, others make her angry, and some unleash scenes such as the one I just described, which leave me with a bitter aftertaste.

So I go on writing in my notebooks, no longer to say what is within me, but in terms of D.'s reactions, and I sometimes soft-pedal things, or else exaggerate my feelings to the point of making them unrecognizable.

I cannot at the time foresee, in my cell of an office in the turret, where I seek refuge when you children are not about, that these notebooks will someday, years later, be published, as the result of a friend's visit. This friend has not yet appeared in our life, but he will soon become one of our few regular table guests. He is a student of literature, who is working on a university thesis on Marcel Proust, having discovered some unpublished material of that writer's. I trust him implicitly, and we spend entire afternoons in my office chatting. I go to sleep early, by ten. He retires late, reading part of the night.

"Don't you have some new manuscript to let me read tonight?" he asks.

Almost always, I have some newly finished novel in the drawer. One evening, after we have moved away from Echandens and I have nothing else to let him read, I remember these notebooks, long since set aside.

"The only thing I seem to have is these notes, which I don't consider very significant, and which are not really interesting."

He takes them to his room with him. And the next day returns them, saying: "You absolutely have to publish this. It's a document of the highest order."

He argues his point so convincingly that I finally am won over, as is usually the case. It needs a title. I feel much younger now than back at Echandens when I was writing these notes.

"Why not call it *Quand j'étais vieux* [*When I Was Old*]?" I suggest.

Because, at Echandens, when I was fifty-seven, I felt like an old man. The book came out, without attracting too much attention. Biographers have mined it, trying to find clues to allow them to reconstruct the real "me." They found them, of course, and many newspapermen did also, without ever suspecting that the better part of what was in those notebooks was written to try to keep a woman, my wife, from slipping into the abyss.

Even today, in 1980, that book, which should have remained unpublished, is quoted more often than my other works, and D. was to make extensive use of it, once our separation became final, to create new legends about me and vilify me.

I am not defending myself. I am merely trying to set down the conditions under which those sometimes exuberant pages were written, and especially with what in mind.

I overlooked mentioning a trip to London, which was to prove significant. A year before, an official BBC representative had come to see us at Echandens with the intention of acquiring rights to fifty-two Maigret stories for television. Following Somerset Maugham's advice, D. had given him the cold shoulder and rejected his offer out of hand.

A few months later, another character showed up, saying that he too represented the BBC. The first one, the one she had turned away, was tall and slim and measured his words, very "British." This second one, whose credentials D. never thought to ask for, was short, very fat, jovial, ruddy-complexioned, always ready to laugh, and made no bones about his love for whiskey.

D.'s negotiations with him took place over a couple of days and over a bottle that was replaced whenever it was empty.

This time, I made sure that I was the one to draw up a draft contract, with several clauses that were nonnegotiable. My terms were fair to the interests of both parties. The rights I ceded the BBC were to apply only to English-speaking countries, with the exception of the United States, and the prints were to be made available to other countries with which I might make separate contracts in my own name. This contract, if memory serves, was to be for twelve years and to cover two showings on any given station.

Now, making trips to great metropolises never worked out well for D. and me, because D., in order to play her part, felt she had to drink and, as during our New York binges while we lived at Lakeville, I had to go along with her, so that such trips remain in my memory as nightmares.

The fellow with the flushed face and the body like a tobacco jar greets us in London and immediately goes into closed session with D.

I think it is on this trip that we meet Simone Signoret and Yves Montand. We have a cordial dinner with them, without ever suspecting that later on Signoret would star in three films based on novels of mine.

This time, or another, we have as neighbors Roberto Rossellini and Ingrid Bergman, with whom we become friends. Their son is the same age as Johnny. His birth had created quite a stir in the United States, where we were then in somewhat the same situation, and I had sent a wire of support to the couple, who were being excoriated by almost the entire press.

Anyway, before we go to bed that first evening, D. decides to show me a contract the BBC has drawn up. She and the little fatty have a date the next morning to continue discussing the terms.

The contract had one peculiarity. Entire passages of it had been crossed out and replaced by bits of typed or handwritten paper pasted over them.

"I'll go through it tomorrow," I said, exhausted from having had to wait for hours.

The fellow brings along cigars, which he constantly smokes. As for the odor of whiskey emanating from him, it is almost as strong as the smell of a London pub.

An endless day begins. Newspapermen keep after me, and I give interviews. Maybe that is when I give that answer to a direct question: "No, I don't like myself! I hate myself."

Which was true at the moment, especially with a hangover. D. and her tobacco jar have lunch in our sitting room without stopping their discussion.

Every now and then, the waiter brings them a fresh bottle, and D. will later inform me, with no little pride: "We decided how certain clauses would read on the basis of who finished the bottle first."

I am, alas, not making this up. At the end of the afternoon, a triumphant and slightly unsteady D., her eyes shining too brightly, holds out the contract to me, crowing: "Jo! I won!"

It is hard to make head or tail of the crossed-out and amended paragraphs, and the hunks of paper stuck over them here and there. I do the best I can. I am reassured by finding that my nonnegotiable clauses have been left intact. Sale only to English-speaking countries, excluding the United States. Rights to make use of the films, in dubbed or subtitled versions, in all other countries to be retained by me for my sole benefit.

"Tomorrow you just have to sign it with the representative of the BBC," she tells me.

"But you just spent the whole day with him."

Confused, embarrassed explanations. It turns out the little tobacco jar has nothing whatsoever to do with the BBC. He is a go-between, having no standing with them except insofar as he has presented a draft contract with me to them.

As in insurance policies and most American publishing or film production contracts, this one is full of clauses in small print, seemingly inoffensive, which are put in there for very good reasons.

I thus find out that our red-complexioned tobacco jar, as agent, collects a hefty percentage. I unfortunately do not pay attention to a strangely worded clause that is hidden behind one of the bits of paper.

The next day, in the reception rooms of the BBC, I sign the document, along with the BBC man—the real one. That afternoon, big press reception at the station. The BBC man announces the news, and I in turn tell how happy I am about it.

I am rather surprised to read in the papers the next day, particularly in the French papers, which were represented at the press reception, big bold headlines such as the ever-recurring CONTRACT OF THE CENTURY, and, in France, A SIGNATURE WORTH A BILLION FRANCS. (At the exchange rate of the period, of course. Because the contract called for payment in pounds sterling, I never did figure out whether that figure was correct or not.)

The films were to be shot in France, in the very locales where my novels take place, and the Welsh actor cast as Maigret, Rupert Davies, would turn out to be perhaps the best inspector of them all. He would become famous overnight, so famous that a future prime minister took him along on one of his election campaigns.

There is just one clause that D. probably did not read any more than

I did, and which I was to become aware of only a dozen years later. It provided that, at the expiration of the contract, all prints and negatives were to be destroyed in the presence of a bailiff, so that today there is no trace left of these fifty-two Maigrets.

I sold the rights to the films in Germany and in most of the countries of Europe and Latin America. I personally handled the contracts for those countries, and the German royalties, in the final analysis, were as great as, or greater than, what I got from Great Britain.

Back at Echandens, we find a noisy château, the air full of dust and the rooms made untenable by the trucks going by right under our walls, on the rocky path, every forty seconds.

Not only has the once-green terrain beyond the railroad track at the foot of our vines been torn up over a surface of I don't know how many acres, but half-tracks and bulldozers almost without number keep crisscrossing it all day long. We finally find out that this huge upheaval portends the building of the largest railroad marshaling yard in French-speaking Switzerland.

The noise is deafening, especially since an iron plate has been put down to cover I don't know what conduits, and every time one of the heavy vehicles goes over it there is a clanking noise that makes us jump out of our skins.

We have to flee, the more so because the new expressway to Geneva, it has now been confirmed, is going to come by right next to the château's vineyards. Should we look for another house, another château, and then modernize it, as is almost always necessary?

I get the idea, for the first time in my life, to build, instead of rebuilding. I had discovered Epalinges when I went there to play golf. Still covered with meadows and planted fields, that region has an amazing view of the French and Bernese Alps, the lake as far as Geneva, where one can make out the fountain on a clear day, and I had fallen in love with it. I ask an architect to come and see us and tell him our plan. I had found out in the U.S., always ten years ahead of Europe, how a house can be built that is soundproof and weatherproof, with the maximum of modern conveniences.

A few days later, we visit a likely plot planted with rape, which, unfortunately, is too small for what I have in mind. But an adjoining plot, belonging to another farmer, is also for sale. I buy both of them, taking options on other adjoining plots.

It is time to leave, children. I have given the architect sketches of my dream house, my first house actually built for me, conceived with my family in mind. I have indicated where the rooms are to be and their approximate sizes.

We go off to Venice, but you, Pierre, will unfortunately not be with us, nor will Nana, who stays with you, Boule, and a few others at Echandens.

The train takes twelve hours to get to the City of the Doges, with a stop of almost an hour at Milan. You are too young, my Pierre, to be made to put up with such a trip, tiring enough for adults.

Babette, who mainly takes care of Marie-Jo, will be with us. So, there are five of us. Even though it meant paying for an unoccupied seat, I thought it better to take a whole compartment, and the trip will be a very good one.

We decided to stay in the principal hotel on the Lido, an island with spacious beaches a quarter of an hour by motorboat from the city. You are both full of wonder as soon as we leave the station in a sparkling motorboat with shining chrome. Your eyes devour all of the boats weaving in and out among the overloaded vaporetti, which are sort of aquatic streetcars, and the romantic gondolas.

Our suite is spacious, the cooking is excellent, and you two are soon acquainted with all the elevator men and bartenders, because you are often thirsty. On the beach, the cabanas are not merely lockers in which to undress, as they are almost everywhere else, but real two-room cabins, laid out in one row facing the sea, and quite far apart.

You quickly become buddy-buddy with two of the lifeguards, who wear wide black straw hats and stay in one place from morning till evening, in their rowboat swaying on the water. The sun has so cooked their skin that the first time you saw them, at a distance, you asked us whether they were blacks.

The morning on the beach, then lunch, either in the hotel dining room or in the open wooden shed on the beach itself.

"We going to take a motorboat, Dad?"

The question pops out of either one of your mouths, or out of both at once. You know whom to go and order it from. Sometimes, your mother goes with us. At other times, she stays in the hotel, because the heat is suffocating and the sun burns her skin.

Like the hundreds of tourists teeming on the Piazza San Marco, you feed the pigeons, who are as numerous as the people but less ridiculous than most of them. We visit the Palace of the Doges, and I hear you, Johnny mine, calling out: "Look at this, Dad!"

We are in the armor room. Under each suit, there is a small printed card. You are attentive to everything, son, and how very conscientious!

"Guess who wore this French suit of armor."

"Louis XIV?"

"Louis XIV didn't wear armor. Well, you might as well know that the man who was small and thin enough to get into that suit of armor was none other than the famous King Henri IV. Read the sign."

I knew he had been small, but not that small, and you look at me triumphantly.

We go for gondola rides and pass under the Bridge of Sighs, the history of which Johnny knows better than I do.

Everyone's mood is perfectly fine. You stuff yourselves with ice cream, my children. Johnny keeps looking for kits for building small sailboats, which he loves to do.

You started out, Johnny, with a patience and punctiliousness that don't seem typical of you, by building the boats sold in Lausanne, at Weber's, in unassembled parts. Then you went on to less simple craft, with two sails and some rigging. Very soon you are doing topsail schooners, then three-masters, after having constructed the Pilgrims' *Mayflower*, down to its last stays and halyards.

Some of your reconstructions are worthy of the ones that old Breton and Norman fishermen succeed, God knows how, in getting inside a bottle. According to Weber's salesman, these boats should take a good week to build. When I tell him you finish one in two evenings, he doesn't want to believe me.

He goes and gets a huge cardboard box. "This one is really intended for adults, because it is very complicated and has a lot of rigging. If your son can do it at all, it should take him a month."

You finished it in four days. Those boats decorated your room until you left, and I think they are still in storage, carefully packed in straw in one or two crates.

Your brother Pierre will go in for building airplanes, which today fill the shelves around his office on Avenue de Cour. He has forbidden anyone to touch or even to dust them.

As for you, Marie-Jo darling, you have now made an important discovery, which you will always remember.

Every afternoon on the terrace of the Lido, six or seven musicians make up a small dance orchestra. You have found yourself a spot near them and are soon on friendly terms. You are a little over seven, but for a long time now in your own bedroom you have had your phonograph and records, just as your brother has in his. You have favorites, one of which is "Tennessee Waltz," which you heard as a baby and to the rhythm of which you like to sway. It looks to me as if you envy the young men and women dancing.

One day, you bashfully approach me. "Would you dance with me, Dad?"

And the two of us waltz off to "Tennessee Waltz," which you asked your musician friends to play. I have to bend down to hold you by the waist, and at times I straighten up and lift you off the floor, light as a feather in your pretty blue-and-white-striped cotton dress, which floats about you.

"Again . . ."

There is ecstasy in your eyes, as well as the great tenderness I have so long known you possessed.

Every afternoon, from then on, we have an almost secret date, at the front table near the musicians, who the minute they see you go into your favorite tune.

This, my little girl, will remain one of my fondest memories, our dances beneath a sun, filtered through an ocher-colored awning, which lights up your cheeks.

People watch you a great deal, as if everyone were sharing in your joy. Or are they just seeing you as a pretty and graceful doll? If so, then they are missing your eyes, which missed nothing, your comments, which show that you are already a real woman knowing how to see, to think, to judge, and, especially, to feel. Since early childhood you have had an extreme sensitivity, and when I see a cloud passing over your brow, I cannot rest until I know the reason for it.

You delight over a little nothing. But also, a little nothing, a word, a miscue, can hurt you to the depths. You don't cry. Nor do you ever ask to be consoled, but it might seem that by this constant turning in on yourself, you are stepping out of the limelight. You become the shadow of a little girl with the look of a big person who is hurt or afraid.

The trip back is hard on you, my little girl. As on our way here, I have taken a whole compartment, in which, from one station to the next, we would soon feel like prisoners. At each stop, people get on who have no place to sit, peasant women with baskets that have chickens or rabbits in them, men weighed down with suitcases or bundles on their way to look for work in Milan or elsewhere.

At the Venice station, neither you nor Johnny can resist the temptation of an ice-cream cone, because it is warm already, at eight in the morning. Is the ice cream what upsets your stomach? You turn pale, your lips tighten. When we ask whether you don't feel well, you just shake your head and try to smile. You hold out for a long time, until you turn to Babette, and mumble: "I'm going to vomit."

No possibility of getting to the toilet, because the crowd, with suitcases and baskets, makes an impenetrable wall. Your mother first thinks of trying to open the window, but then notices the pile of newspapers and magazines we bought at the station. Fortunately! Because you go on painfully vomiting almost until we get to Milan. A newspaper rolled up into a cone or a few pages of a magazine serve as bags.

Between two hiccups, you succeed in muttering: "The curtains."

People are looking at you, among them one fat, friendly countrywoman with chickens. We close the blue curtains on the corridor side, and feel even more like prisoners. Johnny doesn't dare look at you, for fear of being taken with the same thing; he fiercely concentrates on his reading.

We throw the filled cones out the window. Each time, you think you are finished and you try to smile to reassure us. Only to start vomiting again ten or twenty minutes later. A trip that must have remained in your memory, Marie-Jo, as it remained in mine, to the point that later on I turned it into a novel, in which you were not one of the characters.

At Milan, finally, the corridor and a number of the compartments empty out. You are able to freshen your mouth and face with soda water. And so, back home to Lausanne. . . .

We are met by Pierre and Nana, Boule, and the whole household, and you get your color back as well as your joy of living. Didn't we all have a good, peaceful vacation, except for that train trip back?

On our return from Cannes and from visiting the Buffets, I wrote *Maigret et les vieillards (Maigret in Society)*. I am getting ready to start another novel when, a few days after our return, fever keeps me in bed with a terrible bellyache. I palpate myself. I can feel a characteristic stiffness and have our doctor called. I was not wrong.

"You have a very bad appendicitis attack. If I were you, I would consult a surgeon."

"You have to have an operation," the latter says after having palpated me in turn. "I'll call an ambulance."

At eight that night, the anesthetist gives me a first injection. A little later, I am put to sleep with a mask over my face, and I wake up in a room I have never seen before. I feel no pain, no distress. I ring for the nurse and ask what time it is.

"Seven in the morning."

I don't even feel any aftereffect of the anesthesia. "Please be kind enough to hand me my pipe and tobacco, and the matches that are in my pants pocket."

"I don't know whether I should . . ."

"Please do. I am perfectly well. If you don't get them for me, I'll get up as soon as you leave the room and get them myself."

486

In view of my threat, she thinks it best to give me my trousers, in which I find all I need.

A half-hour later, the surgeon, along with the anesthetist and head nurse, come in and find me smoking my pipe.

"This is the first time in my career that I've ever seen a patient smoking a pipe a few hours after I operated on him. Don't you feel nauseated?"

"Not at all."

"Do you know that your appendix was so long that it stretched almost halfway across your back? I'll show it to you, because I've preserved it. At any rate, we caught it just in time. . . ."

A few days later, they tell me I may go home. The doctor merely insists that I spend a few weeks in a quiet, healthful place.

"Versailles, for instance?" I ask. "I know an excellent hotel there, right at the edge of the park."

Why did the name Versailles pop out of my mouth? I had, in fact, seen that hotel only at a distance, hidden in trees. Marcel Achard had spoken to me about it; that's where he hides out when he has a play to write. He told me how calm it was and how comfortable, and said the manager and staff were very nice.

So D. and I are off to Versailles. After two or three days, I am able to go out for walks alone, in the then peaceful and provincial streets of the town. In the afternoons, the two of us walk together in the park, with measured steps, and soon I am strong enough to go by myself to a nightclub, which I believe Achard had also mentioned to me.

People are squeezed in there, one against the other, and I am able to pick out men and women of all kinds, including sober bourgeois from the city mingling with others of a disquieting mien.

The woman sitting next to me, also a respectable bourgeoise, is half drunk. She has left her husband and children because she just felt she needed to escape. "What I may do tomorrow, or in a week," she says, "I don't give a fuck about. Maybe I'll return home, and my husband will forgive me for having run away, because he's not a bad fellow. He has a very important job. I have money of my own too. . . ."

Talking, talking, she orders drink after drink, always double whiskeys, and the bartender keeps an eye on her from a distance, worried and disapproving at the same time.

"Your children . . . You said you had two of them."

"I don't give a fuck about them, either. They'll both turn into men just as self-important and boring as their father. I don't . . ."

She is weaving dangerously, and speaking in an ever sharper tone. I plan to skip out, after paying for the drinks while she has her eyes shut.

"Would you mind taking me back with you? The doormen are used to it. . . ."

A taxi takes charge of us. When we get to the hotel, the woman, whose name I will never know and whom I am never to see again, is asleep and snoring, with her head on my shoulder. The doorman is not the least bit surprised.

"It's nice of you to have brought her back. Sometimes, the cops have to do it. . . ."

In October, after a brief stopover at Lyons to attend a convention of the International Criminology Association, one of the few organizations I actually belong to, I get back to my children, Johnny in his bedroom playing his drums, and Marie-Jo at the piano in the living room.

What a year! I get rid of the obsessive memory of that lost lady stranded in Versailles, who may end up almost anywhere, by writing a novel of which she is the heroine, which I entitle *Betty*.

D. will read this novel more attentively than the others, with passionate interest, in fact, and one day she will throw up to me the fact that I based the character of Betty on her.

It is almost time to start thinking about Christmas and presents, the tree, the traditions that little by little we have fallen into.

Merry Christmas!

57

On January 1, 1961, as usual we wished one another a Happy New Year. How did it turn out? To be a much calmer, more familylike year, to be sure, without the many travels that had separated us the year before.

The trucks keep going by beneath our windows and past the wrought-iron gate of the courtyard. The air remains dusty. But that sustained level of noise does not shock your young ears, accustomed to the more and more vibrant sounds of your records.

I might add that the work sites, encroaching each day closer and closer, have an attraction for you. Our walks, with Mister in tow, often take us as close as possible to the work, where the big machines fascinate you.

I think of Marc a great deal, of the small apartment in which he is learning what married life is like, and I recall that at eighteen, dreaming of it, I had written, as a sort of exercise, some "Tales of Living Together," just as, on a more intimate theme in the same spirit, I had written a series of short tales titled "Coituses." Whatever became of those stories, which Tigy alone has read? I have no idea. They have probably been destroyed. (*No. As I am now revising these pages, in March 1981, Tigy has been kind enough to send me a photocopy of them, and of all the letters I wrote her during my military service and my months of waiting and being down and out in Paris before we got married. Dear Tigy, who never threw out or destroyed anything from our past!*)

Marc does not write us much, nor will any of you, because it takes up a lot of time to try to build a new life. He sometimes phones, as you all will. I nonetheless keep following him in thought, as later I will do each of you.

I know that life is not easy for him, and that is the way I want it to be. When he left us to go with Jean Renoir and start a film career, I made a decision, drew up a kind of charter, not only for him, but also for all you children. In the first place, for myself, the determination not to push you toward this career or that, because each human being, according to his or her own tastes and aspirations, must freely choose the path to follow.

I determined to support you children financially until the age of twenty-six, which in most cases is the outside limit of postgraduate studies, whether you do such work or not, whether or not you are married. I made inquiries about the budget of a middle-class student, in Paris or elsewhere. This was to avoid, children, any of you becoming spoiled, or, most especially, what is referred to as a "playboy," for that is one of my most constant worries.

I don't care whether your bent leads you to become an academic, a craftsperson, or an artist. My allowance will remain the same until the same age, and I would have sent it along also to any one of you who decided to become a "hoodlum."

I come from a family of small craftsmen, and I consider myself a craftsman of the novel. Each of you boys, by the age of two or three, already had a carpenter's workbench, suited to your size, with plastic tools, to be replaced later by a real workbench and authentic tools.

Didn't I have one myself at La Richardière, and then at Saint-Mesmin-le-Vieux? At La Richardière, I even had a country forge, with bellows, tongs, all kinds of irons, and an anvil.

Each of you boys also, at the right time, got a pair of boxing gloves, a punching bag, and I gave you rudimentary lessons. I wanted to teach you in that way, my sons, how to breathe, which is fundamental to all sports, and to be able by footwork and balance to put your whole weight behind a punch. Not to fight—I have never struck anyone—but for bodily discipline and, if need be, self-defense. Each of you had a medicine ball, which I taught you to use so as to develop your chest and muscles.

What I did not teach you was to be well-mannered children. You learned by yourselves, freely, what needed to be learned, including how to use a finger bowl, which I had no idea of when I was sixteen. None of you became a "hoodlum" or a "delinquent," nor even the nonviolent anarchist that I have remained all my life.

I am getting ahead of myself, children, by thinking about your brother Marc's new home in Paris.

Toward the end of 1960, I happened to read a very long article about me and my work by one Bernard de Fallois, whose name I had never heard before, since I stay away instinctively from reviews, magazines, and papers classed as "literary," as well as from groups or associations that claim such a character.

De Fallois's article strikes me because of its familiarity with my work and perception of my intentions. On rare occasions, I have written to a critic to thank him for a favorable article. I write to de Fallois. I mentioned him in the previous chapter, before I actually met him, which happened in January 1961. He tells me that he intends to do a critical/biographical book on me, and asks for an appointment.

So he is our guest at Echandens for some ten days, sleeping in Marc's room, which has become our guest room, without our having changed anything in it since your big brother flew away.

Does de Fallois seem like the literary critic and academic that he is? Very little, to my mind. Rather tall, he does nothing to bring out his height, and his clothes, extremely, almost exaggeratedly, nondescript, show how little he cares for appearances.

Dark-haired, he has dark-brown eyes that look one straight in the face, benevolent, cordial, and almost amused. He can listen to one talk for hours on end, sitting motionless in his armchair, smoking one cigarette after another, ashes falling with the regularity of an hourglass onto the floor. He never changes expression, and I am curious about his smile, which at first reveals his natural benevolence, only to betray later an underlying irony.

Should I say that he asks me a lot of questions, in my strange office in the turret, with the logs burning brightly in the fireplace? Actually, he says very little and I, as usual—as I always resolve in vain not to—do most of the talking.

He makes a great hit with all three of you. While not married, or having any children of his own, he spends a good part of the time with his brother-in-law's large family, who live in the apartment just above his own.

Again as usual, I lay myself shamelessly bare, for I detest poses and affected speeches, which are necessarily artificial.

We become friends. We still are. Breaking with the university and its academic pomp, letting his thesis on Marcel Proust hang in midair, he went into publishing, where, first at Hachette, then at Les Presses de la Cité, he was and continues to be highly successful.

Most of his time with us is spent, not in my office, but on the ground floor, in D.'s domain, where she, with the help of Aitken, supplies the references he requests.

He will make use of them judiciously, with much talent and perspicacity, in a book titled *Simenon*, which appeared in a prestigious collection published by Gallimard. Many books about me have been published, in various languages, many doctoral theses have been written, but almost all that came after Bernard de Fallois's have more or less based themselves on his work.

As soon as he leaves, mid-January, I get going with a Maigret, which is what usually happens to me after a period of tension. I can see by the chronology that *Maigret et le Voleur paresseux (Maigret and the Lazy Burglar)*, begun on January 17, was finished on the 23rd of that month. So it was written in seven days.

This is a turning-point in my work. In the early days, a novel used to take me twelve days, whether a Maigret or not. As I made an effort to condense more, to rid my style of any floweriness or accessory, I gradually went from twelve days to eleven, ten, nine. And now for the first time I was down to the figure seven (as it happens, one of my favorite numbers, after thirteen), which will become a sort of permanent mold in which all of my novels will henceforth be cast.

March 7, I write *Le Train (The Train)*; June 1, *La Porte (The Door)*, both hard novels.

Despite the noisy machinery and the invading dust, I feel in great shape and have time to devote to you children. Was I still living at Echandens? In thought, no, for I was day by day building our future house, my dream house, in which you already held a great place.

I first designed the façade, almost bare and uniformly white, relieved only by the narrow gilt-metal framing of the doors and windows, which, of course, created problems. But isn't that what the architect is there for?

He and I had frequent consultations, during which I courteously but firmly stuck by my guns. Elegant and worldly, he speaks in a muted well-mannered voice, and his behavior is most engaging.

He is not delighted with my sketches. My ideal house, which I have broadly outlined, has in fact the simplicity of the old farmhouses of Picardy and Brittany, and I insist that it have a slate roof.

This is just the opposite of his own tastes. He is afraid of, even shocked by, flat surfaces, and simplicity to him is synonymous with monotony, if not poverty.

As I am what might be called the "master workman" here, he has to give in, which he does gracefully, if unwillingly. According to the strict municipal regulations, we are allowed only so much height, which means a ground floor, a second floor, and a mansard attic floor. We are, however, entitled to cover as much area as we like, and I take full advantage of that.

For the inside, I have a master idea, which will remain as the basis of all the different plans we draw. The building is to be divided into clear sections, so that everyone can have autonomy.

On the ground floor, D. is to get the large corner office, in which board meetings might easily be held. Then a narrow room for file cabinets with doors into both the large office and Aitken's. Another office for a secretary, because I foresee the need for three of them, the photocopying room, and, facing the courtyard, Blinis's office, with the switchboard in it. To the left of the hallway, the long library and the secretaries' lounge.

My office, the smallest one, has doors to a bathroom and the large living room, which in turn leads to a dining room that can seat twenty.

The kitchen is one of the important rooms, with a great central cook-stove, two wall ovens, and I can't recall what else. You must remember, children.

The dining room for the help, next to the kitchen, can easily seat a dozen people.

How about your domains, Johnny, Marie-Jo, and Pierre? First, in the basement, with windows and doors opening onto the garden, a playroom extends the whole length of the house, with white walls and a wood floor specially treated for dancing.

I see the whole thing in a dream. I make sketches. D. and I have a Louis XV boudoir, an almost outsize bedroom, a bathroom with marble floor and walls, the floor black, the walls tan.

Two equally outsize wardrobe closets, which your mother will make much use of, and a massage room, which will also serve as a sick bay and which legend, the media helping, will turn into an operating room. Next to that, a shower.

Your domain, apart from the downstairs playroom, is separated from us only by a landing. As I sketch it, I am imagining it already completed, and that is why I no longer feel that I am at Echandens. Everything will be white, and all over there will be red carpeting. Your rooms and Nana's are in a row, facing south, looking toward the breath-taking panorama of the lake and the mountains.

Starting from D.'s and my quarters, Pierre's room is first. He will sleep alone in it, but a small movable panel will allow Nana, who is in the next room, to look in on him if necessary.

Then, Marie-Jo's room, and Johnny's, and across the hall, facing north, your three bathrooms, one for each of you so there won't be any quarrels.

A door, a landing, and there, for you three, a room set aside for radio, music, and TV.

I was forgetting, Pierre, your own personal playroom, in front of your bedroom, in which you will spend long hours with your little friends, for you make friends easily.

In the left wing, above the six-car garage, bedrooms for the help, two bathrooms. And at the back, a small living room with several armchairs and a TV set.

That, of course, isn't all of it. As long as I am about it, I will build at last—at my age!—a house in which each one has his or her own place, and may also, at will, be alone or join the others.

Almost everywhere except at Echandens, we have had swimming pools. You all love to swim, and your mother and I do too. Our house is at an altitude of some twenty-eight hundred feet, and the snows stay there four to five months each year. A covered pool? Why not made of glass bricks, with a rotunda-shaped glass roof?

"I would really like to afford you the pleasure of going swimming," I say to D. one day.

She will therefore come to the conclusion that I made her a present of the pool and will one day write that it belongs to her.

Dream enough for today. Besides, once my drawings are finished and adapted by the architect, I will no longer discuss the business details with him; your mother will do it in her office.

The architect actually has turned over these details to a younger associate, who will practically become a fixture at the château and from whom D. will be able to get whatever she wants. But doesn't she get whatever she wants from everyone, including me?

"No man ever resisted me!"

And what about women? Didn't she bend them to her whims as well?

A frequent visitor is that elegant leather-goods maker. He may not have resisted her, but he certainly took her, and at my expense to boot.

"He's a very unusual man," D. says to me, in more or less those words. "He's on the edge of bankruptcy, and no one can fill his place. To get over his current problems, he needs . . ." and she quotes a rather round sum. "It's just a loan, you know. . . . He's an honest man, and he'll pay it back."

Her eyes are tender and begging. I give him the money, which does not keep him from going broke, and I never see it again.

The same thing happens with her wardrobe maid, who has a delightful husband, and I am told that after hours he makes himself very useful around the house. They need twenty thousand Swiss francs to complete construction of a house in Italy.

I fall for it. A little later, we discover that this model wardrobe maid, who knows how to do everything, every evening carried off some of our linens, including bed sheets! Fortunately, a lawyer is able to handle this one for us by getting a lien on the Italian house, after threatening criminal proceedings. Our towels and sheets are probably down there.

Marc comes to see us with Francette. D. makes him a present of the black MG that she has almost never driven. I am happy to see my eldest son and his wife drive off at the wheel of this car that was, in a way, my personal toy, although, on seeing them disappear, my heart is a little heavy.

What will be most important, children, will be our vacations on Mount Bürgenstock, which to me will be a subject of wonder, and to you, also, I hope. But first I have to tell you about the cars, the very ones that will take us to that fairy-tale place, from which one looks down on the Lake of the Four Forest Cantons and the white city of Lucerne.

For the first time, that spring, we went to the annual Geneva Auto Show. D. no longer has a car. I stop short in front of the Chrysler display, a magnificent flaming-red car with a new kind of line, which appeals to me.

I ask the salesman about it. He introduces me to Ghia, the famous Italian bodymaker, who created this exclusive model. The price is impressive, but then, isn't the car as well? I buy it for D., giving him a check against Ghia's promise to deliver the car to Echandens as soon as the show closes. D. is jubilant.

We buy another car, smaller and less pretentious, to take you to school in when the weather doesn't require recourse to the less comfortable Land-Rover.

We are passing the Rolls-Royce display when D. whispers to me: "Why not treat yourself to one?"

I had thought of doing that several times in my life, tempted by the smoothness of the silent motor, by the handsome tropical-wood dashboard, by the supple leather of the seats and their comfort. I always resisted this urge because the Rolls had become a symbol, a "status symbol," and I belong to no rank.

No man ever resisted her, she has said, repeated, written. The Rolls-Royce costs only a little more than the Chrysler-Ghia and has the added advantage of lasting ten or twenty years, never going out of style, retaining its market value.

By chance, the Swiss representative of Rolls-Royce recognizes me, probably having seen my picture. "Come in, Monsieur Simenon. Take a seat at the wheel."

I am more and more tempted, and by the time I leave the show I have acquired the Rolls-Royce. This model, which I am to drive for a long time, and my successive chauffeurs will continue to drive for me, and I will keep for ten years without a repair, without a hitch, is called "Blue Mist."

Who will go with me to Mount Bürgenstock? Who will ride in your mother's car? We are taking two nursemaids along—Nana for Pierre, Babette to keep Marie-Jo company. I have gotten the manager to give us half a wing, on the third floor, eight rooms, if I am not mistaken.

The resort is actually made up of three hotels, of which we are in the oldest, the largest, with authentic old masters everywhere. The funicular leading to the lake was built by the father of the present owner, and there is a news kiosk, four or five luxury shops, a mountain golf course, tennis courts, and a well-stocked bar at the exit of the funicular.

We fall into a routine, of which you, my poor Marie-Jo, are to be the victim. The first tennis lesson, right near the hotel, is given at eight in the morning. That is too early for your mother, and Johnny doesn't like the idea. So you make the sacrifice and get up first, to be there at eight, when there is still a slight haze over the mountain, because we are at close to thirty-five hundred feet, I think. I follow you a few minutes later and sit in the stands, where you seek me out with your eyes.

You look charming, your complexion alive, your body lithe and supple in your white skirt and blouse. You have made a conquest of the broad-shouldered pro. He is a former champion of Switzerland and an excellent teacher. When you miss a shot, you turn toward me with a funny expression on your face. When, on the other hand, the pro congratulates you, you share your joy with me by giving me a radiant smile.

Johnny's turn. You go back to the hotel, and I walk over half a mile to get to a curious glassed-in pavilion that attracts me, with its veritable miniature weather station, all the instruments of which are of the highest precision. I consult the barometer, its curve imprinted on a pink band, the thermometer, the hygrometer, and work out my own forecast, because the weather here is what determines what we will be able to do.

A glass of beer standing up near the funicular, looking at the lake and the clouds or the blue sky over the faraway Jungfrau.

Then I watch Johnny play, and D., who comes to take his place, after which I have a daily appointment with the maître d', sometimes joined by the chef. I know each one of your tastes. I know the dishes you won't eat. I consult the menu, and make whatever changes are necessary in it to accommodate each one of you, changes the chef either agrees to or rules out.

Then I climb a rather steep incline to get to a very fine kidney-shaped pool, where we all meet, including Babette and Nana. There is a wading pool for the little ones, barely a foot deep.

You obstinately refuse to put on a bathing suit, my Pierre. After a few days, however, you agree to dip your legs in the water, provided you don't have to take your shoes and socks off. This year, it will go on like that for a whole month, and Nana will be obliged, each morning, to bring extra socks, espadrilles, and pants for you.

On a terrace, in good weather, lunch is served outdoors to those who wish it. The waiters then have to rush out with their setups, dishes, trays, tablecloths, silverware, and also bring the food up a hard, stony path from the hotel's kitchens.

To them, the question of the weather is therefore important, just as it is to our little group. That is why the maître d', knowing that I go each morning to the meteorological pavilion, asks my opinion. I don't take my forecasts seriously. Neither does he, I guess. Yet, every morning, after we decide on the menu, he asks: "What about the weather, Monsieur Simenon?"

I tell him how optimistic or pessimistic I am, or how undecided. The thing becomes a little game between us, and because it turns out that my first forecasts are correct, he starts believing them exactly, which gives me no little worry. The waiters, among themselves, bet on the outcome.

After lunch I rush off to play golf. Sometimes I am accompanied by the pro, a charming young Englishman, who on one occasion gives me a fine lesson in manners. Having missed a shot that normally I always made, I could not resist emitting a loud French *merde*. Which led the young Englishman to comment quietly to me: "That's not very gentlemanly, Mr. Simenon."

I never again swore when I missed a drive or a putt.

I give my old clubs to Johnny, who is taking his first lessons and taking my breath away with his progress.

It is true that in England they say one can't be a golfer if one hasn't started by the age of six. I was thirty when I first played. So I'll always be a duffer, but nonetheless crazy about it, especially on hilly links.

There is a chalet where the golfers can have a drink or eat a bite. Often, Marie-Jo and Babette walk up there to wait for me. A young blonde waitress, with a strong accent, takes a liking to Marie-Jo and, not being too busy, never fails to go out and pick a big pint of wild strawberries for her.

Do you remember that, my little girl? We go back down together. We are very merry in this enchanted landscape and as we walk you eat the strawberries from their cardboard container.

Once in a while, your mother plays with me. She plays seriously, with application, very tense. Her scores are not bad—on the contrary—but next to the pro, she feels humiliated. Doesn't she always have to be best at everything?

When I get back, I shower and change. Almost every afternoon at that time, maybe because both of us are undressed, I get an urge to make love. D. either accepts with resignation or else groans, "No! Not today again . . ."

I go down at dinnertime and know that I will find her at the bar, almost always alone and chatting with the bartender.

Dinner in the great dining room. On July 14, there are little French flags on some of the tables, meaning that the people at them are French. July 21, it will be our turn to have a little flag on our table, and be served a cake decorated with the colors of Belgium.

There is one final habit, which has become my favorite time of the day. A walk as far as the funicular, in the darkness, with only a few lights glowing. You, my children, are the ones who made up this ritual. On the way there, Marie-Jo walks rather far ahead with her mother, while Johnny and I bring up the rear. D. and Marie-Jo wait for us in the dark. Then, it becomes Johnny's turn to walk in front with your mother while Marie-Jo hangs on to my arm.

There is a small band, a bar, a tiny dance floor. The musicians quickly become aware of Marie-Jo's favorite waltz. As soon as we get up from the table, they break into the "Tennessee Waltz." You seem to float through the air around me, little girl, and I never danced with a more radiantly happy partner.

What a wonderful month, my children, even if it did rain and at times there was thunder, almost always in the afternoon.

We were a very tight little nucleus, the three of you and me, with Babette, who was so nice, and our Nana. Was your mother really a part of all that fun? I doubt it, and am somewhat ashamed to say so. But doesn't she have a need to be living her own life, since for the time being she is being deprived of a large household staff and secretaries to boss around?

On September 11, I start to write *Maigret et les Braves Gens (Maigret and the Black Sheep)*. Once again, seven days. Like a race horse, I've found my distance.

58

Toward the beginning of the fall, D. and I hop down to Milan. Every time I have been in this city, I have had lunch or dinner at least once with my old friend and publisher Arnoldo Mondadori, ever since 1935, when Tigy was with me instead of D. He is actually the publisher to whom I have remained faithful the longest, and after his death I will remain faithful to his son and then his son-in-law. Mondadori's firm still brings out my books in Italy.

Short, potbellied, and jovial, welcoming everyone in his loud, gruff voice, Arnoldo sounds like one of the Italian peasants from whom he sprang, and prides himself on having had as a father a small farmer who could neither read nor write. I was acquainted with his family as well. His wife, who patiently followed him throughout his career, even though he had a devastating vitality, is still alive. I remember their villa on Lake Maggiore, in the days when I was still writing dime novels signed Georges Sim or other pseudonyms, and how we challenged one another at boccie, the Italian bowling game, which was still played with big wooden balls.

Mondadori doesn't speak a word of French. I don't know Italian. How did we get along together so well for fifty years and how did we have so many sometimes heroic conversational exchanges?

During this visit, I ask him whether his secretary might be able to find D. an Italian chambermaid. Although our domestic staff includes a faithful "foundation," the chambermaids D. gets from agencies come and go, and she finds that situation hopeless. Most of these maids are used to working for very wealthy foreigners, of course, Middle Eastern emirs, or eccentric Americans, who rent a large estate for a few months' stay on the shores of Lake Geneva.

The secretary, who is bilingual, promises that she will put an ad in *Corriere della Sera,* the most widely read of Italian dailies, and will herself interview the applicants who may seem suitable for D.

Another trip, also very short. Marc has moved. He and Francette now have a less cramped apartment, all the way at the end of Avenue de Versailles in Paris, and he has asked us to come and see it. He will surprise us by introducing his new friends, all young film people, most of them unknown or barely known. Only Roger Vadim among them is an established director. He is accompanied by his new discovery, a Catherine Deneuve with a childlike face who seems completely amazed to be carrying a baby in her womb. Like a little girl who doesn't know what happened to her.

There is also François Truffaut, with a sharp, angular face, young Claude Lelouch, who is still unknown, and, if I am not mistaken, an adolescent Jean-Luc Godard. The atmosphere is warm and friendly. These young people are dreaming of a future that is barely beginning to take shape, and I listen to them discussing the art of film with the enthusiasm with which in my youth we used to discuss painting and poetry. Marc and Francette, not quite used to being married yet, show us around their nest. A comforting evening, which will take its place among my best memories.

I write a new hard novel, *Les Autres (The House on the Quai Notre-Dame),* again in seven days.

Early in December, Mondadori's secretary lets us know that she had found someone she thinks will do. We hop to Milan. After seeing Mondadori in his big office, we go to the secretary's, where there is a young woman waiting for us.

The first thing that strikes me about the applicant selected is the coat she is wearing, a plaid that reminds me of the Burberry coat I liked so much when I first came to Paris and which I still like to wear.

The young woman is standing, neither ill at ease nor arrogant, and I notice that she has a kind of natural serenity. She has an open face, light eyes, auburn hair, and I would not be surprised to find out she is Venetian. She studied French in high school, and understands it, although she speaks it hesitantly. D., more than ever the *grande dame,* interrogates her at length, without at any point succeeding in putting the applicant on the defensive.

Why then, since I have nothing to do with running the household help, do I so wish that she will work out? And why do I have an intuition that this unknown woman will hold an important place in my life? I am not just making up a legend for the fun of it. Teresa herself, years later, when I remind her of this first interview, will find it hard to believe me.

Everything works out. Teresa will come and join us in a few days.

Echandens. Another Christmas, a night slightly more dramatic than earlier ones, since by now D.'s alcoholism is on an ascending scale. Is it her fault? I have been known to drink too, sometimes a lot. It still happens that I do, but when I feel I've had my fill, as I've said, I go off to bed, to avoid endless, more and more violent and vicious arguments.

It almost seems that D. has realized that things have overtaken her, that the role she wanted to play—and which I helped her to play—is not one she can handle. The mail piles up for months on end. When she does decide to dictate answers, she often takes a page or more just to apologize for the delay: sick child, pressing business, important travels. . . . Yet she now has two dictaphones—one in a red leather carrier for herself, the other in the secretary's office. All she has to do is record on a wide tape, slip it into an envelope, and mail it to Echandens. She does do that, maybe once or twice. But she would rather have Aitken come to Paris, Cannes, London, or wherever we may happen to be.

The more she feels inadequate to her task, the more she wants to boss. I sometimes catch sight of Teresa, in a black outfit, with the white soubrette's apron and cap, but I have no idea what her duties are, since D. dresses me down properly if I dare concern myself with the house, even when she finds me in the kitchen, where I go to see my faithful Boule.

D. draws up menus for every day of the week, the way some restaurants do. Monday, I don't know why, is *purée Parmentier* day, which I am sure you remember, children. There is a leg-of-lamb-with-string-beans day, and beef-cutlet day, tartar-steak day, and the day for stuffed eggplant. Never changing! She has no idea what fruits are in season or what fresh stocks there are, because she never does the marketing. But there is apple pie, which Boule always baked wonderfully, with not-quite-ripe apples, lots of cinnamon, and some sweet syrup, American style.

D. each time instructs Boule, who first made it at Lakeville, how to make Virginia ham with pineapple.

I am to find out later, not only from Teresa, but also from others, why the help seem to ignore me. There is a kind of catechism each one of them has to learn when they first come into our employ.

"Monsieur" is not a man like everybody else, but a man who writes and thinks about his novels. The garden is off limits to everyone except the children, because he may be taking a walk there to "think," and meeting anyone might upset him.

No going into his office, or even knocking on the door, not only when the DO NOT DISTURB sign is hung on the doorknob, but at any time during the day, because he may be thinking.

No speaking to him in the hallway or on the stairs, or making the least noise there. No—truly!—no looking him in the face, because that too . . .

These so-often-repeated instructions will come to my ears only much, much later, when people start talking freely to me, as to a human being.

That explains why Teresa looks at me, on occasion, furtively. Do I not seem to her a dark and proud being to whom the rest of humanity barely exists and who keeps himself at a distance from them?

Perhaps, when she unintentionally overhears bits of dialogue between D. and me, she decides that I am a coward, who puts up with anything without protesting. Once again, I can't hold this against D. She is obsessed by the noise and the dust of the trucks. As well as by the future house, the details of which she argues out with the architect's patient and docile right-hand man. She wants to measure up, and the means she employs to do so only further accentuate her disarray.

I timidly suggest, "You're doing too much. You ought to let Aitken handle some of the correspondence."

She looks at me, offended, and replies: "Don't try to teach me what I have to do . . ."

Alas! She does three or four drafts of letters several pages long that could have been answered in ten to twenty lines. And even then Aitken, much more familiar with business than she, has to correct, discreetly, some phrases that might rub the addressees the wrong way.

Didn't I try, in attempting to restore her balance, to give her a high idea of her importance? And doesn't she still, in moments of disarray, with fury in her eyes, cry out in front of the various members of our household staff, as she hatefully looks at me: "I know I used to be a whore, that I still am, that I'll always be a whore, all my life. . . ."

What can one do, or say, especially knowing one will have to carry her panting to bed, and hold the basin for her while she vomits in big spurts, her eyes flooded with tears?

What to do, once again? I am afraid. I keep still, go on preparing on paper the plans for the new house, in which perhaps she will finally be happy.

•   •   •

In February, I have to go to London to co-chair, with the imaginative Rupert Davies, the British Maigret, a formal soirée that amuses me: the pipe makers' annual dinner and ball. I don't know whether Teresa has by now become D.'s "personal" chambermaid, but she goes with us, as does Aitken.

Before we leave, a small event takes place that, like so many other little things, will have far-reaching consequences.

One morning, when I come upon Teresa alone, bending over the dressing table in the boudoir, I get a sudden urge to possess her, and I raise her skirt, without her making a move or uttering a protest. Never in my life —I swear to it—did I ever force any woman, in any way whatsoever, to accept my advances. Nor did I ever indulge in what those of the upper bourgeoisie scornfully refer to as "ancillary loves." To me, a woman is a woman, and therefore worthy of respect, whatever her position or what is referred to by a phrase I detest, "her social station."

I was not aware of the catechism that D. had taught the newcomer. She has heard me come in, come near her, feels my hand on her hip, and does not react when I raise her dress. I can recall the slightest detail. I am barely into her when I can feel her orgasm and, mine being about to be consummated, I withdraw in time. Is the pill already in existence? I have no idea.

She looks at me afterward with expressionless eyes, and I go out of the room both embarrassed and happy. That very evening, Teresa will fill D. in on what has happened. "I am ready to leave right away, if you wish."

D. laughs. "You might as well know, my girl, that if I were jealous of Monsieur, I would have stopped living with him long since."

"But what if he does it again?"

"If it doesn't bother you . . . It doesn't concern me, and you can go right ahead if you enjoy it."

Marie-Jo came in, and D. told her about it.

London is a city that never was any good for D. and me. Too many chances to drink there. The whiskey bottle is always on the living-room table, for the reporters who troop through. This time there are so many of them asking for interviews that one of the most pleasant and efficient women I've ever known comes to our rescue. The Savoy, which continually has celebrities of all sorts as guests, has a very good public-relations office, and she is the strong-willed head of it.

"If you wish, I can screen your calls through my office. I'll make a note of the requests that you can't turn away, and the desk will not let anyone up without my approval."

How precious this woman was to me, because she has at her fingertips the names of everybody in press, radio, and television, not to mention the professional moochers who crash the hotel bar. Come to think of it, this is the evening we meet Simone Signoret. I can remember that well all of a sudden, because she's the one who retied my white tie for me.

An impressive room. I am on the dais with Davies and the governing committee of the association. D. is probably at the table of honor too, but there are so many people that I see her only a couple of times during the ball that follows an excellent dinner and a few speeches, including the toast that Davies and I are there to propose, while smoking our pipes—for here it is quite all right to smoke a pipe while in white tie and tails, and each of us has been presented with one.

In the morning, before D. wakes up, I go to be with Teresa. She does not repulse me, and I still don't know why, considering the unattractive picture of me that had been painted for her. We do not speak to each other. Did we kiss? Our orgasms are synchronous and complete, as they were the first time.

The same day, I learn by cable that I am a grandfather. Marc and Francette have just had a boy, named Serge. Marc has moved again. He now lives on Rue Gros, in the Sixteenth Arrondissement. Is he to have the same kind of nomadic existence I did? Cable of congratulations, and flowers galore. Phone call to the children, who, at their young ages, especially Pierre's, have become uncles and aunt. Marie-Jo is proud of it. Johnny too. Pierre, who is not quite three years older than his nephew, is nonetheless "Unca Pierre."

Back home. In February, I wrote *Maigret et le Client du samedi (Maigret and the Saturday Caller)*. Seven days. In May, *Maigret et le Clochard (Maigret and the Bum)*; in June, *La Colère de Maigret (Maigret Loses His Temper)*. Seven days!

I had traced the plan of each room of the house on heavy paper. I add, to scale, the placing of the various pieces of furniture, to have an idea of the space remaining. The fact is, I detest overfurnished rooms, in which one has to carve out a path among tables, armchairs, stools, and, of course, exotic plants that tickle one's face as one goes by. I like air, lots of air.

I also like to be able, everywhere in the house, to control the amount of sun according to the time of day, so all the windows will be equipped with Venetian blinds, which I became accustomed to in the U.S. Besides the blinds, iron shutters, because I like the house at night to enclose its denizens securely.

I never visited so many antique shops in my life, in both Geneva and Lausanne. I end up being acquainted with all of them, even those hidden away in the smallest side streets. I buy an English desk with drawers on both sides, Louis XV boudoir pieces, a dining-room suite in Adam style, and, for our bedroom, a few fruitwood pieces in Charles X style.

I order from Plymouth, Massachusetts, glass bricks such as I saw in Connecticut. They are made of two hollow pieces, tightly sealed together, which compress a gas that insulates against both heat and sound.

For a long while I expect that I will have to order from America too the kind of storm windows I had at Lakeville, but then we discover accidentally that a Zurich industrialist has acquired the patent for them for Switzerland.

As for the travertine to be used in the hallways, stairways, and several of the rooms, it has to be brought from Italy, since we expect to need an enormous quantity. It is a light marble, yellow, with golden glints and slightly hollow lines. This same travertine long ago was used to build Roman palaces.

Every day, at the time when the shutters are to be closed, I await Teresa's almost furtive passing. There are so many people in the house that our chances to make love without being seen are not very frequent. The sight of her calms me, delights me, perhaps because I feel that she is truly natural. I do not question myself as to how I feel about her. Both of us will go on for years this way, without questioning ourselves. To me, in my quasi-isolation, she is like fresh spring water drunk out of the palm of one's hand. Nothing complicated about her. But nothing rough, either.

Vacation at Mount Bürgenstock, children; the same routine, which we are delighted to fall back into. I have to go more and more often to the bar of the hotel to tell D. that we're all waiting for her at lunch or dinner. I see less and less of her. She spends a good part of her time in the room, phoning Aitken or London or New York, or wherever else.

You are nine, Marie-Jo darling, and while you have remained lithe and graceful, it is no longer quite so easy for me to swing you around to the sound of our waltz.

Pierre is finally willing to take off shoes and socks to go into the nice little wading pool, but insists on keeping on his short pants.

Down below the swimming pool there is a path around it from which, through wide bay windows, one can look up at the swimmers, and you, Marie-Jo, are the one who is most entertained by this sometimes grotesque and sometimes graceful show.

Johnny resumes his golf lessons, with the seriousness and determination he brings to all things.

Tennis, swimming, golf, walk back by way of the path bordered by green meadows with cows grazing in them. The same blonde girl, now a little plumper, still goes out and picks wild strawberries for you, Marie-Jo.

Foundation work has started, and machines just as noisy as the ones at Echandens are digging out the earth, surrounding what will be our house with small mountains. We take you there to have a look, and we will go back often, for you ask a lot of questions.

"Will the swimming pool be the size of that hole?"

"Not quite. There will be some space around the water, paved with nonskid bricks and electrically heated by hidden wires."

"The water won't smell of chlorination, will it?" Marie-Jo is worried because she is allergic to that odor.

"No. It will be purified by electrolysis."

Johnny understands all this, because he is studying physics at school, and fills us in on the system.

I ask them what furniture they would like, because we will be moving very little over from Echandens; what we leave behind will be sold at auction.

Aren't we turning over a new leaf? In a new ambience, won't even D. feel pacified? The new house, to which I am giving all my attention, suddenly reminds me of an old Chinese proverb: "When the house is finished, misfortune comes in."

I reject this idea, which nevertheless will haunt me for a year.

We have to plant trees, and I select birches, which I consider most cheerful because of their fine silvery bark, the lightness of their leaves, and because in winter they don't look like skeleton trees.

This also reminds me of a proverb, not Chinese; it comes to us, if memory serves, from good old La Fontaine: "To build is one thing, but to plant at such an age . . ."

I am fifty-nine. I will be sixty by the time the house is finished. I am convinced I will never see my birches grow as tall as the house.

At the end of September, I make a hop to Paris. A novel is at work within me. I have to get two or three specific details about the Hôpital de Bicêtre. A head nurse asks me whether I can't come back at the end of the afternoon, to see the chief of staff. I shake my head. I plan to fly back the same evening.

"Just tell me whether, from the patients' rooms, the bells of the chapel can be heard."

"The old chapel is still there, but it no longer has any bells."

That upsets the whole idea of my novel. But she fortunately adds: "However, they do hear the bells of the nearby church."

"Does the neurological service treat hemiplegics?"

"There is no one but hemiplegics in this building."

"Does it have private rooms?"

"Just one. Reserved for patients the professor wishes to keep isolated. I can show it to you."

We go through the whole floor.

"Then if that isolated patient's door is open, he can see others go by in the halls, nurses coming and going, can't he?"

"See for yourself."

Fine! I'm almost finished.

"At what time do the nurses have their meals?"

"Eleven-thirty and five-thirty."

"Where?"

"Right here."

I almost overlooked a question that took my nurse-guide by surprise.

"At what time are the garbage cans put out in the yard?"

Even this detail, to me, seems very important.

"At six in the morning. A truck goes around to the different buildings and takes their garbage cans to the yard, against the wall, where the sanitation men come for them."

"Those men in brown, walking around, I take to be incurables."

"Yes. Bicêtre used to be a hospice for . . ."

I know in detail the whole history of Bicêtre.

"They are in that building over there on the left," she adds.

"And the physical rehabilitation services?"

"Come along."

We go into another building, where patients leaning on their crutches, or sitting in wheelchairs, are waiting their turns for their daily exercises. I see apparatuses of all kinds, which I am familiar with, some of them looking like instruments of torture.

When you greet me with hugs on my return, I look at you all with renewed emotion. You have the use of all your limbs in full vigor and your lips are firm, don't hang down, are not motionless, like the ones . . .

October 2, I harness myself to a novel that will be called *Les Anneaux de Bicêtre (The Bells of Bicêtre)*, and finish it only on October 25, after twenty-three days of work. This time, I did not stick with my distance, even though I didn't think I could run beyond it.

Once out of the daze, I find D. more aggressive and more high-strung than ever, and, with that, my fear returns.

"When the house is finished . . ."

I am more determined than ever to give the lie to that Chinese proverb.

59

You are thirteen, Johnny mine, a solid, thoughtful fellow, who throws no more tantrums, as you promised a long time ago. Your eyes are wide open, your look thoughtful. As for you, Marie-Jo, you have just enrolled at the Collège de Béthusy, as your brother did, although entrants are supposed to be ten years old and you are a few months shy of that. Even more than Johnny, you are sensitive to the atmosphere around you, curious about everything, questioning everyone in the house, which now seems to be experiencing an earthquake.

Your mother, my children, is on the point of "cracking up," and our final Christmas at the château is dramatic. Explosions, discouragements that, in D.'s case, translate themselves into harrowing crises, follow one another ever more closely.

She can no longer hold still, always needs someone to talk to, about anything. She sets down figures and more figures, checks the closets of the château to estimate their capacity in cubic meters of clothes, even hats and shoes. Monsieur Coutaz, our cabinetmaker, listens to her for hours, as patient as the architect and his assistant, whom she sometimes wakes up at one in the morning to rehash what they discussed the day before. She wants to do everything, run everything, including the electrical engineer, who will turn out to be as patient as the others.

Do they too feel that she is about to crack up, that she can't continue much longer in this part she is playing? I do my best, without her knowing it, to correct her more extravagant demands. I almost keep out of her sight, since my presence seems to set her off. As soon as I have the bad luck to show up, she provokes me, and, often, I find it hard to remain cool, to keep still, to bow my head, knowing that anything else will bring on an almost wild scene.

In the evening, when those contractors are out of the house, when Aitken is no longer around, when the help are all in their bedrooms or gone home, she fights off going to bed and lingers around your rooms, especially around yours, Marie-Jo, because you resist her the least.

The bouts of alcoholism follow one another, and when I cautiously mention that she might consult a doctor, she replies that she has no faith in any of them.

Between Christmas of 1962 and New Year's, however, one evening she suddenly makes a decision. Without my having suggested it, in a fit of lucidity when she too is frightened by the dizzying slope she is sliding down, she calls an eminent psychiatrist, Professor Charles Durand, a friend who runs one of the most highly regarded clinics in Europe.

I would never have dared mention him to her, or pronounce the words "psychiatrist" or "clinic," but I have long been mulling them over with terror.

Did she actually want me to be there when she phoned him and started to babble on in the way she had more and more been doing lately?

"I just can't go on, Doctor. I'm at the end of my rope. I absolutely have to see you. . . . Yes, right away."

The Prangins Clinic is about twenty miles from Lausanne, on the road to Geneva. Yet the doctor comes over that same evening, and D., who insists that I stay with her, is silent until he gets there. In her insistence that I be present when she sent out that SOS, wasn't there another form of challenge?

The psychiatrist is a reassuring-looking Frenchman, with a soft voice, and his blue eyes encourage one to confide in him. When I show him into the office, D. sharply informs me: "You may leave us."

The doctor had met the two of us several times at friends' and had been able to observe my wife at length.

I go up to the bedroom and pace for an hour. What is she telling him? Not hard for me to guess: what she tells the help, what she tells the children, including you, my ever-so-sensitive little girl: that I keep her swamped with work, that my attitude has been worrying her for a long time, that she has had to fight it out by herself to the bitter end.

Before leaving, our friend says, to me: "Listen, Simenon, it is obvious that your wife really needs complete rest, in peaceful surroundings. I told her so, and she understands. I did not suggest any date for her coming to our clinic. Better let her decide that for herself."

He advances no diagnosis, uses none of the scientific terms that scare people. He speaks more as a friend, with paternal feeling for her.

"Just remember that there will be a room available for your wife and that I will give her my personal care."

D. is standing, cold, motionless, in the center of her office. She looks at me as if she has just played a great trick on me. "Did you hear what he said, Jo? It's up to me, and me alone, to decide when I am to go there! So, not ever, unless I want to."

I go up to our bedroom without speaking the tender words that come to my lips. Whatever I say might prove dangerous. I go to bed, listening for any sound. I am crushed, now that what I had so long been afraid of has come to pass.

A few days go by, and she drinks even more than usual. I understand her, keep out of her way, even when, at eleven at night, I know she is still in Marie-Jo's room. Sometimes today I blame myself for having been a coward.

January 18, Teresa helps her pack her bags, as if she is off on an ordinary trip. She checks everything, not forgetting the rolls of tissue paper or the smallest accessories. I try to stay with her, but she sends me back to my office.

Did she have some liquor brought up? I don't know. She spends the afternoon with Aitken preparing the files she is to take with her to Prangins, along with her Dictaphone. Then she bustles about, giving everyone instructions, loitering still, in the evening, in the children's rooms.

I live through that day in a kind of fog, thinking of the impressive buildings at Prangins we so often glimpsed through their surrounding trees on our way to Geneva.

"Don't you have anything to say to me, Jo?"

"I love you, D."

The only words I can come up with. I have tried so hard and so long to help her, and now I have nothing more to say to her. The verdict has been pronounced, because I know, I understand, that it is indeed a verdict.

"I'll be back home soon. Phone me each morning around ten. You'll be able to see me every afternoon; the doctor promised. Anyhow, I'll be free, free to leave whenever I feel like it. Tomorrow morning, Teresa can come with us and move my things in."

To me, she seems like a phantom, like someone already far, far away, and unfortunately that is the case.

The next morning, she says good-bye to everyone, not overlooking the children, whom she hugs and kisses at length before they leave for school with Alphonse.

I have rarely seen her so calm, so apparently in control of herself.

At Prangins there is a pert little villa called "Sans Souci," the name given it by Napoleon III, who had it built as a nest for his secret love affairs. As distinct from the buildings on top of the hill, it is mainly devoted to "drying-out cures" and convalescents. There are only about fifteen rooms in all. Smiling nurses greet us there, take us to a large, cheerful room with bath, opening onto a terrace. Nothing suggests hospital or clinic. The surrounding park is vast, with lawns and fine trees, swans at the water's edge, and a place for pleasant walks.

"Phone me as soon as you get back home," she instructs me. "And don't forget to phone me tomorrow morning. Phone me every evening too."

The most difficult thing is to act natural with the children at lunch. I do my best to reassure them. I can feel they are watching me intently. What could their mother have told them, those evenings when she lingered in their rooms, especially the last few evenings?

For fifty-one days, exactly, I will be on a new routine. At ten in the morning, I phone D. She quizzes me about everything that is going on at home, even though she knows she will see me at three o'clock. Sometimes I phone our friend Durand, who is taking care of her and tells me she seems quite calm and is talking volubly.

Winter seems endless that year and there is snow in the plain and on the roads, which, although cleared, can be slippery. In the emotional state I am in, I hire an old chauffeur, because I don't feel I can trust my reflexes. We leave early because I won't let him drive fast. Each time, I bring flowers. D. likes that, and I want to spare her the slightest disappointment.

"Do you have your letter?" she asks. The few sentences I write to her every morning before helping Aitken to dispose of the mail, or sometimes meeting with one of the contractors or the architect.

I have some trouble recognizing her. I have no idea whether she is on sedation or other medication. Feverish D., as I knew her to be for so long, is now so calm that it frightens me almost as much as her earlier exuberance did. She speaks to me in a dull and muted, impersonal voice, as if I were a stranger.

I am supposed to leave by five every afternoon, to be home in time for dinner with the children, but she always finds some pretext for keeping me there. She has shown me through every nook and cranny of Sans Souci. We often take a walk in the park, and she tells me about the patients we see. Other afternoons, when the weather is against us, we sit in the sitting room or her room and I do my best to be cheerful.

One day, I go farther than that and, trying to unfreeze her, take her in my arms and lead her to a couch, with no reaction from her. She lets me take her without flinching, without saying a word, without so much as a tremor, and in the face of such a failure, I vow that I will never try it again.

She is living elsewhere. But where? I look for an answer, and one morning I have a semblance of one. She has summoned to Sans Souci a famous lingerie maker from Bern who at one time did work for her. A very stout and determined-looking woman. She has brought two suitcases chock-full of lingerie and laces, and I wait in the parlor for the painstaking fittings to be over.

Back home, I phone her, as promised. Then I put the children to bed at their different times. They are calm and ask fewer and fewer questions about their mother. Yet you, Marie-Jo darling, will ask me one that will warm my heart: "Will we be able to take our vacation at Bürgenstock just the same?"

"Maybe. Probably . . ."

We have a new chambermaid—that is, yet another chambermaid, because, thank God, Teresa is still there. This one is Italian too, Yole, a nice young thing who will mainly be in charge of the children's rooms. She will stay with us for a long time, and will become Johnny's great friend, because he loves to be coddled. When need arises, she will massage his back, or his feet, when he complains of them.

During this confused period, was I having sexual relations with Teresa? I'm not sure. Probably. Yes, certainly, but always hurriedly and without any sentimental demonstrations. I have the feeling that she is watching me, doesn't quite know what to make of me, and is not too sure about herself.

In the evenings, I write a good-night letter to D., which I take to her with the morning one. I never mention in them my confusion, my sorrow, my fear of the future, which is now always with me. Even when, on the fifty-first day, March 10, I bring D. back home.

Durand whispers to me that this is an experiment, but he does not speak of cure, or even of noticeable improvement. Prangins is not a "closed" clinic, but an "open" one, with the patients always free to walk out the gate.

D. decided to come back to Echandens, to her secretaries, the contractors, all the help surrounding her. I drive her and the children to Epalinges, where the work has progressed enough so one can make out the layout of the rooms.

She is disappointed. "Why, the rooms are just tiny!"

The architect and I are almost speechless, and look at one another without understanding, because all the rooms are actually spacious, almost too large.

The foundation of the swimming pool has been started, and Marie-Jo asks in turn: "Will the basin be as big as that?"

And Johnny chimes in: "Will there be a springboard?"

I answer as best I can. That Chinese proverb keeps haunting me. D. has the same feverishness now as before going to Sans Souci and has recourse to the same remedy, which excites her the more instead of calming her down.

Notwithstanding, I write a novel, albeit a rather tragic one, *La Chambre bleue (The Blue Room)*. What else could I do in a house that has ceased to be ours and where there is no place for me except my little medieval office?

June 8, in the sunniest month of Switzerland's year, D. phones to Claude, the one-time hairdresser of the Cannes Carlton, now one of the two or three most fashionable hairdressers in Paris. She asks him to come to Echandens as soon as possible.

He arrives on June 16, and that is when D. most defiantly faces up to me, as if to assert her independence, which I have in fact never threatened.

Her hair which, eighteen years ago in New York, at the height of our passion, or at least of mine, I had suggested she let grow, her hair that she so long was so proud of, is being cut off in a few pitiless scissor-strokes. This is a symbol to me.

The remains of what I had still thought to be love are falling on the rug in small, dark, soft lumps. But she will have them done up into a braid, which, wrapped in tissue paper, will be laid to rest in a long cardboard box.

Strangely, the novel I write at the end of June is entitled *Maigret et le Fantôme (Maigret and the Apparition)*. Yet, like my other novels, it has, in actual fact, nothing at all to do with the drama I am living through.

The novel barely finished, D. suddenly declares that she can't go on living in the commotion of the trucks loaded with dirt, the tractors and bulldozers. She wants to move into town, to stay at a charming hotel run by a man we used to know back in the days of the Lausanne-Palace. We drive her there, with her luggage, Aitken and Teresa assisting.

With one glance, she finds the room too small, tells the owner that she could not put up with it unless the adjoining room were made into a sitting room for her.

The furniture is moved out so it can be turned into a sitting room. D. tells me she no longer needs me, Aitken, or Teresa. We go back to Echandens. Lunch with the children.

At three o'clock, Teresa and Aitken are called. D. is not happy in her two rooms and, while Teresa packs everything up again, she calls Prangins, only to find that they don't have a room for her at the moment. She tries the Hôtel du Golf. Alas, they are all filled up too, and she asks Aitken to put her up in the little apartment in a peaceful neighborhood not far from the lake where she lives alone.

I go there with her and watch while Teresa disinfects the bathroom and makes a bed for her. I am worried. Volubly, D. goes on about the spaghetti she and Aitken will cook.

She seems so high that I suggest Teresa stay and I will have our gardener bring over a cot for her.

That seems to be the best arrangement. But before the cot is on its way, Teresa is back at the château. D. has changed her mind again. She won't stay at Aitken's flat. She'll come back home to sleep, but tells Teresa not to let me know.

Whew! I put the children to bed and am in my office when D. opens the door, calling out, mockingly: "Well? I played a good joke on you, didn't I?"

The next days, she is alternately in the dumps and manic. Nonetheless, to the great delight of Marie-Jo, who uncomprehendingly applauds, she reserves our rooms at Mount Bürgenstock. What can I do but go along?

Our life resumes with more or less the same routine as in the two previous years. Especially for the children and me; D. takes little part in our activities. When she and I are alone, we have nothing to say to one another. She looks at me as if I were a stranger.

In August, ten days or so before we are to return home, Claude Galli-mard comes to see me. For some years, we have been at odds over the interpretation of a clause in our contracts. The clause gives him the exclusive right to publish my works "in standard trade editions." But some of my books have also been published in paperback and book-club editions. He has claimed half the royalties I got for those, which I have not given him. This affair has dragged on for a long time, and Claude, of whom I am very fond, comes now to try to settle the matter once and for all.

When he and I are together, our discussions are friendly. But D. wants to get into the handling of this. She locks herself up in our parlor for a good part of the afternoon, but gets nowhere. Claude comes back in the evening, and she insists that I not be present. Is this the time to confront her? I am too fearful of what the consequences might be.

I go down the hill and spend half an hour at a country dance hall. But I am anxious about what is going on up on the hill. I return to our suite and open the door.

I stop short at what I see. Gallimard is sitting in an armchair, looking embarrassed, which anyone might in the situation. D., in nightgown and robe, has not heard me or seen me. She is kneeling in tears at my publisher's feet.

"I beg of you, Claude, not only for my husband, but for our chil-dren . . ."

"You'd better go, Claude," I say simply.

He goes without a word. We understand each other. I help D., still weeping, to her feet and lead her to our bed.

I will see my long-time publisher again only much later, in a private interview, will prove to him that legally I am in the right, and the whole little matter will be dismissed.

Even though the future now looks dark, I play golf with Johnny; before dinner, Marie-Jo and I go to the neighboring hotel, where she is greeted with the "Tennessee Waltz."

One afternoon, coming back from golf, I am going down toward the hotel, with Johnny and Marie-Jo, if I remember correctly. We are walking along briskly. Just as I am putting my right foot on the first step of the veranda, I feel a violent pain, which makes me stop short for a moment. I did not sprain anything on the links, because I had no trouble walking the mile and a half back to the hotel.

The next day, I am limping badly, and each step is extremely painful. I get an appointment with a specialist in Lucerne, who has my foot X-rayed and does a certain number of tests, after which I am sent to the basement, which strikes me as a kind of inferno. There is a forge, a real one, in operation there, while patients sit waiting, more or less twisted old people, deformed and frightened children, with mothers trying to calm them. I see fittings being done of iron corsets, which are noisily hammered out in the nearby forge.

When my turn comes, they try some iron soles inside my shoes. The blacksmith takes them off and goes back to adjust them. I am finally allowed to leave, in shoes now so heavy they give me a peculiar gait.

"Aren't you limping anymore, Dad?"

"No. But I have the feeling I'm walking barefoot on walnuts."

September 11 to 25, I write *L'Homme au petit chien* (*The Man with the Little Dog*), which is not a happy novel.

On October 20, Marc and Francette bring us little Serge to be baptized, like Pierre, in the tiny church at Echandens by the Catholic priest from Morges, this time without objection.

Marc and Francette are proud of their son, and I am grateful to them for the thoughtfulness of having him baptized here. But the proudest one is you, Marie-Jo, who stand up as godmother, and have prepared yourself for it by learning the entire Credo by heart in Latin. This is no great task for you; like me at your age, all you have to do is read something twice to have it committed to memory.

The godfather is a friend of Marc's whom I had met at his house.

A happy occasion, enjoyed with your Moinat friends, from whom you will soon move away.

The house at Epalinges is just about finished. We attend the installation of the "crown" at the top of the chimney, and, on the tarpaulins covering the still-bare concrete, we hold the traditional housewarming party for all those who helped build it.

The Chinese proverb is still haunting me. October 28, D. decides to return to Prangins, where there is now a room available for her, smaller but pleasanter than her earlier one.

Again I call on her every afternoon with flowers and the various things she asks for. Phone in the morning. Phone when I get back to the château.

"This is going to be long, very long," Durand tells me.

Nevertheless, he lets her out on November 20, and on December 19 our big move takes place. D. has decided to do it all in one day, using as many vans as necessary.

It's a whirlwind. At Echandens, with the help of the entire staff, she supervises the loading of the vans, while I, at Epalinges, show where each piece of furniture is to go.

Pierre has a sore throat and is running a little fever. D., as if in a trance, insists on coming with the last van, carrying him in her arms, a rather pale Teresa sitting next to her.

Everyone is both exhausted and excited.

Very late in the evening, in the office, D. stages a frightful scene, at which Aitken, who is present, is as frightened as I. She threatens to go back to Echandens by herself, wanting no part of Epalinges. I am about to phone Prangins when she slaps me, keeps me from phoning. A little later, after Aitken leaves, Teresa and I carry her to the second floor, where she lies down on the carpet alongside the bed.

And so, our little tribe has moved into the new house, which as yet has no doors. The openings have been covered with tarps, and for a certain period two watchmen make rounds, silently standing guard while we sleep.

Here, in the snow, we celebrate Christmas, my children. Will I have courage enough to pronounce the traditional "Merry Christmas"?

60

You for one, my darling little Marie-Jo, know very well that none of what I am now forced to tell is inaccurate or exaggerated, and that, on the contrary, I on occasion tone down the harsher truths and avoid the repetition of "scenes," which have now become virtually chronic.

Long before me, you had the presentiment that someday I would be forced, for my own sake, for your sake, to write these memoirs, as your final letters indicate, and that is why you left me not only your notebooks, but also your correspondence, your diaries, your poems, and the cassettes you regularly sent me before departing this world.

You are the one I wanted to address in beginning these memoirs, and on the cover of my first notebook your name, "Marie-Jo," written with felt-tip pen, stands as the title.

I thought better of it later, having some scruples. Since I owed you the truth about your birth and your youth, did I not owe the same to your three brothers, and would the three of them not someday worry about their ancestry and the genes they had inherited?

In 1941, when I had only one son, your big brother Marc, for whom I started a history of the family from which he came, that text appeared, in partial form first, under the title *Je me souviens* (I Remember), then, fleshed out, as *Pedigree*. A thick volume, a first one, as I envisioned it, which stopped at the day I turned sixteen. If it did not have a follow-up at the time, the fault lies with the numerous lawsuits brought against me.

This book—these *Intimate Memoirs,* as I quite ordinarily intend to title it—is in a way the continuation of that.

So it was very late, after Marc and Johnny, when you put in your appearance in this screed, which has nothing fictionalized about it, but sticks scrupulously and even crudely to the truth. My recollections are still vivid, although they might reflect some inaccuracies, especially where dates and proper names are concerned, for which I have never had a good memory.

If your brothers are surprised to learn some truths that may have escaped their notice, documents are at their disposal, and nothing of what

I am saying is the product of my imagination. Amazed by the awfulness of some of the things you told me, I confess that I checked them with unimpeachable evidence, which confirmed their reality to me.

It is mainly for you, darling little girl, that I am writing now, without joy, forcing myself day after day to relive some of the agonizing hours you knew so well. It is you who sustain me in this often heartbreaking task.

As soon as we got to Epalinges—as you know better than anyone— your mother refused to sleep in our bedroom. Not only the first night, but almost every one of the none-too-numerous nights she stayed there. My whole concern was for her, her imbalance, which constantly grew worse, the too-painful fate that lay in wait for her. Three times, during 1963, she had appealed to Durand to admit her to Prangins, because she felt she was at the edge of the abyss, and twice she had stayed there.

I was suffering, worrying about her. I didn't yet know that it was over your fate, my darling, that I should have been worrying.

"I *hate* this house!" she had stated the first night.

It was not so much the house, which she had so demanded to be involved in, that she hated. The house was a symbol; her cries of hatred were aimed in fact at me.

Good, shy Dr. Walther came to see Pierre, whose sore throat was nothing to worry about, once or twice a day, in response to your mother's calls. She had a need of someone to open up to, and because of his shyness, his patience, and his kindness, Walther was ideal. She kept him there for hours on end, and this man, not an expert where women were concerned, for a long time erroneously believed what she told him.

Later on, she slept on the couch from Pierre's playroom, which she had set up at the foot of your bed, and for a long time she poured her fantasies out to you.

She waited until your brothers were asleep before calling Teresa, Yole, or whoever else, to bring the couch noiselessly into your room. The house was soundproofed. But it was easy to call anyone from anywhere, through the network of telephones connecting almost all the rooms and the intercoms she had had installed.

Should I, could I, have interfered, and would that not have brought things more quickly to a head?

Very late at night, she talked on and on to you in a monotonous or impassioned voice. I no longer remember exactly what night you furtively slipped out of your room, with her in pursuit. You were light and agile. I saw you, not that first time, but subsequent ones, slim in your light-blue pajamas, running the length of the stairs, the hallways, to hide in the huge attic or the basement.

Your mother sounded a general alarm, calling to all the help to start looking for you.

When you were finally discovered, hidden behind one of the trunks in the attic or crouched in a corner of the basement playroom, you forced a smile, as if the whole thing had been just a game. A game that frightened me when I found out about it by chance and was able to watch it.

For a number of years, in order not to have depressing fits of insomnia, every night before going to sleep I took a harmless sleeping potion my doctors had prescribed, which assured a solid night's sleep. I didn't even know when your mother finally came to lie down at the other edge of our huge bed.

How many times now, at Epalinges, was I awakened by chance, thinking I heard cries, in spite of the soundproofing! I went to find out what was happening. The whole household staff, your mother in the lead, was looking for you. I saw you go out of the house, cross the snowy road in your bare feet, and your mother was the first, barefooted as you, to follow across the icy snow. You were already far away and breathless. You turned your head and took pity, stopped and, retracing your steps, feeling remorse, begged her pardon.

When your brothers got up early in the morning, the help had already put the couch back where it belonged.

I was still hobbling around, because of the arthritis in my right foot. You too, Marie-Jo, like Johnny and several of the help, heard D. say in a pathetic voice to our gardener: "Promise me that you will never leave my husband. Some day soon, he will need you to wheel him around in a wheelchair. . . ."

Like everyone else, you, my little girl, understood that that meant I would soon be an invalid, and I can imagine what those words sounded like deep within you. I was sixty-one and I remember well the picture I had at your age of a man that age. In my first novels, the old people were barely fifty or fifty-five, and I depicted them as decrepit. Today, I can tell an author's age by the ages of his "old people"!

But as soon as we got to Epalinges, the doctors gave me a clean bill of health.

What I didn't know then, but have the proof of today, is that for two years your mother had been advising you to treat me gently "because he is sick," and that she had convinced a good share of the help of this.

On January 10, kind Dr. Walther was concerned about how you looked and your night flights, which your mother had told him about in detail. He phoned Prangins, and Durand sent his closest assistant, Dr. Verlomme, also a psychiatrist. I still have a vivid recollection of that afternoon.

The young psychiatrist asks to talk to you alone, in your room. Walther and I are with your mother, in her large office. We are silent, having nothing to say to one another, while on the floor above you are being "examined." I can still see your mother determinedly walking over to the intercom, to turn it on, which will allow us to hear what is being said in your room as clearly as if we were there with you.

I get up, rush over to keep her from turning it on. Good Dr. Walther starts to blush and opens his mouth to protest against this eavesdropping, which goes against all medical ethics.

She turns toward me, defying me with her dark look. "I am her mother. This is my affair. . . ."

Our pediatrician is too timid to interfere. He lowers his head in confusion and shame as we suddenly hear your self-assured little voice, my little girl.

I try once more, unsuccessfully, to reach the button, to restore your right to privileged communication. I have the feeling that what I am witnessing is mental rape, of which the psychiatrist and you are the unwitting victims. Were not both of you entitled to speak in privacy? I prefer to leave, to go into my own office, where I can't hear any of it.

More than an hour flies by, perhaps two, for Dr. Verlomme is very conscientious about his work, as your mother knows from experience, since he has treated her too.

I have a sort of grudge against him, for a reason that has nothing to do with you. When your mother was at Prangins, Durand turned her care over to him, so they could compare opinions. During her last stay, I met the young psychiatrist once as I was on my way out to my car. We talked for a moment. I did not ask him any questions, because I never ask questions of doctors who are treating members of my family. Isn't it up to them to decide what they have the right to tell?

"I have a piece of advice for you, Monsieur Simenon," he volunteered. "You are stubbornly prolonging a love that has long since gone out of existence. You are speaking of love to someone to whom the word no longer has any meaning. You are uselessly hurting yourself, and it isn't doing any good. Be realistic about it. Look at things squarely, and resign yourself to the raw truth."

I was not ready to hear such words, and I repeat that I held a grudge against him for a long time, too long a time, for years, until I was forced to relinquish what the doctor had called, with an almost mocking smile, my "romantic dreams."

Too bad if that was how he viewed my feelings. I wanted to save her. Today I recognize that I was wrong, and perhaps if I had reacted differently . . .

I will talk about that later on. The psychiatrist and Dr. Walther discuss your case, without the intercom, in your mother's office, which she has left, but not without first trying to stay.

What did she overhear in your confessions, to the extent that you made any—for you always knew how to keep secrets, and kept yours for too many years, paying for it with your life?

Your mother is visibly overwrought while the two doctors hold their consultation. The report they wrote, now before me, proves that you didn't reveal much. They speak passingly of an "anxiety syndrome" with "night terrors, uncontrollable fear of illness and death."

The report goes on: "All of this is due to worry, for the past two years, about her father's condition, and in the last year about her mother's health and 'fragility.' " I did not supply the quotation marks around that ambiguous word "fragility."

"Prescription: Relaxation through bed rest for at least a week, then mountain air and gradual return to activity, depending on her condition."

Durand will soon be telling me, "Your wife has a diabolical intelligence and on occasion I have let her take me in."

The two doctors who signed the report did too, for they added: "Presence of her mother near her indispensable night and day."

She won, which proves to me that you kept your secret, little girl. So she will be able to talk to you until midnight and beyond, about your sick old father, and prepare you for the death of the one you will always remember when you hum, and then when you record, the "Tennessee Waltz." Didn't you wear until the very end a certain ring that was enlarged several times?

You need mountain air? On February 5, your mother drives you there, with the approval of Dr. Walther, who is helpless. She has decided not to stay at the hotel where we were so happy. She prefers to rent a chalet in Villars, where the two of you can live alone, without men—men, whom she is teaching you to beware of, even of your own brothers.

"There'll be just the two of us alone in a tiny little chalet, and we'll do our own shopping, cooking, and housecleaning."

Yes, you do, or, rather, she does, the cooking, for two days, after which she gives up on it and drives you to a hotel for every meal, including breakfast.

During your absence, I don't write, don't try to, but work in the office with Aitken and Blinis.

While I am not ill, I am temporarily handicapped. Before you left, I tore a muscle near the groin, perhaps playing with you children in the snow. It is extremely painful, and an orthopedist fits me with a complicated plaster cast.

You are the one I am continually thinking of, my little girl, you and your mother. If I reproduce here one of the letters I sent you, it is because it is the one you probably reread before killing yourself. Did it bring warmth to your heart? I am not changing a word of it.

Thursday morning

Marie-Jo darling, my prettiest one, my tender love—I feel like adding the sweet word your mother's daddy used to her and which fits you so well too: "my little ray of sunshine" . . . I wish for all your hours to be merry and pink. Alas! it is not within my power to give you happiness all the time, as I try so hard to. I wish for your mother and you to be the two happiest women in the world, radiant beings, always with a little glint of contentment in your beautiful eyes.

Don't hold it against me if I am sometimes so awkward about it. Like Johnny, I too am a big bear with a resounding voice and brusque gestures. That does not stand in the way, believe me, of infinite tenderness.

I am eager to hold you in my arms, to look into your eyes. Maman knows very well that when we look into one another's eyes, we see into the depths of one another's hearts, and then all the clouds disappear. But I don't mean to rush you. Come back only when you really feel like it, when you feel the time has come. You are the one who must know.

Good night, good night, my tender and delicious love. If this letter contained all of my affection, the postman would not be able to carry it.

I hold you softly, softly in my arms and say no more.

Your Daddy

Please share with your wonderful mother everything I have said to you here, which is for her too. I know you are not jealous of her.

Romantic, isn't it? Incurably, I'm afraid. I am not ashamed of it and do not consider it a shameful disease.

D. decides we no longer need our old chauffeur to drive Johnny to school. He is fourteen. So he can go down the steep slope by himself to the trolley bus that goes to Béthusy.

He can be seen leaving in the morning, before daylight, because his class starts at seven o'clock. He doesn't kick, doesn't grouch about it, and, especially, "doesn't throw any tantrums." Good old Johnny!

On your return, as early as February 26, you seemed surprised, Marie-Jo, to see me up and limber, for on that very morning my plaster cast was removed.

"How come, Dad? Are you walking again?"

Had you been told I would never walk again and that the wheelchair was at hand?

Your mother will go on sleeping with you. She has bought you a dog to take the place of Mister, whom we regretfully had to get rid of, because in the last days at Echandens he had begun to terrorize the peasants by killing their chickens and rabbits. Local regulations don't allow unleashed dogs, and I don't fancy seeing our Mister perpetually on a chain, like the dogs hereabouts. A veterinarian, who treated him several times and has a large garden surrounded by walls, adopted him, and I know he will be happy there.

At the same veterinarian's, D. chooses a smaller dog for you, a little Dachshund, unable to kill chickens and rabbits, whom you name Jocky.

Easter is early this year. Vacation is near. D. decides to take you to Cannes, with Pierre and Nana, to our big suite at the Carlton.

There you'll again see Dr. Martinon, now our friend. Always overworked, he will be in for a rather long punishment. Your mother will call him in every evening, sometimes even at night, and keep him till two in the morning. He listens without showing impatience as she unreels a litany of which he knows every chapter and verse.

I suggest to Johnny that the two of us take a vacation, and we leave that very day for Barcelona.

We are a little like two buddies baching it. We discover an unpretentious little restaurant that caters, not to tourists, but to its local habitués. It makes a wonderful paella. Almost every day you want to have your paella. Nor do you get any more tired than I of our walks along the Ramblas and in the shaded little surrounding streets.

One day, we go into a café, a real one, with nothing but neighborhood people. You quench your thirst with a Coca-Cola while I taste the dark local wine, which I find very savory. With the wine, they hand me a saucer with two thin slices of a highly spiced sausage on it, which you like so well you ask: "Dad, couldn't you order another glass so I can have some more sausage?"

We go there at the end of almost every afternoon, after roaming around the port and paying a visit to the covered market, where you are especially interested in the fishes laid out on the floor.

There are big posters announcing a bullfight, with famous matadors, and I can see the glint in your eyes.

"Let's go, huh, Dad?"

The concierge finds us black-market tickets for nice shady seats facing the entrance for the horses and bullfighters. I have seen a bullfight, in the famous old arena at Nîmes, and I have to force myself to take you to this one. When the time for the banderillas and the estocada comes, I allege an urgent need, so as to get away. But you take it all in unflappably.

Good vacation. Each day, I phone Cannes and speak to D. and Marie-Jo. Each evening too, before going down to dinner, I write them a rather long letter.

We all meet again on April 2 at Epalinges, where the swimming pool is not quite completed, because underneath it there is a lot of machinery. So we see it empty, with workers laying in the little sky-blue porcelain tiles. Almost every day, all three of you go to see how far along the work is, anxious to have water in it. The springboard gets set up.

At one end, beneath it, the water will be almost eight feet deep. At the other, blue mosaic steps lead down to a very gradual incline, on which Pierre, at five, will learn how to swim.

A dream, isn't it? But reality is at hand, and no later than April 21 we will have to make an emergency trip to take your mother back to Prangins. She wants all three of you along. Our old chauffeur is driving the Rolls-Royce, which has never had a breakdown. Why is your mother so upset and why with trembling hands does she insist that we go by way of Nyon? I don't have the courage to talk her out of it, for her condition seems more worrisome to me than ever. And in the middle of Nyon, a breakdown—which they say just can't happen—occurs.

I rush out looking for a garage, a mechanic. I don't know much of the town. I walk fast, break into a run. Finally, gas pumps. A mechanic who looks competent and says he's familiar with Rolls-Royces. I get into his pickup, and we ride over to the car. I think I am in the wrong place when I see no D. but only the children and Nana, and our chauffeur peering over the hood.

"Where is Mother?"

"She went to run an errand."

I feel I know where she went and go rushing through streets unfamiliar to me, opening the doors of every café, every bar, every restaurant. I hunt everywhere without finding her.

A last bar, however. And there she sits, looking at me, with a glass in her hand.

"What are . . . what are you . . . doing here?" she mumbles, looking at me with the eyes of a hunted animal.

I take her gently by the arm: "Come on. The children are waiting."

She wavers. I hold her up, looking for the car, which is soon in sight. It seems all that was needed was to press some button or other to get it started again.

We stop outside Sans Souci. A nurse, watching for us, comes over. Taking in D.'s condition with one professional glance, she signals one of her colleagues, and the two together guide D. off to her room.

One of them is soon back to tell us, "She has had a shot. She's asleep."

"When will I be able to see her?"

"You'd better phone the professor late this afternoon or tomorrow morning."

He gives me an appointment in his residential villa, furnished with so much taste, where years before we had spent a friendly evening.

"Do you have bad news for me?"

"Neither good nor bad. It will all depend on how she reacts to the detoxification cure, which we began yesterday."

"A sleeping cure?"

"Yes. Of course, you won't be able to visit her as long as that is going on. Afterward, we'll have to see. . . ."

"Are you pessimistic about it?"

"Neither pessimistic nor optimistic. But I do think I should let you know that this time she'll have to stay on for a rather long time. How is Marie-Jo?" We have a friendly talk. "I would like you to let me know in a few days how your daughter is doing. . . ."

And Marie-Jo worries me too. She doesn't mention her mother to me, to my surprise. Her attitude has changed. Only in minor details, to be sure, but things that seem important to me. Nana and Yole tell me, for instance, that she has started to wash her hands carefully every hour or so, if not oftener, even when they are completely clean.

At the dinner table, she examines her silverware. "Yole, give me another fork. This one is dirty."

And of course there is nothing dirty, or even doubtful, in this house, which journalists will ironically call "sterilized." Yole does not protest, just changes the fork, the knife, whatever.

She examines her food as if with a magnifying glass. I soon hear that in the evening, before falling asleep, she calls Nana or Yole, in a fit of anxiety.

"You have to pull my bed out. There's some dirt under it."

The words "dirty" and "dirt" keep coming back often, too often, like an obsession, and I know enough about the matter to understand the meaning of such repetitions of the same word, especially that one.

I inform Durand about it on the phone, and he takes it seriously, suggesting that we see a Lausanne psychiatrist who specializes in childhood problems.

He informs me that D., who should normally sleep all night and a good part of the day with the shots she is getting, gets up in the middle of the night and goes down to the ground floor to see the nurse on duty. In her room they have found a notebook (which I gave her on one of her earlier trips there), full of recent notes, entered almost daily. The professor is taken aback, for this is the first time he has encountered this behavior.

I do not ask him what she writes in the notebook, because I am too respectful of its privileged character, as I have previously stated.

"But what if the sleeping cure doesn't work?" I am daring enough to ask.

"We'll have to start giving her insulin shots."

That gives me the shivers. I am aware that it means they will deliberately give her carefully controlled comas, a kind of shock treatment, which can be very dangerous. Even fatal, as I have learned from all the psychiatric treatises I have read through the years. I would rather not remember all that I found out that way.

Dr. René Henny makes an appointment for Marie-Jo. When he comes out with my daughter, his face reveals nothing, and we don't discuss anything in front of her. He will phone me in the evening to make a date after hours at Epalinges.

Face to face in my office, he speaks to me, choosing his words carefully, and I feel that the man before me is serious, scrupulous, and questioning himself.

"I must confess to you, Monsieur Simenon, that your daughter's case baffles me. I questioned her a great deal, without pressing her. She answered calmly, intelligently; she has a very lively intelligence. But in the final analysis, I found out practically nothing, I must admit."

He takes his time.

"There is a woman doctor whom I would like to have see her, the best specialist I know of, but she lives and works in Paris. I have no idea whether she would agree to come here. On the other hand, I would not like to prescribe such a trip for Marie-Jo right now. Your daughter is hypersensitive."

The distinguished Parisian doctor does come to Lausanne, and has a long interview with Marie-Jo in the presence of Henny.

I await her verdict with painful impatience. It turns out to be somewhat ambivalent.

"In my opinion, as in that of my colleague Henny, your daughter has hidden away deep within herself, no doubt unconsciously, memories she wants to bury. Her panic fear of dirtiness would seem to confirm that. She is ashamed of something and doesn't want to face up to it. Only a rather long treatment would allow us to get at what is haunting her."

"In Paris?"

"Out of the question. As is also hospitalization. Dr. Henny is perfectly equipped to undertake this job, which is like a deep psychoanalysis, without exactly being one. . . ."

There you are, my darling little girl. You too are a "case." Dr. Henny will not be able to start the treatment until somewhat later. It is now almost August. I—and all of you even more—am still forbidden to go to Prangins, from which I get news by telephone.

The sleeping cure did no good, because of your mother's fierce resistance. Marie-Jo spends a week with her friends the Moinats, at Echandens. You, Johnny mine, are on vacation, and I decide to take you to Paris.

One afternoon at the Museum of Man. But it is the Marine Museum, nearby, that especially impresses you, and we go through it twice.

Every day, I phone Prangins and the Moinats', where Marie-Jo seems to be relaxing and wants to know what we are doing. The week goes by in no time, and we are all back at our swimming pool, now ready, in which you all swim with glee, but not before Marie-Jo makes sure there is no chlorine in the water. Pierre makes his way on water wings, and is very cautious. Nana is learning to swim, on water wings too.

Marc, Francette, who is pregnant again, and Serge come and spend a few days with us.

September. End of vacation. For you, Marie-Jo, two sessions each week with Dr. Henny. He will apply his knowledge and experience to trying to discover the origin of what is troubling you.

61

I feel at fatigue's end, my children, overburdened with emotions that are so heavy and so strong, especially after going back over the last years at Echandens, and the fear I was prey to, our dramatic move to Epalinges, your mother's new departure from home, and, finally, after Marie-Jo got back from Villars, where she was alone with D., her first bizarre actions, which became obsessive.

Today, less than ever do I have the courage to recount in detail and in proper order, as I would have liked to, the events of 1964, which constituted a major turning point in the lives of all of us. At the beginning of 1980, I began this return into the past, and have unfortunately relived it with just as much intensity as at the time, just as painfully, especially as concerns the most tragic episodes, to the point where I am in a hurry to free myself of them.

I hope you will forgive me if I do not give each of you in this chapter the full share he or she deserves, the share he or she holds in my heart and my worries, if I merely get down on paper the most salient memories.

First, the interview I had with the head of Prangins.

"Listen, Simenon, you have to have the courage to face up to things. Your wife is no longer the same woman you believed you knew. She has become a danger to the children, to you, whom she now hates, after having worn herself out trying to be your equal and then your superior. Your very existence stands in the way of her ambitions and will go right on doing so. I'm not saying she'll never be discharged from here. She will leave, some-time, in the near or distant future. She would even have the right to leave here this very day. But not to go back and live in your house. Especially not to live with her children, until they have reached their majority and are mature enough to resist her influence. I am speaking to you as a friend, and you know I am your friend. You have to reconcile yourself to the idea that, henceforth, there is no longer any tie whatsoever between her and you."

I am boiling it all down, for the interview was a long one, a very long one, marked by friendship and wisdom.

"How about Marie-Jo?"

"She is in good hands. You may be assured that she is a normal, intelligent, sensitive child, as my colleague Henny assures me. According to him, she underwent a serious trauma, which we don't yet know about, but which we will have to dig out. She is ferociously turned inward in her effort to keep a secret that is strangling her. One day . . ."

I mumble to him: "Do you know that, since her mother left the house, she has been going to bed early and spending peaceful nights without awakening, without once calling for her nursemaid, without once making an outcry?"

"Henny told me as much."

"No more flights through the house and outside. She is taking lessons to catch up on the time she lost while she was away from school and is determined to return when the new school year begins."

I try to restore to our home all the cheerfulness I had done everything to give it. You may be surprised that I begin with the help, but there are more of them than of you, and they play an important role in our lives.

I call them together and speak to the whole group of them, very simply.

"Listen, my children"—using this term because I am an almost old man while they are young and devoted and I know what they have so long put up with out of attachment to our little family—"each of you knows his own work. You also know the needs of the house. I am not going to give you any orders. From now on, you may organize yourselves as you see fit, and if you have any problems, I am always at your disposal. No more evening 'report.' No more being 'on duty,' each in turn, until midnight. You will eat the same meals that we do, and make any changes in the menus that suit you. I have complete faith in you."

That's all. Immediately, the house becomes more cheerful.

I keep thinking of you, my big Marc, still the dreamer and still so warm-hearted. I almost betrayed you by not inviting you to visit more often with Francette, and then with Serge. I have to make a confession that is hard for me to admit. When you were a child, D. was all attention to you, making up games to play and overflowing with affection.

Until she had a son of her own. Especially until she became Mme Georges Simenon, the one and only, to the exclusion of your mother.

She often complained to me about what was done for you, on the one hand, and for Johnny and then her other children, on the other, and this became a fixation with her. You were no longer, in her eyes, the little boy she had coddled; you had become the intruder. Does that word surprise you? Are you asking why? Because someday you will inherit from both your father and your mother, while her children stand to inherit only from me. She kept repeating to me that it was unfair, that I ought to see lawyers and fix it so this unfairness was repaired. I turned a deaf ear on that. She then resented you even more, and for years you were no longer welcome in the house.

Now that has all changed. Epalinges is your house as much as ours, as well you know, and this very winter we are all going to spend our snow holidays together, then our summer vacation, and it will go on that way for a long time, all the Simenons together.

You, Johnny mine, if you seem to have no friends, it is because you have time only for the two activities you are so serious about, the first of which outweighs the other. You are studying very hard. And when you do finally look up from your studies, you go out and shake yourself off in the garden, in running shorts, bare-chested, and run a number of laps around it at the even pace of serious trackmen. In the swimming pool you will soon be asking me to time you as you swim I don't know how many laps. You are also crazy about music.

You often hop onto your bike and pedal into the forest, where you pick up speed along the paths. This forest and the woodcutters you come across are so attractive to you that one day you will say to me: "Sometimes I wonder whether, when I finish school, I won't become a forester, alone somewhere with just the trees. . . ."

Do you remember, son?

Marc too is a nature lover and each of his moves, as if by coincidence, gets him nearer to it.

In July, I write my first novel of the year, the first one at Epalinges: *Maigret se défend (Maigret on the Defensive)*. After all, my profession is writing, I feel a need for it, and I have remained too long unfaithful to my typewriter.

At the end of September, another novel is at work in me. I want to have it take place in a down-and-out neighborhood of Paris where I used to spend a lot of time, when, often with Tigy, I ventured deep into the most un-wholesome streets by day or by night, because I wanted to know every aspect of the city.

This time, I am concerned with the Quartier Maubert, "la Mouf'," as it is called in argot, that refuge for penniless bums. In 1931, I spent an entire night there, looking for a man who could be photographed for the cover of *Le Charretier de "la Providence" (Maigret Meets a Milord)*. I found him, in the most sinister of those dens for people who have given up all hope, and took him to the studio, where he was photographed next to a rented white horse.

A teeming street, one of the most populous in Paris, and, in my recollection, beyond a gateway open day and night, a paved courtyard, open garbage cans, detritus, the glass-paned shop of a carpenter at the rear, to the right a poorly lighted stairway leading up to two or three floors of sordid hovels.

This is the setting I chose for the novel-to-be, a novel that, although perhaps sordid, I wanted to be optimistic.

Haven't the street and that decrepit building changed with the years? I have to see for myself, as I did for *The Bells of Bicêtre*. So I make a solo jaunt to Paris.

In the afternoon, I find Rue Mouffetard, even more teeming than it once was, with the little peddlers' carts, but also now with shops, the outdoor displays of which take up almost all of the sidewalks. It is a sunny day. I see in my mind's eye a shimmering of colors, I deeply breathe in the aromas of fruit and vegetables, as well as human sweat. I am not able to locate "my" house, the one that sticks in those old memories of mine. Could that be because I first found it in the dark?

Late in the evening, a taxi takes me back to Rue Mouffetard, the driver agreeing to wait for me at the corner. He seems not a little worried, for very unreassuring shadows keep going by in the darkness. I look for my building, finally locate it, true to my memory. I go into the courtyard and up the stairs; the iron rail is very shaky and the worn steps creak under my feet.

On the second floor, a door opens a crack, a bare-chested man looks mistrustfully at me, and I hear voices of children and women speaking Polish. I keep going up, to the top, listening to and inhaling a thick odor of poverty.

I can now return to my taxi. My research is completed. On October 5 I sit down to type and nine days later I put the final period to the novel entitled *Le Petit Saint (The Little Saint)*. When Nielsen asks me what catchline we can put on the white band around the volume, he is surprised to hear me answer, "Well, I finally wrote it."

An optimistic novel, yes, even though so much of it takes place in this apparently hopeless house. For the first time, I have composed a sort of paean to life, a song of hope and appeasement.

Which does not mean that I myself am appeased. I see D. twice in the garden at Sans Souci, and hardly recognize her. Her eyes are fleeting, as if worried, her pasty face has become almost cadaverous, and she now walks and looks like too many others I have seen in this garden. She barely speaks, seems very far off, in a world forbidden to me, and I find it hard to hide my depression from you children.

Durand gives me another appointment. And this time he does it to ask me for another, greater, sacrifice.

"Do you know what is eating away at your wife, Simenon, and perhaps keeping her from recovering? One thought that is unbearable to her, which she mentions to me in every one of our sessions. It's about Boule, who shared your past with you. The idea that Boule is now the mistress of the house, and running it to suit herself, drives her out of her mind."

I protest sharply: "Boule is not the mistress of the house. She . . ."

"I know, Simenon. But nonetheless that has become a fixation, and as long as Boule remains there, there won't be anything I can do for your wife."

"You mean that, after more than forty years, I have to . . ."

"I've stated the problem to you. You'll have to be the one to figure out how to solve it."

I return home completely unstrung. I avoid looking Boule in the eye, Boule who has held such a big place in my life, who has lived through all its phases, including my tough early days in Paris.

In the middle of the night, I phone Marc. "You have a child of two, son. Your wife is expecting another. Would it help you to have Boule come and live with you?"

I don't explain all the reasons to you, my Marc. You are surprised, but enthusiastic.

The next day, I have to have a painful tête-à-tête with Boule. I explain the situation to her in an emotion-filled voice.

"Don't you want me anymore, my fine young gentleman?"

I take her in my arms, do my best to pacify her. "You love children, my little Boule. You took care of mine, who are big now. You adore Marc, and now he has children of his own. . . ."

This is as wrenching for her as it is for me. I can tell that she doesn't fully comprehend the sacrifice I am making.

"From now on, Marc's family and mine will be seeing a lot of each other, we'll be spending all our holidays together. . . ."

She dries her tears, makes an effort to smile, but she will hold this against me for a long time, I know, until she finally forgives me for what she considers to be a betrayal—what, indeed, looks like one.

She will leave as soon as I find a cook, Michel. Pardon me, a "chef," who is also an accomplished pastry cook, and wears the small-checked light-blue trousers and white toque and jacket that are the professional trademarks.

Boule agrees to tell you, Johnny, Marie-Jo, and Pierre, that you are big now, that Marc has a son and is going to have another baby, that they will be needing her, but that none of this is forever, we will all be seeing one another often. . . .

You cry a lot, Marie-Jo darling, because you love Boule, who is in a way your "accomplice," the one in whom you willingly confide, who jealously keeps your "little secrets," even from me. One of her favorite sayings, when insistently questioned, has always been, "I never let the cat out of the bag. . . ."

I resume my place in the office, the "big office," D.'s.

You play a lot with your brother, my little girl, and get along well with him. I mean Pierre, who is now five and doesn't stay still a moment. You ride along the paths on your bike with him, followed by Jocky, who, since you don't pay much attention to him anymore, has become attached to Pierre.

You are gay, full of life, even though at times a shadow crosses your face. We take walks, arm in arm, in the garden and the surrounding paths. All your tenderness has returned, and it is a joy for me to feel your hand holding my arm and at times squeezing it.

I don't ask you any questions. I daily ask them of myself, without finding any answer. What is the secret you have been so fiercely hiding since your return from Villars?

One day, on one of our walks, you open this hermetically sealed door, but just a crack.

"You see, Dad, there is one thing I will never forget, because of which I will always feel dirty. . . ."

"Have you spoken to Henny about it?"

"No. I won't ever say anything about it to him, in spite of all his efforts to draw me out. It's too horrible. It's about Mother. . . ."

You tell me no more than that, and I have too much respect for any human being, and more for my own children, to try to pry that door open.

You will say more about it to Teresa, Nana, Yole, but it will be only in the year 1978, which you will not live out, that they will tell me. By then, I know your secret too, through your letters, the intimate papers you turned over to me, your poems, the cassettes you sent me until just before your death. . . .

You had just died when I received that cassette, and you were not yet in our little garden, cremated with your ring, as you had so insistently requested. I phoned to the head of Prangins, who came over immediately. I played the cassette for him, in an almost hallucinated state.

"It's true," he told me affectionately. "Marie-Jo told me about it. It was the first time in my career that I ever heard so terribly upsetting a confession. I didn't pay full heed to it, because children sometimes imagine things that have no basis. I called her mother into my office. She fought it off a long time before admitting that Marie-Jo hadn't made any of it up. . . ."

"In one of her notebooks, Marie-Jo mentions some sort of 'incest.' . . ."

"To me too she used that word."

We listened to some of the other cassettes together, and I was breathless, feeling like screaming with pain. I begged him to keep those cassettes, lest I be tempted to listen to them again.

Only after nearly two years had gone by did I feel strong enough to ask Durand to return them to me, along with other no less upsetting documents. The need was then born in me to write your story, my darling, to publish your best poems, your quivering letters.

It is now 1980. Two years ago you left us, with a calm, a lucidity, a courage that our psychiatrist friend described as sublime.

At the point that I have reached in these *Memoirs,* you are almost twelve, and I will continue to follow you, to follow all of you, but I have a need, at this moment, to reveal your secret.

You don't hold it against me, do you, darling little girl? You knew I would, didn't you? You wanted me to.

I'm still back at Epalinges, and you still have many years to live. I have a lot left to tell yet, about you and your brothers, about my own life too, of which all of you knew only one aspect.

Your life did not consist of suffering alone, little girl. And it is with your words that I would like to close this period of all our lives, this first phase of Epalinges.

A song, first, which you recorded, along with its title:

Words Made up on the Guitar—For You

> *I never knew how*
> *to drift along*
> *with everything that was nice*
> *and I resisted without knowing,*
> *without understanding why,*
> *with all my strength*
> *against . . . any joy.*

> *I had to suffer gratuitously,*
> *for me,*
> *in order to moan,*
> *in order to have something over which to groan.*

Now, I have already dug so deep
a hole with all my tears
that I could truly bury myself in it.

Yet I think I loved from afar
so many things,
so many people
but there was always something missing,
a taste of dream
a little wonderment.
The tender memories
had to be erased.
Some wounds, it's true,
I had not yet inflicted on myself,
coming to me from other persons
not responsible whom I could never judge
and who hurt me while
thinking that they loved me.

That is perhaps why at this time
I am afraid
as soon as I feel that I too
could love.
I'm afraid of hurting
and for fear of hurting another
I take what is closest,
what is truly within my reach.
Perhaps out of laziness
I take myself.

Comes the obsessional round
of words,
insults and tears,
all caricatures of scenes seen on the stage,
in the movies,
in life,
but amplified a thousand-
a hundred-fold
but even if only twice
that is much too much.
It's no longer anything like a truth,

Sonoma County Library

Sonoma Valley Regional Library

Date: 1/13/2020

Time: 2:34:36 PM

Name: 100212095783

Fines/Fees Owed: $0.00

Important: Starting July 1, HOLDS will

be held for 7 calendar days.

Checked Out: 1

---

oirs : including Marie-J
84982

f 1

no longer anything like sunshine,
no longer anything sweet about it
it's nightmare unending,
truly without a stop,
the tunnel
of almost fifteen years of life
out of twenty-five.

When one thinks—
it hurts—
however you put it
it's still more than half.
So it's no great surprise either
that what remains of the ten years
of other people
sounds like the Tale of Sleeping Beauty,
since actually I was very little
when I already saw myself
as grown.

The guitar?
I no longer even know why.
It seems to play itself
and I am talking by myself too
without knowing how.

My bed awaits
but it is empty,
just my body beneath the cover,
nary a lover.
How would he even dare select me
at this time,
since I've done everything
to get away,
to create all the barriers,
like the ones inside me?
I've put "Off Limits"
on a sign on my brow
but sometimes I forget
and I'm surprised
never to hear anyone call my name.

My name?
What is my name?
Really?
It is made of two syllables
and a hyphen between.

A bridge in my image,
as if there were a bridge softly to cross
to get from one self of mine to the other,
but this bridge,
it makes me dizzy.
I stop in the middle,
I yell,
I fall even before I am falling,
I imagine myself already
down in the ditch.
All this after fifteen years.

What would I like to have again,
only one time,
to see,
love, as before,
to know whether there was anything good,
that I really knew,
normally,
how to feel alongside somebody I loved
too much.
End Part One.
Maybe, The End, period.

Finally, my little girl, that tender, as if pacified, song that you improvised in our little pink house on February 20, 1978, accompanying yourself
on a guitar we did not know you had brought along. It was a few days after
my birthday, a few days before yours.

To a tune known the world over and usually sung at festive occasions,
"Auld Lang Syne," you sang in your warm and moving voice:

> *Until the time we meet again,*
> *for we will meet again,*
> *Brothers,*
> *until we meet again*

536

Let us unite our thoughts.

And you, my Dad, and you, Teresa,
we will meet again soon.
For you, my Dad, I'm singing tonight,
but also for meeting again after the big clouds.
I love you, you know, maybe more than before.
I'll love you all my life.
Yes, you will see, you'll be a hundred
when I myself am fifty
I'm making a rendezvous with you
Across that half a century
And you will see how we all smile
For life will be so fine
For life will be so fine.

You sang us other songs, including "The Flat Country," which is mine, and partly yours as well, yours and all my children's.

Excuse this interruption in the story. I had to speak out, to let you speak out, Marie-Jo.

I promise you that, in a few days, when I get back to these *Memoirs*, I'll find you again, Marie-Jo at eleven, Pierre at five, Johnny at fifteen, and big Marc at twenty-five.

I'll be sixty-one, and we will all be together celebrating Christmas at Epalinges. The first "real" Christmas in our own house.

I could not keep that secret any longer. Don't hold it against me. It was killing me.

Now what I need is a few days of rest, walking with Teresa through our familiar streets, rubbing elbows with the passers-by, going along the shores of the peaceful lake.

I have gotten rid of a weight that was too heavy to bear.

How fine Epalinges will be, next week! And Crans, up there among the white mountains, where we are all going to spend our first winter vacation together!

62

It is the same for 1964 as for other years: if I had to sum it up, I could do so only in images, for my memory works mainly through images, some of them dark and foggy, most of them bright, sunny, vibrant with pure colors.

That year saw some dramatic, even tragic developments, insofar as D.'s fate is concerned. I had been fearing them for a long time, especially the last three years at Echandens and her demented arrival at the house at Epalinges. Many worries also, early in the year, about Marie-Jo.

Still, if I look back on the year as a whole, I find only brightness and light. It is that way with all my recollections, even those of my childhood. Many people I know have a tendency to recall with cruel minuteness the bad times they went through. Without my will having anything to do with it, my brain seems to refuse to record unpleasant images, but is sensitive only to light, sunshine, and joy.

Here is an example. It has to do with a minor incident, but one full of meaning. I think I mentioned it in a few lines: the slap D. gave me at the height of one of her frequent rages. We were in her big office. There were two or three others there, which reminds me that these "scenes" almost never occurred when the two of us were alone.

What set it off? I couldn't say. I mainly see D.'s pale face, disfigured with hatred, her meaningless gesture, her hand or fist landing on my face.

I walked out, to avoid anything worse, and could hear her triumphantly proclaiming, "No man ever resisted me in my life."

I barely remembered these words; only later were they recalled to me by the witnesses. D. confirmed them much later, waving them aloft like a trophy, in a book she unfortunately wrote; "unfortunately," because its consequences were more than dramatic.

I had forgotten the blood gushing profusely from my nose, which I tried with both hands to hold back on the way out. I know I was wearing a yellow sweater. I was forgetting that this sweater, which I still have, was getting bloodier and bloodier as I went along.

I must have gone up to our room. I was also forgetting that shortly thereafter the witnesses to the scene were forced to carry D. up to the bedroom and put her to bed, wracked with hiccups.

In other words, of a cruel and unpleasant event, my brain retained only the image of a hard face, a look, a fist suddenly aimed at my nose.

Of Sans Souci, to which I was rarely admitted, and only for a limited period, just an outline, that of D., somewhat stooped, her face vacant.

As for Marie-Jo, her joy, her vitality, her eyes, which had lighted up again after her mother left, quickly made me forget my days and nights of anxiety, and I was helped by Henny's and Durand's optimism.

The house is cheerful, as I planned, red and white everywhere, with brightly colored paintings in the hallways.

The white-fenced lawn is an ideal place for children to play. I can watch them, join in their games, for the arthritis in my foot is now just a memory.

Twice, I had been back to that Lucerne "smithy," to have my steel soles adjusted. Discouraged, I had mentioned it to our friend Dr. Samuel Cruchaud.

"I had another patient with a problem like yours. He tried everything, and then he went to an orthopedic shoemaker in Lausanne. After taking a cast of his foot, he made him a pair of shoes that look no different than ordinary ones, and from then on he had no more problem."

I discovered the dark, narrow shop, displaying casts of unbelievably deformed feet. A week later, in my new shoes, I walked around without bother or pain. That was sixteen years ago. The same shoemaker still makes my shoes, and I no longer have that arthritis. I sometimes wonder whether I ever actually had it at all.

Boule's departure certainly broke me up, and you children were also upset at being separated from her. But she is with your big brother Marc, taking care of his two children, for Diane was born in October. So Boule remains part of the family.

What most stands out in that year, approaching its end, is our first real Christmas at Epalinges, a Christmas full of joy, without a shadow, except perhaps in some hidden corner of my heart.

Under Johnny's direction, you children decorate the big Christmas tree in the playroom, while I watch and refrain from interfering. This time, it is not a tradition, but a game.

In the evening, with Marie-Jo and Pierre asleep, Johnny helps me arrange the presents around the tree, without sophisticated wrappings, without tissue paper, without ribbons.

If I am not mistaken, Marc, Francette, and their two children arrive early in the morning on December 25. Serge is almost three. Diane, just over two months old, traveled in a heavy cloth carrier and is now wiggling around in one of the playroom's bow windows.

You are aglow, my Marc, at twenty-five, with your blond hair and light, merry eyes. You are bringing a present that will outshine all the others: a skateboard, then unknown in France and still a novelty in the U.S. The playroom, theater-size with a glittering dance floor, is well suited to your demonstrations, which amaze your brothers and sister, as well as me. They try it. You help them paternally.

We are free, children, without hangovers, without red eyes, without any urge to go and sleep it off.

We open the package from "Santa Claus," that good friend of all of ours, my Dutch publisher Abs Bruna, and you all share in the wafers and sweets of all kinds.

Lunch, caviar and traditional turkey, a cake as tasty as it is monumental, and most of the afternoon is spent in the sparkling snow, which crackles under your new sleds and your skis.

The next day we are all off for winter sports at Crans, accompanied by Nana and Teresa.

Teresa, no longer D.'s personal maid, takes care of our quarters. To be sure, D. is not jealous of her on the level of our sexual relations, which she even encouraged. But doesn't the fact that Teresa is along on vacation with the whole family cast some reflection on D. and might it not aggravate her condition?

Dr. Durand had reassured me. "The main thing is, it's time to think of yourself."

"But what about the children? What about Marie-Jo?"

"They'll see no harm in it. Once again, just think of yourself."

So Teresa and I are staying in one room. Johnny and Marie-Jo have their own rooms, with bath, right near ours; Nana and Pierre share another room, also with bath. Marc's little family is staying at nearby Montana, because our hotel was booked solid for the school vacation.

Dream vacation for all of you. Marc, driving our Land-Rover, comes over early in the morning. Nana, Marie-Jo, and Pierre are the first out on the snow. Pierre and Marie-Jo aren't interested in lessons, but go straight out on the easy slopes, tumbling frequently but without hurting themselves. Johnny and Marc prefer going to the steeper runs, at the other end of the little town.

Teresa and I go from one group to the other, walking a great deal in the snow, with the help of spiked sticks, wearing fur-lined boots. We often follow a little trail through the woods that leads to the skating rink, where we find Marie-Jo and Pierre working out under Nana's watchful eye.

Freedom for all of us. We split up and come together again. We are playing out a kind of ballet. Late in the morning, we go with the "young ones" to join the "big ones" at the foot of the ski lift. We window-shop on the way back. We have a long table reserved, at the far end of the dining room, and make sure to get there first so as to be served quickly. The children make friends in no time with the maître d', the captains, and the waiters. Our meals are festive occasions.

When the sun goes down, around four, we all come back, and Marie-Jo takes my arm as she did at the Bürgenstock.

After changing, we meet again in the main parlor to await dinner. Johnny has his own stool at the bar, where he drinks Coca-Colas and treats Marie-Jo to them when she asks him to. In the evening, he often goes night-clubbing with Marc and Francette.

I don't go out without crampons on my boots, and always hold on to Teresa's arm, which no one finds strange.

It is hard for me to speak of our private life, for neither of us makes any mention of it. To be sure, our sexual relations go on more fervently than ever, but when I try to put into words some of the feelings I am beginning to know I have, Teresa hushes me up, and rightly so. What she thinks of me, I have no idea, and will long go on having none. The main thing is that she is here.

For the longest time she had devoted herself to D., as if that were the natural thing to do. She had never been a chambermaid, but accepted that task without protest, applying herself to it so conscientiously that sometimes I was afraid she was on D.'s side against me.

Once, however, last year or the year before, D. had been so aggressive that Teresa's innate dignity moved her to say, "I suppose I'd better go."

"I beg you, Teresa, please stay; I need you too much."

Teresa felt sorry for her and stayed, thank God!

All that is now long past. We are having a real vacation. I skied a great deal in the old days, with Tigy, at Saint-Moritz and in the Tyrol, and even at Lakeville. I've reached sixty-one, when bones knit less well, and after a fall one runs the risk of spending long months in a cast and having aftereffects for the rest of one's days.

I make do with just walking in the snow, morning and afternoon, often again in the evening after dinner. Then we follow a narrow trail that goes below the hotel. I remember one of those evenings. Yellowish lights mark the windows of small chalets, and one can see shadows move across them that remind me of the ones in my adolescence that gave me dreams of life "in double harness."

What nostalgia takes hold of me that night? I can see D., alone among strangers at Prangins, our tumultuous passion of the early months, my desperate effort over so many years to turn us into a real couple. I tried everything, put up with everything—in vain. She is lost to me, and no doubt also to herself. That evening, taken with sudden despair, I decide to end it all. We are walking along a sheer rock. I stop, totter, murmur something like, "I can't go on. . . ."

No empty threat. At that moment, I am determined to put an end to it. Teresa holds me back in time. Fortunately, her arms are strong. From then on, she makes me give up walks along that trail and gingerly guides me toward the brilliantly lighted and crowded streets.

New Year's Eve, which Marc, Francette, and Johnny spend at a night-club. You children, as well as Nana and Teresa, are looking forward to celebrating the new year the next day.

I go downstairs alone, wearing the tuxedo that is obligatory that evening, and while couples dance, I don't stir from my chair, staring at the crowd without seeing it, facing my bottle of champagne in its pail. What am I thinking about? I could not say. I see people kiss one another, exchange wishes, pop balloons, throw streamers and confetti around.

"Spending New Year's Eve all by yourself, Monsieur Simenon?"

I look up in surprise. A man, still young, his face familiar to me, although I can't place a name on it. The woman, very elegant, has a slight American accent with some Italian intonations in it.

"May we drink a toast with you to the New Year?"

I gradually come out of my daze and recognize him as the great actor James Mason, who later, in England, will be cast in the part that Raimu once played in my *Strangers in the House.* The woman with him is an American who was married to an Italian count, and has a son by him who will become a good friend of Johnny's and be a frequent guest at Epalinges. Chance is even more unexpected than that, since James Mason's daughter will also come to visit us, a beautiful, seductive girl, with whom Johnny for a while will be in love.

The year is finally over, dark, almost tragic, at its onset, then gradually filled with children's laughter in the brand-new house where doors are never closed, especially the one to my office. Except when I'm writing a novel and, for three hours at the most, the DO NOT DISTURB sign is hung on the knob.

Professor Durand and his chief assistant suggest that, in view of the lack of results they are getting with D., they have a consultation with some other doctors she trusts.

First, our G.P. and friend Dr. Cruchaud, who is familiar with our life at home and with the children. Another, Dr. Martinon, more or less D.'s confidant, who agrees to come several times to Prangins for consultations. I am ashamed of putting Martinon out so. He nonetheless agrees to take the night train to Geneva, where I stand waiting for him at the foot of the steps at seven in the morning.

These consultations remain like a nightmare to me, because I then live through long anxious hours, hoping each time, against any likelihood, that a miracle will happen.

A fifth doctor, a professor of gynecology, does not take part in these sessions. He is the one who delivered Pierre. His wife and he are frequent dinner guests. He keeps tabs on D. by frequent calls at Prangins, after which he confers with Durand. So there are actually five taking care of D.'s health and looking for any and all means to restore her equilibrium and stability. Did she ever have any stability? Or equilibrium?

After the doctors' consultations, they call D. in, and each one questions her, listens to her as she answers, always volubly. The whole morning is devoted to this. Their conferring goes on until rather late. I pace the walks in the park. Some of the patients are also walking there, alone or in groups, and I am surprised at how many young people there are, students who "cracked up," especially medical students.

Finally, the professor himself comes after me, cordial, putting his hand on my shoulder and leading me into the office, where the others are still in session.

The news is not much different from one time to the next. I will not use the excessively graphic scientific terms. One treatment follows another. I try asking: "What would you think of her taking a trip around the world, with a companion of her own choosing, maybe a nurse?"

"The idea of a change of scenery should not be dismissed out of hand, but it is much too early to consider it."

Martinon's train does not leave till eight-thirty in the evening, if memory serves. I take him back to Epalinges, where the children, especially Marie-Jo, greet him like an uncle. We have a quick dinner, and I drive him back to Geneva.

"You should not entertain any false hopes, Georges. . . ."

He is one of the rare friends with whom I am on first-name terms.

"Do the others agree with you?"

"We are all in agreement. She talks to us a great deal. According to her, you are a monster, my poor Georges. There is nothing she can do about it. You mustn't hold it against her. . . ."

"I don't hold it against her."

"Devote most of your time to taking care of Marie-Jo," Martinon goes on. "I find her much improved. She seems to have regained her gaiety."

"She is working hard at her homework and classes. Often, at ten at night, I have to go and stop her and put her to bed."

"She's a fascinating child. I've read Henny's reports. She has the will to pull out of it, and I am convinced she will succeed. Does she have any girl friends?"

"A number. Anne, the daughter of the farmer at Echandens, spent several days with us. Friends from her class often come to swim in our pool and have a snack with us."

"Does she speak very often about her mother?"

"Almost never. Nor her brothers either, and that bothers me sometimes . . ."

"It's natural, a very wholesome reaction, which I often come across in children."

At the station, I am sorry to see him go. His mere presence is comforting, yet at the same time I reproach myself for putting him to these exhausting train rides, knowing that, barely off the train back in Cannes, he will rush to the hospital, where he is head of the pediatric service, and then to his own office, where young patients stream through sometimes till eleven at night. His wife, Anne, a model of patience, watches over her sainted husband.

From February 25 to March 9, I write *La Patience de Maigret (The Patience of Maigret)*, interrupted at chapter five by a very heavy cold. It is the only one of my novels I have been able to resume and finish after a break of several days. May 28 to June 3, I write *Le Train de Venise (The Venice Train)*, without mention of my little Marie-Jo, who had been so sick in our prison-compartment.

In July, Johnny goes backpacking to Greece with the rest of his Greek class, and sleeps out of doors most nights.

I ask Durand whether this might not be a good time to take the other children, including Marc and his family, on a Mediterranean cruise, and whether D. might not go with us. He has to think it over, and consult his colleagues by phone. He finally gives me a green light. It is an experiment worth trying, but no telling what the outcome will be.

I inquire at a travel agency. They tell me about a cruise on a very modern, virtually new Italian ship, the *Franca C*, which leaves Venice and sails around the Mediterranean and the Black Sea, stopping at Naples, in Sicily, at Athens, Istanbul, Odessa, and Sochi.

I am in time to get cabins for all of us. D. and I will share a two-bed cabin. Nana will come to take care of the youngest children.

Train trip to Genoa, in two compartments. D. seems calm, although preoccupied. In our roomy cabin there will be no demonstrativeness.

On the upper deck there is a swimming pool, in which you children are to be found at almost any time, whenever you are not sunbathing or playing. At Syracuse, we all visit the city, which I know from having made a long stopover there on the *Araldo* in the old days with Tigy and Boule.

The *Franca C* dining room is huge, well lighted, full of reflections, sounds, and good aromas. The meals are copious and appetizing.

D. does not say much, or take much part in family life. She looks at nothing, is impressed by nothing. Ten times each morning, I go up on deck to mix with our various groups of children and adults. The rest of the time, I read in the saloon, where it is cool. Afternoons, around four, part of the deck is shaded, and I play shuffleboard with some of the family.

What is D. doing during this time? Twice she plays on deck, but not with me, whom she seems to be ignoring.

Every evening, there is a bingo game on deck, where it is finally cool, and we all play. Even Marie-Jo, who is just waiting for the time when we are able to dance.

Her mother doesn't seem to be trying to see her. When everyone goes down to bed, including me, she lingers up on deck, and I don't hear her come into the cabin. This worries Marc, who is still very fond of his "stepmother."

One night, he gets up and goes to stroll on deck. It is almost three in the morning. He is surprised to find D., stark naked, in the swimming pool. He tries to get her to put something on and go down to bed, but to no avail.

We are getting near the Dardanelles, one of the most beautiful panoramas in the world. I can in no way foresee what happens there.

The preceding night, D. wakes me. She is naked and slips into my bed, saying simply, "Make love to me."

Only half awake, I look at her with surprise. It has been so long since we have had "conjugal relations," and during those last years at Echandens, she merely resigned herself to them. I can still hear her telling me, "Hurry up. . . ."

This time, she is eager, and—although without desire, I must admit—I do my best to satisfy her.

In vain.

Which earns me a resounding slap, followed by a hook to the jaw. I remain motionless while she dresses and leaves the cabin.

The ship's radiophone operator asks to speak to me the next morning. "I feel I have to tell you about this," he says. "Last night, your wife asked me to get a number in Prangins, Switzerland, on the radiophone."

He seems embarrassed. "Do you know what those calls cost per minute? Your wife finally got her number. She spoke to it for over two hours, pushing me away every time I tried to get her to stop. The conversation was interrupted by sobs, except that at other times she sounded absolutely furious. . . ."

"Did she call Professor Durand?"

"No, she called a Dr. Verlomme, at his home number. I would have liked to tell you then, but she wouldn't let me out of the cabin."

What did she have to tell the young psychiatrist, who had been treating her a great deal, especially recently? I don't know and never will know.

At dawn, we are entering the Bosporus, and I wake you children so you can have the unforgettable sight of the sun coming up and lighting the Golden Horn.

D. is there, leaning on the rail, her face more closed than ever. I try to start a conversation, to get in touch with her. She looks at me with hard eyes, as if I were some stranger intruding on her.

She does not go with us on our visit to the Istanbul market, or to the Great Mosque. Does she even come to dinner with us at the Hilton, where they have such wonderful Turkish cooking? In my recollection she is not at our table. At any rate, she certainly did not join in our conversations.

At Odessa, I lead our little troop onto the big esplanade that looks out over the harbor and the bay. A woman walks by us, and turns back to look. Her little boy, about six, is holding a flower in his hand. She leans over and says something to him. The boy comes over to us, hesitates as he looks at each of you children and grandchildren in turn, selects Diane, who is just beginning to toddle, and politely puts the flower into her hand.

We have lunch at the hotel at which Tigy and I lived for almost a month thirty some years before. You children, Marc, and Francette stuff yourselves on caviar.

What about D.? She seems to have turned in upon herself, no longer belonging to our group, to our family, and Marie-Jo at times glances at her with a worried look.

We are soon in the most famous city on the Black Sea, Sochi, where we take a long walk on the hill through almost tropical vegetation. We get a warm welcome. I buy fur hats, with ear flaps, the kind the Cossacks wear, and little gifts for everybody.

What about D.? Did she stay on board ship? In my recollections, I find her nowhere with us.

Piraeus. Athens. The Acropolis, under a torrid sky. At the Hilton, we get together with Johnny, with whom we had made a date to meet there. He looks terra-cotta-colored and is very excited because he was present at and almost part of a demonstration the day before that was violently broken up by the police.

To be sure, I shared you children's enjoyment, but to me this trip was an experiment that misfired, and D. of her own accord returns to Prangins.

In October, I write *Le Confessionnal (The Confessional)*. I will have written only three novels this year.

D. leaves Prangins temporarily to go to Ottawa, to the bedside of her possibly dying mother. She stays from October 5 to November 4, and her sister sleeps with her in the huge suite recently renovated on the occasion of a visit by the Queen of England. She meets many of her old friends. She phones me every day, just when I am having dinner with you children, so that I have to finish my dinner by myself.

Prangins again. No visitors, no phone calls. The experiment misfired, but at least Marie-Jo is merry and spreads her affection all through the house, in the kitchen as well as the secretaries' offices.

Pierre is now at the same school his sister and brother went to. Johnny is "big," and I treat him like a man.

On November 3, we are going to have a visit from my mother.

63

Yesterday, writing the preceding chapter, I tried to give an overview of an entire year, in spite of myself following a certain rhythm, alternating glowing and dark images, and leaving aside, more or less consciously, events that perhaps also have importance. In these *Memoirs*, I had dreamed of following each of the characters virtually day by day, each of you children especially, whose maturing I have so passionately observed.

That would also involve following those around you, increasingly numerous, which would be quite a challenge. I know that a long time ago writers invented "simultaneism," but then, shouldn't one write in parallel columns, so that the eye might see at one glance how each one progresses as time goes by? That is impossible, and I am forced, once again, to make a leap back.

During Christmas of 1964, which I called our first real Christmas at Epalinges because it was the first that brought together all my children and grandchildren, Marc gave me a big piece of news. Deciding, at least for a while, to stop being first assistant director, he was trying to fly on his own and had conceived and directed his first film, a featurette.

Eric Tabarly, the daring sailor who is still front-page news, had just completed his solo trip around the world. Marc sought him out in Brittany and got him to agree to reconstruct his daily life on his long voyage, this time in front of the camera.

For weeks, they worked at sea, in stormy weather and calm. Tabarly faithfully repeated the gestures of lone sailors, thus reconstituting, by little touches, the routine he followed for so many months, in so many different climes.

Marc was waiting for final prints. In mid-January, he announced to me that he would be coming in a few days, with his reels, to show them to us. I had no trouble in getting a small movie house for a private screening.

Not only the children attend, but also Aitken, Teresa, Yole, and practically our entire household. Marc, inhabitually pale and nervous, waits for our reactions. They are enthusiastic, and I for one am greatly moved by this work, running about an hour, if I remember correctly, which reveals a Marc now fully mature, in control of his medium, capable of a technique I was not expecting to find in so young a film maker.

When we come out, Marc is pacing back and forth, and I embrace him, then walk with him a long time, telling him how proud I am. In order to give him a more tangible proof of my confidence, I add:

"I'll make you a present of the movie rights to my stories in *The Files of Agency O.*"

It is just a minor work, made up of thirteen different tales, but the same characters run through them, and they are therefore quite suitable for a television series.

French TV will buy the films he makes of this book. Then, after failing with American TV, because Tabarly's name is virtually unknown in the U.S., Marc will sell his featurette in Canada and a few other countries. He cast in it an unknown actress, soon to become one of the biggest stars in French films.

Back at the house, we have a joyful dinner, drink champagne toasts to Marc's first film, a date in his career. Marie-Jo and Pierre go to bed. The help go off. Marc and Johnny are still in the dining room when I go into the small bathroom outside my office. All that is missing is a bidet. To clean myself off, I raise my thigh over the washstand. While I am soaping myself, my thigh slides down the porcelain of the washstand. I fall heavily, not backward, but forward. My chest takes the brunt of the fall. I am panting, barely able to breathe, spread out like a crab and trying to reach the knob of the door to open it. The pain keeps me from reaching up high enough. My arm falls back, inert, and I start calling "Help" as loud as I can, forgetting that the house had been soundproofed and that there is little chance anyone will hear me. As a last resort, I do my best to raise myself up on one hand while the other edges up along the smooth door, without finding the knob.

I finally hear Teresa's voice: "Are you in there?"

I then recall that she will have to go and look for a key to open the door from the other side, but her presence, no doubt, gives me the energy to grab the knob and turn it, after which I fall down full length, in a half-faint, quite unaware of what is going on.

I have never seen Teresa lose her composure, whatever the situation. She runs to get the two boys and with their help gets me out of the bathroom, about which Pierre used to say one could walk on its walls or ceiling because they and the floor were all of the same bright-red tiles.

I am not bleeding. I have no apparent wound. While they phone Dr. Cruchaud, I palpate my aching torso, feeling each rib with my finger. I calmly announce: "There are at least six broken ribs. Probably seven."

When Cruchaud gets there, he finds five fractures. While we wait for the surgeon, he does his best to comfort me, but strangely I am not upset. Very lucid, by now. The surgeon, Dr. Pierre Francioli, is also a friend.

"I'd say six ribs," he concludes. And I remember answering, "I'd bet on seven."

He gives me a shot, which starts to dull my pain, as well as my brain, and my last recollection of that evening that started so happily was my whispering to Francioli, who had recently lost his young wife: "You are a widower, Francioli. That must be painful. But it's even more painful, I think, to be a grass widower, a man whose wife is still alive but forever separated from him. . . ."

A suite has been reserved at the Clinique Cecil, where Francioli most often operates and still does today. At ten in the morning, an ambulance comes for me. Teresa rides with me, holding my hand. I grimace at every bump. At the Cecil, before going up to my room, they take me down to a basement, where at that time the X-ray department is located.

Finally, I am back with Teresa in a suite where we are to spend almost three weeks. Francioli is there waiting for me. After studying the X-rays, he says: "You were right, Simenon. The seven ribs are all broken, some of them in two places. What is giving you the most pain is that one of them has touched the pleura, fortunately not very deeply."

"Will this all last a long time?"

"That depends on what you decide. The least painful way to treat you is to enclose your chest in a cast. It will take you a little longer to heal, but . . ."

"What's the other way?"

"There are two others. First, a very tight bandage. A little more painful than the cast, but almost as long."

"The third way?"

"The fastest and most painful."

"An operation?"

"No. That's out of the question. It would, rather, be to leave you just as you are, without anything on your torso. There is every likelihood that you'd be out of here much faster, but I must warn you that you'll have a lot of pain. I can't give you more than three tranquilizing suppositories every twenty-four hours. Four at most. Never any more . . ."

I opt for the third solution, without hesitating.

Our routine is immediately set up. The room is large, and a cot is placed alongside my bed. We have a small sitting room and a bathroom, with an outsize tub square in the middle of it. Naturally, I am in no condition to use that, and Teresa takes care of washing me, which I absolutely refuse to let the nurses do.

For the first time, Teresa and I are actually living together around the clock, except for the half-hour she takes for lunch in the dining room and another for her dinner. No matter how fast she is, those half-hours alone seem long to me.

I am not to stay in bed; quite the contrary. In the morning, she dresses me in street clothes, the way one dresses a child. I shave as best I can and spend hours sitting in my chair, in the sitting room, prior to asking for the first suppository, which I put off as long as possible.

If I have a tendency to worry and groan about anything in my innards, I'm very tough when the trouble is clear, that is, in the muscles or bones. As a child, I often had fractures, or flesh wounds, which I never cried over, so that my poor worried mother thought I was a freak.

How did Teresa sleep on her cot, which must be hard and uncomfortable? She is so close to me I can reach out and touch her.

I have my second suppository just before I go to sleep, keeping the third for the middle of the night, especially the very early morning. I sometimes groan unconsciously and see her standing over me, a little flashlight in her hand.

We never mention love. For years to come, she will forbid me to, just as she interrupts me when I question her about her feelings toward me or question myself aloud about my feelings toward her.

In Mondadori's secretary's office in Milan, I had an intuition that this strange woman in the plaid coat would play a part in my life. I had no idea what one. When, at Echandens, we made love for the first time, I knew that our bodies, at any rate, were in perfect harmony.

Then, at Epalinges, where I was all alone in one wing of the house, I had needed her company in the evening, until it was bedtime. We spoke little and, when we did, it was about the children. She too was a mother, having a big son, who had remained in Italy and with whom she spent almost all her vacations. She understood my children well, almost better than I, especially Marie-Jo, for whom she had infinite tenderness and a natural indulgence.

I have just written, by chance, a word that perhaps tells me what attracted me so much to Teresa. She is perfectly natural, without make-up. She dresses with sure taste, very simply, without regard for the fashion of the day, or for luxury, even less for making an elegant impression.

We have almost identical backgrounds. Her grandfather was a master blacksmith, mine was a master hatter. We are both descendants of craftsmen, the men I prefer above all others, the social category, if you will, that I place above all others. In many an interview, I have characterized myself too as an artisan.

I remain in daily contact with Aitken, who reads the mail to me. I indicate to her what the replies should be, and almost every afternoon she brings them to me for my signature.

Out of discretion, even vis-à-vis the staff of the clinic, Teresa spends a good part of our days in our bedroom, sewing near the window, while I read in the small sitting room. There is just an open door between us, yet I feel even that is too much. I often raise my head to look at her, and the very sight of her relaxes me.

When D. phones me at Epalinges, Aitken tells her I am out, in the city or taking a walk in the country. Aitken then phones me, and I call Prangins. D. and I don't have anything to say to each other. To be sure, she asks about the children, but never listens to my answers. I suspect that she maintains this contact only to assert her presence, her domination, even at a distance, and I am less and less affected by it.

Johnny comes to see me from time to time, affectionate, worried, surprised to find me dressed and sitting up or sometimes walking, holding Teresa's arm, in the corridor. I insist that Marie-Jo and Pierre be told only that I had a slight, insignificant fall and that they be kept away from the clinic. I am afraid its atmosphere might scare them. I speak to them on the phone, making myself sound cheerful and sprightly, so that they won't worry.

Cruchaud shows his friendship by coming to see me every evening after he closes his office.

"Breathe, Georges . . ." and then he puts his stethoscope back in his satchel, saying, "Those lungs of yours are doing all right. . . ."

He tries to build up my optimism, spending over half an hour with me, being affectionate and comforting.

After twenty days, I have virtually no more pain, and Francioli tells me I can go home, that "cuffs" have begun to form around the fractures and that I can go back to normal living, although avoiding any strain on the muscles or brusque movements.

I go back to you children, the office, the walks in the country and in town. In order to avoid being accidentally shoved, I carry one arm in a sling, as a sort of parking light.

I remain in delicate shape and I have occasional spells of sleepwalking. A cot is brought down from the attic, and for a long time Teresa will sleep on it, although there is plenty of space in my big bed. I feel it important, and Teresa does even more strongly, that the children not get the idea that their mother's place has already been taken.

In early April, I take Marie-Jo on a trip to Florence for her Easter vacation. It is her turn, since, the year before, Johnny went with me to Barcelona at the same period. I could not take care of a little girl of twelve by myself, and Teresa comes along. Nana is in charge of Pierre at home.

Florence, with which I am familiar, is my favorite European city, not only because of its incomparable past but also because it remained unchanged after the destructions of the last war.

Marie-Jo is cheerful, relaxed. While she has always shown a pronounced taste for painting, and even a definite talent, she is less than enthusiastic about the old masters of the Quattrocento and Cinquecento. Perhaps the crush of people in front of their works bothered her.

We often have lunch in restaurants with few tourists, and she is delighted with that. Rain sometimes keeps us indoors, and then I go and buy her favorite comics, mainly *Peanuts*, available only in English, and I do my best to translate their humor for her. I am almost as wild as she about Charlie Brown.

Sometimes Teresa takes her to a tea shop, where she goes into ecstasy over the variety of pastries and ice creams she is so fond of. Mornings, she mainly enjoys the shops on the Ponte Vecchio, where I buy her a few corals and embroidered blouses with bright colors.

One evening, we stay up unusually late to have dinner at a nightclub, where she finally turns radiant as I dance with her. I am scarcely aware any longer of my fractured ribs. I just barely feel a slight pain in the chest, at the exact spot where the pleura was touched, and that only on rainy days or when the air is humid.

Many images, almost all warm and colorful, particularly that of my little girl beginning to look like a young lady, with all the aplomb and assurance that go with it.

Did our Easter vacation in Florence leave the same memory with you as with me, my little girl? In the evening, after you were asleep, I would write your mother, because she still wanted to have us on a kind of invisible cord. She demanded her daily letter. It would be a long time before that cord was cut and I felt myself a free man.

Dr. Henny decides that one session of psychotherapy a week is henceforth enough for you. I have no idea whether he has pried out your jealously hidden secret. He did not tell me about it, and I was to discover it only many years later. Alas, my darling! Especially for you!

One more correction to be made to my last chapter. It was not on the way back, but on the way out that we made a stop at Athens, where Johnny was waiting for us at the Hilton, because he went along with us for almost all of our cruise on the *Franca C.*

He got passionately interested in the shipboard game of shuffleboard, as he gets passionately interested in everything, and there were truly epic games between Johnny and Marc and others.

You were mainly interested in Serge and tiny Diane, just as years before you had taken care of Pierre, in your cute nurse's outfit.

At Odessa, Johnny and Marc left us and flew to Moscow. They rejoined us as we were weighing anchor at Sochi, showing up in the midst of the crowd, the streamers and multicolored confetti, and the lively music of the shipboard band.

Am I done with the very eventful year of 1965? Pierre made friends with the three sons of Jeanine, our new chambermaid, who mainly takes care of the children's quarters. His favorite among them is Jean-Jacques, just about his age, and they become inseparable. Pierre at six has a will of his own. He often insists on Jean-Jacques sleeping over. The two brothers also come to play in the garden, the basement playroom, and the pool.

You too, Marie-Jo, will form friendships at school, and at least one of your little girl friends will sleep at our place fairly often.

How could so much happen in one year?

In the offices too, things have changed. For example, D. had insisted that one of the secretaries stay on duty during the lunch hour, going to eat only when the other one returned. I cancel that "guard duty," just as I canceled the help's evening "report," and decide that the secretaries can stop work, not at six o'clock, but at five.

D. refused to grant rights to my works to various Eastern Bloc countries, because they could not export the money due me. I struggled in vain against that position. I write to be read and not to amass money. So I now sign contracts with Yugoslavia, Poland, Hungary, Czechoslovakia, Romania, and Bulgaria, from all of which I will soon be receiving the most enthusiastic and heartfelt letters from readers.

As for Russia, which has not yet signed the Bern Copyright Convention, I have been published there for many years, and printings of five hundred thousand copies are sold out in a single day. What difference if I don't get anything out of it, other than the human warmth, which I appreciate much more than money?

I can finally get around to my mother's visit to Epalinges, where the poor woman felt completely confused. Not only by the size of the house and what she calls its luxuriousness, the swimming pool, the many rooms and nine bathrooms, but also by the freedom my children enjoy. How could she not be surprised, and even indignant deep down, to see them talking so freely, interrupting big people? Hadn't I been raised on "Nice handshake for the gentleman," "Kiss Uncle Schrooten," who had such a hard, prickly beard I refused to kiss him, and "Apologize to the lady"?

The Christian School Brothers also taught me "fine manners," which she finds lacking in her grandchildren.

Poor Maman! Everything here upsets and troubles you.

"Why do you need so many 'servants,' Georges?"

What to answer? It is with the female help that she feels most at home, asking them, "Do you think the house is paid for?" or "Don't you think my son has a lot of debts?"

You never believed in me, Mother. You always worried about me, as if I were bound to come to no good.

I often go to be with you in the garden, where you rest in a deck chair. "What about your wife, Georges?"

She always detested her, and not without reason. She always detested Tigy too, who was guilty of nothing but taking her son away.

I understand you, Mother. I hold no grudge against you; quite the contrary. You had an unhappy childhood. You experienced poverty. You worked a lot, were hard on yourself, always ready to help others.

Was I right to invite you here? You make yourself as small as possible in this excessively large house. I do my best to make you feel comfortable. So does Marie-Jo, who "feels" how upset you are and is sweeter and tenderer with you than with anyone.

The boys are the ones who scare you, with their comings and goings, their often violent games. I think that, for all that I tried, you will be relieved when you take the train at the end of November to go back to Liège. Aitken will go with you as far as Basel, where you have to change trains and might get lost in the huge international station.

I watch you go with a heavy heart, conscious that, whatever I may do, to you I will never be a "good son."

Christmas is coming. I buy Jean-Jacques the same toys I buy Pierre, others for the two brothers, who have now come, in a way, to be part of our household.

Presents for others too, I've forgotten who all, but I know that you will all be together, including Marc and his family, trimming the big tree in the playroom, and the little trees in every room of the house.

Quite a while back I had had a big Chrysler 500, which is now D.'s car, driven over to Prangins, and she is sometimes allowed to use it, to go and have dinner in the Jura with a woman friend. I hear that one evening, on the hill at the top of which the restaurant is located, D. forgot to put on the hand brake or leave the car in gear. Empty, as it luckily was, it rolled down part of the hill and crashed into a wall.

Was that the year, children, that your mother got permission to come for lunch Christmas Day? Possibly. I am not sure. If so, she must have been unhappy to see Marc's family settled in at Epalinges. At any rate, she and I had no head-to-head discussions. And I am sure she must have remained aloof from the general gaiety for the few hours she stayed. Did she wander through the empty offices, no longer hers? Did she go up to what was supposed to have been "our" wing, which she had occupied so little?

However that might be, she was not there at New Year's, because we were already up at Crans, where, from December 26, we had resumed our routine of the preceding winter.

A year is coming to an end, during which I had the visits of many journalists from different countries, and did radio and TV interviews. I can't complain of that. It is one of the side duties of the profession I chose, and I undergo these invasions with good nature.

For I am once again good-natured and am no longer to be found alone and feeling glum in front of a bottle of champagne, so alone and desperate that last year the people at the next table had to take pity on me. They are now friends, both the Italo-American countess and that extraordinary actor James Mason. Having heard, I don't know how, last January, that I was at the Clinique Cecil, wasn't it just like them to pay me a surprise visit and bring me flowers as if I had just given birth? They are not at Crans this year, but I am neither alone nor desperate. My children are with me, and, for the first time, Marie-Jo comes down to the main hall, where she now may drink her first glass of champagne.

For the first time too, after welcoming the New Year with the family, I welcome it, in our bedroom, alone with Teresa.

A new year is beginning: 1966.

64

Evolti has left us, for personal reasons. He is replaced by Jean, a real Swiss, from the canton of Vaud, with a delightful accent, who is familiar with the soil, owning as he does a small farm somewhere in the mountains.

At the far end of the garden, beyond the swimming pool and in front of the hothouse, are a certain number of carefully plowed and fertilized rectangular flower beds, to give us cut flowers in season. I especially like little peppered white carnations, sweet peas, nasturtiums, but to have flowers for the large rooms of the house we need more decorative ones, gladioli, dahlias, and others, which will henceforth be Jean's concern.

In order not to interfere with the children's games, no clump of greenery cuts into the lawn. But at the side of the house and along one side of the swimming pool, spring tulips, the bulbs for which I bring by the hundreds from Holland, make way in summer for geraniums, which I try to have of the brightest red. This will become a tradition, an unchanging routine. As for the frequent mowing of the lawn, it is done by our sophisticated English lawn mower, which becomes the personal enemy of Jean. It is the easiest machine in the world to run. Yet, in Jean's hands, the motor more often than not won't start, and Michel, the cook, Michel to whom no engine is a mystery, has to come out in his high chef's hat to rescue the gardener from his plight.

Other machines scare him too, especially in winter, when practically every morning the two courtyards have to be cleared of snow, an automatic blower that sends out great swirls, which pile up in drifts. They are the delight of Pierre and his little pals, who make igloos out of them—which I check for safety before letting them get into them.

I have bought another machine, set up in the basement near the playroom. It is almost ten feet long and can make four different kinds of ice cream in containers of several quarts. We get the cones in large tin boxes, and in summer we have to replenish them often, when house and garden are increasingly filled with ice-cream-hungry youngsters.

That reminds me of Marc, who, in the U.S., whether in the South, the West, or Connecticut, always brought a gang of boy and girl pals home on days off from school. Marc remains the same: his present home, in the forest of Rambouillet, is invaded every weekend by hosts of friends, whom he welcomes with the same joy and generosity. Everyone knows the door to his home is always open, gargantuan "feeds" will be served up, and those who stay over will always find a place to bed down.

Johnny, on the other hand, remains a loner. Despite the attractiveness of the pool and the playroom, he has never brought home a single friend.

Pierre, starting with Jeanine's sons, will continue, and still continues, to keep up many faithful friendships.

Marie-Jo is the one who will soon fill the house with youth and joyful noise—beginning with her twelfth birthday party, which I planned with Aitken, but alas! was unable to attend, being laid up at that time with broken ribs at the Clinique Cecil.

More than forty girls and boys are invited, on a nonschool day. Aitken typed up the list, with addresses, and rented a bus to go around at the beginning of the afternoon to pick them all up.

This party is followed by many another, to which some of them bring their guitars, electric or not, while others play drums and I don't know what other instruments.

Marie-Jo's vitality is a surprise to me, for whereas she is eager to participate in all activities typical of her age, she is nonetheless determined to get as many 10s (the highest mark) as possible on her report cards.

Sometimes I worry whether that hyperactivity does not mask some deep-seated problems she is trying to get away from. Confidences she made to several members of the household, relayed to me later, seem to bear that out.

When very small, Marie-Jo and Johnny used to play spies. Is Marie-Jo still playing that, but out of some deep-seated need? She knows the hidden corners of the house better than anyone, and she is often to be found walking quietly through one of the long hallways or standing motionless near a door. She must thus have heard, when her mother was visiting, some of the "domestic scenes," in which D.'s voice always becomes vehement, uttering reproaches mixed with insults and threats.

She told three or four of the women in the house, "I'm afraid that someday Mother will kill Dad."

D. has been authorized by Professor Durand (after he consulted with me) to visit home every Wednesday, from lunch with the family until six o'clock.

She arrives around eleven, at first driving her big Chrysler as fast as ninety and more miles an hour, she confesses to me, on the finally completed expressway between Lausanne and Geneva.

She almost always wears dark clothes, has a closed face and slumping shoulders. I see her walk by the office and go get a tall drink, which she brings back there.

I try to start a cordial conversation, feel she is very far away, especially from me, far from all of us perhaps. She scarcely listens to what I have to tell her about the children. She seems to be performing a duty to which she is resigned, and I am always upset to be facing this woman with whom I spent so many years and who now looks at me as if at a stranger.

Her drink finished, she goes back to the end of the hall. I hear her speaking to Aitken or Blinis, and then she comes back, another drink in hand, to sit in the chair facing mine.

At the table, with the children, she gets some color, a little life back, and begins to talk. What can Johnny, Pierre, Marie-Jo think? I never asked them any questions about their mother. It is obvious that they too are trying to establish communication, to create a truly familial atmosphere. Yole waits on us, in her black silk uniform with the little apron, but without the white cap, which I did away with when I again took the household in hand.

When lunch is over, D. gets up and says: "I'll go take my nap in Nana's room." She closes herself in after barking an order at me: "Wake me at four o'clock."

At three, I go down to the office to work with Aitken. At four, I knock on D.'s door, and Teresa comes to help her dress. She then spends about half an hour with Pierre, behind closed doors, after which she is to be found back on the ground floor, in Aitken's office or mine, a drink almost always within reach. Time must drag for her, because she keeps checking it on her wrist-watch.

Did she and I have any real talks during these visits? She announced to me that, when she left Prangins, she would need a "companion," and that she had found one, a rather aged lady of Lebanese high society who, unable to obtain a work permit in Switzerland, was willing to take such a position, since all of her fortune had been left behind.

More consultation among Durand, his assistant, and my two friends Cruchaud and Martinon, whom I still pick up each time at dawn at the Geneva station.

They have tried most of the therapies on her, without success, and for some months will still try to restore some equilibrium to her.

In February I write *Maigret et l'Affaire Nahour (Maigret and the Nahour Case)*, in March *La Mort d'Auguste (The Old Man Dies)*, finished on the seventeenth. I am as yet unaware that this month will expose me to an ordeal more painful than the others, for this time it involves Marie-Jo, whom I cherish above all others—my apologies to her brothers. Isn't she the most vulnerable of my children, and the only girl to have slipped in, as if furtively, between my last two boys?

Dr. Henny comes to see me of an evening, from time to time, always calm and, it seems to me, impenetrable despite his cordiality.

"There is something in her past that she is ashamed of. That's all I have been able to ascertain until now," he says.

"Does it go back to the time she was at Villars with her mother?"

I don't know the truth as yet. Does the doctor know, but is it privileged information? Is he trying, as Durand did later on, to keep me from being too badly wrenched? Henny only answers: "Yes. The first troubles started after Villars."

One visit gives me the sledge-hammer blow I had been unconsciously fearing. Wasn't I right to be concerned about the excessive energy my daughter had been displaying recently?

This time, Henny says, not without compassion: "I would like to try an experiment, to change her surroundings for a while, to be able to observe her surrounded by children with more or less the same problems."

"You mean you want to commit her?" My voice suddenly breaks.

"In Lausanne, I run a home for 'difficult' children. You must under-stand that they live there without any restraint whatever, in a peaceful, agreeable atmosphere. Many of my little patients have been treated there, and come out in the best of shape. I can't promise anything. But Marie-Jo is willing.

"It is an unimposing place, located in the very quiet neighborhood near the Palais de Beaulieu. It has only a score of beds, each in a private room, and the patients have the use of a large garden." It is called "Le Bercail."

On May 30, my little Marie-Jo, that is where I take you, keeping to myself the feelings that are working in me. You, it seems, have become so attached to Dr. Henny that you appear almost happy to be taking his advice. I am surprised, when I go through the establishment, to find it does have a gay, relaxed atmosphere. Yet I am struck by one feature that you appear not to have noticed: all the windows have bars on them and the doors to the rooms lock from the outside.

In a gray-colored corridor, with childish drawings on the walls, we both at the same time notice a wooden gate in front of a tiny room, from which a voice calls out, "Marie-Jo!"

You recognize a boy from your school who used to drive the teachers crazy. The two of you chatter as freely as in the schoolyard.

"See the cage they've put me in? I think they're afraid I'll set fire to their effing joint."

He laughs. You laugh.

"You may come and see your daughter once a week, on Sunday afternoons, between two and five," says the head matron.

I hardly dare glance at your pale face. You squeeze my arm to give me courage. "Don't worry, Dad. I'll be a good girl. Dr. Henny promised he'd come to see me every day."

You see me back to the door, still squeezing my arm. You don't cry. I succeed in not crying either, and after we kiss I run to my car and the tears roll down my cheeks as I drive away.

What did I tell your brothers when I got home? I no longer remember. I reassured them, of course, telling them you would be away only a very short time, something I had no idea of. You are both too young, even Johnny, to be deeply affected, and you return, one of you to his work, the other to his pals and his new nursemaid, Marie-Claire, a nice, tall brunette who used to be a teacher at the Ecole de l'Aurore, which all of you attended.

Nana has gone. She said, quite correctly, that at seven you are too big, my Pierre, to need a graduate nurse.

Marie-Claire watches over you as you play, of course, but also helps you with your homework, drills you in your lessons. She fits into our household very well.

The shock was the more unexpected for having been preceded at Easter vacation time by a week in a Paris as sunny as it had been the first time I set foot there at twenty.

For the last time, Nana had gone with Pierre, Marie-Jo, and me. Johnny was spending the week at Marc's, in Montainville. As I will do henceforth so often, even now in 1980, and you too will do, Marie-Jo (not for so long, alas!) and Pierre, when Marc's house will be the focal point for our family.

We have noisy neighbors in the hotel who play all kinds of instruments. We find out that they are none other than the famous Beatles, all of whose records Johnny and Marie-Jo have, and Marie-Jo is excited.

Together we go to the Museum of Man, and the Marine Museum one day when Johnny is with us.

Especially, we go to Dominique, the fashionable couturier for children of all ages, where I get you reoutfitted from head to foot. It was at this same place that, twenty-one years before, on our way to the United States, Tigy and I had renewed Marc's wardrobe.

It is the end of April. I soon have a phone call from Marc, now twenty-seven. I know he is at the Cannes Film Festival.

Since his recent *Tabarly*, Marc has been busy in television, for which he is preparing the thirteen episodes of my *Files of Agency O*.

I am in my room with Teresa when he calls, and I find his voice hoarse and deep, despite the light tone he tries to put on.

"Don't be worried, Dad. I'm in bed with viral hepatitis, but Dr. Martinon is taking care of me and tells me I'll be back on my feet in no time."

"Are you in a hospital or clinic?"

"No. I'm just in a motel room, on the outskirts of the city, because with the festival going on there's not a room to be had in town."

"Are you alone?"

His voice takes on a triumphant, almost mocking tone.

"You'll never guess who is taking care of me and staying at my bedside. Somebody you used to know."

I can't guess.

"Mylène Demongeot. I bumped into her by chance, and she's more or less taken over as my nurse."

Mylène Demongeot was one of a hundred or more guests at the big party I had given at our Golden Gate villa. Someone stepped on her long dress, which ripped, and D. took her into the bedroom, where Marioutcha repaired the damage. Marc wasn't there. At that time he was interested only in motorcycling and wouldn't attend lunches or dinners where he might have met the most famous directors from Hollywood and elsewhere, as well as many stars.

"Mylène told me the story about her evening gown. And do you know what, according to Russian legend—Mylène's mother is Russian—that is supposed to mean? That one will come back to that house, and stay there for a long time."

Marc is laughing, and it seems to me that I hear a woman's laughter behind his. I phone daily to find out how he is, and his condition is not too serious.

Starting in June, I spend my Sunday afternoons at Le Bercail, where a calm Marie-Jo entertains me tenderly in the garden, soon sprouting its first blooms. Each time, I bring baskets full of fruit and cakes, which she shares with her fellow patients.

When she finally returns to Epalinges, in mid-July, it is to get ready for the whole family's summer vacation at Royan.

Why Royan? I remembered this city, on the Gironde, when it was made up of pretty villas in which the bourgeoisie of Bordeaux got together in the hope of finding the "ideal match" for their sons or daughters. There was greenery everywhere, and white sails slid smoothly over the water, in front of the beach, with its varicolored umbrellas.

That was before World War II. Then, before the invasion, I was instructed to reserve the city exclusively for refugee Belgian diamond cutters.

Three years later, at Saint-Mesmin, there were waves of white planes in a dream-blue sky, and Tigy, Boule, and I would hear muted, faraway explosions. We would wonder whether it was La Rochelle that the Americans were bombing, because its harbor at La Pallice was a shelter for German U-boats. The next day, we would find out it was Royan, which had no military or naval installation, that had been completely flattened.

After the war, I was to hear mayors and casino managers of the coastal cities only half-jokingly say: "The people at Royan are lucky. They're going to have an entirely new, modern city that's going to be hard to compete with."

I expect to be taking my children to a dream city. The only reason Teresa and I are going along is so as not to be separated from them, although somewhat against my better judgment, because for some days I have been afflicted with viral neuritis.

Marie-Claire is with us. Marc, back on his feet, is to bring Francette and the two children to join us. Johnny is in London and will merely stop by.

What a disappointment! This "new city," which its competitors had been afraid of, has lost all its greenery. Straight streets and concrete high rises have replaced the villas.

The hotel is not nearly as comfortable as I had been told. Its ground floor is cheerful enough, especially the dining room, which is partly glass-enclosed and bright. The children fill up on the abundant seafood and spend most of their time on the beach.

My neuritis gives me a lot of pain. Teresa is sharing a small room with me and tells me I moan often. Other times, I get up hoping that taking a few steps, making a few movements, will relieve the pain.

The bathroom is nothing but a shower stall, and it and the toilet are separated from the bedroom by curtains. Teresa can barely fit in the bathroom to give me a head-to-foot sponge bath.

The elevator is almost always out of order, and it is torture for me to have to walk down the stone stairs, which make me dizzy.

The Remblai has turned into a veritable Midway, lined with hot-dog and hamburger stands, the smell of which mixes with the no less greasy odor of the crêpe stands, for crêpes are now the fad. From every little café the sound of jukeboxes is heard.

Marc arrives with Francette, Boule, and the children, but stays only three days; he has to be off shooting somewhere. Johnny, who is with them, goes along with Marc.

I don't believe I ate more than two or three times with my family, who, as usual, were all seated at a long table. Neuritis makes one's whole body hypersensitive. I sometimes drag down to the beach on Teresa's arm, but it is painful for me to walk on the sand, with my feet sinking in, the sun is too strong, and I feel weak.

My friend Cruchaud, in Lausanne, had told me that these attacks generally last twenty-one or twenty-seven days, I no longer remember which. I still have a certain number of painful days ahead of me. At sixty-three, I suddenly feel like a pitiful old man. I am ashamed to take advantage of the care Teresa gives me; she sleeps no more than I, and I guess rather less.

We take afternoon walks on the quiet streets we have located and stop at many antique-shop windows. Two or three times, I go into the casino, where the only game is the simplified roulette game called "boule." I play automatically, indifferent to whether I win or lose.

We discover the fishing wharf, the fish market, in which I recognize familiar images and odors. I feel discouraged and every day am apprehensive about the painful night ahead. I go to bed early but, until a very late hour, we can hear the noisy band from the corner café, where the customers sitting on the terrace dance out of doors.

I decide to escape from this nightmare. I don't feel up to going to Bordeaux to take a plane and change in Paris to get to Geneva before reaching home. Teresa phones the manager of a large garage in Lausanne, who has often worked on my car and in whom I have utmost confidence. He agrees to go and get the Rolls-Royce at Epalinges and drive it to Royan to pick us up.

I go to see Annette, my prewar secretary, who came from Royan and has a fine apartment there, in which she spends her vacations with her sister and brother-in-law. We all drank whiskey. Even me, and it left such a bad taste that even the memory of it turns my stomach. I'm in a hurry to get back to my house, our house.

The chauffeur arrives during the evening, and we leave the next morning around ten. I ask him to go by way of La Rochelle, which is on the way anyway, and I show Teresa the Café de la Paix.

We also go through Nieul, seeing of my old house only the walls of the outbuildings and the small gate opening onto the garden.

I would like this to be a kind of pilgrimage with Teresa. We take the road to Poitiers, which I know so well, then others not familiar to me. I again think of that wheelchair that D. promised the gardener he would someday wheel me in. Am I about to get into it?

My morale is at its lowest ebb. Without Teresa, whom I hang onto, I wonder whether I would have the courage to go on living, I am so weary. We drive along slowly, as I am used to doing. More slowly indeed than usual, because the slightest bump is painful to me.

It is 2:00 A.M. when we get to the door of our house. We have been on the way for about seventeen hours, and Teresa will have to help our Good Samaritan of a driver carry me up to bed.

How did we get through that day? Teresa alone could say, but I prefer not to ask her.

I would like to sleep for a long, long time, a peaceful sleep, without sudden awakenings and without groaning.

To sleep!

65

The house is empty, silent, the first time I have ever found it so. During our annual vacation, we now give all the help the month off. Only Jean, the gardener, and his wife stay in the house to guard the property. For two weeks this woman will do the cooking for Teresa and me. And, for the first time, we will have these meals in intimacy, in the boudoir, since I go about as little as possible.

Aitken is here during office hours, preferring to take her vacation in two halves, one in spring, one in fall.

By good luck, Dr. Cruchaud has just returned from his vacation. I have lost a great deal of weight. He calls in two specialists, and they decide to pep me up with a series of shots. They still delicately speak of viral neuritis. Yet I am completely convinced that what I have is alcoholic neuritis, because during the ordeals I went through I too often had recourse to drink.

I phone the children, whom I left in Royan when I practically fled the place, to reassure them. Boule is with them and I trust her implicitly. Marie-Claire, who has made an excellent impression on me, also contributes to my feeling easy.

During my nightmare stay at Royan, I wrote to D. every night, as she had made me promise to do, and I now wonder what I might have written her, in the feverish state I was in. I will probably never know, because, unlike André Gide, I don't keep carbon copies of the personal letters I write.

In the morning, I go down to the office, the larger one, for I now have two: the one that was formerly D.'s office and the smaller one in which I write my novels. I had replaced D.'s metal furniture with furniture of fine-grained wood and feel more at home in it.

I turn over to Aitken a certain number of tasks I know she can carry out, and she and I talk over publishing, film, and television problems.

The rest of the time, I stay on the second floor. I have forsworn any alcoholic drink, without much effort. Perhaps what partly decided me to was something Teresa told me.

"Do you know that sometimes at night, between groans, you call out?"

Am I then not cured? Have I not succeeded, as Durand and Verlomme so strongly advised me, in cutting the cords that tie me to the past? Will I justify D.'s proud challenge, "No man ever resisted me"?

Thinking myself cured, I now find out that she still pursues me in my dreams, which I was unaware of.

Yet I feel relaxed, after so many years when I was always watching for signs and trying every which way to bring some balance to her.

How peaceful these tête-à-têtes with Teresa! I who have almost always carried the others now allow myself to be carried.

I am sometimes bothered by it, for I realize the weight I thus put on her shoulders. But she protects me so simply, so naturally, as if this were her role in life, that I let myself go.

I have to get over this neuritis and the resulting weakness fast. We came back to the house on August 8. At the end of the month, I am to go to Amsterdam, and then Delfzijl, to be present, with at least forty of my publishers from all corners of the world, at the unveiling of a statue of Maigret, put up at the place where I wrote the first novel of the series, *Maigret and the Enigmatic Lett.* My doctors, especially my friend Cruchaud, waste little time in getting me back in shape.

D. comes to see me, still driving her big white car, and, seeing my skinny figure and sunken face, she does not hide a triumphant smile. No man ever resisted her? I will. I will resist to the very end, refusing to let her destroy me.

I will live, for myself, for my children, with the patient and discreet help of Teresa, for whom I want to live too; I promise myself I will once again be the man I used to be, whom she won't have to carry.

D.'s mother died, perhaps around Christmas, and D. did not request Durand's permission to go to Canada for the funeral. I had had great affection for this woman, whose surface hardness hid a great timidity if not a great modesty.

D.'s sister, Madeleine, comes to see her at Prangins, and they go off together for a two- or three-week trip through Spain. It is one of the psychiatrist's final attempts to achieve a concrete result.

A Spanish marquis, very handsome, with the characteristic haughtiness of old Iberian nobility, comes to see me. He brings a huge and very heavy package, which he opens with true relish. It looks like a book.

It is sumptuously bound in red morocco and I see engraved in golden letters on it: COMPLETE WORKS OF GEORGES SIMENON, surrounded by graceful arabesques. I don't understand. He opens the book, which turns out to be a Pandora's box holding eight smaller volumes, also bound in red, with the same title in eight different languages.

The marquis thought that by surprising me in this way he would get what he wants; he has not come here for nothing. Smoking a Havana cigar, and comfortably seated in one of the new office chairs, designed by Le Corbusier, he explains to me.

"It struck me that it is time to bring out a collection of your complete works, not only in French, but also in the main languages into which you have been translated."

Aitken is present, as she is whenever I am having a "professional" discussion, and we exchange a discreet wink. The marquis, who has a melodious, insinuating voice, is confident that he will succeed.

"This is a very big project, which will net you a lot. I have been preparing it for months with professionals, and I have found, secured, the capital necessary for launching it. All you have to do now is sign the contract I brought."

He takes it out of his expensive attaché case.

I do not touch the document he holds out to me. "Your project," I quietly tell him, "is not feasible. For a capital reason, which you seem unaware of. The countries I am translated in are not all at the same point. In Germany, for instance, where I refused to be published after Hitler came to power, they are a number of years behind, and are not yet ready for Complete Works. In Italy, on the other hand, Mondadori is preparing a very fine edition of my Complete Works, for which I have already seen the designs. In Spain, they are behind too, on account of the war against Franco. In the United States, Complete Works of an author are rarely published, because they don't have enough collectors there, and the biggest publisher in New York told me that the Complete Works of Hemingway, for example, Steinbeck, and even the great Faulkner, simply did not sell. . . ."

He smiles, confidently. "Just read it."

I glance over the contract, which was doubtless drawn up by his lawyers. To my surprise, I find in it none of the usual traps, and in theory it ought to be worth a small fortune to me. He promises that, on signing, I will get a considerable advance.

"Doesn't that tempt you?"

"No. I have always had a principle not to let my publishers lose money on me, even though I am very demanding. I don't want you to be the exception."

"I know what I'm doing, and besides, you certainly can't lose anything on the deal."

This went on for over two hours. I am leery of a man who talks so glibly and shows so much self-confidence.

I finally agree to go along, and he takes a checkbook from his pocket. Then I decide on one last, cautious move, even if it is an affront to his dignity.

"I will only sign it tomorrow, if you still want me to and you bring me a check certified by a Swiss bank."

He doesn't flinch. I was asking for such a bank guarantee because I had had experience with bouncing checks, especially from movie producers.

Never from publishers, it is true, but the marquis is not a publisher. Rather, a sort of promoter, with no track record.

He returns the next day with the certified check. I sign, after warning him one last time. I give the check to Aitken to deposit, and the marquis goes off with his impressive and costly dummy. I will hear little more of him. I will find out via the grapevine that he is circling the globe trying to work out his deal. I had added to the contract a clause stating that after two years it would lapse if the different editions provided for were not underway. I will never again hear from or of this elegant, haughty gentleman.

Aitken goes to Royan to accompany the children on the trip back. They are to leave Boule, Francette, and her two children in Paris, and there catch a plane that will bring them to Geneva.

"But you're all well, Dad!" Marie-Jo cries out on seeing me. "Do you know, I like you even better slim, the way you are now."

Pierre is reunited with his friends, especially his inseparable Jean-Jacques of the pink face and blue eyes. Marie-Jo spends a lot of time in the pool with Marie-Claire. The whole household staff is back from vacation, and Marie-Jo sometimes asks Yole to serve an afternoon snack to her, her brother, and his friends, beside the turquoise water.

Johnny is back too and has started classes again at the gymnase, where he has decided to try for two *baccalauréats* at once, in Greek/Latin and special mathematics, in order to be qualified for any career he chooses. I don't think more than two or three fellows attempt these two tough exams together after only a two-year course.

I ask Cruchaud to go to Holland with us, because I expect it to be a whirlwind trip and don't feel too solid on my feet. So four of us go: Cruchaud, Johnny, Teresa, and I.

Press and photographers are waiting for me, as is Abs Bruna. I am whisked to a small room at the airport, and answer as best I can the questions that pop at me while the flashes of the cameras keep me blinking constantly. Teresa, discreet as ever, waits outside.

Well over forty of my publishers are there, some of them friends whom I am happy to see again, others whom I've never seen before. Old Arnaldo Mondadori has his wife with him and we hug and kiss. Helen Wolff, my old friend, made a special trip across the Atlantic, and Hamish Hamilton has come over from London.

Of course, Sven and Lolette Nielsen are there. I am used to seeing them twice a year at least at Lausanne, first in February, for my birthday, which they never forget. I also am reunited with Bernard de Fallois. I am amazed to see that four people came from Bulgaria. They speak fluent English, and two of them also have excellent French.

Teresa helps me dress. She will have no meals with me, but will eat alone in the dining room. Her attentiveness to me is touching, for I am not used to it and don't feel I deserve such devotion.

A big banquet takes place. Speeches. I give one, impromptu, for I have never known how to write a speech. I give special recognition to Mondadori, the earliest of my publishers, who has been bringing my books out since 1925, when I was writing dime novels, and Italy is the only country in which I have never switched publishers. In France, I have had three. In the U.S., four or five; in Holland, only one, Abs Bruna, but he did not start until the first Maigrets.

Dancing. I think I danced, as well as I could, with old Signora Mondadori. One wine after another, then champagne, liqueurs, and everyone getting red in the face. I give a knowing wink to Cruchaud, sitting with Johnny, to show him my glass contains, and will to the end contain, only water.

I hop from table to table, and finally, very late, am able to get away. How good it is to find Teresa, plain and simple, waiting patiently for me and happy to see me come back in good shape.

In the morning, we are taken off to some reception or other where again there are reporters and photographers.

Dinner, "black tie" again, in a nearby historical château, after a few interviews.

The next morning, a special train, decorated with the flags of the various nationalities, carries us all off to Delfzijl, through the pine woods of Drenthe Province, then canal-checkered Friesland. The city council is waiting for us. They take us onto a very fine boat, which cruises through the estuary, escorted by many sailing vessels. Cold buffet on board. Strangers address me, now in English, now in French, at times in languages I don't even try to understand.

Now where is Teresa? In the train there were four of us in the compartment, in which we were served an abundant and varied Dutch breakfast. Johnny and Cruchaud were with us, and Teresa sat near me. Since then, I've hardly seen her.

But here she comes, bringing me a plate of cold cuts. She has had her eye on me all the time. She also brings me coffee, and then some soda water.

Back to Delfzijl. Flags everywhere. They lead us to the edge of the old canal I know so well. Crowds on the dock. Houses that I recognize. A stone pedestal, a statue so high I am surprised by it, covered with a white cloth.

Five of the actors who have played Maigret are here, including my friend Rupert Davies, who is the only one, at that time, to have played him in as many as fifty-two films.

Blare of trumpets. Local bigwigs. Speeches. I catch a glimpse of Johnny and Cruchaud in the crowd but don't find Teresa, as usual discreetly to the side. A row of photographers, TV cameramen. I am given a rope and told to pull it to unveil the statue.

I pull, but nothing happens. Laughter. I laugh too. I try again. Someone corrects a faulty connection, and when I pull again, down comes the cloth at last, revealing a Maigret who, thanks to the Dutch sculptor, is as close as possible to the way I imagined him, which I alone know.

More trumpets. Applause. Speeches. My turn to say a few words, and the emotion in my voice is real.

The cortege heads for the Pavillon, that restaurant on the bank of the Ems on the terrace of which, over a glass of gin, I thought up the inspector, before starting to write *Maigret and the Enigmatic Lett* on a barge abandoned on the canal.

The four of us get together again on the pink-brick street, and I recount some of the memories of the days when I was twenty-five.

But the crowd is waiting in the restaurant, which has been enlarged. Many students from the nearby University of Groningen have come to greet me. Champagne. Speeches. The reception drags on, and I steal out with Teresa. We stroll down the brick-paved streets and meet Johnny and Cruchaud. A moment's relaxation.

A little later, we are taken to the railroad station. A special—very special —train is there for us. One car is reserved for radio and TV. Music is playing throughout the train, of which one car serves as a dance floor. Technicians are already developing and editing the film shot during the ceremony, which they will show us when we get to Amsterdam.

Food and drinks are served in the compartments. Continual coming and going. Holland gin flows by the jugful. Even Cruchaud and Johnny have succumbed to it.

There is soon dancing, not only in the dance-floor car, but up and down the corridors. Teresa and I are probably the only two drinking nothing, for everything has been provided except drinking water.

At midnight, we pull up, not in the main part of the Amsterdam station, but on a siding closed to the public. The music is still playing, and there is dancing on the platform as we await the showing of the Delfzijl footage. Everyone recognizes himself and others in it. Lots of laughs.

Our plane leaves at nine in the morning. Everyone is downstairs, in the hallway, the lounges, and there are many haggard faces. The various planes will all leave within less than an hour of one another. We are driven there. Good-byes, hugs and kisses.

Teresa and I are alone at the back of the plane. I take a long look at her, very moved. I dare not speak of love, which she has forbidden, but my eyes seek hers out.

Does she understand me as I believe I understand her? We talk only of banal things, but I could swear that, between heaven and earth, after those hurly-burly days, when we kept looking for each other, we are now living through one of the important hours of our lives.

When I speak to her about it years later, Teresa will answer, as my father did to my mother so long ago:

"Well, I'm still here, aren't I?"

She is still here today, so many years later, as I write these lines in our little pink house I have so often written about.

Marc is living with Mylène at Neuilly, in the same building as Francette and his children. He is working on the next episode of the *Files of Agency O.*

Long confab with Dr. Durand. He has had the other doctors in. They had a long interview with D., who is now back at the clinic.

"Listen to me, Simenon. We are all convinced that there is nothing that will change your wife's condition."

"You mean that she is incurable?"

He does not answer, but his expression speaks for itself.

"We have told her that there is no reason for her to go on being treated here, provided: she is not to live with you or the children, and will have the right to see them only for brief periods now and then until they are grown."

"Did she agree to that?"

"Yes . . . And as far as you're concerned, you can get back together with her at that time, if you're bent on suicide."

I understand, but do not react, since I expected this.

"Where will she go?"

"Wherever she wants, so long as it's away from Lausanne and the environs . . ."

"Did she indicate to you what she intended?"

"One of our nurses whom she is rather close to has a small house in the village of Prangins. They seem to have agreed to share it. D. is even talking about how she'll do the marketing, and housework, and cooking."

"As she did at Villars?"

A shadow passes over Durand's eyes.

"It will last for a while, and then . . ."

D. leaves Prangins at the end of September and continues her Wednesday visits to Epalinges. Always about the same. She is driven by a chauffeur from Nyon, who also comes to fetch her.

Marie-Jo reacts to her with a kind of pity but also with something that looks like fear. Much later, I will also find out that she told several people, "Maman scares me."

She scares me too. The humble life she is essaying with the nurse does not delight her. In mid-December, she has a heavy cough, and Cruchaud diagnoses it as rather well developed bronchitis. Did she then spend three or four days at the house in spite of Durand's having forbidden it? At any rate, not with the children. Probably in the music studio, where Marc and Francette and my mother had slept.

She is admitted to the Clinique Montchoisi, run by our friend Dr. Dubuis. She orders two adjoining rooms, since the companion she had mentioned to me before is now on the scene and living with her.

I go to see her. She is in bed, her eyes feverish. The exiled Middle Eastern lady opens a closet to get something and in it I notice two bottles of vodka, one full, the other three-quarters empty.

Soon, Christmas. Marc is with us, with Francette and their children. December 26, the whole family is off to Crans.

Marie-Jo this time agrees to skiing lessons. Marc and Johnny go off skiing by themselves, and except for meals have their own separate activities. They often go out at night and get to bed late. Marc gives skating and ice-hockey lessons to the children on a pond halfway between Crans and Montana.

Noisy meals at our long table, with Boule there too.

Teresa and I, the first ones up, are already out in the snow when the others are having breakfast. Often, in the late afternoons, Marc works, lying on his bed, the pages of his new script strewn around him, his children climbing all over him.

As we did the year before, Teresa and I go from one group to another, arm in arm, and it is good to be alive, good to talk to each other, good to be together, early in the evening, in our bedroom.

Especially since Marie-Jo, now a big almost fourteen-year-old girl, is breathing life in by great big lungfuls.

In October of that year, I was able to write a novel, *Le Chat (The Cat)*, which I had been carrying around with me for several months. And in November, *Le Voleur de Maigret (Maigret's Pickpocket)*.

66

I am surprised, each time I finish totting up my memories for a year, to discover how many events great and small a man may live through in three hundred sixty-five days, and even more so a family, a household such as ours, which keeps growing, though no more children are born into it.

After 1966, too full and often painful a year, I anticipated a calmer one, with little change. But one glance at Aitken's chronology, which in my stride I do not always faithfully follow, shows me that rarely has so much activity occurred around me. You children especially will be the principals in it all; 1967 will mark an important turn in the lives of each of you.

As for D., there is of course change, but I admit I am less and less concerned with it. I even entertain the hope of being permanently cured. Will the future prove me right? I don't yet know.

I see her again at the Clinique Montchoisi, with her very dignified companion. The worst is over for her, so she may leave the clinic at the end of January. For mysterious reasons, she has decided to move to the Hôtel du Golf at Divonne-les-Bains, a town I know only through one evening I spent there with her when we lived at Echandens.

I in no way object to her plan. It is less than ten miles from Geneva, and only some twenty-five miles from Epalinges, where she still visits on Wednesdays.

I am most interested in you children. What was the first animal that began enlarging our household? Johnny's boa constrictor, found who knows where? The pair of caged canaries Pierre wanted because he saw some at his little friends'?

Those animals were to take up a lot of room in part of the house, along with the hamsters Marie-Jo gets me to buy her.

My sons and daughter would seem unknowingly to be following a family tradition. At La Richardière, near La Rochelle, I had raised wolves brought back from Anatolia, wild dogs, a mongoose, and from Malta I had brought back all kinds of exotic birds. In the U.S., Marc had had his own zoo, with snakes, turtles, and I don't know what else.

And now here my big Johnny is walking around the house with a boa constrictor around his neck, to the terror of some of the chambermaids. Even though he locks his boa in when he is out, it keeps escaping, like Marie-Jo's hamsters and Pierre's canaries, which spit grains of bird seed several feet from their cage.

None of this keeps Johnny from working like a demon, for this is the crucial year in which he will take the double *bac* examinations. I can't help admiring his sense of organization. He schedules his studying in detail, allowing himself time for running laps around the grounds, swimming, and soon horseback riding.

Sure of himself, he tells me, "I'll pass, Dad, never fear. I know how many points I have to make in each branch, how many hours I have to devote to each one."

Near Epalinges, at Chalet-à-Gobet, there is a riding club that gives lessons, and its students often ride by our house.

Johnny takes to his lessons so well that soon he can join the riding parties in the forests, and Marie-Jo decides that she too wants riding lessons. I go with her to each lesson. Then there are two of them taking turns, Pierre now having been bitten by it too. I have done enough riding and have remained sufficiently crazy about it to watch their progress with joy, not to mention a certain amount of pride.

On February 19, Pierre Desgraupes arrives with a large TV crew to shoot for the then highly popular program "Cinq Colonnes à la Une" (Front-Page Story), created by my friend Pierre Lazareff, whom I never say no to.

"Here it is, Simenon. I have a script all ready. You have just returned from a trip in your Rolls-Royce. All of your help, in formal uniform, greet you at the door, where they are lined up. I want our viewers to live a real 'Simenon day.' First, your chapter of a novel at your typewriter, on what you call your workbench."

The man has read too many of my interviews, which are never accurate.

"Next, with your three secretaries, in the big office . . ."

"There are only two secretaries now."

574

"Okay, two, then. You go through your mail. You dictate . . ."

"What do I dictate?"

Can he feel I am being sarcastic (I am not trying to hide it)? He makes it snappy.

"Dictate whatever you want. Lunch with the children. Afternoon nap. Walk . . ."

I cut him off. "None of that. First of all, the help never come out to welcome me in uniform. Besides, no one ever saw me do my typing, not even my children, except Marc, when he was very small, in Arizona.

"Anyway, my children don't appear on TV, because I'm not making little monkeys out of them. They do as they please. And, finally, I have no set schedule for my days and there is no such thing as a 'Simenon day.' I am ready to answer whatever questions you want, on camera, to go walking in the snow if you like, although there's nothing very original about that."

He gets up. For an hour, he paces back and forth on the snowy path in front of the house. When he comes back, he says, disgustedly: "Well, then, I'll just question you, but we can't keep the cameras on one subject for an hour or even half an hour, I'll have to have permission to pick up shots, without you in them, in different parts of the house."

They set up the cameras, lights, sound recording. I no longer remember the questions or answers. I never saw the show, or most of the others. The whole crew stays on until Friday evening, shooting I've no idea what. I don't care as long as they leave you children alone.

I never heard again from Desgraupes, who probably has a bad recollection of me. I am not blaming him. Others wanted to show me in the bathtub or shaving!

Marie-Jo is surprisingly busy. In spite of her studies, which she is so devoted to that I have to try to get her to slack off, she gives a big birthday party like the one I planned last year but my broken ribs kept me from attending.

Once again, a city bus to pick up and drop off friends. But they're all bigger now, and it will go on till 10:00 P.M.

Again some forty guests. Johnny and I act as lifeguards. The two of us keep counting bodies in the water to make sure nobody goes under. Yole and Marie-Claire serve ice cream and goodies, and then, in the big playroom, there is a buffet and music and dancing.

Boys and girls no longer dance awkwardly. I take just a glance at them, because I make a point of not embarrassing my children with my presence.

And a miracle happens! Johnny, the overly serious Johnny, who never took part in any party, becomes the life of this one, dancing, playing the drums. It is true that some of Marie-Jo's girl friends already are part of "the budding grove," and Johnny will fall in love with one of them.

Marie-Jo carries on a flirtation too, with a very nice young man who is madly in love with her and tells me she is putting him through tortures by pretending indifference.

So the house grows livelier and livelier, as the children graduate to older ages. Marie-Jo draws and paints a lot, with an instinct that surprises and delights me.

At the beginning of April, I have a visit from the founder and chief operating executive of Editions Rencontre, a house that has specialized in mail-order selling, with great success in both Switzerland and France. He wants to do a bound set, at a very affordable price, of my collected works in French; not in eight languages at once the way my Spanish marquis wanted to do. The latter, as I had foreseen, has defaulted on the contract, and the rights have reverted to me.

"Do you know that my complete works, just counting the ones signed with my own name, run to more than two hundred and twenty volumes?"

"We've already made a list of them. One of your friends, Gilbert Sigaux, has already blocked out the groups, and each volume, on Bible paper, will contain three or four novels."

"Which means more than seventy volumes? Do you think people will really subscribe to that many books at one time?"

"We've taken polls to find out."

He mentions an advance as big as the one from the marquis. I try my best to discourage this man, whom I find very engaging.

"Think it over for several days," he says. "I'll come back next week. . . ."

And he does, just when my best friend Jean Renoir, passing through Europe, is visiting, and Jean, along with Aitken, is present at our interview.

My novels are to be classed, not in strict chronological order, but in two categories: Maigrets and non-Maigrets. Sigaux will get introductions and footnotes. The dummies are very attractive.

I finally dictate to Aitken, to the great amazement of Jean, a short but specific contract, which will turn out to be one of the most lucrative I ever signed.

That evening, Jean and I dine at the Chaplins'. In this house too, the children have begun to leave home and the younger ones are already in bed. Big fire in the fireplace, comfortable atmosphere, a fantastic Charlie, after dinner, telling us, miming for us, literally acting for us the film he has begun to write a script for, which he "lives" before our eyes.

Seated next to him on the big couch, Oona smiles her wonderful smile, all love, sweetness, and, I might dare add, indulgence for her genius of a husband.

In June, I write a nostalgic novel about my good old Paris neighborhood Le Marais, starting at Place des Vosges, which I found had changed. I went to Paris for three days with Teresa, and one after the other I was an impromptu guest on French TV and Europe No. 1.

My health is not great. I am afflicted with aerophagia, and Teresa now openly sleeps in our bedroom, still on her hard and narrow cot. The children know it. They are not unaware that I need her with me, and while we don't advertise what we feel for each other, they can't be unaware of it.

Officially, she is still one of the help, and eats with them, not without evoking some suggestive remarks.

I know that Marie-Jo is jealous of her. She indirectly admits it to me. "Dad, why couldn't I hold the same place in your life that she does?"

From her earliest childhood, she has literally worshiped me, and is trying to keep it up. Yet she is unaware of nothing in human relationships, for she has had a very liberal upbringing, just as her brothers did. Nor is she unaware of certain aspects of Teresa's and my private life together.

Yet, to my great embarrassment, she will go right on repeating through the years, "Why not me?"

What can I answer, when her bright eyes stare so intensely at me?

"You know that can't be, my little girl. . . ."

Then her eyes harden and she walks away.

When D. comes to see us on Wednesdays, all she does is remind Teresa to be sure to take her "pill." D. is not worried about Teresa, but about various women who haunt her nightmares.

In this examination year, your luck, Johnny, hasn't been good. In February, on a snow trip in the mountains with your class, you broke your foot, and after a brief stay in a hospital, you had to wear a cast for a while.

As for Pierre, I am in Italy when he breaks his wrist falling from a horse.

This trip, or tour, of Italy is to last two weeks. It is the result of a promise I made to Mondadori, who organized it. My Maigret novels sell there "like hotcakes," but the Italian intelligentsia tend not to think so much of my other books. Mondadori would like to pull off a great coup, having me lecture at universities and cultural centers.

The tour starts in Milan, where I give three lectures. The first is at the prestigious Piccolo Teatro, which is practially a national institution. I read *Le Roman de l'Homme* (*The Novel of Man*), not yet published but which I had delivered at the Brussels World's Fair. After that, there is a question-and-answer period.

The second Milan lecture is at the French Cultural Center, where I say a few words about the novel and about mankind, the only two subjects I know anything at all about, and then answer as best I can the questions that keep popping at me. In brief, I am imitating the kind of "lecture" I gave at various American universities.

European audiences are not yet accustomed to these impromptu dialogues, and at the beginning I am very much afraid. A young Italian woman sits near me to translate some of the questions. Most of the time, I answer without listening to her, for I have guessed, if not understood, what was asked.

This encourages me for the lecture in the great amphitheater of the University of Milan, filled to the rafters. The students have so many questions to ask me that after more than two hours the rector comes discreetly to whisper to me that the amphitheater is needed for another ceremony and the people are waiting outside.

Everywhere, Teresa succeeds in mixing in with the crowd without letting me know. Sometimes, I catch a glimpse of her in the back of the room. Other times, I don't know she's there. She does not come to any of the luncheons or dinners, and disappears into the recesses of our suite when newsmen or TV people follow us there.

I'm in Milan when I hear of Pierre's accident, and I phone him at the Clinique Montchoisi. He is not the least bit upset by his fall from the horse, and I am amazed to hear him talking sense to me like a little man, even though he is only eight.

The Rolls-Royce takes us to Naples, where we have a wonderful dinner in our suite while outside it is raining buckets. Lecture. Questions. Answers. Reporters and photographers.

By car from Naples to Rome. The Excelsior, with which I have been familiar for thirty years or more, where an official dinner takes place in my honor. More lectures. I doze in the car, mildly numb with fatigue, but as soon as I am facing an audience again, I automatically get back my alertness and assurance.

We decide that, for a rest, we will fly to Venice; at the Gritti, where a hydrofoil drops you at the doorstep, Mondadori has reserved the De Gaulle Suite for us. A newspaperman, who is also a novelist, publishes a much-reported article in which he tells how much our occupying this suite costs.

Lecture. Big super-high-society reception in full dress at the Palazzo Cini, with Count Cini welcoming me at the foot of the steps leading right down to the canal as I step out of the gondola bearing his coat of arms. What

I remember mainly is the numerous frescoes on the walls and ceilings, signed Tiepolo. It is a veritable museum, and the gowns most of the women guests wore could also have been put in a museum. Servants in silk breeches and white stockings, their jackets decorated in gold, keep passing, and what laughter one hears is rare and quickly suppressed. It all reminds me strangely of my childhood, when in a totally different setting my mother would say, "One does not laugh or cough at the table. . . ."

And it would be so good to laugh! All this pomp, which would suit a grand opera at La Scala, seems ridiculous to me, and I am the first to leave.

Teresa's parents live a little over sixty miles away. I suggested to her that she invite them and her son to come and see us. It is refreshing to see them, to look at last upon plain and simple human beings.

The next day I have to stop for a formal luncheon at the estate of the Princess von Furstenberg, née Agnelli. It is a house in baroque style, pleasant, with pleasant people too, generally rather young, and I finally hear some gaiety and can laugh myself.

We leave to catch the Simplon Tunnel train, which will load the Rolls-Royce as well as its passengers.

I am exhausted. Somewhere, halfway, Teresa makes me sit down on a grassy knoll and out of a strange sort of ice-filled packing gets a bottle of champagne, of which she pours me a glass, or two, maybe more, which will allow me to doze, hardly realizing later that our car is up on a moving platform and we, behind a locomotive, are going through the tunnel.

Teresa knows me too well not to know when I can drink and when I can't.

Everyone is in bed when we get home.

In July, my big Johnny passes his two *baccalauréats* with flying colors. He still doesn't know which branch of university studies he will follow. He is attracted to biology, especially oceanography. Where should he study? With his diplomas, he will be welcome at any university in the world.

I make an appointment to see the rector of the University of Lausanne, a famous biologist, several of whose books I have read. He receives me informally. I tell him of Johnny's problem and fill him in on his credentials. I know he is an unconventional man, which many hold against him; his opening speech had created a mini-scandal.

"How old is your son?"

"He'll be eighteen in the fall."

"I'll give you my honest opinion. I've known a lot of young men his age with the same problem, and it is natural at that age not to know which path to take. You know what in our jargon we call a 'sabbatical year'? Well, why not let him have a year of well-deserved vacation? Let him do with that year whatever he wants, wherever he wants . . ."

I buy Johnny his first car, a modest red Mini. And he makes a short trip to Montreal, where he meets his uncles, aunts, and cousins.

Marie-Jo goes to a drawing camp run by her art teacher, whom she calls Kim, for she calls the younger of her teachers by their first names. She also sometimes, in defiance of the rules, smokes a cigarette on the stairs and often, at recess, leaves the schoolyard—which is forbidden—to go to a café-bar at the corner, where she on occasion joins Kim and some of his colleagues. I do not remonstrate with her about this, because I feel she has an imperative need for freedom. Do her teachers feel it too? Some, including Kim, I am almost certain do.

Each year he takes some fifteen pupils to a picturesque spot in Provence, where they live and work quite freely while benefiting from his discreet guidance.

We wait for you to return before leaving on our family vacation, at Vichy. Why Vichy? We have to find a place that is as much fun for the young, including Marc's children, as for their elders. On a trip to Paris, I was attracted by a window display showing a model of the new Vichy, with its parks and especially the Allier River, where all aquatic sports are available, including sailing and water-skiing. There are playgrounds for children. A fine swimming pool is near several tennis courts, and at the end of the riverbank there is even a racetrack. There are innumerable amusements. I lived a good deal in the Allier region, back when I was secretary to the marquis. The cuisine is famous, from the beef of the Charolais to the lamb and poultry, not to mention the no-less-savory goat cheeses. The brochures mention a five-star hotel, in which I reserved rooms.

We get to Vichy in the afternoon. At first glance, the hotel looks like a dowager who has seen better days but, with proper make-up, can still get by.

The manager shows us to our rooms, almost all of which open onto an interior garden surrounded by a terrace. Under the rugs worn thin by the "Vichy ministers," the floor creaks a little, and, to the manager's embarrassment, Pierre blurts out, "Why, this is an old barn, Dad!"

The rooms, while on the old side, are large and bright.

Francette and Boule join us with Serge and Diane. As for Marc, Johnny, and Mylène, they stay for only three days. Marc has to go somewhere to start shooting the first episode of the *Files of Agency O*.

I am informed that Francette and Mylène are living in one villa, which Marc has rented at Saint-Cloud.

Marie-Claire had found a teaching job and left us. Her replacement is a fiery-haired young Dutch girl, lively and always with a laugh ready. In no time, all of the hotel's other guests daily watch for her appearance, each of her entrances being sensational. Her dresses range from apple green to lemon yellow. And the hair ribbon around her strikingly colored hair changes daily, its color each day being more aggressive than the day before.

As everywhere we go, a routine is quickly established, or, rather, routines, each one of us following his or her own.

Except Teresa and me, who will spend the greater part of our time, as at Crans, going from one to the other.

67

Before discussing the life in Vichy of almost our entire tribe, I must relate two things that happened before vacation, and which I was remembering as happening later. First, my mother's second visit, which I had to insist she make. I especially insisted that she be accompanied by some dependable person, for my mother is eighty-seven, and I am a little worried about her taking such a plane trip.

The manager of her local bank branch found her a tall, blond, energetic person, who was also thoughtful with the elderly, to whom she was accustomed.

I go to meet them at the Geneva airport. My mother looks none the worse for the trip. She still smiles somewhat enigmatically and seems happy to be riding again in my "fine coach," as she calls the Rolls-Royce. She is sprightly for her age, very lucid. You children gleefully welcome your grandmother.

I have written her frequently, but it is through my cousin Maria Croissant, two years her junior, that I get real news.

For years I have tried to get my mother to agree to live in her little house, which she was able to buy late in life, with a person to watch over her. She obstinately refuses, claiming she doesn't need anyone, does her own housework, her neighborhood marketing, but Maria tells me in her letters that at times she finds moldy food in the refrigerator.

I confess that I had an ulterior motive in insisting that she come to visit. French Switzerland has a plethora of boarding schools for young ladies from all parts of the world, as well as comfortable, affluent boarding homes in which old people can find an agreeable, serene atmosphere and get all the care they may need. I don't mention this to her right away.

She goes to rest in the music room, getting Teresa to promise she will wake her before me at the end of my nap. She has been up since very early, and we are all convinced she will have a long sleep.

A few minutes before three, Teresa knocks at the door, and a weak voice tells her to come in. She is nonplused to see my mother sitting in an armchair, her face bloody.

"It's nothing, my girl. I just hurt myself a little, but I'm all over it now. Go and wake Georges."

I rush to her. I see the wardrobe lying on the floor. "What happened, Mother?"

Smiling, almost triumphant, she holds out to me four little pink silk bags she has crocheted herself. Each is filled with gold pieces.

"That's the money you gave me, which I never spent. During the war, I hid it under the coal in my cellar. There is a little bagful for each of your children. You never know what can happen. . . ."

In her eyes I find all the pride of the "common people," among whom I was born. Don't I still feel I am one of them? Very touched, I kiss her delicately.

"But what about the blood? And the wardrobe?"

"When I got here, I put those little bags on the top shelf of the wardrobe. When I went to get them, I had to reach up by standing on the bottom, and the wardrobe tumbled over."

"Why didn't you call for help?"

"I handled it all right by myself, as you can see. All I got was some scratches."

Teresa washes her face and finds only apparently superficial scratches, though they bled a lot. I phone Dr. Francioli, who has had occasion to take care of virtually the whole family, but cannot reach him. So I call for an ambulance from the Longeraie emergency room.

"Does anything hurt you?" I keep asking.

"A little . . . Here at the nape of the neck . . . on the shoulders . . ."

The children are in school, for it is June 1 and vacation has not yet started. Teresa and I get in the ambulance with my mother and wait while the doctors examine and X-ray her.

The X-rays show no fracture. At most, a few hematomas. They see no reason to hospitalize her, and I breathe easier.

"What did I tell you, Georges?" she says. "You see, your mother is tough, just like all the Brülls."

I nevertheless reach Francioli. He examines my mother, then joins me in my office.

"No, there's nothing broken," he tells me. "It's a good thing that was a lightweight wardrobe. But I find it hard to understand how, after such a shock, she was able to extricate herself, crawl over to an armchair, hoist herself into it, and wait until three o'clock. I gave her a tranquilizer, because she is going to have some pain in the chest and back. She must already be feeling pain in the rib cage, but won't own up to it. . . ."

He advises me not to leave her alone. Even at night, it would be better to have someone competent watching over her.

I had already thought of that and discussed it with the young secretary who replaced Blinis when the latter got married. Pasquinette, which is what we call the new one, has a landlady who specializes in sitting with old people and invalids. She is supposed to be very sweet.

The landlady will watch over my mother, not only at night but also during the day.

"Don't give those to your children until later, when you are sure they won't waste them. . . ."

Poor Maman! We did not always get along together. She sometimes irritated me. Today, I admire her and will put into the little safe, between my office and the file room, the four little pink bags, which touch me, because they no doubt represent things she did without.

She stays in her room only two or three days. She eats little, and that worries me. But Teresa notices that when, by accident, she is left alone for a moment during lunch or dinner, she finishes everything on the plates.

I remember that when my brother, Christian, and I were children she fed us at home before we went to dinner at one of our aunts', so that we would not make pigs of ourselves, because all the Simenons were big eaters.

In front of the nurse, and Teresa and Yole, who, like me, often drop in on her, she just nibbles. That is due to the "good manners" she was taught and tried in vain to teach us.

June is a superb, luxuriant month. Our birches have grown and shed a luminous, light shadow, especially near the swimming pool, where she is soon spending a large part of the day.

Cruchaud comes to see her. I take advantage of this chance to have a private talk with him about her future.

"I'm worried now more than ever about leaving her alone in her house. For years, I've been begging her to have someone in to help her. Last year, she insisted on repainting her entire staircase by herself. Don't you think she'd be better off in one of these Swiss institutions?"

Cruchaud shakes his head. "I had a long talk with your mother. She talked a lot too. She cherishes her little house 'like the apple of my eye.' Those were her exact words. Any help will just be a humiliation to her. And in the best of all possible institutions, even near here, where you could see her frequently, she would do nothing but dream of her Outremeuse. Generally speaking, anyway, and I've had plenty of experience with it, it is dangerous to transplant people her age. She's already thinking of going home."

"I know. As early as next week . . ."

"Don't try to make her stay. Don't go against her will."

"I'm always afraid of an accident. . . ."

"Better to risk that than try to break her will. Believe me, Georges, I had aged parents, too."

I can still see you, Mother, lying on one of the garden chairs, under the birches, smiling at me as soon as I sit down beside you, with that smile of yours I never did understand.

I bow, heavy at heart, when on July 8 Aitken takes her back by plane to her little house on Rue de l'Enseignement.

Early July, another, very different, visit. My main Russian translator, not without difficulty, succeeded in getting a visa so she could come to see me. She is a professor at the University of Leningrad, and we have been regularly exchanging letters for a long time.

Everything about Switzerland is a wonder to her, and she and I have many conversations in the big office, with Aitken sitting in. She has come with an endless list of questions, which I can't always answer.

She is a cultured woman, of middle age, plump and blond, always smiling. She spends lots of time looking at Lausanne's shop windows, a lot also in bookstores, where she buys piles of books. She hits it off wonderfully with the children.

She is with us until shortly before we leave for Vichy, to which I now get back, along with the routine there.

Teresa is the first one up, leaving our bed without my being aware of it and going to her own room across the hall, where she bathes and dresses before coming, fresh as a daisy, to wake me. From her window, she can see the people "taking the cure," often in pajamas and bathrobes, drinking their first glass of mineral water at the spring, which is right beneath her window.

The food at the hotel deserves all those stars; only the morning coffee is awful, and we rush a few steps away to a rather amazing little bar. It is open almost all night long, catering mainly to the dealers and other help from the Casino. Singers too, especially opera singers, for Vichy's clientele is made up of opera lovers. The bar owner used to sing, and still sings in a chorus, as does his wife, who serves at the counter. Everyone knows everyone else, addresses them familiarly. This is the hour of the day when the streets are washed down, the walks in the parks swept, the little city makes itself up, the hour I have always most liked, from childhood, wherever I have lived.

The air is as light as our mood. We know that dear Boule, also up early, is washing and dressing Marc's children, with whom she sleeps.

Francette sleeps late, and we don't disturb her. Marie-Jo's face is still clouded with sleep when I tiptoe in to kiss her.

Our Dutch girl is making sure Pierre is ready for his first event of the morning. The floor waiters all dance attendance on her. For all her youth, this is an appetizing girl who can't say no to any man.

"Coming swimming, Marie-Jo?"

She yawns. At Epalinges, she was always up early.

"Not right away, Dad. I have a tennis lesson at eleven."

"You have time for a swim before that."

"You all go ahead. I'll join you at the pool."

We all go everywhere on foot, except for Francette, who has kept her car with her. Most often, the four of us go out together. The pool is on the other side of the bridge, which we reach by way of the shaded embankment. Pierre no longer needs water wings, but still doesn't venture into the deepest end. The air is cool, as is the water, there are few swimmers, and there are fine trees around the pool, as there are everywhere in Vichy.

Then we take a walk, while Marie-Jo, after her swim, heads for tennis. Sometimes Pierre has other ideas than walking along the bank. I want each one to do as he or she wishes, without constraint, using his time as his age and tastes dictate.

Saturdays, almost invariably, Pierre goes with us to the other end of town, where the open-air market attracts him almost as much as it does me. The ground floor, with its many rows of vegetables, fruit, cheeses, meat, and delicatessen displays, does not interest him too much. What he wants is to go around the wide gallery, where live animals are for sale. Hens and roosters, in their latticed cages, interest him greatly, although he really prefers the rabbits, of all breeds, which he pets with his finger and teases behind their mesh enclosures.

"Say, Dad, would you buy me a rabbit? They're soft to pet and they look at us with such nice eyes. . . ."

"Where would we keep it?"

"In my room."

"The hotel doesn't allow it. It won't even allow dogs."

Which is true and brought on a small drama. Although there are all kinds of pets at Marc's house, including an owl, a lame magpie, a German shepherd that Marc has trained "for attack," Boule, who is now past sixty and has fine gray, almost white, hair, decided she wanted a pet of her own, an immaculate tiny white dog, with pointed snout and tender eyes, which is always with her.

She brought it to Vichy. Hearing of the hotel's rule, she thought she could hide it in her room. I had to convince her it wouldn't work. So, not without tears, her Pablo, as she calls him, had to be taken to a local vet's for the duration of our stay, and Boule goes to see him with as much emotion as a mother visiting a hospitalized child.

Marc is shooting in the Auvergne, if I'm not mistaken, and Mylène and Johnny are with him.

Teresa and I do a lot of walking. We have always walked a lot and still do, more light-heartedly today. Yet I think we never covered as many miles, arm in arm, as in Vichy.

Lunch brings us all together in the large dining room, where the Dutch girl's entrance is more amazing each day.

In the afternoon, Marie-Jo leaves to go water-skiing, about a mile from the hotel. I take my indispensable short nap. After that, Teresa and I walk, stopping at little neighborhood bistros, where we have coffee or Coca-Cola, depending on the time of day; during our entire stay I drink nothing else.

Pierre has discovered a small amusement park near the water, a miniature county fair. He never tires of shooting the pipes and ducks, throwing balls at the big idiotic-looking cardboard heads. All the games entertain him. We stop by to see him, but our presence makes him nervous.

Around four or five in the afternoon, it is Marie-Jo's turn, not so excited by water-skiing, but whom we always find seated at the bow of the polished mahogany Chris-Craft that tows the skiers. It is run by a tall, well-built, dark young man with a nice face. This is not my time. She and I both know this. She smiles knowingly at me, and Teresa and I go off to explore some new neighborhood.

At the other end of the town, along the river, another park, another spring, and *boules* players, almost all of them retirees. We stop for quite a while, and end up knowing them all by sight. They know us too, and some of them greet us.

We walk and walk. To the hotel. Then there is the happy family dinner.

After that, it's Marie-Jo time, our time, my little girl, but here you don't have to share it with anyone. It is getting dark. The lights in the park go on. A band is playing.

"Happy?"

"Yes, Dad."

I dare not ask her whether her young girl's heart is already beating for the young man who handles his boat so elegantly, and who sometimes, turning the tiller over to a friend, skis so masterfully. We get back to the hotel, where you know I will come and say good night to you. It's too early for that, and, with Teresa, we go to join Pierre, who is involved in a game of Japanese billiards, the rules of which are too much for me.

Teresa and I walk around the bandstand. I am passionately interested in some of the faces, in particular that of a rather thin, very pale woman, whom we see every evening at exactly the same place. There seems to be a dramatic expression in her eyes.

"What do you imagine she's thinking about? What kind of life can she have?" Although unassumingly dressed, she is always in good taste. I can see her in a neighborhood with nice little houses where in the evening all the shutters are closed and streets are empty and silent.

We play at building scenarios, as we do about a man or woman passer-by, about the *boules* players.

The round of the children's rooms, by myself. Starting with the youngest. Candies on the night table. Furtive kisses on the forehead when they are already asleep or pretending to be. Ending up with Marie-Jo, invariably with her covers pulled up to her chin, her eyes closed. I kiss her, tenderly say my good night to her, which she answers in a sweet voice.

Our rather dark little sitting room, where I glance without interest at the local paper. Teresa goes to her room and comes back in nightgown and robe. At ten o'clock I go to bed, as Teresa does too, but here not on any hard iron folding cot. We fall peacefully asleep. Will we not sometimes hear, when we are slow in dropping off, faint steps in the hall? This bothers me, because the hall leads to no rooms but those of the family.

One day, later, Marie-Jo will confess to me that when I thought she was almost asleep, with the covers up to her chin, she was actually fully dressed. She was going out to join Francette, who was waiting for her. The two of them watched for the moment when the thin ray of light beneath our door disappeared. Then they went down the stairs on tiptoe, holding their breath.

Francette's car was at the corner. You went almost every evening to some hot, noisy cabaret or other. You met friends there. But not the handsome fellow in the Chris-Craft. He was a well-behaved local boy who lives in Vichy all year round with his parents.

You will also tell me, little girl, about an amazing rabbit hunt, in some marshy place far out along the river. In three or four cars, you rushed to the spot with headlights glaring, until the rabbit came to a stop, dazzled by the bright lights, and then . . .

Oh, yes, Marie-Jo darling. I don't hold this against you. I don't hold anything against anyone. Here, you are learning games other than the rather innocent ones you played at your parties. I am afraid, afraid for you, just a few months past your fourteenth birthday. But I will preach no sermons, mouth no reproaches. Besides, by the time you confess it all to me, we will be ready to leave. My Marie-Jo is getting emancipated—although not yet all the way, you assure me, and I believe you.

Sven and Lolette come to visit. They are staying at a small, very select hotel hidden deep in one of the parks, where the floors don't creak, my Pierre, and the rugs are not threadbare. This jewel of a place doesn't have rooms enough for our tribe, and, besides, I doubt that they let children come and go noisily through it.

Sven and I take walks in the park, exchanging confidences. He is just about my age and is beginning to feel old. He expects his son Claude to take his place, but his Presses de la Cité group, now encompassing seven publishing houses, has become so large that he is looking for someone to help him run it.

I tell him about Bernard de Fallois, who was hired by Hachette to run their Classical Pocketbook division and is now head of all the company's pocketbooks, having given them a new impetus. Sven has to think about it.

Our two cars come to fetch us and take us back to Epalinges. The help are surprised and amused to see that I am sporting a salt-and-pepper mustache, actually more salt than pepper, and have the look of a phony Englishman. Marie-Jo is the one who asked me to grow a mustache, and I am getting used to it, even getting into the habit of mechanically running a negligent finger over it as I speak.

Johnny, soon back home, makes fun of me in a nice way, quite unaware that one day he will wear a mustache longer than mine, when I have shaved mine off. Which does not keep British newspapers and magazines, even in 1980, from giving precedence to my pictures with the mustache.

In September, after having worked in the large office with Aitken, I remain full of our life at Vichy. With my memories still hot, I write *Maigret à Vichy (Maigret in Vichy)*, in which our enigmatic lady of the bandstand becomes the heroine.

Johnny goes off to Paris, comes back in October, and takes audio-visual English lessons.

Early November, I write *La Prison (The Prison)*.

It is getting close to Christmas, but this year we will not go to Crans. On January 1, we all have lunch in the dining room of the motel at Vert-Bois, which we walk to through the fields, sinking into the snow at every step.

Was D. at that New Year's lunch? Probably, because she is again visiting weekly. If I don't remember her there, it is because I feel freed of her.

Happy New Year, children! Happy New Year to you most especially, Marie-Jo, whom I have been following with concerned tenderness. Happy New Year, Teresa, who has watched over me so much and will have to go on doing it.

At the end of January, I write *Maigret hésite (Maigret Hesitates)*.

In February, Marie-Jo asks whether she can change the light furniture of her room and the yellow curtains that filter in a golden light. My big girl, you choose rather austere pieces in Brazilian rosewood and have me order you a long drawing table, a high stool, a painting easel, all of the same wood, an armchair with black leather cushions, in which I sit at your bedside.

For Christmas, you selected reproductions of paintings by Utrillo, Renoir, Vlaminck, which I have framed, as I have my engravings, my etchings, and my lithographs, in square frames with a thin gilt border.

A year more, and Pierre too will be going to the Collège de Béthusy, like his brother and sister.

Bernard de Fallois comes to see me in March, but I make no mention of my discussions with Nielsen to him, since the publisher has still not made up his mind.

Everything is going fine at home. Johnny is shuttling between here and Paris. In April, I don't know why, I write an American novel based on my recollections of Shadow Rock Farm. I want to call it *The Man on the Bench in the Barn*, which is its English title, but because that does not sound so good in French, they call it *La Main* (The Hand), to my regret.

We are getting close to the events of May 1968, which have become history, and which I will follow with bated breath on radio and television, the more so since Johnny is at the time in Paris. Approaching the barricades out of curiosity, he will get blackjacked by the police.

A blow he will not deserve, since my sons, who were "born with a silver spoon in their mouths," do not share my views. That is their right. I never tried to influence them in anything whatever. It would be unseemly of me therefore to hold this against them.

In June, I write *L'Ami d'enfance de Maigret (Maigret's Boyhood Friend)*, and we decide that we will all meet for our summer vacation this year at La Baule, on the seashore.

68

From La Baule, I am no longer under obligation to phone D. each day, and she makes do with a more or less weekly letter I send to fill her in on the children's doings. It would seem that, on her own, she is moving farther and farther away from us, and I know nothing about her life at Divonne. She is financially independent; although we were married under a separate-maintenance agreement and she has no money of her own, we have always had a joint bank account. I never check on these accounts, except at times to ask Aitken, who gets the statements, whether they are solvent.

So D. has full freedom, and I get only faint echoes of her doings. At the end of the previous year, she spent several weeks at a private hospital, not because she was ill, but to have her nose, which she considered too pointed, shortened. The last time I saw her she was almost pug-nosed. While she was there, she also had cosmetic surgery to fill out her breasts, and to tighten the skin of her belly and, I believe, her buttocks.

The Prangins period is far behind us, and the children ask me no questions, never mention her to me. So I go on this vacation to La Baule with a light heart.

The trip from Epalinges is rather long and difficult. We board a plane to Paris at Geneva. Charming Yole has taken our Dutch parrot's place in looking after Pierre, to the satisfaction of Marie-Jo and Johnny, who also depend on her a great deal. It is her first time on a plane, and she is apprehensive about it, which Marie-Jo finds amusing.

We next have to fly to Nantes, the nearest airport to La Baule. The plane, which seems tiny to us, has only two propellers. We are all piled into a very small space, and the noise of the two engines makes it almost impossible to hear anything. And to think of how easily I feel claustro-phobic! . . . This takes us longer than it took to get to Paris.

Two rented cars are waiting for us at Nantes, and it takes almost an hour and a half to get, finally, to La Baule. We go through the rooms we reserved so long before. Ours, at the very end of the hallway, is a corner room with a magnificent view. The children argue, choose, check the bath-rooms, and also want to see the rooms being held for Mylène and Marc, Boule, Serge, and Diane, who are to come in a day or two.

I remember La Baule from before the war, at the time when my friend André, manager of the Deauville and Cannes casinos, developed this beach and its casino, saying to me, "I wanted to make a miniature Deauville, for my customers' children."

I recognize the familiar couple of miles of fine, light sand, the well-protected bay, the promenade that goes from one cape to the other, but new concrete rental buildings, five or six stories tall, cut off the view of the pinewoods in which can be found some of the old luxury villas, looking somewhat battered.

A few days are enough for us to set up a daily routine. If I attach so much importance to our family vacations, it is because, in the first place, we are all together, Marc's children and mine. Second, each one here is com-pletely free and gives greatest vent to his or her tastes and character. Finally, don't vacations hold a great place among the youthful memories that stay with us throughout our lives?

Also, vacations are when I get my best chance to see the development of my children and grandchildren, as each year, one behind the other, they get closer to their majority.

Marc spends a lot of time playing with his children. They, with Pierre, do calisthenics with an instructor and work out on a very fine Junglegym set up on the sand.

The help will never know about Johnny's pet, his boa constrictor, which he keeps hidden in a suitcase except for the many times when he wears it around his neck on the beach, making the sunbathing young women squeal.

Here again, Teresa will be the first one up. This time, we no longer need an extra room for an alibi. In the early-morning sun, which we daily take advantage of, the tide-washed beach is naked and deserted, except for the beachboys beginning to put up the canvas tents. During breakfast (the coffee here is excellent), we watch a long line of young equestrians and equestriennes go by, their horses sometimes getting their hooves or hocks wet in the clear water. A few little white sailboats begin to leave the har-bor.

Then we walk along the promenade, which takes us to the harbor full of sailboats and motor yachts of all sizes.

A bridge. We are at Le Pouliguen, where there is a real market, with real peasant women, fruit, vegetables, fish especially, fresh from the night's catch, some still quivering. This is a real Breton village, with its traveling peddlers offering dresses, underwear, shoes at unbeatable prices and aggressively going after passers-by. And also a few village bistros, smelling of cider, liquor, and coffee.

Our favorite is a small one that caters to its own habitués, with a hail-fellow patronne brimming out of her corset, old fishermen, peasant women grabbing a bite.

Swimming time changes with the tides. We occupy three or four beach tents. Yole has bought Pierre an inflatable raft, on which he paddles from one of us to another. A little way away, Serge is being serious about his swimming lessons; I discover that he does everything seriously, that his eyes are solemn and questioning.

At low tide, men and women of all ages invade the vast expanse of wet sand with a pail or bag and fill it with mollusks. Some are doubtless professionals, who will sell the delicious shellfish. But what about the others, who often come back with two pails full of shells? Most of them live in little detached cottages they have built after years of scrimping. A neighborhood of common people, Parisian workers, little people among whom Teresa and I like to go walking.

We buy some French bowling balls to play *pétanque* in the sand with one or another of the children or among "big people."

Marie-Jo sleeps late, then hangs around her room and, eyes still filled with sleep, is the last one to come in swimming.

Everyone spends hours in bathing suits, getting tanned. Except me, because that has never appealed to me, and Teresa, who stays with me.

Little by little we get to know all the geography of La Baule, from Pornichet to Le Pouliguen, for we never tire of walking.

The menu is displayed in the main parlor. The children read it or have it read to them before going to their seats at our long table. The cuisine here is more varied than at Vichy, rich in fish and shellfish, which we are all crazy about. Sundays: all the lobster and crayfish one can eat.

Marc can't resist his passion for fishing. He takes the youngsters to Le Croisic and rents a fishing boat with a crew of two. When they come back, exhausted, Marc takes an impressive quantity of fish to the kitchen, and we get to eat some of them.

One day, I am surprised to have an enormous crab served to me. "This is for you alone, sir," the maître d' informs me. "Your son caught it for you, because, it seems, this is one of your favorites. . . ."

That sweet Marc! All of you together get me a present that will be useful to me after swimming: a fine tan terry-cloth jacket and shorts, which I often wear for my walks along the sand.

As for Marie-Jo . . . Except for swimming and meals, we see little of her during the day. She sleeps a lot, and reads a lot in her room, where she likes to hunker down deep in her bed.

However, one tradition dear to me persists. After dinner, she and I still take a walk together. She is tender as ever, hanging on my arm, or, now that she is grown, holding it rather than hanging on it.

Isn't she in the process of changing, of becoming conscious of herself, of little by little making a life of her own?

A different life, which often starts after our walk, when, with her two big brothers and Mylène, she goes to the Casino or to some nightclub frequented by noisy young people. All four of them turn in very late, which explains Marie-Jo's tardiness for the morning swim on the beach, and her afternoon drowsiness, which, however, does not interfere with her playing tennis at five o'clock.

Serge and Pierre build sand castles, planning to enter them in the big contest one of the Paris dailies has organized.

A movie on Rue Charles-de-Gaulle has afternoon children's matinées. You come and go, separate, get back together again. Boule and Yole have their hands full.

Teresa and I set foot in the Casino only once, when I have to be there to take part in a live television show. No, I'm wrong. We also went there one afternoon when they had a show for children and, hiding in the hallway, we watched their reactions.

I buy as a souvenir a coral Buddha about an inch and a half high, which still today is on our mantelpiece. Hadn't Marie-Jo bought a tiny little golden horse in Florence for Teresa, who often wears it on the lapel of her suit?

I am still wearing my mustache, now pure white. I am sixty-five and would like my hair to be white too, but there are just barely a few white streaks visible at the temples.

We all go back to Epalinges the way we came. Johnny is still with us, but not for long; he is about to leave the nest. As for you, Marie-Jo darling, you have just had your last little girl's vacation, but neither of us knows it yet.

I resume my approximately monthly "medic" dinners, which I have been holding for two or three years. Five or six of my doctor friends come with their wives. The most faithful are Cruchaud and Dubuis. In Paris too, on Boulevard Richard Wallace, we used to have some doctor friends in on a Sunday, and Boule would knock herself out cooking. At Lakeville, we had had local doctors as dinner guests. With me, this is a very old tradition.

They all know one another, some of them having graduated in the same class, and the atmosphere is animated. We talk about everything, very little about medicine. When the phone rings, all my guests look at one another: which one of them will have to leave for an emergency?

The big living room is also lively. The wives prefer to sit in the bow windows. These soirées can go on until two or three in the morning, which will not keep any of my guests from being at their offices, clinics, hospitals, some of them even in surgery, by eight o'clock. I admire them, I who have to have my daily eight hours of sleep.

Some other doctors came in the spring, under different circumstances, in which gastronomy was also a factor, although only a very subordinate one.

A Geneva doctor, Pierre Rentchnik, who runs a big medical weekly, thought it would be a good idea to have me interviewed by several of his colleagues, including Cruchaud and Durand, and himself for *Médecine et Hygiène*.

They arrive before eleven in the morning, and on a table in the living room set up an awesome tape recorder, which starts going as soon as we are all seated. For two hours, they bombard me with questions, which I answer as best I can, with complete frankness.

Yole announces that luncheon is served, and I expect a long break. Nothing of the sort. Rentchnik brings the tape recorder and sets it up in place of the bright flowery centerpiece. Our conversation, during the whole meal, will thus be recorded, as it will in the living room, to which we return after lunch and go on until 6:00 P.M.

This is the longest, but the most fascinating, interview I've ever been subjected to. If what I said had been reprinted in full, it would have made a hefty tome. Rentchnik will condense it, publish it in a special issue of *Médecine et Hygiène*, and reprint it as a pamphlet, titled *Simenon sur le gril* (Simenon on the Grill). And the word "grill" is no exaggeration, for, on returning to our room, I have to change my shirt and underclothes, which are soaked, as after every chapter of a novel.

I would like at this juncture to destroy a legend that has had quite some currency. Newspapers have written, both in France and abroad, that while I am writing a novel I do not change shirts, which has led to some jokes on the subject. It is true that each day I am on a novel I wear the same shirt, one bought in New York a long time ago, ample, soft, and comfortable. I take it off, soaked, at the end of the chapter, and I find it ready the next morning, washed and ironed.

Madeleine, D.'s sister, whose sense of humor and sometimes brutal frankness I enjoy a great deal, comes to visit in August. She has spent a long period with D. and tells me how concerned she is. I fill her in on what the four doctors who treated her had said and why they made the decision they did.

The children are fond of Madeleine, especially Marie-Jo. If I am not mistaken, my sister-in-law spends a night with us, and I have a grateful recollection of her friendly, even affectionate, attitude.

Marie-Jo has gone back to school, but I can tell from watching her that she is less and less interested in her studies.

September 16, she goes by herself to Paris to be present at Marc's marriage to Mylène. I could not attend my eldest son's first wedding. I do not attend the second either. I do not believe in marriage. I never have. For family reasons, I got married the first time, in Liège, not only civilly, but also religiously. For other reasons, especially because of the birth of Johnny, I was married to D. in Reno.

I will not attend the weddings of any of my other children either when they marry, if they feel they have to. As for Teresa and me, we need no official benediction, so that I have never considered divorcing D. To say nothing of the fact that Teresa feels no urge to be called "Mme Georges Simenon," or to inherit my worldly goods, should any remain.

There are more than a hundred people at Marc's wedding, held in the park of a château outside Paris belonging to one of his friends. Lambs turn on spits over bonfires. Almost all the guests are young. Many are from the film and theater world, which is Marc's and Mylène's. Johnny is there. But it is not through him that I find out what occurred in one of the château's bathrooms. A Marie-Jo with hardened features will return to me a few days later and tell me about it.

She had retired for a moment to one of the bathrooms. One of Marc's friends came in and sexually abused her, although not going all the way. She will write of this scene later on in the intimate notebooks she entrusted to me.

The following day, or the one after, when she was alone in Marc's apartment, the same friend came in, and, on her brother's bed, this time, fully made a woman of her.

In another notebook, written very much later, Marie-Jo, then nearing the end of her young life, will list the names of her lovers, with naïve comments that will tear me apart: "[So-and-so], a week . . ."; "[X], two months . . ."; "[Y], one time . . ." and so on.

What bothers me about Marc's friend is the comment: "One and a half times." Which means that the act was not fully consummated in the bathroom at the château, during a rather wild night, but was, "one time," that is, one full time, on my son's bed.

It's no fault of yours, my old Marc. You don't have to feel guilty about it.

Whom did Marie-Jo talk to about it at the time? To her oldest brother? The friend is questioned and denies it. Marie-Jo speaks of revealing spots on the bedspread. I have never discussed this with my sons, but I know that, except perhaps for Johnny, nobody believed her.

Teresa and I are in the habit of going down a little path lined with filberts, from which Teresa loves to pick the nuts. This habit began in our very first months at Epalinges. The picture of it came back to me at La Baule, during our walks, and I write—for more than ever I have the need to write—*Il y a encore des noisetiers* (There Are Still Filbert Trees), a novel I consider tender, in which a young girl . . .

In October, Johnny decides to matriculate at the Faculté des Sciences at the Sorbonne, and rents a small unfurnished studio on Rue Ségur, in the heart of the Latin Quarter, a stone's throw from the Seine. He asks me to send him his furniture and all his things.

Once his furniture is gone, I can no longer go through the children's quarters without stopping before his door, now closed. And I say to Teresa, who is as moved by it as I, "The first empty place . . ."

In early December, I hold a debate in Geneva for an audience of jurists, lawyers, charity workers, on a subject that has long been dear to my heart: the need to bring the outdated penal code, which remains more or less as it was forged by Napoleon, into harmony with today's mores. Most countries are trying to do this, but it is so difficult a task that almost all of them are hesitant about it, postponing it, settling for minor revisions for fear of seeing the whole edifice come tumbling down.

On December 12, the principal of the Collège de Béthusy asks me to come and see him, and I know what to expect. He is a courteous man who, on this occasion, displays extreme delicacy.

"You understand, of course, that I want to talk to you about your daughter, don't you? She has a very sharp intelligence, great sensitivity, and has nothing but friends here."

"You may be frank."

"I am aware of her marks. I have questioned her teachers. And it appears certain that she will not pass her term-end exams, the last she is to take here. . . .

"So, I am faced with a problem of conscience, Monsieur Simenon. She could repeat her last term, but I know she is too advanced to be put in with pupils younger than she. As I see it, she would consider this a humiliation, which might . . ."

"I understand, and I am in full agreement with you."

I understand all the better, Marie-Jo, for having been in the same boat as you at your age. I would not have been able to pass those exams either, if our doctor had not advised me to quit school and go to work, my father being incurably ill.

I left the Collège Saint-Servais three months before the exams. As you will leave too. But aren't you gifted in everything, whereas I felt gifted in nothing? I speak to you sweetly, tenderly, that night, and I do believe you were relieved.

Three days later, I had to go to Paris, to have a look at Johnny's studio, which Francette had helped him decorate in a most fanciful manner. In an old building, which Pierre would have called an "old barn," Johnny was almost the only tenant.

The colors were violent, even aggressive. You were happy to be in your own place, son. Teresa and I congratulated you. I remember that all three of us had an improvised bite at the corner bistro where you ate your daily breakfast.

Destinies were being decided, Marc's, Johnny's, Marie-Jo's too, just as today Pierre's is taking shape, and I am thinking of the time when Teresa and I alone will be left in the house, this big house intended for a big family in which . . .

How I need you, Teresa, and your love, for now we do dare speak of love, almost in whispers, behind closed doors.

You will help me, Teresa, watch over the two children left to me, until the day when they in turn leave, and the long hallway leads to nothing but closed doors.

But enough! I was almost forgetting the "Simenon reserve."

69

Having spent six years at Epalinges, I am not yet aware that I will live only three more years in this house that I built for joy and gaiety, built to fill my children's memories with shining images that one day, if need be, might comfort them.

The last three years at Echandens had been dark, sometimes torturous. Our quasi-flight to Lyons with Pierre, still a baby, whom the doctors gave only a fifty-fifty chance to live, at best, with the help of prayers, so crushed me, as I have said, that I had vertigo, which kept me from crossing noisy streets otherwise than in the middle of a crowd, as if I needed protection.

As for D., her state was getting visibly worse, and with a heavy heart I was observing her ever-faster decline, due to reach its paroxysm upon her hallucinating entry into our new house at Epalinges.

Had these repressed worries not little by little sapped my health without my knowing it?

I had no one I could confide in, which might have lessened the too great weight I was carrying, especially in the last years. No one was aware of my fears, my heartbreaks sometimes. Quite the contrary. For my children especially, I forced myself to show a good face, and for D., I often, as in *When I Was Old*, spoke of love and happiness.

My vertigo became more frequent. I began having chest spasms, especially after I broke all the ribs on my left side. The latter have healed, but not back to their original shape. X-rays revealed that my diaphragm now was lying diagonally. I had to go to the hospital to learn how to breathe normally, and every day I had to do breathing exercises under Teresa's supervision.

One afternoon, my friend Cruchaud, and then an enterologist, had to be called in an emergency. I was suffering from a serious intestinal occlusion, and it took the two doctors three hours of effort to overcome it.

From then on, a new phenomenon occurred. With every hard novel I wrote, my digestion became blocked as a result of nervous tension, and every evening before going to bed Teresa had to give me an enema, something I never accepted from any woman. Perhaps because this one was, in total simplicity, a real woman close to nature.

These episodes recall to mind some very old memories, the evenings which, on my first arrival in Paris at age nineteen, I spent writing "for myself" short pieces into which I invested so much intensity that each time before having finished I had thrown up.

I knew, since Cannes, that I had a hiatus hernia. It was then a common thing. I was not worried by it, the less so since I knew from one of my coroner friends that eighty percent of human beings have a hiatus hernia, many of them from birth, without ever being aware of it during their lifetimes.

Mine, alas, from 1967 on, just kept growing, and after examinations as careful as they were painful, a specialist told me: "I have rarely seen 'so fine' a hiatus hernia. Yours, my dear Simenon, is now as big as an orange...."

"Does that explain my attacks of aerophagia?"

"Certainly. And your nervous tension explains your hernia."

"You want to cut it out?"

"That would be too dangerous. I would rather treat you with tranquilizers."

Nor is that all concerning what I call "aches and pains." I sometimes have to get up six or more times a night. All my life I've heard friends talk about prostate trouble. I am not unaware that few men reach old age without having to undergo an operation that was once very painful and leads to sexual impotence.

Isn't that every man's nightmare, when he reaches a certain age? It is, I confess, mine, and I confess also that I attach too much importance to my sexual activities not to be affected by such a prospect.

A urologist gives me further examinations, which show that I do have prostatitis. It is a severe shock to me. I dare not ask, for fear of the answer, whether I will become impotent. I will find out only later, after other treatments. I will then be apprised that, in many cases, including my own, doctors have recently given up excision of the prostate in favor of a sort of curettage which in no way reduces—*quite the contrary*—the patient's virility. Why am I intimidated by doctors, who are also often my friends?

Are all these aches and pains due to the tension I have lived with for so long? Many of them are, at any rate. Even the grippe and bronchitis that keep coming back and become chronic.

Nonetheless, I appear just fine at Epalinges to Marie-Jo and Pierre, as well as the help. If I feel rotten, as I do when I have bronchitis, I stay in my own quarters.

· · ·

Marie-Jo is the one who concerns me more and more and whom I attentively observe. I feel that she has become the "weak link" of the family chain.

The "big ones," Marc and Johnny, are already out living their own lives, and whereas they come to visit often, I do not presume to give them advice. Marc and Mylène are living in the same building as Francette and their two children. He is making out all right in the movie career he chose.

In June, Johnny, having completed his first year of sciences, makes a rather strange confidence to me.

"You know, Dad, what area, it seems to me, is soon going to assume greater, if not the greatest, importance in people's lives?" He seems self-assured, thoughtful, and, to my surprise, adds, "Leisure."

He explains to me how leisure occupies an increasingly large share of people's time and will go on ever more so, as vacations get longer and working hours shorter. In his view, leisure covers a very large area: publishing, films, radio, television, sports. . . .

"What have you decided, then?"

"I would first like to get the feel of publishing."

I allow him to convince me. Sven Nielsen is only too happy to find a spot for him in his ever-expanding publishing empire, and Johnny will spend a year with him, learning the business from the bottom up, from packing and shipping to the corridors of management, by way of all the intermediary departments. Sven will even put him in charge of launching one of my books, and my good Johnny will break new ground, organizing a contest among all the booksellers of France for the best window display, with valuable prizes. Evenings, he takes courses in publishing and bookselling in a school established by the French publishing industry.

Marie-Jo remains my worry. At sixteen she is throwing herself with disquieting frenzy into a number of activities, for which, in fact, she seems definitely gifted.

First, classical dancing, with a onetime star of the Ballets Russes who has a school in Lausanne. Many of the pupils start as early as the age of twelve. To make up for lost time, Marie-Jo takes private lessons instead of the regular classes.

In another establishment, with another teacher, she also is studying modern dance.

She often walks with me in the country. Everything connected with the arts fascinates her. She is tender, so tender that it sometimes scares me.

"What do you think of all this, Dad? I must be a big expense to you, and I'm ashamed of it."

She tells me everything about her private life—everything except her secret, which she will continue to bury in the deepest part of herself. I can guess that it is painful to her and that she is piling up all these activities in an effort to forget.

Evenings, she takes audio-visual courses in English, a language that perhaps reminds her of her earliest childhood and that she will speak all her life, to the point of writing in English many of her poems and songs, and even some of the most confidential letters she will send me.

At the same time she is studying the guitar with a Spanish teacher and plays it several hours a day in her room. Finally, to make up for some of her lack of classical culture, I suggest that she study the history of civilizations. I inquire at the University of Lausanne, and they send a graduate student capable of guiding Marie-Jo through this rather arduous study.

How does she carry off all these activities at once? We are in close, frequent contact, and I do nothing to try to dampen her curiosities. I know too well that what she feels is a deep need to try to express herself in every way, and the most amazing part is that she succeeds in each of these areas that attract her.

Life too attracts her. She goes out at night. I don't keep her from it. One day, I receive a courteous letter from the Geneva police, informing me that my daughter was given a warning in an all-night cabaret in that city, where at her age she was not allowed.

"I ask your forgiveness, Dad."

"I'm not scolding you, little girl. If I showed you the letter, it was only so you would be careful, so you would know that next time you might be in worse trouble."

"I'm a terrible girl, aren't I?"

"You're an adorable girl, interested in everything."

In June, I wrote a novel, *Novembre (November)*, and in September, *Maigret et le Marchand de vin (Maigret and the Wine Merchant)*.

In July, Marie-Jo takes a short Club Med vacation with her best friend of the moment, Véronique, and the latter's mother. Then she joins us at La Baule, where once again we are spending the summer with the whole family, Boule, Yole, and Teresa.

While in Morocco, Marie-Jo hurt her foot and now can't play tennis. Nor does she lunch with us at noon in the big dining room. The hotel has built a kind of bar on the beach at which one can get simple meals. Marie-Jo lives on the beach all day in her bathing suit and, not to have to change, eats at this restaurant-bar.

Except when she has come in too late the night before, after painting the town with her friends. Whereas I am an early-to-bed, morning person, she is an evening and night person.

The day we are leaving, early in the morning, she will come into our room, look out at the bay, the deserted beach, the horses trotting by in single file, and cry out in surprise:

"Is it always so beautiful, Dad?"

Here, she had never once seen the daybreak and now seems to rue the time she wasted.

Teresa and I walk again through streets and on paths now familiar to us; we go along the beach, go swimming, and even spend one whole night awake, for the first time. Shortly after midnight that night, no one knowing at exactly what time, human beings, people like us, are going to walk on the moon. The TV in our small living room will show them to us live as they come out of their contraption, weirdly outfitted.

The children prefer to sleep through it. At midnight, impatient, I decide to shave and get dressed. Yole comes and joins us. When the space images begin to appear, I telephone room service to send up a bottle of champagne. The waiter says, "Never in my life did I serve so many bottles in one night."

All through the hotel, breathless people are watching these human beings setting foot for the first time on the soil of an alien planet.

It is a long telecast. Commentaries continue it until daybreak. Teresa and I, instead of going to bed, go for a walk in the fresh early-morning air. We go as far as Le Pouliguen, where the little bistro at the market is open, its TV set going. Sailors, young and old, are there, commenting on the event, while the women are at work preparing their displays of fish, crustaceans, vegetables, and fruit.

When we do go back to the hotel, we head for the beach, take a swim, and then walk some more, seized by a new kind of excitement, and we will not finally get to bed until naptime.

There is another event while we are on vacation at La Baule, less exciting than the men on the moon. I get a phone call from the assistant manager of the Hôtel du Golf at Divonne. He courteously, but with some embarrassment, informs me that my "wife" is sick, no longer has her companion with her, which I was unaware of, and the hotel cannot keep her under these circumstances.

"What is the matter with her?"

He hesitates, then gives me the name of the doctor who was called in, whom I immediately phone. The doctor is amiable but reticent. "I think all she has is a case of bronchitis. . . . Don't worry, Monsieur Simenon. I think I can take care of her where she is. I'll have a word with the hotel manager. Call me as often as you wish."

That reminds me of another event, also seemingly unimportant, but to which I subconsciously connect D.'s "illness."

In April, she changed chauffeurs. She also changed cars, and I bought her a Commodore, almost as long and wide as the Rolls-Royce, and new to me. She chose the make and model, which came as something of a surprise.

One day when she was visiting at Epalinges, she sat down across from me, in my office. She was more upset than usual.

"You're still my friend, aren't you, Georges? Promise that you'll accept the proposition I am about to make to you. And promise you won't ask me any questions." Then, after gulping down her drink, "This is very important to me, almost a matter of life and death."

"Are you sure you can't tell me more about it?"

"Oh, well! What's the difference? I'll confess the whole thing. I urgently need twenty-five thousand francs."

I am struck by the fact that she sold the almost-new Princess for a song in order to get the Commodore in its place. I am also struck by the defiant look I get from her new chauffeur every time they come, and the fact that he thinks nothing of barging into my office when D. is tarrying there, and saying to her, almost in a tone of command, "It's time. . . ."

She then gets up like an automaton to follow him and disappear inside the car.

"Are you being blackmailed?" I ask.

She cries, answering neither yes nor no. She has always known how to put on the pathos, but this time I feel she means it.

"He wants me to buy him a car just like mine. Don't say no! My whole existence is riding on it."

I sign a check. Yes! What else could I do? And now can you understand why the news of her "bronchitis" is not fully convincing to me?

By phone, the Divonne doctor reassures me. She is better. She can keep her two rooms, with two baths and a sitting room. For herself alone?

Not always, she will tell me laughingly, as if it were a good joke. One evening—in the Casino, I suppose—she met a man who was "very nice," a "real gentleman." I will now let D. speak for herself, as faithfully as I can.

"It was all going very well. I liked this man. After a while, we were having a drink in my room, when he happened to see your picture. He asked me, frowning, 'Do you know him?'

" 'Of course. He's my husband.'

" 'Are you the wife of Georges Simenon?'

" 'Yes.' "

And D. continued, laughing with just a trace of bitterness: "You know what he did? He got up, bowed to me, and said, 'I am sorry that I have to leave you now.'

"You see, Jo, even though we are separated, you are still pursuing me, even through your picture. . . ."

In November, another phone call from the assistant manager at Divonne.

"I'm afraid I must inform you, Monsieur Simenon, that your wife has met with an accident. . . ."

"An auto accident?"

"No. I can't tell you much about it. She was found in her room this morning, wounded, her face bleeding, near a broken bottle. Her doctor was called and he had her taken by ambulance to a clinic in Geneva. She is not in any danger, according to what he said."

"Do you know what happened to her, or when?"

"All I know is that she was in her nightgown. It is my duty to tell you that. I must also add that we do not feel it advisable for her to return to our hotel."

When I keep insisting on more details, he dryly tells me, "If you wish to know any more, just ask the police."

"Were the police called in?"

"I repeat: Just ask the police."

I did not, out of discretion. Doesn't she too have the right to live as she pleases?

I phone the clinic and get her doctor, who reassures me. In a week or two, D. will be back on her feet. She will not go back to the Hôtel du Golf, but to a suite at the Président in Geneva.

Marie-Jo is my main concern from November on, an active, joyous Marie-Jo. She has become crazy about tap dancing, and asks me to get her a dress suit for a show she wants to put on for us. She also has to have a stiff shirt, a butterfly collar, white tie, and collapsible top hat, for her new idol is Fred Astaire.

She is keeping very busy in the big basement playroom, and on the days preceding Christmas she forbids us to come in. She has bought wood, cloth, and pots of paint.

Marc and his family are spending that Christmas at Avoriaz, where at the time all the movie people go. Marie-Jo, Pierre, and Yole are to join them there on December 26.

For the evening of the 24th, Marie-Jo has issued invitations to all of us, as well as a few friends. Was D. there too? Possibly. The whole household staff attends the show.

Now we learn the secret of Marie-Jo's recent busyness. She has built a miniature stage, painted a colored set, and, after giving the traditional French three knocks to signal the raising of the curtain, we hear some familiar music, to which a radiant Marie-Jo appears and does her tap number.

She looks wonderful that way, long and limber, with her stage make-up and her high hat slightly askew.

Loud applause. She dances again, her eyes shining, and I am just as excited as she is. Then she sings, accompanying herself on the guitar.

Teresa and I will be home to celebrate the advent of 1970. The children, big and small, phone each in turn to wish me a Happy New Year.

I cannot keep from feeling sad, for I am apprehensive of the future, mainly for my daughter, but also for D.

This year is going to see another empty place in the house, a second closed door in the children's hallway.

And D. will sink into almost total disorder.

I would like soon to be able to keep myself from telling about the two of them. I am eager to stop torturing myself by reliving these painful years that are becoming too much for me to bear.

If I go on, it is only because I am convinced I must, for Marie-Jo especially, for my children, for my own sake too perhaps.

Just one more effort and I will no longer be telling the tale; it will be Marie-Jo herself, who wanted it, who explicitly turned this task over to me.

I must note that my mother died, at the Hôpital de Bavière, the very place where I used to serve at Mass in the chapel. Teresa and I were at her deathbed for a week, during which she was in peace and did not suffer.

We had succeeded, for her last years, in getting her into a nice rest home, on the Plateau de Herve, where the Ursulines have a farm and a lot of land.

I had had part of a wall knocked down, a bathroom put in, a little sitting room, and, so that my mother might feel at home, I had had her own furniture brought there.

We visited her several times. She was happy, and the Ursuline sisters vied with one another in coddling her.

Her funeral was held in the chapel, where as a child I had been present at so many Masses for the dead. Later on, I was to dictate *Lettre à ma mère* (*Letter to My Mother*), in which I tried to explain for my own understanding everything that, from the beginning of my life, had separated us.

· · ·

Now it is D.'s turn to explain herself at last, in one of her rare moments of lucidity, or sincerity, which, unfortunately, will not last long.

I will summarize a handwritten letter, four pages long, dated January 23, 1971, which deals with the present and the past, confirming what all those little signs had made me fear as early as November 1945.

Starting with "Dear Jo" and ending with "Affectionately again, Denise," it certainly overwhelms me, for in a way it is a kind of painful confession confirming all of the little signs that peppered our years of intimacy and made me want to cure her of her obsessions.

She speaks in it of her "deeper truth," which she says I have doubtless guessed long since, of her destructive rage within an upsetting alcoholism, the risk she ran of doing herself in or of being victim of a cerebral accident.

She is not trying to put on an act, or to use big words. She tells of her life then at Avignon, her fear of cracking up, her wild extravagances, and the indulgence which, because of my concern for her, I had shown.

Finally, she thanks me and begs my pardon, feeling that those words are compatible with her feelings toward me. She embraces me with an affection and an increased friendship that she will never allow to become a burden.

I answer with the following letter:

January 25, 1971

Dear Denise,

I have just read your letter of the 23rd and confess that I am relieved.

For a long time I had been hoping that you would understand and I was worrying myself sick over you. Now, as you say, you have touched bottom and are on the right path. You must remain on it. The cure you are taking at Avignon seems to be doing you an enormous amount of good and, of course, you must not interrupt it.

German TV is here with me. This is one of my last appointments, after which, in a week, if all goes well, I will be able to write my novel.

They want me on the set. I will write you at greater length after I receive the letter you promise me.

Very affectionately yours,

Georges

I have jumped ahead of myself insofar as D. is concerned. In 1970, my true concern is Marie-Jo, who is about to turn seventeen, a few days after my sixty-seventh birthday.

70

Forgive me, my little Marie-Jo, if I leave you for a while at this dawn of the year 1970, which will be so important a turning point in your existence. It is just because of the importance to you, to me too, of what you will live through in that year and the following ones that I wish to clear the ground by some sordid notations, to be able soon to speak of you alone, without being interrupted, without interrupting your own narratives.

So, I must speak of D., D. alone, determined not to allow herself to be forgotten, and using to this end any and all means.

To go back, 1970 marked for her too a turning point of the gravest consequence.

While she is living at the Hôtel Président in Geneva, to which she has been followed by her apparently domineering chauffeur, I offer to buy her an apartment in that city or Lausanne, whichever she prefers, but she is not interested in either of these cities.

She tells me of a villa for sale at Begnins, a village near the French border and Divonne. Why this choice, I will never know. The villa, practically new and with a fine garden, is near and exactly like that of a famous Formula 1 racing-car driver. There are other buyers angling for it, and it is urgent for me to decide quickly. She very much wants it. So, within three days, as she requests, I buy this villa, sight unseen, sight never to be seen. But I take the precaution of buying it in my own name, agreeing to let her have the use of it for as long as she wishes and to be responsible for the improvements she feels it requires as well as furnishing it.

There will be a lot of work to be done on it, for what suits a Formula 1 racer and his family is not necessarily to the taste of D., who will modestly name it, in golden letters: Villa D.

So, Villa D. it is! She has no chambermaid or companion there. The only one who lives there with her, for quite a long time, is a man I did not ever see either, who answers the phone: "Madame Simenon's butler speaking."

So, "butler" it is too! I find out by accident that he is a married Frenchman, whose wife lives in France with his children; and that D. met him at the Président, where he worked as a floor waiter.

This would be of no interest to me were it not for the avalanche of sometimes astonishing bills I receive from suppliers to whom D. went for the furnishing of the villa. One such bill, in particular, surprises and intrigues me. It is for a hundred thousand Swiss francs for just one Oriental rug, which, as I later find out, is moth-eaten, threadbare. The salesman who palmed it off on her didn't waste his time that day.

I pay. Even though D. still has the use of the checkbook on the joint account I opened, for practical purposes, upon my arrival in Switzerland.

No matter. Let her be happy with her butler.

In mid-November, she meets a nurse she knew at Prangins. This nurse, whom I like very much, has now opened, in a small village between Avignon and the Alps, a home in which she takes care of the "maladjusted."

She takes D. down there, and the latter finds a place to stay not far from the city of Avignon, at L'Isle-sur-la-Sorgue. What kind of people will she now be thrown in with? Young people, mostly, more or less bohemian, more or less "outside the mainstream."

But mainly a self-styled former Swiss preacher who has set up an Institute of Human Sciences in an old apartment. I find out—again much later—that he never was a minister, but practices a sort of psychoanalysis without being either a physician or a psychologist. I am never able to get any information about his institute, which no one, even at Avignon, ever heard of.

A first phone call alerts me. It is from a woman cashier at the Crédit Lyonnais bank in Cannes, where I also have a joint account, who says to me: "Monsieur Simenon. I don't know what to do anymore and feel I should let you know. Your wife is 'taking pot shots' at your account."

About the same time, my Lausanne bank lets me know that checks signed by my wife are turning up in piles and that I had better make some provision in order not to find my account depleted, if not overdrawn. Each of the banks advises only one thing: close out the joint accounts and reopen an account in my own name alone.

No need for figures. The total exceeds by very, very much the salary of the president of the Swiss Confederation, and by even more the pay of the prime minister of the French Republic.

I advise D. and let her know what provisions I am making for her. Every three months, an ample alimony check will be sent to her personal account in Nyon, which is near Begnins. I will also pay directly her medical and pharmaceutical bills, her taxes, and the cost of her longer and longer and more and more frequent hospitalizations.

I also agree to honor the fees of the founder-director of the mysterious Institute of Human Sciences, with whom D. is to have psychotherapy sessions for five hours each day. What can she be telling this man? Whatever it is, he takes me to task in a long letter in which he accuses me of all the sins of Israel. I nevertheless honor his fees, which, this time, I will quote: eighty thousand Swiss francs, to be paid not to his own account but to that of his brother, who lives in Switzerland.

Is he the one who brings D. to a moment of lucidity? That may be. This is the time, in 1971, when I receive two letters from D., which, unfortunately only for a short time, raise my hopes. I quoted the first one at the end of the last chapter. Here I will summarize the second, which seems to confirm it.

It is dated March 4, 1971, and speaks of the precipice at the edge of which she was tottering when she started her psychoanalytic treatment.

She has, it seems, forsworn drinking, and understands the "blank" period she underwent as a result of a certain aberration. Her present hope —and it will take time, lots of time—is to overcome all that went before, and she ends the letter with big kisses for all of us.

I feel that now I will have a breather, even though my instinct and my long association with D. prompt me to be on guard against optimism. Besides, I have other concerns, quite innocently caused by my little Marie-Jo.

Yet, I am writing. Because that is a refuge for me? I categorically deny that. I have been writing since I was sixteen, with no ambition other than wanting to express myself, and writing alone is available to me.

In October 1970, a novel, *La Disparition d'Odile* (*The Disappearance of Odile*), which will mistakenly be taken as a reflection of my private life. Intuition perhaps? I don't know and don't try to find out. February 1–7, 1971, *Maigret et l'Homme tout seul* (*Maigret and the Loner*). March, *La Cage de verre* (*The Glass Cage*).

In June, *Maigret et l'indicateur* (*Maigret and the Informer*), which I fortunately finish before the end of the month. For I then receive a letter from D., dated June 23, typewritten this time, the style of which leads me to believe she did not write it all by herself.

This letter comes "Registered, Return Receipt Requested." I smell a threat, and this time I am not wrong.

In it, she makes offensive and vulgar accusations against indubitably honorable third parties, as she will do again seven years later in a book the advertising for which constitutes total misrepresentation, since it uses the catchline "The Marriage of Maigret's Wife."

Was not D. always the exact opposite of the sweet mate of my inspector?

She tells me in the letter that, after her last stay in Switzerland, a representative of a big international press syndicate, which she does not identify, came to see her. He urged her to write a series of articles telling of her life with me. She delayed giving him an answer because she was afraid she might not be able to do it without sounding as though she had some kind of animosity toward me.

After which come pages of reproaches, insults, untruths. The pyrotechnic display of this interminable letter is in a clearly lawyerly style.

It is a proposal for an agreement between us, specifying, in the first instance, that we are never to see each other again.

I am to agree to pay, half to her bank account in Avignon, half to her Swiss bank account, at the end of each month, the sum of forty-eight thousand Swiss francs (or more than half a million Swiss francs per year), starting June 30, 1971, subject to cost-of-living adjustments, allowance for exchange variances, et cetera.

If I agree to this, the "rumors"(?) about me will disappear through the "weight of regained truth"(?). She will forever remain mute about the past and will immediately destroy the manuscript original and the copies of the first two articles she has written.

If I refuse, she will transform—without rancor or hatred—the "public rumors"(?) into "objective news"(!).

The P.S. to this ultimatum demands a "satisfactory answer" at the latest by June 29, failing which she will immediately take "irrevocable steps."

As if with sarcasm, the letter concludes with "Friendly regards."

This time, the desperate little girl of the earlier letters is not only insulting but also threatening, with the precision of a blackmail letter, which is just what this is.

I answer by the following telegram, which, despite my feeling of revulsion, I close with friendly regards:

RECEIVED YOUR LETTER ON FRIDAY JUNE TWENTY-FIVE SHORTLY BEFORE SECRETARIES LEFT STOP IMPOSSIBLE ANSWER BEFORE THE TWENTY-NINTH STOP MOREOVER DO NOT SEE WHAT I MIGHT REPLY TO SUCH A HODGEPODGE OF WILD UNTRUTHS AND THREATS STOP ACCEPTANCE OF THE SIX AMAZING POINTS OF YOUR PROPOSITION OUT OF THE QUESTION STOP GO AHEAD WITH IRREVOCABLE STEPS YOU MENTION STOP FRIENDLY REGARDS   GEORGES

I keep waiting for the promised bombshell, which does not explode. D. has finally shown her hand, and I no longer have any illusions about her. She has declared war. I will not wage it; I will merely defend myself.

Yet, just one remark about this.

In the United States, Tigy's and my divorce agreement provided that not only would I pay her alimony as long as she lived, but also I would carry a life-insurance policy of which she would be the beneficiary. I paid the premiums for nearly two years. During one of our trips to New York, D. met an agent of another company, which, she claimed, offered better terms.

I have always had a distaste for money questions. I let D. handle it, and she spent two whole afternoons with the new insurance agent. Of course, by switching policies, I lost the first two years' payments. But I still had illusions about D.

So I signed the new policy, unaware that D.'s name had been slipped into it. By poetic justice, when I turned sixty-seven and she tried to collect its cash value, the company told her that she was entitled to nothing, that legally only Tigy could collect the money at my death. For, the company having advised me in the interim of this switch of names, I had seen to it that what was done behind my back was rectified.

Henceforth, it would be through the intermediary of amazingly varied lawyers that D. would contact me. And, as was fitting, my lawyer would answer them.

A last letter, however, from her, dated October 18, 1971. More money questions. And, at the end, another threat.

She would be most unhappy, it said, if she had to have recourse to proceedings the repercussions of which would be harmful in the eyes of my readers. It would be distasteful to her to accept the offers of literary contracts received from various sources(?), which would afford her the financial independence I was refusing to give her.

Were her revelations, then, so much in demand? What was she waiting for, to sell them and become "financially independent"?

I answered, again by wire:

YOUR LETTER OF 18 OCTOBER 1971 RECEIVED STOP MY POSITION CONCERNING MONEY PAYMENTS UNCHANGED AS WELL AS THAT ON DIRECTLY PAYING YOUR MEDICAL EXPENSES STOP MARIE-JO IN PARIS WHERE GETTING ALONG VERY WELL STOP TEMPORARILY WITHOUT ADDRESS AS FREQUENTLY CHANGES HOTELS STOP PIERRE IN TOP SHAPE JOHNNY TOO REGARDS   GEORGES

Back to the first lawyer again, but this time not for money or threats.

December 1, 1971

Sir,

Your spouse has consulted me concerning your mutual child Marie-Jo.

Mme. SIMENON specifies to me that you had indicated to her that this child, who is only eighteen years of age, was living at the Hotel UNIVERS, 15 Rue Duperré, Paris (9th).

It turns out that this child remained at this hotel for only a few days and left it for a destination unknown, that the hotel in question is located in a rather unsavory neighborhood between two nightclubs; that your child Marie-Jo was not alone but accompanied by one or several persons unknown.

Under these circumstances, I must demand of you, in the name of Mme Denise SIMENON:

What is the present residence of the child Marie-Jo;

With what persons is she now.

I thank you in advance for your reply.

As is customary in my profession, I would appreciate your informing me of the name of your usual Counsel.

Without going through a lawyer—I as yet have none—I immediately answer:

IN REPLY YOUR LETTER DECEMBER I STOP MY DAUGHTER CURRENTLY OCCUPYING STUDIO AT 8 BOULEVARD DE LA MADELEINE IN PARIS STOP IS IN PROCESS OF MOVING IN STOP AS FOR WHOM SHE FREQUENTS I HAVE NO IDEA STOP CORDIAL REGARDS   GEORGES SIMENON

There will be lawyers after lawyers, in Avignon and Paris, Geneva and Lausanne. Some will refuse to represent her any longer without giving any reasons, which I can guess. At least one, whom she tries to retain, will refuse out of professional ethics, his predecessor not having been paid.

She keeps asking for a million and a half or two million Swiss francs, over and above her alimony, to give her financial independence and assure her "status." She keeps talking about her "status." It is important to her. As it is important to her that she remain Mme Georges Simenon, come what may, which in no way bothers me.

She will cite me before the Civil Court in Lausanne, which she calls upon to supply to her the details of my income, my possessions, and my expenditures.

In such a court, matters are discussed between the judge and the lawyers of the two parties courteously, in technical terms. Unlike Criminal Court, here emotions and outbursts are not tolerated, and the principals are not called upon to participate.

I see her at a distance, and do not recognize her immediately. But I can still see her, dressed in black, her hair almost straight back, getting up to interrupt her attorney and speak for herself, in a passionate voice, making gestures. The judge tries to calm her, to get her to keep quiet. She finally sits down, but jumps up two or three more times to interfere.

Result: She loses her case and has to pay costs.

For eight years, she will keep attacking me in this way, always threatening, sometimes on one ground, sometimes on another, by way of her successive lawyers, but avoiding going to courts, since she no longer trusts them.

The file of her demands has grown so thick I don't have the courage to reread it.

She will cause fantastic rumors about my wealth, mentioning tens of millions, if not billions, of francs.

She reminds me of those aged women, widows or spinsters, in the French countryside and small towns who, on fair or market day in their local administrative seat, pay a call on their "law man." Their final joy in life is bringing suit, whether against a neighbor whose dog has killed a chicken, or over a tree that has grown beyond property lines, or a field in which the surveyors made an alleged mistake of a few yards—anything at all. A contested right of thoroughfare . . . Public insults from a daughter-in-law . . .

It is this "bringing suit" that in the seats of the cantons keeps the "law men" going, and they need not always be law graduates or members of the bar. The old ladies depend on them as on the local faith healer.

The threats of lawsuits started in 1972. I did not give in to one of them. After six years of such "suing," she finally decided to write the much-talked-about book. She did not write it by herself, but with the help of two successive "ghosts," whose names I know. I read the proofs of her book at almost the same time she did.

As for her publisher, a tiny one, not the least bit "world famous," he will go broke a few months later. Did D. at least get paid? Did she finally achieve the "financial independence" mentioned in her letters?

"Lie, lie, some of it is sure to stick," as the saying goes.

In her interviews, she piled it on at leisure, and some of the newspapermen fell for it, even foreign newspapermen, whom she greeted with open arms.

She even appeared on French television, on which I found her pitiful. She moved and talked like an automaton, in a colorless voice, as if drugged.

Was the little girl whom her brothers and sister once called "the Diva" finally having her dream come true?

Did I feel sorry for her? Possibly. But not for long. The furious passions that so long held her in thrall would, more or less directly, have tragic consequences.

Not for me, alas! I have already lived a long life.

But for you, my darling little girl, who sang to me in English, playing on your guitar, "When you are a hundred years old, I will be fifty. . . ."

Now, it is your turn, pretty, fragile Marie-Jo. I have cleared the way.

But the road I am to retrace with you, step by step, from 1970 on, when you were seventeen and I was fifty years older, will be marked by joys and sorrows I will be forced to relive, if I have the strength for it.

At the very least, this time, I will be writing without revulsion.

And with an awful lot of love.

71

Your turn, my darling little Marie-Jo, now that I have rid myself of what was sordid—you would say "dirty"—in my recollections. I did not want to write the story of your life in the same colors; now I can start with a clean palette.

Do you know that it is your life that for more than two years I have been proposing to write, your ardent, pathetic life, which a great heartbreak within me would not allow me to evoke any earlier?

The first two notebooks, of which this is the ninth, had just one name as their title: "Marie-Jo."

But could I write your story without telling the story of your father, your mother, your brothers, those around you? So I thought of another title: "Marie-Jo and Her Brothers."

For the same reason, I dropped that one too, and today, in September 1980, these almost-golden-yellow-covered notebooks as yet have no title on them.

I have four children. I "nurtured" all four with the same attentive tenderness. From your births on, I tried to understand each one of you, to penetrate the fascinating mystery constituted by every human life.

If I give you more space than I do your brothers, my little girl, it is perhaps done unconsciously, because you were, and remain, for your entire life the little girl I always hoped for.

Fate gave me two sons before you, and I was not disappointed in them. Marc and Johnny were greeted with happiness, as, after you, was your brother Pierre. Yet I never lost my hankering for a girl, a little human female whose blossoming I might follow.

Besides, you are the most fragile of my four children, more precisely, the most sensitive, with a sensitivity that sometimes frightened me and made me feel I ought to speak to you only in whispers.

I knew it from the end of your first year, when, through an unfortunate circumstance, at Lakeville, I was unable to stop the car at the corner to hold you in my arms for a moment, the way I did every day as I went to the post office.

This event, though seemingly insignificant, was to characterize all my relationships with you.

You were not only hypersensitive, Marie-Jo, but, as I was to find out a thousand times later on, you had a need for love—not only for receiving it but also for giving it.

All my life, you made me think of a filly, a word you often used later on when, accompanying yourself on your guitar, you sang me haunting Western songs. That is why I have to make an effort today not to use English in speaking to you, as you did whenever intimacy and sentiment were involved.

For cowboys, the term "filly," a young female horse, is the tenderest of words. It evokes the still-untamed and wide-eyed young female, looking at life and people with skittish curiosity, ever ready to break into a slow gallop on her still-frail long legs at the slightest sign of danger.

All your life long, Marie-Jo darling, you reminded me of those fillies. You had their innate sensitivity as well as the need timidly to get closer to other beings to beg for a bit of affection.

I have spoken to you at length about your childhood in these notebooks. You spoke about it too, even in your school compositions, where you revealed yourself without false modesty in some prophetic pages.

Those pages, the ones of your intimate diaries, your letters, your cassettes will come in turn when you tell your own story.

First allow me to tell what I saw, what I experienced with you, often in search of a truth that escaped me and that you yourself would one day reveal. That truth was not known to me in 1970 or in the years that followed. I was feeling my way, making an effort to interpret your half-confidences. If I made mistakes, and disappointed you, I beg you to forgive me, my adorable, susceptible filly.

In 1970, then, you are spending your winter vacation at Avoriaz with your brothers, Boule, and young Yole. My health did not allow me to follow you to that French resort.

I make many phone calls to all of you, of course, but I find it rather difficult to imagine what your life can be like in a furnished apartment with everyone more or less pitching in to do the cooking, or at a nightclub filled with movie people who nightly attract crowds of fans, and you now one of them.

You are seventeen. You have had a first disillusioning sex experience in a bathroom, with a no doubt attractive man, but one who goes from woman to woman sowing children, like a cuckoo, at random. I should so have wished a different initiation for you than the one you thus had, on a night of general madness, between a toilet and a washbowl with a more or less drunken bunch of people coming and going outside the door!

To make it worse, your first lover (how inappropriate the word is in the circumstances!) will deny it before your brothers, make you out to be a liar, a little girl with too vivid an imagination, and I know from you yourself how much that pained you.

At Epalinges, during the parties you gave, you had flirtations with two boys your own age, or barely older, but they didn't go very far, and the two boys were to complain about it for a long time, saying in their letters that you were toying with them. One of them, a very nice fellow, will go on hoping for two years, in vain, and you will nonetheless remain friendly with both him and the other one.

You took private drawing and painting lessons from your teacher at school, and he gave them to you in your room, where the black-leather-upholstered armchair became his. Your room carried his mark, on the days of those lessons, for it retained the sweet smell of his Dutch pipe tobacco. He helps you a great deal in your efforts as a painter. I believe he will also help you through the affectionate friendship he feels for you.

You are trying to find yourself, my darling. You are trying to find yourself in all the meanings of that term. You need contact with others, whose eyes you gravely plumb. You also need to discover your own personality, to know yourself, and that need will pursue you all through your life.

You are the most severe in judging yourself, I have always felt. After a sudden revolt, for instance, most often born of a misunderstanding, you would lock yourself in your room, where, lying on the bed, you would at times spend hours staring at the ceiling, as if that were your punishment.

You will speak of my angers. Please understand that I never felt anger toward you or toward your brothers. Only one woman, as you are only too well aware, sometimes succeeded, deliberately, in making me "fly off the handle."

Of course, once in a while I raised my voice to one or another of you when I was afraid for you. And I was often afraid for you, my little girl, just because of your exacerbated sensitivity.

I was also afraid for your health, when you obstinately avoided sleep, as if you were afraid of it, when you stayed up later and later, and were surprised and unhappy when you were awakened in the morning.

I never asked you to confide in me, any more than I did your brothers, out of respect. In certain periods, you did share confidences with me, of the most intimate sort, with disarming sincerity.

At other periods, you escaped me; I mean you remained closed off from me, as if you resented me, for some reason I did not know and which made me suffer.

I knew that your mother, while she still had a hold on you, went to your room at night and talked to you until very late. And on those evenings she had already spent a lot of time in the office and was never without a load of liquor.

She talked to you about your birth, about how you popped out of her belly "like a cannonball," which gave you the impression that she had been eager to be rid of you. She also told you how she had gone to the hospital, not with toilet articles, as other women do, but with a suitcase full of business papers.

She was proud of that, proud of having phoned her mother in Canada less than an hour after you were born, of having had a long conversation right after that with my New York publisher about I don't know what contract.

You were to conclude, in your child's brain, that you were unwanted, that you had been an unimportant incident, that, once rid of you, your mother was in a hurry to get on with other things, weren't you?

You suffered over it, I know. You spoke to me about it several times. You also confessed to me that she often spoke to you about men, advising you not to trust any of them, because they are nothing but selfish brutes.

You tried to understand yourself, but just as passionately to understand others, especially those closest to you. You made up the game of "spies," which your brother Johnny played with you. Played? Johnny, perhaps, being older, less anxious, didn't take it seriously. To you, it was like a quest, an anxious quest after the truth you hungered for. You listened at doors and, slim and lithe, slipped into the service hatch between kitchen and dining room.

I never reproached you for it, knowing that an almost imperative need to reassure yourself drove you to wander like that, on tiptoe, through the halls, and to stop short, holding your breath, the minute you heard voices.

What did you overhear doing that? Some shouting matches, surely, some of the stormy arguments your mother liked to indulge in, some slaps, some blows, but was I most often the one delivering them?

Perhaps you saw us make love, heard your mother sigh, in resignation, almost in disgust, "Hurry up!"

You were both attracted to men and afraid of them. Kim reassured you through his calm manner and discretion; you admired his patience, his passion for conveying to his pupils his artistic taste.

One day, he took me aside. "Listen, Monsieur Simenon, I am very embarrassed. I feel I'm stealing your money. Marie-Jo's spontaneous talent doesn't need guidance. Most of our lessons is just conversation, often confidences. . . ."

Were you not hanging on to him, Marie-Jo, because the image of your father had been sullied for you?

That too was something I felt, and you confessed it to me later on. I asked Kim please to go on with the lessons, because they were good for you, even, and especially, if they only gave you a release for your heart, which was running over.

On your return from Avoriaz, you can't remain still. You have fallen in love with skiing, which you snubbed at Crans. You ask to go to Montana, near Crans, where there are special winter sports for girls.

I know some people would reproach me for being too lax, for the "permissive upbringing," to use the fashionable term, I gave all four of you. They think it may be acceptable for boys. But, for a girl!

I am not ashamed of it, and I even confess I am not sorry. "Proper upbringing" produces a great many rebels, as in my own case.

I hid nothing from you, Marie-Jo. I left you free, just as I left full freedom to your brothers—for you children will live in tomorrow's world, with tomorrow's morals, which always vary from generation to generation.

I know, for instance, that when you went to Morocco with your friend

Véronique and her mother, you had a young sweetheart. He came to see you at Epalinges, and you received him in your bedroom.

He later disappointed you. Would he have disappointed you as much if you had gone with him to some hotel in Lausanne? Is it necessary to spend a whole night together in order to make love and discover afterward that for one's partner it is just a passing fancy he will brag about as another trophy of the hunt?

You spend a month at Montana. You are enjoying your own youth, no one else's, especially not that of those whose youth is long past except, at times, for the youth of the heart, the very kind that allows me to understand you and give you your head.

I am nonetheless very much afraid for you. You are so willfully stretching the thread of your life that I am afraid it will snap.

Scarcely back home, you are again taking English lessons, trying to get to know thoroughly the language of your early childhood. Tap-dancing lessons. And hours of writing, in your room, in notebooks you later give me that tear me apart.

You know very well, Marie-Jo, that this is no defense of myself, and that I have nothing to apologize for. One doesn't "break" a filly; one tames her little by little, teaching her to live among people, and that requires a lot of love and patience.

On the evening of April 28, you speak to me at length, in intimacy. You accuse yourself of being like your mother, who so often told you you were, and you want to go and rest at Prangins.

But you are nothing like your mother, who was fooling herself while also fooling others all her life.

I have confidence in Dr. Durand and phone him. Somewhat surprised, though less so than I had anticipated, he tells me I can bring you to the clinic the very next day.

I am trying at the moment to speak of it calmly, without showing any emotion. Yet I cannot but remember another departure, a few years before, and now it is my little girl I am taking there.

Durand greets us in a simple, friendly way. All three of us appear calm, as if this were just some fortuitous incident. As soon as I am back home, I phone him.

"Don't get excited, Simenon. I have just had a talk with her. I am almost certain that Marie-Jo is in no way a psychiatric case. I'll see her daily, to reassure her. . . ."

"Is she trying to be like her mother?"

"Rather, to get away from her, to find some shelter. I think she is afraid of her. Call her every morning at around ten o'clock. . . ."

"Can I come and see her?"

"Not right away . . . Let's give her a little time to get rid of whatever it is that's haunting her. . . ."

That year, little girl, we do not go away on vacation, because I want to stay near you. I saw you at Prangins a few times, and I can assure you you are nothing like your mother. You do not isolate yourself. The nurses are already your friends, and you make others among the patients. You speak of Durand as a friend too, the way you used to speak to me of Kim.

In July, the help are all off, so we move into the Lausanne-Palace. Our days go by in walking, almost endlessly, awaiting news of all of you, but of you especially. Of Pierre, whom I have sent to Dinard with Yole. Johnny, Marc, Mylène, the children, are at Cefalù, in Sicily, at a Club Med.

One afternoon, the phone rings. The concierge gives me a jolt when he says: "Mademoiselle Marie-Jo wants to know if it is all right to come up, Monsieur Simenon."

"Of course."

I am taking a nap fully dressed. I rush to open the door and see you before me, tall, thin, slightly pale.

"Am I disturbing you, Dad?"

"Come in quickly."

I kiss you.

"May I go to the bathroom?"

You stay in there a long time. To vomit? When you come out, your face looks better, has more color in it.

"I'm hungry, Dad."

I order you some sandwiches and Coca-Cola. I dare not question you.

You finally open up, to my relief, with a bit of irony. "I took off without telling anyone, Dad. On the way, I thumbed a ride with a man alone in his car. He picked me up, but I didn't know where he was going. . . ."

I dare not ask you why.

"It so happened he was stopping in Lausanne, so I had to get out, and since I was broke . . ."

"Would you have gone wherever he was going?"

"Yes. Are you angry with me?"

How calm you are about it, my little girl, how detached from everything!

"What did you expect to do?"

"What would you expect me to do?"

"Did you have a fight with Durand?"

"No."

"Did you tell him you were leaving?"

"No. The idea just popped into my head this morning. . . ."

"In that case, you have to go back yourself and tell him you plan to check out of Prangins."

"I know."

This is not something that I can handle.

"I will take you back to the entrance to the park. You go in by yourself and tell Durand what you've decided. . . ."

You seem indifferent to everything, darling. You have just become what is called a "runaway." You have to handle this yourself, but I would like to see it work out as well as possible, especially without humiliation.

You eat heartily. You ran away, not only without money, but without taking anything with you.

You ask that Teresa go with us, and we take you to within a short distance of the open gate. I give you a big hug.

"Chin up, little girl. Decide what you want to do, and then tell Durand about it."

"Yes, Dad."

"I'll wait here half an hour, in case you decide to come back. After that I'll be at the Lausanne-Palace, where you know you can always reach me. . . ."

We stay there on the sloping road. I watch your silhouette moving away, very upright. . . .

We must have stayed more than half an hour, then went silently back to our hotel. Later, I phoned Durand.

"Don't worry, Simenon. I saw her. We had a nice quiet chat. She can't quite understand what made her do it. At any rate, it is nothing to be upset about, and she decided of her own free will to stay on here. . . ."

I will not be allowed to visit you for three weeks, but I will nevertheless get word of you daily.

Life has resumed at Epalinges, with a second closed door in the hall, and I go no farther than Pierre's room.

Johnny is traveling in Japan. When he comes back, he tells me about a very powerful motorcycle. It scares me so much I prefer to get him a Triumph VI. He stays at the house only three days, long enough to try out his new car, then happily takes off for Paris.

Marc and his little family have moved to Poigny-la-Forêt, near Compiègne, way out in the country this time, and he is still living there today, very happy ten years later.

621

As for me, Marie-Jo, I have already written *The Disappearance of Odile*, unconsciously foreshadowing things.

I visit you as soon as I am allowed to and find you busy with a staging of Jean Anouilh's *Antigone*, in which at Christmas you are to play an important part, but no parents are invited to see the show.

So we spend Christmas at home with Pierre and his little friends. Then we leave for Crans, where Marc and his family join us and Johnny comes and spends a few days.

What about you, my little girl, always present in my mind? It seems that "over there," you are behaving just as you did at school, that is, as you please, disregarding the house rules.

Have you fallen in love with Durand, as so frequently occurs? You are so familiar with him that he has to turn you over to his assistant, Dr. Verlomme.

I don't know just when you opened up to my friend about your great secret, which finally sheds light on your behavior. At any rate, when I visit you and we walk arm in arm in the park, you seem freed of a great weight, and I feel I have once again found my little girl as she was at the Bürgenstock in the days of the "Tennessee Waltz."

Finally, great joy: June 22, with Durand's blessing I am able to bring you home.

He and I have a long conversation about you. He has grown fond of you. He confirms to me that your case is in no way a psychiatric matter, that in the past you went through an ordeal you resisted as valiantly as possible. He does not mention Villars to me; that is privileged information.

We spend July at La Baule. I give you full freedom there, as I have always done, and as Durand has also advised me to.

This is our last stay there. In two years, the household has been turned upside down and, shortly after we return, it will be completely so, and cruelly.

You have gone back to your room, resumed your occupations. On September 9, I go in to kiss you good night, as I do Pierre, and go to bed suspecting nothing.

Johnny has left for California, to resume a course of study that will see him end up at the Harvard Business School.

In the morning, your door is closed, which does not seem to mean anything, considering your habit of sleeping late.

I go down to my office, and Yole brings me a letter in your handwriting, which I would know anywhere, because it looks so much like you. She found it on your bed when she went to wake you. It is addressed to me.

FOR DAD

Please don't call the police. I won't be away too long!

Thursday, 9:30 P.M.; 9/9/71

Oh! Dad,

I am so upset, my hand is shaking so that I don't know if I'll be able to finish this letter. And then, how to start, what to say, what will I be able to explain to you with my poor words spread on pieces of paper?

When you read this, I will no longer be home, my room will be empty, and . . . I don't know what your reaction will be. But especially don't panic or feel hurt. I am not leaving like "Odile" to commit suicide. I am only leaving because I feel inwardly in a state of instability toward life that would force me to return to the hospital, once again, and I can't stand that idea. Tomorrow, under normal circumstances, I should have been able to decide calmly, with the people who have been taking care of me and helped me, what I should do on the outside, now, if I should keep a room at Prangins or else . . . about a whole future that I can't picture, that terrifies me, and I would surely have "cracked up."

I mentioned this to you yesterday: For the past two weeks I have been feeling myself gradually sort of sinking, have gritted my teeth pretending to myself and to others to be a girl who was getting her balance back, while actually she feels it is slowly slipping away from her.

No, Dad! You see, I've tried. I did all I could during vacation, then after that in Paris, and finally here. Only to come to the bitter, hurtful conclusion that I am far from being cured. I still feel so "strange" at times, so "crazy" [word in English]. I can no longer bear putting up with myself like this, and especially not in front of the people I love, and with whom I so often would have wanted to be otherwise. Nor do I want anymore to be more or less "spared" by caretakers, by beings who are absolutely fantastic and try to pull you through it but with whom it is so hard for you to feel on an equal footing! I can no longer bear the idea of having others see to making me live, that responsibility for oneself being the primary one that any "adult" or "about-to-be adult" should have dignity enough to be able to handle with her own resources. My resources, as it happens, have so far been more than inadequate and that will certainly be no different after I leave. But at least I'll be forced to handle it on my own, and even if I really sink it won't matter anymore because it won't be in front of you, Dad.

You will read all this, and all that I just wrote is so far from what I feel inside myself, which I can't explain, can't make comprehensible.

You know, you're the one who told me this once, when I was small. A wounded or sick animal usually retreats far from his kin, by himself, to get better or die. I too have to be alone, to hide awhile, no longer to confront people I know. I don't care about the eyes of others, the anonymous crowd!

But, you see, I know, I feel that I will still (temporarily?) be unable to do anything really, to undertake anything worthwhile, serious, valid. And as far as I can look back behind me, nothing remains of my past. I find myself empty-handed and so far from closing onto a solid future. I have always been, I know, an empty creature, incapable of any truly rich contact with others, incapable of bringing anything at all to those around me, enclosed in a world far from normal realities, a world that most people cannot comprehend. Thereby I can't (and they can't either) join them. I feel love without being able to communicate or express it, friendship in an ever-unfaithful way because too often occupied with righting a precarious inner equilibrium, once again walled in within myself, far from life itself.

Nothing is coming out, Dad, I "can't" explain, but . . . I need to go away. Too bad if I go down, I sink; after all, that's quite unimportant. Out there, in another city, another country, or here, anyway it's all the same. I'm not able to get cured so I try flight, an unreal flight since wherever I go I will always find I am still with myself, so a stupid flight. But I will be able to drop my arms a little bit without feeling I am losing face with you. I hurt too much, you understand. This fight I have been carrying on since . . . more than seven years, against myself is too hard, too absurd as well. I can't take it anymore, you understand? Or the hospital either. I've spent a year and a half there only to end up today in this state, practically "as before," just as terrified and unable to act "normally." It now seems to me impossible ever to be cured. That's all. So it's not worth spending the rest of my life at Prangins, to suffer there to so little avail.

I am leaving in the hope that in spite of everything new events will force me to change. I am writing you after all as if I thought I would never see you again, or almost, and that is ridiculous. I don't ever expect to be away from you for long, for otherwise I should not be so calm and cold, and other words would come flowing from my pen.

Only, it's true, I don't know what I'll do to keep from feeling really repulsive when I come back. I will have almost "stolen" from you, that's unfortunately the word, nearly 1000 francs for my trip and . . . It's awful, this is the first time in my life I'm taking something this way which belongs to someone else! I can't ask you not to hold it against me, but . . . I don't know how I could have managed otherwise. I . . . I can't ask you to forgive me, that's not possible either, but I'll return it to you one way or another, Dad, and that I swear, on everything that is dearest to me in the world!

I don't have the courage to reread what I wrote, but I am sure that everything I am telling you now is so badly expressed. My sentences have trouble linking up in my brain, my fingers holding the pen are all stiff and my chest is as if on fire.

I only beg you, Dad, not to have the Police look for me. I entreat you. I would prefer anything to being dragged home by the cops after this.

Also explain to Prangins why I'm not at my 11:15 appointment and apologize to Durand for me. At any rate, I imagine you'll let him read this letter and he will understand better than anyone what is torturing me right now.

Forgive me, Dad! Forgive me for what I've been, what I am, for everything that I've spoiled through my fault with you. I love you, but that's something you'll probably never believe and maybe that's what hurts me most of all.

Dad, I will have needed you but did not know how to go after you. All my tenderness has always been inside and never knew how to blossom in front of you. You never saw my love for you. I don't know whether I'll succeed in showing it to you someday.

I embrace you you know and . . . even if this letter is ridiculous, even if it doesn't have the meaning I would have liked to give it, above all don't feel any hurt for me, it's not worth the trouble.

Until soon, with . . . all my love.

Not a word about her mother.

Marie-Jo

How I ever got through that day, my little girl, I have no idea. I remember phoning Durand, who reassured me, telling me this was a predictable reaction and that you will soon surface again.

I feel it is my duty to phone your mother to fill her in, and will deeply regret it. Without a word of it to me, she alerts the Paris Minors' Squad, setting in motion official mechanisms that leave traces.

At six-fifteen in the afternoon, whew! You phone me, to ask me to forgive you, as if that were necessary. You tell me you waited a long time for a night train on the station platform, that you wandered about at dawn, dragging your suitcase, through the streets of Paris, looking for a hotel room. Everything was full.

You finally found a spot in a hotel the name and address of which you give me, in the Second Arrondissement, and I immediately know that you innocently checked into a house of assignation.

I do not entreat you to come home, little girl whom I cherish more than ever. I tell you that I am sending you some money by wire, and ask you to find a different hotel in a less disquieting neighborhood.

I try to make you understand that I am not angry, that at eighteen you're a big girl, free to do as you please, but that your room at Epalinges will always be yours.

I know that you will never live at home again, that my little girl has left the nest in her turn. Had it not been for the discreet and affectionate help of Teresa, I don't know what would have become of me.

Yet, in October, you come to see me for three days. We are both very tender. You confide to me that you have a new love, a young actor you met at a performance of *Oh Calcutta!*, the then-smart show to see, in which for the first time in Paris actors and actresses appear totally nude.

You went again practically every night, for an actor you are really in love with, whose studio you move into. His first name is Roger.

You live together in a bohemian manner, cooking your meals on a hot plate, the way Tigy and I once did.

Even though he gets to bed late, he is up early in the morning to go running in the Bois de Boulogne.

So, there you are, "housekeeping," my darling, and every night you go with your "man," as you proudly call him, to the theater, where you have a regular spot in the wings.

After your good visit, I feel a need to write. It will be *Les Innocents (The Innocents)*, my last non-Maigret novel, though I don't know that yet.

Good night, darling.

Be happy!

72

Do you remember, my little Marie-Jo, one sunny morning, in our big bright parlor, when you were in your first or second year at the Collège de Béthusy? You were wearing a pretty flowered dress and said to me, happily, tenderly: "Are you familiar with the poets, Dad? I have to read a poem in class. What poet do you recommend?"

I looked at the books on the shelves covering almost a whole wall of the huge room, and I handed you a volume by Jacques Prévert, which you smilingly riffled through.

"This one. Listen . . ." And you read me the poem, each stanza of which ended, as I remember it, "and a hundred little raccoons. . . ."

"It's a long one," I objected. "Do you think you can remember it all?"

Half an hour later, triumphantly, you recited it all to me by heart. You wanted to know of another poet, for "later on," and I gave you a copy of the works of Paul Eluard.

How happy I was that day, and how splendid you were!

I can see you now in Paris, in a new studio I found for you on Boulevard de la Madeleine, with your young friend Roger. When you come to see me, in February, you are full of plans. You are no longer thinking of writing or painting, but of the theater, and perhaps film.

"Dad, what do you think of the Cours Simon?"

"It's an excellent school, and a number of our best actors have come out of it."

"Don't you think it would be too expensive?"

She is always afraid of spending too much. To reassure her, I fill her in on a kind of pact I made. I have bound myself to support each child until the age when graduate studies are generally over, whether they are still studying or not.

"You see, Marie-Jo, you may have a clear conscience. You are barely nineteen and still have a lot of time ahead of you. . . . Anyway, where you are concerned, there won't ever be any age limit. . . ."

With what joy you embraced me and what joy you gave me!

Your visits are brief, lasting three days on the average, and you make five that year.

My health leaves something to be desired. Because of my bronchitis, my prostate, my pains just about everywhere, the doctors fill me full of antibiotics and tranquilizers.

At the beginning of February, shortly before your visit, I had written *Maigret et Monsieur Charles (Maigret and Monsieur Charles)*, not knowing that it would be my final novel. In front of you and your brothers I try to put on a brave face, so I won't look too much like a "has-been."

You visit a second time in April, joyful as ever. Once again, this time with Roger, very open and attractive, in May.

You return again in May, then in July with Marc, Mylène, Serge, and Diane. The only one missing is Johnny, still at school in California, although he hops a plane twice during the year to come to Epalinges.

During vacation, Pierre and Yole went on a cruise to Palma de Mallorca, Dakar, the Canary Islands, and North Africa.

Marc went to Canada and Venezuela.

Everyone is on the move, except me, and I try not to mention to you the way your mother is harassing me. Few letters from any of you, but frequent phone calls. Johnny loves talking on the long-distance phone.

It seems as though my worries of the last few years are suddenly weighing me down painfully. My vertigo, especially, gives me trouble, and Teresa and I take refuge at the Clinique Valmont, really more of a hotel than a clinic, above Montreux, with a superb view of a large part of the lake and the Alps, and surrounded by forests in which we can relax by doing a lot of walking.

In September, back to Epalinges. September 18 I go down to my office to set up the yellow folder for a new novel. I close my door at 9:00 A.M. I have to set down the names of my characters, their résumés, their ancestry, sometimes their childhood friends, all the pertinent information, as I've said, of which I usually incorporate only a small part in the book. I have to know it all, to know them; so I make sketches of the layout of their houses, sometimes of the neighborhoods they live in.

On the large folder I have written the name of my main character, which is to be the title: Victor.

What I call my "plots" have never really been that, since I conceived the actions and reactions of my heroes only as I went along, chapter by chapter, learning the solution only when I got to the last page.

It would not work out that way for "Victor." Some two hundred and twenty times before, the system worked perfectly.

The next day, I think about my starting point, as usual, that is, about the "click" that will start my main character on his way toward his final destination. But in the afternoon, I get a phone call from my bank, informing me that your mother, Marie-Jo, is demanding, and ready to pay for, a transcript of all the deposits and disbursements in our one-time joint account. I mentioned this before, meaning that to be the last of her. Now I have to come back to it.

I phone the lawyer. I am sick and tired of fighting, and I recall that she once boasted that she would "smash my pen."

"Tomorrow," I tell Teresa, "if I still feel the way I do today, I will let you know whether or not I will ever write again."

And the next day, still downhearted, I confirm my decision to her.

D. has succeeded in what she wanted for so long a time. From now on she, Mme Georges Simenon, will be the one who writes, and she will try to crush me for good and all.

Has not her dream for a long time been to be the Widow of Georges Simenon, and to take her place in the glorious circle of "Maltreated Widows"?

A little later, I inform Teresa, as she has certainly been anticipating, for we no longer have any need to talk to one another in order to make ourselves understood, of another decision I have made, not hotheadedly, but after mature consideration.

"We're going to leave Epalinges."

Not for some short trip. Forever. Epalinges, conceived for a large family, is no longer suited to the small group we now make up: Teresa and I, Pierre, thirteen, and his faithful Yole.

We find a seven-room apartment in a brand-new high rise in Lausanne, which, through every window, has admirable views of the Parc de Vidy, the harbor, and the lake.

Once ties are cut with a place where I have lived, I am taken with feverish impatience, and within a month the apartment is all fixed up, with furniture from Epalinges.

In October we move, and you, Marie-Jo, will be the first to come and visit us in our new place. What was your reaction? You struck me as nervous, somewhat depressed, and I felt you were probably having some domestic problems.

Pierre is delighted with his room, his study-playroom, his bathroom, the largest of the three we have. He has selected a few paintings, Vlamincks especially; he is homesick for them.

I have a salutary feeling of coming back into myself, into a setting suited to my present size. I am so convinced that I am no longer a professional writer that I instruct Aitken to have my designation changed on all official papers, including my Belgian passport, from "novelist," now no longer applicable, to "without profession," which is more accurate.

The valuable pieces of furniture, paintings, knickknacks, the major part of my library are all sent to storage, where they still remain in 1980.

No sooner are we moved in than Teresa and I leave for Valmont, in a rented car. I sold all five of my cars, in one day. No more chauffeur. No more gardener. No more chef in his high white cap, and no more numerous household staff. When the children come to see me, I will put them up at the Hotel Carlton, at the other end of our avenue.

At the beginning of January, the whole family, on winter vacation at Crans, except for you, Marie-Jo, comes to visit me twice. The second time, I tell them my decision not to write any more novels, and they are deeply concerned. I also tell them that Epalinges is up for sale. I believe I sense a strong feeling for this house in which they were happy, and I soon change my mind about selling it. After all, isn't this house part of what I have to leave to all of you? You can decide later on what to do with it.

On February 5, at Valmont, where we have a pleasant, comfortable suite, I am visited by a Lausanne newspaperman who is also a friend, an erudite academician, to whom, slowly, weighing my words, I impart a sort of message announcing that I have retired from active literary life. I am trying in this way to avoid the more or less "well-meaning" newspaper articles, the rush of interviewers. His article, published in *Feuille d'Avis* (Information Sheet), will be picked up by the wire services and circle the globe.

On February 10, Teresa and I return to our high rise. On the thirteenth, my seventieth birthday, I buy myself something I know only by reputation, a tape recorder, the simplest one I can find, and that very day, without regard to whether or not they will ever be published, I start dictating personal notes, about the walks we take, the small and great joys afforded us.

Two days after my birthday, you come to see us, Marie-Jo, for just twenty-four hours, and we celebrate our birthdays together.

You come back for two days in April, nervous, edgy, and this time I realize that your affair has come to an end. What can I do for you, my darling, I who, because of my vertigo, cannot travel except for the fifteen miles or so between here and Valmont? I hide my physical problems from you as best I can, although several times a night they get me up to pace back and forth.

On June 1, you, for the first time, play a small part in a film. In August, you appear in one of Marc's films, shot in the Corrèze region of France. As for Pierre's vacation, he spends it at Palma de Mallorca, with his pal Christian, and of course Yole.

In 1973, Johnny twice flies from California to Switzerland, and, on one of his trips, takes part in the film Marc is making, as a sound man, while good old Boule is wardrobe mistress.

From one of the balconies of our apartment, through the leaves we can see a small beige-yellow eighteenth-century house, in a private courtyard that is very countrylike. Teresa and I often dream about it. Unfortunately, a doctor has been living in it for twenty-five years; the one next door, which is also part of what was once a great agricultural property, is where my friend and surgeon Dr. Francioli once lived.

Facing what was once the main body of the farmhouse and is now three separate houses, there is a row of stables. Three of these have been made into garages but still have their high iron-girded doors. A horse lives in the fourth.

Valmont, in July and August, long walks in the woods, which bring back a little color to me and let me forget your mother's more and more numerous harassments, but not my fears for you.

You phone me often and at length. You come and see me again in September. You are twenty. Beautiful. At the Cours Simon, you are very popular and your teachers foresee a brilliant career for you. You have everything it takes. Everything except—except I don't know what. The will? Sometimes you have shown ferocious will power, an energy that scares me because it is followed by periods of depression. All of that is what you soon will be saying better than I can, in your own words, in your very personal style.

In November, Teresa, who hardly ever reads a paper, since she is too busy keeping me more or less in shape, happens to see an ad that she shows me with great excitement. A small house is for sale in Lausanne, in an out-of-the-way spot, surrounded by verdure.

We go out on the balcony to look at "our" little house, which seems to be the one described in the ad. I phone the real-estate agency.

"You are at least the thirtieth person to call us since this morning, Monsieur Simenon, but since you are already a client of ours, we will be very happy to give you priority."

We go to see it. One of the ground-floor rooms, very large, has two windows and a large French door opening onto the garden. In that garden, the oldest cedar of Lebanon in the city, more than two hundred and fifty years old.

Dining room, kitchen, scullery. On the second floor, a large room overlooking both garden and courtyard, which can be Pierre's study. Two bedrooms, one for Pierre, the other for Yole, each with bath.

I immediately buy it. All that will need to be done is to turn a part of the excessively long entryway into a bathroom with shower and cut a door through to our study-office-bedroom.

At Christmas, the family gets together at the high rise, all but you, Marie-Jo, around an ample cold buffet. This year, Marc and his family, Boule, and Johnny have decided on Saint-Moritz for their winter vacation. Pierre goes with them, and Yole goes to see her parents in Italy.

A rather sad year-end for Teresa and me, owing to the state of my health and my worries.

Johnny is going back to Harvard Business School. And you, Marie-Jo, where did you spend that year-end? You phone me with good wishes. I know that you are now living on Rue Deparcieux, but I don't dare ask whether you are living alone. You promise to come soon.

The work continues on the little house. We take possession on February 8, 1974, the same day you get here. Our big and very intimate room, in which Teresa and I spend our days and nights, except when we go to the dining room for meals, seems to come as a sort of shock to you.

When Teresa leaves us alone, as she always does, you look at me almost with hardness, and I am afraid to understand. . . .

You say to me indeed, as if suffocating with rage: "Why her and not me?"

"Don't you understand, my little girl?"

"Understand what?"

I point to the bed. "Teresa shares *every part* of my life."

"So?"

I have always been afraid of what I am discovering. You point to the wedding ring you asked me to get you when you were eight. What can I answer? One day, you will speak of incest in relation to your mother, in referring to an unspeakable scene, which was such a trauma to you. And now you are saying . . .

"Whatever she has done for you, I can do as well, can't I?"

Excuse me, Marie-Jo, for relating this scene, which makes me better understand why, henceforth, you are going to have love affairs preferably with much older men.

Often, in Paris, you seek refuge at Marc's, and there our Boule becomes your confidante.

The day after your visit, I have a ridiculous but painful accident. I am not yet familiar with the house we have dreamed about so much and I trip over the doorsill, which I didn't even know was there, fall flat on the tiling.

Teresa bends over and sees me motionless, comatose, one leg twisted. She phones for an ambulance. I am taken on a stretcher to an emergency room that handles accidents.

They finally discover that I have cleanly broken the "greater trochanter" in my thigh, that is, the upper part of the femur, less than an inch from its neck.

Teresa phones the Clinique Cecil, and they send an ambulance for us.

I find I am in the hands of my friend Francioli, who used to live in the house next to ours, in the little paved courtyard, and he tells me that it'll take a while for me to get well. I must especially not move about, even at night, and they put me into a crib-bed which I will not get out of for close to five weeks.

All my personal care is given me by Teresa. Our room is sunny, with a porch on which Teresa puts bottles of Coca-Cola to keep them cool. If I can't sit up, I can at least, resting against my pillows, smoke my pipe, and I am always thirsty.

I panic, however, when the surgeon informs me: "You can no longer expect to take long walks, my dear Simenon. From now on, you'll have to be satisfied with short ones. . . ."

"With crutches? Or a cane?"

"Or on Teresa's arm."

It seems as if this accident even further strengthened the ties that already bound us so tightly. After all, what had I sought after throughout my life, what had I so run after, curious about all women, getting married twice and twice being disappointed, ever running toward a goal I was not aware of and which at last I do know now?

The goal of my endless quest, after all, was not a woman, but "the" woman, the real one, loving and maternal at the same time, without artifices, without make-up, without ambition, without concern for tomorrow, without "status."

I found her without knowing it, by chance, and it took me a long time to realize I had finally reached my goal. For several years now I have no longer indulged in the "hunt for women," not out of lack of appetite or physical capacity. But because I have found one who takes the place of all the others.

I dictate a lot. Teresa, across from me, checks on the proper running of the tape recorder, makes necessary adjustments, signals me when I am coming near the end and should stop.

Do you understand, my little Marie-Jo, that despite all my love for you, despite your adoration of me, you could never play that part in my life? One day, moreover, you will recognize it and will thank Teresa for having made a new man of me.

While we live peacefully in our pink house, as I have begun calling it (the walls of our studio are an orange pink), while our walks get longer and longer, you are taking "total immersion" English courses, that is, speaking nothing but English with your teacher, who is with you from morning till night.

You phone me often, also in English, and I find you more serene. In October, you are going back to your acting classes and, once again, to dancing classes.

As for me, before fall, I have a relapse, with painful vertigo and pains throughout my body. I nevertheless drag along, sleep little at night, getting up often around two in the morning to sit in my chair and drink coffee while I smoke several pipes.

At what point, between June and November, did I find the strength to dictate a new collection that I entitled *Les Petits Hommes* (The Little Men)?

Toward the end of August, I felt better, and we resumed our walks, our little life filled with tenderness.

In November, you come and spend a week with us, my little girl, seven days during which you are calm and loving. You watch our life with a dreamy eye, and you begin to understand what Teresa means to me, even if not yet to love her, as someday you will.

As usual, you sleep at the Carlton, as your brothers do when they are here, as do the few friends who come to see me. You are at home there, and they always keep the same rooms for you, so that it becomes a sort of annex to our house. It is good, my little girl, to see you calm, to hear you laugh, on occasion, reminding me of the way you laughed as a child.

After you leave, I go back to dictating, for my own enjoyment, finally to express freely all the ideas that lay beneath the surface of my novels and enunciate them clearly, which will earn me the hostility of the affluent bourgeoisie and even more that of the right and far right.

At the end of my life I have gone back to simple tastes, the small daily pleasures of my childhood, and Teresa shares them with me. I came into the world, as she did, among what I call the "common people," and more and more I feel that I belong, that I always have belonged, to that milieu of the little people who find peace within themselves. I believe that, despite all my troubles, all my worries about you, my little girl, I spoke of serenity.

And it is true that between two hard blows and in spite of my intermittent ailments, I have found deeper peace, perhaps because I am at last in harmony with myself.

I breathe in all of life about me, feel myself to be in full harmony with nature, in intimate, confident contact with it, as I am with Teresa, who is part of it.

I know that you are reading my *Dictées* (Dictations), Marie-Jo, which have begun appearing, that you have read all my books, from the age of ten on, have reread them several times and made notes in them.

In June of the following year, Johnny graduated from Harvard Business School and had only to choose among the many offers made him. In October, he spends a few days at Lausanne and tells me that he is taking a job with United Artists in their Brussels offices. At twenty-six, he is a serious fellow, concerned, as he always has been, about his future and his responsibilities.

Why, as early as May, little girl, did you voluntarily return to psychotherapy? You tell me little about it, and I avoid asking indiscreet questions of the big twenty-two-year-old girl you have become.

In December, we decide to go and spend two or three weeks at the Montreux-Palace. Winter at Montreux, which is shielded from the winds, is less harsh than in Lausanne. Because of my recent sensitivity to cold, I have bought a huge fur coat, not made of any rare or luxury fur, but plain guinea pig.

I have my tape recorder with me and, between walks, begin to dictate a volume that will be called *A l'abri de notre arbre* (In the Shade of Our Tree), our tree that also shelters so many birds. There are at least six different species, which we can tell apart, although we don't know the names that men have given them. To us, they are just "our birds."

Pierre spends his winter holiday at Crans, but does come to see us at Montreux.

December is calm. For you too, it seems, Marie-Jo darling.

You still live in your studio on Rue Deparcieux. You have had small parts with some distinguished directors, alongside stars of the screen. With some of each, you have affairs, some brief, some more extended, which I know of today in detail, thanks to the intimate diaries, letters, and all the documents you turned over to me.

You spend another two days with us, at Lausanne, in mid-January.

But soon you take refuge at a clinic called "La Villa des Pages," where you spend only your nights, going back home during the day. On May 15 . . .

I no longer have the courage today, my little girl. I am not writing a "suspense" novel. I am living the lives of all of you, especially yours, you the "weakest link," with an intensity I try to cushion with the simplest of sentences, with sometimes superfluous details, which nevertheless give me a chance to catch my breath.

I am too tired tonight. Tomorrow . . .

Good night, Marie-Jo darling.

Tomorrow will be tough!

73

It is a little before 7:00 P.M., and Teresa and I still have dinner at six. We are already away from the table, and give a start when the phone rings, for this is a Saturday, usually an uneventful day.

I freeze when I hear the call is from the Hôpital Cochin in Paris, more precisely its intensive-care unit.

"Is this Monsieur Simenon himself on the line? I must inform you that your daughter, Marie-Jo, is here in our resuscitation room. We have given her preliminary treatment but she is still in a coma. Please don't panic. We are sure we will be able to pull her through, but you probably will want to see her. . . ."

The person at the other end of the line does not know any more than that. The voice is impersonal, and all the questions that rush from my lips get the same reply: "I don't know. The professor will probably be able to tell you more tomorrow morning. . . ."

Pierre, who is seventeen and smart when it comes to pulling strings, finds us two seats on a Swissair flight the same evening. He also calls the George V, which always has a room or a suite for me.

It has been a long time since I last took a plane or train, since I have last traveled anywhere except to go to Valmont. I am having more and more vertigo, and traveling about is painful to me. This evening, I give no thought to that.

As in a nightmare, I wait for the plane, which gets us to Orly around eleven o'clock. I give the address of the Cochin, and we get there about midnight.

"I'll see whether you can visit your daughter," a nurse says. "Usually, no visitors are allowed in the resuscitation room, where she is still undergoing treatment."

How long everything seems to me! She comes back with a doctor who says I can go in alone, and gives me a white gown and cap. I follow him, in an unreal world, through empty silent corridors, while Teresa waits for me in a small room. He opens a door. I see Marie-Jo on a bed, surrounded by strange apparatus. I look at her so intensely that my eyes hurt, and her eyelids open, she sees me, and her colorless lips whisper the one word "Dad."

Her voice is so weak that I guess more than hear it. She takes a certain amount of time to get out, in an equally faraway voice, "You came. . . ."

Her clear, almost transparent pupils express her satisfaction, and I could swear she is smiling that enigmatic smile I have seen before.

"Listen, my little girl. I'm not supposed to be talking to you. Tonight, I am only allowed to see you for a few minutes. You are no longer in any danger, and tomorrow afternoon they'll let me talk to you at greater length. I love you, little girl. . . . Everyone loves you, and you are going to live. . . . Do you understand me?"

Your eyelids flutter. I delicately touch your hand, which seems fragile and diaphanous to me. Our eyes alone speak, communicate, establish something like a warm current between us. I feel a tug at my white gown and I have to leave you in this mysterious room, with two nurses in charge of fending off death.

We still do not know what happened. In the morning, we phone to Marc's. He and Mylène are away, and I don't want to frighten poor Boule, who looks on Marie-Jo as if she were her own daughter. I don't know where Johnny is, because he commutes between Brussels and Paris. I phone Pierre to reassure him. I have to keep busy to keep from thinking.

Since January, Marie-Jo had been taking a rest cure at Villa des Pages, in Le Vésinet, just outside Paris, under the care of Dr. Huchet. During the day, she was free to go home, to her studio on Rue Deparcieux, only spending the night at the villa.

I have to wait till afternoon to find out what happened. Dr. Huchet, whom I reach by phone, knows only that it was not at Le Vésinet, but at Marie-Jo's studio, that the drama took place. From home, she herself called the police emergency service, which immediately took her by ambulance to Cochin. She must have taken a heavy dose of barbiturates, but, before they had a chance to take effect, found the strength to call for help. Huchet has a sympathetic voice and sounds very cooperative.

A taxi takes us back to Cochin. The head nurse receives me, tells me my daughter is out of danger, and that she will have to remain for several more days under the care of two special nurses. She was brought in time—just in time—to this unit, where all the necessary care was immediately given her. I am allowed to see her, not for too long.

Your eyes are open, little girl, and there is almost color in your cheeks. Or am I imagining it? A bit anxiously, you ask: "You're not angry, are you, Dad?"

"Of course not, you darling little idiot . . ."

"I really wanted to, you know. . . . This time, it was on the level. . . . At the last minute, I suddenly had to call for help. . . ."

Your voice is weak, but it is really your voice, and the eyes are yours too, looking me over from head to foot, as if you had thought you were never going to see me again.

"You look funny like that, but I love you, my Dad. . . . Was it very hard on you?"

I don't tell you that it's only by a miracle that I'm still on my two feet, that this trip was the most awful one of my life.

"Are you going back to Lausanne?"

"I have to, my darling. I am in no condition to stay in Paris. . . ."

"I'll phone you as soon as I get back to Le Vésinet. Here, I'm not allowed to. I'm not allowed to do anything. . . ."

Your eyes are heartbreaking, as is the expression on your face. You are all love, and my eyes are all love too. It's as if we were embracing without touching one another, except for shaking hands softly when one of the nurses indicates the visit is over.

"I have an appointment with Dr. Huchet."

"He's a swell guy, a good pal. . . . You know me, Dad . . . I'm always so afraid people aren't going to like me. . . ."

When I leave the room, seeing almost nothing, my ears buzzing, my step hesitant, a young nurse comes over and slips me an envelope with my name on it. She is the one who undressed Marie-Jo when she got here. She found this letter addressed to me and feels she should give it to me directly.

I put it into my pocket, then join Teresa and reassure her, and we go back to the George V. In our suite, I open the letter, which in reality is Marie-Jo's last will and testament, written the same day she attempted suicide, May 15, 1976, and not 1975 as she writes, through an understandable error at so troubled a moment in her life.

I read it with the emotion one can imagine, and even today, in 1980, do not have the courage to comment on it.

STRICTLY PERSONAL!

May 15, 1975

My "big old Dad" whom I love,

I just spoke to you on the phone. I wanted to be sure, before going away forever, that you were all right, that you were happy, and that you wouldn't suffer too much.

You must not hold this against me. There is nothing sad, nothing dramatic about it. Drama is what we play out in life. I don't believe that in death it exists. I am going away because I don't know how to fight on, to accept myself with all my contradictions, to look upon others with peace and fraternally. They still scare me, or else their very being human beings depresses me.

I dreamt too much. After all, I always escaped from the small realities of life, the ones that have charm when one is in harmony with oneself.

I was always a coward. I leaned on those around me, on you, most especially, as if that were due me, without being aware of my selfishness. Little by little, I lost my dignity, the only thing that gives a meaning to existence.

I am ashamed now of sometimes having shown myself too "naked" before you, trying at any price to find a truth of contact that made sense only in my own head.

I made you suffer; forgive me. I've begged your pardon so many times, looking at or patting your pictures on my wall. And crying, of course. I felt I had been struggling with all my strength, since adolescence on, before Prangins, to become someone worthwhile. I go back to a sentence you wrote in *The House on Quai Notre-Dame* that struck me: "I was too ambitious to be part of a group."

Do you understand? In spite of my pessimism, my despondency, I suspected that I had some talents, which would surface someday.

. . . Since last night at the clinic I have been thinking about this letter,

639

and now the words are failing me; everything I wanted to say to you one last time is pent up inside me! . . .

When you do receive it, tell yourself that I am finally very near you, in peace and without further complaint. I will have become your little girl again, who went off arm in arm with you in the sunshine to the bar of the Bürgenstock—the little girl of the Tennessee Waltz. Remember only that about me. Forget the rest—it's better that way—and especially be happy, go on living and savoring every minute as it goes by, with all the sensuality that is in you. That is life: sunshine on bare skin, the look of a passer-by, the scent of a town awakening, two bodies merging without false modesty . . . Especially, to be receptive at every minute that goes by, without thinking ahead to the next. At times, I was able to be like that. I was able to sit on a chair and relax my body, without already tensing it at the idea that I would have to get up again.

I was able to pet a cat as I felt it right near me. I was able to talk to a dog . . .

. . . I never was really able to talk to a person! Now, I have to have the courage of my cowardice, my cowardice of living. I must not fail in this suicide, because that would mean even more care and attention from others.

I no longer want to be a burden to anyone. And since I am not able to love in the way it seems people love . . . I am useless. So why go on living for myself alone, go on fighting to live in this world that causes me so much anxiety, and for which I feel so ill equipped?

You know that when I look at your pictures, some of which go back before I was born, I find myself dreaming of the existence you built for yourself. The fact is, I would have liked then already to be at your side.

I would have liked to prove to you that I was something more than an egocentric being, wallowing in her tears.

It's too late. I've drifted too far, and I'm too old now to crawl into your lap.

I had to interrupt this letter to go see a psychoanalist [sic]. I explained to him what I was going to do and I cried a lot. Why?

I mostly told him how powerless I was to express myself in this letter, which I would want to be calm and lucid.

Dad . . . I don't have to make out a will since I never made any money. Everything is yours. Give my things to anyone you want, my guitar to Serge, if he wants it, because he's rather musical.

In a black-and-white plastic bag under my kitchen sink are all the things I've written and the letters I got from you or others. Will you keep them? As for my notebooks, they are kind of scattered. Some are at the clinic, some in my drawers here, under my panties, also, in my files, with my pictures.

I'm writing fast and badly. I'm afraid I'm going to "fail" again. I'm afraid of being too afraid, at the last minute. But I'll think real hard about you and it will all be fine.

I know you have already decided to be cremated. That you have selected your urn and the place it should be kept.

I am just as terrified of the casket as of fire. So, make up my mind for me, and it will be fine. I only hope, this is my only will, to wear the gold band on my finger until the end. If they have to take it off to autopsy me, put it back on afterward, won't you? This wedding ring is the only thing that counted in my life. Do you understand? . . .

For all the rest, I'm tiptoeing out, so as not to cause any more suffering to anyone and suffer no more myself.

I ache at the idea of leaving you without seeing you again, without seeing the new things you write, knowing what's to become of the family. Provided all of you are happy, that Marc keeps at it and makes good with his films, that Johnny finds happiness in his work, that Pierre goes on being the determined and well-balanced big fellow he is.

That Maman doesn't give all of you too much trouble and excuses me for not having been able to reach her on her birthday. (It was yesterday.)

Enjoy through all your pores your intimacy with Teresa, which I was able so poorly to understand and accept.

Dad, I loved you more than anything else in the world. I'm telling you for the last time. Believe me, I beg of you. That was my only reason for being and it is because I now realize I will never measure up in your eyes, never go back to being someone "clean" that you can have confidence in, that I am disappearing.

I wish you had known me better, I had known you more. I always ran up against my deeper inhibitions, which kept me from communicating.

Here, again, I would have liked to tell you a little of what propelled me into certain ways, and then others, and finally into this vacuum that is no longer bearable. My ideas just aren't clear enough. Too bad, eh?

Together, now, I am sure, we are climbing the mountain and lying down in the grass, with the moon in our hands. There is no more anger, lack of understanding, shame, or weakness.

I am with you and we are happy . . . In addition to "my God," whom I often prayed to, you were my concrete God, the force I clung to . . .

You still are, you are forever . . .

How many "Yum-Yums" can I write you? How many kisses, how many caresses? . . .

I can still smell the aroma of your pipe, I am putting myself in your arms, you are protecting me and I am happy . . .

Be it for me too . . .

your "little girl"
Marie-Jo

P.S. Can I be "repatriated" to Switzerland, so as not to be too far from you?
P.P.S. I've loved Boule, Mylène, Serge, Diane, Francette, Mme L., F., and C. too. If only they could know . . . !

Dr. Huchet comes to see me around six or seven. A young man, likable, frank, and straightforward. We chat for over an hour in a corner of the big empty parlor, this being Sunday. I speak to him of the testament without giving it to him to read, because I respect the "Strictly Personal" my daughter wrote on it.

The doctor has been caring for her attentively. He has noticed that Marie-Jo goes from a period of activity and almost elation to a dark one in which she closes in on herself, as if jealously to keep her obsessions to herself.

Did this depend on her more or less passing love affairs and the disillusionments that followed? More than likely. He is not too concerned about it. For the time being, what she mainly needs is peace, complete rest. He says that, once she is back at Le Vésinet, I may phone her as often as I like. He and I part, each confident of the other.

Teresa succeeds in getting me back home in a fairly pitiful state. We are scarcely settled in when a phone call from Cochin gives me another bit of disquieting news. The very day after we left Paris, Marie-Jo, escaping God knows how from her day-and-night supervision, somehow got to the window and jumped out. Fortunately, her room was on the ground floor, so all she got was some scratches.

She stays at Cochin about a week, after which she returns to Le Vésinet. From there I get news of her through the likable, vigilant Huchet, who has become fond of her.

She is able to talk to me on the phone. She has calmed down. She writes me. Her brother Johnny, as early as the end of May, is back in his Paris studio and goes to see her. Boule also, as well as Marc and Mylène.

After which, for vacation, my whole little clan separates. Pierre and Johnny go to Guadeloupe. Marie-Jo, Huchet feels, can take a vacation if there is someone with her, and she goes to Quiberon, in Brittany, to get some color back in her cheeks. Good old Boule goes with her.

Teresa and I make do with a few weeks at a charming little hotel at

Saint-Sulpice, about three miles from our pink house. I lean less on Teresa's arm. From the terrace, we can see Evian on the other side of the lake and get the idea to end our vacation there.

We occasionally go into the Casino, where, to while away the time, we play a little roulette. One afternoon, while playing listlessly, I am so unspeakably lucky that the other gamblers finally all want to put their chips on the same spaces as mine. Because I don't like money gotten in this way, I now play to lose the pile of chips in front of me. I can't. When dinnertime approaches, Teresa and I head for the cashier's. As I shove the chips out in front of me, there is a sudden fog in my brain. I feel myself falling. I vaguely see feet, legs. The next thing I know I am in an ambulance, then at the hospital, with Teresa by my side.

After lengthy examination, they decide that my sudden faint came from a drop in blood pressure. I have always been hypotensive, with a very slow pulse. This time, however, my pressure went too low, and I am given some kind of shot before being taken back to the hotel.

Teresa phones Cruchaud, and he confirms the diagnosis. He also blames the stormy weather we had during our stay at Evian, the stuffy temperature and comings and goings in the gaming room, which I am no longer able to tolerate.

From August 25 to September 4, we are back at the Clinique Cecil, for a full and exhausting checkup, which turns out to be reassuring. I am now seventy-three, and I can't expect to be fresh and peppy after the successive ordeals I've been through.

September 3, the day before we are to leave the clinic, another alarm. Marie-Jo, at Marc's, has tried to commit suicide again, unless the overdose she took was an accident. She was taken to the hospital at Chartres, where they kept her only overnight.

Boule comes to see us, talks to us a lot about Marie-Jo's ups and downs, which seem to follow the same curve as her love affairs and disappointments. The last so-called suicide, according to Boule, who has her feet firmly on the ground, was just an accidental overdose of medication.

I telephone a lot to Marie-Jo. I write her and she writes me.

On October 25, she decides to go into the Clinique Universitaire, at Rueil-Malmaison. From there, one day when the whole family is away from Paris and she suddenly feels all alone, she writes to her mother. The latter taxis over to see her. What do they say to each other? Marie-Jo will soon tell me about it. One curious detail. Her mother, who always complains of being low in funds in spite of the outlandish alimony I pay her, confesses to Marie-Jo that she doesn't have enough money to pay for the taxi waiting outside, and Marie-Jo has to give her enough to get back to Paris on.

Before that, on September 11 (I apologize for all these flashbacks, but I find it hard, with all the comings and goings, to follow a strict chronology), the whole family, including Marie-Jo, came to visit me in Lausanne and took over a good part of the Carlton. We all got together for a big luncheon in that hotel's excellent restaurant, one of the three best in Lausanne, and everybody talked at once, all as sprightly as could be. Except for Marie-Jo, who was silent, and thereafter prefers to come visit me by herself.

In November, after having consulted Durand by phone, for he knows my daughter better than I, I decide to buy her a studio apartment in Paris.

Johnny has decided to work in Paris too, for the Gaumont film company. Marc's house, at Poigny-la-Forêt, becomes the meeting place for the family.

A busy year, with too many ordeals. That perhaps is the reason, between events, I dictated a lot. In March, I finished *Au-delà de ma fenêtre* (Outside My Window). March-June, *Je suis resté un enfant de chœur* (I Have Remained a Choirboy). Then, practically one right after the other, *A quoi bon jurer* (What's the Good of Swearing) and *Le Prix d'un Homme* (The Price of a Man).

This last book was dictated at Valmont, where I went to convalesce after my prostate operation, the operation that for so many years had been my nightmare. My urologist decided the time had come, and explained to me that he was not going to remove my prostate but eliminate the adenomas by a new procedure.

After only five days, we go home, happy to be done with it. And leave for Valmont, where we spend the Christmas and New Year's holidays. Pierre and Johnny are skiing at Champéry.

Back home. A lot of work with Aitken, who is a wonderful assistant and relieves me of a great share of my worries.

That reminds me of one of D.'s most recent "attacks," by way of her lawyers. She is now making a claim that, from the time we first met, therefore over a period of more than twenty years, she acted as my literary agent, and as such lays claim to no less than twenty percent of everything I earned during this period. That explains why she went after the bank for a print-out of all the deposits to my account.

I never had a literary agent except for a few months when I first got to New York, where I was assured that in the United States authors never negotiated with publishers except through representatives.

D. came to work for me as a secretary, a word that in this case, as in so many others, means stenographer-typist. From the start, she wanted to be more and more important, and if I allowed her to, it was to avoid violent scenes and because I hoped this would restore some equilibrium to her.

She did not write my contracts, something I always did myself. Although she did cook that one up in London with the phony BBC man, over a bottle of whiskey, and filled it so full of erasures and stuck-on corrections that I finally signed it just to get rid of it. It was the only contract I ever lost money on.

End of parenthesis, although I know I am not rid of her and her demands.

Marie-Jo was still at Rueil-Malmaison when I found out by phone that there was a studio available for her, or, rather, two adjoining ones, above the Lido on the Champs-Elysées. She got permission to go and see them. And signed the purchase agreement herself.

I specifically wanted her to feel that this was her own place, fixed up by herself, and if I opted for the Champs-Elysées, it was because I know how she needs what my friend Charlie Chaplin called "City Lights," the nightly coming and going, the busy cafés and nightclubs, in a word, what she has always liked.

For a while there had been a plan to build a three-part house in the country, near Poigny: one part for Marc and his brood, and separate parts for Marie-Jo, on one side, and Johnny, on the other. I rejected this idea because I know how jealous of her independence Marie-Jo is, and she has confessed to me that the country and woods only make her sad.

A passageway has been opened between her two studios, and they now constitute a comfortable apartment, with two baths and a kitchenette.

She left Rueil-Malmaison in February to go into the Marcel Rivière Institute, at La Verrière. Three times a week, by taxi, she went to a psychiatrist, B., for what is more like psychotherapy.

She became attached to this doctor, in whom she confided, somewhat as she did in Durand.

At the end of September, shortly before my operation, she came to Lausanne with Boule for a complete checkup at the Nestlé Hospital, where I was able to see her daily.

In July-August, Marc had taken his family to the United States. He wanted to show Mylène and his children the places he lived in for so long.

Finally, in December, Marie-Jo left the Marcel Rivière Institute, and now seems once and for all to be finished with clinics, rest homes, psychiatrists, and psychoanalysis.

Living at Marc's, she is most often in Paris with Boule, and busies herself furnishing her apartment. I open an almost unlimited account for her, because I want this apartment to become a cozy nest in which everything has been conceived by her for her. I send her the pieces of furniture and various other things she wants, including the full set of my works imprinted with her name, as my other children have received a set imprinted with theirs. She hopes to be moved in by Christmas.

She often phones me, several times a week. Connections with Paris are not very good, my right ear no longer has much hearing, and Marie-Jo doesn't speak very loud. Sometimes I can't understand some sentences. I suggest that she write me, and she does, and then that she buy a cassette recorder, and I receive a number of tapes.

On February 17, Marie-Jo comes to spend a few days with us at Lausanne. She is tender and cheerful. The evening before she is to leave, she has a surprise for us. While the three of us are chatting, she goes out for a moment and comes back with a new guitar.

Sitting on the arm of a chair, facing me, she accompanies herself in the singing of "Tennessee Waltz," our Bürgenstock song, and Brel's "The Flat Country," which to my taste she does even more movingly than that great artist. Her virtually whispering soprano voice moves Teresa and me deeply.

Also, in English, to the music of Bob Dylan:

> How many years of my life have I lost
> Believing I was all alone?
> How many times will it take it to me
> Before I accept what I am?
>
> The answer, I know,
> Is somewhere in my brain.
> The answer is my end I don't find.
>
> How many times will I be on my knees
> Falling down road after road? . . .
> How much part of myself will I break
> Refusing my tenderness and love?
>
> I am scared of the light.
> I try to hide my face.
> I am scared of my own
> Body and mind.
>
> But maybe one day after those years of pain
> I will at last understand?
> Accept that I can't positively repair
> All for what in the past I have failed?

The night I will sleep,
Getting out of my fear,
You will maybe be proud of me?

I will stop to break my tenderness and
Love
And stand on my feet until the end.

When finally in my dreams
I'll see you, Daddy, smile
I'll know that my shame will disappear.

When endly in my dreams
I'll see you, Daddy, smile,
I'll know, know and know,
Yes, that my shame will
Disappear.

What a unique and precious evening!

She sings a lot, and finally confesses to me: "I couldn't bring my old split guitar; it wouldn't have stood the trip. So, this afternoon, I went to our music store and rented this guitar till tomorrow. Since I'm leaving early, I'll appreciate it if you return it. I hope you're not angry with me."

Angry with her? I hug her tightly, holding back my tears.

"You know, Marie-Jo, that you could make singing a career? All you would need, like any singer, is to find a specialist to 'set your voice for you.' I don't know any, but you should easily be able to find out about one in Paris."

I can see that you like the idea. You have given up the movies, in which you had too many sentimental disappointments. You write a lot. You could write your own songs. . . .

We speak about it at length, and when I leave you my heart is full of hope and warm tenderness.

In March, I start dictating *On dit que j'ai soixante-quinze ans* (I'm Supposed to Be Seventy-five).

In April, the whole family comes visiting, except for you. You let me know by phone. You would rather see me alone than with all the others, and say that you'll come toward the end of May.

You do not allow your mother to come into your new apartment.

When she comes to Paris, you go to see her, on May 16, if I am not mistaken, in her suite at the Lancaster.

Since March, as I know from your phone calls and letters, you have had a great weight on your heart. For now your mother has published her "book," which she has been threatening me with for almost six years. I saw it before publication, in a set of proofs that were sent to me. I read them. I could have had the work seized, because it contains more aberrant lies, some of them quite odious, than truths.

Marie-Jo read it, annotated it, and I have that volume before my eyes. She talks to me a great deal about it on the phone, indignant that I should be sullied in this way, begs me not to dignify the libel and publicize it by any reply.

A women's magazine, however, publishes what purports to be an interview with me on the subject. Marie-Jo calls it to my attention, urging me to deny it, since I never gave the alleged interview. It is an old interview, done two years ago, on an entirely different subject, into which the not-overly scrupulous writer slipped a few sentences of his own concoction, which he attributes to me, about the "book."

I wire the editor-in-chief, demanding a rectification. He promises one. Nothing in the next issue.

It is then May 16, the day Marie-Jo calls on her mother, who has been pestering her, and I will hear from an unimpeachable source what happens that evening at the Lancaster. At one moment, an excited D. strips before Marie-Jo to show her the scars on her body left by her various operations.

"You see, my girl, what a woman looks like when she starts growing old? You'll look like that someday too. . . ."

D. leaves the next morning for Avignon. That day, my little girl, you phone me at 11:00 A.M. You seem calm, and at the end say to me: "I love you, Dad. Tell me that you love me too."

"I love you infinitely, my darling. . . ."

"No. I just want you to say, plain and simply: 'I love you.' "

I am upset by this insistence, but I tenderly enunciate, "I love you."

I would like to say more, but you have hung up. In the afternoon, upset by that conversation, I call you back, but get no answer. No answer the following morning either. At 6:45 P.M., Marc's shattered voice.

He tells me that you . . . yes, that you are dead, that you shot yourself in the chest, probably the evening before. He is phoning from your apartment, which is full of police. He had to call the police to open your door, which was locked from the inside.

On your bed, a note for me, in which you ask to be cremated *with your wedding ring on*—I must make sure—and to scatter your ashes in our little garden so you will forever be with me. . . .

I don't have the strength, today, to relive those moments, so I am reproducing here the pages I devoted to them "while they were hot," but as if muted.

You, my darling, are twenty-five and will never be fifty, as in your improvised song.

I am holding a card written, it would seem, on the day you died, before or after that phone call of yours, more likely after, since in it you mention that plain and simple "I love you."

For my "Daddy"
with everything this may perhaps entail that is hard or cruel, according to the circumstances.

I only hope he will understand that "all of this" comes from me alone, that I *wanted it,* and that perhaps at last I have stopped torturing myself.

I love you for the last time, without the "you know" . . . and then the "a lot" which hides the ". . . I dared say I love you! . . . (is that it? . . .)."

Take care of yourself, for me, for all what I was not able to be—(By my own fault.) [Paragraph in English.]

Your little(?)
girl!

You know . . . (I'm going back to "you know" . . .) the most extraordinary thing will be to have had a "Daddy," then a "Dad," to have loved "the man," from afar, like a lover, to have read almost all of "Simenon," with a tight throat, finally to have engulfed all of "the human being," from the little boy until today, through all of those pages and my own memories . . .

A "Gentleman," too, magnificent in his silk suit snatching me away in his arms, carried by the music . . .

A tenderness that I never found anywhere again . . .

Marie-Jo(?)

Extracts from my Dictations

Saturday, May 27, 1978

My darling little Marie-Jo,

Last Saturday for me was the most dramatic day of my life. The whole week has been painful too, and I had the feeling I was holding my breath.

Today, you are at our home, at your home, in our little garden, not far from the cedar you know so well and a lilac in full bloom. Yesterday, your big little girl's body was cremated, and today, beneath a wonderful sun, we sowed your ashes in the grass of our little garden, according to your final will.

We see you through the big window-door. We can talk to you. We know that you are freed, that at last you are without anxiety, and that you no longer have to fear being in what you call a "closed" place.

The sun is warming you. All the birds are chirping cheerily to greet you, and I am no longer weighed down but almost cheerful to feel you at last and forever near me.

This will probably be a very long letter that I will write you in this way, but I will do it little by little in the days ahead.

Today, I just wanted to tell you of my joy, yes, that's right, my joy, because I know that you too are joyful, in knowing that you have finally reached the goal.

Good day, my little girl. Henceforth you will share our existence, in which you will have your place.

You are in the air I breathe, in the light that floods over us, in the throbbing of the cosmos, and in that way you penetrate us from all directions.

Good day, Marie-Jo my pretty.

Sunday, May 28, 1978

Good day, Marie-Jo.

This morning, the first thing I did was to go and say good day to you in the garden, which was even sunnier than yesterday. It seems as if you finally brought on the true spring we had so long been waiting for.

I felt you so present that I expected, I still expect, you to answer me.

We took our first customary walk in the environs, but I cut it a little short because I was eager to talk to you. So many ideas crowd into my head; there are so many things I want to tell you, and I don't know where to start. It's a little like when the orchestra is tuning up or when you yourself let your fingers nonchalantly slide over the guitar before starting a piece.

One recollection has been persistently coming back to me in the last few days, an incident from your earliest childhood, and I no longer remember whether I ever told you about it. You must have been between a year and a half and two. Every morning, your nursemaid took you for a walk in a stroller. Around nine-thirty, having completed my chapter, I jumped into the car to go to the post office for the mail. As if by accident, we almost always met at the same place, about fifty meters perhaps from the private road that led to our house. I would stop the car and pick you up to give you a big kiss, and then we went our separate ways.

One morning, it was impossible for me to stop and greet you. When I got back home, you were limp as a rag doll. Your eyes were closed. Your face colorless. You didn't see anything. You were not crying. You were not talking. You didn't even seem to hear.

Dr. Wieler advised me to pick you up and hug you tight and talk softly to you.

I did, of course, and, with your face almost against mine, I stared at you in anguish, looking for a sign of life. After a few minutes, your eyes opened slightly and met mine. And then, the most extraordinary thing happened. To my great amazement, I saw a slight, very slight, and very mysterious smile steal over your lips.

Five minutes later, still in my arms, you had completely come back to life.

You were just a tiny little girl, and there is a tiny little girl too, who hasn't changed much, even if she did get bigger, sleeping today in my little garden.

I would like to be able to go on chatting with you all day like this but, in a few minutes, Marc and Mylène will be here. I hope, however, that this afternoon I'll be able to have time to go on with our chat. When I talk to you this way, you know, I have the feeling you are listening to me and sometimes that you are answering. Yet, you know very well I am neither a mystic nor a believer.

That doesn't keep you from being here in a way I would swear was real.

Till a little later, darling little girl.

Monday, May 29, 1978
10 o'clock in the morning

My little darling, a quick hello and a big kiss, because in ten minutes a taxi is coming to take me to the lady who is to try on and probably give me my hearing aid. This appointment was supposed to be on Friday, but that day was reserved for you alone.

Do you know that on Saturday, when you moved into our little garden, two beautiful yellow roses, the first of the season, had just opened, as if to welcome you? Two more will bloom between now and tomorrow night and a red rose is on the point of popping. The birds are multiplying too, because the little ones that still have trouble flying come down on the grass with their mothers. They wait patiently, without moving, with their beaks open, for their mothers to put seeds into their mouths.

It is a true renewal and a renewal for you too. I know it, I can feel it. Last week, I was as if crushed and must have looked like a zombie. Now that you are here, have come back to your real home, the whole universe has changed in my eyes, and I feel that henceforth I can never think sad thoughts about you.

We have finally gotten together again forever.

Till a little later, my little girl. The sun is still caressing you softly and wrapping you in delightful warmth.

Same day, 5:15 in the afternoon

My darling,

Marc has just left us to go back to Paris, and tonight Johnny will take his place. . . .

This week was like a waking nightmare and only since you are in our garden have I come back to life. Yet your letter and your messages by way of the tape recorder reassured me, and I understood that you had gone in full serenity. That letter was not read by anyone else and no one has heard your recorded messages either.

I understood that you had reached your decision calmly, several weeks before, and that your departure was a liberation for you.

You finally got rid of (I was going to say "your girl friend") your companion, who was with you day and night and whom you found wherever you looked. Madame Anxiety, as you call her, speaking of her as if she were a person who was inexorably pursuing you.

With unbelievable sang-froid, you got rid of her in the only possible way. Professor Durand, who spent a long time with me Sunday, admires you as much as I do. . . .

The newspapers don't know that, nor does your mother. But I am flooded with telegrams and letters coming not only from friends and acquaintances but from strangers, to whom you have become a sort of heroine. Friday, *France-Soir* published a front-page article with a very big headline. Saturday, again on the front page, there was a big picture of you taken by Gian Carlo Botti. Marc gave me his phone number, and I spoke to him this morning to order all the pictures he took of you.

Wednesday, when we are alone again, Aitken will bring me a big suitcase full of your notebooks, all your papers, books in which you made notes in the margins and which I certainly will keep. I'll talk to you about it after I get a chance to read it all. I'll just say good night, my little girl, for you know our schedule. I am going to close the shutters and in twenty minutes we will sit down at the table. I kiss you hard, very hard and very softly at the same time, with all of my tenderness.

Wednesday, May 31, 1978

Marie-Jo my pretty,

. . . Quite often, during our comings and goings in Lausanne, I would buy you a little girl's piece of jewelry, a necklace of tiny beads, a ring with a colored stone, a bracelet, and so on. Then, one afternoon, you stopped in front of a jeweler's window and, pointing to some wedding rings, asked me to buy you one.

I didn't think at that time you knew the meaning of a wedding band. I just told you that they probably didn't make them your size. We went inside anyway. . . .

And that's how at eight, you proudly wore a gold band on your ring finger.

One day, putting your hand next to mine, you said: "It's just the same as yours."

And only then did I have a still rather vague suspicion that you knew more than I supposed of what wedding rings were for. And when I got the letter in which you expressed your last wishes, I saw that you wanted to be cremated with your wedding ring.

I gave the corresponding instructions, and now, in our little garden, there is a tiny bit of gold in among your ashes.

Which reminds me of another, very faraway recollection. Whenever for one reason or another you had to take off your ring, even for a moment, you refused to put it back on yourself and each time asked me to do it.

I continue getting letters and telegrams, always from a little farther away. Now, they are coming from the United States, pending the arrival of those from Russia or Japan. Some are from people I know, others from strangers. All those who write, or almost all, think I am literally crushed by your departure; I was crushed and speechless for a whole week, and it was hard for me to open my mouth without bursting into sobs. My throat was literally tied in knots, until the Saturday when I finally found you again as I scattered your ashes in our little garden.

What pacified me too were your cassettes, the ones you sent me during the last month and the one found still in your tape recorder. I sensed a kind of serenity in them, if not liberation, and I would not like to appear less brave than you were. . . .

One detail moved me especially. Marc, who was the first one into your place after getting the police to break in, found your apartment in a condition he had probably never seen it in before. All in order, not a thing lying around, not even a cigarette butt. It must have taken you hours to polish everything up so, to do your laundry, iron it, carefully put it away in the closets.

When you phoned me that Friday, your voice was the same as every day and you made no mention to me of a plan you had obviously been preparing for at least a month.

No, I am no longer crushed. I believe I have understood and that, now that you are at last where you wanted to be, you would hold it against me if I cried any longer.

No use in my answering in this way the condolences I receive. People would not understand me, or else they would imagine I have a hard heart, whereas I have never been more brimming over with tenderness.

Thursday, June 1, 1978

Before my nap, I had promised myself I would go back over some memories both very sweet and very sunny, the ones of Bürgenstock.

I had the misfortune to read another interview with your mother, who keeps giving them, and I am more and more nauseated. I don't know whether she goes knocking on the doors of editorial offices, but she is showing wild determination to rack up a record number of interviews. Next to what she is now telling any reporter who wants to hear it, her book seems written in rosy ink. She doesn't stop lying, twisting, and she doesn't spare anyone. Some reporters repeat her words without comment, but there are others, fortunately, who treat all of her accusations without the slightest indulgence and put her in her place.

In the beginning, I didn't give it any importance, but when it goes on day after day, for so long, it ends up turning one's stomach.

I don't always answer, you can rest assured. Anyway, I wouldn't want to give her that honor. If she continues in this tone, she will probably have to go back to a psychiatric clinic, and this time she won't be able to say it is a result of a plot between two doctors and me.

Let's not talk about that anymore. I apologize for having expanded on this, but I have only you and Teresa to whom I can talk with the assurance of being understood.

Same day, this description of the ceremony that followed your return to Lausanne, in the undertaker's parlor:

There were seats on either side of the aisle. On the one side, me with your three brothers. Behind us, Mylène, Boule, and Carole, then Teresa, and finally Kim and Gérard.

To the right, in the first row, your mother and a woman I didn't know. Behind her, a pastor who had been informed that I wanted neither eulogy nor sermon. Finally, in the third row, two more strangers.

None of the people on our side greeted those on the other.

And the next day, at last, before your brothers had arrived at my house, I was able to scatter your ashes in the garden while Teresa sowed tiny grass seeds.

In one of your last phone calls, when you were sending me cassettes you had recorded, some of them sung with guitar accompaniment, some spoken, you said to me:

"See how practical it is. I send you cassettes and you can answer me on cassettes. When I feel like talking to you, all I'll have to do is push a button for you to be in my studio. When you want to hear me talk, you can do the same."

Alas! you never gave me a chance to dictate a cassette to you. But now you are here, right near, and I can talk directly to you. As for you, I have a feeling, stronger every day, that I hear you without needing your voice.

Good night, little girl.

Saturday, June 3, 1978

Hello, Marie-Jo,

My first hello I say to you when I wake up and I wish you a good night when I close the shutters.

When I come back from walking, I nevertheless feel a need to say hello to you again. I can't stay cooped up all day because then I feel a great weight on me. When we got back to the house, a few minutes ago, Teresa said to me: "I bet that all the while we were out, you never stopped dictating."

That's false and it's true. It's false in the sense that I don't prepare what I'm going to say to you. It's true too because from morning to night I am in constant contact with you.

655

Yesterday, I got up the courage to look at the photo albums Aitken brought me from Paris. I don't know whether I've already told you, but she traveled all the way with you. I still have to read your notebooks, all the papers you left, and perhaps listen to your tapes. I hope I'll have the courage to do it this afternoon. Up to now, I've had neither the courage nor the strength for it.

What a beautiful little girl you were! I am sorry I didn't take more pictures of you and I am sorry there are so few of me with you, because I was always the one taking them.

I really discovered you as a young girl, and you were more beautiful than ever, with, however, it seems to me, already a kind of repressed anxiety in your eyes.

When Durand came to see me, I reminded him sadly of the sentence I had said to you on the phone: "This year, it so happens that you have lived a quarter of a century and I've lived three quarters of one."

Durand replied: "Figures always lie. At twenty-five, Marie-Jo had lived a whole life."

I am convinced of that, but I keep wondering at what moment the "Other One," the one you talk about with so much humor and lucidity in one of your recordings, and whom you call "Madame Anxiety," as if that were her first name, moved into your life.

Probably around the time you were thirteen years old, this Anxiety more or less struck up a companionship with you. She revealed her presence by small, still-discreet signs. For example, forty or fifty times a day, you felt a need to wash your hands. And in the evening, before going to bed, you suddenly had the sheets changed even though they had just been put on that morning, and a careful check had to be made under your bed.

It is true that you overworked yourself, since this was the time when you accepted no mark in school that was less than perfect.

A woman psychiatrist specializing in children's ailments was brought from Paris, and after she saw you, you asked to be sent for several weeks to a delightful little clinic in which you were completely comfortable. It had a nice name, Le Bercail. You came back from there more relaxed, but your mother was showing signs of more distressing disturbances and had already been at Prangins for two years.

It is probably the fact of having seen these disturbances that caused your own trouble.

Some of the scenes, indeed, were enough to tear apart the hypersensitive little girl you were.

I believe, and all the doctors agree, that that is where we have to look for the birth of Madame Anxiety. . . .

Perhaps it was because you were just too gifted that this Madame Anxiety began to dog your footsteps.

Today, my soul is aching, my darling, and I kiss you with all of my very old tenderness.

Sunday morning, June 4, 1978

My tiny little Marie-Jo,

I should have written: "My tiny little and great big girl both at once."

Yesterday, not without apprehension, I finally read a part of the papers you left, and I went from discovery to discovery, until my hands were trembling.

I knew that you had suffered during the greater part of your life, but I had never imagined so intolerable a suffering, and I keep wondering how you stood it for so long.

If I understand correctly, the months preceding your decision were the hardest, until in the last month you arrived at a sort of serenity in despair. Those two words seem to contradict one another, but you must understand what I am trying to explain to myself.

When you were still very young, you were already an idealist as well as being greedy for life and eager for tenderness.

Many betrayed you, and some more than others, because they were closer to you, brought you to your final gesture. (I wonder why I am writing "some," in the plural.)

All yesterday afternoon, I suffered with you, for you, and more than ever I understand why you decided so long ago, for you had already written me about it several years ago, that you wanted to rest in my little garden.

But living step by step your prolonged stations of the cross was almost too much to bear.

I went to say hello to you this morning, as I always do and as I will go on doing. But I wonder whether in the days ahead I will feel up to doing it every day.

Don't be angry with me. I am a very old father. I was also your friend and I tried to be the confessor you so sorely needed.

Unfortunately, I don't have the detachment of a professional confessor.

In a little while, after taking a walk, I will go on reading, because, as long as I have the strength for it, I am determined to go through all of it.

Even your photograph albums, which I leaf through with both admiration for my little girl and rage toward those who were unable to hold a hand out to her, when indeed they did not finish her off.

Excuse me, Marie-Jo, for my bitterness this morning. I anticipate that it will be worse tonight and in the days ahead, for I still have a lot to read and to find out about.

You still have my tenderness, which I have always dedicated to you. It is not very much. You needed an absolute gift your Dad was not able to give you.

I embrace you, my little big Marie-Jo, having only the consolation of knowing that you are beyond suffering.

Monday, June 5, 1978

My little painful one,

I have just spent two days reading and rereading the confidences you wrote with me in mind over several years, and which I was never aware of. Reading them has been a nightmare to me, as a great part of your life was, even more painfully, to you, while you struggled so valiantly against your phantoms.

I always wondered "how" it all started. I had a sneaking suspicion but no certainty and had never questioned you on the subject.

Your mother had just come temporarily out of Prangins and took you for a vacation of a little less than a month to Villars. And it was when you came back from there that you showed the first signs of obsession. Now, I know why.

Later, she took you to Cannes, which didn't help any; quite the contrary.

I will say no more. I will no longer relate to you your life as I have lived it, for you know it better than I, and I will keep to myself the small and large secrets you have confided in me.

Knowing at last, I love you only the more tenderly for it, and I admire you for having held out for so long.

I still have to read the notes you wrote in the margins of *Un oiseau pour le chat* (A Bird for the Cat) [her mother's book]. In reality, you were the bird that was sacrificed, but I never was the cat; you understood that.

I am emerging from these two days completely at a loss, yet feeling myself closer to you than ever, for, as in the song Gabin sang, "Now I know."

I love you, my little girl, and I am happy that, at last, you are at peace.

Your Dad

End of Dictations.

I still have to tell you, my darling little girl, that after two years, the seals remain on your door.

About a year after your death, your mother was present at the inventory, along with a notary, two lawyers, an expert, and a court clerk. On this occasion, the seals were removed from your room, with Aitken representing me. That is when your mother was seen nosing around everywhere, around your still-bloodstained bed, ordering pieces of furniture moved away from the walls to make sure there was nothing behind them, opening closets and drawers, while all those present wondered how they were supposed to react.

The seals were put back.

In 1980 (as today, in March 1981), they are still there, the apartment remaining as you left it, because your mother refuses to accept your three brothers as your sole heirs. She insists on getting her share—by far the biggest one, a half—and letting them split the other half.

The legal maneuverings have been going on for two years. Your mother is stubborn.

As for me, I will not give in, and you understand why, my darling little girl, don't you?

You are still in our garden, where someday I will join you.

Au revoir, little girl I love.

Now, it is your turn to tell, and you will do it better than I, who no longer have either the courage or the strength to.

[signed] Georges Simenon

Memoirs written from February to November 1980.
Revised in February and March 1981.

Marie-Jo's Book

Your book, my little girl, that you so
wanted to write and that you wrote and
sometimes sang in your always tender,
sometimes cheerful, often painful manner.

Today I am keeping my promise and
publishing it.

Dad

The Little Gray Cloud

A little gray cloud was traveling in the sky, carried along by the winds. It was a beautiful dark gray with bluish glints, but heavy with tears and sorrows, and did not look like it admired the landscapes that spread out at its feet.

That's because it was very unhappy, this baby cloud! It would have liked to make people happy, and see them gay and satisfied; but all it could do was displease them and everybody groaned as it went by.

Some went inside for protection, making sure all the windows were securely closed, and sighed: "Hmm, now it's going to rain again!"

Others, who absolutely had to go out, put on boots and overcoat, quickly opened their umbrellas and, as they waded through the puddles of water, blew their noses noisily.

Of course, the sadder the little cloud was with the result it got the more it cried, and the heavier the rain that it sent down!

And it went on this way for months and months. The days went by, and the little cloud got dark, dark, sometimes even frighteningly black. It was driven by the strong, impetuous West wind that carried it ever farther.

One day when it was going across Southern Italy, in one of those desolate, extremely dry regions, the little cloud suddenly lent an ear to laments that seemed to be coming from below. Strangely this voice was not grating and full of anger as usual but sad and yearning.

"So, I am not the only one to cry," thought the little cloud, with surprise. "Let us go and see what this is about."

But, first, it had to get permission from Mr. Wind, which was not easy.

"Please, dear West Wind," the baby cloud softly asked, "couldn't you make a little detour to carry me down there? It sounds like someone is crying."

"If you think your laments are not enough for me, you are wrong," Mr. Wind nastily answered.

"Oh, please," the baby cloud begged, "just once."

"All right, all right!" the wind grumbled.

And it started to blow as hard as it could toward the farmhouse that could now be seen, driving the little cloud before it.

And what did they see? A poor peasant looking in despair at his dried-up fields.

"Oh, if it would only rain at least once my crops would not be completely lost," he was saying with a short sniffle.

"But there is no use hoping, it never rains around here. How am I going to feed my wife and children if I have nothing to sell this month?"

"Par . . . Pardon me," the little cloud timidly began, having heard it all, "I could bring you a lot of rain if you wish."

"Honest to God?" asked the peasant, his eyes already shining with joy.

"Honest to God," answered the baby cloud. "All I have to do is cry for it to rain. And your poverty makes me so sad that that won't be hard!"

And he cried abundantly. His tears were good for the earth, which drank up this water eagerly.

Then, on the final sob, the shower stopped.

"Oh, thanks, thanks," cried the farmer. "Look how fine my crops are now. Some fine rays of sunshine on them and I will be able to harvest them and find a buyer."

Baby cloud also was all happy. For the first time, it had brought someone pleasure.

When, all of a sudden, the peasant's face clouded over: "If you leave now, it will never rain here again and the soil will dry out again."

"That's true," sighed the little cloud, and with that he let a few more tears escape.

"Incidentally," he suddenly cried out, all cheered up, "if I stayed here you would never be poor again, because I would make it rain."

And, turning toward Mr. Wind:

"Could you leave me here, and go on your way by yourself? You could just say 'hello' to me as you went by, but without carrying me any farther?"

The little cloud's eyes began to beg:

"Say, do you agree?"

"Well," the West Wind hemmed, "it's against the rules. But seeing as I will find plenty of other clouds to come with me . . . It's a deal!"

"Yippee!" shouted baby cloud kissing it. "Thank you very much. Good-bye and see you soon!"

"Until next time!" called the wind. And it blew up its cheeks and went away.

That is how the little gray cloud always stayed up over the farm. When the soil dried out, it was so sad that it immediately poured out a good beneficial rain. And when on the contrary the earth was not thirsty, it was so happy that it did not cry anymore and let the sun take its place for a few days.

Controlled in this way, the two kinds of weather did wonders. The good peasant became the richest farmer in the region and thereafter lived quietly with his wife and children.

And the little gray cloud was happy too. At last his job made sense!

THE END

1966
Château of Echandens, 13 years old

The Life of a River

I am a little river not even having the honor of being mentioned on the map of the world. I came out of the earth in a grotto on a mountainside, so thin and lanky that my mother, a big rock among so many others, does not stop petting me all the way along the road to light, to liberty. I still feel her rough and fleshless fingers touching me going by, in a silent, unhappy adieu. But I, being all wild with joy at the idea of the trip I was about to take, did not even stop to lick her with wavelets and continued selfishly on my way. Nothing more could arrest the thirst for adventure that pushed me forward.

I soon got to the exit. The brilliance of the sun dazzled me. All around me there were forests of firs and pastures then, above it all, the mountains with snowy peaks.

Such a spectacle certainly did not leave me indifferent, but far from delaying me I rushed down the rocky slope, jumping from stone to stone, avoiding the big rocks. The fresh and crisp air was good for me and I was visibly growing bigger.

I finally got down to the valley and my wild drive slowed down little by little. I was even quite breathless when I got to the approaches of a little village in the region.

The inhabitants must have been afraid of me for they had built, along my flanks, a low stone wall, the whole length of the hamlet. Yet I had no hostile thought in my head and found this work superfluous. I was still ignorant of the spring rain that swells your stomach in a few hours and makes you overflow into the fields quite against your will.

It was only a few kilometers beyond the village that I made the acquaintance of this traitress.

The sky, so blue at the exit from the black hole of my birth, was getting darker and darker. The mountains dewed by the dawn three hours before now disappeared under a thick fog. Heavy drops first merged into my body. Then the shower broke. Sheets of water beat down on me, piercing me through and through. The wind raised the rain up and threw it in bunches against the leaves of the trees, which bent under the strength of the shock. The peasants hurriedly took in the hay which they had just mown and had already taken so long to dry!

A strange sensation took hold of me. A sensation of lightness and intoxication. I did not realize that I was swelling at a terrifying rate, that the rain water adding to me made me overflow the path I was supposed to follow. I now found that I was halfway between the fields and the route I had set for myself. And nothing to do about it! An untamable force kept driving me on out. In a few minutes I would reach the isolated farmhouse over there, whose occupants had closed doors and shutters, but would not be able to hold me back.

I was terrified at the idea of the disaster I was going to commit. I tried to brake my pace. I was actually struggling against myself and it would have taken a miracle or else that . . . And that is what happened. The rain suddenly stopped. The wind had driven back the larger clouds and the only ones left were very small insignificant ones, a grayish white, which the sun would soon get through.

I had finally stopped moving ahead. And I was even returning at top speed toward my cozy little bed. I had the feeling I was deflating like a punctured inner tube, a feeling just as intoxicating as the previous one. Unfortunately, in my flight, I left parts of myself here and there, in the random hollows and bumps. For the moment they made little puddles but they would soon dry up in the sun. I could do nothing for them, although this gave me a kind of painfully empty feeling in the stomach. An hour later I was back to normal rhythm, leaving behind me the bad memory of that unintentional experience. The others were right: one must be wary of the rain, that pitiless executioner!

I don't want to tell you all my adventures, although they are one as interesting as the next. It would take too long! Too long also to describe to you in detail all the landscapes that paraded before my eyes. But try to imagine at times lush prairies of high grass, with peaceful, stupid cows whose bells ring far away, at other times entire fields of fruit trees standing against a blue, light, vaporous sky.

I especially admired, as I went by the sunsets, bright red at the horizon, then turning from aggressive yellow to a more restful yellow, and ending in this slightly whitish blue. These indescribable splendors took my breath away and I slowed down for a time. Finally, tearing my eyes away from this wonderland of nature, I started forward again fast, ever faster, carrying with me clumps of earth and small pebbles.

Time went by in this way, taking me from one village to the next, crossing rockfalls, flowing under bridges. And then one day . . . I suddenly saw before me a blue sheet that seemed endless and the brilliant reflections of which, provoked by the sun, dazzled me. This stretch so close to my own character and so beautiful would, as I guessed in getting closer to it, be my grave. The path I was following led straight to it and appeared to drown in the salt waters. My thirst for adventure had shown me many wonders which I would never again get to see. The sea, from which I was now only a few meters away, was going to carry me far away from solid ground and clean air.

Then, after a last look toward the landscapes that were so dear to me, I let myself be carried off by my destiny. I had the impression I was going down into a bottomless, infinite pit. A delicious feeling of coolness took hold of me as, becoming part of me, a huge wave closed over me, and I thought I was disappearing forever.

Innocent that I was! At that very moment, completely astonished, I was again reliving the grotto of my childhood, my mother's silent adieu and the brightness of a new sun. I was reliving the rain and the cows and the moonlight nights. Finally the sea and that bottomless hole. I closed my eyes and smiled. I had been renewing myself for a long time already and had not realized it!

THE END

November 19, 1968

It was a Thursday. Sullen weather, fog, or rather a kind of drizzle, which, as soon as one went out, soaked through your clothes, wet you through and through. It was cold.

We had finished eating. She was taking her time in leaving. She could not find her coat, looked everywhere for her keys, her bag.

"Will you still be here at three o'clock?"

"No," he said, "I'll be gone already. But I'll be back early in the evening, after my appointment."

Was he eager also for her to have closed the door, for the two of us to be alone at last? And was he as embarrassed as I, now that her steps grew more distant? I could feel inwardly that "it" would take place, that he would do it. But it was vague. In fact, for me, it was not to go that far.

He sat down on the couch:

"Everything okay?"

I smiled at him.

"I'm a little tired but . . . that seems to be the way I always am."

He smiled too. I found him handsome. A lot of charm especially. Yet he was forty, could very easily have been my father. When I was with him I didn't realize it, at any rate tried to forget it. I had sat down across from him, near the table, and he was holding my hands. I was too far away for this to be a comfortable position but I didn't move, I didn't dare. Before, I had always remained a little stiff with him, without any initiative in my movements. I don't know why.

We stayed that way a long time. He talked about his painting, his wife, his kids. That should have been enough to bring me to my senses. On the contrary. I was sinking deeper into a dream, a compact and agreeable atmosphere. He was becoming more tender as he talked. So was I.

"Sit over here."

I obeyed mechanically, yet with the slightest tightening in my chest. Was it . . . ?

I was awkward, became even more so when he placed his lips on mine. Yet I was used to it. This was not the first time. But I was confusedly realizing that this time would not be like the others, that I would do nothing either to avoid that.

I had quickly lost control of myself. I felt his breath growing stronger. He had unbuttoned my pants and I let him go ahead without resistance. I should have understood that it wasn't the same for him, that . . .

"Come on."

He was leading me gently toward the bed. I was submerged in a wave of tenderness, my ideas surrounded as by a thick fog and . . .

We made love. Badly. It didn't happen the way I had imagined it. The last time, surprised at my virginity, he had stopped in time, had not dared go beyond mere touching. And since I had felt nothing at all, in my naïveté I had been afraid I was not normal.

Now again I was afraid. There had been no real gestures of tenderness, no blossoming of a true love. It was purely . . . mechanical. At the start, it hurt, after that it got nice, nothing more.

At the moment and especially later on, I tried to make myself believe that I was full of love, truly, that I had lost all sense of things and him, had merged myself into him.

It wasn't that. Perhaps I also have a very literary idea of it. But I was thinking too much for it to be real, the image I had of him was so crude as to be indecent. Finally, he was too concerned with his own personal pleasure to be really sincere.

He had broken away immediately afterward to make sure no one was coming, and I had gone toward the bathroom. My make-up was no longer very sharp, my hair was tousled. But my eyes were calm, perhaps a bit befuddled?

"You'll have to leave, now."

"Yes."

I sighed. He looked nicely at me and I went over to him. I was trying to keep from thinking, looking wildly for excuses for myself. I must not allow myself to doubt him. Otherwise, what I had done made no more sense.

He embraced me, kissed me. I felt engulfed in his arms. So comfortable! Was it, for him, too? . . .

"Tell me, do you really love me?"

I was caressing his hair, running my fingers softly over his lips.

"I adore you!"

I believed it. A little. But that little was enough for me. I was happy, now. He was mine. I felt him to belong to me entirely. I drove her from my mind. Nothing existed but the two of us.

"You'll come back this evening? Promise?"

"Promise!"

He grazed my mouth one last time and closed the door.

She would be back before long. The bedspread had to be straightened out, the cushions rearranged.

I was relaxed. Never had I felt so relaxed. I lit a cigarette, lay down on the couch. A kind of joy, mixed with melancholy, invaded me. I was especially proud of having made love for the first time. I was not aware of how ridiculous it was. I was bigger now, more of a woman. I had become a woman, that was what was important. And, at that thought, I held my cigarette differently, my gestures became slower, which I thought to be more graceful. These thoughts remained hazy in my mind. I was just trying to believe in my love, in him, as hard as I could. To believe that I was capable of loving.

It is late. Past midnight. Tomorrow, I'll be bushed and I'll do my work badly. No matter!

I was sad this evening. I felt empty, slightly disheartened. Over everything. I've been holding this in for a month and it's hard. To no one would I dare confess that I am afraid of not having loved totally. I've tried to persuade myself of it, but the feelings I had were superficial and ephemeral. The fact is, I cheated to myself, driven forward no doubt by curiosity. One evening, one night, enveloped in sweet and tender music, I may feel myself in love . . . but perhaps with just anybody. And it is so easy, during, after, to embellish the facts, at the cost of losing in this way something one will never recapture again!

At any rate, he never saw me again. I try not to think of him, especially not to feel contempt for him. For I hold it against him a little, but I am not sorry for what happened. It's more subtle than that, too hard to explain. It's my fault anyway. I should not have thrown myself into his arms. He took advantage of it and, as far as I am concerned, he was right to.

THE END

1969
Epalinges, 16 years old

My big Dad,

I felt such a need to talk to you a little while ago. About nothing at all. And then about my almost daily behavior toward you. You don't realize that I adore you. You can't realize it because I don't know how to show it to you and most often hide it behind not very nice manners. I don't know why. Well, yes, maybe . . . Everything I'm going to tell you in writing, I already tried to explain to you without being able to. After all, I am not very gifted for that, I stumble too easily. You also think I'm "playacting." That may be, but in that case unconsciously (most of the time!).

I'm having trouble right now finding a good balance, "my" balance. That, you know. That's what makes me turn inward, think only of myself. It is said that true balance is found only between two people. I'm not yet able to do that, as far as I am concerned. It is said that it is obtained to the extent that one tries to help that of others, or just to help them. I can't. I try, whatever you may say, to be not only nice, but to show the respect I have for my neighbor, to "think" of him. Then I am artificial, seeing myself more or less act as if in a mirror—or else, on the contrary, it destroys the little bit of stability I have acquired.

That is not exactly what I wanted to express. What I mean is that I need, so far as possible, to feel that I am pretty, loved by others in order to be gay and agreeable. And that is hard. Most often, I find myself ugly, full of faults that others criticize. I instinctively stiffen and turn back in on myself. What a number of hours a day I can spend partly loathing myself, in disgust, partly crying, feeling myself powerless to do any better! "What a number of hours" is perhaps overstatement, but often. Of course, that means crying over myself (and perhaps reveling in it) which is never very good! Anyway, "I try," you can be sure of that, but I know that as long as I have not found a stable "self," I will not succeed in thinking more of others.

Look! An example! I know very well that I give everybody a pain in the ass before going out in the evening. I can't do otherwise. With difficulty! It's awful! I always need something or other at the last minute to feel physically "right," ready to wipe away one of my complexes for the evening. The times when on going out, I see how ugly I am in the mirror, and inside myself, I don't have a good time, am disagreeable or cold. All my enmity toward myself pours out over others. I close in on myself. I could cry at times like that. (I cry later in my room!) That's the ridiculous part. I have such a need to be loved, and do so little for it!

All that I've just written really shows character all right: centered on myself. I always tell myself by way of reassurance that, with inferiority complexes like mine, one can't afford to put on airs. And yet, in a certain measure, I think one can. Right after having experienced them deeply, one has a tendency to go too far the other way, to reassure oneself and then, really believing in it for a while. That's when one becomes execrable. When I feel pretty, I feel it too much, am too sure of it, and after having dragged on the lower floors, I suddenly place myself much too high. I "inflate" myself as the saying goes. Others feel it, won't stand for it and are right.

How the few words I wanted to write you have carried me far away from the ideas I wanted to express.

First of all that I love you deeply. (That's how I started my letter and that was right, a good start. Unfortunately . . . afterward . . .) And then that, so many times, I would like to snuggle into your arms and let myself go, crazy as I am, with all my faults, without your judging me. I have such need of you, of your strength, of your love. Need of being able to express myself freely, without this damned modesty of mine, without this reserve, this stiffness that I stupidly feel whenever I am with you, this feeling especially that, whatever I may do, you will not find me natural. I know that I may be coquettish with my brother, unable to tease, to act a part perhaps from time to time, but a gay, funny, mischievous part (which I nevertheless have spontaneously, some days, with my friends). That's the somewhat big-girl part of me. But there is also the very little one, as I said above, who would still like to be able to be cuddled just as when she really was. It's no longer possible and I don't know anymore. I've lost the freshness (if I had it, really, long ago!). Especially now when I am feeling guilty toward you, and especially toward myself. Guilty conscience. It's true! You're right. At home, I do my work badly, without any discipline whatsoever. My other classes are okay. Although twice, I've canceled dancing lessons, alleging the teacher wasn't available. That's not real, real nice. It all comes from lack of will power. Without wanting to make a joke, from lack of the will to find the will power! The worst is that I hurt myself as much as I do you.

Proof! You know, the day when Marc and Mylène were still there, when you were sick and in your bedroom. The two of us talked. For once,

I had succeeded in making contact, which I do so infrequently, through my own fault. A Friday. I had just missed dancing, because I was all in and didn't have the guts to go there anyway. At the end, kissing me, with a pat on the shoulder, you said to me: "Just the same, you're a swell gal." And I thought I had to turn it into a joke: "That happens to me now and then!" You laughed. That made me happy. Your eyes were laughing too, and so were mine. I had my father's esteem, I was happy. Then, as I was leaving, the idea that I had lied to you, that I had not deserved that very trust hurt me so! For once that your daughter was "okay," or at least you thought so, it wasn't true. I felt like confessing it all to you and then, out of cowardice, I didn't say anything. Out of cowardice! Yes! because I'm not long on courage. I dare to write you this story now, with sincerity, agreed, but being conscious just the same, way down deep inside me, that you won't say anything now after several weeks. In itself, that is no longer worth a thing.

Crazy, what f. . .ing stupidities I can write! And with such importance too! But I would like to tell you once again that this lousy work is in part due to fatigue. This fatigue of course because I go to bed late, which is not really an excuse. Especially, once again, it's due to a lack of stability, because of a vague anxiety, an impression of insecurity, that I keep putting off the time to go to bed. If I put out the light at that moment, I find it hard to fall asleep, so sleep poorly anyway. I need to dream a little, awake, to build around me agreeable and reassuring situations, think of or latch onto (in this case, the verbs are synonymous) people, places perhaps slightly artificial but in some way "protective." To run away, in a word, from certain realities which I find it hard to accept, out of weakness. And to fall asleep at last in that little world I have created. This is not romanticism; it is vitamins and sleeping pills all at once. In the evening, I am often tense especially if I have been alone all the time before, without going out. A little logy too, because of the cigarettes. It's my only way of relaxing: to surround myself with a fake but warm and agreeable atmosphere and nothing else.

It's very complicated. I will always be unable to explain it clearly. Anyway, you did understand it, didn't you? It is surely not so difficult to comprehend as I imagine. I am the one who can't make head or tail of it!

All of that, not so that you will forgive me (what I am, what I seem, and how I act). So that I may feel closer to you from now on, so I can know a stupid girl like me has a terrific "poppy," whom she adores and with whom she would simply let herself go if only she found his arms . . . (Got to point out that she's near-sighted. One point in her defense!) . . . and if the arms are opened to her.

There. Seven pages of imbecilities, but sincere I think, such as they are.

I kiss you very hard, my Dad. Have a good trip and read this only when you find time. Because it isn't worth wasting even minutes over this. (It's so badly written anyway!) With a big yum, yum. I hug you in my arms till I squeeze you to death . . .

Till Friday.

Your little girl

Marie-Jo

1970

Prangins Clinic, 17 years old

November ?, 1970

Night had already fallen. All around, the violent lights of the city, the neon signs and traffic signals going from red to green gave her a sort of slight dizziness, a rather disagreeable feeling of floating.

Despite the rush-hour denseness of the six o'clock traffic, the squeaks of tires against the pavement seemed far away to her. Perhaps because of the enveloping darkness, full of dim shadows, which prevailed beyond the electric glows and muted the noises?

The taxi was moving off, leaving behind the headquarters buildings, rapidly turning the corner to go up the street that led to the intersection.

She crossed her legs, pulled slightly at the creases in her trousers, and finally found a comfortable position. But that did not mean she relaxed. Her muscles were tense and almost hurt. Her head was heavy. Heavy with all the memories that rushed back into her mind at the sight of the familiar décor.

And besides, the car heater must have been badly set. The heat, inside, was suffocating. So that, curiously, despite the November cold, it smelled of humid clothing and sweat. The smell of the woman next to her, especially, bothered her. She sighed and her lungs contracted painfully as they let out a long breath of air.

How long was it, now? More than six months, at least! Yes, six months since she had last gone along these roads, seen these cafés, these movie posters. A strange sensation, undefinable in its complexity, took hold of her, and now it was in every fiber of her being that she hurt. Not with one of those purely physical sufferings, which the brain records and can localize, but a dull ache, as if radiating from inside, which oppressed her by its intensity. An ache for which so many things were responsible.

Just the music, to begin with. Although half drowned out by the noise of the wind against the car body, it reached her, soft, languishing, enveloped her in confused, troubling images, reminding her of the times in her life when she had been happy.

Her eyes began to smart and she had to make an effort to hold back the tears. She gritted her teeth and her fingers contracted in an almost imperceptible motion to make fists. She absolutely had to hide her distress, however deep it might be. And protect her internal collapse.

For weeks she had been using up all her energy, her will power, in making herself appear closer and stronger. She had no right to collapse at the mere thought of a past no longer connected to anything, which had broken off with her already, long before she suspected it.

She then caught herself whispering, "Someday perhaps . . . you'll go back home." Her lips moved softly, as if to say yes. Why then at the same time did a slight fog of tears have to come and dissolve shapes and mix colors before her eyes?

She was suddenly afraid of having spoken too loud and looked fearfully toward the nurse. But the latter, although right next to her, had obviously heard nothing.

She promised herself she would be more careful. From talking so much with herself, in her room, she had created an automatism for herself she was no longer sure she could control when her thoughts went deeper.

She smiled bitterly: wasn't this one more step forward toward quiet madness?

Others, perhaps, found it hard to understand her. But to her it seemed quite natural to talk out loud like that within the four walls of her room, to make sounds vibrate so that, breaking the surrounding silence, they in a way became company for her. Sometimes, the four walls, the floor and the ceiling formed a kind of box in which she found herself trapped. Then, concentrating on the echo of her own voice, she would forget her prison and lose herself soon in the exclusive universe of her suffering.

It was so simple. And so familiar. She had ended up calling those moments "crises" and she could predict almost with certainty when the next one would occur.

As just now, for instance, when she felt overcome by that unbearable anxiety and the suppressed sobs were searing her throat. She tried to keep control of herself, wept silently, holding herself back at each new spasm so as not to cry out. The little sentence danced around in her head, obsessively: "You'll go back home again." She wanted to moan, like a wounded animal. An urge to vomit added to this dizziness and her jaws were so tight that the muscles must have been bulging on either side. She forced herself to open her mouth slowly by wetting her lips. For they would soon be there and she would have to smile! Control herself behind that smile. That was the best way, she had recently discovered. Toward the doctors and toward herself. First by cheating a little, by playing a part, until the latter became like a second reality. Like just plain reality, perhaps? And that forced her to maintain a certain dignity.

As much as possible, at any rate, she would try from now on not to analyze too much. For fear of mixing things up even more, or, worse, discovering the limits of her intelligence and her inability to find answers. For fear of these nauseas, too, which took hold of her as soon as she looked at herself too crudely. For fear of the truths, quite simply. At any rate one could not expect of her that someday she would achieve perfect objectivity toward her own image. So?

"Someday you'll be happy, you'll see. You'll know what it is to be yourself. Someday . . ." She now softly nurtured her dream, as back home, in those moments of depression, she liked to let her fingers run through the fur that covered her bed. That soft, silky, quasi-sensual contact pacified her even in her tears. It was something like her dream. It hurt her and comforted her in turn.

She closed her eyes and let herself go to the suffering and relief so strangely intermingled. Perhaps she wallowed in this state or it was a means of escape from . . . She shook herself, reopened her eyes. She must not! If only out of reserve. And not toward the others, this time, but toward herself. It was too easy to declare oneself irresponsible! With her, the mechanism still operated in time, her instinct for self-preservation threw the alarm before it was too late. Until when? Would she not soon be putting it to sleep as she got stuck in her torpor? Would she not get to be like those ghosts that wandered through the antiseptic hallways whom she rubbed elbows with each day? They too had perhaps one day decided, more or less deliberately, to "throw in the towel." They had turned off the alarm signal forever. In order to do that, no need even to disconnect anything, as she had just found out. All they had had to do was close their ears for a certain length of time, until the sounds no longer awakened anything in them . . . Total impermeability to the echoes of the outside world.

Outside the window, suddenly, her eyes caught some familiar shadows. They were arriving. The smile automatically took its place on her lips, without her even having to try. She opened the car door. She was coming out of a dense fog and, thrown into the sharp evening air, she realized how far, a little while ago, she had gotten from reality. A few mists nevertheless remained in her mind, but these would take longer to dissipate, she knew. She could not keep from turning toward the sleeping countryside before going through the door, which was then bolted behind her.

"Someday, you'll go back . . ." The little sentence still resounded within her, the sole hope capable of nourishing her daily struggle and making her silently accept all the humiliations. It would still keep resounding that way in her heart as long as needed.

She slowly went up the stairs behind the nurse, checked herself as she was about to waver and had to grab hold of the banister. She was exhausted as after a long physical effort, at the end of her nervous energy. She forced herself to breathe deeply to regain her lucidity.

The doctor was up there in the office, waiting for her. Once again she would have to weigh her words, open herself a little more at each one of them, lay herself still barer. She had become used to it, and, there too, despite a certain shame she sometimes felt, and even though it was not expected of her, she kept forcing herself to smile. That was her temporary refuge, before being able to collapse, alone at last, in her room and let everything come out, with no one to see!

"Someday, with sunshine all around . . ." She tightened her fists . . . "You will know PEACE." She crossed her fingers as if to underline her thought and knocked at the door.

THE END

677

1971
Paris, 18 years old

Letter to one of her doctors

Tuesday, October 2, 1971

It is 9:15 P.M., my record player is softly playing a tender Tahitian song and I suddenly feel like writing you before going out to dinner.

Just back in Paris a week, four to five days of anxiety and hypernervousness, difficulty in adapting, even depression. Then very softly, on tiptoe because still very new, since Sunday, an approach to equilibrium, a relaxation of my whole being in movement, in contacts, in "life."

(It's the way it always is when one finally relaxes that one realizes the extreme and superfluous tension of the days before, the anxiety and unconscious depression which nonetheless motivated our reactions.)

I am appalled to see the extent to which I was "out" to a significant share of reality on leaving Lausanne. I felt it confusedly since I discussed it with you, but once again I was cut off behind that "wall," those "blinders" we are both familiar with.

I am sorry now about not having been at ease enough within myself to look around me, not having been able to leave with a more definite picture of the house, Dad, Pierre, at not having left more "easily." Too bad! It was a great step to take, an "elephant's step for an ant."

Until the very last minute I was probably afraid of not being able to make it and . . . I held my breath! It tenses you to hold your breath: you turn white, then red, sometimes blue; you are no longer yourself as a result, and . . . you don't feel at ease! All it takes once more is a first breath of air and . . . ! It's instinctive, it's what I did, first with still slightly contracted lungs, and then now freely. I am happy, I believe. At any rate in comparison to the last years I've lived through. I am now gaining confidence in myself, sitting quietly among people, timidly discovering myself as I discover them, stumbling at times, awkwardly, but sooner or later finding a support so as to straighten up. A real, solid one, more easily unmasking the artificial, fabricated one which will collapse very quickly, and me surely with it. Happy? Yes, I believe so. For the first time in . . . ever so long (!) I dare again use that word, slowly discover its meaning for me. I say for me, since each one gives it his own meaning, and this word exists only in the ideal or to the degree that one believes in it.

With R. last night, I used it for something wonderful, which I had thought still unattainable to my being. In love-making simply, since for the first time I experienced coming with the other one, and I accepted myself as a woman, and accepted him, fully.

I am expressing myself poorly, again and always. It's too bad! I would like to find sentences completely true in their simplicity to explain to you, to make you feel this . . . moment of my life. The whole mixed-up beginning of my letter was just to get to this, and if I took my pen in hand tonight it was to tell you that . . . this something wonderful that I could no longer really believe in had at last come to pass! And all that this implies by way of overwhelming difference within me, in the depths of my being, the change, the joy, the . . . I don't know! All the words I will be able to write will be empty by comparison. It was fine, tender . . . ! ! ! ! ! !

Yesterday afternoon, R. and I had gone to Marc's, at Rambouillet. It was sunny, we felt fine, like sweethearts, and I was happy to be going again to see Boule, who, even though Marc and Mylène are still in Italy (for a short subject), had been back at the house for two days. Francette was there, of course, with the kids, since she's still waiting to be able to move into her new house. But, unlike other weekends, there were no other invasive people, none of those other friends, and the house was calm and hospitable, Francette relaxed and therefore "nice" to me. I believe the country can never seem more beautiful than when one goes there to escape for a while from the teeming of Paris.

For the first time too, we were spending a day just as a "couple," the two of us, without dragging our other friends along. And in the car, both on the way out and back, it was terrific to feel we had "our intimacy."

After the theater, in the evening, again with friends around us, but after the relaxation of the afternoon, laughing with them was a pleasure again. We had a guitar, and all of us, five, six, maybe more, went up to Sacré-Coeur, by way of the little streets behind Pigalle. On the steps we sang, with Paris at our feet and the full moon over our heads. Paris was not only at our feet, but I think it quite simply belonged to us.

R. and I went back home, arm in arm, and the hotel room was there for us, nice and warm after the brisk cold outside.

All of that for the atmosphere, as I believe that everything that happened yesterday contributed to relaxing me, to letting me be myself, and no doubt allowed me at last to experience that wonderful happiness in R.'s arms. My last unconscious reticences, which I retained within the deepmost part of me, no longer existed; there was really then only R., me, him I felt I loved and desired with all my being, him I finally wanted to abandon myself to completely. And then . . . Everything . . . and nothing. The feeling that every being experiences at the paroxysm of love, a strange desire to cry afterward although one knows that one has never been happier, that this is precisely too total, too strange a peacefulness, with the feeling of living perhaps for the first time at the same rhythm as the earth, and the world itself is there, nice and warm, palpable between your hands.

There. How stupid, all of those phrases, those inadequate phrases! They're so "nothing" alongside it, of course! I just needed to write them to you because . . . that night which has just changed so many things for my life, I owe to myself, without any doubt, but I owe it to you certainly . . . very much as well. Right?

I know that you will be happy, content, for me, that to a third party such a letter would seem ridiculous, if not incomprehensible but that you will understand.

I believe that all that, through these words and even by way of these lines, through all you may feel that is hidden behind and unfortunately inexpressible, had to be shared with you, that it is the revelation of the "woman" I am able to be that is important, this first revelation which will afford me so many more.

Well, there! I no longer know quite what to say. Surely a lot of other things; better to explain to you my life in general currently in Paris.

I nó longer feel up to it, now. Wow! Eleven o'clock! I must quickly go and eat before meeting R. at half past eleven when the show lets out!

So . . . this perfectly stupid letter, embodying in spite of everything I believe the full measure of attachment, affection and immense confidence that I have for and in you.

I kiss you (very hard!)

Your Marie-Jo

P.S. You are over your head in work, as I am only too well situated to know, and I don't want excessively to hope for a reply. But just a tiny word, even dismissive? It will give me so much pleasure!

Looking forward to seeing you again, this winter, between trains!

M.-J.

November 3, 1971

"Bonsoir Daddy, Bonsoir Maman."

After the kisses, it was necessary to go up the stairs as fast as possible to the bedroom, back tense and chilled at the idea of the large "Christ," on his cross, who, tonight perhaps, like all other nights, would try to get out of the picture to run after her.

He had never been able to as yet, of course, but today? . . . He looked so horrible, all naked and bloody, with his beard and his long hair all over his face! And that picture of suffering would surely end by dragging her along into that horror.

She never stopped being afraid until the door to the landing was well closed behind her. Huddled deep in her bed, she finally succeeded in forgetting it and resuming her place in reality, savoring the relief she felt after this daily fright. Perhaps she even kept it up unconsciously just so as to be able to accede to this well-being? Only, at three, she was still too young to try yet to analyze it.

That age, to her, meant Cannes, the big house at the top of the hill, in the middle of the pines, with the wrought-iron gate, at the entrance, framed in mimosas that had given it its name, "Golden Gate."

The swimming pool, too, of which the only recollection was connected with her brother Johnny falling into it with all his clothes on on his bike, in the midst of the water lilies in the small basin. A red bike, which later she was to consider to be tiny, but which at the time was still much too heavy for her, and she of course forbidden to make use of it.

She had a bizarre image of the short-sleeved gray shirt dripping with water, and her brother's amazed look, coughing and spitting while the governess bawled him out.

That was about all as far as the house was concerned. Of school, at Cannes, one fact remained nevertheless blistering in her memory, because directly concerning her. At school where, as she had been told later on, she was already in a class with pupils twice her age, having refused to remain more than one day at the school called nursery.

It is true that in this class of "big kids," she didn't really take the lessons and that, based on them, she was given work within her grasp.

And it was right in the middle of one of those lessons that, all alone in her corner, facing drawing paper and some pots of colors, and wanting herself to answer one of the questions, she had made too brusque a gesture to raise her hand, with the disastrous effect of overturning all of the ink on the desk and shoulder of the schoolmate seated in front of her.

Even now she could stop that picture in front of her eyes, see again the varicolored spot getting bigger and stretching out immeasurably, as desperately slowly as in the movies, when the reel runs in slow motion.

The anger of the teacher, itself, had been mild compared to the apprehension she had first felt of it, and this panic fear over the reaction of a big person had been the first to engrave itself in her memory.

It was beginning to make sense only now. Now when, at more than nineteen years of age, before her unwholesome anxiety about people and things and the better to control it, she was trying to understand its reasons through her past.

Wasn't it strange that the latter should bring back to her only painful and paralyzing feelings, however far back in her childhood she went? When those are the very ones, according to the psychologists, that time should most easily erase. Or at least transform little by little to make them less definitely disagreeable.

She called them her "traumas." "Small" and "large," for she could classify them that way by categories, by order of size, or, as here, in their chronology.

By order of importance, the "accident" of course came at the head of the list automatically. But that took her less far back; when she was already five or six years old, and it was no longer Cannes but Echandens, a little village between Geneva and Lausanne: big plane trees have now replaced the pines; the château and its two turrets, the colonnaded house. She wears her hair a little longer, and regularly gets it all tangled playing boys' games. No more swimming pool, but an immense park enclosed within a high wall that she daily shinnies up. Not for the exercise or to show off, but to go furtively across the way, despite father's forbidding it, to buy some candy. The grocery-tobacconist's is at the corner a little farther away, at the end of the bend.

And it was just at this dangerous turning, at the foot of the great tree which, from the garden and because of its many branches, makes the climb so much easier, that the two motorcycles so unfortunately bumped into each other.

In the dust and pine needles, they skidded under the dining-room window and finally stopped upside down on the gray stones.

That, she knows too only because she has been told about it, since in fact she saw nothing, and even refused to see any of it.

What she was able to reconstruct in her imagination was doubtless much more awful than reality, but that too she is still too young to understand.

The face of the cook, suddenly appearing between the doorjamb and the door, was in itself something quite out of the ordinary.

Then, the choppy words she uttered in order to attract her mother's attention little by little awakened her anxiety.

"Madame, Mister (the dog, a superb royal standard poodle, an integral member of the family), Mister is sick. Come quick!"

Her mother had already understood something unusual was happening. She had probably also already made the connection between the dust she saw come up outside the windows a few minutes before with the repeated and unusual brakings that between two mouthfuls, in spite of oneself, one had to hear. Not so unusual however as to be troublesome, hushed by the thickness of the storm windows. Nothing over which to stop eating.

Only there, there are two motorcyclists lying on the road and bathing in their blood, and that's what the cook finally gets across to them, too upset to lie under the avalanche of questions that Véronique and her brother keep asking her.

And now that her mother is losing her calm, hurrying to call an ambulance, now that a mob attracted by the shouts is crowding against the foot of the wall, Véronique, for her part, is seized with panic.

It seems to her that her universe has suddenly shrunk, to be nothing more than a powerful vise pitilessly crushing her.

She can breathe now only with difficulty, sees things more and more confusedly through all this agitation, and it seems to her she is going to scream.

She calls mother, wants to know what her brother sees through the windowpanes, why, when he turns away, he looks so pale.

He had the courage to look. He saw and no longer imagines a horrible nightmare.

While she hesitates. She would like to, yes, she "must" see for herself. But they are too hard, those few steps to be taken from the table to the window, and she resists her mother, who presses her, shoves her, herself bewildered by her daughter's reactions.

But then, why is she so insistent on making her see the awful spectacle, the bodies surely mangled, the liters of blood and of twisted metal?

She can see them only too well, as a matter of fact, in her head. She can't take it anymore, after "seeing" them so much, so she screams.

"I'm explaining to you what's happening, Véronique. There is nothing anymore, I assure you. For your own good, you have to look. They are just hurt a little . . . They are being taken in an ambulance . . . There, they're gone! The police are cleaning up the few traces of blood on the ground. And there's nothing so tragic about it. The water looks a little pink, that's all. Like in the movies, you know?"

Véronique has closed her ears, refuses to hear with all of her tensed-up being, shrinks in the arms, full though they are of tenderness, dragging her away toward the bad dream.

She is going to cry. She cries, letting go all at once of that untenable tension that was oppressing her. She still turns away, instinctively, and the harder, the more pressing her mother becomes.

When she finally does lean over, breaking her final resistance, there is nothing left but a slightly shiny spot still glinting in the sunlight.

The road has gone back to its everyday look, as if nothing had happened. Nothing but the horrible nightmare from which she is extirpating herself with difficulty, painfully, as after too great a physical effort.

Only, while there is nothing left at the bottom of the wall, nothing but that spot, which she no longer sees for staring at it too intently, that "nothing" is just what will never be able to erase what she keeps engraved in her mind.

She is still not able to recover, again be secure, dares not accompany mother and Johnny down there, as far as the policemen and, in a final mad flight from the images pursuing her, she runs for refuge into her father's arms.

These images that violated her protective cocoon hit her despite the family nucleus that until then she had thought so tight, so solid.

"And what if 'they' come back, Daddy?" Yes, what if "they" were to come back, bring the stretchers up into the living room, deposit the livid bodies at the foot of the large armchair, and ask her father to hang on to her so as to take care of them? . . .

"Oh, Daddy . . . Daddy, I don't want to!"

The little arms have gone rigid around his neck, avidly begging for a little strength and gentleness. Her blond head is lying against the protective chest, the last tears flowing to the sound of words so well spoken to console her.

Then her hiccups grow less frequent, a relaxation of all her nerves, which slowly unknot, comes slowly to submerge her, freeing her at last.

At the same time that she hears her mother's footsteps on the stairs, that Johnny, triumphant, comes over to her and takes her hand, in an awkwardly protective manner.

His eyes are all shiny with an immense pride: he's seen it all, he has. He wasn't scared. Well . . . hardly! And he even told the policeman what he knew about it.

They are all around her now; she's nice and warm inside and it's good.

She would be perfectly satisfied if she weren't in some confused way slightly ashamed, as when you're not really sick and you ask to be allowed to stay in bed anyway.

Then she smiles, in order to feel less foolish, and sniffs one last time, before making her entrance into difficult forgetting.

"Paris"

THE END

For you, little Daddy
[Title in English]

Just remember, for a while
There was sunshine everywhere,
You and I were just a smile
And it was all part of us there.

Your big steps went too fast for me.
I held on to your arm desperately.
Your tender eyes were full of glee,
Your light eyes that were looking at me.

Our long walks on that vacation,
Do you remember, Daddy mine?

That fully blossoming sensation
Of love we felt one day so fine?

When both of us wanted to dance
And you pressed me to your chest
To the tune that was our romance,
Our "Tennessee Waltz," the very best.

We were really sweethearts two,
You seemed so strong as you held me
And we were so happy too.
You remember, Daddy, do tell me?

Just remember for a while
There was happiness everywhere.
You and I for a little while
Had a future that seemed so fair . . .
. . . But it had no room for us there!

THE END

Friday, August 5, 1972

Dear ol' Dad [in English],

I am at Saint-Jean-de-Luz since Wednesday afternoon at five, the weather is superb and I . . . I'm super–"sick as a dog"! Yesterday, in spite of an already healthy cold, I tried just the same to go swimming but today I judged it more prudent to stay in bed all day. I don't think I have any temperature, but I'm coughing a lot, as usual with me in such cases, and it would be stupid to let myself in for bronchitis or tonsillitis. So I'm taking care of myself, all alone in the room that R.'s parents put at our disposal, looking enviously at the sea through the window. No matter! I just hope this won't last all through vacation!

Last Monday and Tuesday were spent in preparing to leave and I went to the "Fleas" to pick up a few last things. Only, an awful storm hit Paris late Monday, and I got soaked to the bone. When I took the train to Rambouillet at 9:00 P.M., my clothes were still stuck to my body and I didn't get to have a good hot bath till ten o'clock. That was a little late!

Everything packed, we left Rambouillet by motorcycle at five in the afternoon. Roger and I were each wearing at least three or four sweaters, besides our leather jackets, under the nylon fishermen's coveralls we bought the day before for the rain and wind. The sky was still not very inviting, but R. and Marc had talked it over the day before and found it too involved to get the motorcycle loaded on the train. We kicked ourselves, once we got going! After an hour it started to rain, naturally, and in spite of all our gear, the icy moisture got in everywhere; we were frozen.

At seven, we stopped at Vendôme, in a little hotel where it took over an hour to get some hot water. It was getting to be a joke, by this time!

I was completely knocked out by the road, with a terrible skull ache from the wind beating on my face during the whole trip, and the buckets of water splashing wholesale on my shoulders. R. gives them our clothes to dry and we go to bed right after eating.

We were up at six-thirty, to try to go faster than the rain, since it only started to fall, we were told in the region, around ten o'clock every morning.

Only our clothes were still wet, the porter at the hotel having found nothing better, in this weather, than to put them outside to dry! (It wasn't funny anymore, but ludicrous!)

Fortunately, the farther west we went, the clearer the sky became, and the first rays of sunshine appeared around eleven o'clock. We had ridden quite far by then, and at one, we reached Bordeaux where, a few kilometers farther along the road, we stop to eat. In a rush, because more clouds were reappearing, threatening us with a few raindrops which, very fortunately, we left behind. Finally, at five in the evening, we pulled up in front of the house, at the seashore, in which R.'s parents have a permanent lease on the top floor, facing the beach: two bedrooms, bath, small vestibule, all very clean, very "nice." Not to mention a little gas-ring in a corner for cooking.

So, here we are! A terrific blue sea, an extraordinary location, a few days to bronze in the sun, but a fine grippe keeping me in the room! No need to wonder how I caught it!

I'm a little low tonight, of course, feel a bit weakened by staying in bed, so . . . I've written you. My first letter since vacation began! Proving that there's some good side in everything, right?

I haven't been able to get to the post office yet to phone the secretaries my address, and I don't think I'll need any money yet. I'm saving the maximum right now and I still have my two-thousand-franc monthly allowance untouched, despite what I had to spend to get ready for the trip. If I should be short before leaving for Corsica (assuming I'm no longer sick!) I will then send a telegram in a hurry from the Côte d'Azur, where, according to our plans, we ought to be spending several days.

I'll try to get to phone you soon too, so as to give you some news by word of mouth.

In the meantime, this letter written any old which way, I believe, and my mind slightly foggy from medicines, but full of the immense tenderness that I am sending you across France.

I love you and kiss you very hard.

A "hu-u-u-ge" YUM-YUM.

Your "little"

Marie-Jo
"Saint-Jean-de-Luz"

?/?/1972
to a friend

You said to me the other day: Come on, write me a song. As if it were as easy as pushing a button!

Since then though I search my mind,
Look through it time after time,
Silly ideas are all I find
Or else words that just won't rhyme.

So I write and I erase
And once again I try my hand,
Calling myself to my face
Names you alone could understand.

I found my inspiration, see!
I'll start with the shimmering sea.
Nuts! I kidded myself all along,
Plagiarizing a Charles Trenet song.

That's no subject for me.
You might say I'm all at sea.
But then love will move me to
Some words that I might make do.

"Theirs was more than a great love.
"Time flew by, heavens above!
"And they never saw it go,
"Lying together in the snow."

That would move a cow to tears
Or else I'll watch the trains go by.
You were right, all of my fears
Of stupidity were justified.

So why should we complain,
Why not do like all the rest,
The singers of a very plain
Kind of song that seems the best?

You will get your song, old chum,
On this summer's hit parade.
It may make you look like a bum
But you'll have it, enough said!

"Pigalle"

THE END

October 13, 1972

He is a little drunk and he knows it, zigzagging slightly on the sidewalk, in this walk he determined would never end, all alone in the evening air.

The sky, above him, seems a prisoner of the rows of houses that make such a cutoff on either side of the street.

Just a starry band toward which he raises his head, to which he appeals because it perhaps represents an all-powerful god, a supreme reality which, by its existence, reassures him about himself, makes him less miserable over being a man.

He does not wonder why he is here, outside, nor what drove him into this cold humidity. It doesn't matter anymore. He is conscious of only one thing: he has reached the end, the end of his anxieties. He has gone full circle, merged with the center of the universe, in his slow, painful step.

He killed "the other one," for good! The one who questioned himself, who hesitated, the one who was so afraid. He left him there, in a puddle of water, under a lamppost, and he went far away, so far he will never be able to hope to come back.

But why come back, now that he has understood? What every being wants to have he now has in himself, with a new and irrevocable certainty.

Painful too. But at last he is free, liberated from the taboos of this world and his own weight. Free, since he has become integrated into infinity, has dizzily coupled with the slow, imperceptible movement that rules all of nature in its perpetual renewing.

He can no longer doubt: his heart is beating to the same rhythm as the endless passing of the days. He needs now only to feel he is living fully, with a henceforth inviolable concept: absolute faith, one truth, beyond despair, far beyond the humid fog that enveloped his eyes.

Those bitter tears that he had shed before accepting being a man, in his total humility.

"Poigny-la-Forêt"

November 19, 1972, 11:25 P.M.

I know the time, because I've just told it to the three guys sitting right next to me, which made me look at my watch. Otherwise I should certainly not have thought of it.

I know that I still have a very long time to wait until the others come out of the movie, a very long time to spend alone with myself in this café.

Yet, there are people there, all around, those guys sitting a meter away at the next table, and they are so far away at the same time, in another universe to which tonight I no longer know the entrance, as if it were inaccessible.

My near-sightedness is a big contributing factor. I see them only in a funny kind of fog, made even thicker by the veil of tears I cannot hold back.

Why cry? A feeling of sorrow for myself, fatigue or real suffering? Real to me at any rate if only in "my own" reality. But why does it go on being so different from that of the "others," why does my "truth" always reach a breaking point that keeps it from coinciding with theirs? . . . Or am I just imagining that again? I no longer know. Not tonight. Anyway, I have never really been able to answer all these self-analyses. Lose myself in them, yes. As in a dense labyrinth from which logic is inextricable.

Nevertheless I feel that I am lucid, in almost any circumstances whatsoever. Even in the most complete depression. Only, that lucidity is still one of my own truths, knocked off center like the rest by an obligatory lack of objectivity.

Like tonight. Everything remains "real" around me, only my receptivity is different. I no longer perceive things in the same way; I feel as if they are very far away, from where they no longer reach me, or else they do too hard, in an exacerbated manner: they assume an importance I would not give them in another frame of mind.

It all turns into long monologues with myself, sentences thrown out into the night, as just now, up to the stars, so distressing and attractive at the same time. To a "god" I still keep somewhere within myself to find comfort in through tears too long held back. A need. The idea of a reassuring presence, even infinitely far away, in this universe which without him I just cannot conceive, and who is there every time I call him, every time I can no longer face up to myself alone and his existence allows me to accept myself more simply. His existence which gives a raison d'être to mine, explains it perhaps, allows me to believe in a certain ending, in the fullest blossoming of the being, even beyond life, in a total love which through him exists, and which he must help us someday to attain, without letting us know it yet in this world.

Happiness, quite simply. This poor word which here can seem only derisory, without true resonance because so inaccessible, must find its fulfillment "elsewhere."

This "god" rocks me in his arms, as tenderly as Dad would do if he were with me and I dare ask him to, in a solitude I know to be so much like all other solitudes which people the world and only makes me feel mine to be greater, pacifies me in the warmth brought to me by his belief itself, in this wonderful idea that someday all I will need do is lie down for all my being to be absorbed into the infinite and couple with the primal movement. Not in death properly speaking, allied to oblivion, but in its complete antithesis: the discovery of true existence, of which I will at last be able to reach the paroxysm, in the absolute.

"Archi-Duc"

THE END

Oh Dad, if only you could be here, near me, could take me in your arms as you did when I was small and make me forget everything. Forget everything so as to start over afresh, as if washed clean by you of all this past in which I am stuck and am no longer able to get out of. This past which carries on my present, because I myself have not sufficiently changed. Will surely never be able to change. The proof: occupied as I am in writing these few lines, in an undeniable need, in turning myself around myself, inside of problems I create for myself.

I would so like to be able to be born, now, to have before me a brand-new, still spotless life.

Daddy, tell me that someday . . . Someday, as I used to repeat in my prison, hanging on to the bars that turned me into a captive animal. Someday . . .

But nothing will ever be able to be really wonderful.

That is only the memory of one of my childhood dreams.

"Archi-Duc"

THE END

November 22, 1972

She comes in, walks slowly onto the empty stage, on which no distinct shapes can be made out. Just the suggestion of a dark hole, bottomless, limitless.

A voice is heard, first muted, coming from very far away, then more and more audible until finally it is completely close, as the scene progresses.

THE VOICE, *simply stating a fact.*
You are all alone.

SHE
I think so, yes . . . All alone.

You don't look around you enough. There are people, a whole lot of people teeming around you and you don't look.

SHE, *with a quick look around.*

I've looked, already. But there's nothing, no one.

Explaining.

Everybody, that's the same as nobody. A person is still all alone.

THE VOICE, *very gentle.*

You are surely right . . . As far as you are concerned. But it's your own fault just the same. One can tear oneself away from solitude. It is hard to do, but one can. One has to want to, very much . . . And it's easier just to give in to it.

SHE, *violently.*

But I'm not giving in to it. It just so happens, I'm not accepting anything.

Suddenly humbler.

That is why I have to be with you.

She goes toward the hole, slowly, starts to make a gesture and goes on in a whisper.

SHE

But it's so hard to let yourself fall. Just like that, without anyone to give you a shove for a start. (*Louder, getting progressively more animated, almost comical.*)

SHE

Oh, boy! If someone only gave me a tiny little shove (*she starts a gesture*), I could fall so easily!

Serious again.

SHE

Only there is never anyone who will help you. Some because they don't understand or don't want to understand, others because they are afraid. And there are some who would like to fall themselves, and even one who does from time to time. But to give the little bit of a shove to someone who is asking them to, that they never do.

THE VOICE, *almost amused, still very gentle.*

That's rather normal, don't you think? One doesn't help someone to die. At least . . . not someone who asks them to when he seems to be alive.

SHE, *in a revolt full of despair.*

But I can't go on living. And that's what you too don't want to understand. I don't know how one is supposed to go about it, living "their" life. They themselves have complicated it so! They complicate it for the fun of it!

A pause, then becoming softer.

SHE

I'm sure that's not what you wanted either at the start. (*More and more bitterly.*) They, of course, tried to, for sure, and hard, too! But they didn't know what path to take to get to where you wanted them to go. What you had merely outlined, they were not able to carry forward, as simple as that. And they are feeling their way on every path, in every direction, without ever discovering the end, although that's what's most visible, right under their feet. And even if they were to discover it there would always be some who would block their way to it, for personal advantage or because they resented not having been first.

Her voice gets stronger as she grows angrier.

SHE

And you, you knew all of that, long before they even suspected it. And you didn't do anything; you still aren't doing anything. You made the outline, sure, lightly put in the pencil strokes needed to build it. But without even wondering whether they were able to firm them up and finish the picture. Because you forgot to go on, with them and to stay with them so as to guide their hands, what perhaps was supposed to be a masterpiece will never be anything more than a lousy amateur's daubing.

She stops breathless, very red-faced and somewhat embarrassed at having gone so far. She turns slightly away from the supposed direction of the voice.

THE VOICE

Are you so much in need of the absolute? You must surely know that that goes against what I wanted to create. And that I made all of you human on purpose, so that you might always hope to reach something, even beyond your best effort. But "hope" only.

Even more gently, if that is possible.

That is what life is, for you as for them. Your life which rests only on hope. Once you have accepted that, that you decide to face up to it, maybe then you may begin to know a semblance of happiness and by that very fact a small bit of absolute.

SHE, *almost harsh.*

So you ask us to nibble gently at life, little bit by little bit, nice and easy, without hurrying. Without wondering whether one day we'll be able to swallow it all. All that I really want is one mouthful, just one! But it has to be an enormous one, and tasty when I chew it, even if after that there are to be no others. No longer to have to hesitate between each one, to hesitate stupidly while being apprehensive about the possible taste of the next.

She once again goes toward the hole,
determined, very erect, strengthened.

SHE

After that, I will be able to let myself fall without any problem and without anyone having to push me. To join you of my own free will, and not because my legs will no longer carry me, because I have lost my strength, reduced and tottering at the edge of the hole. To fall before more bitter mouthfuls come and spoil the aroma of the first.

She adds much more gently, as if it were a final prayer.

SHE

Those are the existence and the death that my whole being wished for. "Wished for," because it is already too late, isn't it? And that is why I ought to have jumped a little while ago. Before being tempted to hope, to wait resignedly like the others for the slow coming-on of old age.

THE VOICE

You lack courage. That's the only real explanation for your distress. You lack courage, courage, courage . . . (*The voice goes on repeating, obsessively, and goes off into the distance, appearing to drown in the infinite.*)

SHE, *suddenly scared, looking everywhere for the voice.*

Stop . . . Don't say that! Stop . . . but come back! Don't leave me, not now! Go on telling me, talking to me . . . please. Or else I'll be really alone!

The voice remains silent and she collapses, prostrate.

You don't know how much I need . . . I . . . *(She stops, not finding any word, repeats:)* I need . . . *(Violently, crying out.)* I don't know what it is! But I need it just as much as I need to drink, eat, and sleep.

A pause, then as if to herself.

SHE

This isn't the first time. When it came over me, I tried drinking but it wasn't thirst, eating but it wasn't hunger, sleeping, making love too. But that still was not what my being was hankering for. The demand remained within me, more imperative than anything in the world. So painful, so deep . . . inconceivable.

She adds softly, without believing it.

SHE

The need to be born, perhaps, to be born to life which I do not know.

She weeps, smoothly, without sobs. Like a child, for she has the fragility of one.

The voice, very far away, begins speaking again.

THE VOICE, *almost lovingly.*

What you needed was me.

SHE, *vigorously shaking her head.*

No, because you were there. I called you and you came to me. Always. Remember. *(A pause. She adds.)* But that was not enough.

THE VOICE, *without reproach, simply stating a fact.*

I know. Because it wasn't me you were calling, not to my arms that you were holding yours out. To those of another. Your father or another. I was only a substitute. To allow you to let yourself go . . . for a while. To a pretense of tenderness. And that is only right. Since on my own I do not exist, but only in the mind of one who believes I do.

SHE, *too surprised to go on crying.*

Yet you are the very essence of all life, the spark that engenders all of nature, the process of its eternal renewing.

No, that is not I. That would be too easy. Besides, you just named them and those exist as such, for no one ever invented anything. I am only the explanation of it all, manufactured after the fact in the imagination of men.

SHE, *panicking, desperate.*

But you're talking to me. And a little while ago, when I blamed you for creation, for your too-imperfect world, you yourself told me . . .

THE VOICE, *interrupting her without harshness.*

I answered because today you believed in me. I "am" because you believe. My voice exists, since it touches your senses and your mind, but it exists right now only in your imagination. At different moments, it converses with every human being, but it always remains subjective and ephemeral. I am but the transposition of a second yourselves, and I die each time all of you no longer need that.

SHE

I don't understand.

THE VOICE

Yet, the little I know and have been able to explain is within you, in a you still unexplored, of which you are only suspecting the importance. On it depend most of your actions. You call that the unconscious. You will still have occasions to be in touch with it, but from such a distance. My voice was merely one of those transpositions, and that is why you can't understand. Or else, it would merge with your intelligence and I don't believe that is possible.

SHE, *repeating, wild-eyed.*

I don't understand . . . I don't understand. (*She is livid, and, without realizing it, has gotten much closer to the hole. Now, she is at its very edge.*)

THE VOICE, *human for the first time, abandoning its almost-unreal gentleness.*

You have no right to fall, not now. And you know it.

SHE, *as if sleepwalking.*

I don't understand . . . I don't . . . *(With a sudden start, but her eyes still feverish.)* And I don't want to understand. Since I can never reach you, at least let me reach peace, Peace, PEACE! *(She has jumped, with a final cry which grows dimmer and soon gives way to a deep silence.)*

Nothing moves on the stage. Only the hole has closed, noiselessly, and one no longer even knows where it was. Everything seems to be over when the voice resumes, one last time.

THE VOICE, *very gentle again, without any irony.*

You forgot that this was only a dream. The struggle is not over. It begins again now, even as you are waking up and I am going off to sleep. To be silent at last. And there will be a little peace anyhow: when I have completely disappeared in the first mists of the morning, to reappear again only the next time you are asleep.

"Archi-Duc"

THE END

November 25, 1972

Letter to X.

I am writing with this tiny little hunk of pencil that I was using to doodle with while I was waiting for you, just now. I couldn't find anything else to trace these few lines with, these few words with which I would so like to be able to make up a fine love poem. Alas, I don't have the talent for that. And how to explain what I am feeling here, right now? You have just closed the door behind you and I didn't even get to say *au revoir*. Rolled up in my warmth and the covers, I didn't dare move, for fear of breaking that feeling that is so sweet and so painful at the same time: the feeling of belonging to you completely. And never to be able to more so than a few moments ago, when you made love to me, when my whole being vibrated to the tiniest impulses of your body, to the slightest beginning of a caress, to the mere movement that let me hope for one. Yet you took me no differently from usual. And you certainly didn't feel that "something" new which was what made me want to cry.

I did cry, anyway. Cried those tears that are the most agonizing, because they are entirely internal, without drops and without sobs. And that seem then to tear up your chest and can only stay inside you, without escape anywhere.

Because of a tenderness I must have imagined, a new warmth of your body upon mine, a sweeter penetration, which turned an instant into a wonderful moment.

The revelation perhaps of a true love, of the offer, without restriction, of all of my being to yours? of surrender.

What you have no way of knowing is that this is the first time I have felt this. For the first time I came into your arms allowing myself to go to the very fulfillment of my pleasure.

I loved you, simple as that, was able to love you like a lover, and all that on top of my love.

"Pigalle"

THE END

December 4, 1972

What idiocies I've already written in this notebook! And here I am tonight with pen in hand again, after only yesterday having sworn to myself that I would no longer let myself indulge in this belated adolescent crisis.

I've let Marc read a few passages of it. And he was the one who compared them to the torments of pubescent girls. He also who was first to concede that, if I was going through them now, it was perhaps because when I was sixteen, behind disinfected bars, I had not been able to grow up normally.

I know it all so well! Just as I know I too often use it as an excuse. For my weaknesses, my weekly lack of will power. I rest upon that past suffering, which so easily in my eyes becomes the explanation for all my shortcomings. Especially the one that was, as it is most difficult for me to conceive, a purely "gratuitous" suffering. Caused exclusively by myself.

But isn't that after all what always happens, and for anybody? Aren't we ourselves always the ones to whom we owe our hurts, in our manner of filtering events, receiving them, so they can best affect us? Even when other people are involved. Merely because we have our sensitivity open to all emotion.

Am I stating it badly? That's getting to be a habit! And it matters so little, after all.

If I felt like writing tonight, before going to sleep, it was first of all on a very specific subject. On something which, when it happened, scared me a little. To realize that a little nothing was enough to make me lose control of myself, to have felt myself literally at the limit of "self-control" [word in English].

Tonight. At the Archi-Duc. Across from J., with his *pastis* in his hand, standing next to my barstool, raising his glass laughingly at I can't remember what joke.

Then the hurt, yes, that something that makes it impossible for you to breathe without pain, a yen to cry, a bitter taste between gritted teeth, at the same time as a repressed anger, a sudden need to externalize a deep suffering in a cry or a gesture.

The glass, at the level of my eyes, his smile right at the edge of the yellowish liquid, and the urge to make the inconsiderate gesture, to strike, to grab the glass and dash it to the ground.

Idiotic. Completely! Bad literature, I was about to say. Perhaps at the very limit, at times like that, we watch ourselves acting or thinking and then some ill-digested readings come back up to the surface and . . . Pseudo-romantic readings! And all so terribly true, just the same, at the moment.

My jaws that I felt closing so hard, so tightly, to contain the impulse, to hold back the tears as well, or the outcry.

There, that's all! After that I left, I couldn't do anything else. To get swallowed up in the Métro, escaping from the beating rain, to walk very fast, not listening to his steps, behind, which must be following.

To sit down. Hoping against hope, and resenting that I hoped, for his presence next to me on the bench. Then his unclear outline edging into the corner of my eye, at the limit of my field of vision, because unable to look him in the face.

Words. Let out, like that, without seeming really to have a meaning, so far away from the deep truth which was twisting my stomach all at the same time.

The Métro, at last. The intentionally different compartments. The brief idea, perceived for an instant, of childish behavior. The fugitive reminiscence of childhood quarrels. The desire almost to smile, not to take seriously these few minutes of life which perhaps might be considered, later on, only as a simple parenthesis.

Then the steps up, the outside, again, but this time right in front, barely three paces away, his back turned, undecipherable.

The hurt, again. The tearing, inside, that burns so.

A sidelong glance, a last impulse, this one dominated too. The one to throw oneself into his arms, to mumble apologies, to accept everything, whatever it might be, from the other with a smile.

And then I had already turned left, knowing that he would not follow, that it was not his direction. It was too late.

And he, what had he lived through during those few minutes? Perhaps absolutely nothing corresponding to what I had felt?

The burning, ever a little deeper. And then the comforting and tender sound of some music, the accompaniment of a guitar at first far away and nostalgic, at the other end of the hall.

The imperative need then to hang on to that for a few instants, to accept its human warmth and its refuge.

A tall blond fellow who was singing, an unknown voice but a warm one made to pacify. I sat down on the floor. And little by little I felt the sorrow easing off, the burning seeming less sharp and burrowing away somewhere inside of me where I was able quietly to start putting it to sleep.

Hope. Tomorrow was so close. Tomorrow when maybe he . . .

Why write all this, now? It doesn't mean a thing. But I realize to what an extent it liberates me, purges me, a little like confession.

I am only afraid of continuing to take myself too seriously. I'm sure of it, as a matter of fact. And I always have.

So I just promised myself, sitting on the floor, in among the cigarette butts, the bits of punched tickets and the drafts of air, not to attach too much importance to things. To try pushing the buttons, to open myself out, at last, to look "outward." In the middle of all those strangers passing by whose feet I saw first, before I raised my head.

I feel better. I'll make it . . . someday!

"Pigalle"

THE END

December 1972

Here I am! In my room, barely five minutes after having left you. You could feel reassured!

J. . . . I said this to you at B.'s but I feel the need to say to you again: forgive me. For having cracked up before you, not having been able to keep myself from crying when I detest that kind of weakness and usually always succeed in controlling myself. I was too tired!

When you were drinking at the bar I had already gone to lie down in the back room in order to get rid of stomach cramps that were too persistent. I was washed out but was too eager to spend two hours with you to mention them to you. I should have, nothing would have happened!

S . . . That's not what I wanted to write. I would just like to carry on a real conversation with you, without recourse to paper and pen. To feel your presence. The illusion this way can only be imperfect but at least I am pushing back the moment when I will find myself alone with myself and the memory of this evening.

I would like . . . to ask you not to walk out on me, not right away, not . . . now. That would be worse, you know. I can no longer conceive of it. I can no longer imagine my current life without you, without thinking of you, without your presence, one of your kisses or your hand on my shoulder.

So . . . Don't take this away from me unless it be to relieve yourself of all responsibilities for my fits of the blues. Don't do it, unless it were to be for you a true relief, a true desire. I beg you and hate myself for begging you like this, without any start of dignity but . . . I don't know how I could go on with what I've just barely started in my life, in class, among my friends, to find a semblance of balance, if I had suddenly to block you out of my thoughts and I am not asking you to assume any of those responsibilities toward me that you are so wary of . . .

I don't know what to say beyond that. I would like to be able to tell you the extent to which you have become indispensable to me but I also know the fear you feel, the uneasiness, faced with such a feeling.

I am so sure I love you . . . totally, being far from the mere egotistical feeling you seem to imagine. You understand . . . I know what it means to hang on to a being without loving him since I did it for more than a year with R. I can compare . . . and that's not the way I was! My being did not vibrate at contact with him as it does with you; I did not feel this tenderness and this need to impart it to him, always and forever, without ever being sated. I could let my body go in a certain degree of pleasure, of course; physical desire sometimes came over me. But never this mad pleasure, untranslatable and almost unbearable, that I have known with you; it's so different! I am for the first time giving myself totally to a human being, to you, and it is through this total gift of myself to the you whom I love that I accede to this pleasure. Isn't this love? But then what is it!?

I feel myself now accepting you entirely, as the man I already know, the one I am only discovering and even the one I don't yet know but accept in advance. For this is no longer a simple "carnal" desire, it has become

. . . a "whole." No more disgust possible, no sudden revulsion . . . I accept you, fully, entirely, tired, sick, fat or not fat, the way you are. Do you understand? I despair a little of ever being able to translate into words what I am feeling. But do you understand just the same . . . a little bit?

I was saying: I accept you, as you are, so will also succeed in accepting your behavior, in our relations as in other things. I am still lacking a certain amount of stability, a little of the strength to do it, as this evening. But I'll succeed in changing, surely. In no longer going against your wishes to be alone, in considering normal the sawtooth course of our strange affair, your intermittent desires, if I am sure that they really do exist. If I am sure that in a sense you are fond of me. Then I will be there when you want and will be able to wait. I promise you. Weren't things better this week already? Only because of the fatigue, just too much, and the cold did I let myself go. It won't happen again. I accept, if you still wish it, and only if you do wish it, of course; and perhaps it can all be wonderful just the same. Right?

This is too stupid! I almost feel as though I'm asking you to do me a favor and don't like to show myself in such an aspect of humility! I am so convinced that I am unable to retain anyone's "*enduring*" affection, attachment or attention. I know myself too well! And then I say to myself that just the same there had to be something that kept you with me for our affair to have endured until now and that comforts me a little. Or else . . . maybe you were too lazy a man to look elsewhere and were just satisfied to keep what was comfortably at hand? It hurts me and that's too bad. It's my own fault. I too am lacking a kind of courage. We're even, anyway!

My eyes are closing, I am no longer seeing what I'm writing. Am I even really writing? Everything seems so strange to me, tonight, hazy, perhaps I'm dreaming and tomorrow I would be able to forget all of this. I hope so . . . so hard!

These poor words so badly translate all that I am feeling! It's enough to drive one to despair.

Only one last time: you still do want me a little, you're willing, aren't you, J.? Tell me so . . . quick, very quick . . . I'm waiting, squeezing you very hard against me.

You know . . . I love you perhaps as much as my father and that's more than I would ever be able to say about it to anyone . . .

. . . Marie-Jo

"Pigalle"

703

1973
Paris, 19 years old

January 25, 1973

My good old Dad,

It's been days and days now that I've been trying in vain to write you, without succeeding. The words don't come, the sentences get lamentably mixed up and I end up quitting right after the first few lines.

I can't go on anymore, Dad. That's a terrible thing to say, to confess, and especially to you. Everything seems to me in a nightmare to be beginning again the way it did two years ago. I find myself again at the same static, negative point, after a brief, ephemeral period of blossoming.

Anxieties coming from everywhere and nowhere, the progressive inability to relax, to let myself be "me" among others, my inability especially to shake this new wall, these new blinders which suddenly, or perhaps insidiously, without my being able to feel it coming on, have once again separated me from a certain everyday reality and from practically everybody.

But why, for goodness' sake, why?? . . . ! Really, by now, I ought certainly to know the recipe, the antidote to all my fantasies! That antidote which for two years, day by day, I was patiently taught to record, to practice, in the hope that it might remain forever in some small corner of my brain, right nearby, and that at the slightest alert the trigger would be tripped and help me in overcoming any new onset of nightmare.

So? . . . All that for nothing, really? For me to have forgotten it, in spite of all the trouble it took for me to get it, or that, more precisely, after a year of application, it already prove ineffective?

When I think of it, Dad, I grit my teeth, close my fists and punch, randomly, against the wall, the wardrobe or on my pillow.

That's all "cheap dramatics," I know, amateur playacting, and especially expressed that way. But I can't get rid of this anger, or of my powerlessness in face of a self I am unable to understand, get tired of understanding and despair of ever controlling.

A great fatigue, as well. In an idiotic struggle that no one appears to be able to imagine, all too real to me, but exclusively in my own mind.

Dad, if you could . . . But no, you have no magic wand, of course, you never did have and not even in those first moments when I would most have needed it.

It's not your fault, it's . . . one being's unadaptability to life as it seems to be lived by everyone else. It's . . .

It gets all mixed up, as usual. Maybe even more so tonight because I can't keep from crying. From feeling sorry for myself, as you say! But what about when one can't do anything else?

I've been looking for . . . a good ten years now, for the recipe that would finally allow me to live normally, for the road to take to free myself from all that's holding me back. I had the impression I was running, till I lost my breath, and I just stayed in one place, lamentably! Oh and then . . . What good explaining! I'm angry at myself for bringing you this added trouble, when all I want is for your life to be one gigantic sunshine and that a little of that sunshine come to you from me.

A dream too, but this one wonderful. A dream I hang on to desperately on evenings of crisis and despair. A dream filled with the confidence you might have in me, of a pride, so tiny, you might feel in me. A dream in which I would be your little girl, just that, facing you, without any image from the past coming stealthily between us.

But that dream is idiotic! I end up wanting to believe in it too much and new disillusionments just become bitterer. Time going by becomes so many barriers between it and me, and already we no longer have "our" house.

I should have started a lot sooner, when I was still under your wing. Taken advantage of the extraordinary chance offered me by life alongside you. I let it get away. I did nothing, or so little, to discover you, and that is what I will never forgive myself for.

Yet I was living near you full of curiosity about you, of desire to go ever deeper in order to find the man, beyond my father whom I adored and defied, out of necessity. I might have; all the circumstances appeared to come together to allow me to do it. And I remained enclosed in my own problems, my phobias, finally spending the last two years of my childhood behind a barrier of medical histories and white gowns.

I'm weeping over it, Dad. Twenty a month from now, to the day, and twenty years of a black hole filling my memory, or worse, memories marked by maman in an indelible way. No place in them for you! Except at brief intervals perhaps, but too brief for them not to seem to me now almost unreal.

Do you understand why I am hurting? What I have retained of you, in my past? A single, a unique moment of happiness: our vacations at Bürgenstock. I hang on to that desperately, as if in the end it might wipe away all the others.

I don't want to speak about it again and I must especially not try to relate it. All I need to do is feel the gold ring on my finger, which since then has never left me.

But did you already think of it, Dad? In your angers that reproached me for my coldness, my possible lack of love. Did you really never think of it? I was little at the time, then later tending to be dreamy, disorderly. But I never lost it, will never be able to lose it. To me, it's . . . an amazing taste of sunshine and coolness in my mouth, a sign of love and I was about to say a certain purity. Will you think of that, someday, Dad?

I should not be writing all this. One should not want to try to express things that, while very simple, nevertheless on paper become almost immodest.

THE END

May 22, 1973

My big Dad,

Right now I am in the optician's waiting room for the second fitting of my contact lenses. It will last three hours and, having nothing else to do, I'm using the time to write you.

I didn't get to finish the list I told you I started last week. As usual because on reading it I notice that everything is much too mixed up and poorly expresses my deeper thoughts.

I prefer starting another, even if I fall into the same excess.

I have just spent two calm, quiet days at Marc's with Bou-Boule, resting and taking advantage of the country for a weekend. With the desire to stabilize myself, to continue reinforcing my equilibrium and my health, that were so precarious at Christmas.

I've resumed my activities. Monday, that is yesterday, rehearsals at class, my calls at the prefecture for my work permit, appointments with the dentist or others.

All this in the hope of improving myself, of soon feeling myself "like new," without any kind of little problems. It's long, and hard, I've already written you that, and a painful feeling of loneliness weighs on me sometimes. Only I say to myself that this is necessary, take a deep breath and start off again toward the conquest of a new self, which seems so reticent at the idea of coming out. I also discover that I have abilities I was unaware of, try to use them to the maximum and to lean on them. To give myself confidence in myself.

I think of you often. That gives me courage. The determination you showed throughout your existence in building something with your own hands, in never allowing yourself any weakness toward yourself. I'm getting a later start, under obviously different conditions, which ought to be easier; perhaps I will achieve a result even if it is long in coming? I am applying myself to it as you see to the utmost, for the first time with so much will power. I am becoming more demanding in my way of life, allow myself many less indulgences.

I have the disagreeable and wonderful impression at the same time of "molting," of renewing my skin, of gradually sloughing off the old one to make way for a new, finer one.

What results is an immediate discomfort that is slightly painful, confronting the questions that suddenly loom before me without my being able to answer them as yet. An uncertainty. A fear of becoming just what I wouldn't want to be, of not using what I have that is most valuable and, on the contrary, what I don't much like about my person. For my behavior sometimes surprises me, facing certain small everyday events. I have trouble relating them to me. They surprise me and I then reject them while ordering myself to take a different attitude, which I believe better. Only . . . if that is to go against my own self, must I still force myself to it? It's disconcerting . . . I am "looking for" myself with the fear that I will discover myself! We spend a whole life "finding" ourselves, don't we? And yet, can we really look back at ourselves at a certain age with the satisfaction of having completed a few well-determined stages? I hope so. As you wrote so well: the profession of man is a hard one. That's a sentence I must never forget.

I'm talking idiocies, am I not? What's more, I'm not very clearly seeing what I'm writing, because my contact lenses still aren't quite adjusted to my vision. The fitting won't be over for another two hours and, since the weather is nice, I'll use the time to go strolling outdoors, watching the passers-by, something I rarely do because I don't see clearly.

I love you, my Dad, and I rejoice at the idea that I will be seeing you soon, with vacation approaching, like a big and perhaps finally smiling, relaxed girl.

I hug you tightly to me so as to become imbued with all your tenderness . . .

your little

Marie-Jo

Friday, June 15, 1973

My big old Dad,

I'm writing you from a funny place: in the parking garage on Rue du Colisée, across from Marc's office, after midnight. Very funny, isn't it? I'm waiting for them to go back out to Poigny and spend a quiet weekend before the extra-heavy week ahead of me starting Monday.

I did not get discouraged, as you are going to see, and set myself uninterruptedly to work on my famous scene from [Jean-Paul Sartre's] *Dirty Hands,* in preparation for the competition that I then *perhaps* (?) hope still to be accepted for. I'll know that Wednesday morning, after the elimination audition that will take place Tuesday night. I've got my fingers crossed, but I think that at any rate, whatever the result, the main thing will be to have done my best, in full conscientiousness toward myself.

I've gone on, since my last letter, with that difficult struggle against the undisciplined and "lost" Marie-Jo that you have known most often. She is gradually beginning to quiet down, even if that sometimes requires a great effort on my part. I am at last convinced that one day I'll win out. That one day I'll be able finally to forget that lost adolescent girl, landing in Paris at seven o'clock one October morning, almost two years ago now, having broken with life, her family, having broken with any semblance of reality. Unable to open her eyes a little and find her way on her own through this jungle even the simplest laws of which escaped her completely. I must become an "adult," it's about time, and am doing my best to.

Marc's film will no doubt help me a great deal. For a month I will have a chance to follow the calling that fascinates me, or, rather, to learn it, from its a.b.c., under conditions that put all the trumps in my hand, as well as a few small responsibilities. I'm not far short of jumping for joy! I am quite determined to make the most of this month of August!

Wow! It really smells stuffy in this garage. I am sitting at the wheel of the car, the paper on my knees, Bob Dylan is mutedly singing on the mini-cassette and I'm still waiting for Marc and Mylène, who went off to dinner and forgot to leave me the address of the restaurant.

That doesn't matter. I'm quite comfortable just the same, in the intimacy of the words I am sharing with you and this music that is enveloping us both, very softly.

I may telephone you before you get this letter, Tuesday probably. I nevertheless wanted this little tête-à-tête because I know the importance you attach to them and the consideration they represent in your eyes. For me too. I am only in a hurry for them not to take place any longer in writing but face to face.

In the meantime I hug you tightly to me, harder if that's possible than all the previous times . . .

Your little

Marie-Jo

Thursday, July 5, 1973

My big old Dad,

I'm writing you from my little café, the unchanging Archi-Duc, where I rarely set foot anymore. That's why I wanted to get back into its atmosphere a little, without feeling myself a part of it any longer.

Many things have come to pass in a week, many things I no longer thought could happen these days.

The competition, that I talked to you about on the phone, then the audition at the Théâtre Antoine Saturday afternoon first, later Tuesday evening, which did not give me complete satisfaction since another girl, at the last minute, got the part instead of me. That doesn't matter. I am conscious of having "put up a good fight," and you can't have everything at once.

The most important thing happened last night, on Chabrol's shooting, where I celebrated my baptism of floodlights, other spotlights, and movie camera. With an adorable crew and in a delightfully relaxed atmosphere.

I had terrible stage fright, as you can imagine, and am waiting to see the rushes to be able to say I am fully satisfied with my brief appearance as a soubrette, at the door of my "cathouse." Just because it is brief is no reason for it not to be good, and I find it hard to imagine how I must come out on film. We'll see. The three days in August will be more exciting, since I'll be in the center of a huge squabble among Maurice Gerrel, Fabio Testi, and Vivianne Romance, whom you used to know at Cannes, it seems.

There it is, my Dad. I expect to make a hop next week to Valmont, to kiss you and smell the odor of your pipe, which I miss.

I love you, very, very much . . .

. . . your little

Marie-Jo
"Archi-Duc"

September 16, 1973

My big Dad,

I'm taking time to write you at last, taking advantage of this sunny Sunday afternoon, when I'm lazing on a café terrace on the Champs-Elysées while waiting for the 5:00 PM movie show.

I feel a bit lonesome, my best pal being busy elsewhere today, and I'm trying really gently to fill up this day while avoiding too much melancholy. For I miss that wonderful vacation I just had, the rough mountains of the Cévennes and its sharp air, the atmosphere on the set, feverish or relaxed but always fascinating.

How many things I saw and learned! And I hope to keep them sufficiently intact in memory so as to be able to call on them later when necessary for my work.

I was happy, I think, truly, and for the first time in a sustained discipline. A little lonely, yes, as always, as now. Lonely among the others because of having no one beside me to love. Maybe that will come someday and I just have to accept for now living my own life, for "myself," without being able to share it.

Where was I? At my return to Paris, my professional contacts. I wrote to Lecoq, am expecting his answer next week, when I will also go to see Lee Strasberg's assistant so as to compare their two methods and determine which is the more likely to toughen me up for the profession.

The sun is beating down in spite of a small breeze, I am in the process of digesting and find myself dozing off over my sheet of paper.

It's good, the hot air on one's skin, all the passers-by who are so fascinating to observe, very different one from the other, in the way they walk, the way they carry their heads, their smiles or their frowns. It's amusing. You played this game before me and it followed into your novels. This is also the best schooling for me, when I will be obliged to understand them before I am able to portray them.

That's it, Dad. Soon time for the film, a few more gulps of Coca-Cola and the end of these lazily filled pages. I didn't write anything very intelligent but . . . isn't it better that way? I let my being relax alongside you, almost in your arms, leaving my problems for later on.

I love you, my Dad, very . . . very much. It's good to be alive today, maybe tomorrow too, soon in Lausanne as well.

A thousand Yum-Yums . . .

Marie-Jo

October 7, 1973

My big Dad,

This time I'm writing you from a big brasserie near the Etoile while waiting again for movie time. Every Sunday I take advantage of it now, when it's not on weekdays, in my free moments. The more pictures I see the more other ones I want to see and it's becoming a veritable passion. I didn't know before that I had such a yen for film, but . . . It's a good sign, isn't it? And besides . . . I've already attended three of Voutsines's courses this week, with increasing enthusiasm as I went on finding Stanislavski and Strasberg at the root of his teaching. Anyway, I was accepted right away as a pupil, after having gone up on the stage with two or three "new ones" like me, and worked the exercise called "sense memory," which you must be familiar with. He told me it was "very, very good" [quote in English], and that he was surprised to see how the very first time I was able to follow my "object" step by step, without getting ahead of myself, letting myself be carried by my imagination. A good start, as you see, in which no panic or anxiety interfered with my concentration. I'm beginning to know how to relax since last summer and that's what is most important to me right now: no longer to undergo events but to control them, while taking my time. With "discipline"!

I'll let you smile over that last word, because I've taken my time getting around to it, haven't I? It's not perfect yet but I feel that I organize my days much better and by the same token find I have a much greater receptivity toward life.

So, Dad [words in English] . . . I spent three wonderful days with you, last week, and I wanted to write you that. I felt myself very close, in full mutual confidence, and the fact that you let me listen to part of your recording touched me a great deal. Especially what you said on it. Next time

I'll try to wear a dress when I come and see you and leave my ever-present blue jeans in Paris. Maybe that way I'll have the illusion of again becoming the little girl who hung onto your arm to go dancing?

I love you, my Dad, so deeply that I would never be able to express it fully. You are a wonderful father, you know, the kind thousands of little girls must dream of having. And I have you, I'm lucky, and it's as your little girl that I snuggle right up against you as I say to you, till soon . . .

. . . Marie-Jo

October 27, 1973

My big Dad,

It's not Sunday but only Saturday, and still I feel the need to write you, perhaps because I'd organized my free day at the movies, without waiting for tomorrow, and that that now is associated with a short intimate moment in your company.

Contrary to other times too, this is not afternoon but already my usual bedtime: 10:00 P.M.

I still have before my eyes images of the film I have just seen, as extraordinary in its form as in its content: *The Master and Marguerite* by Alexsander Petrovic, in which Ugo Tognazzi acts with rare truth and finesse.

I was in a hurry to get up this morning. As soon as I was dressed I rushed to the nearest news kiosk to get . . . a great disappointment! On account of the strikes, the magazine *Grazia* had not come in and I will have to wait until Tuesday before being able to read the article about me that is in it. I'm telling you this with a wink: don't forget to buy the issue dated "October 26," in which you will be able to admire your daughter! . . . (hmm!)

Apart from that . . . a somewhat upsetting week, full of joy as well, which allowed me to see C. again during some long evenings, he being in Paris for a week.

An agreeable surprise, with nevertheless a slight bitter aftertaste, for it obliged me to go back to too many memories I had thought erased.

And then . . . it somewhat shook up the new structure of my life, my almost too well established "discipline," my set schedules. Made me also more powerfully feel the loneliness in which I have taken refuge since last summer and, although knowing it is necessary, temporarily, brought me a sudden nostalgia for neglected contacts.

It also led me to "take my bearings again," and from that I now better

712

understand my present attitude. Why I felt this need to sweep away everything around me so as to start clean, even though that meant I would be without external supports. I believe I am looking for a "central kernel," a consolidation of my being in which, as in a building, carefully, stone by stone, I try to raise myself on solid and independent bases. Toward what . . . ? Toward the sun, way up there in the sky, or toward a few terrifying clouds heavy with rain? I have no way of knowing. But at least, if I apply myself conscientiously to the scaffolding, I will better be able to withstand eventual rough weather.

I am going through a period I know is transitory, but which is necessary for me to reach . . . "something else," something fuller, richer, and which, without this stage, I would not be up to living through intensely.

I have the feeling I'm "hibernating," not in my work, which remains active, but in my relationships with those around me, so succinct that they thereby become almost nonexistent.

There it is! Many, many silly things, for you, my poor Dad, who are going to try to read them through to the end. This will not be my "best" letter, as you so kindly defined the last one, but . . . they are at least a few confidences, a few questions asked in my life that I am happy to share with you.

I have confidence, you know. That's quite new for me and surprising, but I believe I am beginning to see how to go about my "little way in life," doing the best I can. And, I do believe, if for a moment I stop to ask myself: "WHY?" a fleeting ray of sunshine or your image in my mind will be enough to allow me, with a shrug of the shoulders, to set out again with the idea of taking upon myself to see it through, out of simple loyalty to myself.

I love you, Dad, I would love to live near you through all kinds of wonderful moments, to see again more often in your eyes that tenderness and that warmth which would warm my whole being. You have so many things to teach me . . . When will I have the time to take them in?

This little movement of my hand over your forehead, as a caress . . .
your little

Marie-Jo

November 15, 1973

My big Dad,

I'm writing you today from Marc's office, in a somewhat excited atmosphere because tonight we are going to the premiere of Guy Bedos and

Sophie Daumier. Marc is thinking about his tux, Mylène about her evening gown, me . . . about my jeans!

No! The atmosphere is mostly somewhat unusual, because we had to have a picnic in the cutting room, transformed for the occasion into a refectory. The wholesalers' strike, of course, and no restaurant open, even on the Champs! So, since we had no desire to fast! . . .

You must be wondering if I'm not slighting my work with all of this. Don't worry! [In English.] I'm continuing my classes very dutifully and starting dance again next week, to limber up a little.

Because . . . I have a big piece of news for you: tomorrow I'm signing a contract for the Granier-Deferre film. Six to ten days of shooting, between December 28 and January 16, two or three scenes with Alain Delon himself! Enough truly to "launch" me, if I prove up to it, and that is why I plan to force myself for a month to follow a preparatory "training program" so as to be in top shape. Final exception tonight, when I will probably get to bed somewhat late, then, after that, and until I hear the word "speed," "discipline," "discipline," "discipline"! I really want to give myself every advantage this time!

That's it, my Dad. Perhaps I may also get, in between, something in the film of Michel Audiard, whom I met personally yesterday. But on that score, nothing definite yet. We'll see.

There's more and more noise around me now and I have to hurry and go change for tonight.

I kiss you "on the run" but always with the same tenderness.

Your little

Marie-Jo

November 23, 1973

My big Dad,

I'm writing you again from Marc's office, where I am quieter today, with less commotion than last week.

I've just come back from class, which lasted almost five hours, but without a single minute of boredom. It's really fascinating!

I am going full-out with my "discipline," right now, and immediately feel more relaxed. That's the best remedy for that excessive tension I was under not so long ago, and didn't as yet know how to control. The thing is that I not only have to be in shape for the Granier-Deferre picture, but before that, on December 13, for a day's work with Chabrol, who is hiring me again for a TV drama. And this time I will have to carry it off in a little three- or four-minute scene, exactly twenty-four lines of dialogue. What makes me happiest is to see that a director, who already used me, last summer, considers me good enough to play a larger part. That gives me renewed confidence in myself, with the desire to go quickly from progress to progress, through hard work. Finally, the contract pays 600 francs "net," which is enormous for TV. Meaning that Bébors, my "agent," now feels I can command more than the union scale: 350 francs.

And then . . . I'm supposed to make some tests Tuesday or Wednesday for another TV serial, for consideration for one of the leads. If that works out, and I take it, it will have me working steadily from January 16 (end of the Granier-Deferre schedule) to the beginning of April.

But none of that is set yet and I'll give you news of it as soon as possible. Apart from that . . . well, I went back to dance yesterday afternoon and today I am completely stiff!

I made prudently sure to join the beginners' classes, but I now see how rusty I am and will have to suffer for a while yet before getting back to being as limber as I was at fifteen.

That's it. This is all (and a lot, I believe) for this little conversation, my Dad. Thanks for your wire but I confess I am impatiently awaiting a letter in which you might talk to me at greater length. As far as paying for the dancing classes, I'll make arrangements directly with Aitken, if you agree, of course.

How I wish I didn't have to talk to you about that, especially just before telling you that I always think of you very much, and that it is often your presence in my mind that supports me in my professional endeavors.

I love you, my Dad, perhaps even more deeply as I grow up and try to become an adult in my turn. It's hard but . . . you made it all right, didn't you?

With all my tenderness in a great big YUM-YUM . . .
your little

Marie-Jo

December 21, 1973

My big Dad,

A long letter will follow, soon, but I absolutely wanted to drop you a line for Christmas. I still think of you just as much, Dad, and I'm afraid that if I keep telling you that you'll grow tired of it. Fortunately this remains only thoughts and they can't all reach you there, because then how I'd take you over would be something else!

On this Christmas Day I would like you to know that, in spite of the distance, I will tell you of all my tenderness and all the happiness, truly, all the wonderful sundrenched things I wish you to live through next year. Maybe I'll be able to bring you some of them myself? I don't know yet how I'll find them. I'll try . . . as hard as possible. To have the feeling I deserve you, my Dad.

I love you, don't know how to write it anymore, would like to repeat it to you infinitely. At the same time I know that one must never say it too much, just whisper it, so that one's mouth can be filled with all the savor of those words as it pronounces them. So I whisper it to you, say it to you very softly, don't even say it to you but allow this love to quiver somewhere within me, to slip into a look from my eyes into your eyes. In a caress of my hand on your shoulder. In the contact of this pen with this paper. Seizable only by you.

And a kiss on your brow, my Dad, for you whom I would like always to keep as I saw you in my childhood.

I lov . . . No! Nothing more. I don't want to write anything else that might, through words, tarnish what I feel.

Christmas has become a commercial celebration, without soul, pumped up by advertising.

The real Christmas is the one that lives in me when I hold you in my arms . . .

. . . your little girl

Marie-Jo

December 1973

My Dad,

There now. A poor year-end with an even poorer balance sheet. Very few things accomplished in these twelve months of existence.

Words, here, nothing but words, words that I begin to hate because they escape from me and I have the feeling I no longer know how to handle them. No longer the way I used to. Was it an illusion, then, or did I really succeed in making them live a little? Doubtless they expressed more faithfully than today my emotion or my realizations of things.

I took stock, a little while ago. That is to say, I put some music on, thinking I would dream, escape for a moment into sweet nostalgia. I was not able to let myself go. I suddenly felt the full weight of all the tension in my being, the latent anxiety that grips it and that I anesthetize day by day. I projected myself into the coming week and saw myself lowering my arms before you. Because I have no energy left. I find myself, after a year, like a puppet whose mechanism someone forgot to wind up and who, in a pose that is grotesque for being so uncomfortable, is suspended in mid-movement.

What was I trying to write, exactly? My pen doesn't work with my ideas either anymore. I find it hard to move it forward and the sentence it traces, at the instant it traces it, has already become foreign to me, as if dead on the blank page.

So I was saying: balance sheet at year-end: almost zero. That, at least, allowing for the "almost," is clean and precise. I have not made any progress in my attempts at being an actress and worked little or not at all at my classes.

For the past two months I've been circling myself, sniffing at myself, nauseating myself by continually smelling my own odor and thereby forgetting what the slightest other smell is like. Maybe, in the long run, it is a pleasure to destroy myself this way in a few seconds of thoughts and then to spend hours, after that, weeks or a year, in pasting the pieces together again. At any rate it keeps me busy. It hardly leaves me time to do anything else. And it always brings me back to the same spot, to the same lame picture of my personality which needs only a draft of air to scatter it all about again.

To say that I'm fed up with it is saying little. To say that I am conscious of indulging myself in a certain kind of self-destruction is quite true. To say that I have the means of undertaking other measures in my life would no doubt also be accurate but only by adding that I have not yet found them.

The proof! At the very most I just suspect them. And what makes me furious, really, is to feel that I am capable of going straight ahead when I am zigzagging and bumping into the wall! A question of balance.

March 1, 1974

Oh how lone it is tonight
To be walking home again
In the deep dark of the night
To my old familiar pen.

No one waiting for me there,
Nor anyone for whom to care.
Music to be listened to,
Music for me to be rocked to,
A god refound again, who
Is the only one I talk to.

I should have grown accustomed to
This old skin I drag around,
At least be able to make it do,
Forgetting how it gets me down.

Oh how lone it is tonight.
What if I were to change my tone,
Escape the darkness of the night
And find an "elsewhere" of my own?

With someone waiting for me there,
Someone for whom I could care,
Someone to be listened to,
Someone who would rock me too,
A love discovered that is new
And I could merge myself into.

But then how can I ever shed
This old skin that I drag around?
Since it and I are forever wed
I'll have to keep it for my own!

Oh how lone it is tonight.
Lone will be tomorrow too.
I had hoped for hope in sight
But lost it. Now what can I do?

"Montparnasse"

THE END

April 19, 1974

My big Dad,

Long time since I wrote you, isn't it? It was better, I think. It allowed me to forget the last idiocies I sent you pompously committed to paper.

How anxious I am to read your "book." I'm dying of curiosity and impatiently awaiting the first proofs. I am happy especially to have felt you to be in top shape at the other end of the wire, last Monday, satisfied with your revision. I once again have a "novelist Daddy" and . . . I was proud of it!

I told you on the telephone: I've thought a great deal, recently, have tried "to take stock" and make a balance sheet of my first eight months in the world of the cinema. I think it is more interesting for me this year to give up a chase after small parts and work quietly in my corner with a view to getting better.

I don't feel that I am capable yet of assuming a leading role, and just to go on "emoting" before a camera wouldn't help me much anymore. A break of a year doesn't seem too much to me. Twenty-two isn't too old an age to make a debut in a career, especially if the trumps in my hands become stronger in the meantime. It's up to me to see to that and to take the right road for it!

And then . . . (don't laugh, promise?) I would like this year to try out my abilities as a scriptwriter or author, to write on the level some stories that go beyond my usual seven or eight pages of anecdotes. To see whether I might be able to consider, later on, devoting myself to it full time. I need to, want to. Is that enough? There too I have a lot to prove to myself. There it is, my Dad. I'm not telling you about my immediate project which, I hope, will soon take shape as a scenario I'll let you read. I'd like it to come as a surprise so quickly . . . I'm saying good-bye before my pen is tempted to write you more about it.

With all my love . . .

. . . your little Marie-Jo

July 11, 1974

My big Dad,

It is 11:45 at night. I'm writing to you from the movie house I am working in, outside the doors to the auditorium, on the poorly upholstered chair for the use of the usherettes. I am waiting for the show to come to an end, that is to say, 1:00 A.M. Then, I'll still have to check to make sure nobody left any belongings behind, double-lock the emergency exits, give the ticket seller's cash to my boss after having rechecked the amount. At last, I'll go and change in the narrow little closet that is our cloakroom and, quickly, very quickly, go to bed. Work resumes again tomorrow at 1:30 P.M., with an extra late show at half past midnight . . . Oof! A tough job, thankless because looked down upon by most people and harder to do than first appears. I admire the ones among my co-workers who have been keeping at it year after year!

I was lucky, besides: there are six of us here, sharing the work in two theaters and I immediately felt that I had been accepted into the bosom of the group in a very nice way. In two weeks, when I quit, I will probably be leaving behind some real friends.

And then . . . I'm saving money. Sou by sou I've put aside more than 1,000 francs, in a wallet I keep just for that. My first driving lesson was conclusive, my instructor seems very indulgent and crazy about your books.

In a word, I am living at a new kind of rhythm, at times trying. But it forces me to follow an iron discipline and allows me each day to discover a fragment of a life I was not aware of. I find with surprise that I am avidly observing those around me, deeply absorbing the ambient atmosphere. I think less of my own little person, no longer have time for that, and by the same token feel a strange sense of relief.

I'm eager to see you again, my Dad. We'll talk all this over face to face and I'll be able to hold you tenderly in my arms . . . Soon!

I love you

your little girl

Marie-Jo

October 10, 1974

My big Dad,

I got your letter the day before yesterday but haven't found any free time in which to write you. I chase after productions, I go to my dance every evening and I try too, very timidly, "to hatch" that Christmas tale of mine.

Anyway . . . here I am in front of this sheet, all yours, ready to answer you. With my pen. That really is a lot more practical than dipping my finger in ink.

Your reproaches hurt me. I don't think I deserve them. I was deeply upset, in fact, by the news of all your problems, and filled with rage at hearing that maman was going on with her petty intrigues.

Why didn't I dare speak to you openly about that, even in writing? Perhaps by a sort of "discretion," I can't find any other words for it. Money questions are important, in life. I know that. At least I am beginning to find it out. However, it is difficult for me to judge a situation that I don't know well, in an area in which I have no competence, and to understand especially the future consequences that will result from it.

You know . . . I love you as you are, my father, alive, with your good pipe smell, the inflections of your voice, your way of taking your handkerchief out of your pocket and blowing your nose. I love you for all that you taught me or, more precisely, for what I was able to absorb, as a bad pupil. I hope I'm up to, someday, totally espousing your way of seeing Man, with that indulgence that people generally accord only to children, forgetting that at any age, deep inside oneself, one always remains a little boy. I have this somewhat bitter certainty that life is too short to allow us to mature as we should, that it is only an eclipse, and that at the end of the road we all find ourselves very far away from our aspirations. Isn't that the theme that constantly comes back in your books? That good dumb bastard of a human being who, after much travail, suddenly realizes almost by accident that he was never able to reveal himself to others and even less to himself!

I admire your ability to sniff around you, to capture the instant of "reality," devoid of any pathos, and to translate it later onto paper without setting yourself up as judge.

I love you and I admire you, now as in the past. I do not want to project myself into future situations, suffer over them in advance. Thinking of the money that your work brings you makes me gnash my teeth. That's not what is important to me. If you have some, all the better; I wish that you would always have enough to live well, comfortably. The important thing, nonetheless, is what you were able to create in millions of pages and which, for its part, will never lose its value, I am sure of it. The essential resides in the dimension of your characters, in their truth. Not in the jingling of the coins they drag around in their pockets! I am grateful to you for still helping me in my existence, for paying for my gropings in the area I have chosen. But I don't look upon that as something due me. And if, tomorrow, you found yourself obliged "to cut me off," as in your case as a young artist in Paris, I would be quite able to earn enough to buy me a camembert! That's something quickly learned, whatever people say. When there is no other possibility one adjusts without realizing it, on the spot. Anyway, there are thousands of people, around me, who get along on a hard-boiled egg a day. Why not me? My stomach is no different from theirs, so far as I know!

You see, Dad, I am ready for all the hardships and am exaggerating on purpose to prove it to you. By reserve, simply, by a very stupid reserve, I would so have preferred not to speak of all this again, of this idea of inheritance that haunts you and that, to me, is unbearable. If it were legal, feasible before a notary (and maybe it is?), I would immediately sign a renunciation of all goods I might be entitled to later on. To the advantage of Maman, for instance, if that's what she'd like, not out of charity but because I don't care! And that would prove to you that I am sincere when I tell you I love You, naked, the man, my "Dad," for the love you gave me and your advice for my adult years, for all you led me to discover, to feel, about life, by trying to hold to nothing but "pure" truths.

Let's not talk about it anymore, O.K.? Soon, very soon, I'll be earning my living; I'm going to hurry up, I'll do double duty. I will accept the facilities you tender me as long as you feel you can afford to. Someday when necessary, don't hesitate to stop them. I will go on walking; you'll see, it won't be any worse. In spite of my having one leg shorter than the other, I don't limp! So?

Just one more thing: another very simple reason had kept me from writing you sooner. I was afraid. Afraid that you would once again consider my letter to be too "literary," of an excessive romanticism, piling on sentences of prefabricated lyricism. I was afraid that you might feel it not to be very sincere, in the same way as the stories of mine that you read, and that you might not believe me.

That's it. Today, at least I won't correct a thing. I leave as they are the repetitions, the overlaps and the bad French. Too bad if my words come out "poor." I have lots and lots of tenderness in me and right to the tips of my fingers, you might feel it in a caress, but it's my fountain pen that doesn't have much. Can you hold that against it?

My Dad . . . someday, in your arms, fully the two of us, in a total comprehension one of the other and mutual trust, I will finally have "earned" my living! . . .

your little girl

Marie-Jo

November 29, 1974

"Essay on Anxiety"

One o'clock in the morning. Muted music, at floor level, this notebook on the floor too and me lying on my belly on it. Only the little lamp in the corner behind the loudspeaker, on the carpet, gives me light. The radiator, in the other corner, gives off its heat . . . that ought to be enough and yet . . .

Anxiety is there, incessantly present. She fills the whole room, she spreads over the walls, she rises within me with the passing hours. She is stifling me. Even though she has for long been part of my daily life I still can't get used to her. And every time I come home, when as I open the door she invites me to share her loneliness, I am seized with a desire to flee.

Would it not be enough to turn my back, to lock the door again and melt away outside in the darkness of the streets? No, of course not. Since, by all evidence, I carry her away with me; she follows me everywhere, like a faithful companion.

She is in my belly, she is in my head, she has taken over a being and, at home, in the evening, she simply is the first one to come in through the keyhole. That is why I at first think she is waiting for me, that she never leaves the room. She slips in through the hole just ahead of me, wafted on a draft of air and, in the same way, when I leave, slips out on my heels.

· · ·

1:00 A.M. Music at floor level, my notebook on the floor and, on top of it, my body lying on my belly. A little light: the little lamp in the corner, behind the loudspeaker, to light up the three of us. The four of us, I beg your pardon. How can I forget it? My anxiety, in full force, fully devouring, more robust than ever. She got her health by taking mine from me. So she is flourishing, naturally. As she grows she fills all of the room, then she swells, spreads over the walls, comes to offer herself even in my bed, where soon, in the shadow in which she tantalizes, she penetrates me until the final tearing apart. Never sated, suffocating in my skin, she suffocates me with her. And, even though I have long been used to her embrace, her triumphant laugh crushes what still remains of my poor intelligence and each time drags me ever farther away into the echoes bouncing back from oblivion.

1975
Paris, 22 years old

March 3, 1975

My big Dad,

Here's the letter, as promised. I had you on the phone just now but I still have a little time left, exactly an hour and a half before my dance class. Besides, I'll have to take myself by the hand to go there. But I will go! I have to, don't I?

Since I left Prangins, almost four years ago now, I have lived from day to day, pretending to take life as a game but recognizing that in it there was something so serious and so important, so irremediable too, that I kept putting off the time when I would have to settle into it for good, build myself a future and make my choices.

I kept making up excuses for myself. Hadn't I been ill? Wasn't I still disturbed in my physical and moral equilibrium?

So I declared myself a "convalescent," reassured by the pampering that word suggests and the idea of time being left hanging between two parentheses, without any link to the future.

I was young. I kept telling myself: later, someday, soon I will truly start living. As for "right away," of course, I felt myself unsuited to get going! I was afraid, as even today I am afraid. Afraid of the responsibilities that determine one's existence, afraid of losing a "virginity" by calling myself adult.

In sum, I was living in expectation of another life, the one that I described as "real" while very softly calling to it. I grazed it with the tips of my fingers like a timid animal, as if to tame it. Get it accustomed to my smell. I contemplated it from afar but with envy, with love, because it attracted me so that it made me dizzy, and pushing it away, refusing to let myself espouse it forthwith, was as painful to me as it was necessary.

"Existence" . . . : a dream! A dream for later on, a dream that would concretize the woman I was going to become, that "someone" I would fashion night and day with determination. A dream inaccessible to the little girl of today, who ran the risk of soiling it through her awkwardness and impetuosity.

So I left Marie-Jo between her two parentheses and stubbornly kept repeating to her that, in this refuge of waiting, she would not grow old.

It is not always easy to play at being blind. My skin fitted me less and less comfortably. Nevertheless, I just had to move, to stretch, to get some air!

So, without going too far, I stuck the end of my nose outside. I did some movie work, I mumbled through classes and at producers' offices. Quite sincerely, for the camera attracted me, the spotlights dazzled me and, inside of me, behind my mask frozen by stage fright, a voice whispered to me: "someday, in all this light, you will reveal yourself to others and to yourself. You will explode, you will carry far above their heads the cry you are holding back, which is searing your throat. You will be 'YOU' for the first time."

"Someday" . . . Not now. Never now. I braked my desires, I took refuge in small parts, in my timidity, in my lack of assurance.

I was marking time in my anxiety. The anxiety of BEING "right now," in the present minute. Every morning I rejected the mug I saw in my mirror.

Didn't I like myself? It was because I wasn't ready! Once again I would hide then; to divert myself, I would try retouches which, by dint of being imperfect, only accentuated my despair. When did I realize, exactly? It seemed to me that I was gradually awakening from a long sleep. I looked behind me and contemplated ad nauseam those four years of my life sunk in the depths of time. My existence had grown old without me, without my realizing it. I thought it was brand new, quite sheltered in its little dream corner, when in fact it was already displaying, in broad daylight, the manners of a whore. I shrugged my shoulders, or at least acted as if I had. One had to accept it, didn't one? And finally decide which road to take among the thousand that lay ahead.

I am still hesitating. Everything scares me. They all imply the loneliness, the egoism of glory or the bitterness of defeat. Unless I were to change courses, to take myself off in another direction? I discovered a path, outside the roads. It goes toward a "somewhere" that it invites me to share: X. and his love, my love and him. Or, rather than use the word "love," those almost invisible bonds that are growing tighter between us and the balance I feel when I am with him.

Is that, in the final analysis, the choice to be made? But what if this "we two" were only one more illusion? What if later on, when it is really too late, I were to discover that I had made a mistake?

When will I be able to decide? To face myself lucidly enough to recognize my possibilities and no longer only my desires.

I get dizzy, I spread myself around, I play at living life but don't live it. I'm afraid and I set up dreams. I would like it if nothing were serious, especially not irremediable. I know that one false step is all that is needed to bring it all down. So I hide away from reality and hang on to the derisory. I rush toward a "Claude," an "Alain" or some other, so long as they are not X. and nothing forces me to make a commitment to them. By dint of putting the spontaneous to sleep I get to forget who I am. I just pretend to be.

Am I right to question myself this way? Must we at any cost know where we are swimming to? It may be enough to let oneself drift with the stream of existence and . . .

I would so like you to tell me, Dad! But how can one be answerable for another's destiny? Someday, at the end of the road, one remains alone to live out the ending. Alone as well to experience the total unfolding and still to wonder about the "whys" of such and such a meander.

Oof! It does one good to write, to pour oneself out, even in a confused manner, as in this letter.

It is in the image of my problems, in my image. Smeared and stupidly sentimental!

For now, I am continuing my coming-and-going in Paris. In the long run, perhaps I will succeed in making it mean something . . . ?

I love you
your little girl

Marie-Jo

April 3, 1975
(first psychoanalyst)

My "big Dad,"

My new psychiatrist being on vacation, I'll only see him in a week. I am really impatient to get going with my analysis. I feel a vital need of it, the need to learn how "TO BE," totally. And starting out to discover oneself is to go out equally toward others, in a deeper and more objective approach.

. . . X. arrived last night but is leaving again Sunday already. Something unexpected in his work which at the same time cancels our "short vacation."

I'm not in pain over it. I have been making do for too long with "pseudo-vacations," ever since I got out of school, to tell the truth: over six years. Isn't it finally time for me to start making something of my existence? Seriously, and on solid bases, which I have to construct.

Tomorrow morning I will go out and buy a wooden table and a chair. I will then, as of next week, enter upon my writing discipline, parallel to my analysis and a bodily reeducation. What numbers of pages I dream of blackening! The result doesn't much matter. Whether it turn out good or bad, the important thing will be to fill my paper day after day and to rid myself of those phantoms embedded in my mind. Phantoms created in my childhood, in my adolescence, all the ones that still haunt me today.

I want to confront them once and for all in harsh light, tear them out of the "fuzziness," the "soft lighting" that protects them and which they wrap themselves up in as in an aura of anxiety. I want to demystify their power, that power which I myself imprudently gave them, without realizing it, by playing around too often with my imagination . . .

. . . I am writing fast on the corner of a counter as I gulp down my morning hot milk. It is ten o'clock and I have an appointment in five minutes.

The start of a good or a bad day? It is gray and cold in Paris, and before long it will be raining. Up to me to heat up my own personal sun as the hours go by, to color the sky a softer gray. The chills in the air are not disagreeable. Provided one lets oneself go with them by unleashing the nervous tension. We always nurture it exaggeratedly, the way most of the time we waste our energy on futilities.

We know so poorly how to live! We aspire to believing, to developing, but we refuse to go along at the same rhythm as existence. By what right do we complain, then, that we are suffocating in the same setting? We do nothing to try to change it. Deep down within us, it reassures us . . . Too bad if it turns our stomachs! . . .

. . . The Human Being is strange. He continually tries to avoid nature and its laws of harmony, he tries so little to understand its essence and become part of it. Merely because he is afraid? . . . Oh la, la! I'm really late! I forgot to wish you a "Happy Easter," according to tradition. I was at La Rochelle with Marc and the "little family." I thought of calling you and then . . . You don't mind? [Sentence in English.] . . .

. . . My Dad! . . . I whisper my "Dad" and that word carries within itself much more than I could ever write . . .

your "little girl"

Marie-Jo

P.S. Beyond the father and the man that I loved in you, I have recently discovered a sort of intimation of a "friend." Something that looks a little like complicity, something new in watermark behind our conversations. I am getting closer to you, I am understanding you better, I would like always and even more until . . . until we are "adult" and "adult," one facing the other . . .

M.-J.

I love you, my Dad, I have my ring on my finger and I feel real close, real close to you, in this oh so wonderful feeling of confidence and tenderness . . .

your little and
big girl

Marie-Jo

April 15, 1975

My "big Dad,"

As early as last Thursday and until late in the night I devoured *Un homme comme un autre* (A Man Like Any Other). I wanted to write you my impressions of it right away but I was too torn and everything was racing around in my mind.

During the weekend, I wielded the paintbrush a little at Poigny to help Marc in his work and only today have I gotten back the calm needed to talk to you about it.

What to say exactly? That it's a very fine book? . . . That, you must suspect, even if you're not sure of it.

The first part especially, in your descriptions of your youth, of your discovery of life, is as full of images and odors, as dense as your best novels with "characters." One could believe you are once again putting yourself into the skin of another and that, instinctively, you divine his emotions. You reconstruct his world.

As the pages went on, a desire came over me to know always more about him, that "other one," to meet him on the platform of a bus and go off with him to the seas of the north. I kept forgetting that "HE" was you, a you of long ago, and that while he was still alive in the deepest part of your memories and your impulses as a man of today, it was hard for me to make him out there.

Perhaps for brief moments, yes. In a flash of the eyes or a suddenly peculiar mimicry which, without one's knowing why, is different than usual. We all have a tendency to stop at the simple external aspect, at the bodily envelope that is wearing out, or at the picture of a father we have made for ourselves once and for all and to which we allow very few concessions. We are afraid of digging further and upsetting our nice little comfortable idea. We remain blind.

I was blind (or, rather, wanted to be) above all on a point of your private life and its most important one: your attachment to Teresa. You speak of the "resistance" your children feel toward her. That's true. As far as I am concerned I never accepted her and often for ill-defined reasons that came out of my subconscious.

I fully realize now how selfish I was: I wanted you all for me, open to me whenever I needed you, available to my little girl's whims. I wanted "my" Dad exclusively. I would not recognize the man of another love.

But again, why did you never present her to us, show us Teresa in her real place? Was it out of shame? Did you hope we would guess it all on our own? We weren't able to. She had no clear position alongside you. She no longer was, since Epalinges, a simple chambermaid; she slept in your bed but addressed you as "Monsieur," and, in front of us, you spoke formally to one another. She accumulated the titles of governess, practical nurse, companion, all more than approximations in relation to the truth. And then, from time to time, in a moment of forgetfulness or inattention, you addressed her familiarly in one single sentence, which overthrew all the conceptions we had admitted.

I sound like I'm accusing you, Dad. That's not it at all. If I were to accuse anybody it would first of all be me and my lack of understanding, my jealousy, my selfishness. Perhaps it was we who, through our attitude,

729

drove you to this dissembling, to this playacting composed of white hospital gown, formal address and "Monsieur" and which, considering the bonds between the two of you, was a mockery.

From now on I will accept Teresa better. I can't go on rejecting her and loving you all at the same time, since she is part of you. I feel like saying: in the future, I'll take it all! My Dad, the man, as well as his love for another woman. I have such a need to encompass you in your entirety!

I'm shooting my mouth off, am I not? This sounds like a letter from a woman to her lover or husband. I am only your daughter but I admit that it delights me to forget it for a moment and to show myself to you from my "female" side. With a wink.

The second part of your book disconcerted me. I think that to understand it well one would have to read in order everything that you have dictated up to the present, in other words, the other four volumes to come. I have the feeling that you are trying to find yourself for the first time, that you are trying your hand at analysis but without really daring to, you who before lived mainly by instinct, pouring out into your characters the bothersome overflow of your unconscious. Writing a book was the equivalent of an enema. You cleaned yourself out yourself and, without wishing to be too aware of it, you wiped away the dust. The components of that dust meant little to you, as well as its provenance. You quickly made a gift of it to imaginary "others" and, a dust harsh with rain or golden in the sunshine, it impregnated the pages with its reality. If you had analyzed at a younger age (as I have a tendency to) the "whys" of your impulses, your desires or your refusals, would you have written? By creating, you were freeing yourself of everything bothersome, everything that creates anxiety because one has not understood it or gotten close enough to it. It was not in your nature to dissect things, to look at them under a magnifying glass, that would have been too terrifying. So you stored them up in a bunch, without sorting them out, and instinctively in your books threw out whatever affected your own equilibrium.

What am I trying to get at, exactly? . . . I don't trust my own degree of intelligence or its abilities. I am only twenty-two, I haven't lived through a tenth of your experiences. Moreover, I don't have your talent, and I would like to describe my feelings to you with much more humility.

I was struck by how much, at your age, you still hesitated on the subject of yourself, as much as I do on my side, if not more. I was frightened by the difficulty you had in discerning Yourself in existence, all alone, without the help of your imaginary worlds since you ceased writing. I was hanging on to illusions. I thought that at the end of a life one had at least some of the answers about one's own identity. And then I was conscious of a man, "Georges Simenon," who was still timidly trying to find himself at seventy-two. A man who amazed himself by pronouncing his own name, surprised at hearing it resound for the first time in his own ears. But are you stammering it or articulating it? . . . To me, your voice goes about it with a strange kind of naïveté. It's enjoyable, it delights me, but it scares me a little too . . .

I'm shooting my mouth off more and more, hmm? Like you, it seems to me I feel an abundance of truths that, however, I never succeed in unraveling completely. Those almost palpable truths, within reach, yet always elusive!

. . . "Monsieur Simenon," You "the man," my Dad, I love you and I admire all of you . . .

your little girl

Marie-Jo

May 29, 1975

My "big Dad,"

Back in Paris. I'm resuming my little daily humdrum routine and trying to do it with more conviction. In a little while, I'll go over to 101 quai de Branly to consult the ads for foreign employment. The organization handling this is called the "C.I.D.J." I don't know just what the initials stand for but I know it has something to do with exchange of students between different countries.

My fear of leaving is just as great as my need to. But, even ill at ease inside my skin, I feel protected by my habits. I have no one to see in particular, no real friend, but I nevertheless know some names, some faces, some distant silhouettes to which I can hang on. All I have to do is phone to exchange a banal good-day. It is true also that the loneliness seems even heavier after the conversation is over.

For the weekend I'll surely go to Marc's. He is leaving with Mylène for Brussels on Sunday, and I'll be alone in tête-à-tête with Boule, in the intimacy of the memories I will ask her to tell me about. I will share your youth again, your long voyages, your making your way through life. And, just as one gets the pieces of a puzzle together little by little, I will be bringing the picture of the man that you were more and more out of its haziness.

Does that really help me in understanding the man you are today? Will I soon succeed in establishing a precise image? . . . And why does that seem so indispensable to me? The truth is, I have no idea! I only know that thinking about you dissipates some of my dizziness while appeasing my anxieties. I fill the vacuum with your imaginary presence.

. . . I would so like to do and no longer to dream. Get myself going otherwise than like an automaton. Is there something essential in the way one lives life that I am unable to assimilate? Is it because of that that my reason for being eludes me, because I run after it that it divorces itself from reality? . . .

I spoke to you of tenderness, recently. I can spend hours petting a cat or Marc's bitch, or even the smooth wood of my stairway banister, but I lose all spontaneity in an embrace with a man. A barrier pops up, uncrossable. My emotions scatter and my gestures no longer correspond to their original impulses. I become a caricature of what I am feeling and which is suffocating in the deepest part of me without even coming up to the surface. Is that why I ache? For all that has been piling up for years in my belly that I am powerless to externalize? Like a monstrous pregnancy that would never come to term! . . .

. . . I'm not writing you a letter. I picked my pen up with the idea of at last starting a short story, some recollections, anything at all. And then I realized I had nothing to say, nothing or too much, which is the same thing, so I gave up trying to collect my thoughts. After all, I feel in front of a blank page the way I do in front of a man. I'm afraid to let myself go, to show myself in too great nudity. I am just as afraid of it as I desire it! Isn't our faith in the act of love intimately connected with our belief in existence? From disillusionments to disillusionments, I seem to have lost both. I convinced myself little by little that I was frigid, that I was as incapable of giving as of receiving. Then, behind my tense mask, it doesn't matter whether I laugh or cry, I'm the only one to know about it. One quickly gets tired of feeling things only for oneself. Soon, I'll be just as indifferent to myself and the vacuum will permanently take over in my place.

S . . . ! Excuse me for running on so! I have to struggle against my defeatism but I feel like a boxer who, after having carefully put his gloves on, can't find his punching bag anymore. What can he punch instead? His own face? . . . At the risk of knocking himself out! . . .

You are very good to me, Dad, maybe even too indulgent. Did you, at twenty-two, have someone to hold you up when you lost your footing? Certainly not your mother, nor Tigy. How did you succeed in keeping your balance? . . . I know the answer: you wrote something other than what I have just written. You looked elsewhere than at your own umbilicus . . . My God, if only Maman had been able to keep from giving me one at my birth! . . .

your little girl

Marie-Jo

September 28, 1975

When one loses contact
Or guesses one never had it
When one senses a pulsating life
But one does not live it
When it remains inaccessible
Like an alien heart
Like the beating of the blood
In a stranger's veins

When one bumps into one's prison
Into one's own barriers
At the limits of oneself
Which one cannot ever cross

When one suffers inwardly
Till one wants to explode
To yell a final yell
Like the one at one's birth
To let die a rale
A murmur fading away

When one thinks of diving
Into the abyss of no return
Or one dreams of sunshine
Of simplified love

When one reaches for unity
When one no longer doubts
And one begs for the peace
Slipping through one's fingers

Covered by all the problems
Which are only mirages
Smothered in the dust
Piling up in our brains

When one turns toward God
And one tries to believe
When one finally kneels
Arms already crossed
As if to hug the void
The desert of a life
In which one had been nude

When one is disgusted
With lights with crowds
With the agitation
That keeps us on the go

When one loses the illusion
Of making any mark
On the passing on earth
Of one man among the others
But one persists even so
In going toward "elsewhere"
Elsewhere than oblivion
Elsewhere than the absurd
Especially "somewhere"
That will reassure us

When one blinds oneself
So as not to stumble
Before all the meaninglessness
That we accumulate

When we make ourselves deaf
To the words that hurt
The inevitable lies
Or truths too "true"

When we stand mute
Despite fears and desires

Because we are ashamed
And that cannot be said

When one looks at oneself
Upside down in the mirror
When one checks the image
Deformed and negative
Deprived of spontaneity

Contrary to nature
Which breathes at its rhythm
Unaware of the vanities
Careless of appearance
Of cheating on details
Of trying to retouch
Like a has-been actor
As all of us do
In the constrained gestures
Of the world of human race

When we use up our lives
To recake the mask
To repaint the smile
That has no more charm
To tint the looks
That have lost their shine

When man persists still
In envying appearances
The superfluous arrogance
The mimicry of chieftains
The gildings of the envelope
Often with nothing inside
With no message to deliver
Without reply requested

When one knows that time
Will yellow its corners
Make the glue run
and erase the address

When our children soon
Bored with reading us
Will make paper dolls
Out of what is left

We will finally be free
To make room for them
And we will dissolve ourselves
In the Peace of the stars!

"Poigny-la-Forêt"

THE END

October 8, 1975

This is it, my Dad. 10:20 P.M. I no longer want a thing. It's all over.

I'm writing you as a final obligation, but will not reread what I write, won't scratch anything out, won't look for any new words. I've come to the end of embellishments as I've come to the end of my desires and sufferings.

I won't cry either. That was all right "before." When it still freed me from my anxieties, from my excessive nervous tension.

Now I'm "at the end of my rope," hunkering down into the bottom of the hole, curled up in some thick sticky darkness, in my odor which irritates and obsesses me, but which I can't get away from.

I might perhaps have been able to write you more concretely, last night, when total vacuum had not taken over my entire brain.

It's too late. Words are empty as my head, so poor they're transparent. I have to extirpate them one by one from my pen which refuses to obey me, already inert beneath my fingers.

I no longer believe in anything.

My past has been nothing but lies.

I've wasted my life getting to realize that.

I've lied to others by lying first of all to myself.

Thanks to a small share of sincerity, I built some dreams I wanted to be true.

For me to fight *against* the world seems monstrous; *for* the world, the crowd, utopian and devoid of interest.

For me to fight for or against myself seems to me undisentanglable and enervating.

I didn't yet know, in trying to make myself proof against suffering, that at the same time I would become proof against the little joys with which happiness begins.

In twenty-two years of life, I accomplished only one step, the first, endlessly undertaken forward then backward, in the movement of a pendulum imprisoned within its clock. From one foot to the other I stayed on the same spot. I trampled a little spot of earth without even leaving my trace on it. I trampled in vain in the fixed landscape of a stage set.

People turn my stomach, they no longer amuse me, they no longer move me to pity. When I bump against them as I go by, I recognize in them my own frailties, my shames, the hypocrisies that disgust me. They return my own image to me and I am tired of being pleased by it or avoiding it by turning my eyes away. How I would like to apologize to them for my also being one of their mirrors and deforming their features until they become unrecognizable.

I've had enough of it. I can't go on. I've tried, I believe. How long? In full consciousness of what I was doing, in a daily struggle, at least twelve years. Almost half of my existence! Isn't that enough? Isn't that enough for drawing up a balance sheet and laying down arms?

I've destroyed some of my dreams, others destroyed themselves, unable to survive reality.

I've repressed my fears, my desires, my needs, I've disturbed people for very little and displaced a lot of air for nothing. I've wept tears that already no longer exist although they contained all of myself.

I've emptied my body of its impulses, my heart of its outbursts, my being of its warmth and the necessary minimum of human tenderness.

I no longer exist. The place is free for a successor. Someone courageous, less intransigent, someone having two lungs to breathe with and not a slab of cold marble by way of a rib cage.

My God, forgive me. I did not know how to love, either life, or people, only my own person ad nauseam.

Make my father be happy, as well as my brothers and the man who recently stood by me without my giving him [anything] in exchange,

I'm dropping it all, I have no more dignity, no will power. I see no more reason for being and refuse to go on making up new ones for myself.

Thanks for everything, my God . . .

Marie-Jo

F.,

I'm seeing you tomorrow, that's wonderful. Wonderful too to have heard your voice on the phone Tuesday, for the first time since I've been at the clinic.

You spoke to me a great deal about efforts, will power . . . There comes a stage, which I know all too well, where those words no longer mean anything. I mean: when of my own volition I asked again to be institutionalized, Monday, I was no longer able to live normally, to act the way others do, to feel anything right.

A dichotomy occurred within my brain, making me temporarily really "crazy," enclosed in my universe, which was no longer in any way reassuring. Imagine a universe of haziness, of questions without answers, repressed aggressiveness, waking dreams with a morbid aftertaste.

My life was caught between two walls: the oblivion before my birth and the one after my death, which seemed to be getting closer to one another at top speed before my spectator eyes, so as to fuse together and leave nothing but a shrunken outline of my existence.

November 24, 1975

Clinic: 10:30 P.M.

Dad. I haven't finished *Des traces de pas* (Traces of Footsteps) yet. I read half of it, then, last night, too curious, I leafed through some passages at the end where I found myself.

Your accident . . . The terrible scene of the day before, my powerlessness to communicate to you . . . not violence, not hatred, only so selfish a love that it would not admit your way of living "as a couple."

No doubt, I watch myself live and my sentiments may be theatrical. But they're all I have. Without my poses, if poses they be, I am nothing. I have told too much about me, opened myself too much to you, in a bad way, a one-way way, with my eyes turned inward. But my blind eyes were trying to see you, Dad, that was my torture. I had only one more step to take to be with you, I felt it . . . one step in the dark that I just couldn't take.

I looked for you too, I wanted to understand you, as much as I look for myself, as you feel your way to try to understand yourself.

I have nothing in my life. Nothing except . . . Leave me the power of the ring on my finger, let me believe in it, leave me my dream, egocentric, I know, but leave me that little mixture of you and me.

Let me love you without always asking yourself whether I am sincere. Let me . . .

Can you trust me and not have doubts? . . .

Dad. Three letters, your name, my past and the vacuum in my hands. your little girl

Marie-Jo
"Villa des Pages"

November 26, 1975

6:00 P.M. I'm waiting for this evening's medication so I can finally go to sleep and stop thinking "consciously."

Right now, I'm thinking as I speak, as if the words were saying themselves in a low voice inside my head, as if they inscribed themselves in printed letters right behind my eyes and bumped up against the linings of my skull.

I take up my pen to communicate them as they come to the outside world, so that they will finally escape from inside me in the illusion of a contact.

I am too lonely. How can I be helped by being put nicely in a practically bare room, without my being told what to do, without medication, with only my own presence for company?

For the last six months, I have of my own volition locked myself within myself with a sort of complaisant despair. I have played with the workings of my brain as one toys with a decaying tooth, and I threw my ideas out at the top of my voice against the walls of my room. They didn't bounce back, I heard no more echo. I was crying in a vacuum. I was calling God, and trying to believe in him, long enough to calm down. I was making conversation with pictures of my father and I was trying to see him all-powerful again, as in my childhood.

"Villa des Pages"

January 7, 1976

Bonjour, Monsieur
Just say "bonjour"
Why yes, it's me
Don't you recognize me? . . .
Don't go away, Monsieur
Since I told you it's me! . . .

In the streets, the lights
In this concrete box
He bumps into the city
He bumps into passers-by.

He looks like a drunk
Puffing away in the dark
It does him no good
To hang on to people's clothes.

Bonsoir, Madame
Just say "anything"
Why yes, it's me
Don't you recognize me?
Don't go away, Madame
Since I swear to you it's me! . . .

In the stream of the crowd
That is drowning in Paris
In the moving shadows
On the shiny pavement

He gets lost in the round
And he runs like mad
Ignored by these people
He is howling to.

Messieurs, Mesdames
Just say "anything"
It's me, the man
So don't go away . . .
All of you, I exist
So recognize me! . . .

He showed his mug
With the tears drying on it
Then his wide-open hands
And then he collapsed.

A circle was formed
Waiting for the police
Faces with empty eyes
He could see from below.

Mister Policeman
Just say "why"
Of course, it's me
Don't you recognize me?
I'm going to get up
You'll see standing up
I haven't changed.

Pardon, what did you say?
My name? . . . My address? . . .
Just wait a second
It's silly, I've a hole . . .
A black hole in my head . . .
Just a second, please . . .
Just let me . . .

I am . . .
My name is . . .

I live at . . .
Why are you arresting me?

All of you, answer!
Do you recognize me?
So, go on, tell him
Tell it to him for me! . . .
My lord . . . my head . . .
I've forgotten it all . . . !

"Poigny-la-Forêt"

THE END

January 11, 1976

I would like the sun
In the palm of my hands
When it rises from a night
During which I haven't slept.

I would like its rays
Like water in my mouth
When a window reflects
The colors of my room.

I would like to roll up
In the warmth of their light
When I'm standing naked
In front of my window.

I would like to hold
Within my fingers tight
The shiny little grains
That make up the dust
Rising up in the air
From rug to ceiling.

I would like to prolong
This enjoyable moment
When, by closing an eye,
My hands in big close-up
Are wedded to the roundness
Of the sun growing bigger
Right at the tip of my nose
As it turns the sky blue.

                                        "Lausanne"

                                        January 30, 1976

If you go toward life
Without feeling others
Without raising your head
Without meeting their eyes

If your walk straight ahead
Leads you blindly on
Incessantly to draw
The circle of prisons

Make a little effort
To hold out your hand to me
To recognize in me
Someone like yourself.

If you have an ailment
Planted deep in your heart
That makes your nights weep
And your daytimes drown

If you disdain embrace
Without going on
To try to seek in love
What your being expects

743

Make a little effort
To hold out your hand to me
To recognize in me
Someone like yourself.

If you lose the idea
Of what you really are
With just a gaping hole
By way of memory

If you endlessly fall
As passing time goes by
Deep in the glaucous water
Into which your blood flows

Make a little effort
To hold out your hand to me
To recognize in me
Someone like yourself

If in the deepest dark
Of your gnawing madness
Each mirror reflects
The face of your fear

Phantom of life
Ignored by happiness
If you see yourself dying
Do not cry out

For I will have the courage
To survive for you
If I feel that confidence
Has driven out your despair.

I owe you a secret
I have lived your anxiety
I know your ailment
You know, I'm like you.

And if it's not too late
We can try together
To invent a sun
To make love to us.

"Poigny-la-Forêt"

THE END

(No stroke of genius, eh? . . . Too bad!)

February 4, 1976

My Dad,

I'm sending you, as promised, a short text I recently wrote, in the guise of a song. That's why you'll find a refrain in it, as well as the number of "feet" identical everywhere. I don't think it's any good. It's only one try among others, "copy" for the sake of "copy." I try to write as often as possible and even when I don't feel a need to. Just to be "working."

. . . I hope that Teresa is quietly getting over her operation and that she will soon be back on her feet. I hope especially that this hasn't put too much of a crimp in your little daily pleasures.

I, for one, am in a hurry to be rid of winter. I want to see a real hot sun again, but without forgoing my activities in Paris. I still have quite a few "bench marks" to lay out in order to build up my life and be able to take a vacation without a guilty conscience, without feeling I am running away from myself or from my problems.

That's it, my Dad. I think a lot of you every time I feel myself giving way. I say to myself: "He succeeded in jumping over the obstacle, why not me?" And I try in my turn . . .

With all my tenderness . . .
your "little girl"

Marie-Jo

February 19, 1976

I wanted so many things
When I was very little

So much purity and Love
So much sun in my eyes
With the big strong arms
Of a Daddy mine alone

I dreamed of smiles
Of clouds in the sky
I looked at the moon
That I held in my hands
And in the evening blue
I spoke to the stars

I would have wanted, Daddy,
To give the world to you
All that was quivering
In the depths of my heart
The warmth of a Love
To be shared with you.

"Poigny-la-Forêt"

THE END

April 24, 1976

My Dad,

My own Dad . . . My big Dad. The Dad of my childhood, of Tennessee Waltz. The Dad of later on, when I cuddled up on his lap. The Dad of now, so tender, and yet to whom I can't explain a thing. No more contact possible! I am a prisoner of a self I no longer understand, no longer control. I am living in a vacuum, without memory, without impulses, without resiliency.

Oh Dad! On this afternoon I am at home washing my hair before going to see Dr. L. Afterward, I'll take the express train directly to the clinic. They let me out for the day. I nonetheless am living there for the time being, and no doubt for a good long time.

It is two o'clock. I have just gotten here to the mess of my studio. I put on a record, I looked at your picture and . . . I cried.

I called to you, the way I used to do when I was little. I promised you I'd do everything to pull out of this, so that you can finally be proud of me.

How much work on myself before being able to renew contact with others! I am living in the anarchy of my body and my head. I am walled-up alive in fantasies that the sun can no longer even break through. I am suffocating in my madness. I would like to cry out and I don't know how to talk, to write correctly anymore. I would like a caress but am unable to reach out for it.

Am I going to get well, tell me? Oh! Tell it to me in strong terms, have faith for me.

Someday, I'll fully regain your arms, as a big girl you are no longer afraid of.

Someday . . . When will it come, when I've been waiting for it so long? . . .

I love you, my Dad. I beg you whatever happens, whatever becomes of me, don't forget that. Always remember my infrequent real smiles and drive my tears out of your memory. They should never have existed. Why did I let them take hold of me, as well as my anxiety? . . . Why was I never able to live, even when I had you right near me?

A caress as big and hot as the sun, a kiss on your forehead, a hand on yours and peace all around . . .

your "little girl"

Marie-Jo

May 15, 1976 [misdated 1975]

[This STRICTLY PERSONAL letter appears in Chapter 73, pages 639–642.]

A brain that's broken down
A body drawn and quartered
An anxiety in prison
All the sobs suppressed.

That is all that is left
Of my being gone mad.
My suffering escapes me
And moans in the night.

My heart has no more hope.
I wish it would stop
Knocking so in my head
All splattered with black.

A whole world of dreams
Has gnawed my entrails out.
I am sinking into nowhere
Into a pit of fire—(without end)

I'm going back to the void
Becoming dust once more.
I ask now of death
To put an end to my fate.

"La Verrière"

October 6, 1976

My big Dad,

The monotony of hours interminably dragging on. Waiting for tomorrow, Sunday, when I will at last go out for a few hours with Johnny.

Waiting too for the verdict of the psychologists, Tuesday, who have already seen me twice and will then let me know the treatment I am to take. Psychodrama? Group analysis? Individual psychotherapy? . . . That last possibility scares me. I can't very well see what good would come from a short-time one-on-one with a doctor I will change once I am on the outside. Why not start in right away with B.? Answer: my medical contacts are supposed to stay within the clinic.

I'm despairing a little. For two weeks, they had me under observation. I had the feeling I was marking time without any help, except for the friendly and comforting contacts with the nurses. With some of the patients, too, but so many of them already go out on weekends or spend their days going around town. The corridors then are empty and I haven't anybody to talk to.

Some personal improvement, just the same: I've tried to overcome my nervous bulimia. And then, while I still sleep quite poorly, it is almost wholly without drugs. I do everything I can to get back to normal sleep.

There. I try to paint, can't do it. I try to write, find it hard to do. Too many interferences in my brain to give free rein to my inspirations. Yet it's not the desire to express myself that is lacking. I choke with bottling everything up within me, in anarchistic disorder. Will I someday "look like" me? Have I ever been "normal"? I can sense a throbbing life, rich in colors, in movements, full of zest. I feel it vibrating behind the opaque screen that is walling in my being and making me blind. I suffer from being outside an existence some of the odors of which I feel, at times, that I can smell. If only I could understand myself at last, I would be able to dive into it naked, freed of the weight of my fantasies, the way one dives into clear water following the current. I would open myself to others, I would be able to love them . . .

And my love for you would be even greater, more serene, simpler, without selfishness or romanticism. I often hurt, because I deify you and thereby you become inaccessible. When I can have you again in the image of my father, I will at last have won. I will be real close to you, in a reality better than the dreams of the past . . .

your "little girl"

Marie-Jo

November 10, 1976

Often before my eyes
There appears the image
Of a past so present
It would fill pages
If I had the courage
To speak again of then.

The summer of our vacation
Do you remember it too?
When the sun far away
Died away without complaint.

749

The shadows growing longer
All was quiet in the air
A very warm caress
As we went along together
We two arm in arm
To the bar that now was dark.

The music was playing
For just the two of us
A waltz, a secret
That drew us to the floor.

I raised my head up high
I looked into your eyes
And read your tenderness
And then I hugged your arms
For you were going too fast
For my very little steps.

I could feel the dizziness
That was taking hold of me
I was inside your warmth
And laughed for all to see.

Then we went for a drink
And I had my orange juice
It was so hard to climb
Up on the big bar stool.

Before we went away
You gave them a wink
And had them play again
The waltz that was our own.

We were hearing it still
In the darkness outside
When we had to go back
Toward our own hotel.

It's true, I was small
Only seven years old
Pretending to be your wife
I could forget Maman.

"Le Vésinet"

November 15, 1976

My big Dad,

10:30 A.M. I'm waiting for the doctor in charge of this floor who will work out my week's schedule with me. Maybe I'll be allowed to go out Wednesday or Thursday with Boule to buy a winter coat? I also want to go to the hairdresser's, to indulge my vanity, essential to keep from going to seed.

A rather good encounter, last Friday, with my psychotherapist. A few sessions will probably be enough to make me see the "whys" of my rejection of past analyses. So, soon, I will be ready to meet B., without having to worry about running into any lack of common grounds.

Your letter gave me a lot of pleasure. Not only by the immense tenderness in it, but because of what it allows me to glimpse of my future, in a concrete way.

I was afraid I would be taken up for a long time with lodging and organizing problems. Thanks to Aitken's experience, as soon as I am up and about, it will be easier for me to fit into life again. After that, I'll get down seriously to studying English and typing, with a view to making sure I have a real profession. I am not wholly ruling out, I'll confess, some new attempts at movies and writing. Later on, when I have acquired solid bases and the certainty of earning a living, I'll try a few more experiments. I have too much need to externalize myself and the artistic milieu is the only one that really allows that.

At any rate, I'm well aware I'm starting from scratch. I have to rebuild, learn everything. I have to acquire my independence, and mistakes at twenty-three are no longer permitted. I will be responsible for my choices. In what area, finally, will I best be able to fulfill myself? I hope to find that out through psychotherapy.

In the meantime, I'm improving slowly, with the means at hand. I try to keep as active as possible so as not to get stuck in monotony. In the clinic, days all are too much alike. So I make a point of painting, even if what I do is bad. I play the guitar and I write. Nothing any good, just any old thing, the important part being mainly to resume contact with the proper meaning of words and to connect them once again to my ideas.

My Dad, I finally do want to believe in life, in its everyday reality, good or bad. My dreams of the absolute were merely an escape. Now I want to get the feel of the "true" . . .

your little girl

Marie-Jo

November 19, 1976

Two drops
One a tear
One of blood.

Two drops mixing together
Diluting and disappearing.

In the tear, the whole of a lifetime
One man's progress, his blood oozing out.

The tear was the color of the moon
The blood was sunset red.

"Rueil-Malmaison"

November 20, 1976

Am I alone being held a prisoner
By a self I cannot face?
Am I alone imploring a father
To protect me in his great embrace?

"Rueil-Malmaison"

1977
Paris, 23 years old

January 1, 1977

My "big Dad,"

I'm going to phone, in a little while, and wish you a "Happy New Year" [in English]. Nevertheless I feel a need to write you, because the day is going monotonously by and I feel a bit homesick.

I am allowed to "go out," this weekend, but have no place to go, nothing to do, all alone in Rueil or Paris. The "little family" is spending the weekend at a château two hundred kilometers from Paris and I didn't have the courage to go so far to them.

So, there it is. I'm just "hanging around," as the saying goes. I did my exercises this morning, a good walk in the park and then . . . After lunch, the afternoon is long! . . .

Last night, I woke up around half past twelve and whispered tenderly to you all my wishes for harmony and sunshine in the new year.

I'm still struggling; I haven't lost courage, even when a kind of loneliness, a lack of warmth or nearby affection weighs heavy on me. I'm anxious to be well enough to see some of my friends again soon, to see "YOU" again.

The weather is fine today, the air was mild, outside, the colors of the trees bright and shimmery.

Now (it's quarter to five), the sky is turning pink up over the houses and under my window I hear some children playing on roller skates. Well now! . . . All of that breathes of life, so why speak of monotony? . . .

I'm seeing B. again next Friday at 4:00. I'm delighted at the idea. I have the feeling that we understand one another and am looking forward to the next encounters to be sure of it. That way, I'll finally be able to go into analysis, empty out the overflow of my skull, get back to being who I am or maybe just find out, at any rate improve.

Hurry with those pictures, to have you "concretely" on one of my walls, to see you scold me when I get one of my fits of spleen. It's time to forget Baudelaire! . . .

Just now, your voice on the phone. What a pleasure to hear you and know that you are better. I didn't think my drawings were any good. You encourage me to go on, as I hope soon to be writing more often "for myself," and something other than poems. I don't have enough spontaneity, I get hung up over style and so does the flow of my thoughts.

I have a thousand ideas for tales, short stories. I'm just afraid to undertake them.

Dad, Daddy, my own "father" [word in English], you "Mr. Man," I love you just as much as I am fighting to come finally to life. I reach out toward you as I do toward life, more and more utterly, and I open myself to it at the same time as to your arms . . .

your "little"

Marie-Jo (Yum-Yum 77!)

January 16, 1977

My "big Dad,"

How long have I left you without news? I don't remember. I've had a tough couple of weeks, with a return of anxiety and great lassitude. My fatigue is due, of course, to the fact that I wasn't sleeping more than five hours a night for the past two months. The anxiety, I suppose, comes from this new year opening up before me and making me dizzy, afraid of failure, mainly of not making it with my psychotherapy.

Yet my last two sessions with B. were positive. We both feel we will get along perfectly and soon be doing good work together. Another one or two "getting-to-know-you's" and . . . on with the job! . . .

I'm sleeping better, but only with the aid of stronger drugs, Neuroleptics that I don't trust. They make you wake up feeling dull, with diminished reflexes and lucidity. A feeling of drowsiness not far from neurasthenia. Anyway . . . this is only temporary, long enough to relax me, to get me back in shape.

You see, I was afraid of telling you about it, that you might be depressed or sad. Don't be. Little regressions like these are often the prelude to a greater step forward. So I remain optimistic, in spite of my present disarray. The clouds will soon go away. I keep my fingers crossed and think of you; you sustain me, across the mountains, if only through the golden ring I softly caress.

I love you, my "Dad," I need you and hope someday to be of help to you in turn, through my presence and my tenderness.

Everything works out, the pieces always get put back together again. But not too fast, or there's a danger of spoiling some of them . . .

Yum-yum . . .

your "little"

Marie-Jo

May 2, 1977

My big Dad,

I don't know how to write anymore, excuse me. That's one of the reasons for my long silence. And then . . . I keep fighting off nightmares, what with my contradictions, my bulimia, my insomniac nights . . .

I do everything I can to improve with B. but it's not very fast. I'm marking time. I despair at times and call to you in tears, at night, deep in my bed. You gave all of yourself that you could to help me. You can't do any more. Simply, I am just not up to your presents. My apartment remains empty and I wonder whether I'll ever see the day it is lived in. My thoughts dribble away, my memory is fading, my body doesn't always obey me, tense as it is with anxiety and refusal to accept it as it is.

I forget who Marie-Jo is. I don't know the monster who has taken her place. I suffer for nothing, gratuitously, for want of knowing how to live.

Dad, write me a little note, any old thing. I need it. I'm even losing the hope of seeing you again someday.

I long for your arms, your love, to cuddle up in your confidence. Recall security to me. Does it still exist? How does one find it?

I hurt, you know . . .

your "little girl"

Marie-Jo

July 12, 1977
[Letter in English]

I would have liked to live in Beauty, Peace and Harmony, to know Love again, to come in Love for the first time, with tenderness, before I die.

It's already too late. No more feelings in my heart, just emptiness. My brain is broken and my body lost somewhere, very far from me. I stop to fight, to suffer for nothing. I have spent my life to destroy myself and at last

I won! I am so week now that I can't even make one more step. My destiny is there. I have to follow it. Why do I still have to breathe, with so much pain and tears.

Please, Dad, make me die. I have nothing more to say. Maybe just "bye" to my father, the only person I thought I had loved completely. It was in fact just a dream, another illusion, because I was not able to understand myself well enough and so, not able to understand him either. Sorry, Father, I have lost you, killed you forever. I stop to exist at the same time. I'm not so sure that love ever existed somewhere else than in my imagination.

Forgive me Lord for all that I have made wrong, but I've lost my strength!

I have failed. Pardon me.

Take my life in your big universe . . . I hope to join the stars, the moon, the dark blue sky so beautiful . . . Will you give me that chance? . . .

I don't have my place in the world anymore! In fact, I've never had it! It's like a game, too hard to play, too complicated. And I am a bad actor.

Me? Who's "me"? "Me" was maybe never born! "Me" was dead before, many centuries ago. It was nobody, nothing. The dark is going to cover the page and the story will end here!!!!

Marie-Jo

July 14, 1977

Monday green. Wet of grass. Clouds of rain. Seven days before my eyes. Discouraging green.

Tuesday orange. Juice of fruit. Rays of sunshine. Fall of evening. Refreshing orange.

Wednesday red. Dried-up blood. Dying horizon. Opaque color. Suffocating red.

Thursday yellow. Acidity. Absence of light. Nerve-racking yellow.

Friday brown. Autumn. Cozy fireplace. Reassuring brown.

Saturday gray. Light haze or fog. Transparency. Melancholy. Old-time gray.

Sunday white. Vertiginous void. Anxiety surfacing. Space beyond comprehension. Silent white.

"La Verrière"

October 23, 1977

I love you without daring to touch you
Not knowing how to make myself yours
So I take refuge in my prison
For fear that I might soil you.

I would like to tear away your mask
And finally discover your real face
Through which I might recognize my own
And so dissipate all my nightmares.

Sketch of my childhood
Pastel faded with time
Unconscious of your adult presence
I refused to grow up along with you.

And yet I might have tamed you
Had I but buried the imaginary
But I was never able to get across
Your threshold opening to the horizon.

You who are the life of any man on earth
You are still within me when I think I'm far away

You keep entreating me to choose your way
While I scatter myself in every letter of your name.

"Poigny-la-Forêt"

October 25, 1977

There are no words I still know how to pronounce coherently to express the "overflowing" emptiness that immobilizes me in the unreal. All logic escapes me, all power of concentration, analysis and synthesis. The numerous exacerbated sensations I have experienced have canceled one another out by adding up too quickly into too great a contradiction. For the past two weeks, I have been living in two cycles, interchangeable from one hour to the next. Nonrecognition of myself, along with the fantasies of what I imagine I am or more precisely what I am not, and the sudden dynamism, at the limits of nervous tension, which makes me reopen my eyes on a world perhaps(?) more accessible. I lecture myself with gritted teeth. I shove myself forward (toward what? it hardly matters!) for the sole purpose of walking, even backward. For fear of finding myself paralyzed with anxiety, incapable of reacting, even by shaking my head. I am at the limit of burying myself alive. I reject my name, my money (my father's), my femininity, my place alongside others and in outside life. I go on walking without a goal, without creating anything, fleeing all responsibilities.

I am derailing. Certainly more than I even imagine. I am taking myself off onto a siding, to park my narcissistic suffering there.

November 12, 1977

My "big Dad,"

Finally a letter! . . . Everything happens! I hope that your convalescence is progressing well and that I will soon see you again in the same top shape as on my last trip.

Where are you with your writings? What are the titles of the last volumes still to appear? I admit being frustrated by not knowing and I forget to contact Annette to ask her for the last volume being printed. I have an intuition that they are more and more dense and condensed, deeper. I have the conviction that they will soon be the climax of your lifework.

I'm trying, between "downs," to discipline myself in writing. To write something other than "me" and always "me." I so want to get to a "tale," a "short story," "novellas." Am I really able to or is this just one more illusion?

You know what would be my dream? That you write me a "little story" for Christmas, that would be my present, something between the two of us which would be to me, not an example, but a stimulus. And then maybe I will send you one back and . . . It's only a dream. Don't feel obliged to make it come true.

I love you, "Monsieur Simenon—my Dad." And I am certain now that my whole life will be influenced by your work. Up to me to turn that into a "good" influence.

It is time for me to start getting ready for my final "release." Dr. M., who has treated me so far, leaves December 20. I hardly feel like staying here long after he goes, starting over with another whom I won't know and in whom I'll probably have less confidence.

The whole thing is not to overestimate my strength and to act without nervousness, without rushing things through some headstrong decision. I have to settle in calmly, without exhausting myself, with the support of B.

I have to make the decision and stick to it. Because prolonged hospitalization also has its dangers. I am losing the notion of outside reality, getting afraid of it, falling asleep in a false "securitization." Click! It is beginning to happen to me and all I need now is a good kick in the buttocks to project me forward.

To be in my apartment for the New Year?

Oh yes . . . I would so like to!

Why not say it positively, then?

I want it! There it is, it's said. Now to make it concrete . . .

your "little girl"

Marie-Jo

December 22, 1977

My "big good old Dad,"

How beautiful life is, son-of-a-bitch! How good it is to see, even if somewhat fuzzily, without glasses and without "dark." For the past two hours, I have been breaking in my contact lenses with delight, like a little Christmas bonus ahead of time.

I painted, last night, I planed planks, I washed, put away, and then

. . . I'm typing on the typewriter, to get myself used to it, old things to file away, pending having NEW ONES! I . . . I'm just plain living. And I really think (I cross my fingers!) [in English] that this Christmas is the one that will see a new birth. (Of me. Of Jesus I don't know.)

Thanks to you, my Daddy, thanks to your patience, to all that you have given me, to your trust in me, especially, in letting me make my own decision about my independence.

There will still be clouds, for sure. But I await them in full awareness, from now on, ready, if need be, to stand up on the tips of my toes and look out over them . . .

I love you with a capital A, you know, the one in Amour and Amusement, and even more so in my "dAd" . . .

Merry Christmas and Happy New Year [in English].

your cApital little girl

Marie-Jo
"Lido"

———

1978
Paris (Lido), 24 years old

———

January 16, 1978

I don't want to see anymore, hear anymore, speak anymore, just one last time to feel the throbbing of space grazing my skin.

After that I'll remain on my knees on the sidewalk of an evening, and I'll wait for the moon until it comes down into my hands.

At the hour of my death, I will in this way be without any more anxieties, shame or request. In the middle of the crowd continuing to go round, I will leave the world without breaking the circle, cautiously and without noise, as if it were nothing. Outside already, for good and forever, I will have the peculiar smile of losers, the smile open toward something else [than that] of the winner in it: the secret, the invisible, that which is inside and suddenly goes quiet, getting back to the source of well before birth, joining through the end the bit of beginning. When the unique coupling is consummated again, in a palpable silence of Peace and Harmony, when the outsized universe becomes human again, within reach of man suddenly transformed, transported beyond his norms, his shapes and limitations, returning to the central nucleus that engendered him.

I will perhaps have written a thousand books inside my head, danced on stages with spotlights for the blind, before those strangers, other people, apparently won over. I will have seduced them by imitating the whores, guided by the false information of distorting mirrors.

I will have wept especially over a thousand deaths of my father, all except the real one, a thousand imaginary ones, and moaned over my life, out of inability to become part of it.

An air bubble in the throat makes no noise. Yet it is the explosion of the being discovering himself, at the time of the adieu, at the curtain fall, when he has to leave himself as he gives up his name.

"Lido"

Cassette recorded by Marie-Jo, in English

"When I Was Alone"

"Lido, January 1978"

[*Beginning barely audible*]

> The music . . . and see how . . .
> I am just going to play it again . . .
> I don't care. It's already almost midnight . . .
> . . . at home . . . my dinner . . . everything and
> I haven't done . . .
>
> Put the record on and after maybe to just have
> a piece of quiet.
>
> [*Solo of Indian flute, then Marie-Jo speaking over it*]

Somebody who would see me now, he would think
I am really crazy and he would be right,
because I am.

He would think my mind's lost, anything and
nowhere,
any way . . .

I would like now to say no!
I don't want more.
I am not made for the life.
You gave it to me, Lord,
but I don't know what to do with it.

It may be something too, I mean or too big
for me or too simple. I try always to find
something more complicated.
I am always searching, searching, but
troubles and troubles again,
and that's why I bother every people, everybody.
You know that, Lord, don't you, since I am born.
You know why
When I am lying like that on the floor
I feel that all the rest is not more important,
that all the rest is just a bullshit.

And there is no reason to be in a hurry like
we are all the time, to run and to make forward . . .
We are losing our time and life, running after
something that does not exist, that will never
exist, that you are the only one to have
and we'll never know when nor how you've got it.

I don't like to talk on the microphone.
It's not the same. I have the impression to look
at myself in front of a mirror.
That's why I want to cry
and will not, I can't. I'm still waiting away
for tears. I don't know when I will have the
courage to see my father.
He will see that I am not well; it's not the

same like the telephone because when I call him
he cannot see me and I can try to have a clear
voice, I can find my words and I can say to him
it's always okay and that I am happy.
It's what he does by his own also.
He always tries to seem better than he is
on the phone I mean . . . Lord!
Do you realize that?

At first, I will have to wake up at seven o'clock
tomorrow morning, to be ready for my contact
lenses, to try to wear them and after I will have
to go to talk with B. again.
I'm sure it won't be enough . . . I am sure I will
forget the main things, the most important one.
I would like to . . . I don't know what . . . maybe
not to wait until my 30th years old to disappear.
When I try to be better
I feel one way or another, like that last
weekend,
because all my efforts seem so natural for others,
in fact they are,
it's not normal that they are so hard to me.

Now it's cold on the floor.
I would like to have your hand in mine
just like this on my head
to take all bad thoughts that there are in,
take it like this in your fingers
and to throw it away
by the window
to throw it in the space.

I don't know what I will do,
I am scared of myself again,
I am ashamed too for my brothers
to look like I am.

It hurts also, I mean . . . in my head and my
stomach and my legs.

· · ·

I would like to be able to write, for example,
to write a story or even just a letter
for my father.
I am scared too in front of the page and
I don't have no more ideas in my head, my broken mind.

There is nothing more, just a dark hole again,
like when I was younger.
It seems to repeat years after years,
always the same thing
always the same old step before to fall down,
it's harder and harder after, too, to wake
up again, to try to walk, if nowhere.

You know why the moment I have the impression
to bother everybody around me, first Mylène and
Marc, they have their work and it is important.
Johnny, too, because he is somebody now, and
I am quite nothing.
I will be never nothing, I mean nobody.
Why?
Because I don't know my name,
Because I never recognize Marie-Jo
or I don't want to recognize her.

I would like to . . . to get peace, Lord.
Peace . . . peace . . . You know what I mean
when I say PEACE, don't you?
It's really like the moon in the sky,
or like a piece of sunshine or
like when you breathe and you have the
impression it's for the first time in the world.
You know why
I would like to be able to do things by my own,
not to be always obliged to call somebody
like my father or somebody else, to say:
I don't know how to do,
I need money,
I have this appointment
I have to be in it and I have to work for him . . .
It's not true.

That's not what I want.
THAT'S NOT WHAT I WANT.
It's like for my lessons.
I try to have some English lessons
or type machine lessons and
I don't want to be secretary.
I know that's wrong to say that
but I don't want to be in an office for the
rest of my life.
It does not interest me.
I don't want to be closed in a business.
I, I . . .
O Lord, I am really sure what I try to get
in that fucking life don't exist.
It's not made for human beings.
It is nowhere.
It's too hard to try to have it in ourselves.
It's a question of imagination,
to try to imagine it days after days,
to try to be cool all the time,
to try to accept all the time, all things,
to try to smile and say I am Okay
and I don't care about . . .
Because in fact I care.
I suffer [*she sobs*].
God never knows why that . . . I am searching
so hard, this why that I repeat all the time
to you and for what you can't answer.
It would be too easy to have the answers,
to know the truth.
Truth [*she cries*]
The truth for what happened between my father
and my mother,
for what happened exactly
in front of my father and me.
Why I have always cried like that
and why I have always felt that I was . . . well . . .
I don't know but I was somebody strange and not
like the others . . . I don't know, Lord . . . I
don't want no more.

. . .

I made that crazy thing and I beg you pardon
for that. I have called the doctor this morning
and he said he will come at eight o'clock this
evening and I have waited, I've been waiting
until twenty past nine. And after I was so
scared and so hungry that I have run to just
eat bullshits and sugars and everything and
I have just put a note on my door with my excuses.
But it's not enough. It was stronger than I
that needing to eat food, just sugar and what
I don't like and I hate in fact,
just to be sick and to vomit and after
to lie on that floor and to be able to talk
to you.
I am sure now it comes so often, it's . . . it's
the fourth time it happens since I am out of the
clinic. I am sure it will come sooner and sooner
and now I'll be fat again or else I will die
and I will vomit once or . . . because I vomit
all the time blood and I shit blood too and all
this in troubles. I can't be worth physically
like that and mindly either.

I'll put the record player again just to hear
my music and after I will shut . . . I will shut
the microphone because I don't want to . . .
I can't be free; it's like if it would be
something else with me in my jail in that room
and it's an unagreeable impression.

I like to see the red light, American player
I give it was a warmer red light,
somebody, something, I mean, soft and nice.

[*Plays the same record as at start*]

O play it again
Game to my game [?]
O wake up and I will
Or go to the bottom and I will see me in front

of the mirror and try to be better.
Now it's my trousers [?] . . .
Maybe I will eat.
Maybe it'll happen and I fall down on my knees
just on the sidewalk like that, in the middle
of every all people around.
And I will say I can no more.
Don't help me, I don't need help.
Just say to you that I can't more.
You don't have to care about.
You don't have to call a doctor.
No S P L O [?], nothing.
Just want to stay on the sidewalk
on my knees and wait until I die,
to see that moon,
my head [*she cries*]
and wait until when I will stop breathing.
I'll be able to catch it in my hands,
the moon,
or else it's the same,
the same in dreams,
something round, round, pure
and natural.

O Jesus
if it continues like that I don't know, I . . .
you know . . .
I do not even see
I will get out of life by myself.
Just hope that you will,
you will take it on me soon.
I am too tired.
There is too much to do to be able to be useful
for people. I have so much to learn again.
Too much to learn to control myself
to be able to build for others.
I will try to fight again but if it's with
no more conviction, or not enough, I . . .
You know, don't you, what I mean?
I move, I don't know where.

I don't make a move
when moving.
But I need a Kleenex just to . . . just a
cigarette. Those cigarettes which will kill me.

I know one thing too, and that's
I am sure to never live long enough
to be really in love with somebody,
to make the world with somebody
and to be really happy and catch the moon
like I know.
I will never be able to get that instant to
my father, to see him without shame or fear or
anything like that, just to be me, and he him,
and just don't say anything but to look at
each other and to be friends and confident
of ourselves.
It's not possible . . .
Walls . . . my record player . . . You, Lord,
You know so much about my feelings for
my father and my family and all the people
that I like, that I think that I like, but
you are the only one; you don't have the
single ideas on that because I can see it
through my attitude because I look closed
all the time.

O Lord

I think I might . . .
I would like to have a big fever,
to be able to say just I am sick . . .
and not sick in my head, no,
just sick in my health.
Just give me one . . .
to pay attention,
for me it's not the same if I have something;
for instance they are used to see me sick
and they always think it's in my head first
and that's true.

I can't even just have a cold like somebody else,
like, like they have.
For me a cold is first a thing to say to my
psychologist.
You see why I am tired to death but I know
when I will wake up and try to go to bed,
after, I won't . . . I won't sleep very well.
I am too tired.
It's not a . . . I mean it's . . . oh you understand
what I mean, don't you?
I don't want to explain it again . . .
I don't want to explain
It's in myself but I can't explain it.
It's in myself and that's all [*she cries*].
It will never get away.
It's a part of me, and I will die with it
but I will never be able to live with it.
It's worse than a cancer or something like that,
It's . . . I don't know what it is.
I don't know that's a fear.
It's no longer a fear, it's more complicated.
It's also on you . . .
You know that's like a game
that you've lost . . . a game.
Even if you . . . you have to start it
you know that you've lost
and there's no reason for you to continue to play it
because it was wrong even when you . . . you made your
first step,
the first step was wrong
and you can't change it;
it will always be wrong.
You can try to run after that
but the first step was wrong when you've started.
You fall down sooner or later
and my first step was . . . I don't know when.
Not when . . . when I was dancing with you, father,
because I am sure at that time it was all right.
I am not sure you remember it . . . the same that
I remember [*she cries*];

that dance, that special music that I don't have
here, is the only thing I've got in my life,
my price [*or* Paris?], all the rest with my
mother, after with you, Daddy, and Teresa . . . it
was wrong.
Like a big mistake, or a big lie, or a big
misunderstanding.
I would like to be able to be naked in front
of you,
I mean naked my brain and that you would be
able to see everything in that would be okay for
you and you won't mind and you would agree with.
I would like that it would be possible
to be with people like that.
Just to feel [like?] others,
I mean to feel right others and
to know when they are tired or when they . . .
to know it and to just act
like we have to to be in harmony,
no discourageance more,
no talkings,
no problems,
I mean no fight.
Maybe no more languages,
just a feel with the skin, the body,
with the eyes . . .
O for me it's hard because I don't see
with my eyes. I am sure I am almost blind.
I'm able sometimes
to feel all right,
short times but
I am unable to . . .

I don't like this apartment . . .
just right now . . .
I heard a knocking at my door and
I was afraid . . . Naturally, it can be
just somebody in the hall
or some people that just try to get fun knocking at
my door,
but I don't feel secure . . .

Anyway, even if they can come in here, in that
room, they will never come in my jail
because for them that room will be just a room,
a piece or maybe they can steal some things
or I don't know.
For me it's a box,
four walls, four . . . that's just a box
and I am in it.
I have always been in boxes, the smaller
the boxes, my head and my stupid brain, which
does not work more or refuse to work,
like if something would be blocked forever.
You know what, Lord.
It's already quarter to one
and I have such a headache.
Nothing more in my stomach.
I have to stop to complain,
stop to talk to the microphone and
searching my words because when I am not
just in front of you I can't find my words anymore.
I am sure to make many mistakes and to be
not understood by other people than you,
but even if I make mistakes in English
it's our language and you understand it.
You understand all the languages on the earth
and in the universe.
You have the secret of that universe.

February 18, 1978

First of all man, all alone, unique point. And then, on earth, another
man all alone, unique in himself too but already a "second" point. Two
minuscule spots move beneath the sun, with the darkness of their two
shadows besides.

And then, on the concrete, the darkness grows. This is the multitude
of other unique beings, beings unaware of one another, a crisscrossing of
spots and shadows, the shadows making spots as if to mark off the space and
the spots were mistaking themselves for their shadows, beneath the no-

longer-visible sun. The anxiety is collective for the solitudes crowding one another. Each unique point claims to be more unique still. It tries to hide from itself, from its identity; it knows it will never be the others and turns them into random abstractions and finally washes ashore on the sphere of a world turning without revealing why.

The pinheads burst, they stick into each other's backs, and the shadows throw all the compasses off by covering the noonday sun with darkness.

And then, one day, the man-point, the nth spot casting a shadow on the preceding spots, the man-point raises up his pinhead and tries, all by himself, to see farther on. He thinks he sees his shadow disappearing at noon, and then shortly all those of the other assembled men. A unique work lies before the similar points: on the texture of the earth there then begins a wonderful weaving, a very simple design with juxtaposed spots, married one to another and merged into one color.

Men have the earth for their unique possession, they free themselves of the self enslaving the Earth.

"Carlton," Lausanne

February 20, 1978

For you, my Dad, whom I saw and heard so poorly, for want of being organized and making myself available.

Yet there have been moments of smiles, even of laughter, and that by itself promises me, in a short time after I have made more progress, comfort and harmony in your little bed-sitting room, with Teresa to smile upon us too and keep me, when I get too noisy, from exhausting my good "old Daddy" [words in English].

Three quarters of a century against one quarter.

One day, you'll see, it will be a century against a half and it will really be fascinating and funny to get together again!!! shaking our heads over the future of mankind, so small but so rich in themselves if only they "really" wanted to do good! . . .

your "little old"

Marie-Jo
"Figuiers 12"—Lausanne

Dad,
TONIGHT . . .
It was a bit of the moon, the dream moon of a slightly mad poet, that I gave you, from my insides, from my emotion, all that I am with promise of becoming . . .
I am happy.
Do you know why, hmm, tell me?
I found you again, simple as that . . .
And that's more than any present in the world.
your little

Marie-Jo
"Lido"

March 2, 1978

"Daddy-Daddy,"
Tennessee Waltz, at last! Like a secret anniversary present, last Wednesday, when I was going by Champs-Disques, I asked, without believing it possible, whether this song was still available anywhere.
It is sung the way we used to hear it at Echandens on your old 78 rpm, alas, broken since then . . .
Today, the magic of this waltz sends me back to the sunshine, to the savory taste of that vacation, so curiously lived "as a twosome" between six and seven at night.
I did not know, at the time, that this tune would later symbolize a conception of tenderness and love of life, an indispensable theme to walks at day's end, all dawdling, arm in arm, with the wild strawberries on a few knolls. My good-luck hymn of well-being with "the other one," when the "You" becomes "I" before it is "We" . . . A magnificent Monsieur in his evening dress, a Monsieur who smells good when he has me in his arms on the floor, who smells of his pipe and the freshness of shaving, with the softness of his vest against my cheek, this Monsieur who is my Daddy, unique, irreplaceable. My first man to love, the one that a lover, someday,

will have to compete with. This sweet well-being "of the twosome" in my seven-year-old heart keeps coming back to my over-twenty-year-old woman's body, reaching out to make a couple with a male, a companion . . .

Yes, but shhh! . . . No more words, no more writings. Listen, Daddy, the Tennessee Waltz! And then, if you wish to, after that, to make me happy, dance a step or two and take Teresa's hand. You will be back in Bürgenstock, will share our sunshine with her, our joy, a smile, the tinkling of an ice cube in a glass of orange juice.

There will always remain a little something unique in our recollection, a kind of involuntary selfishness. A bit of a secret deep in our breasts, down where it keeps warm and where it goes on reliving endlessly. A tiny bit of a secret for you and me, a "we" that goes on to the notes of the past . . .

I love you . . .

Marie-Jo

[She quotes the words, in English.]
(But I've not lost you, Daddy! Hey?)
Your little "old girl" [last two paragraphs in English]

Marie-Jo
"Lido"

March 13, 1978

My Dad-Daddy,

Quickly a little letter, to show you I'm not forgetting you, despite my antibiotics and suppositories! What sh . . ! Bronchitis, a good sinusitis, a little fever, and, for bonus, a few gynecological pains . . . It's really just what you like and what I am wild about myself for the start of a season!

Too bad, hmm? . . . My morale is holding out and I hope very quickly to be carrying out all the plans I recently made for myself.

Lots of contacts already made, as concerns "jobs" [word in English] likely to pay me half a "minimum wage" per month.

Anyway, I had started recording a tape for you, with my songs to the guitar. Unfortunately, I had to stop while in full swing, my voice sounding curiously like the heartsick croakings of a lovelorn toad . . .

Oh well! A week from now, if I behave myself on the "tobacco" side, I hope to be back in shape.

I am reading and rereading you: *Tant que je suis vivant* (As Long as

774

I Am Alive). And I'm waiting to have my mind entirely clear to write you all the impressions that submerge me when I steep myself in Simenon.

There are too many, almost. I have to get to sort them out in order to put them to you better. What stands out, of course, is the stature of a big "simple fellow," so complete in his simplicity that he can, sometimes, be irritating, a man so "human" that he seems to burst out of his bounds, always at the far end of paroxysms that are frightening, that totally overwhelm the everyday, that everyday that is everywhere so compact with an atmosphere that fills your life after having filled your books.

A personal worry: will you get to the end of the self-analysis that you have undertaken, first as the outline for a picture, as a sketch of no consequence, but the lines of which, dictation after dictation, on their own engender other lines, demand a precision you perhaps never intended.

After having stuffed yourself on "man" to the point of sweating, after having projected him in your books in a reality so dense it became unbearable, you come back to the one who seemed to have been forgotten, unconsciously repressed: Georges Simenon, plain and simple. Through "man laid bare" whom you have been going after all your life, hadn't you somewhat fled from the image of your "You," also laid bare? . . .

I admire you for trying, all by yourself, to undress him, without exhibitionism but without shame either. Simply with some modesties, some intimate taboos which may, at first glance, be taken for dishonesties. But if you someday achieve a bareness of yourself as complete as that of one of your books, that day, my Dad, will be . . . Not the consecration of a genius, in the usual terms and the lack of measure that that entails. Something no longer quite fully "human." No! You will have succeeded in attaining the essential, on an "against the grain" path contrary to the normal curves of life: from the man in the street who was everyone except "you" (especially through your image, it's worrisome so . . . quick a novel! I hurt, it's hard . . . why? . . . Because I keep running away from myself along all the pages which however, endlessly, bring me back to myself? . . .), you come back toward this "you," you look for him, little by little you put him into question again . . . He this time will be your starting point, opening toward the others. Men, and no longer man in the singular who, having become a character, was a palliative in your solitary creation for the lack of true communication with that indispensable recognition of your own image.

your little

Marie-Jo

What am I waiting for? . . . At six o'clock in the morning, after two sleepless nights of bulimia that engender four kilograms more on the scale, I am tottering as I go back and forth in my room, my belly heavy with a "vomit" that won't come up, looking like a pregnancy I will never have.

How many discoveries during my deliriums, last night, at dawn, before dozing off a bit in the daylight. And then how many clicks in my skull, of revolt and shame, of sorrow too on reading the book my mother has just written.

I have just finished it, my stomach ready to burst with the gorging I did to find a cowardly palliative for my anxieties. (Bulimia to cover up the other internal "shit" and vomit, with the illusion of expelling it from myself.)

They will redouble, moreover, in a little while in front of my mirror. I wanted to know, at last. A share of truth, to discover, through her story, images corresponding to those of my childhood, of my own lived version of that drama.

There are few. I lived mine outside of her rails, outside of my father's too, as if we had only been three runaway locomotives, speeding on, parallel, chasing after one another, but defying the rules of simple logic, which clearly demonstrated that in this way we could never come together.

Yesterday, at this same time, I was bawling myself out aloud, louder even than usual, begging my "you," that other "me," to answer the questions of my past. I was certain I would commit suicide during the next hour. So I could without fear bring the worst back up to the surface, without its affecting me in a future that would no longer be. It is practically impossible for me to transcribe my monologues now in these pages, for they are in English, my child's English. As it is just as hard for me to dictate my feelings to a tape recorder, because it cuts off the free passage of my unconscious speech, by taking on the aspect of a labored, studied English. Things, after all, have always been supports to me, an auxiliary, all projections of myself.

It is with them that I built my universe, the universe of Love, of warmth, of tenderness and touching, as well as the one of aggressiveness, poison, cruelty and shame. It was a chair that first made me discover the secret pleasure of my sex. It was also what engendered my first shame. A leaf, in a bush, was symbolic of nature, of Peace and the recognition of my being on earth. But it was also the bearer of little red fruit, symbolic of a poison that, perhaps, was going to take away my life when, after touching it, I would lick my fingers.

This doesn't come from my mother. Not in my recollections, at least. I had "my things" that brought me my fantasies long before she ever spoke to me of her own universe of madness. I was already abnormal. I already had a God and, already, I felt my body in conflict with my mind, the rejection of myself in actions that shamed me. Need to sully myself in my own eyes, to debase myself, to be nothing anymore and especially not Marie-Jo. I can still see, at school, about five years old, the little snots from my nose that I picked out with my fingers, during class. I never had a handkerchief and, by this habit, artfully maintained, I made an ever-bigger circle, around my seat, of little viscous grains that fell to the floor. The picture is still there, in my head, as clear as a photograph.

In the same way, in class, when nervous fatigue became too upsetting, imperceptibly I moved around on my seat in such a way as to revive, in a flash, that special warmth in my crotch. Can it be, really, that the teacher and my schoolmates never noticed anything? On the other hand, a ray of sunshine that fell in a slant over a rumpled sheet of paper became, for the time a difficult class lasted, the little dog that carried me off to its wonderful world, far from arithmetic and closed walls.

Seven o'clock. I'm not getting anywhere. Not by writing. I have to sleep finally, but first of all, and this will be the hardest part, I have to try to vomit a little.

Noiselessly, because Mylène and Marc are sleeping in the next room. Afterward . . . I give myself until tomorrow to recover, without feed and without sobs.

To deflate all my flesh too that's been puffed up by my overdoing things. Otherwise . . . I will certainly have to disappear, won't I? Instead of endlessly dragging around my own hatred, which can only run off onto others.

There will never be any answers. And yet, something has happened, something between Maman and Dad, the Why of both their books. Unfortunately these books are stuffed with those lies that are the truth to them and that will bring me only additional discomfort, if not panic.

How, why did they separate in such a way? Why was I caught between the two of them?

———

March ?, 1978
Cassette recorded by Marie-Jo, in English

———

. . . how it works. It's not easy, I mean that machine
there but I think you must make it better than
next, last, I mean. I'd like to have another
micro, but I don't have it. Bull shit!

[*She yawns*]

I don't know really how to do it. I am just lying
down on my bed and I hear the birds outside;
they sing; it is quite beautiful. In fact,
I don't care.

Let me see . . . I vomit three quarters of an hour
before and now I would have to sleep a little
bit to be okay for this afternoon when I will
be in front of you.

I thought that I had many things to explain on
that microphone. I have no more ideas now,
I don't know how to say them, it does not come
more in my head.

Yesterday, yesterday night it was really crazy.
I was really hating myself harder than I've ever
been. I saw the doctor and I was completely out
because I slept only one hour in the morning.
It was on Wednesday morning. Wednesday night I was
completely out when I saw him. Well it was maybe a
little bit of shame to show myself in that condition
but in fact I was so sure to soon really make a suicide,
I mean to kill myself, that it was no more

important to take pills to try to cure myself and
when he went away, when he left me, I was a little
bit anxious for sure but I just decided to eat
again and I keep my food like to punish myself more,
also because I was tired and it was very tiring
to try to vomit, especially now when I have no more
reactions and my stomach does not function very
well to try to push all that food away.
It's funny what I said. I cried a little bit
here in my music, but it was not like usual.
It was out of anything real, in another
dimension maybe, I don't know how we say in
English, it was the first time also I spoke
with my mother, I mean to my mother, and I was lying
down on the floor with my hands just under my stomach,
and I said to her, I can't find the words
now, the words were all right, I said: [Text incomplete.]

Not only just that image, it is not the worst,
but all what you told me, all the phone calls
when we were at the mountain and the phone calls
with Daddy and when after you cried you were
crying and telling me that you . . . I was tiring
and I was sick. It's not only that. I spoke to
the night also and I said:
"I have known how much it can be beautiful,
I know this, but now I am out, because I have
ruined my body, I have destroyed it better than
we can do and now for me it's no more possible.
And then now tonight through my window, I was . . ."
I opened the window in my bathroom and I shut
all the lights inside of the apartment and it
was no moon for sure because there is no moon now,
but no stars either and only that it was just not
dark blue as it has to be; it was something
yellow but gray at the same time, a sick gray,
a sick yellow, a sick color, like smog, and it
was coming maybe from the lights of the streets
all around, from the avenues, but it was like,
like if the sky would have been covered with a
wall, and I had to imagine the moon up through

that dead gray color and my stars and all
the . . .
and I felt involved again. I don't know how
to explain it . . .
Say those . . . what I have got in my life, what
I've got really nice from you. Just a smile,
a smile that maybe you don't remember, the time
you opened the door downstairs and you were
going I don't know where; I don't remember. It
was important, just before to go with your bicycle,
and you just opened the door and you smiled
to me and . . . No! It was when you went to buy
your, to make your shopping, and it was nice
outside, nice weather; it was sun and it was
great and spontaneous, and . . . Oh, I stop
because I can't explain all this, like I won't
be able to explain it in front of you in six
hours, something like that.

Oh, that's only shit, I am plenty of shit and
all what I am able to do is shit also, to make
shit all around me.

I don't care, and I have to
disappear. I can't continue that way for my own,
trying to get some instant of pleasure, and just
for all the other moments when I suffered and
when I can't do things right for my family and so
and so [*she sighs*] I am completely obsessed
by the money, to get money and to don't be in
front of that jealousy with Marc and Mylène and
Johnny and to have much more than they have, ah!
[*she sighs*] then I stop and see their next . . .

April 11, 1978

My "big good old Dad" and "Daddy,"
Your phone call, this morning, warmed my heart. You seemed, between the words, to understand so well my present disarray, lost as I saw

myself, recently, in the confused and "inexact" past of D.'s book, in your past so deep but heavy with suffering in *Quand j'étais vieux* (*When I Was Old*), and then, in your already-"past" present of *Tant que je suis vivant* (*As Long as I Am Alive*), recalling only in 1978 the thoughts of my Dad in 1976.

All of this shook me up in certain entirely new arrangements that I was trying, with so much difficulty, to acquire with B. in my suddenly "extra-hospital" life.

On December 6, it was as a fearful Baby that I left the clinic, and two years of institutionalization which, by lasting any longer, might work against me, might lock me up forever inside the unreal. So I had to get out, even, like a "Baby," unstable on my legs and expecting the worst "on the outside," after having understood that no more good, outside of myself, would come to me from any hospitals, whatever they might be. Even if I were to fall on my face, and perhaps for good, let it at least be in life while I persisted in struggling for some kind of dignity. It was more than hard. My worst enemy was myself; I needed at all costs to tame it, to demonstrate to it, by way of at times almost hysterical "*self*-bawlings-out," that it had no real reasons to go on destroying itself, that some qualities, even if rare, were still within this me and that they absolutely had to be exploited as a palliative against the shortcomings. I swore oaths, several during these four months, oaths by which I demanded of myself friendship for myself and for others, patience, as few "judgments" as possible, at any rate. A whole lot of indulgence!

All these oaths were sworn only to dissolve from week to week and they had to be continually renewed, recalled to this Marie-Jo who was destructive out of disgust, desperate at seeing herself, days on end, tirelessly going around in a circle, despairing of getting back a little of her personality, the one she might at last dare show to others, share with others, and not all the mud, the dirt, the horror that she always saw in it, and, in this refusal to accept it, bringing it thereby to be odious to her friends, intolerant, because so ill at ease in this still-unknown skin! . . . Poorly known!!! January saw me mainly leaning on the shoulders of Marc and Mylène, Boule and . . . on your money too Dad, which shames me the worst. Unable "really" to get organized, I sometimes paid twice as much as necessary for some of the apartment expenses. This shame, again, was one more reason for the destructive Marie-Jo to go on with her depredations. She dragged me into a complete anarchy of schedule, of appointments to make and keep, of hours needed for sleep. I was living most of the time in contradiction with time, getting my equilibrium back only by lucky random grabs, which very quickly turned into "illusions."

In February, after seeing you, I finally hoped to be able to accept m more and (my apartment was just about finished! . . .) with a man who seemed to love me too, who was often at my place to help me and . . . at last! . . . I was starting off again in life. I would make up a definite program, begin to make contacts, find out about classes and about . . . about too many things!!! Coincidence? . . . The man left on vacation just about the same time as D.'s phantoms appeared in her book.

I read. I reread. Then I made notes so that this new trauma might at least help with my spychotherapy [sic] work. I reread you fully. I compared. I spent nights of delirium in which my fantasies, as if liberated, came out of my subconscious to keep me company. I gritted my teeth. I knew that in this way I was finding out about a lot of things, a lot about this deeper "Me," usually unconscious, but which all of a sudden seemed almost legible.

I was writing everything, frenetically, all my discoveries, all the images, all . . . all my despairs, in the final analysis. Because it was TOO MUCH!!! I was becoming worse than a "monster"; all of my past, thus laid bare, revolted me. And the sessions with B. were not long enough to allow me to put each thing back in its place, in a more correct, more rigorous analysis . . .

[*Unfinished*]
"Lido"

April 14, 1978

My Daddy,

Quick, before the "family" leaves to go to you, this short note.

A "long long" letter is in the works. Too long to finish today. But I promise you you'll get it next week.

So . . . I'm feeling better, truly. I'll spend my Saturday quietly tomorrow with Boule. And I'll breathe a little country air, after having "locked myself up" in my problems. I was wrong to see maman, last week. I didn't know her neurotic "truth" would upset me to such a point.

I love "you," you know, so much! Will you always remember it? . . .

Till soon, whenever you want, when we can be quiet and it can be good walking in the sunlight! . . .

Yum-Yum, a real whole lot and . . . have a good time with all of them. You'll see Serge . . . He's terrific. What a great guy!

Marie-Jo
"Lido"

"My Daddy,"

A small rotten snapshot and had fun coloring it— A gadget! . . . (didn't try to get a resemblance, don't look for any! . . .)

For tape No. 1, I started on side No. 2 (side two) [two words in English]. But nothing of interest, except maybe some "little dog bayings to the moon." (My own, the bayings, I mean, like a strange lullaby. I didn't think it was recording yet. Fact is, all I've done here, I did voluntarily ignoring the mike, convincing myself that the machine wasn't turned on. Which played tricks on me: all the last part of side 2, with "The Flat Country," is practically inaudible, even with the volume full up— Your poor ear . . . Won't it be put to the torture? As a present, this is really good! . . .)

Side one [in English], 1st tape: new or improvised poems on old themes from drafts a little over two years old— So, not my current mood, never fear! . . .

Alternation of Tahitian, American, and a little more classical tunes . . .

"*Jeux interdits*" [Forbidden Games]—(oh, so badly played)!

On the other tape, almost virgin, just an attempt to put words to "Blowing in the wind"—and then, lucubrations starting, again from illegible drafts of two or maybe three years ago.

Nothing any good.

Only authentic thing, in my eyes: the improvisations. When I speak to you, in spite of the "squeaks" and "squawks," but so inaudible because of the amplifier that I'm really afraid you won't ever understand any of it . . .

Yet, it was at last something "real"
and so full of you! ! !

Marie-Jo

Text of cassettes
accompanying letter of May 10

This recorded tape is for you, Daddy, and don't hold it against me if at times you don't hear well; it's because the tape didn't work. So at times you'll have to set very very loud, especially on the other side and maybe on this side too, at the maximum, and maybe then you'll have to glue your ear to understand, but I hadn't the courage to do it over because, first of all, I admit to you I did this with a tiny little machine because I hadn't the courage to take out the big one, and besides, I did this being tired but thinking so much of you, and I said to myself that it was worth the trouble and that even if it was bad it was still a little bit of my presence that you can always cut off by pressing the button. But it's not as if I was there. When I am there you can't press a button and make me disappear like that. You at least have to say to me: Marie-Jo, be a good girl; I have to be quiet a little. So then, you'll press the button and I am not there anymore and then you can press the button again and I'll be there. So it's practical, isn't it? And then maybe you'll be able to send me a little message the same way. We'll mutually press our buttons and that way we'll each have a little of both of us whenever we want, before we see each other for good, without any more buttons. Buttons are for pants, buttons are for suits, buttons, they're all right from time to time for heads like muttons—to make a rhyme—but not for life forever and all the time. OK?

Fine, I'm going to try a song again. I don't know what you like, but before that I'll quick have to listen to it, have to make a little stop to find out if it recorded. OK?

[*Accompanying herself on the guitar, she sings in English "You Are My Sunshine."*]

I just want to tell you, you who may be anyone or anything, a star in my window, a street light, an elevator door, why not, or you the tree, or all those unknown faces, all those around me, you, listen:

I ache, tonight, ache in my being, tired of living my life so stupidly, like those in false comfort, like those in alcoholic illusions, of being there eating richly while others, others outside, have nothing, nothing to eat, nothing even to say: I'm eating poor. Like the food, I waste my time, and time does the same to me because it gobbles me up too. It gobbles up my existence because I leave it to it, because it gets away from me, because I can't be master of it or am not master of it anymore, if it can be said that once I was able to master it.

I ache for love, ache in my skin, my nerves at the quick, head empty, or too full. Those are words that we've all used so much that they're empty too, empty by dint of trying to be filled up.

I'm telling all this to you now, for all those I won't tell it to. All the things that I'll leave alone, right in their places, their places that they have found and that I don't for anything want to take away from them. On the contrary, I love things perhaps, instead of human beings, because, precisely in their places, they are, they represent, everything peaceful, everything that doesn't move, that accepts being there and that one can touch, caress, without making it run away and without, without torturing, without bumping it.

To you who won't even be my lover tonight, not even a companion, nothing of what I expected, as a child, simply my pillow no doubt, a little bit of warmth tonight, you who in fact will be absent, for want of having gone to meet you. You whom I know to be everywhere in fact in the world, whom I know to be plural when I want you singular, to you, I say good evening to you; in fact forget that I ache; that'll make me forget too.

To sleep in your arms, Josephine, to sleep within the gaze of your single eye, so lively, so bright, blue as the sky before nightfall, circled with depth as when night is falling. To sleep in your arms, little elephant. My childhood from before my bad childhood, my childhood all sunshine and laughter, racing through the woods, my childhood of cows and chickens, wheat fields and chestnuts, my sunshine of wine presses and my naked feet, my childhood with a garden of my own, a secret, beneath a felled tree. Little elephant, I told you everything tonight, I covered you with tears that in fact were only mine, old lady's tears already, dirtying your oh so dusty plush because you come back to me from far away. From a furniture warehouse that becomes repository of the past. I caressed you with my uncreating hands, empty hands, no longer good for anything, good only to smooth down your ears and maybe soon to sew in your eyes. No not maybe, soon, yes, I promise you. The one you're missing, the one in which you fall asleep. But you know, Josephine, all the glint of that missing eye has added itself to the other which becomes even sweeter, benevolent, sometimes mysterious, but always conciliating.

Little elephant, make me sleep, make me dream for real at night when it's allowed and drive away the dreams of daytime when they're forbidden.

[*Accompanying herself on the guitar, Tahitian songs with Tahitian words: 1. "Tahiti," 2. "Eh ma doudou," 3. "Na teva Ohé Ana."*]

I unscrewed my head
And I dug a hole
In the mud of the earth,
Had it all over my hands.
Then I sat me down,
My head on my knees,
Right next to the hole
where I was going to bury it.

I thought I was seeing for the very last time
This part of me that had made me suffer so.
I looked at my eyes, which were sobbing still,
And I saw that my mouth was opening to speak.

"You have nothing left to say,"
I whispered to it.
"I don't want to hear you moaning any more about my past."
That waxen face, perfect reflection of my own,
Allowed itself a grin that I took to be a sneer.

"So, I disgust you?"
I asked of it.
"Well, it's mutual then,
Because I abhor you.
You made me sick with all your illusions.
You always cheated me, by scrambling my thoughts.
You truly applied yourself, oh yes, to forgetting my name,
To cutting me off from the world, from all truths.
You destroyed my body, through all those years,
Forcing on it your rhythm of a compass gone wild.
My revolt today should come as no surprise.
I invite you to taste the hell I have endured.
You're no longer at all like me, no longer of my blood.
So carry off to your grave this monster
You wanted to be mine."

I had spit these words out in my blind rage
With so much violence I was suddenly afraid
My head no longer had the strength to reply.
Its features became set as it heard me cry.
It rolled without noise to the crook of my arm
Looking for some warmth like a tiny kitten.
I didn't know what to do. I was ashamed of us.
And then in the hole in my neck
There came a draft of air.
So I shivered and put my hand on my head
in distress,
Quite worried about myself.

"Go on, don't take it to heart.
I made a mistake.
Your place really is up there
At the top of myself."

I screwed my head back between my two shoulders.
With my foot I closed the hole of its coffin.
I felt very funny.
I was almost dizzy,
An aftertaste of tears
Buried in my chest.

At last I understood that beyond disgust
There was tenderness in a corner of my skull,
And I smiled, timidly, thinking of my head,
And I felt the smile coming out of its eyes.

On a walled road with a drop on either side,
On a road that is blocked,
The man all alone walks, exhausted.
A sign farther on with these words:
"No exit, turn back."

Turn back to what, the man wonders.
Go back the other way on the road to the past,
Mark time again in all those lost years,
Then start all over again after digesting them?

The man tottered. He becomes blind.
His brain is sinking in the blanched sun,
In the dust of this road,
This road to nowhere.
Going backward is absurd.

But understand, dear God, I no longer have the time.
I've chucked up my past,
I've fled the stink of it.
If I don't have this road,
Then where will I go?

Everything fogged over. Before his eyes already
And inside his head
And from his mouth a strange tick-tock, tick-tock is heard,
An obsessive tick-tock.
The tick-tock of time,
The one that makes the world run,
The one that made him run on this road
For nothing,
The one that recalls death
To come in his name.
The man has lost his shadow
In spite of the blanched sun.
He no longer has a self.
He is alone without his double,
His earlier companion,
When he falls in the dust.
His identity escapes and sinks in farther on
And is not afraid to flee.
And the man wants to yell to call it back,
To get it to . . . to stay.
But the image has trembled because of the drops of sweat,
Because of the mixture of dream,
For the man can no longer think.
He no longer hears the obsessive tick-tock,
The tick-tock of his mouth,
That of one already . . . already dying.
The identity, the timid identity,
Comes back toward the shape on the road.

The shadow comes back down, slides under the man.
It comes back, like a velvety rug,
For him to retrieve a little softness,
In this abandon, in the last one
That finally carries him elsewhere,
Even if it isn't by way of the road,
By some other, by a return to the past,
Even if it is now in a somewhere else,
He will never have been able to imagine.

[*On guitar alone: two melodies*]
End of tape, my Dad.

———

Cassette

———

Eleven-year-old Poem

Thunder's rumbling
Rain is falling
Sky is darkening
Flash in distance

Trees are shaking
Flowers are bending
Clouds are advancing
A little rabbit
It's a real deluge coming down now
Like the Good Lord having fun just like a kid.
He surely thinks he's gone back in time
To when men fought for their damsels with devotion,
Riding up on their horses in coat of mail.
He is acting just like Don Quixote
With his windmills.
Charging his rival,
Lance point thrust out,

Very lordly, he goes forward,
And looking very determined.
Oh, you'll have her, your damsel in distress,
Oh Lord king of the Heavens,
But only, only for her,
See how it's raining,
How it's raining.

You're really a little rascal
Doing only as you see fit.
See how the hay is now
Lost perhaps to the peasants?
No, do not feel broken-hearted.
We like you a lot all the same.
Anyway, listen to the bells ringing.
They're carrying on like that for you.
So, laugh, laugh, laugh,
Like the big kid that you are,
For after all, you've really deserved
This little party we're giving for you.

[*Sings to guitar accompaniment*]

This is just *au revoir*,
My friends,
This is just *au revoir*.
Because we'll meet again,
My friends,
It's just an *au revoir*.
It's just an *au revoir*,
My friends,
It's just an *au revoir*.
Because we'll meet again,
My friends,
It's just an *au revoir*.

[*To the same tune*]

Maybe it is just good day,
Maybe just good night,
Because you know so well, my Dad,

I'll be back with you, right.
Sometimes at night when I'm alone
I whisper little words
And then when it is very late
I just give you a kiss.
Of course that's only in my head
And you are not aware,
Except perhaps that in your dream
I am a little there.
Yes, it is just a good day,
It is just a good night,
And it will be all laughs,
And yes, especially,
All joy when I
Come back there to see you.
I'll explain all the things that you
Perhaps never understood,
Everything that took me such a long time,
Almost a quarter of a life,
To be able to understand,
Through a very long travail,
And then, you know,
Nothing's ever done,
Especially when one starts to think
About problems and about oneself,
Hoping someday in that way
To be with all the rest again,
To be back with you, my Dad,
So this is not an *au revoir*,
No, it's just a new hello,
And soon again in your arms
I'll be back with you.

"The Flat Country":
    With the North Sea
    Just like . . .
My mistake, my mistake, that's awful. I'll start over. I have to start over.
Tired, hmm? Don't worry about it [sentence in English].
[*Seductively*]
    With the North Sea
    Just like us . . .

791

That can't be! It's starting again. Shit.
Let me pull myself together, hmm? Just a second.
[*With a Provençal accent*]
     With the North Sea
     As if unique . . .
[*She drops Brel's words and just hums the tune, then goes back to Brel's words.
At the end of the song, she whistles to her guitar accompaniment, then to that same
tune, sings:*]
     I'll never have but one Daddy.
     He is just terrific.
     With a Daddy I won't ever forget,
     With a Daddy who's in all my memories,
     With a Daddy I'd like to see again,
     With a Daddy I'd like to cater to,
     A little as if he were,
     As if he were a little kid,
     Like children both of us.
     Like two children
     Both of us,
     Together laughing
     At the sun,
     Forgetting the gray
     Of every day,
     Forgetting the gray
     Words sometimes say,
     Forgetting the gray
     Of words sometimes in the way,
     In the way,
     In the way.

     That is why we must stay quietly,
     Listening to the waves so quietly
     And thinking that far away
     The sea is going out
     To join up with the light
     from which all of us have come,
     A light that feels good on one's skin,
     Just like it feels so good
     To feel the rays of sunshine,
     Feel the wind,
     Feel all of nature,

And to feel in the eyes of another,
of one's father, a little love,
Which out of reserve we call affection,
and then out of reserve don't call anything at all.
We forget, we can no longer say: I love you.
Because that's of another time,
That is made for women,
That is made for lovers.
So we say: I love you a lot, you know,
That little "you know" to hide the "lot"
and to cover up "I dared say I love you."

[*Accompanying herself on the guitar, she whistles "Where Have All the Flowers Gone?"*]

End of this part and unfortunately very very badly recorded. Excuse me, Dad. OK?

Cassette marked "STRICTLY PERSONAL"

[*First side: Statement only, which I take to be "Song, my own words"* + *"improvised" ramblings*]

I'm going to try a new song, but I don't know it at all because I made up words to the tune of Bob Dylan's "How Many Roads Must a Man Walk Down, etc." and it's the same tune but the words are mine. This is the first time I'm singing it, so I'm afraid I may make a few little mistakes. Anyway, that's not too serious!
[*In English:*]
How many years of my life have I lost
Believing I was all alone? Yes and
How many times will it take me
Before to accept what I am?

The answer, I know,
The answer is on my brain.

The answer is mine
But I don't find.

How many times will I be on my knees,
Falling down road after road?
I am scared about the light,
I try to hide my face,
I am scared about my own body and mind.

But maybe one day after those years of pain
I will at last understand?
Accept that I can't positively repair
All what in the past I have failed?

The night I will sleep,
Getting out of my fear,
You will maybe feel proud of me?
I'll stop to break my tenderness and love
And stand on my feet until the end,
When endly in my dreams
I'll see you, Daddy, smile,
I'll know that my shame
Will disappear.

When endly in my dreams I'll see you, father, smile,
I'll know that my shame will disappear.
The answer is mine,
Is somewhere in my brain.
The answer is mine
But I don't find.

When endly in my dreams,
I'll see you, Daddy, smile,
I'll know that my shame
Will disappear.

[*Hums, then whistles, accompanied by the guitar, then, very softly:*]
The night . . .
Sleep . . .
Getting out
My fear.

You will maybe
Be proud of me
When endly in my dreams
I'll see you, Daddy, smile.
[*In a more determined tone:*]
I'll know, know, know and know,
Yes, that my shame
Will disappear.

Cassette

Ah, music at ground level. My notebook on the floor, just below, and, above, my body lying on my belly. Is it really my body? Wait, I'm feeling. Yes. Yes yes, I believe, at least it looks like it. Even examined closely in the light. Because I have a light, there in the corner, behind the loudspeaker; it is illuminating the three of us, the music, the notebook and me. Oh excuse me! Oh all my apologies. All four of us I ought to say. How could I have forgotten? Oh yes how? And why did I catch myself when at last I had succeeded in ignoring her presence. Oh well, never mind, hmm!

Fine. She is here. Much too much, even. One would think that the whole business is just for her. I'm talking . . . don't you know? . . . I'm talking about my anxiety. But don't you know her? Ah! You sure are lucky. Fine! But then I have to introduce you. Excuse me, if you please. She would be offended otherwise, you understand? Uh, well, there it is. Oh no, hmm, now that it's done, don't you try ducking out like that. Ah, you're not going to run away, now; are you scared? Scared of my anxiety, but that's ridiculous, you see. You know, you couldn't be any more scared than she is. On that score, she's really unbeatable. Myself, for example, in all this time, I've never been able to outdo her. So, in the distress sector, hmm, no way to beat her by a single degree. Anyway, one might believe that . . . I don't know . . . that she spies on me, that she examines me, and then, then she trembles. So I tremble too. Inside, I say to myself: holy shit, I'm trembling more than she is, right? No, not at all, not by any means. There've been several checks. No change. Always the same. It's not funny, you know. Once at least when

795

I was on grounds where I thought I could prove myself . . . well no, there, not a chance. But, you know, it's not really her fault. Got to be sorry for her, see. At the beginning I had said to myself: First I'll hide all the mirrors. No more mirrors, could be she'll be less scared. Because maybe it's as with animals; anxiety, it sees itself in a mirror, then it gets scared because it doesn't really know what that is. So, no more mirrors, no more nothing. And then I see her, there in the corner, warm and cozy, quiet like me, then . . . Bang, something hits me all of a sudden. So I say to myself: Shit, what is that? Ah, it was the walls, that is, one of the walls. Well, not really so much a wall. Oh well, look, just imagine: she was all alone, she didn't have any mirror and so, just the same, she had to go and project on the wall the image she had of herself and bing! same old thing. Only there it kind of went in the wrong direction and hit me smack in the face. Well, that was one I didn't appreciate, because, okay, well, all she had to do was be objective, because it's a known fact that when the shot and when the reflection, after, the reflection . . . I mean that the transfer is subjective, so it can make a mistake in its trajectory, so then, I can understand, but . . . ah, that wasn't the first time what kind of a load did I take all over my head, hmm? Well, after, I tried having it out a little with her, because if she could receive a little too, then she'd leave me alone. But what was the worst part about it was that I was beginning to look at the walls too. And then all of a sudden: Bang! Boom! Bang! It hit. Oh well, I smiled the tiniest bit because on account of me I wasn't objective anymore, not at all; well, there was my whole subjective falling down on her. So once again we had a draw. *(Sigh)* After all, without Anxiety there, well, I'm telling you this now because I think, and I hope, she's not hearing, okay, so what should I do? Well, I mean to say, yes, I was talking about the three of us, my notebook, my music and me, but the music, it's there to make me forget that in my notebook I'm not writing anything, and besides, my lying on top of it doesn't do much. So, that's when I look at my Anxiety and then I say to myself: "Couldn't you maybe write a little too? Well instead of making reflections off the wall, do them in my notebook at least."

I had no sooner said that than bing! I get something in my eye. It was a letter. That is, I mean a letter of the alphabet, and it just jumped like that boom! into my eye. So I look at the letter: it was an M. Well, yes, I must have written my name like that without knowing why, for want of writing anything else. Well, all the other letters went in too, hmm, all in the same eye. So then, because I had almost enough of it, I *(sigh)*, I wrote Anxiety. I said to my self at least that'll go to her. Well no, bang! in my other eye. And then that isn't all, because there were other pages underneath. And then that was just unbelievable. One might have thought there was a storm, and all the words began to waltz, to waltz, to waltz, and it wasn't in my eyes anymore they came; it was really right into my own head. Well into my thoughts, into my brain. Poof! So can you feature that, me, who'd already had so much trouble getting them out, putting them on paper, now the paper had to send them back to me by way of that other one there. And they pounded into my brain as fast as they had come out. It was miserable.

I don't know why I'm telling you all this; after all, you, you don't care a shit about it. Well, you got your little dog, so it keeps you company. What is his name? [*She bursts out laughing.*] Ho, that's cute, Loulou! Hello, Loulou. Ah, but I haven't had the honor of being introduced. Loulou? Ah! Monsieur Loulou, and Loulou Dog. That's very nice. And there are never confusions, that way? When somebody calls Loulou, then he goes, or when, or else you, you go when it's he they're calling, right? I'm saying that, you know, because, well, the same thing happened to a pal of mine. Oh, I think he was off the wall, like me with my anxiety. He had a dog, and one night he says to me:

"I take him out, there, as usual. I take the leash because in the neighborhood one didn't have the right, well, one couldn't go out without the leash, because the cops wouldn't let you. The cops, you know, I've had it up to here and then some," but I wasn't listening anymore because he was talking politics and at the time I didn't know much about that.

He says, "Okay, I take on the leash, we go toward the usual lamppost. Well, we stay there a little while as usual, time enough for . . . Then I go back home. I close the door. Then I see my dog scratching, scratching at the door, and moaning and I say to him:

"Come on now, don't pull that on me; after all, you just peed, and . . . then, just when I'm bawling him out and I say the word 'peed,' I look at my fly and I see it's unbuttoned. Poor fella, I say; I hadn't even realized I was the one who peed against the lamppost; he must have been knocked for a loop. I had acted as though, as usual . . . Crazy, hmm. Oh but then, I was going nuts too."

Anyway, that's to show you that there are things unbelievable like that that happen sometimes.

Good, well, well I'm going, I'm going to let you go. Just say good-bye to my companion here. Maybe that'll make her happy. Oh, happy I don't know, because she doesn't know what happy is. Imagine! Anxiety. Anxiety everywhere. So anxiety even when it's a little bit happy, it's no longer happy. It's nothing. She rejects everything. Everything, everything, everything. Maybe she won't even say good-bye to you.

"Well, well, aren't you going to say good-bye to the gentleman? You . . . hmm . . . what are you going to say to him?"

You see, she doesn't want to answer. Oh watch out! Shit! See that? Yes, that's it, I knew it. She has . . . well yes, the dog jumped out of the window. You know that's not serious; we're on the ground floor. He'll come back, he'll come back.

"Hey, come here, come here, come here, come here, Loulou, come here. Jump jump through the window, come back in, jump through the window. Hey there, listen, hey! Hey! You must be high or something! What are you doing? You're not the one I told to jump!"

Well, now the two of them are gone. You're not very amusing, you, you know; truly, you're shooting your mouth off. Oh, and cut that out with the walls, cut it out with all of that, cut it out with the words . . . I've had it up to here as well, you know. Go on, get out. You've got the keyhole, there, isn't that enough for you, no? You don't need a lot of room. You take up a lot, yes, but you don't need much room just the same if you want to go in or out. Ah, at any rate, it's as if I was talking to some wind. Couldn't you make a deal, say? for tonight. Because I've been putting on an act also. Anyway, you know it. Oh, no need to smile. [*She sighs.*] Put on a little act for yourself tonight. Imagine that . . . look, with your letters try to make another word. Hmm? With an x and a y . . . oh, you're missing some others, but don't you think you could turn it into the word tenderness? For one night. Just one. You know, that one could jump right up at us. Wouldn't hurt a bit. Try! You willing, eh? Let's write: tenderness, in the notebook. Come on, help me. Come on. Write: Tenderness. And that would really be something nice to lie down on. OK? Well then, good night. Good night! I'm putting out the light.

[*Free, "live" improvisation of a story*]

It was early morning.
Yes, I remember it very well, you know.
One of those early mornings over Paris
that have been so often described,
with some haziness,
little droplets of rain
and then the cold
on your trench coat
gray as the rain.
A strange kind of trench coat, anyway,
out of fashion.

For someone of my age
we were young,
both of us.
We had maybe been drinking a little,
oh, a little like anyone else.
Afterward, to wipe out the night,
we had had a croissant
each,
that is, each had had a half.
We really weren't hungry.
We really wanted something else,
were hungry for something else,
not even for love,
that is, not that kind of love,
the love in bed,
the love of embraces.
What we wanted
was to put in concrete form the empty words
that we had spoken,
glass after glass,
empty words in the night,
even hollower in the early morning,
words on which the little rain
bounced up
and then wiped them away.

I remember, with a smile you took my hand
and then, how come I didn't understand?
You said to me:
"Okay, well, so long! I'm going back to . . .
I'm going back to my wife, over there."

You said your wife with a little laugh.
She was only your then companion,
Just one of those girls.
But certain words, you never used,
perhaps out of modesty,
and you said "wife" with something like pride,
still, despite your confusion.

                    •   •   •

It's true, you said to me:
"She's waiting for me over there."

I went out
and saw your back
in your trench coat
crossing the bridge.
Then I went away
in another direction.
What I didn't know
was that the wife,
waiting for you over there,
was not on the other side of the bridge.
It was the Seine down below,
and that you had jumped,
that nobody,
not even me—I was in the Métro—
that nobody had heard a thing,
and that by chance later on
like a big fat fish,
like all those no longer in the river,
a fisherman had brought you in.

You had said:
"No one can understand."
But had I been paying attention,
it so turns out,
with that smile,
I would have known, have understood:
You were speaking of . . . of all the others
out of contact with all those others still.
You were speaking of a whole world
imposing itself, on the contrary, on the same world.
Billions of mirrors
bouncing back their images
without hearing the cries, the calls,
stopping up their ears
so as not to hear the suffering
clinging to the image, the image
of the actors.

I no longer very well know, you see
But . . . I think that even if I hadn't kept you,
kept you from jumping,
even if, rather, I hadn't helped you
not to jump,
I would have understood for myself,
perhaps a little bit for all those others,
I would have understood why tonight
I'm talking to a hazy face
no longer quite yours anymore.

I'm talking nonsense about myself.
I have the feeling I can still see your legs
on the parapet.
I have the impression of feeling the movement,
and the movement I feel is the one
that is struggling within me,
very much the same,
ready to act,
ready to destroy me.
I will not need the Seine;
there are other ways
already planned,
in fact, for a very long time.
Maybe already
that very morning
when the two of us were talking . . .

Don't you find now, say,
that it was stupid?
You who by now
perhaps
have found some whys,
some hows?

Perhaps . . .
Perhaps you do know, say,
now, when it is too late,
what all of us might do

with our lives
so they too should be exactly like
a thrill of understanding,
a burst of . . . in the eyes, that shimmers
and then comes back to the other,
some furtive but very real contacts.
All those contacts that
for good and all
would destroy all the make-believes.

[*Another "strange story"*]

Just the same it's a strange story.
I must tell it to you because . . .
Oh, it's a story that didn't appear
in the papers, with good reason.
Nobody else . . . fact is, nobody
knows it but me.

It was told to me by a pal.
If I now feel free to talk about it,
it's because he's gone far away
and I don't think he'll ever come back.

I'll gloss over some details because
they're all connected with who he is,
with his private life, and might permit
recognizing him if by chance one day you
too were to go very far away and then, very
far away by chance, you and he were to meet.

Anyway, he was somebody . . . from what is called
a good family, but in fact from a very bad
family as well,
you know, people who drank,
people who underwent quite a few stays
in psychiatric hospitals for
nervous depression, for . . . you know, all
the everyday, normal life, which all of us

know and . . . which we are not spared.
It has become commonplace anyway.

But for him, no.
Obviously, his family to him was the
center of the world and no matter how he tried
to compare, to look at things around him,
he hadn't yet gone very far away.
As it happened, he thought he was perhaps
responsible
or else in the opposite way useless,
that he had no place there
or that he had too much.
Now, to the story. He had moved to
Paris. He had a not bad studio, which I
visited, by the way, and that's how I
got mixed up in all the circumstances that
make up this story.

And he bought a phone-answerer. He said to me:
"You know, with the life we're leading these
days, it's a very useful thing; if I go out,
I know who calls me," and so on, and so on.

The fact was, he wasn't doing much and
he knew himself, and when he talked to me,
even if he tried to smile and despite the
agitation that he tried to whip up in himself so
as to whip it up around him too, he didn't believe
in it really.

Anyway, during his nighttime tours, which were
mainly to escape his nothingness, to try
to forget it or not recognize his
usefulness, he was always afraid, with a terrible
anxiety, that he might not know if that answerer
was answering properly, because he had had some troubles
at first, and, he had tried
to figure out approximately at what time
people might have phoned.

So, to accomplish this, for instance, we would come out
of the movies and he would say:
"Excuse me, I'm going to phone myself."
It was, besides, an expression that he found
to be rather amusing, and so he'd make his call
and then come back.

Fine! And even when he wasn't with me, I
know he'd do this often, and constantly when
he was not at home for two or three hours
at a time.
It sometimes even happened that he made
five or six phone calls which he had
to listen to later and which were
all in his own voice, coming from himself.

In the beginning, it was all right except for the
drawback, between the other phone calls,
of always hearing oneself talking to oneself.
It was a reference point.
And then, I saw that, more and more, things
were not going well. He did any old thing.
He drank, or he ate at any
hour. He knew that his life style was
destroying him. He was closed off and hardened completely,
he who before still had that sensibility
quite evident to others even when
it revealed itself in possibly aggressive
ways. And from day to day, I couldn't
recognize him anymore.
Nobody could recognize him.

And I wanted to question him. I'd
say to him:
"Is this on account of your family,
on account of So-and-So? Or So-and-So?" and all that,
and he answered me:
"No. It's on account of me."

That, of course, was during long discussions
that we had had, and all of us were
in agreement in saying that the main sources
of our sufferings, our personal sufferings,
were always just ourselves.
So, in the beginning, this way of answering
me seemed to me quite normal and synthesized
in five words all our long, very long
dissertations.

Then one day he added:
"It's on account of my answerer."
"On account of your answerer?"
"Yes, after all, on account of my answerer."
That's all.
Since then he never added a thing.
He never ungritted his teeth.

And it was truly terrifying. We never saw
him except in eclipses. He might have been a tramp.
A tramp with money, because in spite of it all
he always found some, and he who before
had been a nice little sponger, was sponging
still off people, although they
didn't like it very much.

When he went away without warning, nothing
at all, it was by accident that I was led to going
to his studio. I was one of the few
who had a set of his keys. Which, incidentally,
allowed me later on to take care of some of
his business, about which I've still heard nothing.

And all those tapes were still intact.
The answerer tapes. I listened to them.
I could not now reproduce
the way they were spoken, but just think
that, to set them off, he would start in:
"It is now ten pee em. When you get back

home, you'll know. Okay?"
And then hang up.

Little by little, he actually seemed to
be encouraging himself, saying to
himself:
"Don't forget, you have to do this, you
have to do that. Do it. Be nice,
do it . . ."

There was so much tenderness in his
beseeching, so much comprehension,
so much . . . I don't know how to say it . . . it was
full of emotion. As if he were talking
to a sweetheart, to . . . It was . . . It was
extraordinary, and the sweeter the words, the
sweeter the messages to himself became,
the tougher at the same time he himself
was becoming.

It was in a . . . in an answer tape,
in some . . . in some breaks in the
answerer that I understood why.
He swore at himself in reply, knowing well
that when phoning from the outside he wouldn't
be able to hear those insults. He forthrightly
insulted himself. Called himself all kinds of names. I
wouldn't dare repeat them, as much out of regard for him
as because he is now very far away, and
if someday you go very far away you might
perhaps run into him. And this strange dialogue
from himself to himself went on all those months.
On the day before he went away I
got some answer to the riddle. His
last phone call—phone call
from outside, to himself—was even
filthier than all the answers that he
gave himself when he got home. Just that, made
from the same mold, yet it went very much
farther. It was a challenge. A terrifying challenge . . .

•　•　•

It meant dragging through the mud whatever still
might be he, hope to be he. And that just
left him no more hope. That couldn't
leave him any anymore.

I tried to find an answer tape that might
have been from the next day, that is, the day
on which he left, just before he left. And I
looked for a long time, a very, very long time.

I always came back to the earlier insults but . . .
but no reply to that last entreaty
which came from outside, to those last
blasphemies, and that is where all of a sudden I
came upon a whisper. I had to amplify it
very, very loud, and I distinguished these words
as in a dream.

He was saying:
"OK, you've won.
I know now how far I can go. And
I also know that I can take it and that
in taking it, I'll go beyond."

Did he go beyond, did he get over, that barrier
in himself the way he went across borders?
He knew that when he packed his bag, he put himself
inside. But I think that it is as a man,
as a human being, for the first time that he
was conscious of carrying himself farther. Farther,
where maybe someday you will go and where I hope,
at any rate through no fault of mine, you will meet him.

A live story. Made up as I went along too.

Marie-Jo

Cassette
Words Made up on the Guitar . . . For You . . .
[This poem is included in the main text at pages 533–536.]

Cassette

Words for you

I say good night to you again, my Dad,
A good night and many good days
and good evenings,
all the length of . . . as many as there be,
lots, lots, lots of sunshine for you
and I'll always be there a little if you
just wish
in a glint beside the window.
When you take a walk midst a chirping
of birds, any old place, I'll be slipping
into the landscape, which I will at last know how
to find and appreciate.
I'll be all right.
You'll have to say I'll be all right.
You'll have to think it, because I
am sure of it. It will be true.
And I'll go on loving you in little
winks like this every time that
something sparkling or nice takes place
anywhere around you.

Take care of yourself
Don't forget it. [Two lines in English.]

[*She sings, accompanied by her guitar, in English:*]

Waiting
I'm waiting to
I'm waiting to die
Before to pass away

Waiting for the stars in the sky
To go with their eyes[?]

I'm waiting for the high moon
Before to cry and die
I'm waiting for the high moon
Before to pass away

It'll be soon the end
And the end of my body
And my arms will be down
I will lay down
Under the ground

But no tears in my eyes
No more words in my mouth
O no,
I'll be in the silence
Forever well in the nature
I'll be in the high moon
Up in the sky
In the peace

[*She whistles a tune, accompanying herself on the guitar, then continues to sing in English with guitar accompaniment:*]

It's like another sort of good-bye
Another love's good-bye
Or maybe it's also like to say
I will love you
Forever
I will remember always
Your face
Your smile
Your smell
Your pipe
And also
The dance when
I was
Really young

I will always remember
The dance but
My fingers are wretched tired
To play more
On a
Guitar

[Songs improvised with guitar, in English]

When all these days will know, these days will know, these days,
When all these days

When you will see me
When I will come to you
When you will see me
I'll be to you
There won't be problems more
It will be just the end of my silly past
And I will be for the present
And I will be for the present

When the moon will take me in its arms
When the moon will be high in the sky
I will go to see her
And to follow her away
When she will go to sleep
Under the roof [?]
When you will see father
It will be the end

You will see my smile
For the end of my past
And even if I can't find her with the real life
I'll find myself forever in the moon in her arms
Her arms, the moon, the high moon of the dogs
When they cry in the night all alone
I'm like a dog all alone in my apartment
When I see the high moon behind my window

I want to cry and I even can't
I want to say: Take me
She doesn't seem to understand
Or maybe she does not hear
One day I know she will hear me
When this time my world will be for the first time
Enough okay with a meaning for her
With a meaning for a tenderness like I say
That she is all the tenderness of all the years
And that she is more tender than my own Daddy
I know will never find your warnings
When, when I was a child I was in your arms
But that time over my past will never come more
And I have to forget my dreams when I will see the moon.
O high moon, o high moon, o high moon
You will hear me. Please you will take me
Please you will take me
See my heart does not work like it has to work
See my mind does not work like it has to work
All my body, all myself is already broken
I know that I can't survive in that world
Of silly people
It's not me or the people
It's only I all myself but I project all my image

Oh no! *(then she drops the song and says:)*

I just want to sleep and all forget
I'll join the high moon tonight
She'll take me with her for the big sleep
When she will disappear soon and go back to the dark.

Moon don't forget me
Take me as soon as it is possible
I am already tired to death
I just hope to be without fear
When trying for me to let my body and my mind here
And to go with you through the space.

Moon, high moon, I have loved you
maybe more than anybody else in that world

Except my father
But say moon, my father can't be in your image
When I try through your face to see his face
Anyway it's not possible because I can't even imagine the pipe
You are a lady so you don't smoke
He's a man, he smokes a pipe
That's why even if I love you so much without pipe
You'll never be him.

I will never forget that smell when I was his child, you know,
And when I was dancing with him during those beautiful vacations
It was like, like a big dream. It's also a feeling, a feeling to peace,
A feeling to be included forever in the universe, to breathe the real
Air on the rhythm of the nature.
I just hope when I'll join you that I will feel that again even if it's in
Another way. Because when I'll be in the space again like before my
birth
Maybe I'll find again that feeling to be included in something bigger
Than everything even cleverest men here can imagine and I have told
you
So many things especially about my father, maybe sometimes when we
won't
Be sleeping, maybe I will sleep, but you will wake up one night like
you
Do every month, maybe when you will be up high in the sky you will
say to
Him some words very kindly, very softly only for himself, you will say
to
Him all those words that he has never heard because he was too far
from me
And I said it at night
Moon, you are like a round balloon you know,
Like a big ball, and when I see you round like this
So brilliant, white in the dark you seem to be so soft
To touch and so good to have in my arms.

Don't forget me like I'll never forget you
Please remember that I have no pain

.

In fact I don't suffer and the day I will join you
Will be, I think so, the heavens.

OK? I hope you keep, the message for [?] death [*almost inaudible*]

———
1978 (undated)
———

You, Daddy, my "Lord and Father" [line in English],
I apologize for writing you this letter, when my senses are already betraying me and I am today going under forever. Why tell you this, why hurt you through my pain? For one last contact, as true as it possibly can be in spite of my delirious universe that cuts me off from reality.
I am wiped out, physically worn out and morally destroyed. I have lost track of myself somewhere in my head and my body, in the outsize space of my anxiety and my past illusions.
I would like, Dad, for you to divine only, behind these incoherent words, the oh so painful Love I have had for you. From afar, in the whispering in my pillow, or in my desperate sobs yearning for your arms. I was running after a dream I knew was impossible: I felt myself a "woman" for you, my aim of "becoming" was only in terms of you. To find you again younger, the young man from before I was born, or little boy I might have conceived. I might have recognized myself in you, have come to fruition in the reflection in your eyes. [Rest of letter in English.]
"Save me Daddy"—I'm dying—I'm nothing more, I don't see my place —I'm lost in the space, the silence of the death. Forget my tears but please, believe in my smile, when I was your little girl, many years ago.
Be happy for me—Remember my Love, even if it was crazy.
That's for what I've lived and for what I die now—

Marie-Jo

———

1978 (undated)

———

My Dad,

If you only knew! All that I'm not saying, all that you won't and shouldn't ever be able to know.

So as not to hurt you even more, to the point of disgust, perhaps?

I so skillfully shoved myself down into a self-conditioned madness, skillfully nurtured during these last months, that, and I am only now realizing it, even if I wanted to reverse matters, start over by shaking my head, it would be too late.

It is already feeding on itself, even though I myself, beforehand, consciously engendered it. It walks all around me all by itself, at an infernal rhythm, like that of Voodoo dances or exorcism cults, even though, quite the contrary, nothing can exorcise me anymore. I still ache a little. I had so big, so heavy an ache that I no longer felt it; I was too overwhelmed. At brief moments only, as compensation for one final little joy, for the savor of a memory that won't let itself be forgotten, I experience like an open wound, like the dismembering of my being, the interminable hours of my suicide by degree and my debasement.

I'm afraid only that my madness may grow too great before my real end, and I still don't have the courage to make myself disappear properly. When . . . ? Always tonight, tomorrow . . . One more reprieve. An excuse for digesting my bulimic meals before making the necessary gesture.

I'm not crying anymore. Chuck myself up in my head more than in my stomach. I yell without breathing, I talk with my eyes closed.

God. If only someone had the kindness, the charity (too bad about pity, at the point I've reached I accept it) to fire the shot for me, as wonderfully as in "They Shoot Horses, Don't They?" my fetish film.

Someone else's hand at the last second, after the acceptance and my eyes on the sea, at sand level.

God, yes!

If only someone would put an end to me! But who ? . . .

Marie-Jo

May 18, 1978

I ask only (if that's still possible?) to be cremated but that, with what is left of me (somewhere in a "garden" in Lausanne?), they don't forget to leave me my wedding ring . . .

Thanks

M.J.

I am no longer asking to be pardoned. I suppose it is not possible, in front of so cowardly an act, to pardon? . . .

P.S. Is it all right if one scatters *a little* of my ashes out in the open? . . . So as not to remain imprisoned *completely* in something "closed" but to join with the wind and . . .

"Poetry" no doubt!!!

Marie-Jo.